Désirée

MARSEILLES, 1794

My name is Bernardine Eugenie Désirée. They call me Eugenie; I should much prefer Désirée.

I have met a young man with a very interesting face and the most unpronounceable name—Boonopat, or Bonapart, or something like that.

'It is our sacred duty,' says Napoleone, 'to instil into all the European peoples the ideas of Liberty, Equality, and Fraternity. And if necessary we must do it with cannon!'

Yesterday I had my first kiss. His face was quite close to mine, so close that I trembled and involuntarily closed my eyes. Then I felt his lips pressed tightly on mine, until suddenly —I don't know how it happened, it was not what I wanted to do—my lips parted.

CONTENTS

PART I

THE DAUGHTER OF A SILK
MERCHANT OF MARSEILLES

MARSEILLES, at the beginning of Germinal,
Year II. (The end of March 1794 by Mama's
old-fashioned reckoning.)

I think a woman can get her way better with a man if she has
a well-rounded figure. So I've decided to stuff four handkerchiefs into the front of my dress to-morrow; then I shall look
really grown up. Actually I *am* grown up already, but nobody
else knows that, and I don't altogether look it.

Last November I was fourteen, and Papa gave me this lovely
diary for my birthday. It's a shame really to spoil these beautiful white pages with writing. There's a little lock at the side of
the diary, and I can lock it up. Even my sister Julie won't know
what I put in it. It was my last present from dear Papa. My
father was the silk merchant François Clary, of Marseilles;
he died two months ago, of inflammation of the lungs.

"What shall I write in that book?" I asked in perplexity
when I saw it on the table among my presents. Papa smiled
and kissed me on the forehead: "The story of Citizeness
Bernadine Eugenie Désirée Clary," he said, and then a troubled
look came into his face.

I am starting my future history to-night, because I'm so
excited I can't get to sleep. So I slid softly out of bed, and I
only hope Julie, over there, won't be awakened by the flickering
of the candle. She would make a terrible to-do.

I'm excited because to-morrow I'm going with my sister-in-
law Suzanne to see Deputy Albitte and ask him to help Etienne.
Etienne is my brother, and his life is in danger. Two days ago
the police suddenly came to arrest him. Such things do happen
in these days; it's only five years since the great Revolution, and
people say it's not over yet. There are many guillotined every
day in the Town Hall square, and it's not safe to be related to
aristocrats. Thank goodness, we haven't any fine folk among
our relatives. Papa made his own way, and he built up Grand-
pa's little business into one of the biggest silk firms in Marseilles.

Papa was very glad about the Revolution, though just before it he had been appointed a Purveyor to the Court and had sent some blue silk velvet to the Queen. Etienne says the velvet was never paid for. Papa almost cried when he read to us the first broadsheet proclaiming the Rights of Man.

Etienne had been managing the business since Papa died. When Etienne was arrested, Marie, our cook, who used to be my nurse, said quietly to me: " Eugenie, I hear that Albitte is coming to town. Your sister-in-law must go to him and try to get Citizen Etienne Clary set free." Marie always knows what's going on in town.

At supper we were all very dismal. Two places at the table were empty—Papa's chair next to Mama and Etienne's next to Suzanne. Mama won't let anyone use Papa's chair. I kept thinking of Albitte and crumbling my bread into little balls. That annoyed Julie. She is only four years older than me, but she wants to mother me all the time, and it makes me furious.

" Eugenie," she said, " it's bad manners to crumble your bread."

I stopped making bread balls and said:

" Albitte is in town."

The others took no notice. They never do when I say anything. So I said it again:

" Albitte is in town."

At that Mama said: " Who is Albitte, Eugenie?"

Suzanne was not listening: she was sobbing into her soup.

" Albitte," I said, proud of my knowledge, " is the Jacobin Deputy for Marseilles. He is staying a week and will be in the *Maison Commune* every day. And to-morrow Suzanne must go to him: she must ask him why Etienne has been arrested, and insist that it must be a misunderstanding."

" But," Suzanne sobbed, looking at me, " he wouldn't receive me!"

" I think—I think it might be better," said Mama doubtfully, " for Suzanne to ask our lawyer to see Albitte."

Sometimes my family disgust me. Mama won't have a jar of marmalade made at home unless she can give it a stir, and yet she will leave a matter of life and death to our silly old lawyer. I suppose many grown-ups are like that.

" We must see Albitte ourselves," I said, " and Suzanne, as Etienne's wife, is the one who should go. If you're afraid, Suzanne, *I'll* go, and I'll ask Albitte to release my big brother."

" Don't you dare go to the *Maison Commune*!" said Mama at once. Then she went on with her soup.

" Mama, I think . . ."

" No, I will not hear of it," said Mama, and Suzanne began sobbing into her soup again.

After dinner I went upstairs to see whether Persson had got back. You see, in the evening, I give Persson French lessons. He has the sweetest horse's face imaginable. He's terribly tall and thin, and he's the only fair-haired man I know. That's because he is a Swede. Heaven only knows where Sweden is— somewhere up by the North Pole, I think. Persson showed me once on the map, but I forget where. Persson's papa has a silk business in Stockholm, and the business is somehow connected with ours here. So Persson came to Marseilles for a year to get experience in Papa's business. Everyone says you can only learn the silk trade in Marseilles. So one day Persson arrived at our house. At first we couldn't make out a word he said. He declared that he was talking French, but it didn't sound like French at all. Mama got a room ready for him in the attic; in these unsettled times, she said, it was better for Persson to live with us.

I found Persson had come in—really he is such a respectable young man—and we sat down in the parlour. Usually he reads to me from the newspapers, and I correct his pronunciation. And once more, as so often, I got out the old broadsheet about the Rights of Man that Papa had brought home, and then Persson and I listened to each other reciting it, because we wanted to learn it all by heart. Persson's equine face grew quite solemn, and he said he envied me because I belonged to the nation that had presented these great thoughts to the world.

" Liberty, Equality, and the Sovereignty of the People," he declaimed. Then he said: " Much blood has been shed to establish these new laws, so much innocent blood. And it must not be allowed to have been shed in vain, Mademoiselle."

Of course, Persson is a foreigner, and he always calls Mama ' Madame Clary ', and me ' Mademoiselle Eugenie ', in the family though that is forbidden; we are both just *Citoyenne* Clary.

Suddenly Julie came into the room. " Would you come for a moment, Eugenie," she said, and took me to Suzanne's room.

Suzanne was sitting huddled up on the sofa, sipping port-wine. Port-wine is supposed to be strengthening, but I am never given a glass, because young maidens do not need strengthening, Mama says. Mama was sitting next to Suzanne, and I could see that she was trying to look energetic. When she does that, she looks more frail and helpless than ever; she

9

hunches up her narrow shoulders, and her face seems very small under the little widow's cap she has worn for two months. My poor Mama looks much more like an orphan child than a widow.

"We have decided," said Mama, "that to-morrow Suzanne shall try to see Deputy Albitte. And," Mama added, clearing her throat, "you are to go with her, Eugenie!"

"I am afraid to go alone, among all the crowds of people," Suzanne murmured. I could see that the port-wine had not strengthened her, only made her drowsy. And I wondered why I was to go with her, and not Julie.

"Suzanne has made this decision for Etienne's sake," said Mama, "and it will be a comfort to her, my dear child, to know that you are with her."

"Of course you must keep your mouth shut," Julie hastened to add, "and let Suzanne do the talking." I was glad that Suzanne was going to see Albitte. That was the best thing to do, the only thing, in my opinion. But since they were treating me like a child, as usual, I said nothing.

"To-morrow will be a very trying day for us all," said Mama, getting up. "So we must go to bed soon."

I ran into the parlour and told Persson that I had to go to bed. He packed up the newspapers and bowed. "Then I will bid you good night, Mademoiselle Clary," he said.

I was at the door when he suddenly murmured something. I turned back.

"Did you say something, Monsieur Persson?"

"It's only——" he began. I went over to him and tried to see his face in the dusk; I did not bother to light the candles as we were going to bed. I could just see Persson's pale face.

"I only wanted to say, Mademoiselle, that I—yes, that I shall soon be going home."

"Oh, I am sorry, Monsieur; why?"

"I have not yet told Madame Clary, I did not want to trouble her. But you see, Mademoiselle, I have been here for a year and more, and they want me in the business in Stockholm. And when Monsieur Etienne Clary comes back everything will be in order here. I mean, in the business as well; and then I will go back to Stockholm."

It was the longest speech I had ever heard Persson make. I couldn't quite understand why he told me before the others. I had always thought he didn't take me any more seriously than they do. But now, of course, I wanted us to go on talking. So I went over to the sofa and indicated with a very ladylike gesture that he was to be seated next to me. As soon as he sat down, his tall frame folded up like a pocket knife; he rested his elbows on his knees, and I could see he didn't know what to say next.

" Is Stockholm a beautiful city?" I asked politely.

" To me it is the most beautiful city in the world," he answered. " Green ice-floes sail about in Mälar, and the sky is as white as a sheet that has just been washed. That is in the winter, but our winter is very long."

His description did not make me think Stockholm particularly beautiful. I wondered, too, where it was that the green floes were sailing about.

" Our shop is in the Vester Longgatan. That is the most modern shopping centre in Stockholm. It is just by the Royal Palace," Persson added proudly.

But I was not really listening, I was thinking ' about to-morrow ', and thinking ' I must stuff some handkerchiefs into the front of my dress and——'

" I wanted to ask you a favour, Mademoiselle Clary," I heard Persson saying.

' I must look as pretty as I can,' I was thinking, ' so that for my sake they will release Etienne.' But I asked politely:

" What is it, Monsieur?"

" I should like so much," he faltered, " to keep the broadsheet about the Rights of Man, the one Monsieur Clary brought home. I know, Mademoiselle, that that is a presumptuous request."

It was indeed. Papa had always kept the broadsheet on his little bedside table, and after his death I had taken it for myself.

" I shall always treasure it, Mademoiselle," said Persson.

Then I teased him for the last time: " So you've become a Republican, Monsieur?"

And once more he wouldn't say. " I am a Swede, Mademoiselle," he replied, " and Sweden is a Monarchy."

" You may keep the broadsheet, Monsieur," I said, " and show it to your friends in Sweden."

At this moment the door flew open and Julie cried angrily: " When are you coming to bed, Eugenie? Oh," she added, " I didn't know you were with Monsieur Persson. Monsieur, the child must go to bed. Come along, Eugenie!"

Julie was still scolding me when I had put almost all my paper curlers into my hair and she was in bed. " Eugenie, your behaviour is scandalous. Persson is a young man, and it's not proper to sit in the dark with a young man. You forget that you are a daughter of François Clary. Papa was a highly respected citizen, and Persson can't even speak decent French. You will disgrace the whole family!"

'What rubbish,' I thought, as I snuffed out the candle and got into bed. 'What Julie needs is a husband; if she had one my life would be easier.'

I tried to sleep, but I could not stop thinking about to-morrow's visit to the *Maison Commune*. And I kept thinking, too, of the guillotine. I see it so often when I am trying to go to sleep, and then I dig my head into the pillow to drive away that memory, the memory of the knife and the severed head.

Two years ago our cook Marie took me secretly to the Town Hall square. We pushed our way through the crowd that swarmed round the scaffold. I wanted to see everything, and I clenched my teeth because they were chattering so. The red tumbril brought up twenty ladies and gentlemen. They all wore fine clothes, but dirty bits of straw clung to the gentlemen's silk breeches and the ladies' lace sleeves. Their hands were bound with rope behind their backs.

Sawdust is spread on the scaffold round the guillotine, and every morning and evening, after the executions, fresh sawdust is put down, but in spite of that it is always a terrible reddish yellow mess. The whole square smells of dried blood and sawdust. The guillotine is painted red like the tumbrils, but the paint is peeling off; for the guillotine has been there for years.

On that afternoon the first person brought in was a young man who was accused of being in secret correspondence with enemies abroad. When the executioner jerked him on to the scaffold his lips were moving; I think he was praying. He knelt and I shut my eyes; I heard the blade fall. When I looked up, the executioner was holding a head in his hand. The head had a chalk-white face; the eyes were wide open and staring at me. My heart stood still. The mouth in the chalky face was wide open as though about to scream. There was no end to that silent scream.

I could hear confused voices round me; someone sobbed, and there came a high-pitched giggle. Then the noise seemed to come from far away, everything went black before my eyes, and—well, yes, I was horribly sick.

I felt better then, but people were shouting at me for being sick: I had spoilt someone's shoes. I kept my eyes shut so as not to see the bleeding head. Marie was ashamed of my behaviour, and took me out of the crowd; I heard people abusing us as we passed them. And ever since then I often can't sleep for thinking of the dead staring eyes and the silent scream.

When we got home I couldn't stop crying. Papa put his arms round me and said: "The people of France suffered for hundreds of years. And two flames rose from that suffering: the flame of Justice, and the flame of Hatred. The flame of Hatred will burn down and be extinguished in streams of blood. But the other flame, the sacred flame of Justice, little daughter, can never again be completely extinguished."

"The Rights of Man can never be abrogated, can they, Papa?"

"No, they can never be abrogated. But they can be temporarily suppressed, openly or secretly, and trodden under foot. But those who trample on them will incur the deepest blood-guilt in all history. And whenever and wherever in days to come men rob their brethren of their rights of Liberty and Equality, no one can say for them 'Father, forgive them; for they know not what they do', because, little daughter, after the Declaration of the Rights of Man they will know perfectly well what they are doing!"

When Papa said that, his voice was quite changed. It sounded—yes, really, it sounded just as I should expect the voice of God to sound. And the more time has passed since that talk with Papa, the better I have understood what he meant.

I feel very close to Papa to-night. I am afraid for Etienne, and a little afraid of the visit to the *Maison Commune*. But at night we are more easily frightened than in the daytime.

If only I knew whether my life's story will be happy or sad! I want ever so much to have some experience out of the ordinary. But first I must find a husband for Julie. And, above all, Etienne must be got out of prison.

Good night, Papa! You see I have begun to write my story.

24 hours later. (How many things have happened!)

I am the disgrace of the family!

On top of that, so much has happened that I don't know how I can write it all down. First of all—Etienne has been released, and is sitting downstairs in the dining-room with Mama, Suzanne, and Julie, and he is eating away as if he'd been kept on bread and water for a month, instead of only three days.

Secondly, I have met a young man with a very interesting face and the most unpronounceable name—Boonopat, or

Bonapart, or something like that. Thirdly, downstairs they're all furious, calling me a disgrace to the family, and they have packed me off to bed.

Downstairs they are celebrating Etienne's return, and though it was my idea to see Albitte, I am being endlessly scolded, and there's no one with whom I can talk about the future and this Citizen Buonapar, impossible name, I'll never remember it— there's no one with whom I can talk about this new young man. But my dear good Papa must have foreseen how lonely you can be if you are misunderstood by everybody, and that is why he gave me this diary.

To-day began with one to-do after another. Julie told me that Mama had decided that I was to wear my odious grey gown, and that *of course* I must wear a lace fichu tight round my neck. I fought against the fichu, but Julie shrieked: "Do— you—think we shall let you go in a low-necked dress like a— like a girl from the port, let you go to a government office without a fichu?"

As soon as Julie had gone I hastily borrowed her little pot of rouge. For my fourteenth birthday I had a pot of my own, but I hate it, it's such a childish pink. Julie's 'Cerise' suits me much better. I dabbed it on carefully, and I thought how difficult it must have been for the great ladies in Versailles who used thirteen different shades one on top of another to get the right effect. I read about it in the newspaper, an an article on the Widow Capet, our Queen who was guillotined.

"My rouge! How often must I tell you not to use my things without my permission!" said Julie crossly as she came back into the bedroom. I quickly powdered my whole face; then I damped my forefinger and smoothed my eyebrows and eyelids —they look much nicer when they are a little shiny. Julie sat on the bed and watched me critically. I began to take the paper curlers out of my hair. But they got caught in my curls, I have such horrid stubborn natural curls that it's a terrible business to coax them into smooth corkscrews hanging down to my shoulders.

We heard Mama's voice outside: "Isn't that child ready yet, Julie? We must have something to eat now if Suzanne and Eugenie are to be at the *Maison Commune* by two o'clock."

I tried to hurry, but that only made me clumsier than ever, and I simply could not get my hair right.

"Julie, can't you help me?"

Honour to whom honour is due. Julie has the light touch of a fairy. She finished doing my hair in five minutes.

14

"In one of the papers I saw a drawing of the young Marquise de Fontenay," I said. "She wears her hair in short curls, and brushes it down on to her forehead. Short hair would suit me too."

"She only does it to let everyone see that she was only rescued from the guillotine in the nick of time! But she won't have cut off her hair till she left the prison. She must have had long hair, and her elaborate frisure, when Deputy Tallien first saw her in prison. But," Julie added like an old maiden aunt, "I should advise you, Eugenie, not to read newspaper articles about the Fontenay."

"You needn't be so condescending and superior, Julie, I'm no longer a child, and I know quite well why Tallien got a pardon for the beautiful Fontenay, and what his object was. And so——"

"You are impossible, Eugenie! Who tells you all these things? Marie in the kitchen?"

"Julie, where *is* that child?" Mama called. She sounded annoyed.

I pretended to be tidying my fichu and stuffed the four handkerchiefs into my frock. Two on the right and two on the left.

"Take out those handkerchiefs at once! You can't go out like that," Julie said, but I pretended not to hear her, and impatiently pulled open one drawer after another looking for my Revolutionary cockade. Naturally I found it in the last drawer of all. I fastened it on to what seemed to me a most seductive handkerchief bosom. Then I ran downstairs with Julie to the dining-room.

Mama and Suzanne had begun to eat. Suzanne had her cockade on. At the beginning of the Revolution everyone wore a cockade, but now they are worn only by Jacobins, or when people are going to see someone in a Government office, or a Deputy. Naturally, in troubled times, for example last year when the Girondists were being persecuted, and there were wholesale arrests, no one dared to go out without the blue-white-red rosette of the Republic. At first I loved those rosettes showing the national colours of France, but now I don't like them any longer. I think it's undignified to pin one's convictions on to one's frock or coat lapel.

After dinner Mama got out the cut-glass decanter of port-wine. Yesterday Suzanne had a glass, but to-day Mama filled two glasses and gave Suzanne one and me one.

"Drink it slowly," she told me, "port-wine is strengthening."

I took a big gulp; it tasted sticky and sweet, and all of a sudden it regularly warmed me up. It made me very cheerful, too. I smiled at Julie, and then I saw there were tears in her eyes. She actually put her arm round my shoulders and pressed her face against my cheek. "Eugenie," she whispered, "take care of yourself!"

The port-wine was making me very lively. For fun I rubbed my nose against Julie's cheek, and whispered: "Perhaps you're afraid that Deputy Albitte might seduce me?"

"Can't you ever be serious?" said Julie irritably. "It's not just a game going to the *Maison Commune*, with Etienne under arrest. You know they——" She stopped short.

I took a last good gulp of port-wine. Then I looked straight at her. "I know, Julie, I know what you mean. Usually the near relatives of arrested men are arrested too. No doubt Suzanne and I are in danger. And you and Mama are in danger too, but as you are not going to the *Maison Commune* you two won't be on show. And so——"

"I wish I could go with Suzanne." Her lips were trembling, but she controlled herself. "But if anything happens to you, Mama will need me!"

"Nothing will happen to us," I said. "And if it did, I should know that you are looking after Mama, and that you will try to get me out. We two must always stick together, mustn't we, Julie?"

Suzanne did not speak on our way into the centre of the town. We walked very fast, and she did not look to right or left, even when we went past the fashion shops in the Rue Cannebière. When we reached the Town Hall square she suddenly took my arm. I tried not to see the guillotine. The square still smelt of fresh sawdust and dried blood. We met *Citoyenne* Renard, who for years had made Mama's hats. She looked round timidly before nodding to us; she had evidently heard that a member of the Clary family had been arrested.

A great crowd were loitering in the entrance to the *Maison Commune*. When we tried to push our way through, someone caught hold of Suzanne's arm. Poor Suzanne shook with fear and grew very pale.

"And what do you want, *Citoyenne*?"

"We wish to speak to Citizen Deputy Albitte," I said quickly in a loud voice.

The man, I decided he was the porter at the *Maison Commune*, let go of Suzanne's arm. "Second door on the right," he said. We pressed on through the dimly lit entrance, found the second door on the right, opened it, and were assailed by a confused roar of voices and a horridly stuffy atmosphere.

At first we did not know what to do. So many people were sitting and standing in the narrow waiting-room that you could hardly move. At the far end of the room was another door, at which a young man stood on guard. He wore the costume of the Jacobin Club; he had a high collar, a huge black cocked hat with a cockade, and a silk coat with very fine lace cuffs; he had a walking stick under his arm. I thought he must be one of Albitte's secretaries, so I caught hold of Suzanne's hand and tried to push through to him. Suzanne's hand was trembling and as cold as ice, but I could feel beads of perspiration on my forehead, and I was vexed with the handkerchiefs inside my dress, for they made me hotter than ever.

"We want, please, to see Citizen Deputy Albitte," Suzanne murmured when we came up to the young man.

"What?" he shouted at her.

"To see Citizen Deputy Albitte," Suzanne stammered.

"Everyone in this room wants to see him. Have you sent in your name, *Citoyenne*?"

Suzanne shook her head. "How do we do that?" I asked.

"Write out your name and business," he said. "People who can't write get me to do it for them. That costs——" he glanced appraisingly at our clothes.

"We can write," Suzanne said.

"Over there on the window-ledge the *citoyenne* will find paper and a quill," said the Jacobin youth. He might have been an archangel at the gates of Paradise.

We pushed through to the window-ledge. Suzanne quickly filled up a form. Names? *Citoyenne* Suzanne Clary and *Citoyenne* Bernadine Eugenie Désirée Clary. Purpose of visit? We stared at each other in perplexity.

"Write the truth," I said.

"Then he won't see us," Suzanne whispered.

"He'll make inquiries anyhow before he sees us," I urged. "Things are not exactly simple here."

"Simple, no, indeed!" Suzanne moaned as she wrote: "Purpose of visit: concerns arrest of *Citoyen* Etienne Clary."

We then struggled back to our Jacobin archangel. He glanced casually at the paper, barked "Wait," and disappeared behind the door. He was gone, it seemed to me, for an eternity. At last he came back and said: "You may wait. The Citizen Deputy will receive you. Your name will be called out."

Soon afterwards the door was opened, someone gave the

archangel instructions, and he shouted "*Citoyen* Joseph Petit." I saw an old man with a little girl get up from the bench by the wall. I quickly pushed Suzanne toward the two empty places. "We had better sit down, it will be hours before it's our turn."

Our situation had improved enormously. We leaned back against the wall, closed our eyes, and wriggled our toes in our shoes. Soon I began to look about, and I noticed our shoemaker, old Simon. I thought of his son, young Simon with the bow legs, and how gallantly those bow legs had marched in that company eighteen months ago.

I shall never forget that march. Our country was being pressed on all sides by enemy armies. The other countries would not tolerate our proclamation of the Republic. It was being said that our armies would not be able to hold out much longer against those superior forces. But one morning I was awakened by singing under our windows. I jumped out of bed and ran on to the balcony, and I saw, marching past, the *Volontaires* of Marseilles. They were taking three cannon from the fortress with them, because they did not mean to appear before the Minister of War in Paris empty-handed.

I knew many of the marchers. There were the apothecary's two nephews, and, Heavens! shoemaker Simon's bow-legged son, exerting himself to keep pace with the others! And there was Léon, the assistant from our own shop: he had not even asked permission, but had simply enrolled and gone off. And behind Léon I saw three dignified young men in dark brown clothes: Banker Levi's sons; the Rights of Man had given them the same civil liberties as all other Frenchmen. Now they had put on their Sunday best to go to war for France. "*Au revoir,* Monsieur Levi," I shouted, and all three Levis looked up and waved.

The Levis were followed by our butcher's sons, and then came in serried ranks the workmen from the docks. I recognised them by their blue linen blouses and the clatter of their clogs. And they were all singing

Allons, enfants de la patrie. . . .,

the new song, which became famous overnight, and I sang with them.

Suddenly Julie was standing next to me; we picked flowers from the rose-trees growing round the balcony and threw them down.

"*Le jour de gloire est arrivé . . .*" came up to us in a roar, and the tears ran down our cheeks. And below, Franchon, the

18

tailor, caught two of the roses and laughed up at us. Julie waved back at him with both her hands, and called excitedly: "*Aux armes, citoyens, aux armes!*"

They still looked like ordinary citizens in their dark coats or blue linen blouses, their patent leather shoes or wooden clogs. In Paris only some of them were given uniforms, because there were not enough to go round. But with or without uniforms, they beat back the enemy and won the battles of Valmy and Wattignies—the Simons and Léons and Franchons and Levis. And now the song they sang as they marched to Paris is being played and sung all over France. It is called the *Marseillaise*, because it was carried through the land by the men of our city.

When I was thinking of those scenes, the old shoemaker had pushed his way through to us. He shook hands with us eagerly but with embarrassment, and we felt that he wanted to express his sympathy. Then he turned hastily to the subject of leather soles, which can scarcely be procured, and he went on to talk of the tax relief for which he wanted to ask Albitte, and of his bow-legged son, from whom he has had no news. Then his name was called, and he took leave of us.

We waited for hours. Sometimes I closed my eyes and leaned against Suzanne. Every time I opened them the rays of the sun came more aslant and a little redder through the window. Now there were fewer people in the room. Albitte seemed to be cutting short the interviews, for the archangel was calling out new names more often. But plenty of people who were here before us were still waiting.

"I must find a husband for Julie," I said. "In the novels she reads the heroines fall in love when they are eighteen at the latest. Where did you meet Etienne, Suzanne?"

"Don't bother me now!" Suzanne said. "I want to concentrate on what I must say in there." She glanced at the door.

"If I ever have to receive people, I shall not keep them waiting. I'll give them definite times to come, one after another, and receive them at once. This waiting is dreadful!"

"What nonsense you talk, Eugenie. As if you would ever in your life—what did you call it?—be receiving people!"

I fell silent, and grew sleepier still. Port-wine makes you gay at first, I reflected, then sad, and finally tired. But it is certainly not strengthening.

"Don't yawn, that's rude," Suzanne was saying.

"Oh, but we are living in a free Republic," I murmured sleepily, but I woke up with a start because another name had

19

been called. Suzanne put her hand on mine. "It's not our turn yet," she said. Her hand was still cold.

At last I really fell fast asleep. I slept so soundly that I thought I was in bed at home. Suddenly I was disturbed by a light. I did not open my eyes; "Julie," I seemed to be saying, "let me sleep, I'm tired."

A voice said: "Wake up, *Citoyenne*." But I took no notice, until someone shook me by the shoulder.

"Wake up, *Citoyenne*. You can't go on sleeping here!"

"Oh, leave me alone," I grumbled, but then I was suddenly wide awake. I was startled, and pushed the strange hand from my shoulder. I had no idea where I was. I was in some dark room, and a man with a lantern was bending over me. For heaven's sake, where was I?

"Don't be alarmed, *Citoyenne*," the strange man said. His voice was soft and pleasant, but he spoke with a foreign accent which made me sure I was having a bad dream. I said I was not afraid, however; "but," I added, "where am I and who are you?"

The strange man stopped shining the lantern in my face, and now that the light was closer to him I could see his features more clearly. He was a really handsome young man, with kind dark eyes, a very smooth face, and a very charming smile. He was wearing a dark suit and a cloak over it.

"I'm sorry to disturb you," the young man said politely, "but I'm going home, and I'm closing Deputy Albitte's office."

Office? How had I got to an office? My head ached and my legs felt like lead.

"What office? and who are you?" I stammered.

"It's Deputy Albitte's office. And my name, as this seems to interest the *citoyenne*, *Citoyen* Joseph Boonopart, secretary to the Committee of Public Safety in Paris, seconded to Deputy Albitte as his secretary during his journey to Marseilles. And our office hours were over a long time ago; I must lock up, and it's against the law for anyone to spend the night in the *Maison Commune*. I must therefore ask the *citoyenne* very kindly to wake up and leave."

Maison Commune, Albitte. Now I knew where I was, and why. But where was Suzzane? I was at a loss.

"Where is Suzanne?" I asked the friendly young man.

At that his smile broadened into a laugh. "I have not the honour to know Suzanne," he said. "I can only tell you that the last people who came to see *Citoyen* Albitte left here two hours ago. I am the only person left in the office. And I am going home now."

"But I must wait for Suzanne!" I insisted. "You must excuse me, Citizen Bo—ma——"

"Bonoparté," said the young man, politely helping me out.

"Well, *Citoyen* Bonoparté, you must excuse me, but here I am, and here I must stay till Suzanne comes back. Otherwise there'll be a terrible to-do when I get home alone, and when I confess that I lost her in the *Maison Commune*. You can understand that, can't you?"

He sighed. "You are monstrous persistent," he said, as he put the lantern on the floor and sat down next to me on the bench. "What is this Suzanne's surname, and what did she want from Albitte?"

"Her name is Suzanne Clary, and she is my brother Etienne's wife," I told him. "Etienne was arrested, and Suzanne and I came to ask for his release."

"Just a moment," he said. He got up, took the lantern, and disappeared through the door at which the archangel had stood guard. I followed him. He was bending over a large writing-desk and looking through some documents.

"If Albitte received your sister-in-law," he explained, "your brother's dossier must be here. The Deputy always asks for the papers in the case before talking to the relatives of arrested men."

I did not know what to say, so I murmured: "The Deputy is a very just and kind man."

He glanced up at me mockingly. "Above all a kind man, *Citoyenne*. Perhaps too kind. And that's why *Citoyen* Robespierre of the Committee of Public Safety commissioned me to assist him."

"Oh, so you know Robespierre?" I said without thinking. Heavens, here was someone who knew Deputy Robespierre, who will arrest his best friends to serve the Republic!

"Ah, here we are, Etienne Clary," the young man exclaimed in satisfaction. "Etienne Clary, silk merchant of Marseilles, is that right?"

I nodded eagerly. "But in any case," I said, "his arrest was a misunderstanding."

Citizen Bonoparte turned to me: "What was a misunderstanding?"

"Whatever it was that led to his arrest."

The young man put on a grave air. "I see. And why was he arrested?"

21

"Well, we don't know," I admitted: "But at any rate I can assure you that it was a misunderstanding." Then I thought of something. "Listen," I said eagerly. "You said you know *Citoyen* Robespierre, the Commissary for Public Safety. Perhaps you can tell him that Etienne's arrest was a mistake and——"

My heart stood still. For the young man shook his head slowly and seriously. "I can do nothing about this case. There is nothing more to be done. Here—" he solemnly picked up a document—"here is the decision, entered by Deputy Albitte himself."

He held the sheet out to me. "Read it for yourself!"

I bent over the document. But though he was holding the lantern quite close I could make nothing out. I saw a few hastily written words, but the letters danced before my eyes.

"I am so troubled, please read it to me," I said, and I was close to tears. He read out:

"The matter has been fully explained and he has been set free."

"Does that mean——" I was trembling all over—"does that mean that Etienne——?"

"Of course! Your brother is a free man. He probably went home to his Suzanne long ago, and is now sitting with the rest of the family enjoying his supper. And the whole family are making a fuss over him and have entirely forgotten you. But— but—what's the matter, *Citoyenne*?"

I had started helplessly weeping. I couldn't stop, the tears ran down my cheeks, and I wept and wept; and I simply could not understand why, for I wasn't sad, I was inexpressibly happy, and I didn't know you can weep for joy.

"I am so glad, Monsieur," I sobbed; "so glad!"

It was obvious that this scene made the young man uncomfortable. He put down the dossier and busied himself with things on the desk. I dug down into my 'Pompadour' handbag, and looked for a handkerchief, but I found I had forgotten to put one in. Then I remembered the handkerchiefs in the front of my dress, and I reached down into the open neck. At that moment the young man looked up, and he could hardly believe his eyes: two, three, four little handkerchiefs came out of my frock, like a conjuring trick.

"I put them there so that people should think I was grown up," I murmured, because I felt that I owed him an explanation. I was terribly ashamed. "You see, at home they treat me as a child."

"You are no longer a child, you are a young lady," Citizen Boonopat assured me at once. "And now I'll take you home. It's not pleasant for a young lady to walk through the city alone at this time of night."

"It is too kind of you, Monsieur, but I cannot accept—" I stammered in embarrassment. "You said yourself that you wanted to go home."

He laughed: "A friend of Robespierre permits no contradiction. We'll have a sweetmeat each, and then go."

He opened a drawer in the desk and held out a paper bag to me. In it were cherries dipped in chocolate. "Albitte always keeps bonbons in his desk," he told me. "Take another chocolate cherry. Good, isn't it? Nowadays only Deputies can afford bonbons like these." The last sentence sounded a little bitter.

"I live on the other side of the city, it would be very much out of your way," I said guiltily, as we were leaving the *Maison Commune*. But I did not want to refuse his company, for it's quite true that young ladies cannot be out alone in the evening without being molested. Besides, I did so like him.

"I am so ashamed of having shed tears," I said a little later. He pressed my arm and reassured me: "I understand how you felt. I have brothers and sisters too, and I love them. And, indeed, sisters of about your age."

After that I no longer felt in the least shy. "But Marseilles is not your home?" I asked him.

"It is. All my family, except one brother, live here now."

"I thought—well," I said, "your accent is different from ours."

"I am a Corsican," he said, "a Corsican refugee. We all came to France a little over a year ago—my mother, my brothers and sisters, and I. We had to leave everything we possessed in Corsica, and escaped with our bare lives."

It sounded wildly romantic. "Why?" I asked, breathless with excitement.

"Because we are patriots," he said.

"Does Corsica belong to Italy?" I inquired, for my ignorance is beyond belief.

"How can you ask such a thing?" he replied hotly. "For twenty-five years Corsica has belonged to France. And we were brought up as French citizens, patriotic French citizens! That's why we could make no terms with the party that wanted to hand over Corsica to the English. A year ago English

23

warships suddenly appeared off your coast; you must surely have heard of it?"

I nodded. Probably I heard of it at the time, but I had forgotten all about it.

"And we had to flee. Mama and all of us." His voice was grim. He was like a real hero in a novel: a homeless refugee.

"And have you friends in Marseilles?"

"My brother helps us. He was able to get Mama a small Government pension, because she had to flee from the English. My brother was educated in France. At Brienne, at the military school. He is a General."

"Oh!" I said, speechless with admiration; I felt one should say something when told that a man's brother is a General! But as I could find nothing more to say, he changed the subject.

"You are a daughter of the late silk merchant Clary, aren't you?"

I was very surprised. "How did you know that?"

He laughed: "You needn't be surprised. I might tell you that the eyes of the law see everything and that I, as an official of the Republic, am one of those many eyes. But I'll be honest, Mademoiselle, and admit that you yourself told me: you said you were Etienne Clary's sister. And I learned from the documents that Etienne Clary is the son of the late François Clary."

He spoke quickly, and when he does that he is liable to roll his r's like a real foreigner. But, after all, he is a Corsican.

"By the way, Mademoiselle," he suddenly said, "you were right. Your brother's arrest was indeed due to a misunderstanding. The warrant for the arrest was actually made out in your father's name—François Clary."

"But Papa is no longer alive!"

"Quite so, and that explains the misunderstanding. It is all down in your brother's dossier. Recently an examination of certain pre-Revolution documents revealed that the silk merchant François Clary had petitioned to be granted a patent of nobility."

I was astonished. "Really? We knew nothing about that. And I don't understand it; Papa never had any liking for the aristocracy. Why should he have done that?"

"For business reasons," Citizen Bonaparté explained, "only for business reasons. I suppose he wanted to be appointed a Purveyor to the Court?"

"Yes, and once he sent some blue silk velvet to the Queen,

I mean to the Widow Capet in Versailles," I said proudly. "Papa's silks were famous for their excellence."

"His petition was regarded as—well, let us say as entirely unsuited to the times. That's why a warrant for his arrest was issued. And when our people went to his address they found only the silk merchant Etienne Clary, and so they arrested him."

"I'm sure that Etienne knew nothing about that petition," I declared.

"I assume that your sister-in-law Suzanne convinced Deputy Albitte of her husband's innocence. That is why your brother was released; and your sister-in-law must have hurried to the prison at once to fetch him. But all that belongs to the past. What interests me," he continued, and his voice was soft, almost tender. "What interests me is not your family, Mademoiselle, but you yourself, little *Citoyenne*. What is your name?"

"My name is Bernadine Eugenie Désirée. They call me Eugenie; I should much prefer Désirée."

"All your names are beautiful. And what shall I call you, Mademoiselle Bernadine Eugenie Désirée?"

I felt myself blushing. But thank goodness it was dark, and he could not see my face. I had a feeling that the conversation was taking a turn of which Mama would not have approved.

"Call me Eugenie as everyone else does. But you must come to see us, and in front of Mama I'll suggest that you should call me by my Christian name. Then there won't be any trouble, because I believe that if Mama knew——"

I stopped short.

"Are you never allowed to take a walk with a young man?" he inquired.

"I don't know. So far I've never known any young men," I said without thinking. I had completely forgotten Persson.

He pressed my arm again and laughed: "But now you know one—Eugenie!"

"When will you call on us?" I asked.

"Shall I come soon?" he rejoined, teasing.

But I did not answer at once. I was full of an idea that had occurred to me a little earlier: Julie! Julie, who so loves reading novels, would be enthusiastic about this young man with the foreign accent.

"Well, what is your answer, Mademoiselle Eugenie?"

"Come to-morrow," I said, "to-morrow after office hours. If it is warm enough we can sit in the garden. We have a little summer-house, it's Julie's favourite place in the garden." I considered that I had been extremely diplomatic.

25

"Julie? So far I have only heard about Suzanne and Etienne, not Julie. Who is Julie?"

I had to talk quickly, for we had already reached our road. "Julie is my sister," I said.

"Older or younger?" He sounded keenly interested.

"Older. She is eighteen."

"And—pretty?"

"Very pretty," I assured him eagerly; but then I wondered whether Julie would really be considered pretty. It is so difficult to judge one's own sister.

"You swear it?"

"She has lovely brown eyes," I declared, and so she has.

"And are you sure your mother would welcome me?" he asked with diffidence. He did not seem sure that Mama would be glad to see him, and, quite frankly, I wasn't sure either.

"I am sure she would welcome you," I insisted, for I was determined to give Julie her chance. Besides, there was something I wanted myself. "Do you think you could bring your brother, the General?" I asked.

Now Monsieur Boonopat was quite eager. "Of course. He would be delighted, we have so few acquaintances in Marseilles."

"You see, I've never seen a real General close up," I confessed.

"Well, you can see one to-morrow. True, at the moment he has no command, he is working out some scheme or other. Still, he is a real General."

I tried in vain to imagine what a real General would be like. I was sure that I had never met a General, and, as a matter of fact, I had not seen one even at a distance. And the pictures of the Generals in the days of the *Roi Soleil* are all of old gentlemen with huge wigs. After the Revolution, Mama took down the portraits of them in the parlour and stacked them in the attic.

"There must be a great difference in age between you and your brother," I said, for Monsieur Boonapat seemed very young.

"No, not very much difference. About a year."

"What!" I exclaimed, "your brother is only a year older than you, and a General?"

"No, a year younger. My brother is only twenty-four. But he is very clever, and full of amazing ideas. Well, you'll see him to-morrow yourself."

Our house was now in sight. The road was lit up from the

26

ground-floor windows. No doubt the family had been at supper for some time.

"That is where I live, where the lights are."

Suddenly Monsieur Boonapat's manner changed. When he saw the fine white house he was less sure of himself, and quickly said good-bye. "I mustn't keep you, Mademoiselle. I am afraid your family will be anxious about you. Oh, no, don't thank me. It was a great pleasure to escort you, and if your invitation was seriously meant, I shall take the liberty of calling to-morrow in the late afternoon, with my young brother, that is to say if your mother does not object, and if we should not be disturbing you."

At that moment the front door was opened, and Julie's voice pierced the darkness: "There she is, by the gate!" Then she called impatiently: "Eugenie, is that you, Eugenie?"

"I'm coming in a moment, Julie," I called back.

"*Au revoir*, Mademoiselle," Monsieur Boonapat said as I ran up to the house. Five minutes later I was being told that I was a disgrace to the family.

Mama, Suzanne, and Etienne were at supper; the meal was over and they were having coffee when Julie brought me in in triumph. "Here she is!"

"Thank God," Mama said. "Where have you been, my child?"

I glanced at Suzanne reproachfully. "You must have forgotten all about me," I complained. "I went to sleep and——"

Suzanne was holding Etienne's hand. She put down her cup indignantly. "Well, I never! First she goes fast asleep in the *Maison Commune* and leaves me to see Albitte alone, and now she wants to blame *me*!"

"When you left Albitte I think you must just have forgotten me!" I said.

"But where have you been all the time?" Mama asked. "We sent Marie to the *Maison Commune*, but it was closed and the porter said there was no one there, only Albitte's secretary. Great heavens, Eugenie, to think that you walked through the town alone, at this time of night! The things that might have happened to you!"

Mama picked up her little silver bell and rang it. "Bring the child her soup, Marie!" she said.

"But I wasn't alone," I said, "Albitte's secretary was with me."

Marie gave me my soup, but before I could begin Suzanne burst out:

"The secretary? That rude fellow at the door?"

"No, he was only a messenger. Albitte's secretary is a charming young man who knows Robespierre personally. At least, he says he does. By the way, I have——"

But they would not let me finish. Etienne cut me short: "What is his name?" he asked.

"It's a difficult name, and I didn't catch it properly—Boonapat or something like that. He's a Corsican. By the way, I have——"

"And you came alone, at night, with this stranger?" Etienne shouted, playing the stern father. First they had fussed because I had come home alone, and now because I hadn't.

"He is not a stranger, he introduced himself to me," I said. "His family are in Marseilles. They are refugees from Corsica. By the way, I have——"

"Go on with your soup, or it will be cold," said Mama.

"Refugees from Corsica?" said Etienne contemptuously. "Probably adventurers. Adventurers, that's what they'll be!"

I put down my spoon to defend my new friend. "He has a very respectable family," I said. "And his brother is a General. By the way, I have——"

"What is his brother's name?"

"I don't know. I suppose it's Boonapat too. By the way, I——"

"Never heard the name," Etienne growled. "But the officers are being appointed indiscriminately, and the Generals are nobodies!"

"By the way," I got in at last, "I wanted to say——"

"Go on with your soup!" Mama insisted.

But I refused to be interrupted any longer. "By the way," I repeated, "I have invited them both for to-morrow."

Then I started quickly on my soup, because I knew how they were all looking at me in horror.

"Whom have you invited, my child?" Mama asked.

"Two young gentlemen. *Citoyen* Joseph Boonapat or whatever it is, and his young brother the General."

"That has got to be stopped," Etienne shouted, banging the table. "We don't want a couple of escaped Corsican adventurers we know nothing about!"

"And it's not proper," said Mama, "for you to invite a chance acquaintance in a Government office. That is not the way to behave. You are no longer a child, Eugenie!"

"That is the first time anyone," I exclaimed, "has told me I'm no longer a child!"

" Eugenie, I am ashamed of you," said Julie.

" But these Corsican refugees have so few friends in the town," I ventured. I hoped Mama would sympathise.

" What do we know of them? Out of the question!" Etienne grunted. His recent experiences had set his nerves on edge. " You are a disgrace to the family!" he shouted.

" Etienne, she's only a child, and doesn't realise what she has done," said Mama.

That upset me entirely. " Please understand," I said, " once for all, that I am neither a child nor a disgrace!"

There was a moment's silence. Then Mama said with all the imitation sternness she could put on: " Go to your room at once, Eugenie!"

" But I'm still hungry, I've only begun my meal," I protested.

Mama's silver bell rang again. " Marie, please serve Mademoiselle Eugenie's meal in her room," she said. Then she turned very kindly to me: " Go along, my child, have a good rest, and just think about the way you have been behaving. It has distressed your mother and your good brother. Good night, my child."

Marie brought my supper up to the bedroom, and sat on Julie's bed.

" What's amiss? What's upset them all?" she asked sympathetically.

When we are alone Marie always calls me *tu*; she is my friend and not a servant. After all, she came to us years ago to be my wet-nurse, and I believe she loves me as much as her own natural son, Pierre, who is being brought up somewhere in the countryside.

I shrugged my shoulders. " It's all because I've invited two young men for to-morrow."

Marie nodded thoughtfully. " Very clever of you, Eugenie. It's time Mademoiselle Julie met some young men."

Marie and I always understand each other.

" Shall I make you a cup of chocolate?" she whispered. " From our private store?" For Marie and I have a private store of delicacies which Mama doesn't know about. Marie gets the things from the larder, without asking.

After I had drunk the chocolate, when I was alone, I began to write it all down. Now it's midnight and Julie is still downstairs. It's horrid of them to leave me out.

Julie has just come in and is beginning to get undressed. Mama has decided to receive the two gentlemen to-morrow.

The invitation could hardly be cancelled. So Julie told me, as if it was nothing. "But I've been told to tell you that it will be their first and last visit."

Julie standing in front of the mirror rubbing cream on her face. The cream is called Lily Dew. Julie read somewhere that even in prison the Dubarry always used Lily Dew. But Julie will never be a Dubarry. Now she is asking whether he is handsome.

"Who?" I asked, pretending to be stupid.

"This gentleman who brought you home."

"Very handsome by moonlight. Very handsome by lantern light. But I've not yet seen him by daylight."

That's all I could tell her.

MARSEILLES at the beginning of Prairial. (The lovely month of May, says Mama, is almost over.)

His name is Napoleone.

When I wake in the morning and think of him, my heart lies like a heavy lump in my breast, from sheer loving. (I lie with my eyes shut, so that Julie shall think I'm still asleep.) I didn't know you could really *feel* love—I mean, bodily. With me it's like something tugging round my heart.

But I had better tell it all just as it happened, starting from the afternoon when the two Buonapartes came to see us. As I had arranged with Joseph Buonaparte, they came the day after my failure to see Deputy Albitte. They came late in the afternoon. Etienne is not usually home by then, but he had shut up the shop and was waiting in the parlour with Mama, so that the young men should see at once that our home is not without a male protector.

Nobody had spoken more than a few words to me during the day, and I could see they were still vexed with my *bad behaviour*. After dinner Julie had disappeared into the kitchen; she had decided to make a cake. Mama said there was no need; she was still full of Etienne's idea of ' Corsican adventurers '.

I went into the garden for a bit. Spring was in the air already, and I found the first buds on the lilac trees. Then I asked Marie for a duster and did some dusting in the summerhouse—in case, I thought. When I went in with the duster I saw Julie in the kitchen. She was taking a cake-tin out of the oven; her face was burning and her forehead damp with perspiration, and her hair was just ruined.

"You're going the wrong way about it, Julie," I blurted out.

"Why? I kept exactly to Mama's recipe, and you just see if our guests don't like it."

"I didn't mean the cake," I said, "I meant your face and your hair. You'll smell of the cooking when the gentlemen come, and——" I paused—"for heaven's sake give it up, Julie, and go and powder your nose. That's much more important."

"What do you think of that, Marie?" said Julie, irritated.

"If you don't mind my saying so, Mademoiselle Julie, I think it's quite right," said Marie as she took over the cake-tin.

In our room Julie did her hair and carefully put on some rouge, while I stood at the window and looked out.

"Aren't you changing?" Julie asked in surprise. But I didn't see any real need for it. Of course I quite liked Monsieur Joseph, but in my mind I had already betrothed him to Julie. As for his brother the General, I could not imagine him taking any notice of me. Nor had I any idea what you talk about to a General. I was only interested in his uniform, though I hoped he would tell us about the fighting at Valmy and Wattignies. 'I do hope,' I was thinking all the time, 'that Etienne will be courteous and amiable; and that it will all end well.' As I looked out of the window I got more and more troubled about it. Then I saw them coming! They were having a lively discussion as they came along. And I was inexpressibly disappointed!

Well, there! He was a little man, shorter than Monsieur Joseph, and Joseph himself is only middle-sized. And he had nothing striking on at all, not a single star, or ribbon of any order. Only when they reached the gate did I see his narrow gold epaulettes. His uniform was dark green, and his top-boots were not polished and not even a good fit. I couldn't see his face because it was hidden by an enormous hat, with nothing on it but the cockade of the Republic. I didn't dream that a General could look so drab. I *was* disappointed.

"He looks very poverty-stricken," I murmured.

Julie had joined me at the window, but she kept behind the curtain. I suppose she didn't want the two citizens to see how curious she was.

"Why do you say that?" she said. "He looks very handsome! You can't expect a secretary at the *Maison Commune* to be very spick and span."

"Oh, you mean Monsieur Joseph? Yes, he looks quite elegant; at all events someone seems to brush his boots regularly. But look at his young brother, the General!" I sighed and shook my head. " Such a disappointment! I had no idea that there were such undersized officers in the army."

" What did you think he would be like?" Julie asked.

I shrugged my shoulders. " Why, like a General. Like a man who gives you the feeling that he can really command."

To think that all that happened only two months ago! It seems an eternity.

When Julie and I went into the parlour, the two brothers jumped up and bowed almost too politely, not only to Julie but to me too. Then we all sat, stiff and strained, round the oval mahogany table. Mama was on the sofa, with Joseph Buonaparte next to her. On the other side of the table sat the poverty-stricken General, on the most uncomfortable chair in the house, with Etienne next to him. Julie and I were between Mama and Etienne.

" I have just been thanking *Citoyen* Joseph Buonaparte," said Mama, " for his kindness last night in seeing you home, Eugenie."

At that moment Marie came in with liqueur and Julie's cake. While Mama filled the glasses and cut the cake, Etienne tried to make conversation with the General. " Is it indiscreet, *Citoyen Général*," he asked, " if I inquire whether you are in our city on official business?"

Joseph answered at once for the General: " Not at all. The army of the French Republic is a people's army, and is maintained by the citizens' taxes. Every citizen, therefore, has the right to know what is being done by our army. Am I not right, Napoleone?"

The name Napoleone sounded very foreign. We couldn't help all staring at the General.

" You may ask anything you like, *Citoyen* Clary," the General replied. " I, at all events, make no secret of my plans. In my opinion the Republic is only wasting its resources in this endless defensive warfare on our frontiers. Wars of defence merely cost money and bring in neither glory nor the means of replenishing our exchequer. Thank you, Madame Clary, thank you very much." Mama had handed him cake on a plate. He turned back to Etienne: " We must go over, of course, to offensive warfare. It will help the French finances, and will show Europe that the people's army has not been defeated."

I had been listening, but without understanding. His face was no longer concealed by his hat, and though it's not a

32

handsome face, it seems to me more wonderful than any face I have ever seen or dreamt of. And suddenly I understood why I had been attracted the day before to Joseph Buonaparte. The brothers resemble each other, but Joseph's features are not so strong or compelling as Napoleone's. They only suggest the stronger face for which I was longing. Napoleone's face carries out that suggestion.

" Offensive warfare?" I heard Etienne ask in dismay. We all sat in dead silence, and I realised that the young General must have said something startling. Etienne was looking at him open-mouthed. "Yes, but, *Citoyen Général*, has our army, with its very limited equipment, as we are given to understand——"

The General waved his hand and laughed. "Limited? *That's* not the word! Our army is a beggars' army. Our soldiers at the frontiers are in rags; they march into battle in wooden shoes. And our artillery is so wretched that you might suppose that Carnot, our Minister of War, thinks he can defend France with bows and arrows."

I bent forward and looked hard at him. Afterwards Julie told me my behaviour had been *dreadful*. But I couldn't help it. Especially I was waiting to see him laugh again. He has a thin face with tightly drawn skin, very sunburnt, and surrounded by reddish-brown hair. His hair comes down to his shoulders; it is not dressed or even powdered. When he laughs his drawn face suddenly becomes very boyish, and he looks much younger than he really is.

Then I started: someone was saying to me: "Your health, Mademoiselle Clary." They had all raised their glasses and were sipping the liqueur. Joseph had put his glass close to mine; his eyes were sparkling, and I remembered what we had said the day before: "Oh," I had told him, "call me Eugenie as the others do." Mama raised her eyebrows in annoyance, but Etienne was too wrapped up in his conversation with the General to hear.

"And on what front could an offensive operation be carried out with advantage?" he was asking.

"On the Italian front, of course. We shall drive the Austrians out of Italy. A quite inexpensive campaign. Our troops will easily supply themselves in Italy. Such a rich, fertile country!"

"And the Italians themselves? I thought they were loyal to the Austrians?"

"We shall set free the Italian people. In all the provinces we conquer we shall proclaim the Rights of Man." Though the subject seemed to interest the General, I could see that Etienne's objections bored him.

"Your garden is wonderful," Joseph Buonaparte said to Mama, looking through the glass door.

"It's too early yet," Julie ventured, "but when the lilac is out, and the climbing roses round the summer-house——"

She stopped in confusion. I could see she was losing her composure, for lilac and rambler roses do not come out together.

"Have the plans for an offensive operation on the Italian front taken definite shape?" Etienne asked. He would not drop the subject; it seemed to fascinate him.

"Yes. I have almost completed the plans. At present I am inspecting our fortifications here in the south."

"So Government circles are determined on an Italian campaign?"

"*Citoyen* Robespierre personally entrusted me with this tour of inspection. It seems to me to be indispensable before our Italian offensive begins."

Etienne clicked his tongue, a sign that he was impressed. He nodded. "A great plan," he said, "a bold plan." The General smiled at Etienne, and that smile seemed to captivate my brother, though he is such a hard-headed business man. Etienne said eagerly, stammering like a schoolboy: "If only that great plan succeeds, if only it succeeds!"

"Have no fear, *Citoyen* Clary, it will succeed," the General replied, getting up.

"And which of the two young ladies would have the kindness to show me the garden?" asked Joseph.

Julie and I both jumped up. And Julie smiled at Joseph. I don't know just how it happened, but two minutes later we four found ourselves in the leafless garden, without Mama and without Etienne.

It is only a narrow gravel path that leads to the summer-house, so that we had to go two by two. Julie and Joseph went in front, and Napoleone and I followed. I was racking my brains for anything I could say to him, I was so eager to make a good impression on him. But he seemed too buried in thought to notice our silence. And he walked so slowly that Julie and his brother got farther from us. I began to think he was deliberately dawdling.

All of a sudden he said, "When do you think my brother and your sister will be married?"

I thought at first that I must have misheard him. I looked at him in astonishment, and I could feel that I was flushing.

"Well," he repeated, "when will they be married? Soon, I hope."

"Yes, but," I stammered, "they have only just met. And after all we have no idea——"

"They are just made for each other," he declared. "You know that too."

"I?" I looked wide-eyed at him.

"Please don't look at me like that!" he said.

I was so upset that I could only look down. And I was becoming furious with him.

"But," he persisted, "you yourself were thinking last night that it would be a good thing for your sister to marry Joseph. After all, she is at the age at which young ladies generally become betrothed."

"I didn't think anything of the sort, Citizen General!" I declared. Then I had the feeling that in some way I had compromised Julie. I was no longer angry with Napoleone, only with myself.

He stood still, and turned to face me. He was only half a head taller than I, and he seemed pleased to have found somebody he didn't have to crane up to.

It was getting dark, and the grey spring twilight was dropping like a screen that shut us off from Julie and Joseph. The General's face was so close to mine that I could still see his eyes; they were sparkling, and I was surprised to find that men, too, have long eyelashes.

"You must never have any secrets from me, Mademoiselle Eugenie. I can see deep into the hearts of young ladies. Besides, Joseph told me last night that you had promised to introduce him to your elder sister. You told him, too, that your sister is very pretty. That was not true, and—you must have had a good reason for your little fib."

"We must go on," I said to that, "the others will be in the summer-house already."

"Shall we not give your sister a chance to get better acquainted with my brother before she becomes betrothed to him?" he asked softly. His voice sounded very gentle, almost— yes, almost like a caress. His accent seemed foreign much less often than his brother's.

"Joseph will very soon be suing for your sister's hand," he told me quite simply. It was so dark now that I could only see his face dimly, but I could tell that he was smiling.

"How do you know that?" I asked, puzzled.

"We talked about it last night," he replied, as if that were the most natural thing in the world to do.

"But last night your brother had never seen my sister," I retorted, outraged.

Then he very gently took my arm, and the contact sent a thrill all over me. We went slowly on, and he talked with such tender intimacy that we might have been friends for years.

"Joseph told me of his meeting with you, and he mentioned that your family are very well-to-do. Your father is no longer alive, but I assume that he must have left considerable dowries for you and your sister. Our people are very poor."

"You have sisters too, have you not?" I remembered that Joseph had mentioned sisters of my age.

"Yes, three young brothers and three young sisters," he said. "And Joseph and I have to provide for Mama and all of them. Mama has a small pension from the State, because she was treated as a persecuted patriot after her flight from Corsica. But the pension does not even pay the rent. You have no idea, Mademoiselle Eugenie, how dear everything is in France."

"So," I said, freeing my arm, "your brother only wants to marry my sister for her dowry?" I tried to speak without heat, but I was hurt, and my voice shook with disgust.

"Why, how can you say that, Mademoiselle Eugenie! I think your sister is a very charming young lady, so kind, so modest, with such lovely eyes—I am quite sure that Joseph likes her very much. The two will be very happy together."

He began to walk faster, as if we had exhausted the subject. But I warned him that I should tell Julie what he had just admitted.

"Of course," he said. "That is why I have told you everything so carefully. Yes, tell Mademoiselle Julie, so that she shall know that Joseph will soon be suing for her hand."

I was horrified. 'How shameless,' I thought, and I imagined Etienne sneering 'Corsican adventurers!' "May I ask," I said coldly, "why you are so concerned about your brother's marriage?"

"Sh! Don't shout! You will realise, Mademoiselle Eugenie, that before taking up my command-in-chief in Italy I should be glad to see my family rather better settled. With his experience as politician and political writer, Joseph may forge ahead if he no longer has to work as a subordinate employee. As soon as I have gained my first victories in Italy, of course I shall look after all my family." He paused. "And—believe me, Mademoiselle, I shall look well after them."

We had come to the summer-house. "Where have you been, General," Julie asked, "with the child all this time? We have been waiting for you and Eugenie." But we could see that she and Joseph had forgotten all about us. They were sitting close together on a little bench, though there were plenty of chairs there. Besides, they were holding hands; I suppose they thought we wouldn't notice it in the dusk.

We all went back then to the house, and the two brothers said they must be going. But at that Etienne spoke up. "My mother and I would be very pleased if the Citizen General and Citizen Joseph Buonaparte would stay to supper with us. It is a long time since I had an opportunity of so interesting a talk." As he said that he looked quite appealingly at the General; he seemed to be ignoring Joseph.

Julie and I ran up to our room to do our hair. "Thank goodness," she said, "they have made a good impression on Mama and Etienne."

"I must tell you," I said, "that Joseph Buonaparte will soon be suing for your hand. Principally because," I added, but I had to stop, my heart was beating so, "because," I said when I could finish the sentence, "because of the dowry!"

"How can you say such a hateful thing!" said Julie, with her face flaming. "He told me how poor his family are, and of course," she added, tying a couple of little black velvet bows in her hair, "he could not marry anyone without means, as he has only a small salary and has to help his mother and the children. I think that is very noble of him—Eugenie!" she exclaimed, breaking off, "I won't have you using my rouge!"

"Has he told you already that he wants to marry you?"

"Whatever put that idea into your head? Why, all he talked about, of course, was just things in general, and his young brothers and sisters."

On our way down to the dining-room, where they were all crowded round our two guests, Julie suddenly put her arm round my shoulder and pressed her face against mine. Her cheek was very hot. "I don't know why," she whispered, kissing me, "but I am so happy!" She's surely in love, I said to myself.

As for me, I was quite calm. But I did have that curious tugging round my heart. 'Napoleone,' I thought—'a strange name.' So that's how you feel when you're in love. Napoleone!

All that was two months ago. And yesterday I had my first kiss; and yesterday Julie was betrothed. The two events belong together somehow, for while Julie and Joseph were sitting in the summer-house Napoleone and I were standing by the hedge at the bottom of the garden, so as not to disturb those two. Mama has told me always to spend the evenings in the garden with Julie and Joseph, because Julie is a young lady of good family.

Since that first visit the two brothers have been to see us almost every day. It was Etienne's doing—who could have believed it? Signs and wonders will never cease, and it was he who invited them to come. He can never have enough of his talks with the young General. Poor Napoleone, how terribly they bore him! Etienne is one of those people who value a person according to his success. When I revealed that the two Buonapartes were Corsican refugees, he refused to have anything to do with them, and called them 'adventurers'. But ever since Joseph showed him the cutting from the December *Moniteur* in which his brother was gazetted Brigadier General, Etienne has raved over Napoleone.

Napoleone had driven the English out of Toulon. That is how it happened. The English are always meddling with our affairs, and they are indignant at our condemning our King to death, though Napoleone says it is scarcely a century and a half since they did just the same to their own King. And now they, the English, had formed an alliance with the Royalists of Toulon, and had occupied the town. So our troops laid siege to Toulon. Napoleone was ordered there, and in no time he did what his seniors had been trying in vain to do: Toulon was stormed, and the English fled. Then it was that the name Buonaparte appeared for the first time in the Army Orders, and Napoleone was promoted Brigadier General. Etienne, of course, pestered him to tell him the whole story of the victory at Toulon, but Napoleone says there was nothing in it. It was only a matter of a few cannon, and he, Napoleone Buonaparte, knew perfectly well where to put cannon and which way to point them.

After his success at Toulon, Napoleone went to Paris, to try to see Robespierre. Robespierre is the most powerful man in the Committee of Public Safety. That committee is our Government. To get to the great Robespierre he had first to see the lesser Robespierre, the great man's brother. Robespierre—the real one—thought Napoleone's plans for a campaign in Italy were excellent; he discussed them with the Minister of War, Carnot, and asked him to entrust Napoleone with the preparations for the campaign. Napoleone says that Carnot falls into a rage whenever Robespierre interferes with his Ministry, because it is no concern of Robespierre's. But nobody dares to contradict Robespierre, for he has only to sign a warrant and anyone is sent straight to the guillotine. Consequently Carnot received Napoleone with a show of friendliness, and took over the Italian plans from him.

" First," said Carnot, " go and inspect our fortresses in the south; I will give your ideas careful attention, *Citoyen Général*." But Napoleone is quite sure that his plans lie pigeon-holed somewhere in the Ministry. Robespierre, however, will soon arrange, Joseph thinks, for Napoleone to be given the supreme command in Italy.

Etienne and all our friends hate that man Robespierre. But they do not say so aloud, it would be too dangerous. It is said that Robespierre has made the members of the Revolutionary Tribunal give him secret reports on the attitude of all the officials in the State service. Even the private life of every single citizen, they say, is watched. Robespierre has declared that every genuine Republican has a duty to live a moral life and to despise luxury. Recently he actually had all the brothels in Paris closed. I asked Etienne whether brothels are a luxury, but he said angrily that I mustn't talk about such things. And no dancing is allowed in the streets any longer, though that was a pleasure everybody enjoyed on public holidays. Etienne has absolutely forbidden us ever to criticise Robespierre in front of the two Buonapartes.

Etienne talks to Napoleone of scarcely anything but the Italian plans. " It is our sacred duty," says Napoleone, " to instil into all the European peoples the ideas of Liberty, Equality, and Fraternity. And if necessary we must do it with cannon!" I always listen to these talks, so as to be with Napoleone, though they weary me terribly. The worst is when Napoleone begins to read the Handbook of Modern Artillery to my brother. That happens sometimes, and Etienne, the stupid, thinks he understands it all.

But when we are alone he never talks about cannon. And we are very often alone together. After supper Julie always says: " Don't you think we ought to take our guests into the garden for a bit, Mama?" Mama says " Go along, children!" and we four, Joseph and Napoleone and Julie and I, disappear in the direction of the summer-house. But before we get there, Napoleone generally says: " Eugenie, what do you say to a race? Let's see which of us can get first to the hedge!" Then I lift up my skirt and Julie cries " Ready—steady—go!" Then

Napoleone and I set off hot-speed for the hedge. While I run to it with my hair flying and my heart beating wildly and a stitch in my side, Joseph and Julie disappear into the summer-house.

Sometimes Napoleone wins the race, and sometimes I do, but then I know that Napoleone lets me. The hedge is just up to my breast. Generally we lean close together against the foliage; I rest my arms on it and look up at the stars, and then Napoleone and I have long talks. Sometimes we talk about *The Sorrows of Werther*, a novel by an obscure German writer named Goethe, which everybody has at present on the dressing-table. I had to hide the book, because Mama won't let me read love-stories. But I was disappointed with it. It's the story, sad beyond belief, of a young man who shoots himself because the young lady whom he loves marries his best friend.

Napoleone is quite enthusiastic about the book. I asked him whether he could imagine himself committing suicide because he was crossed in love. " No," he replied, laughing, " because a certain young lady whom I love won't be marrying someone else." But then he looked sad and gazed earnestly at me, so I hurriedly changed the subject.

But often we just lean against the hedge and look at the quiet meadow beyond. The less we talk, the nearer together we seem. Then I imagine that we can hear the grass and the wild flowers breathing. Now and then a bird sings somewhere in melancholy tones. The moon hangs in the sky like a yellow lantern, and while I look at the slumbering meadow I think: ' Dear Lord, let this evening last for ever, let me go on for ever leaning against him.' For although I have read that there are no super-natural powers, and the Government in Paris has set up an altar to Human Reason, I always think ' Dear Lord ' when I am very sad or very happy.

Yesterday Napoleone suddenly asked, " Are you never afraid of your destiny, Eugenie?" When we are alone with the sleeping meadow, sometimes he uses the familiar *tu*, although not even betrothed lovers or married people do that nowadays.

" Afraid of my destiny? No," I said, " I am not afraid. We don't know what the future holds in store for us. Why should we be afraid of what we don't know?"

" It is a strange thing that most people declare that they do not know their destiny," he said. His face was very pale in the moonlight, and he was looking into the distance with wide-open eyes. "For myself, I think I do. I know my destiny. My star."

" And are you—afraid of it?" I asked.

He seemed to be reflecting. Then he said quickly, " No. I know I shall do great things. I am the sort of man who will build up States and guide their course. I am one of the men who make world history."

I stared at him, amazed. I had never dreamed that people could think or say such things. Suddenly I began to laugh. At that he shrank back and his face was distorted. He turned quickly to me.

" Are you laughing, Eugenie?" he murmured. " Laughing?"

" Please forgive me," I said. " It was only because I was afraid of your face, it was so white in the moonlight, and—so aloof. When I'm afraid, I always try—to laugh."

" I don't want to give you a shock, Eugenie," he said, tenderly. " I can understand your getting frightened. Frightened —of my great destiny."

We were silent again for a while. Then a thought occurred to me. " Well, I too shall make world history, Napoleone!"

He looked at me in astonishment. But I persisted, trying to express my thought. " World history consists, after all, of the destinies of all people, doesn't it? Not only men who sign death warrants or know just where to place cannon and which way to fire them. I am thinking of other people. I mean those who are beheaded or shot at, and in fact all men and women who live and hope and love and die."

He nodded slowly. " Quite right, my Eugenie. But I shall influence all those millions of destinies of which you speak. Do you believe in me, Eugenie? Do you believe in me, whatever happens?"

His face was quite close to mine, so close that I trembled and involuntarily closed my eyes. Then I felt his lips pressed tightly on mine, until suddenly—I don't know how it happened, it was certainly not what I meant to do—my lips parted.

That night, long after Julie had snuffed out the candle, I could not get to sleep. Then Julie's voice came out of the dark: " Can't you sleep either, little one?"

" No. It's so hot in the room."

" I've something to tell you," Julie whispered. " A very great secret; you mustn't tell anyone. Anyhow, not till to-morrow afternoon. Will you promise?"

" Yes, I promise," I said, wildly excited.

" To-morrow afternoon Monsieur Joseph Buonaparte is coming to talk to Mama."

Was that all? " To Mama? What about?"

"Gracious, aren't you stupid! About us, of course, about him and me. He wants—well, what a child you are! He wants to sue for my hand!"

I sat up in bed. "Julie! That means you are betrothed!"

"Sh! Not so loud! To-morrow afternoon I shall be betrothed. If Mama makes no objection."

I jumped out of bed and ran across to her, but I bumped into a chair and hurt my toes. I cried out.

"Sh, Eugenie! You'll be waking everybody." But I had got to her bed. Quickly I snuggled under the warm eiderdown and excitedly shook her shoulder. I could not think how to show her how glad I was.

"Now you are a bride, a real bride! Has he kissed you already?"

"You can't ask that, child. A young lady does not let herself be kissed until her Mama has agreed to the betrothal."

"Why," I said, "he must have done."

Julie was nearly asleep. "Perhaps," she murmured.

Then I made my head comfortable on Julie's shoulder and went to sleep too.

LATER

I think I'm tipsy. Just a little tipsy, very nice, very pleasant. Julie has become betrothed to Joseph. Mama sent Etienne down to the cellar for champagne. It's champagne that Papa bought years and years ago, to be kept for Julie's betrothal. They are all sitting on the terrace still, discussing where Julie and Joseph shall live. Napoleone has just gone to tell his mother all about it. Mama had invited Madame Letitia Buonaparte and all the children for to-morrow evening. Then we shall get to know Julie's new family. I do hope Madame Letitia will like me; I hope—no, I mustn't write it, or it won't happen! Only pray for it and secretly believe it.

We ought to have champagne often. Champagne tingles on your tongue and tastes sweet, and after the very first glass I couldn't stop laughing. After my third glass Mama said, "Nobody must give the child any more!" Suppose she knew I had already been kissed!

This morning I had to get up very early, and till now I had no chance to be alone. So as soon as Napoleone went away I ran up to my room, and now I am writing in my book. But my thoughts are running about and bumping into each other, each of them, like so many ants, carrying a little load. Ants

42

drag along pine needles, twigs, or grains of sand; my thoughts each carry a little dream of the future. But they keep dropping them, because I have been drinking champagne and can't concentrate.

I don't know why it is, but I had quite forgotten that our Swede, that Monsieur Persson, was going away to-day. Since the Buonapartes have been coming to see us I have not had much time for him. I don't think he likes Joseph and Napoleone. When I asked him what he thought of our new friends, he only said that he found it difficult to catch what they said, because they spoke so quickly, and besides that their accent was different from ours. That showed me that the Corsican accent is too difficult for him.

Yesterday afternoon he told me that he had packed everything and was going by the mail coach to-day. I determined, of course, to see him off, for I really like his equine face, and besides it is fun going to see the mail coach off. You always see different people there, and sometimes ladies in Paris gowns. But then, of course, I forgot Persson and his preparations, because, after all, I had my first kiss to think about.

Luckily I remembered Persson's departure the moment I woke up this morning. I jumped out of bed, put on my shift and my two petticoats, scarcely gave myself time to tidy my hair, and ran down to the dining-room. There I found Persson having his farewell breakfast. Mama and Etienne were hovering round him and doing all they could to make him have a good breakfast.

The poor man has a frightfully long journey ahead of him. First to the Rhine and then through Germany to the Hansa city of Lübeck, and from there by boat to Sweden. I don't know how many times he has to change coaches to get to Lübeck. Marie had given him a picnic-basket with a couple of bottles of wine and a roast chicken and hard-boiled eggs and cherries.

Etienne and I went with Monsieur Persson to the mail coach. Etienne carried one of the travelling-bags and Persson struggled with a big parcel, the other bag, and the picnic-basket. I begged him to let me carry something, and at last he reluctantly gave me the parcel, saying that it contained something very precious: "The most beautiful silk," he confided to me, "that I have ever seen in all my life. It is silk which your poor papa bought and intended for the Queen at Versailles. But events prevented the Queen——"

"Yes, really royal silk," said Etienne. "And in all these years I have never offered that brocade to anyone. Papa always said that it was only suitable for a court dress."

"But the ladies in Paris still go about elegantly dressed," I objected.

"The ladies in Paris are no longer ladies!" Etienne retorted. "Besides, they prefer quite transparent muslins. Do you call *that* elegant? No, heavy brocade is no longer worn in France to-day."

"Well," said Persson to me, "I have ventured to buy the silk. I have been able to save a great part of my salary from Messrs. Clary, and I am glad that I have been able to spend it on this material. It will remind me——" he gulped in his emotion—" it will be a reminder of your dead Papa and of the firm of Clary."

I was surprised at Etienne. He cannot sell this heavy brocade in France. It is certainly very valuable, but at present it is quite out of fashion, so that he cannot sell it, and he has worked it off on Persson. Naturally, for a great deal of money; the firm of Clary has certainly made a good profit out of this deal.

"It was not easy for me to dispose of this material," Etienne said candidly. "But Monsieur Persson's country possesses a royal court, and Her Majesty the Queen of Sweden will need, I hope, a new State robe, and will appoint Monsieur Persson a Purveyor to the Court."

"You must not keep brocade too long, silk goes to pieces," I told Monsieur Persson, as a well-informed daughter of a silk merchant.

"This material will not," Etienne declared. "There are too many gold threads woven in."

The parcel was quite heavy, and I held it in my two arms, pressed against me. Although it was still early, the sun was hot, and my hair was sticking damply to my temples when at last we reached the mail coach. We had come rather late, and so could not spend long in farewells. The other passengers had already taken their seats in the coach. Etienne, with a sigh of relief, lifted in the travelling-bag he had been carrying and set it down on the toes of an elderly lady, and Persson almost dropped the picnic-basket as he shook hands with Etienne. Then he entered into an excited discussion with the postillion, who had placed his luggage on the roof of the coach. Persson told him that he would not let the big parcel go out of his sight and would keep it on his knees all the time. The postillion objected, and in the end the coachman lost patience and shouted: "Take your seats!" The postillion jumped up to the box and sat next to the driver and blew his horn. At last Persson got awkwardly into the coach with his parcel. The coach door was slammed to, but Persson opened it again. "I shall always hold it in honour, Mademoiselle Eugenie," he shouted. Etienne, shrugging his shoulders, asked, "Whatever does that mad Swede mean?"

"The Rights of Man," I replied, surprised at myself, because my eyes were brimming. "The broadsheet on which the Rights of Man are printed." As I said it I thought how pleased Persson's parents would be to see his equine face once more, and I thought that man was passing for ever out of my life.

Etienne went into the shop, and I went with him. I always feel quite at home in the silk shop. I always did feel entirely at home. As a little girl I had often gone there with Papa, and he had always told me where the different rolls of silk came from. I can also distinguish the various qualities, and Papa always said that it was in my blood because I am a true silk merchant's daughter. But I think it is just because I so often watched Papa and Etienne passing a piece of material between their fingers, apparently crumbling it and then looking with their eyes screwed up to see whether it would crush easily, whether it was new or old material, and whether there was any danger of the material soon becoming brittle.

Although it was early in the morning, there were already customers in the shop. Etienne and I greeted them courteously, but I noticed at once that these were not important customers, only citizenesses who wanted muslin for a new fichu or cheap taffeta for a coat. The ladies from the great houses in the environs, who in the past had given big orders to our firm at the opening of the Versailles season, are no longer to be seen. Some of them have been guillotined, many have fled to England, but most have gone 'underground', that is to say they are living under false names in some place in which they are not known. Etienne often says that it is a great disadvantage for all craftsmen that the Republic does not arrange balls or receptions. For that the terribly stingy Robespierre is to blame.

I went to and fro in the shop for a while, helping the customers to feel the various materials and persuading them to buy bright green silk ribbons, because I had the feeling that Etienne wanted to get rid of them. Then I went home, thinking as always of Napoleone, and wondering whether he would put on a gala uniform for our celebration of Julie's betrothal.

When I got home I found Mama very excited. Julie had

confessed to her that Joseph was coming in the afternoon to talk to her. And now she felt unequal to the situation. At last, in spite of the heat, she went into the town to consult Etienne. When she came back, she had a headache, lay on her sofa, and asked to be called as soon as Citizen Joseph Buonaparte had come.

Julie, on the other hand, was behaving as if she was crazy. She was going up and down the drawing-room, groaning. Her face, too, was quite green, and I knew she was ill. Julie always suffers from stomach-ache when she is very excited. In the end I took the restless soul into the garden with me, and we sat in the summer-house. The bees were humming in the rambler roses, and I felt sleepy and very contented. Life is so simple, I thought, when you really love a man. Then you belong only to him. If I were forbidden to marry Napoleone, I should just run away with him.

At five o'clock there arrived a gigantic bouquet, with Joseph hidden behind it. The bouquet and Joseph were taken into the drawing-room by Marie; then Mama was informed, and the door of the drawing-room closed behind the two. I put my ear to the keyhole to try to catch what Joseph and Mama were murmuring. But I could not make out a word.

"A hundred and fifty thousand francs in gold," I said to Julie, who was leaning against the door with me. She shuddered.

"What do you mean?"

"Papa left a hundred and fifty thousand francs in gold for your dowry, and a hundred and fifty thousand for mine. Don't you remember that the lawyer read that when Papa's will was opened?"

"What does that matter?" said Julie peevishly, pulling out her handkerchief and wiping her forehead. Heavens, what a comic picture is a bride-to-be!

"Well, are we to congratulate you?" said someone behind us, laughing. Napoleone! As soon as he had come he leaned against the door with us. "May I, as a future brother-in-law, share the intolerable suspense?"

Julie's patience broke down. "Do what you like, but leave me in peace!" said she, sobbing. At that Napoleone and I went on tiptoe to the sofa and sat down silently. I was fighting against hysterics, the whole situation was so idiotically absurd. Napoleone poked me gently in the side. "A little more dignity, I should like to suggest, Eugenie!" he whispered, pretending to be cross.

Suddenly Mama was standing in the doorway, saying with a shaky voice, " Julie, please come in."

Julie rushed into the drawing-room like mad, the door closed behind her and Mama, and I—threw my arms around Napoleone's neck and laughed and laughed.

" Stop kissing me," I protested, because Napoleone had at once seized his opportunity. But in spite of that I did not let him go—until I thought of the gala uniform. I got a little away from him, and looked reproachfully at him. He had on the same threadbare green uniform as usual, with its shiny back.

" You might have put on your gala uniform, General," I said. But I was sorry at once for saying that. His tanned face grew quite red. " I have none, Eugenie," he confessed. " So far I have never had enough money to buy one for myself, and all we get from the State is a tunic—the field-uniform I am wearing. We have to pay for the gala uniform with our own money, and you know——"

I nodded eagerly. " Of course, you are helping your Mama and the children! And a second uniform would be quite superfluous, wouldn't it?"

" Children, I have a great surprise, a very great surprise for you!" Mama stood in front of us, laughing and crying at the same time. " Julie and Joseph——" Her voice quivered. Then she regained composure. " Eugenie, fetch Suzanne at once! And go and see whether Etienne has come home yet. He promised me that he would be here punctually at half-past five."

I rushed up the stairs and told the two of them.

And then we all drank champagne. It was getting dark in the garden, but Joseph and Julie no longer bothered about the summer-house but just talked about the home they would set up in one of the suburbs. Part of Julie's dowry was to serve for buying a nice villa. Napoleone went away to tell his mother all about it. And I came up to my room to write it all down.

Now my nice little bit of tipsiness is all gone. I am just tired, and a little sad. For now I shall soon be alone in our room, and I shall never be able to use Julie's rouge again and surreptitiously read her novels. But I don't want to be sad, but to think about something cheerful. I must find out what day is Napoleone's birthday. Perhaps the pocket-money I have saved up will be enough for a uniform. But—where do you buy a gala uniform for a General?

Napoleone has been arrested. Since last night I have been living in a nightmare.

Meanwhile the whole town has been wild with joy; there is dancing in front of the Town Hall, and band after band of musicians are marching past. The Mayor has arranged the first ball for two years.

Robespierre and his younger brother were outlawed and arrested by the other Deputies on the ninth of Thermidor, and dragged next morning to the guillotine. Everybody who had been associated with him in any way is now in terror of arrest. So far ninety Jacobins have been executed in Paris. Joseph has already lost his position, which he owed to Napoleone's friendship with Robespierre's brother. Etienne says he will never forgive me for bringing the two Buonapartes into our house.

Mama wants Julie and me to go to the Mayor's ball. It would be my first ball, but I'm not going. I cannot laugh and dance when I don't even know where they have taken Napoleone.

Until the ninth of Thermidor—no, really until the tenth—Julie and I were very happy. Julie was working hard on her trousseau, embroidering hundreds of letter B's on cushion covers, tablecloths, sheets, and handkerchiefs. The wedding is due to take place in about six weeks. Joseph came every evening to see us, and often brought his mother and the children. When Napoleone was not inspecting a fortress somewhere, he would look in at any time of the day, and sometimes his two handsome A.D.C.s, Lieutenant Junot and Captain Marmont, came with him.

But I was not a bit interested in the interminable talk about the political situation, so that I have only now learnt that some two months ago Robespierre decreed that Deputies could be arrested like other people by any member of the Committee of Public Safety. They say that many Deputies are very frightened because they have grown rich on bribes. The Deputies Tallien and Barras are said to have become millionaires.

Suddenly Robespierre had even the beautiful Marquise de Fontenay arrested, the lady whom Deputy Tallien set free some time ago and who since then has been his mistress. Nobody knows why she was arrested; perhaps it was just to annoy Tallien. People Tallien and Barras were afraid of being arrested for taking bribes; at all events, they organised a big conspiracy with a man named Fouché.

At first, this news was simply not believed in Marseilles. But when the newspapers arrived from Paris there was wild excitement. Flags were hung out, the shops were shut, and everybody made a round of visits. The Mayor did not even wait for confirmation, but at once released all the political prisoners. At the same time, the fanatical Jacobins were quietly arrested.

Napoleone and Joseph were terribly agitated when they came to see Etienne; they went into the parlour with him. After they left, Etienne was very bad-tempered: he told Mama that those 'Corsican adventurers' would be getting us all into prison. Napoleone stayed with me for hours in the summer-house, and told me that he would have to change his profession. "You can't expect an officer," he said, "in whom Robespierre took an interest to be retained in the army." I noticed for the first time that he took snuff.

Junot and Marmont came every day to meet Napoleone secretly at our house. They could not believe that he would simply be struck off the army list. But when I tried to comfort him and told him what Marmont and Junot had said, he shrugged his shoulders and just said, "Junot is an idiot. He's a faithful soul, but he's an idiot."

"But you always say he's your best friend!"

"Of course he is—absolutely faithful and devoted; he would go to his death for me. But he hasn't any sense—he's an idiot."

"And Marmont?"

"Marmont is very different. Marmont sticks to me because he is sure that my Italian plans will bring success in the end. Bound to!"

But everything has happened differently from what we expected. Last night, when Napoleone was at supper with us, we heard the approach of men on the march. Napoleone jumped up and rushed to the window; he never sees a squad of soldiers but he must find out what regiment they belong to, where they have come from, where they are going, and what is the sergeant's name.

The tramping stopped in front of our house; we heard shouting, and then the crunching of the gravel in the front garden; finally there came a hammering at the front door.

We all sat as if turned to stone. Napoleone had come away from the window and was looking at the door, with a pale drawn face. He had crossed his arms.

Then the door was flung open, and Marie and a soldier burst into the room together.

"Madame Clary!" Marie began, but the soldier cut her short. "Is General Napoleone Buonaparte in this house?" he shouted.

Napoleone calmly went up to the soldier, who clicked his heels, saluted, and said, "Warrant of arrest against Citizen General Buonaparte!"

He handed a paper to Napoleone. Napoleone held it close to his eyes.

"I'll bring a light," I said, jumping up.

"Thank you, my love," said Napoleone, "I can read the order quite well."

Then he put down the paper, looked hard at the soldier, and went up to him and tapped him on the button below the collar.

"Even on hot summer evenings," he said, "the sergeant's uniform is required to be buttoned up. What stupidity!"

While the soldier fingered his uniform in embarrassment, Napoleone turned to Marie.

"Marie," he said, "my sword is in the ante-room; will you please be so kind as to hand it to the sergeant."

Then, bowing toward Mama, he said, "Please forgive this disturbance, *Citoyenne* Clary!"

Napoleone's spurs clinked as he went out. Behind him tramped the sergeant. We did not move. Again we heard the crunching of the gravel in the garden; then the soldiers marched away. Not till then did Etienne break the silence.

"Let us go on," he said, "there's nothing we can do."

He picked up his spoon.

When we came to the joint he remarked, "What have I told you from the first? He is an adventurer, sponging upon the money of the Republic!"

And when we came to the dessert he added, "Julie, I regret having given my consent to your betrothal to that man."

After supper I slipped away through the back door. Although Mama had had the whole of the Buonaparte family here several times, we had never been invited by Madame Letitia to go there. I had a good idea why that was. The family live in the poorest quarter of the town, just behind the fish market, and Madame Buonaparte may well have been ashamed to let us see her poor refuge. But now I wanted to see her. I must tell her and Joseph what had happened, and talk about how to help Napoleone.

I shall never forget that journey through the dark narrow lanes round the fish market. At first I ran like mad; I felt that

50

I must not lose a moment; I only slowed down when I was coming to the Town Hall square. My hair was all damp, and my heart was thumping painfully.

There was dancing in front of the Town Hall, and a tall man with his shirt-collar open caught me by the shoulder and roared with laughter when I pushed him away. One person after another tried to stop me; sticky fingers touched my arms, and suddenly a girl exclaimed, " Look, there's the little Clary girl!"

It was Eliza Buonaparte, Napoleone's eldest sister. Eliza is only seventeen, but that evening, painted and powdered and with dangling earrings, she looked much older. She was hanging on the arm of a young man whose fashionable high collar hid half of his face.

" Eugenie!" she called after me, " Eugenie, won't you let my partner give you a drink?"

But I ran on, into the narrow unlit lanes leading to the fish market. There I was in the midst of a darkness filled with a giggling and shrieking throng. A hubbub of love-making and quarrelling came out of all the doorways and windows, and courting cats were miauling in the gutter.

I breathed more freely when I reached the fish market; there were a few lights there, and I began to get the better of my timidity. Soon I was ashamed of it, and also of the fine white villa with the lilac trees and rambler roses that was my home. I crossed the fish market, and asked where the Buonapartes lived.

I was directed to the dark entrance of a lane: the house was the third on the left. Joseph had once told me that they had a basement dwelling.

I came to some narrow steps that led down to a basement, stumbled down, reached a door, and found myself in Madame Buonaparte's kitchen.

It was a big room, lit only by a candle in a broken saucer. The smell was dreadful.

Joseph was sitting at the table, in a crumpled shirt, without a neckerchief, reading newspapers by the light of the candle. Opposite him, the nineteen-year-old Lucien was bending over the table, writing. Between the two was a dish with the remains of a meal. At the back, in the dark, clothes were being washed; somebody was scrubbing hard, and water was splashing. The heat was unbearable.

" Joseph!" I said, to attract his attention. He jumped up.

" Has somebody come?" asked Madame Buonaparte, in broken French. The scrubbing stopped, and Napoleone's mother came into the light, wiping her hands on a big apron.

"It's me, Eugenie Clary," I said.

At that Joseph and Lucien started up. "For heaven's sake, what has happened?" Joseph asked.

"They have arrested Napoleone."

For a moment there was deathly silence. Then Madame Buonaparte cried out, drowning Joseph's voice:

"Holy Virgin, Mother of God! I saw it coming, I saw it coming!"

"Terrible," exclaimed Lucien.

They gave me a rickety chair to sit on, and I told them what had happened.

Then Louis came in from another room: he is seventeen and very fat. He listened apathetically.

I was interrupted by loud howls; the door flew open, and little Jerome, Napoleone's ten-year-old brother, burst in; behind him ran twelve-year-old Caroline, shouting at him the most picturesque quayside curses and trying to get something he was cramming into his mouth. Madame Buonaparte gave Jerome a box on the ear, and screamed at Caroline in Italian. She took away Jerome's tit-bit. It proved to be a stick of marzipan; she broke it into two and gave half each to the combatants. Then she shouted:

"Quiet! We have a visitor!"

That drew Caroline's attention to me, and she exclaimed:

"Oh la, la, one of the rich Clarys!"

She came up to the table and sat on Lucien's knee.

'What a dreadful family,' I said to myself, and then I was sorry for saying it. They cannot help being so many or so poor. And they have nothing but their kitchen to live in.

Joseph asked question after question. "Who arrested Napoleone? Were they really soldiers? Not police?"

"No, soldiers," I replied.

"Then he won't be in prison, but under military arrest somewhere," said Joseph.

"What difference does that make?" groaned Madame Buonaparte.

"A tremendous difference," Joseph explained. "The military authorities will not let a General be simply executed; first they will court-martial him."

"You have no idea, Signorina," said Madame Buonaparte, "how dreadful this is for us." She brought a kitchen stool and sat down close to me, and put her damp work-worn hand on my arm. "Napoleone is the only one of us who is earning regularly, and he always worked so hard, and saved every

52

centime and gave me half his pay for the other children. It is dreadful, dreadful."

"Anyhow, now he can't make me go into the army," growled fat Louis. He was quite triumphant.

"Shut your mouth," Lucien shouted.

The fat boy was now seventeen, and he had never done any work. Napoleone wanted to make him a soldier, so that there should be at least be one mouth less for his mother to feed. I cannot imagine how Louis could march with his flat feet, but perhaps Napoleone meant to put him into the cavalry.

"But why," Madame Buonaparte asked, "why have they arrested him?"

"Napoleone knew Robespierre," Joseph murmured. "And he had let his plans be transmitted to the Minister of War by Robespierre."

"Always those politics," Madame Buonaparte complained. "I tell you, Signorina, politics have been the ruin of my family! My children's poor Papa was always mixed up with politics, and he was always losing his clients' cases, and he left us nothing but debts. And what did my sons talk about all day long? About getting acquainted with prominent people, getting to know Robespierre, getting an introduction to Barras—they go on like that all the time. And look at the result!" She banged the table in vexation.

I looked down. "Your son Napoleone, Madame, is a genius," I said.

"Yes—unluckily," she retorted, looking at the flickering candle.

I looked up at her and Joseph. "We must find out where Napoleone is," I said, "and then we must try to help him."

"But we are so poor, and we don't know anybody with influence," Madame Buonaparte moaned.

"The Military Commandant of Marseilles," said Lucien, "must know where Napoleone has been taken." The family look up Lucien as a poet and an unpractical dreamer, but it was from him that the first useful suggestion came.

"Who is the Commandant of Marseilles?" I asked.

"Colonel Lefabre," said Joseph. "And he cannot bear Napoleone. Quite recently Napoleone told the old Colonel what he thought about the fortifications here: they are in shocking disrepair."

"To-morrow," I heard myself saying, "I'll go to see him. Madame Buonaparte, would you get together some under-clothing, and perhaps some food, and do it up into a parcel

53

and send it to me early to-morrow? I'll ask the Colonel to give it to Napoleone. And then——"

"Thank you so much, Signorina," said Madame Buonaparte excitedly, "*tante grazie!*"

At that moment we heard a splash, a shriek and a long howl, and Caroline cried out happily, "Mama, Jerome has fallen into the wash-tub."

As Madame Buonaparte lifted the boy out of the tub and cuffed him, I got up to go. Joseph disappeared to get his coat and see me home. Lucien murmured, "It is very good of you, Mademoiselle Eugenie; we shall never forget it."

I felt rather frightened at the prospect of going to see that Colonel. As I said good-bye to Madame Buonaparte, she told me that she would send Polette to me with the parcel next morning. She started at the name. "Polette!" she said. "Where is she? She went out with Eliza to a friend over the way, and was going to be back in half an hour. And the two girls have been out the whole evening!"

I remembered Eliza's rouged face. No doubt she was enjoying herself with her partner in some tavern. But what about Polette? She is just my age.

Joseph and I went silently through the town. I was thinking of the evening when he first saw me home. Was that really four months ago? That was when it all began. Until then I had been a child, although I thought I was grown up. To-day I know that you are not really grown up till you fall in love.

"They can't possibly guillotine him," said Joseph, as we came to the villa. "The most they will do is to shoot him."

"Joseph!"

So that was what he had been thinking about on our long silent walk. 'He doesn't love him,' I said to myself, 'he actually hates him.'

"But we belong together," he said, "Napoleone and I and the others. We stick together."

"Good night, Joseph!"

"Good night, Eugenie!"

I slipped in without being noticed. Julie was in bed already, but the candle was burning on her bedside table. She had been waiting for me.

"I suppose you were with the Buonapartes!" she said.

"Yes," I replied, as I undressed. "They live in a cellar, and Madame Letitia was washing shirts at that late hour, and Jerome, that dreadful imp, fell into the wash-tub. It looks as if the two girls, Eliza and Polette, go out at night with men. Good night, Julie—sleep well!"

At breakfast Etienne told us that Julie must put off her wedding, as he was not going to have a prisoner's brother as a brother-in-law. It would be a humiliation for the family, and very bad for the firm's reputation.

"I'll never let my wedding be postponed!" said Julie, in tears. Then she locked herself in our room.

Nobody spoke to me about the affair, because nobody but Julie has any idea that I belong to Napoleone. Except Marie; I feel sure she knows everything.

After breakfast Marie came into the dining-room and beckoned to me, and I followed her into the kitchen. Polette was there with the parcel.

"Quick, let's go before anybody sees us," I said to her. Etienne would have had a fit if he had known I was going with a parcel for Napoleone.

I have lived all my life in Marseilles, and Polette only came here a year ago, but she knows her way about much better than I do. She knew exactly where to go to find the Colonel Commandant. She talked all the way. Her hips swayed so that her scanty blue dress swung to and fro. She walked very erect, and thrust out her breast; it is much bigger than mine, though we are of the same age. She kept passing the tip of her tongue over her lips, to keep them damp and shiny. Polette has the same narrow nose as Napoleone; her dark hair is twisted into a thousand little curls and tied up with a blue ribbon; her eyebrows are thinned and picked out with charcoal. I think Polette is lovely, but Mama doesn't like me to be seen with her.

Polette talked all the time about the Marquise de Fontenay, the new Madame Tallien. "The Parisians are all wild about her and call her Notre-Dame de Thermidor; she was brought away in triumph from the prison on the ninth of Thermidor, and Deputy Tallien married her there and then, and just imagine—" Polette opened her eyes wide, breathless with excitement—"just imagine, she is wearing dresses without any petticoat! She goes about in a quite transparent dress, and you can see everything! Everything, I tell you!"

"Where did you hear that?" I asked, but Polette took no notice.

"She has raven-black hair and raven-black eyes, and she lives in a house in Paris called the Thatched Cottage. The walls inside are covered with silk. There she receives all the famous politicians every afternoon, and I have been told that if you want anything from the Government all you need do is to tell her. I have been talking to a gentleman who only arrived yesterday from Paris, and this gentleman——"

" And this gentleman?" I repeated, in suspense.

" I made his acquaintance. The way you do make people's acquaintance, don't you? He was looking at the Town Hall, and I happened to be passing, so we got into conversation. But not a word about it—do you swear you'll say nothing?"

I nodded.

" Good," said Polette. " You swear to it by all the saints in heaven. Napoleone cannot bear my talking to strange gentlemen. He is a regular old maid on that subject. Tell me, do you think your brother Etienne would give me some material for a new dress? Something pink and transparent. That's the Command Office. Shall I come in with you?"

" I think I had better see him alone. Wait for me, won't you? Promise!"

She nodded gravely, and crossed the fingers of her right hand over the thumb. " I'll say a Paternoster. It can't do any harm."

I went in with the parcel. In the Command Office I heard myself asking the orderly to announce me to Colonel Lefabre. My voice sounded hoarse and strange.

The Colonel was sitting at a big desk in a big, bare room. At first, in my agitation, I could not speak a word. The Colonel had a red-faced cube of a head, with a stubbly grey beard, and he wore an old-fashioned perruke. I laid the parcel on the desk, and gulped in desperation. I just could not think what to say.

" What is that parcel, *Citoyenne*? And who exactly are you?"

" Pants, *Citoyen* Colonel Lefabre, and my name is Clary."

His pale blue eyes looked me up and down. " A daughter of the late silk merchant François Clary?"

I nodded.

" I've played cards with your Papa. Very respectable man, your Papa." He kept his eyes on me. " And what am I to do with the pants, *Citoyenne* Clary?"

" The parcel is for General Napoleone Buonaparte. He has been arrested. We don't know where he is. But you, Colonel, will know. I think there's a cake in the parcel. Underclothing and a cake."

"And what has the daughter of François Clary to do with the Jacobin Buonaparte?" the Colonel asked slowly and solemnly.

I flushed up. "His brother Joseph," I said, "is betrothed to my sister Julie."

"But why does not his brother Joseph come here? Or your sister Julie?" His pale blue eyes looked gravely at me. I felt sure he knew everything.

"Joseph is afraid. The families of arrested persons are always afraid," I managed to say. "And Julie now has other troubles. She is crying because Etienne, our big brother, has decided not to allow her to marry Joseph Buonaparte. All," I said with indignation, "all because you have arrested the General, *Citoyen* Colonel!"

"Sit down," was all he said.

I sat on the edge of a divan by his desk. The Colonel took snuff, and looked out of the window. He seemed to have forgotten me. Then suddenly he turned back to me.

"Listen, *Citoyenne*," he said. "Your brother Etienne is quite right. Of course he is. A Buonaparte is no match for a Clary, for a daughter of François Clary. A very respectable man he was, your poor Papa."

I said nothing.

"I don't know this Joseph Buonaparte. He's not in the army, is he? As for the other man, that Napoleone Buonaparte——"

"*General* Napoleone Buonaparte," I said, looking straight at him.

"As for that General, it was not I who arrested him; I only obeyed an order from the Ministry. Buonaparte has Jacobin sympathies, and all officers of his way of thinking—I mean all extremists—have been arrested."

"What will they do to him?"

"I have no information as to that."

The Colonel seemed to consider that the interview was over, so I got up. "The underclothing and the cake," I said, pointing to the parcel. "Could you give them to him?"

"Nonsense! Buonaparte is no longer here. He has been taken to Fort Carré, near Antibes."

I was not prepared for that. They had taken him away, and I could not get to him.

"But he must have a change of underclothing," I insisted.

The Colonel's face swam before my eyes; I wiped away the tears, but others came. "Can't you send the parcel to him, Colonel?"

"Now tell me, little lady, do you imagine that I have nothing to do but look after the underclothing of a scamp who is allowed to call himself General?"

I began to sob. He took snuff again; the scene seemed to upset him a good deal. "Do stop crying," he said.

"No," I sobbed.

He came away from his desk and stood in front of me. "I told you to stop crying," he roared.

"No!" I sobbed again. Then I wiped the tears away and looked at him. He was standing close to me, in obviously sympathetic perplexity. That made me cry again.

"Stop!" he shouted, "stop! Well, as you won't leave me in peace, and as you—very well, I'll send one of my men to Fort Carré with the parcel, and ask the Commandant to give it to that Buonaparte. *Now* are you satisfied?"

I gave him a tearful smile.

I was just going out when it occurred to me that I had not thanked him. I turned round. The Colonel was looking doubtfully at the parcel.

"Thank you very much, Colonel," I whispered.

He looked up, cleared his throat, and said, "Listen, *Citoyenne* Clary. I'll tell you two things, in confidence. To begin with, this Jacobin General won't have his head chopped off. Secondly, a Buonaparte is no match for a daughter of François Clary. Good-bye, *Citoyenne.*"

Polette came back part of the way with me. She poured out a flood of trivial talk. Pink silk she wanted, transparent. Madame Tallien, they said, was wearing flesh-coloured silk stockings. Napoleone would enjoy the cake. It had almonds in it. Did I like almonds? Was Julie really getting such a huge dowry that she could buy a villa for herself and Joseph? When should I be talking to Etienne about the silk, and when would she be able to go to the shop to fetch it?

I hardly listened. What the Colonel had told me was running in my head like a jingle.

'A Buonaparte has no right at all
To wed a daughter of François Clary.'

When I got home I learned that Julie had got her way. Her wedding is not to be put off. I sat with her in the garden and helped her to embroider monograms on serviettes—a prettily curving B.

58

MARSEILLES, end of Fructidor. (Middle of September.)

I don't know how Julie spent her wedding night. Anyhow, the night before was terribly exciting, for me at any rate.

Julie's wedding was to be very quiet, with nobody present but our family and all the Buonapartes. Mama and Marie had been busy, of course, for days, making cakes and fruit creams, and on the night before the wedding Mama nearly broke down, she was so afraid things might go wrong. Mama is always worried before a party, but they have always been a great success.

It was decided that we should all go early to bed, and that Julie should have a bath. We have baths much more often than other people, because Papa had such modern ideas, and Mama makes sure that we go on doing what he wanted. So we have a bath almost every month, in a tremendous wooden wash-tub which Papa had made for the purpose in the laundry cellar. And as it was the night before Julie's wedding, Mama shook some jasmine scent into the bath water, and Julie felt like the late Madame Pompadour herself.

We went to bed, but neither Julie nor I could sleep, and so we talked about Julie's new home. It is outside Marseilles, but no more than half an hour's drive from us.

Suddenly we kept quiet and listened. Under the window somebody was whistling " *Le jour de gloire est arrivé!* "

I sat up. It was the second verse of our Marseilles song. And after it came at once Napoleone's signal. When he came to see us he always gave me that signal when he was still a long way off.

I jumped out of bed, pulled back the curtains, threw the window up, and leant out. It was a very dark night, sultry and oppressive. There was a storm brewing.

I screwed up my lips and whistled. There are very few young ladies who can whistle; I am one, but unluckily people don't approve of the gift, thinking it is ill-bred.

" *Le jour de gloire——* " I whistled.

"*—est arrivé!* " came from below.

A figure that had been standing close to the wall of the house moved out of the darkness and stepped on to the gravel path.

I forgot to shut the window, forgot to put on my slippers, forgot to put something round me, forgot that I had only my nightdress on, forgot what is proper and what isn't proper! I ran like mad down the stairs, opened the front door, and felt the gravel under my bare feet.

Then I could feel somebody's lips on my nose. It was so dark, and in the dark it's no good trying to see where to kiss.

There was thunder in the distance.

He pressed me to himself and whispered:

"Aren't you cold, *carissima?*"

"Only my feet," I replied, "I haven't any slippers on."

At that he lifted me up and carried me to the steps leading up to the front door. There we sat, and he wrapped his cloak round me.

"How long have you been back?" I asked.

"I have not got back yet, I am only on my way," he said. I leaned against him, and felt the roughness of his uniform on my cheek. How happy I was!

"Was it very horrid?" I asked.

"No, not at all. How good of you to take the parcel!" he said, stroking my hair with his lips. "It reached me with a covering note from Colonel Lefabre. He told me he had only sent it for your sake. I demanded to be brought before a court-martial, but I was not allowed that right."

"A court-martial! But that would have been dreadful!"

"Why? I should have been able then to explain to some senior officers what it was really all about. I could have told them of the plans I had left with that ass, Carnot, the Minister of War. They would at least have taken notice of that. Instead of that——" He moved away a little, and rested his head on his hands. "Instead of that, my plans are gathering dust in some pigeon-hole. And Carnot rests content with a precarious defence of our frontiers!"

"What are you going to do now?"

"They have set me free, because there is nothing against me. But those gentlemen at the Ministry don't like me. They will send me to the dullest sector of the front, and——"

"It's raining," I said, interrupting him. Big drops were falling on my face.

"No matter," he said, surprised at my mentioning it, and he told me of the horrid things they do to a General they want to be rid of. I drew in my legs and wrapped the cloak closer round me. It thundered, and a horse neighed.

"My horse, I tied it up to your garden fence," he said.

It began to rain more heavily. There was a flash and a clap

of thunder alarmingly close, and the horse neighed desperately. Napoleone shouted something to it.

A window opened about us. "Who's there?" Etienne shouted.

"Come into the house," I whispered to Napoleone, "we shall be soaked."

"Who's that?" roared Etienne.

Then we heard Suzanne's voice:

"Shut the window, Etienne, and come over to me, I'm frightened!"

"There's somebody in the garden," Etienne replied, "I must go down and see what he's up to."

Napoleone went under the window. "Monsieur Clary, it is I, Napoleone."

There came another flash. I saw for a moment his thin slight figure in his scanty uniform. Then it was pitch dark again, there was a crash of thunder, and the horse tugged at the reins. Now it poured in torrents.

"Who is that?" Etienne shouted into the rain.

"General Buonaparte," Napoleone shouted back.

"But you are in prison!" Etienne retorted stupidly.

"I have been set free," Napoleone explained.

"But what are you doing here, General, at this hour?"

I jumped up, caught up the cloak, which came down to my ankles, and joined Napoleone.

"Don't stop here, it will be the death of you," Napoleone whispered.

"Who are you talking to?" Etienne shouted. The rain had abated, and now I could tell how his voice was shaking with fury.

"He's talking to me!" I called back. "Etienne, it's me, Eugenie!"

The rain had stopped. A very pale moon came out timidly between the clouds, and showed us Etienne in his nightcap.

A hiss came from the nightcap: "General, you owe me an explanation!"

Napoleone shouted up to him. He had put his arm round my shoulder. "I have the honour," he said, "Monsieur Clary, to request the hand of your younger sister."

"Eugenie, come in at once!" Etienne ordered. Behind him we could see Suzanne's head. It looked rather funny in its countless curlers.

"Good night, *carissima*," said Napoleone, kissing me on my cheek, "until to-morrow's wedding breakfast." His spurs rattled as he went along the gravel path. I slipped indoors, forgetting to give him back his cloak.

Etienne was standing at his bedroom door in his nightshirt, holding a candle. I slipped past him barefooted and wearing Napoleone's cloak.

"What would Papa have said!" Etienne growled.

Julie was sitting up in bed. "I heard it all," she told me.

"I shall have to wash my feet, they are all gritty," I said, taking the jug and pouring it into the basin. When I had finished I got back into bed, spreading the army cloak over the counterpane. "It's his cloak," I said to Julie. "I shall have such lovely dreams under it."

"*Madame la Générale* Buonaparte," murmured Julie thoughtfully.

"If I'm lucky, he will be thrown out of the army," I said.

"Gracious! that would be awful!"

"Do you think I want a husband spending all his life at the front? No, let them dismiss him! Etienne can make use of him in the firm."

"You'll never get Etienne to do that!" said Julie, snuffing out the candle.

"I suppose you're right," I said. "What a pity! But Napoleone is not likely to take any interest in the silk trade. Good night, Julie."

Julie was almost late at the registrar's office. We could not find her new gloves anywhere, and Mama declared that you can't get married without gloves.

When Mama was young everybody was married in church, but since the Revolution people have had to go for the ceremony to the registry, and very few couples trouble to go on to a church or find one of the few priests who have sworn allegiance to the Republic. Julie and Joseph, of course, had no intention of bothering about that. Mama has been talking for days about the bridal veil she had; she would so have liked Julie to wear it. She told us, too, about the organ music you heard at a proper wedding when she was young.

Julie has put on a pink dress with real Brussels lace and red roses, and Etienne got a Paris business friend to hunt for some pink gloves for her and send them to him. Now we couldn't find those gloves anywhere. The wedding was to be at ten o'clock, and it was not till five minutes to ten that I found the gloves under Julie's bed. Julie rushed off with them, followed by Mama and the two witnesses.

Julie's witnesses are Etienne and Uncle Somis. Uncle Somis is one of Mama's brothers, and he comes to all the funerals and weddings. They found Joseph and his witnesses, Napoleone and Lucien, waiting at the registrar's office.

I simply had not had time to get dressed, as I had had all the hunt for the gloves. I stood at our window and called out " Good luck!" to Julie, but she didn't hear. The carriage was covered with white roses from the garden, rather faded; it did not look at all like an ordinary hackney coach.

I had given Etienne no peace till he brought me home some sky-blue satin from the shop for a new dress. Then I insisted that Mademoiselle Lisette, our dressmaker, should not cut the skirt too full. But I'm sorry to say it's not as close-fitting as in the Paris fashion-plates, and I'm laced round the waist and not close up under the breast like Madame Tallien in the pictures showing her as 'Madame de Thermidor', the goddess of the Revolution. Still, I think my new dress is wonderful, and I feel like the Queen of Sheba, when she was tricked out for King Solomon. After all, I am a fiancée too, though Etienne seems to look upon that as nothing but a troublesome midnight rumpus.

They arrived before I was really ready, I mean the guests. Madame Letitia was in dark green; her hair was simply combed back, and bunched on her neck like a countrywoman; there is not a single white hair to be seen in it.

Eliza had thick paint on her face, and looked as garish as a tin soldier; she was wearing all the ribbons she had been able to wheedle out of Etienne in the last few weeks. Polette looked very pretty in a dainty little pink muslin dress. (Heaven only knows how she got Etienne to give her that material, the most modern there is!) Louis had untidy hair and obviously felt like a fish out of water. Caroline had had her face washed, and her hair was actually in order. That dreadful child Jerome began asking for something to eat the moment he arrived. Suzanne and I gave liqueurs to those over fourteen.

Madame Letitia said she had a surprise for us all. " A wedding present for Julie?" asked Suzanne, for Madame Letitia had not given Julie anything. She is dreadfully poor, but she might at least, I thought, have made something by hand.

Madame Letitia shook her head, smiled mysteriously, and said, "Oh no!" We wondered what she could have brought. Then it came out: yet another of the Buonapartes! He was her step-brother, an uncle named Fesch, only thirty years old, an ex-priest. But there is nothing of the martyr about this uncle

Fesch, and so in these anti-clerical days he has retired from religion and gone into business.

"Is he doing well?" I asked. Madame Letitia shook her head. She hoped Etienne might persuade him to enter the firm of Clary.

Uncle Fesch came in a few minutes; he had a round jolly face, and was wearing a clean but shabby coat; he kissed Suzanne's hand and mine, and praised our liqueur.

Then they all came in from the registry. The first to appear was the carriage with the faded white roses, and Julie and Joseph and Mama and Napoleone got out. In the second carriage were Etienne, Lucien, and Uncle Somis. Julie and Joseph ran up to us; Joseph threw his arms round his mother's neck. The rest of the Buonapartes crowded round Julie; then Uncle Fesch put his arm round Mama, who had no idea who he was. Our Uncle Somis gave me a resounding kiss on my cheek and then patted Eliza. Then all the Clarys and all the Buonapartes formed such an excited cluster that Napoleone and I had a chance of a good long kiss—till somebody next to us coughed in disgust. Etienne, of course!

At the breakfast the bride and bridegroom sat between Uncle Somis and Napoleone, while I found myself squeezed in between Uncle Fesch and Lucien. Julie's cheeks were flaming with excitement and her eyes were sparkling, and for the first time in her life she looked really pretty.

Immediately after the soup, Uncle Fesch tapped his glass, because as a former priest he felt he really must make a speech. He spoke for a long time, very solemnly and very tediously, and as he considered it politically inadvisable to mention God he gave praise to 'Providence'. We owed to Providence, he said, this great happiness and this good meal and this harmonious gathering; we owed them all entirely to the great and beneficent rule of Providence.

Joseph winked at me and then smiled at Julie; Napoleone began to laugh. Mama's eyes were brimming more and more the longer Uncle Fesch preached; she turned them on me, full of emotion. Etienne, too, looked at me, but wrathfully, because the Providence that had brought Joseph and Julie together, and had so intimately united the Clary and Buonaparte families, was, without any question—I, Eugenie.

After the toast, Etienne made a speech; it was brief and bad. After that we left Julie and Joseph in peace.

We had just come to Marie's wonderful marzipan cakes with

64

crystallised fruits on them, when Napoleone jumped up. Instead of politely tapping his glass, he thundered:

" Attention for a moment! "

We all sat up, coming to attention like startled recruits, and Napoleone told us, in short little sentences, how happy he felt to be able to take part in that family celebration. But he owed that good fortune not to Providence, but to the Ministry of War in Paris, which had suddenly, without any explanation, released him from arrest. Then he paused, and looked at me, and I knew what was coming—and I was very worried about what Etienne might do.

" So I will take this opportunity," he resumed, "when the Clarys and the Buonapartes are joined together in a family celebration, to tell you all that——"

His voice had dropped, but we were all so quiet that it was easy to tell that it was shaking with emotion.

"—that last night I sued for the hand of Mademoiselle Eugenie, and that Eugenie agreed to become my wife."

There came a storm of congratulations from the Buonapartes, and I found myself being hugged by Madame Letitia. But I looked across at Mama. Mama seemed to have had a shock; she was not at all glad. She looked away and turned to Etienne, and Etienne shrugged his shoulders.

At that moment Napoleone went up to Etienne, holding his glass, and smiled at him. It is wonderful what power Napoleone has over people; for Etienne's thin lips parted, and he grinned and clinked glasses with Napoleone.

Polette hugged me and called me ' sister '. Monsieur Fesch shouted something in Italian to Madame Letitia, and she replied happily " *Ecco!* " I think he had asked her whether I was to have as big a dowry as Julie.

Amid all the excitement and emotion nobody had been watching Jerome, and the imp had been able to stuff into his mouth whatever he could find room for. Suddenly I heard Madame Letitia cry out, and she dragged away a green-faced Jerome. I took the two on to the terrace, and there Jerome surrendered all his ill-gotten gains. He felt better then, but it was quite impossible for us to take coffee on the terrace as we had intended.

Soon Julie and Joseph said good-bye to us all, and got into their decorated carriage to drive to their new home. We all went with them to the garden gate, and I put my arm round Mama's shoulder.

" Don't cry, dear Mama," I said.

Then came more liqueur and cakes, and Etienne gently told Uncle Fesch that he could not take another assistant into the firm, as he had already promised to take in Joseph and probably Lucien. Finally all the Buonapartes left, except Napoleone.

We walked round the garden, and Uncle Somis, whom we only see at weddings and funerals, asked me when I was going to be married. At that Mama turned to Napoleone, with tears in her eyes.

" General Buonaparte, will you promise me one thing?" she said. " Will you put off the wedding till Eugenie is sixteen? Will you?"

" Madame Clary," Napoleone replied, smiling, " that is not for me to say, but for you yourself, and Monsieur Etienne and Mademoiselle Eugenie."

But Mama shook her head. " I don't know how it is, General Buonaparte," she said, " you are so young, and yet I have the feeling——"

She broke off and looked at him with a wry smile. " I have the feeling," she resumed, " that people always do what you want. They do at all events in your family, and, since we have known you, in my family as well. So I turn to you. Eugenie is still so young; do please wait till she is sixteen!"

In reply to that, Napoleone silently lifted Mama's hand to his lips. And I knew that that was a promise.

On the very next day Napoleone received orders to proceed at once to the Vendée to take up the command of an infantry brigade under General Hoche. I sat on the grass in the warm September sunshine and watched him tramping to and fro, pouring out his indignation at that shabby treatment. The Vendée! To hunt Royalists hiding there! A few starving aristocrats with their fanatically loyal peasants!

" I'm an artillery specialist, not a gendarme!" he exclaimed. Up and down he went, with his hands behind him. " They deny me the triumph of a court-martial, and now they propose to bury me in the Vendée, like a Colonel on the eve of retirement! They are keeping me away from the front, to commit me to oblivion!"

When he was full of wrath there was a yellow gleam in his eyes.

" You could resign," I said softly. " I could buy a little house in the country with the money Papa left for my dowry, and perhaps some land with it. If we manage carefully and——"

He stood still and looked at me.

"But if you do not care for that," I continued, "you might perhaps join Etienne."

"Eugenie! Are you mad? Or do you seriously think I could settle in a farmhouse and keep fowls? Or sell ribbons in your brother's shop?"

"I did not want to hurt you, I was only thinking what we could do."

He laughed heartily. "What we could do! What the best General of Artillery in France could do! Don't you know that I am France's best General?"

Then he began walking silently up and down. In a few moments he said:

"I'm riding away to-morrow."

"To the Vendée?"

"No, to Paris. I'm going to talk to the people at the Ministry."

"But isn't that—I mean, in the army don't you have to do exactly what is ordered?"

"Yes, yes indeed. If one of my soldiers disobeys an order, I have him shot. They may have me shot when I get to Paris—I shall take Junot and Marmont with me."

Junot and Marmont, his A.D.C.s since Toulon, are still in Marseilles, without employment. They regard his future as their own.

"Can you lend me any money?"

I nodded.

"Junot and Marmont cannot pay for their lodgings. Like me, since my arrest they have received no pay. I must settle their bill at the inn. How much can you lend me?"

I had been saving up for a gala uniform for him. There were ninety-eight francs lying under the nightdresses in my chest-of-drawers.

"Give me all you can," he said, and I ran up to my room and collected the money.

He put the notes in his pocket. Then he pulled them out again and carefully counted them.

"So I owe you," he said, "ninety-eight francs."

Then he put his arms round my shoulders and embraced me. "You will see that I shall persuade all Paris: they must give me the Command-in-Chief in Italy. They have got to!"

"When will you be starting?"

"As soon as I have paid my A.D.C.s' bill. Don't forget to write to me often; at the Ministry of War in Paris; the letters will be posted on to me at the front. Don't fret."

"I shall have lots to do. I have all the monograms to embroider on my trousseau."

He nodded eagerly. "B, B, B, *Madame la Générale* Buonaparte."

Then he untied his horse, which, to Etienne's annoyance, he had tied again to our garden fence, and rode away into the town. The slim horseman in the quiet road between the villas looked unimposing and very solitary.

PARIS, twelve months later: Fructidor, Year III. (I've run away from home!)

There's nothing more disagreeable than running away from home. I haven't seen a bed for two nights now, and my back aches because I've been sitting in the mail coach for four days without interruption. I feel sure I'm black and blue all over; stage coaches are so horribly badly sprung. And I haven't any money for the return journey either. But I don't need that. After all, I've run away from home and I've no intention of going back.

It's only two hours since I reached Paris. It was getting late, and in the dusk the houses all looked the same, grey houses with no front gardens, houses, houses, nothing but houses. I had no idea that Paris was so big.

I was the only one in the coach who had never been to Paris before. That wheezing M. Blanc who got into the coach two days ago, going to Paris on business, took me to a hackney coach, and I showed the driver the slip of paper on which I had written Marie's sister's address. All the money I had left went on the fare, and then the driver was rude because I couldn't give him a tip.

The address proved right, and, thank God, Marie's relatives, Clapain by name, were at home. They live in the outbuildings of a house in the Rue du Bac. The Rue du Bac can't be far from the Tuileries; we drove past the Palace and I recognised it from the pictures. I kept pinching myself to make sure I wasn't dreaming but was really in Paris and had really run away from home.

Marie's sister, Madame Clapain, was very kind to me. At first she was quite overcome at seeing the daughter of Marie's mistress. But then I told her I had come in secret, to settle some business, and I had no money; Marie had said that perhaps—

At that Marie's sister stopped being overcome and said I could stay with her. Was I hungry? And how long did I want to stay?

I said I was very hungry, and gave her my bread ration card because, on account of the bad harvest, bread is strictly rationed and food of any sort is dreadfully dear. As for how long I was going to stay I had no idea, perhaps a day or two, perhaps—

She gave me something to eat, and then Monsieur Clapain came home. He told me that their rooms were part of the outbuildings of a former aristocratic mansion. The mansion had been confiscated by the Government, but because of the housing shortage the municipality had divided the outbuildings up into small dwellings and let them to big families.

The Clapains are an enormously big family. Three small children were crawling about the floor, and two more came running in for something to eat. The kitchen where we had our meal was so full of babies' nappies hanging up to dry that it was like being in a tent.

Immediately after the meal Madame Clapain said she was going for a walk with her husband. She could hardly ever do that, she said, because of the children. But now I was there she could put the children to bed and go out for a bit. When the children were all in bed, Madame Clapain put on a little hat with an ostrich feather rather the worse for wear, Monsieur Clapain scattered a whole little bag of powder over his almost bald head, and off they went.

All of a sudden I felt dreadfully alone in this huge town and so I rummaged in my travelling-bag, just for the company of my familiar possessions. At the last moment I had put in the diary, and now I took it out and turned the pages over, and read how everything had happened. After that I set to work, with a splayed quill which I found on the kitchen cupboard next to a dust-covered inkbottle, on this account of my running away from home.

It is a whole year since my last entry. But then, so very little happens to a grass widow—or rather to a grass fiancée, with her husband-to-be away in Paris. Etienne found me some cambric for handkerchiefs and nightdresses, damask for table-cloths, and linen for bedclothes, and took the cost out of my dowry. I stitched innumerable finely curved B's, pricking my fingers times without number, and sometimes I visited Madame Letitia in her cellar dwelling, and sometimes Julie and Joseph in their charming little villa. But Madame Letitia could only talk about the way everything got dearer and dearer and how Napoleone hadn't sent her any money for ages. And Julie and Joseph never did anything but look deep into each other's eyes, and say things I could never understand, and giggle—evidently very happy but a bit idiotic. All the same, I went there quite often because Julie always wanted to know what Napoleone had written to me and gave me Napoleone's letters to Joseph to read.

Unfortunately, Napoleone didn't seem to be doing at all well in Paris. A year ago he arrived there with his two A.D.C.s and Louis—he had taken that fat youngster with him at the last moment to help Madame Letitia. And of course there had been a tremendous fuss at the War Ministry because he hadn't gone to the Vendée as he had been ordered to. He just talked about his Italian projects until, simply to get rid of him, the Ministry sent him to the Italian front, but only as an Inspector, not as Commander-in-Chief. To the Italian front he went, only to be cold-shouldered by most of the Generals or told not to interfere. At last he fell ill with malaria and returned to Paris. When he turned up again at the Ministry, the War Minister raged at him and showed him the door. After that Napoleone was on half pay for some months and then he was simply dismissed from the Service without a pension.

A dreadful situation! We just couldn't imagine what he was living on. He pawned his father's watch, but that couldn't have lasted him longer than three days. He couldn't keep Louis any more, and forced him to enter the army. At times Napoleone did some casual work in the War Ministry, drawing maps and damaging his eyesight. His torn trousers were a great worry to him and he tried to patch them up himself, but the seams kept on bursting. He applied for a new uniform, but the Government would not allot one to a dismissed General. In despair he went where everyone goes nowadays who wants something: to the 'Chaumière', the 'thatched cottage' of the beautiful Madame Tallien.

At the moment we have a Government called the Directory, nominally a council of five Directors. But Joseph maintains that only one of our Directors really counts—Director Barras.

Whatever happens in the country, Barras comes to the top. (Like filth floating in the harbour, I sometimes feel. But perhaps one shouldn't talk like that about the Head of the Nation, or at any rate one of our five Heads.) This man Barras is an aristocrat by birth, but he managed to turn Jacobin in good time, and so he has been none the worse. Then, together with Tallien and a Deputy called Fouché, he overthrew Robespierre and saved the Republic from the 'tyrant'. And after that he moved into an official residence at the Luxembourg Palace and became one of our five Directors. A Director has to see all the important people, and as he isn't married Barras has asked Madame Tallien to throw open her house every afternoon to his guests, or, which comes to the same thing, to those of the French Republic.

A business friend of Etienne's told us that at Madame Tallien's champagne flows very freely indeed, and that her salon is always full of men who have grown rich through the war, and of speculators who buy up cheaply all the aristocratic mansions which the State has confiscated and then sell them at a huge profit to the *nouveaux riches*. There are also many entertaining ladies there, friends of Madame Tallien's, said this man, but by far the most beautiful women are Madame Tallien herself and Josephine de Beauharnais.

Madame de Beauharnais is Barras' mistress, and she wears a narrow red ribbon round her neck to show that she is related to a 'victim of the guillotine'. That is no longer a disgrace but a high distinction. This Josephine is the widow of the General de Beauharnais who was beheaded, and that means that she is a former countess.

Mama asked Etienne's friend whether there were any decent women left in Paris at all, and he answered:

"Oh yes. But they are very expensive!"

He laughed, and Mama sent me to the kitchen for a glass of water.

One afternoon Napoleone called at Madame Tallien's and introduced himself to Madame Tallien and Madame de Beauharnais. They both thought it dreadful that the War Minister would not give him a new command or even a new pair of trousers, and they both promised to get him the new trousers at all events. But first he would have to change his name a bit. Napoleone sat down at once and wrote to Joseph.

"By the way, I have decided to change my name and I advise you to do likewise. No one in Paris can even pronounce Buonaparte, and from now on I am calling myself Bonaparte. And of course Napoleon instead of Napoleone! Please address my letters accordingly and tell the family of my decision. After all, we are French citizens, and I want my name to go down as a French name in the Book of History."

So he was no longer Buonaparte but Bonaparte. His trousers

were still torn, his father's watch was pawned, but he still thinks of making history.

Joseph, like the ape he is, must needs change to Bonaparte as well, and so did Lucien, who got a post in St. Maximin in charge of a military depot and has begun to write political articles. Joseph sometimes goes off as a commercial traveller for Etienne and brings home some good orders, which, Etienne said, should put some fat commission into Joseph's pocket. But Joseph doesn't like being called a traveller in silk goods.

During the last few months Napoleon's letters to me have become rare, though Joseph gets one twice a week. Yet at long last I have been able to send him the portrait he wanted. It is a dreadfully bad painting, I must say. It gives me a snub nose, and I don't believe for a moment that mine is really like that. But I had had to pay the painter in advance, and so I took the painting and sent it to Paris.

He didn't even thank me. His letters have become quite empty now. They still begin with *Mia Carissima* and end with a hug. But as to our wedding date, not a word! Not a word about my being almost sixteen! Meanwhile he writes pages and pages to Joseph about the fine ladies in Madame Tallien's salon. ' I have come to realise,' he wrote in one letter, ' the important part that really distinguished women play in a man's life, women of experience, women of understanding, women of the great world.' . . . Oh, how that hurt me!

A week ago Julie decided to join Joseph on a long business tour. Mama cried a lot because one of her children was going away on a real journey, so Etienne sent her to stay for a month with Uncle Somis, to give her a change. Mama packed seven travelling-bags, and I took her to the stage coach for her four hours' journey to Uncle Somis' place. At the same time Suzanne found she felt rather ' run down ', and badgered Etienne into taking her to a spa. Thus it came about that Marie and I were left alone in the house.

One afternoon I was sitting with Marie in the summer-house: that was the afternoon of decision. It was one of those autumn days when the roses are all gone and the leaves are etched sharply against the pale blue sky, and you feel that something is fading away, dying. Perhaps that is why not only silhouettes are so sharp and clear but thoughts are too: anyhow, as I was stitching another ' B ' on a napkin I suddenly dropped it and said :

" I must go to Paris. I know it's mad and the family would never hear of it. But I must go."

"If you must, then go," said Marie, who was shelling peas. She didn't even look up.

Without taking it in, my eyes followed a green and golden insect crawling over the table.

"What could be simpler?" I said. "We're alone in the house. I could take the mail coach to Paris to-morrow morning."

"You've got enough money, anyhow," said Marie, and exploded a thick pod of peas with her thumb. The little crack of the explosion did not disturb the insect on its way across the table.

"Well, it'll probably be enough for the journey if I stay only two nights at a hotel. The two other nights I might be able to spend in the parlours of the coaching inns. They might even have a bench or a sofa."

Marie looked up at me for the first time.

"I thought you had more money than that," she said, "under your nightgowns in the chest."

I shook my head. "No, I—I lent most of it to someone."

"And where are you going to stay in Paris?"

The insect had reached the edge of the table. I turned it round carefully and watched it crawling back the way it had come.

"In Paris?" I pondered. "I really hadn't thought of that. It depends, doesn't it?"

"You have both promised your mother to wait for the wedding till you are sixteen. And in spite of that you want to go to Paris now?"

"Marie," I blurted out, "if I can't go now, it may be too late and there may be no wedding at all!"

For the first time I had said right out what until then I had hardly dared to think.

Marie went on bursting pea pods. Then she asked:

"What's her name?"

I shrugged my shoulders. "I don't know, really. Perhaps it's Madame Tallien, perhaps it's the other one, Barras' mistress, Josephine, who used to be a countess. I really couldn't say. But, Marie, you mustn't think any the worse of him for that. You see, he hasn't seen me for ages. But—let him set eyes on me again!"

"Yes," said Marie, "you're right. You've got to go to Paris. Long ago my Pierre joined up and he never came back to me. And there I was with Little Pierre and no money at all, and so I had to go to the Clary family as a wet nurse. I wrote

73

to Pierre and told him everything, and he didn't even bother to answer. Yes, I should have tried to go and see him."

I knew all about Marie's sad story, she has told it to me so often.

"He was too far away," I said, "you couldn't have got to him."

The green and golden insect had reached another edge of the table.

"You go to Paris," said Marie. "You could spend the first few nights with my sister, and then we'll see."

"Yes, we'll see," I said, and getting up I put the insect down on the lawn. "I'm going to town now to ask about the mail coach to-morrow morning."

The family had taken all the good travelling-bags and I only found an old and very shabby one. I packed it in the evening, and did not forget to put in the blue silk gown which I had been given for Julie's wedding. It is my most beautiful frock. I'll put it on, I thought, when I am going to call on Madame Tallien to see him again.

The next morning Marie went with me to the coach. I passed along the familiar road to town as in a dream, a very beautiful dream in which I knew I was doing the right and only possible thing.

At the last moment Marie gave me a big medallion made of gold. "I have no money," she murmured, "I need my wages for Little Pierre. Take the medallion, it's real gold. It's from your mother, the day I weaned you. You can easily sell it, Eugenie."

"Sell it? Whatever for?"

"For the return journey," Marie said, and turned away quickly.

And so, for one, two, three, four endless days my bones were shaken in that wretched coach, along a never-ending dusty road, past fields and woods, through villages and towns. Every three hours there came a sudden jolt that threw me against the bony shoulder of the lady in mourning on my right. The jolt meant a change of horses. Then on and on again. And all the time I was thinking of how I would go to Madame Tallien's and ask for General Bonaparte. And then I would say, 'Napoleon, I know you haven't the money to come to me, so I've come to you, because we belong together!'

This strange kitchen, Marie's sister's, is full of unfamiliar shadows. I haven't seen the furniture by daylight, that's why.

74

Will he be glad? Of course he will! He'll take my arm and introduce me to his fine new friends, and then we'll go away to be alone, walking about since we have no money to sit in a coffee-house. And perhaps he may know someone where he can put me up till we've had Mama's consent to the wedding. And then we'll get married, and then—

Ah, they are coming home, Monsieur and Madame Clapain. Let's hope they have a reasonably good sofa on which I can stretch myself, and to-morrow—to-morrow, to-morrow, how I am looking forward to to-morrow!

PARIS, twenty-four hours—no, an eternity later!

It's night-time, and I'm sitting once again in Madame Clapain's kitchen. Once again? Perhaps it isn't ' again ', perhaps it's just ' still ', and I haven't been away at all from this house and the whole of this day was nothing but a bad dream and perhaps I may yet wake up. But did not the waters of the Seine close over my head? It was so near, I remember, the lights of Paris danced a minuet on the waves and in their dancing seemed to beckon me on, and I did bend over the cold stone side of the bridge and maybe I did die and float down the river, floating, floating and no longer feeling any more. Oh, if only I could die!

But no, I'm sitting at an unsteady kitchen table and my thoughts go round and round. Every word and every face comes back to me now whilst outside the rain beats against the windows.

It has been raining all day long. Before I had reached Madame Tallien's house I was soaked through already. I had put on the beautiful blue silk gown. But walking through the Gardens of the Tuileries and then on along the Rue Honoré I discovered that by Parisian standards it was quite old-fashioned. Here the women wear dresses that look like shirts and are held together under the bosom by a silk ribbon. They don't wear fichus either although it's autumn now, and they only drape a flimsy scarf around their shoulders. My tight sleeves, which come down to the elbows and have laced edges, look quite impossible. Apparently one no longer wears sleeves, only shoulder-clasps. I felt ashamed because I looked like a real provincial.

It was not difficult to find the ' Chaumière ' in the Rue des Veuves. Madame Clapain had told me exactly how to get there, and although in spite of my impatience I kept stopping and looking into the shop windows of the Rue Honoré I reached my goal within half an hour. To look at it from outside the house gives a rather modest impression. It's hardly bigger than our villa at home, built in rural style and thatched. But through the windows you can see the sweep of brocade curtains.

It was early yet in the afternoon, but I wanted to have my surprise ready in good time and to be waiting in one of the reception rooms by the time Napoleon would arrive. I knew that Napoleon went there almost every afternoon, so that this was the best place to meet him. And I also knew that anybody could enter here where Madame de Thermidor keeps open house, because he wrote so to Joseph.

Outside the house a lot of people were hanging about who stared with critical eyes at everybody approaching the ' Chaumière'. I looked neither left nor right but went straight to the gate, opened it, entered and ran right into the arms of a lackey. He wore a red silver-buttoned livery and looked exactly like any of the lackeys in the pre-Revolutionary aristocratic houses. It was new to me that the dignitaries of the Republic were allowed lackeys in livery. Which reminds me, by the way, that Deputy Tallien himself used to be a servant.

This fine flunkey then looked me up and down and asked in an arrogantly nasal voice:

" What do you want, citizeness?"

This question was the last thing I had expected, and so I only managed to stammer:

" I should like to—to go inside! "

" I can see that," said the lackey. " Have you an invitation?"

I shook my head. " I . . . I thought that—well, that anybody might come in here."

" You did, did you?" the fellow grinned, his eyes becoming more and more insolent. " The Rue Honoré and the Arcades of the Palais Royal are good enough for the likes of you, dearie! "

I felt myself turning puce in the face. " What—whom do you think you are talking to, citizen?" I managed to bring out, nearly overcome with shame. " I've got to get inside because I've got to see someone in there."

But he simply opened the gate and pushed me out. " Order from Madame Tallien: ladies not allowed in except when accompanied by gentlemen. Or perhaps you claim to be a personal friend of Madame's?" he added in his most contemptuous voice, pushing me out on to the street and banging the gate.

And there I was, among the curious mob on the pavement. Meanwhile the gate opened and closed all the time; but some girls had forced themselves in front of me so that I couldn't see who the guests of Madame were.

"It's a new arrangement," said a girl with a thickly rouged face to me, and winked. "Only a month ago we were all allowed in without the slightest difficulty. But then some foreign paper wrote that Madame Tallien's house was no better than a brothel. . . ." She bleated rather than laughed and her mouth showed more gaps than teeth between purple-painted lips.

"It's all the same to her, but Barras said that one had to keep up appearances," said another one from whom I shrank back in horror because of the awful pus-filled sores in her chalk-white powdered face. "You are a new one, aren't you?" she asked me, looking pitifully at my old-fashioned dress.

"Barras! Don't talk about Barras!" Purple Lips bleated once more. "Two years ago he had to be satisfied with Lucille at twenty-five francs a night. To-day he can afford the Beauharnais! That old she-goat! Rosalie, who got in there" —her pointed chin jerked towards the house—"the day before yesterday with her new friend, wealthy Ouvrard, told me that that Beauharnais woman is having an affair now with a real youngster, an officer who knows how to press her hand and look deep into her eyes. . . ."

"Fancy Barras standing for that!" marvelled Pustule Face.

"Barras? Why, he doesn't mind, he even wants her to sleep with the officers! All he cares for is to be on good terms with the Army people because some day he may have to depend on them. Besides, he's probably sick of her already. Josephine, always in white, and nothing but white. That old bitch with grown-up children. . . ."

A young man intervened here: "Her children are twelve and fourteen years of age. Not much grown-upness there. By the way, Theresa spoke in the Assembly to-day."

"You don't say, citizen!" The two girls at once turned their whole attention on the young man. But he bent over to me and asked:

"You're not from Paris, citizeness? But you probably read in the papers that lovely Theresa is the first woman ever to have addressed the National Assembly. To-day she talked about the necessary reforms in the education of young girls. Are you interested in all that, citizeness?"

He smelled abominably of wine and cheese and I withdrew a bit from him.

"It's raining, let's go into a coffee-house," said Purple Lips, looking encouragingly at the young man with the abominable smell. But he stuck to me.

"It's raining, citizeness," he said.

Yes, it was raining. My blue frock was all wet and, besides, I felt cold. The young man touched my hand as if by accident, and at that moment I knew that I couldn't stand it any longer.

Just then another cab drew up by the gate. With both elbows I forced my way out of the group of loiterers, ran like mad towards the cab and right into a man wearing an army officer's greatcoat. He had just got out of the cab, a dreadfully tall man, so tall that I had to raise my eyes in order to see his face. But since he had pulled his three-cornered hat down over his eyes I saw nothing but a gigantic nose.

"Please forgive me, citizen," I said to the giant, who shrank back in astonishment from my attack, "please forgive me, but I should like to go with you."

"You would like what?" he asked, taken aback.

"Yes, I'd like to go with you for a moment. Ladies are only allowed into Madame Tallien's house if they are in the company of gentlemen. I've got to get in there, you see, I've got to—and I have no gentleman to escort me in."

The officer looked me up and down and didn't seem to like the prospect. Then, suddenly coming to a decision, he offered me his arm and said:

"Come on, citizeness!"

The lackey in the hall recognised me at once. He looked at me with indignation and then bowed deeply to the giant and took his greatcoat whilst I inspected myself in a tall mirror. Wet strands of hair were hanging into my face, and as I rearranged them I found that my nose was shiny. But there was no time to powder it because just then the giant said impatiently:

"Well, are you ready, citizeness?"

He was wearing a beautifully tailored uniform with thick gold epaulettes. When I lifted my face to see him properly I noticed that the small mouth under his striking nose was curled in disapproval. Quite obviously he was annoyed because he had given in and taken me along. And now it occurred to me that most likely he took me for one of the prostitutes outside the gate.

"Please forgive me," I murmured, "I didn't know what else to do."

"Conduct yourself decently in there and don't let me down," he said severely, made a stiff little bow and once again offered me his arm.

The lackey opened a white double door and we entered a big room crowded to the walls with people. Another lackey seemed to shoot out of the floor in front of us and looked at us questioningly. My escort turned to me abruptly:

"What's your name?"

I didn't want anybody to know of my presence, and so I only whispered my Christian name, "Désirée."

"Désirée who?" he asked, annoyance in his voice.

I shook my head. "Please, please, just Désirée."

So he told the lackey curtly, "Citizeness Désirée and Citizen General Jean-Baptiste Bernadotte."

"Citizeness Désirée and Citizen General Jean-Baptiste Bernadotte!" the lackey announced into the room. The people standing near us turned round, and a dark-haired young woman in a gown that seemed to consist of yellow veils at once left her group and glided towards us.

"How lovely to see you, Citizen General! What a marvellous surprise!" she twittered and stretched out both her hands to the giant. A searching glance of her great dark eyes ran over me from top to bottom and stopped for a fraction of a second on my dirty shoes.

Meanwhile the giant bent down over her hands and kissed—no, not her hands but her white wrists. "You are too kind, Madame Tallien," he said. "As always when Fortune allows a poor soldier from the front a sojourn in Paris, my first call is here at Theresa's magic circle!"

"As always the poor soldier from the front deigns to flatter. And he's lost no time in finding company either, I see. . . ." Her dark eyes scrutinised me once again. I attempted a little bow, but its only result was that Madame Tallien lost every shred of interest in my poor little person and calmly interposed herself between the General and me.

"Come on, Jean-Baptiste," she said, "you'll have to say how-do-you-do to Barras. He is sitting in the garden-room with that horrible Germaine de Staël—you know, old Necker's daughter who scribbles novels all the time—and we've got to relieve him. He'll be delighted at your . . ."

And then I saw nothing but my giant's back and the yellow veils over her otherwise naked shoulders. Other guests came between us, and there I was quite by myself in Madame Tallien's glittering salon.

I took refuge in a window niche and surveyed the room. But I couldn't see Napoleon anywhere. There were a lot of uniforms there, but not one as shabby as that of my fiancé.

The longer I stayed the deeper I crept into the protecting window niche. Not only was my dress impossible but my shoes too appeared quite ridiculous to me. The ladies here didn't wear proper shoes at all, just soles without heels, tied round the feet with narrow gold or silver straps so that the toes were left free, and the toe-nails were painted pink or silver.

I could hear a violin playing in one of the adjoining rooms. Servants in red uniforms moved among the guests balancing trays full of enormous bowls, glasses and snacks. I gobbled a smoked salmon roll, but the taste was lost on me because of my excited state. Then two gentlemen came into the window niche and stood near me talking without paying any attention to me. They talked about the people of Paris who wouldn't put up much longer with the rise of prices and would riot soon.

" My dear Fouché," one of them said, taking snuff with a bored air, " if I were in Barras' place I'd shoot the mob to bits."

" For that you'd first have to find someone ready to do the shooting," the other one remarked.

Thereupon the first man, between two snuff boxes, jerked out the sentence that he had just seen General Bernadotte among the guests.

The other one, the man called Fouché, shook his head. " Bernadotte? Never in your life. But what about that little wretch who keeps hanging round Josephine these days?"

At that moment someone clapped his hands, and over the general murmur I heard the twitter of Madame Tallien's voice : " Everybody to the green room, please! We have a surprise for our friends."

I went along with the crowd into an adjoining apartment where we were so tightly packed that I couldn't see what was going on. All I could take in was the green-and-white striped silk covering the walls. Then champagne was handed round and I too was given a glass. We had to press together still more closely to let the lady of the house make her way through. Theresa passed quite close to where I stood, and I saw that she had nothing on under the yellow veils. The dark red nipples of her bosom showed quite clearly. How indecent it was!

She had taken the arm of a gentleman whose purple frock-coat was embroidered with gold all over. He was holding a lorgnette to his eyes and gave an impression of extraordinary arrogance. Someone murmured, " Good old Barras is getting fat," and I realised that I was in the presence of one of the five masters of France.

" Form a circle round the sofa please! " Theresa called out. Obediently we arranged ourselves in a circle. And at that moment I saw him!

Where? On the little sofa. With a lady in white.

He still wore the old down-at-heel boots, but his trousers were new and immaculately pressed and new too was his uniform jacket, a jacket without either badges of rank or medals. His lean face was no longer tanned but almost sickly pale. He sat there stiffly and stared at Theresa Tallien as if the salvation of his soul depended on her. The woman by his side was leaning against the back of the sofa, her arms stretched out and her small head with its tiny curls thrown backwards. Her eyes were half closed, the lids painted silver, the long neck shining up provocatively white out of a narrow dark-red velvet ribbon. And then I knew who she was : the widow Beauharnais. Josephine!

A mocking smile played round her closed mouth, and we all followed the glance of her half-open eyes : she was smiling at Barras.

" Has everybody got champagne? " asked the voice of Madame Tallien.

The small figure in white stretched out her hand, someone gave her two glasses and she held out one towards Napoleon : " General, your glass! "

She was smiling at him now, a very intimate, somewhat pitying smile.

" Citizens and citizenesses," came Theresa's voice loud and shrill, " I have the honour to make an announcement to our friends which concerns our beloved Josephine."

Theresa obviously enjoyed the scene. She was standing quite close to the sofa, holding her glass high, while Napoleon had got up, looking at her in great embarrassment. Josephine, however, had once more thrown back her childlike curly head with its painted eyelids.

" Our beloved Josephine," Theresa continued, " has decided to enter again the holy state of matrimony. . . ." A suppressed titter sprang up somewhere and Josephine absent-mindedly fingered the red velvet ribbon round her neck. ". . . to enter again the holy state of matrimony and . . ." Here Theresa made an eloquent pause and looked across to Barras who nodded to her. ". . . and engaged herself to Citizen General Napoleon Bonaparte."

"No!"

I heard the scream exactly as everybody else did. Shrilly it seemed to cut the room in two and to hover for a moment in the air, followed by an icy silence. Not till a second later did I realise that it was I who had screamed.

The next moment I found myself in front of the sofa, saw Theresa Tallien shrink away terrified, smelled her sweetish scent and felt on me the stare of the other one, the woman in white on the sofa. But consciously I saw only Napoleon. His eyes were like glass, transparent and expressionless. A vein was quivering on his right temple.

We faced each other for what seemed to be an eternity. But perhaps it was no more than the fraction of a second. Only then I turned my eyes to the woman.

I saw her silvery eyelids. I saw the tiny wrinkles round the corners of her eyes. I saw her lips painted deep red. Oh, how I hated her! With one sudden lunge I threw my glass of champagne at her feet.

The champagne splashed on to her frock. She screeched hysterically. . . .

I found myself running for all I was worth, running and running, along a rain-drenched street. I had no idea how I had got out of the green room, the white room and the hall, past the guests who recoiled from me in horror, past the servants who tried to seize me by the arm. I only knew that suddenly a wet darkness enveloped me, that I ran along a row of houses, that I turned into another street, that my heart was thumping like mad and that like an animal, instinctively, I was running in the direction I wanted. And then I reached a quay, stumbling and slipping on the wet stones all the time till a bridge loomed up before me. The Seine, I thought, the Seine, oh good, good! And then I stopped running, walked slowly across the bridge, leant over and saw thousands and thousands of lights dancing on the water, up and down with the waves. How merry it looked! I bent forward over the parapet, the lights danced up towards me, the rain pattered. Never before in my life had I been so alone.

I thought of Mama and Julie and how they would forgive me once they knew the whole story. In any case Napoleon was probably going to report his engagement this very night to Joseph or his mother.

That, I suddenly realised, was the first clear thought in my brain. It hurt so much that I couldn't stand it. So I put my hands on the edge of the parapet and tried to pull myself up and——

Yes, and at that moment someone gripped me hard by the shoulder and pulled me back. I tried to shake off the strange hand and shouted, "Leave me alone, leave me alone!" But I was seized by both arms and dragged away from the parapet. I struggled as hard as I could to tear myself free, but it was no use. It was so dark that I couldn't even see the face of the man who dragged me off. For sheer despair I sobbed and panted and I loathed the sound of the man's voice which I heard over the noise of the rain, shouting:

"Quiet now, quiet. Don't be a fool! Come, here is my cab."

There was a chaise standing on the quayside.

I continued to struggle desperately, but the stranger was far stronger than I and pushed me into the cab. He sat down by my side and called to the coachman:

"Drive off, never mind where. Just drive."

I sat as far away as possible from the stranger. But then I noticed that my teeth were chattering with the wet and the excitement and rivulets were streaming from my hair across my face.

A hand, a big warm hand came towards me and searched for my fingers.

I sobbed. "Let me get out! Let me, please. . . ." At the same time I clung to this strange hand because I felt so wretched.

"But you asked me yourself to be your escort," the voice came out of the dark of the carriage. "Don't you remember, Mademoiselle Désirée?"

I pushed his hand away. "I—now—I, I want—to be alone."

"Oh no, you asked me to accompany you to Madame Tallien's. And now we'll stay together till I see you home."

His voice was very quiet and really very agreeable.

"Are you this General—this General Bernadotte?" I asked. And then everything came back to me with perfect clarity and I shouted:

"Do leave me alone. I hate Generals. Generals have no heart."

"There are Generals and—Generals!" he said, and laughed.

I heard something rustling in the dark and a coat was laid across my shoulders.

"Your coat will be soaked," I said. "I am wet from the rain, wet through."

"Never mind," he said. "I was expecting that. Wrap yourself up well."

A memory seared through me like fire, a memory of another General's coat, of another rainy night. That night Napoleon asked for my hand. . . .

The carriage rolled on and on. Once the driver stopped and asked a question, and the strange General answered:

"Go on, never mind where."

And so we rolled on, and I kept sobbing into the strange coat. Once I said:

"What a coincidence that you happened to pass over the bridge just then."

"Not a coincidence at all. I felt responsible for you because I brought you among those people. And when you ran away so suddenly I followed you. Only, you ran so fast I preferred to hire a cab and keep on your track. But I wanted to leave you alone as long as possible."

"And why were you so awful then and didn't leave me alone?"

"Because it was no longer possible," he said calmly, and put his arm round my shoulders. I was dead tired and weary and didn't care any longer what happened. Driving on, just driving on, I thought, and never to have to get out again, never to see again, to hear again, to speak again, I thought. . . . And so I put my head on his shoulder and he pulled me closer to him.

I tried to remember what he looked like, but I couldn't disentangle his face from all the many faces I had seen that night.

"Do forgive me," I murmured, "that I let you down so badly at Madame Tallien's."

"That doesn't matter in the least," he said, "I am only sorry —for your sake."

"Do you know," I confessed, "I deliberately splashed the champagne over her white frock. It leaves stains." Suddenly I started crying again. "She is so much more beautiful than I . . . and such a great lady. . . ."

He held me very tight and with his free hand pressed my face against his shoulder. "Yes, cry, my child, cry. It'll do you good."

I wept as I had never wept before. I just couldn't stop. I

wept and sobbed and moaned, and all the time I pressed my face into the rough cloth of his uniform.

" I shall ruin your shoulder-padding with my crying," I said once, sobbing.

" Yes, you'll do that all right," he answered. " But don't let that trouble you. Cry if you feel like it."

We must have been driving through the streets of Paris for hours and hours, and all the time I cried so much that in the end I could cry no longer.

" I'll take you home now. Where do you live?" he asked.

The Seine came back to my mind and I said: " Drop me here. I'll walk home."

" Oh! Walk home? In that case we'd better drive on," he said dryly.

I took my head from his shoulder. It felt no longer comfortable because I had cried too much on it and it was too wet now. A question occurred to me.

" Do you know General Bonaparte?" I asked.

" No. I've only seen him once before in the War Minister's ante-room. I didn't like him."

" Why not?"

" Don't know why. These things, likes and dislikes, can't be explained. You, for example, I like."

We fell silent again after that. The cab rolled on through the rain which in the light of a street lantern made the pavement shine with many colours. My eyes hurt and I closed them and let my head rest against the back of the seat. Then I heard myself say:

" I believed in him more than I have ever believed in anybody in the world. More than in Mama. More than in, or rather different from the way in which I believed in Papa. I just can't understand. . . ."

" There are many things you don't understand, my girl!"

" We were to be married in a few weeks' time. And he never so much as mentioned that. . . ."

" He would never have married you, my little girl, never! You see, he has been engaged for years to a wealthy silk merchant's daughter in Marseilles."

I gave a start, and at once his hand closed warmly and protectively round my fingers again.

" You didn't know that either, did you?" he continued. " The Tallien told me this afternoon. She said that our little General abandoned a big dowry in order to marry Barras' ex-mistress. Bonaparte's brother is married to the sister of this fiancée from Marseilles. But, as things are now, a former countess with good connections in Paris is more important to him than a dowry in Marseilles. You see, little one, you'd have been the last girl in the world for him to have married."

Evenly and almost comfortingly his voice came through the dark. At first I didn't understand what he was driving at and I asked him:

"What are you talking about?"

Frantically I tried to get my thoughts into some sort of order, at the same time clinging for dear life to his hand, which, at this moment, was the only warm thing in my life.

"My dear little girl, I am sorry that I have to hurt you so much. But it is better that you should know everything. I know exactly how it feels, but—it can't get worse now. That's why I told you what the Tallien told me. First there was a rich middle-class girl and now there is a countess with excellent connections deriving from her amorous past associations with one of the heads of our State and two gentlemen of the Supreme Command of the Army. But you, my dear, you have neither connections nor a big dowry."

"How do you know?"

"One can see that. You are only a little girl and a very good girl. You don't know how the great ladies behave and what goes on in their salons. And you haven't got money either, otherwise you'd have slipped a note to Madame Tallien's lackey and he'd have let you through. Yes, you are a decent little thing and . . ."

He stopped. And then, quite unexpectedly, he burst out, "And I want to marry you."

"Let me get out, at once. I won't let you make fun of me," I said, and knocked on the window. "Driver, stop! Stop!" I shouted, and the cab stopped.

But the General shouted even louder, "Drive on at once!" and the carriage immediately got going again.

"Perhaps I didn't express myself properly," the General's voice came somewhat hesitantly out of the dark. "Please forgive me. I never have a chance of getting to know young girls like you. And—Mademoiselle Désirée, I really would like to marry you."

"In Madame Tallien's salon there are plenty of ladies who have a preference for Generals," I said. "I haven't."

"You don't believe, do you, that I would marry cocottes— sorry, Mademoiselle, ladies like that?"

I was too tired to answer, too tired to think. I still didn't understand what this man Bernadotte, this giant of a man, really wanted from me. In any case, what was the good? My life, I felt, was finished. The cold of the night made me shudder in spite of his big coat, and my silk shoes, soaked and heavy, hung like lead on my feet.

"Without the Revolution I shouldn't be an officer now, Mademoiselle, let alone a General. You are very young, but perhaps you remember that before the Revolution no one not belonging to the aristocracy could get beyond the rank of captain. My father was a lawyer's clerk and the son of a very humble artisan, Mademoiselle, and I had to work my way up. I joined the Army when I was fifteen, was nothing but a sergeant for many years, and then step by step—well, anyway, I am a Divisional General now. But perhaps you think I am too old for you? . . ."

What was he saying? 'You'll believe in me whatever happens, won't you?' Napoleon asked me once. A great lady with connections and painted eyelids! Of course, I thought, I understand you, Napoleon, I do. But it'll break me . . .

"I asked you an important question, Mademoiselle."

"I am sorry, I didn't hear it. What did you ask, General Bernadotte?"

"I asked whether, perhaps, I am too old for you?"

"But I don't know how old you are. And what does it matter, anyway?" I said.

"It matters a great deal indeed. I may really be too old for you. I am thirty-one."

"I'm going to be sixteen shortly. But I am so tired. I should like to go home now."

"Of course. Forgive me, I am so inconsiderate. Where do you live?"

I gave him the address and he told the cabman.

"Won't you think over what I asked you?" said the General. Then his voice came more hesitantly through the dark, "I shall have to be back in the Rhineland in ten days' time. Perhaps you could give me an answer by then?" And quickly he added, "My name is Jean-Baptiste Bernadotte. For years I have saved up part of my salary. I could buy a little house for you and the child."

"Child? What child?" I asked involuntarily. The things he said were quite beyond my comprehension.

"Our child, of course," he said eagerly, and felt for my

87

hand again, but I withdrew it quickly. "I want a wife and a child," he continued, "have been wanting them for years, Mademoiselle."

At that my patience gave out.

"Do stop," I said, "you don't know me at all."

"Oh yes, I do," he said and it sounded very sincere. "I believe I know you better than your family knows you. I have so little time for myself, I am always at the front, you see, and therefore I can't visit your family for weeks at a time and—well, I can't take you out for walks and all that sort of thing, the things you are supposed to do before you propose. I have to decide quickly and—I have decided!"

Oh God, he means it, he means it! He wanted to use his leave to get himself married, to buy a house and . . .

"General Bernadotte," I said, "in any woman's life there is room for only one great love."

"How do you know?"

"Well, I . . ." Yes, how did I know? "You can read it in all the novels, and it is certainly true," I said.

At that moment the brakes screeched. We had arrived at the house of the Clapains in the Rue du Bac. He opened the door and helped me out.

There was a lantern over the house door. As at the gate of Madame Tallien's house, I raised myself on my toes to see his face. He had beautiful white teeth and a strikingly big nose.

I gave him the key borrowed from Madame Clapain and he unlocked the door.

"You live in a noble house," he remarked.

"Oh, only the servants' quarters," I murmured. "And now, good night and many thanks, many thanks for—everything."

But he did not move.

"Do go back to your cab," I said. "You'll be wet through. And you can make your mind easy, I'll stay at home all right."

"Good girl," he said. "And when may I come for your answer?"

I shook my head. "In any woman's life—" I began saying, but he raised his hand. Then I broke off and said instead, "Really, General, it won't do! Really it won't! Not because I'm too young for you but, you can see for yourself, because I'm far too small!" And with that I rushed into the house and banged the door to behind me.

When I reached the kitchen of the Clapain family I was no longer tired, only numb. I couldn't sleep now, I'd never be able to sleep again, never. . . .

And therefore, at this moment, I'm sitting at the kitchen table, writing, writing, writing. The day after to-morrow this Bernadotte fellow will come here and ask for me. I certainly shan't be here any more. Where I shall be forty-eight hours hence I don't know. ...

MARSEILLES, *three weeks later.*

I have been very ill: a cold, sore throat, a high temperature and what the poets call a broken heart. Illness enough.

I sold Marie's gold medallion in Paris and got enough money for it to get home. And at home Marie at once put me to bed and sent for the doctor because of my temperature. The doctor of course couldn't understand why I had got a cold because there hadn't been any rain in Marseilles for days. Marie also sent for Mama, who returned without delay to nurse me. Up till now no one has found out that I was in Paris.

At the moment I am lying on a sofa on the terrace. They wrapped me up in countless blankets and said that I was looking pale and dreadfully thin. Joseph and Julie, who came back yesterday, are expected to visit us to-night. I hope they'll allow me to stay up.

Now Marie comes running on to the terrace waving a paper in her hand. How excited she seems!

General Napoleon Bonaparte has been appointed Military Governor of Paris. Riots in the capital have been suppressed by the National Guard.

At first I couldn't read at all, the paper trembled badly in my hand. But then it steadied and I could read in comfort. Napoleon, the paper said, has been made Military Governor of Paris. An infuriated mob wanted to storm the Tuileries and to tear the Deputies to pieces. Driven into a corner, Director Barras handed over command of the National Guard to General Napoleon Bonaparte, the man who had been sacked by the Army. On his appointment he demanded *carte blanche* from the Assembly and got it. After that he ordered a young cavalry officer by the name of Murat to collect some guns, and these he placed along the northern, western and southern sides of the Tuileries so that they covered the approaches along the Rue Saint-Roche and over the Pont Royal. The mob was not deterred by the sight of the artillery and kept on advancing till a voice with an edge as sharp as a knife ordered, 'Fire!' A single cannon-shot sufficed to drive the mob back. Now every-thing was quiet again, and the Directors Barras, Lareveillière, Letourneur, Rewbell and Carnot expressed their gratitude to the man who had saved the Republic from new disorders and appointed him Military Governor of Paris.

I tried to think it all over. A conversation in the window niche of Madame Tallien's house came back to my mind: ' If I were in Barras' place I'd shoot the mob to pieces, my dear Fouché.' ' For that you'd first have to find the man ready to do the shooting.'

One cannon-shot was enough, then, and it was Napoleon who did the shooting. He gave the order for the guns to fire, at whom? At the rioting mob, the paper said. Who were the rioting mob? Probably the wretches who were living in cellars and couldn't pay the inflated price of bread. As to cellars, Napoleon's mother, too, was living in one. ' Your son is a genius, Madame Buonaparte.' ' Yes, unfortunately,' she answered.

Someone interrupted me, and so I am now writing in my room.

As I was still pondering over the news I heard Joseph and Julie come into the living-room. They arrived far earlier than expected, and through the terrace door, which wasn't quite shut, I overheard Joseph saying:

" Napoleon sent a courier with a long letter and plenty of money for Mama, and I asked Mama through a messenger to meet us here. You don't mind, Madame Clary, do you?"

Oh no, Mama didn't mind at all, on the contrary, she said, she'd be very glad to see her. And meanwhile wouldn't they like to say how-do-you-do to me out there on the terrace? I was, Mama added, still very poorly.

But Joseph seemed to hesitate and Julie started to cry and to tell Mama that Napoleon had written to Joseph of his engage-ment to the widow of General de Beauharnais. And there was also, I heard Julie say, a message for me that he always wanted to remain friends with me.

" Oh God, oh God!" Mama exclaimed, " the poor child!"

At that moment I heard Madame Letitia, Eliza and Polette enter, and everybody talked at once, till Joseph's voice started to read out something. That must have been the letter of the new Military Governor of Paris.

Later he and Julie came out on to the terrace and sat down with me. Julie stroked my hand whilst Joseph in obvious embarrassment said something about how autumnal the garden looked already.

"May I congratulate you on your brother's success, Joseph?" I said, pointing to the letter which he was nervously crumpling between his fingers.

"Thank you, thank you," he said. "I'm afraid I have some news for you, Eugenie, which Julie and I regret. . . ."

"Never mind, Joseph, I know," and when he looked puzzled I added, "You see, the door to the living-room was open and I heard everything."

I had hardly finished my sentence when Madame Letitia happened on the terrace, looking very bellicose.

"A widow with two children," she exclaimed, "a widow with two children and six years older than my boy! And that is the kind of daughter-in-law Napoleone dares to bring me!"

I remembered Josephine in that room at Madame Tallien's house: silver-painted eyelids, babyish curls, sophisticated smile. And here was Madame Letitia with red calloused hands and the scrawny neck of a woman who had spent her life washing her children's clothes and preventing them from getting into mischief. Her bony fingers were closed round a wad of bank-notes. Aha, I thought, the Military Governor of Paris has lost no time in sending his mother a part of his Governor's salary.

A little later I was put on the divan in the living-room and heard them discuss the great events. Etienne brought out his best liqueur and emphasised how proud he was to be related to General Bonaparte. But Mama and Suzanne bent their heads over their needlework and said nothing.

"I am quite well again, really," I said. "Couldn't you let me have one of my napkins which I had started to embroider for my trousseau? I want to get on with my monograms."

The serviettes were brought and I started another series of B's which made them all feel awkward when they noticed it. Suddenly I had the feeling that one phase of my life had come to an end, and so I said into the silence that had fallen on us:

"I don't want to be called Eugenie any longer. My name is Bernadine Eugenie Désirée and I like Désirée best of all. Couldn't you call me Désirée?"

They looked at each other with concern. I felt sure they thought I had gone out of my mind.

ROME, three days after Christmas in the Year V. (Here, in Italy, they still go by the pre-Republican calendar and say: Dec. 27th, 1797.)

They've left me alone with the dying man. His name is Jean Pierre Duphot, a General on Napoleon's staff. He arrived in Rome to-day in order to propose to me, and then, two hours ago, a bullet hit him in the stomach. There was nothing he could do, the surgeon said, and so we put him on the sofa in Joseph's study.

Duphot has lost consciousness. His breath sounds like so many little sobs, and a thin trickle of blood comes from a corner of his mouth, so that I have to fold a serviette round his chin. His eyes are half open, but they see nothing. From the adjoining room I can hear the murmuring voices of Joseph, Julie, the doctor and two Embassy secretaries.

Joseph and Julie left the room because they don't like seeing a man die, and the doctor went with them. This Italian doctor thinks it far more important to be introduced to His Excellency the Ambassador of the French Republic in Rome and brother of the conqueror of Italy than to attend some unimportant staff officer on his deathbed.

I don't know why, but I have the feeling that Duphot will regain consciousness once more although I realise like the others how far gone he is already. Therefore I have fetched my diary and have begun writing in it once again after all these years. I shan't be quite so alone now. My pen scratches away on the paper, and that at any rate means that the sobbing death-rattle from the sofa is no longer the only sound in this room.

Since I saw Napoleon—only his mother now calls him Napoleone, the rest of the world speaks of him as Napoleon Bonaparte and speaks of hardly anything else—well, since I saw him that time in Paris I have never set eyes on him again. To this day no one in my family knows of that encounter. He married Josephine in the spring of the next year with Tallien and Director Barras as his witnesses at the ceremony, and as soon as he was married Napoleon paid all the widow Beauharnais' dressmakers' bills. Two days later he went off to Italy—as Commander-in-Chief! And within the next fortnight he had won six battles!

The sound of the dying man's breathing has changed: it has

become quieter. And his eyes, instead of being only half open, are wide open now. I called his name. But he did not hear me.

Yes, within a fortnight Napoleon had won six battles and the Austrians evacuated Northern Italy.

I can't help remembering our evening talks by the hedge. So Napoleon has really founded States. The first he founded he called Lombardy, the last the Cisalpine Republic. He made Milan the capital of Lombardy and appointed fifty Italians to administer the State in France's name. Overnight there appeared on all public buildings the words: ' Liberty, Equality, Fraternity '. Then the people of Milan had to hand over a big sum of money, three hundred horses and their most beautiful works of art, and all that Napoleon sent to Paris, but of course not without deducting the pay of his troops which the Directors in the past had always left unpaid. Messrs. Barras and Co. in Paris didn't know whether they were on their heads or their heels. Money in the exchequer, Italy's most beautiful horses drawing their carriages, and valuable paintings in their reception rooms! There was one painting in particular to which Napoleon drew the attention of Paris. It's called ' La Gioconda ' and its painter was a certain Leonardo da Vinci: there is a woman in it, Mona Lisa they say is her name, and this woman smiles with her lips closed. Her smile reminds me of Josephine's. Perhaps Mona Lisa had bad teeth just like the widow Beauharnais.

At the end of it all something happened which no one had thought possible. As one knows, the French Republic had separated itself from the Church of Rome, and as a result the Roman Catholic clergy beyond our frontiers have always cursed the new France from their pulpits. But then suddenly the Pope approached Napoleon in order to conclude a peace treaty with France. When that came out people crowded into Etienne's shop to listen to his story of how Napoleon years ago had confided to him his great plans. For he, Etienne, was not only General Bonaparte's brother-in-law but also his very best friend. . . .

I have been sitting with Duphot again for a while and held up his head a bit. But it's no use. It doesn't make his breathing any easier and he keeps on fighting for breath. I have wiped a drop of bloodstained foam from his mouth and I notice that his face is waxen yellow. The doctor whom I called in told me in broken French that it was an 'interior hæmorrhage' and then went back to Joseph and Julie. They, for all I know, may be talking about to-morrow's reception. . . .

Apparently even before the treaty with the Vatican had been concluded the Government in Paris had become uneasy. Why? Because Napoleon drafted and signed all agreements with the Italians whom he had 'liberated' himself without ever bothering to ask the Government whether the conditions he imposed were acceptable to it. That exceeded, so the Directors seem to have grumbled, the powers of a Commander-in-Chief, it had no longer anything to do with the conduct of the war but fell under the heading of 'Foreign Policy' and was of such importance that they would have to send professional diplomats out to his headquarters to advise him. . . . At that Napoleon wrote out a list of names of men whom, he suggested, they should give the title and powers of an Ambassador of the Republic and despatched to Italy. The list was headed by the name of his brother Joseph. And that was how Joseph and Julie came to be here.

At first they had gone to Parma, then as Ambassador and Madame Bonaparte to Genoa, till at last they arrived in Rome. And, by the way, they had come here not directly from Marseilles but from Paris. For hardly had Napoleon become Military Governor of Paris than he wrote to Joseph that the capital offered him far better chances than a mere provincial town.

I can see now that whatever happens Napoleon will always find some profitable job or other for Joseph. At first it was the modest position of a secretary of the *Maison Commune* in Marseilles. Then, in Paris, he introduced him not only to Barras and his lot of politicians but also to army contractors and those newly rich who had made their money in property deals, and so Joseph too began to join this particular racket. He bought confiscated aristocratic mansions auctioned off cheaply by the Government, and re-sold them at several times their purchase price. Etienne explained to me that this type of business is flourishing now because of the housing shortage. Within a short time Joseph had made enough money to buy a little house for himself and Julie in the Rue du Rocher.

When news of the victories in Italy came—the victories of Millesimo, Castiglione, Arcola and Rivoli—Joseph's standing in Paris at once improved tremendously. After all, wasn't he the elder brother of that General Bonaparte whom the foreign

papers call 'the strong man of France' and our own the
'liberator of the Italian people', of that man whose lean face
now adorns coffee cups, flower vases and snuff-boxes in all the
shop windows? On one side of these cups, vases and boxes
you can see him in glossy paint, partnered on the other side by
the French flag. No wonder that the Government at once
acceded to the request of its most successful General and
appointed Joseph Ambassador!

Joseph and Julie moved into their first Italian marble palace.
Julie was very wretched there and wrote in despair to ask if
I couldn't come and join them, and Mama agreed. And since
then I have been moving round the country with them from
one palace to another, living in dreadfully high-ceilinged rooms
with floors of black-and-white tiles and sitting about in pillared
courts full of innumerable fountains whose curious bronze
figures squirt their water from all sorts of apertures.

The *palazzo* we inhabit at present is called the Palazzo
Corsini. All the time we are surrounded by clanking spurs and
rattling sabres because Joseph's staff consists of nothing but
officers. And to-morrow is the day of the biggest reception
which Joseph has given so far, a reception for the 350 most
important citizens of Rome. For the last week Julie has not
been able to sleep; her face is as white as a sheet and there are
black rings under her eyes. Julie, you see, belongs to the type
of women who are all of a dither if they have only four guests
for dinner. But every day we are at least fifteen at table now,
and on top of that Joseph arranges receptions for hundreds
of people every few seconds. Although a whole battalion of
flunkeys, cooks and chambermaids buzzes through the house
Julie feels solely responsible for the whole affair and hangs
round my neck at short intervals sobbing and moaning that
most certainly everything would be in a sorry mess. In that
respect she's Mama's true daughter.

Duphot has moved again. For one second I had hoped that
he would regain consciousness, for in that one second he
looked at me with clear eyes. But almost immediately after
they clouded over once more, and now he is fighting for breath
again, spitting blood and sinking deeper and deeper into the
pillows. What wouldn't I give, Jean Pierre Duphot, if I could
help you! But I can't.

In spite of battles and victories and peace treaties and the
making of new States, Napoleon found time to keep an eye on

his family. From the very beginning of his Italian campaign his couriers brought money and letters to Madame Letitia in Marseilles. He made her move into a better house and send Jerome, that street urchin, to a decent school. For Caroline he found a very exclusive girls' boarding-school in Paris, the very school where his stepdaughter Hortense de Beauharnais receives her education. Well, well, how the Bonapartes have gone up in the world! And how furious Napoleon was because his mother had allowed his sister Eliza to marry a certain Felix Bacciochi! Why this hurry, he wrote, and why, of all men, this lazy hopeless wastrel of a music student, this Bacciochi?

Eliza had been going about with Bacciochi for a long time, always hoping that he would marry her. At last, after the news of the first victories in Italy, Bacciochi proposed and was promptly accepted. After the wedding Napoleon began to fear that Polette too might bring someone into the family whom he thought unsuitable, and therefore he insisted that Madame Letitia and Polette should pay him a visit at his headquarters in Montebello. And immediately after their arrival there he married Polette off to a General Leclerc whom none of us had ever heard of.

What I did not understand and what I found rather disagreeable was the fact that Napoleon, in the middle of all the world history he was making, had not forgotten me either. He seemed to have taken it into his head that he had to make amends to me for something or other. And so in complicity with Julie and Joseph he sent men along as candidates for my hand in marriage. The first to arrive was Junot, his former adjutant in his Marseilles days. One day Junot, tall, fair and charming, arrived in Genoa, steered me into the garden and clicked his heels. " I have the honour," he said, " to ask you to marry me." " No, thank you," I answered. " But it was Napoleon's order," he good-naturedly insisted, and I remembered what Napoleon had thought of Junot: " a loyal man, but stupid." I shook my head and he rode back to headquarters.

The next candidate was Marmont, whom I had also known in Marseilles. Marmont did not ask me directly but hinted at it with delicacy. Again I remembered what Napoleon had said about his friends. This one, he judged, wanted to be in on his, Napoleon's, career. There Joseph Bonaparte's sister-in-law would certainly serve this purpose well, I thought. It meant being a member of Napoleon's family, even doing Napoleon a service and incidentally marrying a handsome dowry. I answered Marmont's delicate hints with a ' no ' just as delicately embroidered. But after he had gone I complained about it to Joseph. Couldn't he write to Napoleon and tell him to spare me the marriage proposals of his staff officers?

"Don't you understand," said Joseph, "that Napoleon considers it a distinction for one of his Generals to be married to his sister-in-law's sister?"

"I am not a medal to be awarded to a deserving officer," I objected, "and if this sort of thing doesn't stop I'm going back to Mama."

This morning Julie and I were sitting, in spite of the cool weather, in the pillared court of our palazzo. For the thousandth time Julie and I were studying the names of the Italian families of the high aristocracy who were to come to the Embassy to-morrow night. Joseph joined us there. He was holding a letter in his hand and talked casually about this and that, as is usual with him whenever something that he finds unpleasant has happened. Suddenly he said:

"Napoleon has seen to it that we get a new military attaché. General Jean Pierre Duphot, a very charming young man."

I looked up. "Duphot? Didn't a General Duphot report to you once in Genoa?"

Joseph was pleased. "Of course," he exclaimed, "and he made quite an impression on you if I remember right, didn't he? Because, you see, Napoleon writes that he hopes that Eugenie—please forgive me, he still speaks of Eugenie instead of Désirée—that you would take pity on this very lonely young man. And therefore . . ."

I got up. "Another marriage candidate? No, thank you! I had thought that that was really over and done with." Going to the door I turned round to them: "Write to Napoleon at once that he is not to send this Duphot or whatever his name is on any account."

"But he's here already! He arrived a quarter of an hour ago and brought Napoleon's letter."

I was furious and banged the door to behind me. I like banging doors. In these marble palaces it sounds like an explosion.

I didn't go down for lunch, to escape Duphot. But I put in an appearance for the evening meal. It's too boring to eat by yourself in your room. Of course, they had given the young man the seat next to me. Like a slave Joseph always does exactly as Napoleon wishes.

The young man didn't get more than a few cursory glances from me. I had an impression of a man of medium height with a big mouth horribly full of white teeth. These white teeth irritated me because he kept laughing at me all the time.

Our conversation was frequently interrupted. We are used to people standing about in crowds outside the Embassy and shouting " *Evviva la Francia! Evviva la Liberta!*" all the time, with an occasional " *A basso la Francia!*" mixed in. Most Italians are enthusiastic about the ideas that our Revolution and our Army have brought to them. But the heavy costs of our occupation and the fact that all their officials are appointed by Napoleon seems to embitter many. At all events, to-night the noise outside sounded different from other nights, louder and more menacing.

Joseph told us why. Last night some Roman citizens had been arrested as hostages because a French lieutenant had been knifed and killed in a tavern brawl. And now a deputation of the Town Council of Rome was waiting outside to speak to Joseph. An enormous crowd had gathered to watch the proceedings.

" Why don't you see them?" asked Julie. " We could have waited with the meal."

Joseph explained—and the gentlemen of his staff nodded their agreement—that that was quite out of the question. He wasn't going to see anybody, because the whole affair was no business of his but that of the Military Governor of Rome and had been the Governor's from the very beginning.

Meanwhile the noise outside kept growing, and finally there were blows on the door.

At that Joseph shouted:

" My patience is at an end. I'll have the mob dispersed. Go to Military Headquarters," he told one of his secretaries, " and demand that the square outside the Embassy be cleared. I can't stand that din any longer."

The secretary left, and General Duphot called after him: " Better be careful and go out by the back door!"

We continued our meal in silence. Before we had reached the coffee stage we heard the sound of horses. So they had sent a battalion of hussars in order to clear the square. Joseph got up at once and we went with him outside on to the balcony on the first floor.

The place below looked like a witch's cauldron. There were thousands and thousands of heads, and thousands and thousands of voices clamouring stridently. We couldn't see the Council Deputation anywhere. The excited mob must have pressed it against the portico of the house. The two sentries down there were standing motionless outside their boxes, and I had the impression that at any moment the crowd would trample them into the mud. Joseph made us all go back quickly into the room, where we pressed our faces against the panes of the high windows. He was as pale as death and kept chewing his lower lip, and his hand trembled as it played nervously with his hair.

The hussars had surrounded the square. Like statues they sat on their horses, rifles at the ready, waiting for the order. But their commander was apparently still undecided about it.

" I'll go down and try to reason with the crowd," Duphot said.

" It's useless, General, don't do it," said Joseph imploringly. " Don't expose yourself to the danger. Our hussars will . . ."

Duphot smiled and showed his white teeth. " I am a soldier, Your Excellency, and used to danger. Besides, I'd like to prevent unnecessary bloodshed."

And so, his spurs clanking, he went to the door. Before he reached it he turned round and, if you please, tried to catch my eye! I turned quickly away towards the window. So that's what it was: for my sake he indulged in this piece of bravado! In order to impress me he went down to face the raging mob unarmed and alone.

' How senseless,' I thought, ' how senseless! Junot, Marmont, Duphot, what have I got to do with them?'

At that moment the door was being opened downstairs. We opened the window a fraction in order to hear better. The clamour grew weaker, but it sounded as threatening as before. Someone yelled: " *A basso . . . !*" and once more: " *A basso . . . !*" We couldn't see Duphot yet. Then the crowd withdrew some way to make room for him, and he came into view raising his hands to ask for silence. And it was then that a shot rang out, followed immediately by the first salvo from the hussars.

I rushed out of the room and down the stairs and tore the door open. The two sentries had picked up General Duphot, holding him up under the arms. His legs dangled lifelessly to the ground, his face with the twisted mouth hung to one side, and his eternal smile was frozen to a grin. He had lost consciousness. The two soldiers dragged him into the hall and his spurs clanked as his legs trailed over the marble tiles.

" Take him upstairs!" I heard myself say. " We'll have to put him somewhere upstairs." As I was saying this, white distraught faces appeared around me: Joseph, Julie, the fat

99

Councillor to the Embassy, and Minette, Julie's chambermaid. They made room for the two soldiers to carry Duphot up the stairs. Outside all had become quiet. Two salvoes from the hussars had been enough.

I opened the door to Joseph's study, which was nearest to the staircase. There the two sentries laid Duphot on a sofa and I pushed some cushions under his head. Joseph, who was standing by my side, said that he had sent for a doctor and that perhaps it mightn't be as bad as it looked.

I saw a damp stain on his dark-blue uniform in the region of his stomach.

" Open his tunic, Joseph," I said, and Joseph obeyed with clumsy and nervous fingers. There was a light red circle of blood on his white shirt.

" A stomach wound," said Joseph.

The General's face had turned yellow and there was a jerky kind of sob coming from his wide-open mouth. At first I thought he was crying, till I realised that he was fighting for breath.

When the Italian doctor, a thin and shortish man, arrived he was even more wrought up than Joseph. It seemed to have been a great stroke of luck for him to be called to the French Embassy. He said at once that he was a great admirer of the French Republic and of General Napoleon Bonaparte and, as he was opening Duphot's shirt, he mumbled something about these regrettable incidents to-day and about irresponsible elements at the bottom of them.

I interrupted him and asked whether he needed anything. He looked up in confusion and it took him a moment or so before he remembered.

" A drop of lukewarm water, please. And perhaps a clean cloth."

He began to wash out the wound. Joseph went up to the window and Julie was leaning against a wall on the verge of being sick. I took her out of the room and told Joseph to look after her, which he did, greatly relieved that he need not stay.

" A blanket," said the doctor, " could you get me a blanket? His limbs are quite cold already. He is bleeding to death, you know. Inside him, Mademoiselle, inside him."

We spread a blanket over Duphot.

" There is nothing we can do now, Mademoiselle. How terrible! A man of such exalted position!" he said, and his eyes went over the gold braid on Duphot's uniform. And so, having done his duty, he quickly made for the door through which Joseph had disappeared. I went with him.

In the adjoining room Joseph, Julie, the Councillor and some secretaries sat together round a big table talking in whispers and sipping port. Joseph rose and offered the doctor a glass, and I could see how the Charm of the Bonapartes enveloped the little Italian in a haze of bliss. He stammered:

"Oh, Your Excellency, brother of our great Liberator . . ."

I went back to Duphot. At first I had something to occupy me: with the help of napkins I tried to wipe away the thin trickle of blood down his chin. But I gave it up soon because the blood never stopped trickling. In the end I spread the napkins round his chin over his tunic. All the time I tried in vain to catch his eye, and when I had done what there was to be done I fetched my diary and started to write.

I must have been sitting here for many hours. The candles are almost burned down. But from the next room there still comes the gentle murmur of voices. No one wants to go to bed before . . .

A moment ago he came to at last.

I heard a movement from the sofa, kneeled down by his side and put my arm under his head. His eyes rested on my face, taking it in, for a long time. Obviously he didn't know where he was.

"You are in Rome, General Duphot," I told him, "in Rome, in Ambassador Bonaparte's house."

His lips moved and spilled out blood-flecked foam. I wiped it away with my free hand.

"Marie," he managed at last to say, "I want to go to Marie."

"Quick," I said, "quick, tell me, where is Marie?"

His eyes were clear and alive now and they asked a question. I repeated therefore:

"You are in Rome. There have been riots in the streets. A bullet hit you in the stomach."

He nodded almost imperceptibly. Yes, he had understood.

I tried to think quickly. I couldn't help him, but perhaps I could help her, Marie?

"Marie, what's Marie's surname? And where does she live?" I asked in as urgent a tone as I could muster.

Fear came into his eyes. "Don't," he brought out, "don't—tell—Bonaparte."

"But if you are going to be ill for a long time we must

101

inform Marie. There's no need to tell Napoleon Bonaparte." I smiled at him with the smile of a friendly accomplice.

"Must—marry—Eugenie, Bonaparte said, and——" The rest of the sentence was inaudible. Then the words became clearer once more: "Be sensible, little Marie—always look after you—after you—and little George—darling, darling Marie——"

His head fell to one side, he pursed his lips and tried to kiss my arm. He thought I was Marie. He had explained to her exactly why he wanted to leave her and her little son: to marry into Bonaparte's family, which would mean promotion and undreamed-of possibilities. . . .

His head now felt as heavy as lead on my arm. I lifted it a bit. "Give me Marie's address, I'll write to her," I said, and tried to catch his eye once more. For a second his gaze became clear again: "Marie Meunier—36—Rue de Lyon—Paris," he said.

His features had suddenly sharpened, the eyes lay deep in their sockets and beads of perspiration stood on his forehead.

"We shall always look after Marie and little George," I said. But it didn't reach him any more. "I promise," I repeated.

Suddenly his eyes grew wide and his lips twisted convulsively. I jumped up and ran to the door. At the same time a long moan came after me and then died away.

"Come, doctor, come at once!" I heard myself call.

"It's all over," the Italian said after he had bent cursorily over the sofa.

I went to the window and drew back the curtains. The grey and leaden light of dawn crept into the room. Then I put out the candles.

In the other room they were still sitting round the table. The servants had lit fresh candles, and the room with its air of festive illumination seemed like an abode in another world.

"Joseph, you must cancel the reception," I said.

Joseph started up. He seemed to have fallen asleep with his head on his chest: "What—what's that? Oh, it's you, Désirée."

"You must cancel the reception, Joseph," I repeated.

"That's impossible. I've expressly arranged that——"

"But you've got a dead man in your house," I explained.

He stared at me with furrowed brows. Then he got up hastily. "I'll think it over," he said, and went out. Julie and the others followed him.

When Julie and Joseph reached the door of their bedroom Julie stopped and asked:

"Désirée, may I lie down in your room? I am afraid of being alone."

I did not object that, after all, she had Joseph and would not be alone, but simply said:

"Of course you can sleep in my bed. I want to go on with my diary anyway."

"Diary? Do you still write your diary? How strange!" she said with a tired smile.

"Why strange?"

"Because everything is so different now. So quite, quite different!"

She sighed and lay down on my bed without taking off her clothes. She didn't wake up till lunch time.

Some time during the morning I heard the sound of hammering. When I went down to find out I saw that they were putting up a stage in the big reception room. In one corner Joseph was directing the work in Italian. At long last he had found an opportunity to speak his mother tongue. When he caught sight of me he came and explained:

"This is going to be the stage. From here Julie and I are going to watch the dancing."

"Stage? For the reception to-night?" I asked in astonishment. "But you can't go on with it, you can't!"

"Not with a dead body in the house, you're right. That's why we had the—hm, the remains of the late Duphot taken away. I've had him laid in state in a cemetery chapel, in as ceremonious a state as possible because, after all, he was a General in the French Army. And we must go on with the ball as a matter of course. It's even more important now than ever, because we have to show that law and order reign in Rome. If I cancelled it the whole world would say at once that we are not masters of the situation. Whereas the whole thing was really only a minor incident, however regrettable, you understand?"

I nodded. General Duphot had left his mistress and his son in order to marry me. And in order to make an impression on me he had exposed himself rashly to a raging mob and had been killed. But of course all this was only a minor though regrettable incident.

"I have to talk to your brother, Joseph," I said.

"Which one? Lucien?"

"No, the famous one, the General. Napoleon."

Joseph tried to hide his surprise. All his family knows that up till now I've anxiously avoided meeting Napoleon.

"It concerns General Duphot's family," I explained curtly, and left the room in which the hammering of the workmen made so much noise.

Returning to my room I found Julie awake and in tears. I sat down on the edge of the bed; she put her arms round me and sobbed and sobbed.

"I want to go home," she cried, "home! I don't want to live in these strange mansions. I want a home, like everybody else! What are we doing here, in this strange country where they want to kill us? And in these awful draughty castles? And in these high rooms which make you feel you are in a church, not in a house? We don't belong here, I want to go home!"

I pressed her to me. It took the death of General Duphot for her to realise how unhappy she was here.

A bit later there came a letter from Mama from Marseilles. We read it crouching side by side on my bed. Mama wrote in her tidy slanting hand that Etienne had decided to move to Genoa with Suzanne in order to open a branch there of the firm of Clary. In these days a French business man would have particularly attractive opportunities there and, so she wrote, the silk business would always be carried on best from Italy. She, Mama, would of course not stay behind by herself in Marseilles but she would go with Etienne and Suzanne to Genoa, and she hoped that I would soon find a good husband although I should for heaven's sake not allow myself to be hustled. As to the house in Marseilles, Etienne intended to sell it. . . .

Julie had stopped crying. Deeply shaken we looked at each other.

"Then we shan't have a home any more," she murmured.

I felt a lump in my throat. "You'd never have gone back to our villa in Marseilles in any case," I said.

Julie stared towards the window. "I don't know, I don't know. No, of course, I wouldn't. But it was so lovely thinking of the house, the garden and the little summer-house. You know, in all these months that I have been moving about here from *palazzo* to *palazzo* and feeling dreadfully wretched I have always kept thinking about it, always. Never of Joseph's little house in Paris, no, always of Papa's villa in Marseilles!"

There was a knock on the door. Joseph came in, and Julie at once started weeping again. "I want to go home," she cried.

He sat down on the bed and took her in his arms. "You shall go home," he said tenderly. "To-night we get the great reception over and to-morrow we leave. For Paris! I've had enough of Rome."

He pressed his lips together and his chin down on his chest. It made it look like a double chin. Perhaps he thought he made a more impressive figure that way.

" I shall ask the Government to give me another and, maybe, more important position," he said. " Are you looking forward to our home in the Rue du Rocher, Julie?"

" Yes, if Désirée goes with us," said Julie in a voice half choked with sobs.

" I'll go with you," I said. " Where else should I go?"

She looked up at me through her tears: " Oh, we'll have a lovely time in Paris, you and Joseph and I. You can't imagine, Désirée, what a marvellous city Paris is! And such a big city, too! Those shop windows! And the thousands of lights which the Seine reflects at night, no, you simply can't imagine it because you've never been there yet!"

Julie and Joseph left the room to make arrangements for our departure, and I fell on my bed. My eyes were burning with lack of sleep.

In my thoughts I imagined the conversation I was going to have with Napoleon, and I tried to remember his face. But all I saw with my mind's eye was the unreal glossy face which smiles at you now from every coffee cup, flower vase and snuff-box. And then this unreal face disappeared in its turn before the lights that dance on the waters of the Seine at night, those lights which I shall never be able to forget.

PARIS, end of Germinal, in the Year VI. (Old people abroad would say April 1798.)

I've seen him again!

We had been invited to a farewell party. He was going to embark with his army within a few days for Egypt, to unite East and West there by the Pyramids and to turn our Republic into a world-wide Empire, as he told his mother. Madame Letitia listened to him calmly and afterwards asked Joseph whether they were trying to conceal from her that Napoleon suffered at times from attacks of malaria. It seemed to her that the poor boy wasn't all there. . . . But Joseph explained to her, and also to Julie and me, that it was by the Pyramids that Napoleon would smash the English and their Empire to pieces.

Napoleon and Josephine live in a small house on the Rue de

la Victoire. It used to be the house of the actor Talma, and Josephine bought it from his widow in the days when she used to glide on Director Barras' arm through Theresa Tallien's salon. At that time the street was called the Rue Chatereine; but after Napoleon's victories in Italy the City Council renamed it Rue de la Victoire in his honour.

To get back to the farewell party: it was incredible how many people forced themselves into the small and undistinguished house, which has only two small rooms besides the dining-room. I am still confused even now when I recall all the faces and voices.

Julie had made me almost ill during the morning by asking me every few seconds with tender concern if I was excited and if I still felt anything for him. I was excited, naturally, but I really couldn't say whether I still felt anything for him. 'When he smiles,' I thought to myself, 'he has me in the hollow of his hand,' and therefore I rather hoped that he and Josephine would still be furious with me because of the scene that day in Madame Tallien's house. Again and again I reflected that he'd probably hate the sight of me now and so certainly would not smile at me. I almost hoped he would hate me.

I put on a new dress, yellow with a red underslip, and I used a bronze chain which I had bought once in an antique shop in Rome, as a belt. The day before yesterday I had my hair cut short. It is the new fashion which Josephine introduced, and now all ladies of fashion copy the way she brushes her babyish curls upwards. I can't do that with my hair; it's too heavy and thick for that, and I have no elegant curls. So I put my hair up and held it together with a ribbon. 'But,' I thought, 'whatever I do, by the side of Josephine I shall always look like a little country cousin.'

The new frock was cut very low, but I no longer need handkerchiefs to stuff into my bosom. Just the opposite: I've made a resolution to eat fewer sweets, otherwise I'll get too fat. My nose, however, is still a snub nose, and that, unfortunately, it will remain to the end of my days. Which is particularly sad now, because since the conquest of Italy everybody is in raptures about ' the classic profile '!

At one o'clock, then, we drove up to the house in the Rue de la Victoire and entered the first of the two small rooms, which was already full of Bonapartes. Madame Letitia and her daughters live in Paris now, and the whole family meets quite often. Yet at every reunion the Bonapartes greet each other with kisses and embraces. I was pressed first to Madame Letitia's bosom and after that vigorously taken into Madame Leclerc's arms. Madame Leclerc was that little Polette who before her marriage declared that Leclerc was the only officer of her circle for whom she felt absolutely nothing. As Napoleon, however, thought that her many *affaires* would injure the reputation of the Bonaparte family, she had to marry him all the same. He is a short-legged, pouchy and very energetic man who never laughs, and looks as if he could be Polette's father.

Then, with her husband Bacciochi, there was Eliza, horribly painted and boasting all the time of the great position which Napoleon had found for her musical husband in one of the ministries. And Caroline, and Josephine's daughter, fair, angular Hortense, who had been allowed out of their exclusive boarding-school for the day, were there, huddled together on a fragile little chair and giggling at Madame Letitia's new dress of heavy brocade which reminded one of the dining-room curtains.

Among the noisy and excitable crowd of Bonapartes I noticed a thin, fair-haired and very young man with the sash of an adjutant round his uniform. His blue eyes stared a trifle helplessly at the beautiful Polette. I asked Caroline who he was and she, almost choking with giggles, managed to tell me at last that he was Napoleon's son!

The young man seemed to have guessed that I was asking about him. He made his way through the groups towards me and introduced himself: "Eugene de Beauharnais, personal adjutant to General Bonaparte."

The only ones who hadn't put in an appearance yet were our hosts, Napoleon and Josephine. But now a door was flung open and Josephine put her head through and called: "Do forgive me, my dears, do forgive me! We've only just got back. Joseph, would you mind coming out for a moment? Napoleon wants to speak to you. Make yourselves at home, my friends, I'll be with you in a second." The next moment she had disappeared.

Joseph followed her out, and Madame Letitia, annoyed, shrugged her shoulders. Everybody started talking again. But suddenly they all fell silent because someone in the next room seemed to be having an attack of hysterics. A fist banged a table or a mantelpiece and one could hear the smashing of glass. At the same time Josephine slipped into the room where we were standing aghast.

"How nice," she said, "to find the whole family together,"

and smilingly she went up to Madame Letitia. Her white gown clung tightly to her delicate figure, a dark red velvet scarf hung softly and loosely round the naked shoulders and made her girlish neck appear very white.

"Madame, you have a son by the name of Lucien, haven't you?" Josephine asked Madame Letitia.

"My third son, yes. What's the matter with him?" Madame Letitia answered. Her eyes were full of hatred for this daughter-in-law who didn't even take the trouble to remember the names of her brothers- and sisters-in-law.

"He wrote to Napoleon that he had married," said Josephine.

"I know," Madame Letitia answered and her eyes grew narrow. "Do you mean to say that my second son does not approve of his brother's choice?"

Josephine shrugged her delicate shoulders and smiled: "Sounds like it, doesn't it? Just listen how he is shouting!" The attack of hysterics next door seemed to amuse her a lot.

The door was thrown open and Napoleon stood there. His lean face was red with fury. "Mother, did you know that Lucien has married the daughter of an inn-keeper?"

Madame Letitia looked him up and down. Her eyes went from the reddish hair which fell untidily to the shoulders, over the deliberately plain uniform which, it was obvious, must have been tailored by the best uniform maker in Paris, down to the points of his highly polished, narrow and very elegant boots.

"Well, Napoleon," she said, "what is it you don't like about your sister-in-law Christine Boyer from St. Maximin?"

"You, all of you, don't you understand me? An inn-keeper's daughter, a village wench who every night in an ale-house waits on the farmers of the district? Mother, I don't understand you."

"As far as I know, Christine Boyer is a very good girl and has a very good reputation," said Madame Letitia, letting her eyes stray for a moment over Josephine's small white figure.

Suddenly Joseph's voice rang out: "After all, we can't all marry former—hm—countesses!"

At that I noticed Josephine flinch almost imperceptibly, but her smile grew wider. Her son Eugene flushed to the roots of his hair.

Napoleon swept round and stared at Joseph. One could see a little vein pulsating in his right temple. After a moment he passed his hand across his forehead, turned abruptly away from Joseph and said cuttingly:

"I have the right to expect suitable marriages from my

brothers. And you, Mother, I want to write to Lucien at once to tell him to get a divorce or to have his marriage declared void. Tell him that I demand it. Josephine, can't we eat yet?"

And at that moment our eyes met! For a fraction of a second we looked at each other. There it was, the dreaded, hated and yet so badly longed-for meeting! Quickly he left the doorway, pushed the angular Hortense out of his way and took my hands:

"Eugenie! How glad I am that you accepted our invitation!"

His eyes never left my face. He smiled, and his lean features were filled with youth and the glow of life, as on that day when he promised Mama that he would wait for our wedding till my sixteenth birthday.

"How beautiful you've become, Eugenie," he said. "And you're grown up, quite grown up!"

I took my hands out of his: "I am eighteen now, after all," I said, and I thought I sounded gauche and not very sure of myself. "And we haven't seen each other for years." Well, that at any rate sounded a bit better.

"Yes, it's a long time, far too long, Eugenie, isn't it? The last time, let me see, where did we meet the last time?" He cast another glance at me and then broke out laughing. His eyes sparkled as he remembered our last meeting, finding it very funny indeed, very funny.

"Josephine, Josephine," he called, "you must meet Eugenie, Julie's sister. I've told you so much about Eugenie."

"But Julie told me that Mamemoiselle Eugenie prefers to be called Désirée," Josephine said as she came nearer and stood beside Napoleon. Nothing in her Mona Lisa smile betrayed any recognition of me. "It was very kind of you to come, Mademoiselle."

"I should like to have a word with you, General," I said quickly, and his smile froze. He probably thought that I was going to make a scene, a sentimental childish scene. So I added: "It's about a rather serious matter."

Josephine hastily put her arm through his. "Dinner is ready," she announced, "do come and sit down, please!"

At the table I found myself between that boring Leclerc and shy young Eugene de Beauharnais. Napoleon talked carelessly and addressed himself mainly to Joseph and Leclerc. When we had finished the soup he hadn't even started it. I remembered that in his Marseilles days this desire to talk overcame him only intermittently, and when it did he spoke in jerky sentences supported by dramatic gestures. Now he was speaking very fluently and with great self-assurance and did not seem to want any objections or replies. When he began to talk about 'our arch-enemies, the British' Polette emitted a moaning: "Oh God, now he's off on that tack again!" and we were treated in great detail to all the reasons why he did not want to go on with the invasion of Britain. He had, he explained, made a comprehensive study of the coast round Dunkirk and had had the idea of building flat-bottomed invasion barges which could land in small fishing ports, as the big ports suitable for berthing men-of-war were too heavily fortified.

"Bonaparte, we've all finished our soup. Do start yours!" I heard Josephine's gentle voice. 'So,' I thought, 'she calls him Bonaparte instead of Napoleon and she doesn't "thou" him. Perhaps that is aristocratic etiquette; I wager she never called her first husband anything but *Monsieur le Vicomte*!'

Napoleon hadn't heard her admonition. He bent over the table towards Leclerc, who was sitting opposite him: "Imagine," he exclaimed, "imagine, Leclerc, by air! To be able to transport whole battalions by air across the Channel and drop them at strategic points in England! Battalions, provided even with light artillery transported by air!"

Leclerc opened his mouth to say something, but shut it again.

"Don't drink so much and don't drink so quickly, my boy," Madame Letitia's deep voice boomed across the table.

Napoleon put his wine-glass down at once and hastily began to eat. A silence fell for a few seconds, broken only by Caroline's senseless giggling. Then we heard Bacciochi, to whom the silence must have felt uncomfortable, say:

"Pity your grenadiers couldn't grow wings!"

Napoleon at once started up again and turned to Joseph: "You never know," he said, "I may yet be able to attack by air. Some inventors came to see me and showed me their plans of giant balloons capable of carrying three or four men and of keeping afloat in the air for hours. Highly interesting, full of fantastic possibilities!"

At last he had finished his soup and Josephine rang for the next course, chicken and asparagus sauce. As we were eating it Napoleon explained to Caroline and Hortense what the Pyramids were. Then he went on to tell the assembled company that, in Egypt, he was going not only to destroy Britain's colonial power but also to liberate the Egyptians.

"My first Order-of-the-Day to my troops—" bang, his chair had fallen over because in his excitement he had jumped up and pushed it back and run out of the room. Within a second he returned carrying a closely written sheet. " Here, you must hear this: ' Soldiers, forty centuries look down on you!' That," he said, turning to us, " is the age of the Pyramids. This Order-of-the-Day will be published there, under the shadow of the Pyramids. To continue: ' The people in whose midst we find ourselves are Mohammedan. Their credo runs: God is God and Mahomet is his prophet——' "

" The Mohammedans call God Allah," interrupted Eliza. She had started to read a lot of books in Paris and liked to show off the knowledge she had acquired.

Napoleon frowned and brushed her interruption aside. " I'll work the details out later," he said. " Here is the most important passage: ' Don't raise your voices against their faith. Treat them, the Egyptians, as you've treated Jews and Italians. Show the Muftis and Imams the same respect which you have shown to priests and rabbis '." Here he paused and looked at us. " Well?"

" It's fortunate for the Egyptians that under the laws of the Republic you are to liberate them for the cause of the Rights of Man," Joseph said.

" What do you mean by that?"

" That the Rights of Man are the guiding principles of this Order-of-the-day. And they didn't come from your brain." Not a muscle moved in Joseph's face as he said that, and I remembered for the first time in years what I had felt in Marseilles: that he really hated his brother.

" You've said that very beautifully, my boy," said Madame Letitia's voice soothingly.

" Please do eat up, Bonaparte," urged Josephine, " we're expecting a lot of people after dinner."

Obediently Napoleon crammed the good food into his mouth.

I happened to notice Hortense at this moment. This child— no, at fourteen you're no longer a child, don't I know!—well, this awkward youngster Hortense, who didn't at all resemble her lovely mother, never took her somewhat protuberant watery eyes off Napoleon, and there were hectic patches of red on her cheeks. I realised Hortense was in love with her stepfather, and I found this thought sad and depressing rather than funny. Eugene interrupted and said:

" Mama wants to drink your health."

I raised my glass to her, and smilingly, slowly, she raised hers and drank. When she put it down again she winked at me. I knew exactly what it meant: she remembered . . . the day at Madame Tallien's . . .

We went to the other room for coffee. There were a lot of people waiting there who wanted to wish Napoleon luck and God-speed. I had the feeling that all Madame Tallien's former clients were now trying to force their way into Josephine's little house. Men in uniform were quite numerous, among them my intended suitors Junot and Marmont, whom I gave a wide berth. I heard them tell the ladies laughingly that once in Egypt they would have their hair cut short. "We'd look like Roman heroes," they insisted, "and besides it'll keep the lice away." One very smart officer with wavy dark hair, sparkling eyes and a flat nose told Madame Letitia that it was Napoleon's idea.

"I don't doubt it, General Murat," she answered, "he's always full of mad ideas."

She seemed to have taken a liking to this young officer whose blue tunic was covered with braid and his white trousers with gold embroidery. I think Madame Letitia is rather fond of colourful southern splendour.

A little later Joséphine told three young people to get up from a small sofa to make room for an important guest. This was no other than Barras, one of the five Directors of the French Republic, in gold-embroidered purple uniform, and a lorgnette in his hand. Joseph and Napoleon Bonaparte at once took the seats on either side of him, and over their shoulders leaned a thin man whose peaked nose seemed familiar. Of course, he was one of the two men whom I had seen in the window niche at Madame Tallien's, a certain Fouché, I believe.

Eugene, perspiring madly, apparently thought it his job to find chairs for the guests. Without any warning he pushed fat Eliza and me down on to two chairs immediately in front of the sofa on which Barras was holding court. He also found a gilded arm-chair for 'the Minister of Police', M. Fouché. But when an elegant young man with a slight limp and an old-fashioned powdered wig approached our group Fouché immediately jumped to his feet again. "My dear Talleyrand," he exclaimed, "won't you sit down with us?"

They talked about our Ambassador to Vienna, who was on his way home. Something sensational seemed to have happened in Vienna. I gathered from the conversation that, on an Austrian national holiday, the Ambassador had flown the flag of our Republic and that thereupon the Viennese had attacked the Embassy to tear the flag down.

All that was new to me. I never have the chance to read a paper because of Joseph, who, as soon as they arrive, takes them away and reads them in his study. And if later on Julie and I want to see them we find that Joseph has cut out all the important articles and taken them to Napoleon to talk them over. So I never have an inkling of what goes on in the world. This incident had apparently happened almost as soon as we had made our peace with Austria and installed an Embassy there.

"It seems to me, M. Talleyrand," said Joseph, "that you shouldn't have sent a General to Vienna as our Ambassador but a professional diplomat."

Talleyrand raised his thin eyebrows and smiled. "Our Republic does not as yet dispose of sufficient professional diplomats, M. Bonaparte. We have to call in auxiliaries from outside the diplomatic service. You yourself helped us out in Italy, didn't you?"

That went home. So Joseph was only an 'auxiliary diplomat' in the eyes of this M. Talleyrand who, it appeared, was our Minister for Foreign Affairs.

"And in any case," I heard the nasal voice of Director Barras say, "in any case, this man Bernadotte is one of our ablest men, don't you think so, General Bonaparte? I seem to remember that at one time in Italy you needed reinforcements very urgently, and the Minister for War ordered Bernadotte to take the best division of the Rhine Army to Italy. And how did this man from Gascogne manage it? He crossed the Alps in the depths of winter with a whole division within ten hours, six for the ascent, four for the descent! If I remember correctly a letter from you, General, written at that time, you yourself were most impressed by this feat."

"No doubt Bernadotte is an excellent General," said Joseph, shrugging his shoulders, "but a diplomat? A politician?"

"I believe he was quite right in showing the flag of our Republic in Vienna. Why should the French Embassy not hoist its own standards when all the other buildings showed their flags?" Talleyrand said thoughtfully. "After the violation of the extra-territorial status of our Embassy, General Bernadotte left Vienna at once. But I feel that the apology from the Austrian Government will arrive in Paris even before he arrives. In any case, there was no one better suited than he for the post in Vienna," he concluded, examining the polished finger-nails of his small hand.

A barely perceptible smile showed on Barras' blueish, somewhat bloated face as he pronounced Bernadotte a very far-sighted man with great political acumen. Then he added, dropping his lorgnette and fixing his gaze on Napoleon, whose lips were pressed together and in whose temple the little vein was pulsating: "A convinced Republican, this Bernadotte, determined to destroy all the enemies of the Republic, both external and—internal!"

"And what will be his next appointment?" broke in Joseph with obvious jealous impatience.

Barras' lorgnette sparkled in the light as he answered: "The Republic needs reliable men. I imagine that a General who started his military career as a private soldier is bound to enjoy the confidence of the Army. And as he happens to enjoy the confidence of the Government as well it could only be natural if——"

"He were in the future to become Minister of War!" That was the voice of the man with the peaked nose, Fouché, the Minister of Police.

Before Barras could say any more Theresa Tallien, in a very thin Venetian lace blouse, appeared before him. "Our beautiful Theresa," he smiled, and rose heavily to his feet.

Theresa motioned him to sit down again. "Don't get up, Director," she said. "And look, there's our Italian hero! Isn't it a charming afternoon, General Bonaparte, and doesn't Josephine look charming? I am told that you are taking little Eugene along with you to the Pyramids as your adjutant? May I introduce to you M. Ouvrard, the man who supplied ten thousand pairs of boots for your Italian Army? Ouvrard, here he is in person: France's strong man!" The rotund little man who followed in her wake bowed deeply.

Eliza dug me in the ribs: "Her latest boy friend! Army contractor Ouvrard! Not so long ago she was still living with Barras whom she had stolen from Josephine. Did you know that? But now that old fool sticks to the fifteen-year-olds. An uncouth chap I find him! His hair is dyed, of course. No one has hair as black as that."

All at once I felt I couldn't stand it any longer on this chair next to the perspiring, odiously perfumed Eliza. I jumped to my feet and pushed my way to the door in order to find a mirror outside in the small hall where I could powder my face.

The hall was half dark. Before I got to the candles flickering in front of the tall mirror I had a fright. Two figures leaning close to each other in a corner suddenly separated. One of them was in a white gown.

"Oh, I am so sorry," I said.

The white-gowned figure came forward into the light of the candle. It was Josephine.

"Sorry? Why?" she said, smoothing her babyish curls with a fugitive movement of her hand. "May I introduce M. Charles to you? Hippolyte, this is Joseph's charming sister-in-law, sister-in-law of my brother-in-law, that's our relationship, is it not, Mademoiselle Désirée?"

A very young man, certainly not more than twenty-five years of age, bowed slickly.

"This is M. Hippolyte Charles," continued Josephine, "one of our youngest and most successful—well, what? What do you do, Hippolyte? Oh, of course, Army contractor! One of our youngest Army contractors . . . !"

Josephine laughed and obviously found it all very amusing. "Mademoiselle Désirée," she added, "is an old rival of mine."

"Victorious or vanquished rival?" inquired M. Charles.

Before he got his answer we heard the clanking of spurs and Napoleon's voice from the door:

"Josephine, Josephine, where are you? All our guests are asking for you."

"I wanted to show Mademoiselle Désirée and M. Charles the Venetian mirror which you gave me in Montebello, Bonaparte," said Josephine calmly, taking him by the arm and pulling him towards M. Charles. "May I introduce to you a young Army contractor? M. Charles, here at last your greatest wish will be fulfilled: you may shake the hand of the Liberator of Italy!"

Her laughter sounded enchanting, and at once the signs of exasperation in Napoleon's face vanished.

"You wanted to talk to me, Euge—Désirée?" Napoleon said to me.

Quickly Josephine put her hand on the arm of M. Hippolyte Charles: "Come along, I must go back to my guests."

We were facing each other alone in the flickering candlelight. Nervously I started fishing for something in my bag, whilst Napoleon went up to the mirror and stared at his own face. It looked hollow and full of shadows in the uncertain light.

"Did you hear what Barras said a moment ago?" Napoleon spoke abruptly. He was so immersed in his thoughts that he talked to me in the intimate manner of the happy times of the past without noticing it.

"I heard it, but I didn't understand it. I know so little of these matters."

He continued to stare into the mirror. "'Internal enemies of the Republic,' a nice expression! It was meant for me. He knows that I could——"

He broke off, contemplated attentively the play of light and shadows on his face in the mirror and chewed his upper lip. Then he went on: "We Generals saved the Republic. And we Generals keep it alive. We might easily take it into our heads to form our own Government. . . . They beheaded the King and the Crown rolled into the gutter. All one need do is to pick it up. . . ."

He spoke like someone dreaming. And exactly as in days gone by, at first I felt fear and then a childish desire to laugh off the fear.

He swung round unexpectedly and said in an acid voice: "But I am going to Egypt. I leave it to the Directors to wrangle with the political parties, to let themselves be corrupted by Army contractors, to choke the French economy with worthless money. I am going to Egypt and shall plant the flag of the Republic——"

"I am sorry to interrupt you, General," I said. "I have written down here the name of a lady, and I ask you to give orders that she is to be provided for."

He took the chit out of my hand and read it close to the candles. "Marie Meunier, who is that?"

"The woman who lived with General Duphot, the mother of his son. I promised him that both should be provided for."

He dropped the chit and said with a gentle regret in his voice: "I felt sorry for you, very sorry. You were engaged to him, Désirée, weren't you?"

I felt like shouting into his face that I had had enough of this miserable comedy. But I only brought out hoarsely:

"You know quite well that I hardly knew Duphot. I don't understand why you torture me with these things, General."

"With what things, Désirée?"

"With these marriage proposals. I've had enough of them, I want to be left alone."

"Believe me, only in marriage can a woman find the fulfilment of her life," said Napoleon unctuously.

"I—I'd like to throw the candlestick at you!" I managed to jerk out, and I clenched my fists to prevent myself from really throwing things at him.

He came up to me and smiled, that fascinating smile of his which once upon a time meant everything to me. "We are friends, are we not, Bernadine Eugenie Désirée?" he asked.

"Will you promise me that Marie Meunier will be paid a pension for herself and her child?"

"Oh, here you are, Désirée! Get ready, we must be off!" That was Julie, who entered the hall at this moment with Joseph. When they saw Napoleon and me they stopped and looked at us in surprise.

"Will you promise, General?" I repeated.

"I promise, Mademoiselle Désirée." He took my hand and kissed it quickly. Then Joseph stepped between us and with a lot of back-slapping took leave of his brother.

PARIS, four weeks later.

The happiest day of my life started for me in the same way as all the other days. After breakfast I took the small green watering-can and began to water the two dusty palm trees in the living-room which Julie had brought home from Italy. Joseph and Julie, still sitting at the breakfast table, were discussing a letter, and I only listened with half an ear to what they were saying.

"You see, Julie," said Joseph, "he has accepted my invitation!"

"For heaven's sake, I haven't prepared a thing!" said Julie. "And whom else are you going to ask in? Shall I try for some cockerels? And what about trout in mayonnaise as hors-d'œuvre? Trout is dreadfully expensive just now, but . . . You ought to have told me before, Joseph."

"I couldn't be sure whether he'd accept my invitation. After all, he's only been in Paris for a few days and is inundated with invitations. Everybody wants to hear from him in person what really happened in Vienna."

At this point I went out to refill the watering-can. When I came back Joseph was just saying:

"—had written to him that my friend Director Barras and my brother Napoleon had told me so many pleasant things about him and I should be happy if I could welcome him to a modest meal in my home."

"And strawberries with Madeira sauce as a dessert," Julie was thinking aloud.

"And so he accepted! Do you know what that means? It means that personal contact with France's future Minister of War has been established! Napoleon's most particular desire is being fulfilled. Barras makes no secret of the fact that he wants

117

to hand the War Ministry over to him. Old Schérer was like so much wax in Napoleon's hand, but we haven't an inkling of what Bernadotte is going to do. Julie, the food must be really first-class, and——"

"Whom else shall we ask?"

I took the bowl of roses from the centre of the breakfast table and carried it into the kitchen to renew the water. On my return Joseph was just explaining:

"A small dinner in the family circle, that's it. That'll give Lucien and myself the opportunity to talk to him as much as we want. So: Josephine, Lucien, Christine, you and myself." Seeing me he added: "Yes, and of course our little one. Make yourself beautiful, Désirée, to-night you'll meet France's future Minister of War."

I am bored by all these 'small family dinners' which Joseph has been giving all the time in honour of some Deputy, General or Ambassador. They are always arranged in order to spy out political behind-the-scene secrets and to send them red-hot in endless epistles by special courier across the sea after Napoleon, who is on his way to Egypt.

Joseph so far has not accepted—or received—a new ambassadorial appointment. He seems intent on staying in Paris to be 'at the centre of things', and since the last elections he has even entered the Assembly as Deputy for Corsica, which island, since Napoleon's victories, has naturally become very proud of its Bonapartes. Lucien too, independently of Joseph, has stood for Corsica and been elected. A few days ago, almost immediately after Napoleon's departure, he moved to Paris with his wife Christine. Madame Letitia had found a small apartment for them, and there they live precariously on Lucien's pay as a Deputy.

Lucien belongs to the extreme Left. When he was told that Napoleon expected him to divorce his wife he nearly split his sides with laughing. "My military brother seems to have gone off his head!" he shouted. "What is it he doesn't like about Christine?"

"Her father's tavern," said Joseph.

Lucien laughed. "Mama's father only had a farm in Corsica, and a very small one at that!" Suddenly he became thoughtful, frowned, and said to Joseph: "Don't you think that, for a Republican, Napoleon has very peculiar ideas?"

Almost every day we read Lucien's speeches in the papers. That thin, blue-eyed, brown-haired fellow seems to be a great orator. It's impossible to say whether he really likes these 'small family dinners' which are given for the sake of good connections or whether he only comes so as not to offend Joseph and Julie.

As I was putting on a yellow silk dress Julie slipped into my room. With her usual introductory phrase: "If only nothing goes wrong! . . ." she threw herself on to my bed. "Why don't you put the brocade ribbon in your hair? It suits you," she said.

"Why!" I said, searching in my drawer among ribbons and combs, "why should I? There won't be anybody there of any interest to me."

"Joseph heard that this future Minister of War is supposed to have said Napoleon's Egyptian campaign was nothing but midsummer madness and the Government should never have allowed it," said Julie.

In a fit of bad temper I decided not to put anything at all in my hair but simply to brush my curls upwards and try to keep them up with two combs. I grumbled at Julie as I was doing my hair: "These political dinners bore me to tears."

"Josephine at first didn't want to come," said Julie. "Joseph had to explain to her how important it would be for Napoleon to be on good terms with this rising man. She's bought a country house, Malmaison, and she was going out there with some friends for a picnic."

"And she's right, too, in this beautiful weather," I said, looking through the open window into the pale blue evening, which was full of the scent of lime trees. I almost hated the unknown guest of honour who kept me in the house. At that moment we heard the sound of a carriage driving up to the door, and Julie rushed out of the room with a last "If only nothing goes wrong!"

I didn't feel like going down and welcoming visitors. Not until I heard a babel of voices and got the feeling that they had all arrived and Julie was waiting for me did I overcome my reluctance. When I had reached the door to the dining-room and put my hand on the door-handle it occurred to me that I could have gone to bed and said that I had a headache. But it was too late then. The next moment I would have given anything for it not to have been too late and if I had really gone to bed with a headache.

A man was standing with his back to the door. But I recognised that back at once, the back of a giant of a man in dark blue uniform with big gold epaulettes and a broad sash in the colours of the Republic. Joseph, Julie, Josephine, Lucien and his wife were standing around him in a semi-circle holding liqueur glasses in their hands.

I couldn't help standing by the door like one paralysed and staring in confusion at the broad-shouldered back. But the family circle found my conduct rather strange. Joseph looked at me over the shoulders of his guest, the eyes of the others followed Joseph's, and at last the giant himself noticed that something strange was going on behind his back, interrupted himself and turned round.

His eyes grew wide in amazement. My heart beat so wildly that I could hardly breathe.

" Désirée, come on, we're waiting for you," said Julie.

At the same time Joseph came to me, took my arm and said: " This, General Bernadotte, is my wife's little sister: Mademoiselle Désirée Clary."

I never looked at him. Like someone in a daze I kept my eyes fixed on one of his bold buttons, felt vaguely that he was politely kissing my hand and heard from a long way away Joseph's voice saying:

" We were interrupted, General. What was it you were going to say?"

" I—I'm afraid I really don't remember what it was."

I would have known his voice among a thousand others! It was the voice from the bridge across the Seine in the rain, the voice out of the dark corner in the cab, the voice at the door of the house in the Rue du Bac.

" Sit down, please," said Julie.

But General Bernadotte did not move.

" Sit down, please," Julie repeated and went up to Bernadotte. At that he offered her his arm. Joseph, Josephine and all the rest of us sat down with them.

The ' small family dinner ' given for reasons of political expedience took a course very different from the one Joseph had mapped out for it.

As arranged, General Bernadotte was sitting between the hostess and Josephine, and Lucien had taken Joseph's place beside Julie so that Joseph could sit exactly opposite General Bernadotte and direct the conversation. But the General seemed a little absent-minded. Mechanically he began to occupy himself with the hors-d'œuvre, and Joseph had to raise his glass twice to him, before he realised it and responded. I could tell by his face that he was thinking hard, that he was trying to remember what he had been told that day in Madame Tallien's house: about Napoleon and his fiancée in Marseilles, a young girl with a big dowry who was Joseph Bonaparte's sister-in-law, and about Napoleon's desertion of fiancée and dowry. . . . So immersed was he that Joseph had to speak to him three times before the guest realised that we all wanted to drink to him. Hastily he raised his glass.

He remembered his duties to the lady by his side and turned to her abruptly: "How long has your sister been living in Paris?"

The question came so unexpectedly that Julie at first was taken aback and did not quite understand what he was driving at.

"You are both from Marseilles, aren't you?" he asked again. "What I mean is, has your sister been living in Paris for a long time now?"

By now Julie had collected her wits. "No," she answered, "only for a few months. It's her first stay in Paris. And she likes it here very much, don't you, Désirée?"

"Paris is a very beautiful town," I said awkwardly, like a schoolgirl.

"Yes, as long as it doesn't rain," he said, regarding me intently.

"Oh yes, even when it rains," put in Christine, the inn-keeper's daughter from St. Maximin, eagerly. "I think Paris is a fairyland town."

"You are quite right, Madame. Fairy tales happen even when it rains," Bernadotte said solemnly.

Joseph began to fidget. After all, he had not lured the future Minister of War into his house with all the powers of persuasion he could muster simply to discuss the weather and its influence on fairy tales. He took the initiative and said with an important air, "I had a letter from my brother Napoleon yesterday."

But Bernadotte didn't seem to be interested at all.

Joseph continued, "He writes that the journey is going according to plan and that the British Fleet under Nelson hasn't even let itself be seen yet."

"That's probably due more to your brother's good luck than to his good management," Bernadotte said good-temperedly, and raised his glass: "To General Bonaparte's health! I am very much in his debt!"

Joseph didn't know whether to be pleased or offended by this.

Bernadotte's whole conduct left no doubt that he felt himself to be the equal of Napoleon in rank. It was true, of course, that Napoleon had been Commander-in-Chief in Italy, but meanwhile Bernadotte had been an Ambassador and he knew as well as the rest of us that he was meant to be Minister of War.

Things began to happen as the cockerels were served, and Josephine of all women was the prime mover of it all. For some time I had felt her watching General Bernadotte and myself. I don't believe that there is anybody else in the world who can sense the tensions and the invisible forces working between a man and a woman to such an extent as Josephine. Up till now she had been quiet. When Julie talked about this being my first stay in Paris her thin eyebrows went up and she regarded Bernadotte with great interest. It was certainly possible that she remembered Bernadotte as having been present that afternoon at Madame Tallien's house. . . .

At last she found the opening she had wanted to replace Joseph's conversational topics, which ran on political and military lines, by something more to her liking. Inclining her head with its babyish curls, she winked at Bernadotte and asked:

"It can't have been very easy for you as Ambassador in Vienna, can it? I mean because of your being a bachelor. Haven't you often missed the presence of an Ambassadress in the Embassy?"

Firmly, Bernadotte put down his knife and fork. "Indeed I have, indeed! I really can't tell you, my dear Josephine—I may call you Josephine, may I not, as in those days in your friend Madame Tallien's house? Well, I really can't tell you how sorry I was not to be married. But," and now he turned to the whole assembled company, "but I ask you, ladies and gentlemen, what am I to do?"

Nobody knew whether he was joking or in earnest. There was an embarrassed silence round the table till at last Julie forced herself to remark with awkward politeness, "You haven't found the right one yet, General."

"But yes, Madame, I have! Only she disappeared again, and now——" He shrugged his shoulders as if he were in a kind of humorous dilemma and looked at me laughingly.

"And now you simply go and look for her and propose to her," Christine exclaimed. She did not find the conversation at all unusual but was quite at home in it. In her father's ale-house in St. Maximin the young fellows of the village used to talk to her about very much the same kind of difficulty.

Bernadotte grew serious. "You are right, Madame," he said. "I shall propose to her."

With that he got up, pushed his chair back and turned to Joseph: "Monsieur Joseph Bonaparte, I have the honour to ask you for the hand of your sister-in-law Mademoiselle Désirée Clary." He sat down again without taking his eyes off Joseph.

There was a deathly silence. A clock could be heard ticking, and perhaps, I thought, my heartbeat too echoed in everybody's ear. In desperation I stared down at the white tablecloth.

At last Joseph spoke. "I don't quite understand, General Bernadotte. Do you really mean that?"

"I do."

Again the deathly silence fell.

"I—I think you ought to give Désirée time to think over your proposal."

"I have given her time, Monsieur Bonaparte."

"But you've only just met her," Julie said, trembling with excitement.

I looked up. "I should very much like to marry you, General Bernadotte."

Was it I who said that? A chair fell over with a great clatter, curious and stupefied faces stared at me intolerably, I don't know how I escaped from the dining-room. I only know that I found myself sitting on the bed in my room, crying, crying.

After a while Julie came in and pressed me to her and tried to calm me down. "You needn't marry him, darling. Don't cry, don't cry."

"But I must cry," I sobbed, "I must. I can't help it, but I'm so happy, so happy that I simply have to cry."

Before I went down again—they were all in the living-room now—I washed my face in cold water and powdered it. But Bernadotte said at once, "You've been crying again, Mademoiselle Désirée."

He was sitting next to Josephine on a sofa. But Josephine got up and said, "It's Désirée's place next to Jean-Baptiste now."

I sat down next to him, and then everybody talked at once to overcome their embarrassment. There was some champagne left over from dinner, and as the dessert had been forgotten in the agitation over the course of events we ate it now. The strawberries and Madeira sauce helped me over the first frightful moments.

Bernadotte was not in the least embarrassed but radiated good temper all round. After we had eaten the dessert he turned to Julie and asked politely, "Do you mind, Madame, if I take your sister for a drive?"

Julie nodded understandingly: "Of course not, my dear General! When is it to be? To-morrow afternoon?"

"No, I rather thought, now."

"But it's dark now!" Julie objected in dismay. No, it wasn't done for a young girl to go for a drive with a gentlemen in the dark.

I got up and said with determination to Julie, "It'll only be a short drive. We'll be back soon." Then I left the room so quickly that Bernadotte didn't even find time to say good-bye properly to everybody present.

His carriage, an open one, was standing outside. We drove through a spring evening filled with the scent of lime blossom. When we got nearer to the heart of the city its lights sparkled so brightly that we couldn't see the stars any more.

All the time we hadn't spoken a word. As we were rolling along the bank of the Seine Bernadotte called to the coachman, and the carriage stopped close to a bridge.

"That's the bridge. Remember it?" said Bernadotte.

We got out, went side by side to the middle of the bridge and leaned over the edge. The thousand lights of Paris were dancing up and down on the waves of the river.

"I went several times to the Rue du Bac and asked after you. But the people there didn't want to tell me anything about you!"

"Yes, they knew that at that time I was here secretly and without permission," I said.

We went back to the carriage, and he put his arm round my shoulders. My head just came up to his epaulettes.

"You told me that night that you were far too small for me," he said.

"Yes, and now I am smaller still! I was wearing shoes with high heels then and they're quite out of fashion now. But perhaps that doesn't matter."

"Perhaps what doesn't matter?"

"That I am so little."

"It doesn't matter at all. Just the opposite!"

"How do you mean 'just the opposite'?"

"I like it."

On the journey back I pressed my cheek against his shoulder. But the epaulettes scratched rather a lot.

"This awful gold stuff bothers me," I murmured crossly.

He laughed. "Yes, I know, you don't like Generals."

It struck me all of a sudden that he was the fifth General who had proposed to me. Napoleon, Junot, Marmont, Duphot:

I decided to forget about them. I preferred to have my cheek scratched by the epaulettes of the fifth, named Bernadotte.

When we arrived back we found that all the guests had gone meanwhile and there were only Julie and Joseph left.

"I hope you'll come to see us here often, General," said Joseph.

"Daily——" I said, and stopped. Then, resolutely, I went on and brought out his name for the first time: "Daily, won't you, Jean-Baptiste?"

"We have decided to get married very soon. You won't raise any objection?" Bernadotte asked Joseph.

Of course, we hadn't talked about the wedding at all. But as far as I was concerned I would have married him then and there.

"I shall start to-morrow looking for a pleasant little house," Bernadotte continued, "and as soon as I have found one to our liking we'll get married."

Something he had said and I remembered ran like a sweet little tune through my mind: 'For years I have saved up part of my salary. I could buy a little house for you and the child.'

"I shall write to Mama at once," I heard Julie say. And Joseph added, "Good night, brother-in-law, good night. Napoleon will be very pleased about the news."

As soon as Bernadotte had gone Joseph exclaimed at once: "I don't understand this at all. Bernadotte is certainly no man of rash decisions!"

"Isn't he a bit too old for Désirée? He's at least——"

"In the middle thirties, I should say," Joseph estimated. Turning to me he said, "Tell me, Désirée, do you realise that you are going to marry one of the most important men in the Republic?"

"The trousseau!" Julie cried, "what about the trousseau? If Désirée is really going to get married soon we'll have to do something about the trousseau."

"We don't want this man Bernadotte to say that the sister-in-law of a Bonaparte was married without a first-class trousseau," Joseph said, and looked at us solemnly.

"How long will it take you to get everything ready?"

"As far as the shopping part of it goes, that's quickly done," said Julie. "But the initials have to be embroidered on the linen."

At that point I intervened in the excited talk: "But the trousseau is all ready in Marseilles. All we need do is to send word to have it despatched here. And the initials are all on." -

"Yes, yes, of course," cried Julie, with eyes as round as saucers for sheer surprise, " Désirée is right, the initials are all on, B——"

"Yes," I smiled going to the door, " B, B, and nothing but B!"

"The whole thing seems very peculiar to me," murmured Joseph with suspicion in his voice.

"If only she's going to be happy!" Julie said softly.

Happy, happy, oh how happy I am! Let me tell it to all the world, you, God in Heaven, you, lime trees in the street, you, roses in the vase, how happy I am!

PART II

THE WIFE OF
MARSHAL BERNADOTTE

SCEAUX near PARIS
Autumn of the Year VI (1798).

I was married to General Jean-Baptiste Bernadotte on the 30th of Thermidor in the Year VI of the Republic at seven o'clock in the evening at the registry office in Sceaux, a suburb of Paris. My husband's witnesses were his friend Antoine Morien, a captain in the cavalry, and the Recorder of Sceaux, Monsieur François Desgranges. I for my part had no option but to ask Uncle Somis, who, as a matter of principle, never misses a family wedding, and, of course, Joseph to be my witnesses. At the last moment Lucien Bonaparte turned up at the registry office, so that I appeared with three witnesses in tow.

After the ceremony we all went to the Rue du Rocher, where Julie had prepared a magnificent feast. (I should add that everything went according to plan, but it had cost Julie three sleepless nights!) So as not to offend anybody, Joseph had asked all the Bonapartes living in or near Paris. Madame Letitia repeatedly expressed her regret that her stepbrother Fesch, who had returned to his priestly office, had been prevented from coming. At first Mama had intended to come from Gonoa for the wedding. But she had been ailing a lot lately, and therefore the journey was considered too strenuous for her in the summer heat. As for Jean-Baptiste, he hates all kinds of family festivities, and as he has no relatives in Paris he only brought his old friend Morien along. My wedding therefore was completely dominated by the Bonapartes, for whom Uncle Somis, a slow, comfortable provincial, is no match. To my astonishment Joseph had asked at the last minute General Junot and his wife Laura, the daughter of a Corsican friend of Madame Letitia's whom he had married at Napoleon's wish. Junot, a member of Napoleon's staff, was in Paris for a short time to report to the Government on Napoleon's entry into Alexandria and Cairo and his victory at the Battle of the Nile.

I felt dreadfully bored during the wedding breakfast. It began very late. The late evening hours are the fashionable time now for getting married, and therefore Joseph had arranged for the ceremony to take place at seven o'clock. That made everything else late. Julie had wanted me to stay in bed the whole day before going to the registry office so that I should look as rested and as pretty as possible. But I had no time for that. I had to help Marie put away our cutlery, which we had only bought the day before. Besides there's always so much to do when one furnishes a house.

Only two days after Jean-Baptiste and I had become engaged he turned up to say that he had found a suitable house. I had to go there that very moment to look at it. It is a small house in the Rue de la Lune in Sceaux, 3, Rue de la Lune, to be exact. On the ground floor we have the kitchen, the dining-room and a small closet in which Jean-Baptiste put a writing desk and piles of books. Every day he comes along with more books and we have called the closet ' the study '. On the upper floor there are only a beautiful bedroom and a tiny chamber. Then there are two small offices, bedrooms for Marie and Fernand. Marie was imported into our ménage by me, Fernand by Jean-Baptiste.

Marie and Fernand quarrel all day long. Mama had wanted to take Marie with her when she moved to Genoa, but Marie refused. She didn't tell Mama what she was going to do but simply took a room in Marseilles and worked as a cook at family celebrations of people who were proud to have ' the former cook of Madame Clary ' working for them. But I knew that, although she had never said so in so many words, she was simply waiting. The day after my engagement I wrote her a short note: ' I am engaged to General B. of the bridge of which I once told you. As soon as he's found a suitable house we shall get married, and if I know him he'll find the house in twenty-four hours. When can you come?' I never had an answer to that letter. But a week later Marie arrived in Paris.

" I only hope Marie will get on with my Fernand," said Jean-Baptiste.

" Who is your Fernand?" I asked, startled.

It came out then that Fernand came from Jean-Baptiste's home town, Pau in Gascony, went to school with him and joined up at the same time. But whereas Jean-Baptiste was being promoted all the time, Fernand only just escaped being thrown out of the Army scores of times. Fernand is small and fat, his feet hurt him when the Army starts marching, and his stomach aches horribly when the battle begins. It isn't his fault, of course, but it's very disagreeable for him. All the same he wanted to stay in the Army to be near Jean-Baptiste. He has a passion for polishing boots and knows how to remove the most persistent grease stains from tunics. Two years ago he was given an honourable discharge from the Army so that he could devote himself entirely to the boots and stains and the creature comforts of Jean-Baptiste. When he was introduced to me he defined himself as ' the servant of my General and schoolmate of Bernadotte '.

As soon as Marie and Fernand set eyes on each other they started quarrelling. What about? About Fernand stealing from the larder and about Marie using his twenty-four shoe brushes and wanting to wash the General's underclothes without asking his, Fernand's, permission, and so on. . . .

When I saw our little house for the first time I said to Jean-Baptiste, " I shall write to Etienne to pay over my marriage portion to you."

Jean-Baptiste sniffed contemptuously: " What do you take me for? Do you think that I am going to build our home with my wife's money?"

" But, Joseph——"

" I must ask you not to compare me with the Bonapartes," he said sharply. Then he took me laughingly by the shoulders and said, " My little one, all Bernadotte can buy you to-day is a doll's house in Sceaux. But if ever you feel like wanting a mansion——"

At that I nearly screamed: " For heaven's sake, anything but that! Promise me that we are never, never going to live in a mansion, please!"

I remembered with horror those long months in the Italian *palazzi*, and the thought came to me that people were speaking of Bernadotte as one of ' the coming men'. His epaulettes looked ominous to me. " Promise me," I implored him, " never a mansion, never!"

He gazed at me. His smile faded slowly from his face. " We belong together, Désirée," he said. " In Vienna I lived in a splendid palace. But to-morrow I may be ordered to the front and then I shall have nothing but a camp bed in the open. And the day after my headquarters may be moved to a castle, and if I asked you to join me there, would you refuse?"

We were standing under the big chestnut tree in our future garden. ' Soon we'll be married,' I thought, ' and I shall try to be a good wife and to keep everything beautiful and in apple-pie order. That's what I want, this tiny house with the chestnut tree and the overgrown flowers beds.' But then the thought of what I wanted was followed by the ghastly images of high-ceilinged rooms, marble tiles and lackeys always getting in the way.

"We shall be very happy here," I said in a murmur.

But he was insistent. "Would you refuse?" he repeated.

I nestled up to him. "I shan't refuse," I said, "but I shan't be very happy in a castle."

When I was kneeling in front of the kitchen cupboard on the morning of my wedding day putting away the white china, Marie asked, "Aren't you excited, Eugenie?" A few hours later, when Julie's maid was trying to coax my obstinate hair into Josephine's babyish curls, Julie remarked, "Strange, I do believe, darling, you are not at all excited."

I shook my head. Excited? Why should I be excited? Since that fateful moment in the dark cab, when Jean-Baptiste's hand was the only bit of warmth left in my life, I have always known that I belonged to him. In a few hours' time I should put my signature on a piece of paper in Sceaux Registry Office and with that confirm what I have been certain of for so long. No, I wasn't excited at all.

After the ceremony we had the wedding breakfast, which, as I said before, was such a boring affair. Most of the talk, apart from Uncle Somis' toast to the bridal couple and some revolutionary oratory from Lucien, was about Napoleon's Egyptian campaign. Jean-Baptiste was heartily tired of this subject, but Joseph and Lucien had taken it into their heads to try to convince him that the conquest of Egypt was one more proof of Napoleon's genius.

"I think it out of the question," said Jean-Baptiste, "that we can hold Egypt permanently. And the British know it and so they don't bother to engage in a colonial war with us."

"But," Joseph put in, "Napoleon has taken Alexandria and Cairo already and won the Battle of the Nile."

"That won't disturb the British greatly; properly speaking, Egypt is not under British but under Turkish suzerainty anyway, and the British consider our troops as no more than a passing inconvenience——"

"At the Battle of the Nile the enemy suffered 20,000 killed, we not even fifty," interrupted Junot.

"Magnificent," added Joseph.

Jean-Baptiste shrugged his shoulders: "Magnificent? The glorious French Army under the leadership of its inspired

General Bonaparte and with the help of modern heavy artillery killed 20,000 half-naked Africans who hadn't even boots on their feet. Really, I must say, a magnificent victory of the gun over the bow and arrow!"

Lucien opened his mouth to say something, but then hesitated. He looked sad when he said at last, " Killed, in the name of the Rights of Man."

" The end justifies the means," said Joseph. " Napoleon will carry his conquests farther and drive the British out of the Mediterranean region."

" They wouldn't dream of challenging us on land," declared Jean-Baptiste. " Why should they? They have their fleet, and not even you will deny that it is far superior to our own Navy. The moment they destroy the ships which carried Bonaparte's Army across the sea——" Jean-Baptiste broke off and looked at each of us in turn: " Don't you see what is at stake? Any moment now a French Army may find itself cut off from its base. And then your brother with all his victorious regiments will be caught in the desert like a mouse in a trap. The Egyptian campaign is an insane game of poker and the stake is far too high for our Republic."

I knew that Joseph and Junot were going to write to Napoleon that very night that my husband had called him a poker player. What I did not know, however, nor anybody else in Paris for that matter, was the fact that sixteen days before, the British under the command of a certain Admiral Nelson had attacked the whole French fleet in the Bay of Aboukir and almost completely wiped it out. Further, since that day Napoleon had been trying desperately to establish contact with France, failing which, he saw that his soldiers and himself would be bound to perish in the burning desert sands. No, nobody could possibly know that on my wedding day Jean-Baptiste Bernadotte foretold exactly what had in fact already happened.

At this stage of the discussion I couldn't help yawning, which is not a very decorous thing for a bride to do. But then, I was getting married for the first time in my life and didn't really know how to behave. Jean-Baptiste noticed it, rose and said:

" It's late, Désirée. I think we ought to go home."

There it was, for the first time, this so personal phrase, ' We ought to go home ' . . .

At the bottom end of the table Caroline and Hortense looked at each other darkly and started to giggle. My comfortable

Uncle Somis winked at me and patted me as I was saying good-bye to him. " Don't be afraid, little one," he said, " Bernadotte won't eat you."

We drove in the open carriage to Sceaux through a sultry late summer's night. The stars and a round yellow moon seemed to be within arm's reach, and I felt that it might be no accident that our house stood in the Rue de la Lune, Moon Street.

When we entered the house we saw the dining-room brightly lit. Tall candles were burning in the silver candelabra, a present from Josephine and Napoleon. On the table we found a bottle of champagne and glasses and a bowl full of grapes, peaches and marzipan cakes. But the house was silent and there was not a soul to be seen.

" That's Marie's work," I said, smiling.

" No," said Jean-Baptiste, " Fernand's!"

" But I know Marie's marzipan cakes," I said, and ate one.

Jean-Baptiste regarded the bottle thoughtfully. " If we drink any more to-night," he said, " we'll have a dreadful headache to-morrow morning."

I agreed and went to open the glass door leading out into the garden. The scent of roses hung in the air and the chestnut leaves glittered silvery at the edges. Behind me Jean-Baptiste extinguished the candles one by one.

Our bedroom was quite dark. I felt my way to the window and drew back the curtains to let the moonlight in. Jean-Baptiste meanwhile had gone into the little room next to the bedroom and I heard him rummaging for something. Perhaps he wanted to give me time to undress and go to bed, I thought, and felt grateful to him for his consideration. I undressed quickly, went to the wide double bed, found my nightdress spread out on the silk cover, put it on, slipped quickly under the blanket—and screamed at the top of my voice.

" For heaven's sake, Désirée, what is it?" Jean-Baptiste was standing by the bed.

" I don't know. Something pricked me horribly." I moved. " Ow, ow, there it is again!"

Jean-Baptiste lit a candle, and I sat up and threw the blanket back: roses! Roses, roses with prickly thorns!

" What idiot——?" Jean-Baptiste started shouting, and then stopped as we stared at the rose-strewn bed in confusion.

I collected the roses as Jean-Baptiste held up the blanket. The bed was full of them, there seemed to be no end to roses and thorns.

"It's probably Fernand's doing," I murmured. "He wanted to give us a surprise."

But Jean-Baptiste would have none of that: "Of course it wasn't Fernand, of course it was Marie! Roses, I ask you, roses in a front-line soldier's bed!"

I put the roses on the bedside table, from which they spread their heavy scent. Suddenly I realised that Jean-Baptiste was looking at me and that I had nothing on but a nightdress. Quickly I sat down on the bed and said, "I am cold. Let me have the blanket back." Immediately he let it drop on me.

It was unbearably hot under the blanket. Yet I covered myself up to the ears and kept my eyes shut, and so I didn't notice that he had put out the candle.

Next morning it came out that Marie and Fernand for the first time had agreed on something. They had agreed to adorn our bridal bed with roses and they had, both of them, forgotten about the thorns.

Jean-Baptiste had taken two months' leave to spend the first weeks of our married life with me. But from the moment that the news of the annihilation of our fleet at Aboukir reached Paris he had to go to the Luxembourg Palace almost every morning to attend, with the Minister of War, the council meetings of the Directors.

He had hired a stable near the house and put two horses in it. Whenever I thought back to my honeymoon weeks I saw myself in the late afternoon standing by the garden gate and waiting for Jean-Baptiste. And as soon as a distant clip-clop of hooves became audible my heart would start beating madly and I would say to myself for the thousandth time that within a second or two Jean-Baptiste would round the corner on one of the horses, that he was my husband really and truly and for ever and that I wasn't dreaming, wasn't dreaming at all. . . . Ten minutes later we would sit under the chestnut tree and drink coffee, and Jean-Baptiste would tell me all the things that would be in the *Moniteur* next morning and also all the things that must not become known on any account. And all the time I would blink contentedly into the setting sun and play with the chestnuts lying about in the grass.

The defeat at Aboukir electrified our enemies. Russia was getting ready for war again, and the Austrians, who only a short time ago had apologised to our Government for the insult to our flag, yes, the Austrians too were once more on the march and nearing our frontiers from Switzerland and from Austria.

The Italian states under French sovereignty which Napoleon had so proudly founded received the Austrians with open arms, and everywhere our armies were in panic-stricken flight.

On one of these afternoons Jean-Baptiste was particularly late in returning. As he jumped off his horse he told me, " They've offered me the Supreme Command in Italy. I am to stop the rot and at least attempt to hold Lombardy." We drank our coffee, as evening was falling. After that he fetched a candle and many sheets of paper into the garden and started writing.

" Are you going to accept the Command?" I asked once, feeling afraid, much afraid of I don't know what.

He looked up. " I beg your pardon? Oh, I see. Yes, I'll accept if they accept my conditions. I am just drafting them." And on went his pen over sheet after sheet.

Afterwards he went into the house, and there he continued writing. I put his supper on his writing desk, but he didn't notice it and went on writing.

A few days later I heard by chance from Joseph that Jean-Baptiste had handed in to Director Barras an excellent memorandum concerning the Italian front. In it he had stated exactly the number of troops he needed to hold the front and to garrison the rear areas properly.

But the Directors could not agree to his conditions. More men were conscripted, but there were no weapons or uniforms to equip them. Under the circumstances Jean-Baptiste refused the responsibility for the Italian front. So Schérer, the Minister of War, took over the Command himself.

One day two weeks later Jean-Baptiste appeared at home suddenly about lunch time. I was just helping Marie to bottle plums when I saw him, and I ran into the garden to meet him.

" Don't kiss me," I warned him, " I smell of kitchen, we're bottling plums, so many that you won't get anything but plums for the whole of the winter."

" But I shan't be here to eat your plums," he said, and went into the house. " Fernand," he shouted, " Fernand, get the field uniform ready, pack the saddle bags. We leave at seven to-morrow morning. At nine o'clock you'll take my luggage——"

I didn't hear the rest, he had disappeared into the house, and I was left by the garden gate.

The whole of the afternoon we spent in the garden. The sun had lost its warmth. Withered leaves covered the lawn. Yes, it had turned into autumn overnight. I had my hands folded in my lap and listened to his words and the sound of his voice. Sometimes he spoke to me as to a grown-up person, and then again softly and tenderly as if I were a child.

"You've always known, haven't you, that I would have to go to the front again. You've married a soldier, after all, and you are a sensible woman, you must calm yourself and be brave——"

"I don't want to be brave," I said obstinately.

"Listen, Jourdan has taken over the command of three armies, the Army of the Danube, the so-called Swiss Army and the Observation Army. Masséna is going to try with the Swiss Army to hold back the enemy at the Swiss border. I am in command of the Observation Army and I am moving up to the Rhine, which I am going to cross at two points, near the Fort Louis du Rhin and between Speyer and Mayence. I demanded thirty thousand men for the conquest and occupation of the Rhineland and they've been promised. But the Government won't be able to keep its promise. Désirée, I'm going to cross the Rhine with a make-believe army, I shall have to beat the enemy with a make-believe army—are you listening, my little one?"

"There's nothing you cannot do, Jean-Baptiste," I said, and I was almost in tears.

He sighed. "The Government unfortunately seems to be of the same opinion as you and will let me cross the Rhine with a bunch of miserably equipped raw recruits."

"'We Generals saved the Republic and we Generals keep it alive'," I murmured, "Napoleon once said to me."

"Naturally! That's what the Republic pays its Generals for. There's nothing peculiar in that."

"The man from whom I bought the plums this morning abused the Government and the Army for all he was worth. He said, 'As long as we had General Bonaparte in Italy we won all the battles and the Austrians begged for peace. As soon as he's away to carry our glory overseas everything is upside down.' Strange, the impression Napoleon's campaign has made on simple people."

"And that Napoleon's defeat at Aboukir has been the signal for a sudden attack of our enemies seems to have escaped your greengrocer. And that Napoleon won battles in Italy but never fortified the conquered territories sufficiently seems to have escaped him too. Now we shall have to hold the frontier with ridiculously small army contingents whilst colleague Bonaparte is sunning himself with his excellently equipped Army on the banks of the Nile and everybody thinks him the strong man!"

"'A King's crown lies in the gutter, and all one need do is to pick it up'," I murmured.

"Who said that?" Jean-Baptiste almost shouted the question.

"Napoleon."

"To you?"

"No, to himself. He was looking into a mirror at the time. I was only standing next to him by chance."

After that we were silent for a long time. Darkness fell, and I could no longer see his face.

The silence was broken by Marie's furious yelling from the kitchen. "I won't have pistols cleaned on my kitchen table. Take them away, at once!"

We heard Fernand answer in a soothing voice, "Do let me clean them here. I shall put the bullets in outside."

"Take them away, I say," Marie kept on yelling.

"Do you use your pistols in battle?" I asked Jean-Baptiste.

"Very rarely, since I've become a General," he answered out of the dark.

It was a long, long night. For many hours I lay alone in our bed and counted the chimes of the little church of Sceaux, knowing that downstairs in the study Jean-Baptiste was bending over maps and marking them with thin lines and crosses and circles. At last I must have fallen asleep, for suddenly I woke up terrified, feeling that something dreadful had happened. Jean-Baptiste was asleep by my side. My startled movement woke him up.

"What is it?" he murmured.

"I had a dreadful dream," I whispered. "I dreamt that you were riding away—riding to a war."

"I am riding to a war to-morrow," he answered, with the front-line soldier's ability to be wide awake at once as soon as he is woken up. "By the way," he continued, "I want to speak to you about something. Tell me, Désirée, what do you do during the day?"

"Do? What do I do? How do you mean? Yesterday I helped Marie with the plums. And the day before yesterday I went with Julie to her dressmaker, Madame Berthier, the one who fled to England with the aristocrats and has come back now. And last week——"

"Yes, but what do you *do*, Désirée?"

"Nothing, really," I said in confusion.

He put his arm under my head and pressed me to his

shoulder. "Désirée, I shouldn't like you to have too much time on your hands when I'm away, and so I thought that you should take lessons."

"Lessons? I haven't had lessons of any kind since I was ten."

"That's why," he answered.

"I went to school when I was six, together with Julie. It was a school kept by nuns in a convent and all convents were dissolved when I was ten. Then Mama wanted to teach me and Julie herself, but it never really came to anything. How long did you go to school, Jean-Baptiste?"

"From my eleventh to my thirteenth year. Then they threw me out."

"Why?"

"One of our teachers was unfair to Fernand."

"And so you told him what you thought of him?"

"No, I hit him."

"I'm sure that was the only thing to do," I said, and snuggled as close up to him as possible. "I thought you'd gone to school for years and years because you are so clever. And the many books you are always reading. . . ."

"At first," he said, "I simply tried to make up for lost time. Then I learnt what they teach you in officers' training schools. But now I have to get to know a lot of other things as well. For instance, if you have to administer occupied territories, you have to have some idea of commerce, of law, of—but anyway, they aren't the kind of things that you need to know, little girl. I thought you should take lessons in music and deportment."

"In deportment? D'you mean dancing? But I can dance. I've danced at home in Marseilles every year on Bastille Day in the Town Hall square."

"No, I didn't mean dancing. Young girls used to learn quite a few other things besides dancing in their boarding-schools. How to bow, for example, or how to invite your guests with a motion of your hand to move from one room into another——"

"Jean-Baptiste," I interrupted him, "we've only got the dining-room! If ever one of your visitors should want to go from the dining-room to your study what need is there for me to make elaborate gestures with my hand?"

"If I am made Military Governor at some place or other then you'll be the first lady of the district and you'll have to receive innumerable dignitaries in your salons."

" Salons!" I was full of indigation. " Jean-Baptiste, are you talking again about castles and mansions?" And I bit him in the shoulder.

" Ow, stop!" he shouted, and I let go.

" You can't imagine," he said, " how, at that time in Vienna, all the Viennese aristocrats and the foreign diplomats waited for the moment when the French Ambassador would compromise his Republic. I am sure they prayed to high heaven that I would eat fish with the wrong knife. We owe it to the Republic, Désirée, to conduct ourselves impeccably." After a while he added, " It would be lovely if you could play the piano, Désirée."

" I don't think it would be lovely."

" But you are musical!"

" I don't know about that. I like music very much, yes. Julie plays the piano, but it sounds awful. It's a crime to play the piano badly."

" I should like you to take piano and also a few singing lessons," he said with determination. " I told you about my friend Rodolphe Kreutzer, the violin virtuoso, didn't I? He went with me to Vienna, and he brought a Viennese composer to me in the Embassy. Wait a moment, what was his name? Oh yes, Beethoven. Monsieur Beethoven and Kreutzer played to me many an evening, and I've regretted it ever since that, as a child, I was not taught to play an instrument——" he broke into laughter: " But my mother was glad if she could find the money to buy a new Sunday suit for me." He became serious again, unfortunately. " I do want you to take music lessons. I asked Kreutzer yesterday to give me the address of a music teacher. You'll find it in the drawer of my writing desk. Start on them and write to me regularly how you're getting on."

A cold hand seemed to claw at my heart. Write to me regularly, he had said, write, write, write. Nothing left but writing. . . .

A leaden grey morning light came in through the curtains. I stared at them, I could recognise their colour and pattern clearly. But Jean-Baptiste had fallen asleep again.

Someone hammered at the door. " Half-past six, *mon Général*!" That was Fernand's voice.

Half an hour later we were having breakfast, and for the first time I saw Jean-Baptiste in his field uniform. Neither ribbons nor medals nor sashes relieved its severe dark blue. Hardly, however, had I taken a sip of my coffee when the dreadful business of leave-taking began. Horses whinnied, people knocked at the house door, unfamiliar voices spoke and spurs clanked. Fernand opened the door: "The gentlemen have arrived, sir!"

"Show them in," said Jean-Baptiste, and the next moment the room was full of officers I had never seen before. Jean-Baptiste introduced them casually as 'The gentlemen of my staff,' told them that I was delighted to meet them, and then jumped to his feet: "Ready," he said, "let's go!"

He turned to me: "Good-bye, my little girl. Write often. The War Office will send your letters on to me by special courier. Good-bye, Marie! Look after your mistress!"

With that he went, and all the staff officers disappeared with him. I wanted to kiss him once more, I thought. But the room filled with the grey morning light all at once, started to swirl round me, the yellow flames of the candles on the table flickered strangely, and then all went black.

When I came to I was lying on my bed. A repusive smell of vinegar surrounded me, and Marie's face hung close to mine.

"You've fainted, Eugenie," said Marie.

I pushed the compress with its nasty smell of vinegar away from my head. "I wanted to kiss him just once more, Marie, just to say good-bye, you know."

SCEAUX near PARIS, New Year's Eve between the years VI and VII. (The last year of the 18th century is just beginning.)

New Year bells have torn me out of my terrible dream, the bells of Sceaux village church and the distant ones from Notre-Dame and the other Paris churches. In my dream I was sitting in the little summer house in Marseilles and talking to a man who looked exactly like Jean-Baptiste, but I knew he was our son and not Jean-Baptiste. 'You've missed your deportment lesson, Mama, and your dancing lessons with Monsieur Montel,' my son said in the voice of Jean-Baptiste. I wanted to explain that I had been far too tired for that. Just then the horrible thing happened: my son shrank, he got smaller and smaller and finally was only just a dwarf, not even knee-high. The dwarf, my son, clung to my knee and whispered, 'Cannon fodder, Mama, I am nothing but cannon fodder and I am ordered to go to the Rhine. I myself rarely use pistols for shooting, but the others do—bang bang!' He was shaking with laughter all the time. A mad fear seized me, I wanted to grab the dwarf to protect him. But he kept slipping from my grasp and under the white garden table. I bent down, but I was so tired, oh so tired and sad. And suddenly Joseph was standing by my side and held out his glass to me: 'Long live the Bernadotte dynasty!' and he laughed bad-temperedly. I caught his eyes, and they were the scintillating ones of Napoleon. At that point the bells struck up and I awoke.

Now I am sitting in Jean-Baptiste's study and have only just managed to find an inch of room among the tomes and maps for my diary. From the streets I can hear merry voices, laughter and tipsy singing. Why is everybody in such good humour when a new year begins? I myself am so unspeakably sad, firstly because Jean-Baptiste and I have quarrelled by letter, and secondly because I am so afraid of this new year.

Well then, let me tell you. The day after Jean-Baptiste's departure I obediently went to the music teacher whom this Rodolphe Kreutzer had recommended. He is a small very thin man who lives in a very untidy room in the Quartier Latin and has draped very dusty laurel wreaths all over his walls. The first thing this little man, whose breath smells abominably, told me was that it was only because of his gouty fingers that he was forced to give lessons. Otherwise he would devote himself entirely to his concerts. Could I pay for twelve lessons in advance? I paid, and then I had to sit down in front of a piano and learn the names of the different notes and which key belongs to which note. Going home after the first lesson I felt dizzy in the carriage and was afraid I might faint again. But I got home, and since then I have been going to the Quartier Latin twice a week. Also I hired a piano to practise at home. Jean-Baptiste wanted me to buy the instrument, but I thought it a pity to spend all that money.

Every day I read in the *Moniteur* that Jean-Baptiste is marching triumphantly through Germany. Yet although he writes almost every day he never mentions the war. On the other hand he never forgets to ask how I am getting on with my lessons.

I am a very bad correspondent, and therefore my letters are always short and I can't put in what I really want to tell him so badly, that without him I am very unhappy and that I am longing for him. He now writes like an old uncle! He stresses the importance of continuing my 'studies', and when he realised that I didn't even want to start them he wrote: 'Although I very much want to see you again I set great store

140

by the completion of your education. Music and dancing are essential things, and I do recommend some lessons with Monsieur Montel. However, I notice that I am giving you too much advice and I finish for to-day by kissing your lips. Your J.—Bernadotte who loves you very much.'

Was that a lover's letter? I was so annoyed about it that in my next letter I didn't mention his advice at all and didn't tell him either that I was now having lessons with this Monsieur Montel. God alone knows who recommended this man to him, this perfumed ballet dancer, this cross between a bishop and a ballerina who makes me curtsey 'gracefully' to invisible dignitaries, walk up to equally invisible old ladies and conduct them to an invisible sofa whilst all the time he hops around me to check the effect. One might almost think that he was preparing me for a royal reception, me, a convinced Republican.

As I had written nothing about my lessons in deportment the courier brought me one day the following letter from my Jean-Baptiste: 'You say nothing about your progress in music, dancing and other subjects. While I am so far away I hope that my little girl will make the best of her lessons. Your J.—Bernadotte.'

This letter came on a morning when I was particularly wretched and in no mood for getting up at all. I was feeling very lonely in the wide double bed, didn't even want to see Julie when she called, didn't want to think about anything at all. Then the letter arrived. The letterhead of the official notepaper which Jean-Baptiste uses for his private correspondence as well says: *République Française,* and underneath, *Liberté—Egalité.* Why, I clenched my teeth, why should I, the daughter of a worthy silk merchant from Marseilles, be educated into a 'fine lady'? Jean-Baptiste, I thought, is probably a great General and one of the 'coming men', but for all that he comes from a very humble family, and anyway, in a Republic all citizens are equal and I don't want to come into circles where you direct your guests about with affected gestures of the hand.

I got up and wrote him a long, furious letter. I cried as I wrote it and the ink ran. I hadn't married a preacher, I said, but a man of whom I thought that he understood me. And as for that man with the odious-smelling breath who made me do finger practice and that perfumed Monsieur Montel, they could go to the devil, I had had enough of them, enough, enough. . . .

Without reading the letter through I sealed it quickly and told Marie to get a cab and take it immediately to the War

Office to be passed on from there to General Bernadotte. Of course, next day I was afraid that Jean-Baptiste would be really angry. I went to Montel for my lesson and afterwards practised scales for two hours on the piano and attempted the Mozart minuet with which I want to surprise Jean-Baptiste when he gets home.

I felt grey and sad and forsaken, as sad and forsaken as our garden with its bare chestnut tree. A whole week crept by till at last Jean-Baptiste's answer came. 'You have not told me,' he wrote, 'you have not told me yet, my dear Désirée, what it was that offended you in my letter. I do not at all want to treat you like a child but like a loving and understanding wife. All I said should have convinced you that——' And then he started off again on the completion of my education and told me unctuously that one gains knowledge 'by hard and persistent work'. In the final sentence he wrote: 'Write and tell me that you love me!'

This letter I haven't answered yet, for something has happened meanwhile which made any further letter-writing impossible.

Yesterday morning I was, as so often before, sitting by myself in Jean-Baptiste's study twirling the globe on a little table and wondering about the many countries and continents of which I knew nothing. Marie came in and brought me some broth. "Drink that," she said, "you must eat things now that'll make you strong."

"Why? I am very well. I'm even getting fatter all the time. The yellow silk dress hardly fits me round the waist now." I pushed the cup away. "Besides, I hate greasy things."

Marie turned to go. "You've got to force yourself to eat. And you know quite well why."

I was startled. "Why?"

Marie smiled, came suddenly back to me and made to take me into her arms: "You do know, don't you?"

But I pushed her away and shouted at her, "No, I don't! And it isn't true either, I know it isn't!" With that I ran up to the bedroom, locked the door behind me and threw myself down on to the bed.

Naturally the thought had occurred to me, of course it had. But I didn't want to admit it. 'It can't be true,' I thought, 'it's quite out of the question, it—it would be dreadful if it were true. It can happen that for some reason or other one can miss a period, or even two in succession, perhaps even three. It can happen, can't it?'

I hadn't told Julie anything about it, for if she knew she'd drag me to a doctor. And I didn't want to be examined, I didn't want to be told that——

And now Marie knew it. I stared up to the ceiling and tried to think it out. It's something quite natural, I told myself, something quite natural, all women have children. There were Mama, and Suzanne, and—well, Julie has been to two doctors already because she so badly wants children and hasn't got any yet. But children are such a dreadful responsibility, one needs to know such a lot oneself in order to bring them up and explain to them the things that are right and the things that are wrong. And I know so little myself. . . .

Perhaps it would be a little boy with dark curly hair like Jean-Baptiste himself? And perhaps one day this little image of Jean-Baptiste would be killed in the Rhineland or Italy like so many of the sixteen-year-olds whom they are conscripting even now to defend our frontiers? Or perhaps he himself would use a pistol and kill other people's little boys?

I pressed my hand on my stomach. Was there really a new little human being in there? What a preposterous thought! But at the same time it flashed through my mind that it would be *my* little human being, a little part of my own self, and for the fraction of a second I was happy. Then I tried to see it differently. *My* little human being? No, impossible, no man can be owned by another man. And was there any reason why my son should always be able to understand me? What about me and Mama, for instance? How often do I find her views old-fashioned, how often do I tell her white lies! And precisely the same thing would happen between my son and myself: he would lie to me, find me old-fashioned, be annoyed by me. You little fiend in my body, I thought angrily, *I* didn't ask for you to come.

Marie knocked on the door, but I didn't open. I heard her going back into the kitchen, heard her returning and knocking again. This time I let her in. "I warmed the soup up for you," she said.

I asked her: "Marie, at that time when you were expecting your little Pierre, did you feel very happy?"

Marie sat down on the edge of the bed. "No, of course not," she said, "I wasn't married, you see."

Very hesitantly I said: "I heard that you—I mean if you don't want children you can—there are women, I mean, who could help you."

Marie looked at me very intently. "Yes," she said slowly,

143

" there are. My sister went to a woman like that. She has too many children as it is and doesn't want any more. Yes, and afterwards she was ill for a long time. And now she can't have any more children. And she will never be really right again either. But great ladies such as Madame Tallien or Madame Josephine, they are sure to know a proper doctor who would help. But it's against the law, you know."

She paused. I lay with eyes closed and pressed my hand to my stomach. It was flat, quite flat, my stomach.

" So you want the baby done away with?" I heard Marie ask.
" No!"

I shouted it involuntarily. Marie got up and seemed satisfied.

" Come, eat your soup," she said tenderly. " And then write and tell the General. He'll be pleased."

I shook my head. " No, I can't write things like that. I wish I could say it to him."

I drank my soup, dressed, went to Monsieur Montel and learned some more dancing steps.

This morning I had a great surprise. Josephine came to see me. Up till now she had only been twice, and every time together with Julie and Joseph. But from the way she behaved there was nothing to show that there was anything unusual about her sudden visit. She was magnificently dressed in a white frock of thin woollen material, a short very close-fitting ermine jacket and a high black hat with a white feather. But the light of the grey winter morning was not kind to her features: when she laughed it showed up all the many wrinkles round her eyes and her lips seemed very dry and unevenly painted.

" I wanted to see for myself how you are getting on as a grass widow, Madame," she said, and added, " We grass widows must stand by each other, must we not?"

Marie brought hot chocolate for us grass widows, and I asked politely: " Do you hear regularly from General Bonaparte?"

" No, not very regularly. He's lost his fleet and the British have cut his communications. Only now and then a small ship manages to get through the blockade."

I had nothing to say to that. Josephine looked round and saw the piano. " Julie has told me," she remarked, " that you are taking music lessons."

I nodded. " Do you play the piano?"

" Of course," said the former viscountess, " I have played since I was six."

"I'm also taking dancing lessons," I went on. "I don't want to disgrace Bernadotte."

Josephine took one of the marzipan cakes. "It's no simple matter to be married to a General—I mean a General who is away, in the war. Misunderstandings arise so easily when you are separated."

'Heaven knows she's right,' I thought, and remembered my stupid exchange of letters. "One can't write everything one wants to write," I said.

"Exactly!" Josephine agreed readily. "But there are always other people who interfere and write malicious letters. Joseph, for example, our brother-in-law." She pulled out a lace handkerchief and put it to her lips. "Joseph, let me tell you, wants to write to Bonaparte to tell him that he called on me yesterday at Malmaison and found Hippolyte Charles there—you remember Hippolyte, don't you? That charming young army contractor?—well, that he found Hippolyte there in his dressing-gown. So he wants to bother Bonaparte, who has other things to think of just now, with a trifling thing like that."

"Why in the world does Monsieur Charles want to walk about Malmaison in a dressing-gown?" I really couldn't understand why he chose this type of clothing for his visits.

"It was nine o'clock in the morning," said Josephine, "and he hadn't yet finished his toilet. Joseph's visit was a surprise, you know."

I didn't know what to say to that.

"I need company, I can't stand being left to myself so much, I have never been alone in all my life," she said, and tears came into her eyes. "And as we grass widows must stand together against our brother-in-law I thought that you might have a word with your sister. Perhaps she could influence Joseph not to say anything to Bonaparte."

So that was what she wanted. "Julie has no influence whatever on Joseph's actions," I said truthfully.

Josephine looked frightened. "You refuse to help me?"

I said that I was going to a New Year's Eve celebration at Joseph's house to-night and that I would have a word with Julie. "But you mustn't expect too much, Madame," I added.

Josephine was visibly relieved. "I knew you would not desert me, I knew! Tell me, why do I never see you at Theresa Tallien's? A fortnight ago she had a baby. You simply must come and see it." Walking towards the door she turned round once more: "Life isn't too boring for you in Paris, Madame, is it? We must go to the theatre together some time. And please, tell your sister that he can write to Bonaparte as much as he likes, only I'd rather he omitted all mention of the dressing-gown!"

I drove to the Rue du Rocher half an hour earlier than expected. Julie, in a new red frock which didn't suit her at all, fluttered in confusion across the drawing-room, arranging and re-arranging the little silver horse-shoes which she had put on the table to ensure a happy new year for all of us.

"Louis Bonaparte will be your neighbour at table," she said. "The fat fellow is so boring, I really don't know whom else I dare bother with him."

"I wanted to ask you something," I said. "Couldn't you ask Joseph not to mention the dressing-gown to Napoleon, I mean the dressing-gown of this gentleman Charles at Malmaison?"

"The letter to Napoleon has gone. Any further discussion is useless," said Joseph, entering at this moment. He went to the sideboard and poured himself a glass of cognac. "I wager Josephine came to your house to-day to ask for your good offices. Is that right, Désirée?"

I shrugged my shoulders.

"It's a mystery to me why you are on her side instead of on ours," Joseph continued indignantly.

"Whose do you mean by ours?" I asked.

"Mine and Napoleon's of course."

"You are not concerned in it at all. And Napoleon in Egypt can't undo what has been done. It would only grieve him. Is there any need for that?"

Joseph looked at me with great interest. "So you are still in love with him! How touching!" he scoffed. "I thought you had forgotten all about him!"

"Forgotten?" I was amazed. "How can you ever forget the first time you were in love? Napol n himself, good God, I hardly ever think of him, but the wild heart throbs, the happiness and all the pain and suffering that followed it, I'll never forget those!"

"And that's why you want to save him a great disappointment now?" Joseph appeared to find this conversation amusing. He poured himself another drink.

"Yes. I know what such a disappointment feels like."

Joseph grinned. "But my letter is on its way already."

"In that case there's no sense in continuing to talk about it."

Joseph meanwhile had poured out two more drinks. "Come

on, girls," he said, "now let's wish each other a happy New Year, you must put yourselves into a cheerful mood. Any moment the first visitors may arrive."

Obediently Julie and I took the glasses. But I had not even touched the cognac when I suddenly felt very sick. The smell was repellent to me, and I put the glass back on the sideboard.

"What's the matter with you?" Julie exclaimed. "You're green in the face."

I felt beads of perspiration on my forehead, dropped on to a chair and shook my head. "No no, it's nothing. I feel like that so often now." I shut my eyes.

"Perhaps she is going to have a baby," I heard Joseph say.

"Impossible. She would have told me," Julie contradicted him.

"If she's ill I'll have to write and tell Bernadotte at once," said Joseph.

Quickly I opened my eyes. "Don't you dare, Joseph! You won't breathe a word. I want to surprise him."

"With what?" both of them asked at the same time.

"With a son," I said, and suddenly I felt very proud.

Julie knelt down by my side and took me in her arms. Joseph said, "But perhaps it's going to be a girl."

"No, it'll be a son," I declared. "Bernadotte is not a man for daughters." I rose from the chair. "And now I'm going home. Don't be annoyed, please, I'd rather like to lie down and sleep into the new year."

Joseph had filled the glasses again, and he and Julie drank my health, Julie with tears in her eyes.

"Long live the Bernadotte dynasty," Joseph said, and laughed.

The joke pleased me. "Yes, let's hope for the best for the Bernadotte dynasty," I said. Then I left for home.

But the bells wouldn't let me sleep into the new year. Now they've finished, and we've been in the Year VII for quite a while now. Somewhere in Germany Jean-Baptiste is celebrating the New Year with his staff. They may even be drinking my health. But I'm facing the new year alone.

No, not quite alone. Now there are two of us wandering into the future; you, my little son as yet unborn, and I, and we hope for the best, don't we? For the Bernadotte dynasty!

SCEAUX near PARIS
17th Messidor of the Year VII
(Mama would probably write July 4th, 1799.)

My son arrived eight hours ago.

He has dark, silky hair. But Marie says he'll probably lose his first hair anyway.

His eyes are dark blue. But Marie says that all newly born children have blue eyes.

I am so weak that everything quivers before my eyes, and they would be very annoyed if they knew that Marie had given in and secretly brought me my diary. The midwife even thinks that I shan't survive, but the doctor says that he'll get me through all right. I've lost lots of blood, and they've somehow managed to raise the lower bedposts to stop the bleeding.

Jean-Baptiste's voice comes from downstairs.

My dear, dear Jean-Baptiste.

Jean-Baptiste!

My beloved Jean-Ba——.

SCEAUX near PARIS
One week later.

Now not even that giantess, my midwife, believes that I shall die in childbirth. I am sitting in bed propped up by many cushions, Marie brings me all my favourite dishes, and in the morning and evening France's Minister of War sits by my bedside and gives me long lectures on how to bring up children.

About two months ago Jean-Baptiste returned out of the blue. After New Year's Day I had taken myself in hand and written to him again, short notes and not at all loving ones, because I did want him back so badly and at the same time was so angry with him. I read in the *Moniteur* that he had taken Philippsburg, which was defended by 1500 men, with a force of 300, and that he had taken up his headquarters near a town called Germersheim. From there he went on to Mannheim, conquered the city and became Governor of Hesse. He governed the Germans of this territory according to the laws of the Republic, prohibited flogging, put an end to the ghettoes and received enthusiastic addresses of thanks from the universities of Heidelberg and Giessen. There must be some very strange races about: as long as you don't conquer them they think themselves for unknown reasons to be cleverer and better than anybody else in the world. But once you've beaten them they're full of unimaginable weeping and gnashing of teeth, and many of them maintain that secretly they've been on the side of their enemy all the time!

After his victories Barras recalled Jean-Baptiste to Paris.

One afternoon I was sitting by the piano as usual practising the Mozart minuet which by now wasn't going too badly when I heard the door open behind me. "Marie," I said, "this is my surprise for our General, the minuet. It doesn't sound too bad now, does it?"

"It sounds wonderful, Désirée, and it is a very great surprise for your General!" said Jean-Baptiste's voice, and he took me in his arms. After two kisses it was as if he had never been away.

As I was laying the table I tried to think how to tell him about our baby coming. But his eagle eye misses nothing, and quite suddenly he asked:

"Tell me, my girl, why didn't you write that we were going to have a son?" He, too, never thought for a moment that we might have a daughter!

I put my hands on my hips, frowned and tried to look annoyed: "Because I didn't want to trouble my preacher! You'd have been desperate at the thought that I might be forced to interrupt my education!" I went up to him: "But, my dear General, you may be easy in your mind: your son may not be born yet, but he has already started his lessons in deportment with Monsieur Montel!"

Jean-Baptiste at once forbade me to take any more lessons. If he had had his way he wouldn't have let me out of the house, so concerned was he about my health!

Although all Paris talked of nothing but the political crisis caused by the Royalists on the Right and the Jacobins on the extreme Left and feared new riots, I myself noticed very little of it. The chestnut tree blossomed white, and I sat under its broad branches sewing baby-clothes. Julie, who came every day and helped with the sewing, sat with me, hoping that I should 'infect' her: she wants a child so badly, and she doesn't mind at all whether boy or girl. In the afternoon Joseph and Lucien Bonaparte came round quite often and talked at Jean-Baptiste.

Apparently Barras made an offer to Jean-Baptiste which he indignantly rejected. Barras is the only one of our five Directors who matters, and all political parties are dissatisfied with their more or less corrupt practices. Barras had the idea of exploiting this dissatisfaction, getting rid of three of his co-Directors and then carrying on the Directorate with Sieyès, an old Jacobin. As he was afraid that his projected *coup d'état* might lead to riots he asked Jean-Baptiste to assist him as his military adviser. This Jean-Baptiste refused. Barras, he told him, should stand by the Constitution, and if he wanted a change in it he should put it before the Assembly.

Joseph thought my husband crazy. "You," he exclaimed, "with the help of your troops could be the dictator of France to-morrow!"

"Quite!" said Jean-Baptiste calmly, "and I want to avoid that. You seem to forget, Monsieur Bonaparte, that I am a convinced Republican!"

"But it might be in the interests of the Republic if in critical times a General were at the head of the Government or, at any rate, backed it up," said Lucien thoughtfully.

Jean-Baptiste shook his head. "A change in the Constitution is the business of the representatives of the people. We have two Houses: the Council of Five Hundred to which you, Lucien, belong, and the Council of Ancients to which you may one day belong when you reach the age necessary for membership. It is they who have to decide about the Constitution, but certainly not the Army or one of its Generals. However, I'm afraid we are boring the ladies. By the way, Désirée, what is that funny thing you are working on?"

"A jacket for your son, Jean-Baptiste."

About six weeks ago, on the 30th Prairial, Barras succeeded in inducing three of his co-Directors to retire. Now he, together with Sieyès, was the master of our Republic. The dominant parties of the Left demanded the appointment of new ministers. Our Minister to Geneva, a Monsieur Reinhart, replaced Talleyrand as Minister of Foreign Affairs, and our most famous lawyer and gourmet, Monsieur Cambacérès, took over the Ministry of Justice. But as we are involved in war on all our frontiers and can defend the Republic in the long run only if the Army is thoroughly reorganised, everything depends on the choice of the new Minister of War.

Early in the morning of the 15th Messidor a messenger appeared from the Luxembourg Palace to order Jean-Baptiste to go at once to see the two Directors. Jean-Baptiste rode away, and I sat the whole morning under the chestnut tree. I was annoyed with myself, because last night I had eaten a whole pound of cherries at one sitting, and now they were rumbling about in my stomach and making themselves more and more disagreeable. Suddenly I felt as if a knife were thrust into my body. The pain only lasted the fraction of a second, but after it had gone I sat there paralysed. Oh God, how that hurt! "Marie," I called out, "Marie!"

Marie came, saw me and said: "Up into the bedroom with you! I'll send Fernand for the midwife!"

"But surely, it's only last night's cherries!"

"Up into the bedroom!" Marie repeated, and pulled me up. The knife-thrust pain did not come again, and, relieved, I went upstairs. I heard Marie despatching Fernand, who had returned from Germany together with Jean-Baptiste. "At last he's of some use," she said, coming back into the bedroom with three sheets, which she spread over the bed.

"I'm sure it's only the cherries," I said obstinately. But I hadn't finished speaking when the knife thrust again and pierced me right through from the back. I screamed, and when the pain had passed I started to weep.

"Aren't you ashamed of yourself? Stop blubbering!" Marie shouted at me. But I could tell by her face that she was sorry for me.

"I want Julie, I want Julie!" I wailed. Julie would pity me, and I did so want to be pitied.

Fernand arrived with the midwife and was sent straight away to Julie.

Oh that midwife! That midwife! She had examined me a few times during the last few months, and there had always been something uncanny about her. But she appeared to me like some giantess out of a tale of horror. She had powerful red arms, a broad red face and a real moustache. The wierdest thing, however, was that this female grenadier had painted her lips heavily under the moustache and wore a coquettish white lace cap on the untidy grey hair.

The giantess looked me over carefully and, I thought, contemptuously.

"No hurry," she said, "with you it'll take a long time."

At the same time Marie said that she had hot water ready down in the kitchen. But the giantess said: "No hurry! Better put some coffee on the fire!"

"Strong coffee, I take it? To cheer Madame up?" inquired Marie.

"No, to cheer *me* up," said the giantess.

An endless afternoon passed into an endless evening, the evening into an endless night. A grey dawn came and hung over the room for an eternity, then followed a burning hot morning which seemed to last for ever, then another afternoon, an evening, a night. But by then I could no longer distinguish the times of day. The knife thrust through me without interruption, and as from a great distance I heard someone scream, scream, scream. In the intervals between the thrusts all went black before my eyes. Then they poured brandy down my throat, and I was sick and could not breathe, sank back into blackness and was torn awake again into horrible pains.

Sometimes I felt that Julie was near. Someone kept wiping the perspiration from my forehead and face: My shift stuck to me, and then Marie said in her quiet voice: " You must help us, Eugenie, you must help us!"

Like a monster the giantess bent over me, the flickering candlelight threw her shapeless shadow against the wall. Was it the same night still or was it the next? " Leave me alone," I cried, " leave me alone," and my fists beat the air around me wildly. They all shrank back, and then Jean-Baptiste sat on my bed, held me tightly in his arms, and I put my face against his cheek. The knife was thrusting again, but Jean-Baptiste did not let go of me.

" Why aren't you in Paris in the Luxembourg Palace? They sent for you, didn't they?" I said in a strange, panting voice during a short spell of painlessness.

" It's night," he said.

" And they didn't tell you to go away to another war?"

" No, no, I am staying here now, I am now——"

I didn't hear the rest of what he said: the knife was at work again, and a wave of immeasurable pain closed over my senses.

A moment came in which I felt actually well. The pain had ceased, and I was so weak that I couldn't think. It felt like floating along on waves, floating along not seeing anything. But I heard. Yes, I heard! " Hasn't the doctor come yet? If he isn't here soon, it'll be too late!" This was spoken by a voice pitched high in excitement, a voice strange to me. But why a doctor? I was all right now, I was floating along on waves, the waves of the Seine with the many lights dancing up and down. . . .

Someone poured burning hot, bitter-tasting coffee into my mouth. My eyes blinked, and I noticed that it was the giantess who spoke in that excited high-pitched voice. " If the doctor isn't here within a minute——" I heard her say. Funny, I should have thought it impossible that such a mighty woman could have a voice like that. But why this fuss about the doctor? The worst was over now, wasn't it?

But it wasn't, it was only beginning.

I heard voices from the door. "Please wait in the living-room, your Excellency. Calm yourself, your Excellency, I assure you, your Excellency——"

Excellency, Excellency? What was an Excellency doing in my room?

"I implore you, doctor——" That was Jean-Baptiste's voice. Jean-Baptiste, Jean-Baptiste, you must not go away. . . .

The doctor gave me a camphor injection and told the giantess to prop me up by the shoulders. I had come to again and saw Julie and Marie standing on either side of the bed holding candelabra.

The doctor was a small thin man in a dark suit. I couldn't see his face, but I saw something flashing in his hands. "A knife," I screamed, "he's got a knife."

"No, only a forceps," said Marie calmly. "Don't scream, Eugenie!"

But perhaps he had had a knife after all, for once again the dreadful pain pierced my body exactly as before, only faster, faster, faster still and finally without any interruption whatever till I felt that I was torn here, torn there, torn completely to pieces. I fell into a bottomless pit, and all went black again.

Coming to, I heard the giantess's voice again, but now as coarse and indifferent as before: "She'll be finished soon, Doctor Moulin."

"She might get through, citizeness, if only we could stop the hæmorrhage."

Something was whimpering somewhere in the room. I should have liked so much to open my eyes, but the lids were like lead.

"Jean-Baptiste, a son, a wonderful small son," sobbed Julie.

And all of a sudden I could open my eyes, wide. Jean-Baptiste had a son. Julie held a little white bundle in her arms, and Jean-Baptiste was standing next to her. "I didn't know how small a small child is!" he said in amazement, turned and came to my bed. He knelt down, took my hand and put it against his cheek. It felt unshaven and wet, yes, quite wet. So Generals too could weep?

"We have a wonderful son," he said, "but he is still very small."

"They always are, in the beginning," I said with difficulty.

Julie showed me the bundle. A face as red as a lobster could be seen among its white coverings. Its eyes were closed and it had an air of being offended. Perhaps it hadn't wanted to be born?

"I must ask everybody to leave the room. The wife of the Minister of War needs rest," the doctor said.

"The wife of the Minister of War? Does he mean me, Jean-Baptiste?"

"Yes, I became France's Minister of War the day before yesterday."

"And I haven't even congratulated you on it," I whispered.

"You were busy," he said, and smiled.

Julie put the bundle into its cot. Only the doctor and the giantess were left with me in the room, and I fell asleep.

Oscar!

It was quite a new name to me. Os—car. . . . Really and truly, it didn't sound too bad. It was supposed to be a Nordic name, this Oscar, and that's what we called our son.

It was Napoleon's idea. He wanted to be godfather. The name Oscar occurred to him because he was reading the Celtic songs of Ossian in his desert tent. When one of Joseph's talkative letters to Napoleon reached him with the news of my pregnancy, he wrote back: "If it is a son Eugenie must call him Oscar. And I want to be his godfather!" Jean-Baptiste, who, as the father, had some say in the matter after all, he didn't mention at all. But Jean-Baptiste, when we showed him the letter, smiled.

"We don't want to offend your old admirer, my little girl," he said. "As far as I am concerned he can be our boy's godfather, and Julie can represent him at the christening. The name of Oscar——"

"It's a dreadful name," said Marie, who happened to be in the room just then.

"It's the name of a Nordic hero," put in Julie, who had brought Napoleon's letter.

"But our son is neither Nordic nor a hero," I said, and looked at his tiny face in my arms. It was no longer red but yellow from jaundice. But Marie insisted that most new babies get jaundice a few days after their birth.

"Oscar Bernadotte sounds good," said Jean-Baptiste, and there the matter ended as far as he was concerned. "In a fortnight's time," he added, "we shall leave here, Désirée, if you agree."

A fortnight later we were going to move into a new house. The Minister of War is obliged to live in Paris, and therefore Jean-Baptiste bought a small villa in the Rue Cisalpine, between the Rue Courcelles and the Rue du Rocher, quite close to Julie.

The new house wouldn't be much bigger than the little house in Sceaux. But at any rate it would give us, apart from our own bedroom, a proper children's bedroom, and downstairs we would have not only a dining-room but also a reception room, so that Jean-Baptiste would have somewhere to entertain the officials and politicians who often come to him in the evening. Up till now our social life has gone on in the dining-room.

I myself am now on top of the world. Marie cooks all my favourite dishes, and I am no longer so dreadfully feeble. I can even sit up in bed without any help. Unfortunately, however, I have too many visitors, and that is rather a strain. Josephine called and even Madame Tallien and that authoress with a face like a full moon, Madame de Staël, whom I only know very casually. Besides, Joseph solemnly handed me a novel he has written which makes him feel like a great writer. Its name is *Moïna* or *The peasant girl from Saint-Denis*, and it is so boring and sentimental that every time I start reading it I fall asleep. But Julie never stops asking me: "Isn't it wonderful?"

I know, of course, that all the visits are not meant for me personally nor for my son Oscar but for the wife of the War Minister. This moon-faced woman Madame de Staël, who, by the way, is the wife of the Swedish Minister but doesn't live with him, this Madame de Staël told me that France at last had found the man to put her affairs in order, and that everybody regarded Jean-Baptiste as the real head of the Government.

I read Jean-Baptiste's Proclamation which on the day of his appointment he addressed 'To the Soldiers of France!' It was so beautiful that I cried as I read it. 'I have seen your dreadful privation,' Jean-Baptiste said in it, 'and I need not ask you whether you know that I have shared it. I swear to you that I shall not give myself a moment's rest till I have found for you your bread, your clothing and your arms. And you, comrades, you will swear to me that you are going to defeat once again the dreadful coalition against France. We shall stand by the oaths we are taking.'

When Jean-Baptiste comes home at eight o'clock in the evening from the Ministry he eats his meal by my bedside, and then he goes to his study, where he dictates to his secretary till deep into the night. And at six o'clock in the morning he is on his way again to the Rue de Varennes where the War Office is housed at the moment. I know from Fernand that the camp bed down in Jean-Baptiste's study is quite often not used at all. I think it awful that my husband is supposed to save our

Republic single-handed. And to crown all, the Government hasn't even enough money to buy arms and uniforms for the 90,000 recruits whom Jean-Baptiste has in training, and there are stormy scenes between him and Director Sieyès.

If Jean-Baptiste could at least be left alone in the evenings when he wants to work at home! But there are always people coming and going. Jean-Baptiste told me only yesterday that the representatives of all the parties are doing their best to get him to support their side.

One evening, just as, weary and exhausted, he was gobbling down his evening meal, Fernand announced that 'a Monsieur Chiappe', who didn't want to say what he had come for, was waiting downstairs. Jean-Baptiste rose hurriedly and ran down to get rid of this mysterious Monsieur Chiappe. After a quarter of an hour he was back in our room, his face red with fury.

"This Chiappe," he said, "has been sent to me by the Duc d'Enghien. The cheek of it! What Bourbon impudence!"

"And who is the Duc d'Enghien, if I may ask?"

"Louis de Bourbon Condé, Duc d'Enghien. He is the ablest member of the Bourbon family, works for the British and is somewhere in Germany. If I seize power and give France back to the Bourbons they want to make me Constable of France and goodness knows what else. The impudence of it!"

"And what did you answer?"

"I threw him out. And told him to tell his chiefs that I am a convinced Republican."

"Everybody says that it's you who really governs France now. Could you overthrow the Directors and become Director yourself, if you wanted to?" I asked cautiously.

"Of course," said Jean-Baptiste calmly, "of course I could. The Jacobins even proposed something like this to me, the Jacobins and some of our Generals. I need only say the word and they would make me Director and give me much greater powers than the Directors have now."

"And you refused?"

"Naturally. I stand by the Constitution."

Just then Fernand announced Joseph, my brother-in-law. Jean-Baptiste groaned. "Really, that's the last straw! Well, Fernand, let him come in."

Joseph came in, and bent first over the cot and said that Oscar was the most beautiful baby he had ever seen. Then he wanted Jean-Baptiste to go down with him into the study. "I should like to ask you something and it would only bore Désirée," he said.

Jean-Baptiste shook his head. " I see so little of Désirée, I prefer to stay here with her. Sit down, Bonaparte, and be brief, I have plenty of work to do yet."

So they both sat down by my bed. Jean-Baptiste took my hand in his, and its light touch sent a feeling of serene confidence and strength across to me. I closed my eyes.

" It concerns Napoleon," I heard Joseph say. " What would your attitude be should Napoleon wish to return to France?"

" I should say that Napoleon could not return as long as the Minister of War had not recalled him."

" Bernadotte, let's be perfectly frank: a commander of Napoleon's importance is, at this moment, completely wasted on the Egyptian front. Since the destruction of our fleet the campaign there has more or less come to a standstill. The Egyptian campaign therefore can——"

" Be called a fiasco, which is precisely what I prophesied."

" I hadn't intended to express myself quite like that. However, as no decisive developments are to be expected in Africa, it would perhaps be possible to use my brother's abilities on other fronts to greater advantage. Besides, Napoleon is not only just a strategist. You yourself know his interest in organisation, and he could be of great help to you here in Paris reorganising the Army. Moreover,"—here Joseph hesitated and waited for Jean-Baptiste to say something, but Jean-Baptiste remained silent. So Joseph went on: " You know that there are quite a number of plots being hatched against the Government?"

" As the Minister of War I am not quite ignorant about that. But what has that got to do with the Commander-in-Chief of our Army in Egypt?"

" The Republic needs a—needs several strong men. In times of war France cannot afford party intrigues and internal differences."

" If I understand you right you are suggesting that I am to recall your brother to deal with the different plots, are you not?"

" Yes, I thought that——"

" To deal with conspiracies is a matter for the police and for no one else."

" Quite, if the conspiracies are directed against the State. But I can tell you that influential circles are thinking of bringing about a concentration of all positive political forces."

" What do you mean by ' concentration of all positive political forces'?"

"For instance, if you yourself and Napoleon, the two ablest men of the Republic——"

Bernadotte cut him short: "Stop talking nonsense! Why don't you say simply: 'In order to free the Republic from party politics certain persons are contemplating the introduction of a dictatorship. My brother Napoleon wishes to be recalled from Egypt in order to apply for the position of dictator.' Why don't you simply say that and have done with it, Bonaparte!"

Joseph, disagreeably surprised, cleared his throat. Then he said: "I've seen Talleyrand to-day. The ex-minister thinks that Director Sieyès would not be disinclined to support a change of the Constitution."

"I know exactly what Talleyrand thinks, I also know what some of the Jacobins want, and I can even tell you that above all the Royalists have pinned all their hopes on a dictatorship. As for me, I have taken the oath to the Republic and I shall be loyal to our Constitution whatever happens. Is my answer clear enough?"

"You will appreciate that a man like Napoleon is bound to be driven to despair by his enforced idleness in Egypt. Moreover, my brother wants to settle some important private affairs here in Paris. He wants to divorce Josephine, whose unfaithfulness has wounded him deeply. If my brother in his distress decided to return without your authority, what would happen then?"

For one moment Jean-Baptiste's fingers closed round my hand with an iron grip. Then they relaxed and I heard him say calmly: "In that case I, as the Minister of War, should be compelled to court-martial your brother, and I suppose that he would be condemned as a deserter and shot."

"But Napoleon, the great patriot that he is, can no longer, in Africa——"

"A Commander-in-Chief has to remain with his troops. He led them into the desert, and he has to stay with them till they can be brought back. Even a civilian like you must realise that, Monsieur Bonaparte."

After he had finished, an uncomfortable silence reigned in the room.

At last I said: "Your novel, Joseph, is a most exciting book."

"Yes," he replied with his usual modesty, "everybody congratulates me on it."

He rose and Jean-Baptiste accompanied him downstairs.

I tried to get some sleep. In the uneasy state between sleeping and waking I recalled a little girl racing a nondescript thin

158

officer till they stopped by a moonlit hedge. " I, for example, I know my destiny," the officer said and the young girl giggled. " You'll believe in me, Eugenie, whatever happens, won't you?"

I felt certain, suddenly, that Napoleon would return from Egypt. Some day he'd simply turn up and overthrow the Republic if he had the chance. He doesn't care for the Republic nor for the rights of its citizens, and he just doesn't understand men like Jean-Baptiste, he never has and he never will. I remember what my father said: " My little daughter, when-ever and wherever in days to come men deprive their brothers of their right to liberty and equality no one will ever be able to say of them: ' Lord forgive them for they know not what they do '."

At eleven o'clock Marie entered, took Oscar out of his cot and put him to my breast. Jean-Baptiste came up too. He knows that Oscar gets his supper at this time.

" He'll come back, Jean-Baptiste," I said.

" Who?"

" Our son's godfather. What are you going to do?"

" If I get the necessary powers I'll have him shot."

" And if you don't?"

" Then he'll take them himself and have me shot. Good night, my girl."

" Good night, Jean-Baptiste."

" And don't think of it any more. I was only joking."

" I understand, Jean-Baptiste. Good night!"

PARIS, 18th Brumaire of the Year VII. (Abroad they would say November 9th, 1799. Our Republic gets a new Constitution!)

He did come back!

And to-day he brought about a *coup d'état* and became the head of France's Government a few hours ago!

Several Deputies and some Generals have already been arrested and Jean-Baptiste said that we may at any moment expect a visit from the State Police. It would be dreadful, unimaginably dreadful for me if my diary fell into the hands of the Police Minister Fouché and of Napoleon himself. How they would laugh! Therefore I've decided to write down every-thing that's happened at once and then hand it over to Julie to keep for me. She, after all, is the new dictator's sister-in-law, and surely he'll never let his police search *her* house?

I am sitting in the drawing-room of our new house in the Rue Cisalphine. In the dining-room next door I can hear Jean-Baptiste pacing the floor, up and down and up and down. " If you have any dangerous papers let me have them," I shouted to him. " I'll take them to Julie to-morrow with my papers."

But Jean-Baptiste answered: " I have no—how do you put it?—' dangerous papers.' And Napoleon knows quite well what I think of his treasonable action."

Fernand was rummaging about the room, and I asked him whether there were still many people standing outside our house in silent groups. He said there were.

" What do these people want?" I wondered.

Fernand put a new light into the candelabrum and said: " They want to see what's going to happen to our General. I'm told that the Jacobins wanted our General to take over the command of the National Guard and——" He scratched his head thoughtfully and noisily and was obviously asking himself whether to tell me the truth or not. " Yes, and people think that our General will be arrested. General Moreau was arrested some time ago."

I am preparing myself for a long night. In the adjoining room Jean-Baptiste keeps pacing the floor, I write on, the hours pass slowly and we wait.

Yes, Napoleon returned quite unexpectedly, exactly as I had thought he would. Four weeks and two days ago an exhausted courier dismounted from his horse in front of Joseph's house and announced: " General Bonaparte, accompanied only by his secretary Bourrienne, has landed at Fréjus in a tiny freighter which slipped through the British blockade. He's hired a special coach and will be in Paris at any moment."

. Joseph got dressed hurriedly, fetched Lucien, and both brothers went and took up stations in front of Napoleon's house in Rue de la Victoire. Their voices woke Josephine, who, when she heard what was happening, put on her most fashionable dress, dashed into her carriage and drove like fury through the southern suburbs to meet Napoleon. She hadn't even wasted any time on make-up, she did that in the carriage. She had only one aim, to get to Napoleon before Joseph saw him and to try at all costs to prevent a divorce. But hardly had her carriage driven off when Napoleon's chaise drove up to the house in the Rue de la Victoire. The two carriages had missed each other by a few moments. Napoleon jumped out, the two brothers ran to meet him, and there was a lot of back-patting.

They went into the house and withdrew into one of the small rooms.

Round about midday Josephine returned exhausted from her futile journey and opened the door to the room where the brothers were in conference. Napoleon looked her up and down: "Madame," he said at last, "we have nothing more to say to each other. I shall take the necessary steps for a divorce to-morrow, and shall be obliged if meanwhile you will move into Malmaison. In the meantime I shall look round for a new house for myself."

Josephine broke into violent sobbing. Napoleon turned his back on her, and Lucien took her up to her room. After that the three brothers continued their conference for hours, and later on were joined by Talleyrand, the former Minister for Foreign Affairs.

Meanwhile the news spread quickly through all Paris that Napoleon had returned victoriously. Crowds gathered round his house, soldiers turned up and shouted "*Vive Bonaparte!*" and Napoleon showed himself at the window and waved to the crowd. All the time Josephine was sitting in her bedroom weeping wildly; her daughter Hortense tried to calm her down and gave her camomile tea.

It was not till the evening that Napoleon was left alone with his secretary Bourrienne. He dictated letters to innumerable Deputies and Generals in order to notify them of his safe return. Later on Hortense appeared, still angular, thin, colourless and timid, but already dressed like a young lady. The long somewhat pendant nose gave her an air of precociousness.

"Couldn't you go and talk to Mama, Papa Bonaparte?" she said in a whisper. He brushed her aside like a fly.

He did not send his secretary away till midnight. As he was still debating with himself where to lie down for the night—Josephine was still occupying the bedroom—he heard loud sobbing outside the door. He quickly locked it. Josephine continued to stand there, outside his door, and weep for two full hours. At last he opened. Next morning he woke up in Josephine's bedroom.

Julie, who had it from Joseph and Bourrienne, told me all this. "And do you know what Napoleon said to me?" she added. "He said to me: 'Julie, if I divorce Josephine all Paris will know that she cheated me, and I'll be the laughing-stock of Paris. If I don't divorce her, you see, all Paris will know that there is nothing to blame her for and it was all malicious talk. At the present moment I must not, on any account, make myself ridiculous.' A strange attitude, don't you think, Désirée?"

There were other things she had to tell me: "Junot, too, has come back from Egypt and so has Eugene de Beauharnais. Almost every day officers of the Army in Egypt land secretly in France. And according to Junot, Napoleon left a fair-haired mistress behind in Egypt, a certain Madame Pauline Fourès whom he called 'Bellilote'. She is supposed to be a young officer's wife who had accompanied her husband to Egypt in disguise. Just imagine! When Napoleon got Joseph's letter about Josephine—you remember the letter, don't you?—he ran up and down in front of his tent for two hours, then sent for 'Bellilote' and dined with her."

"What became of her?" I asked.

"Junot, Murat and the others say that he handed her over, together with his command of the Army, to his second in command."

"And what does he look like?"

"The second in command?"

"Don't be stupid, Napoleon, of course!"

Julie became thoughtful. "He's changed, you know. Perhaps it's something to do with the way he's doing his hair now. He had it cut short out in Egypt, which makes his face look plumper and his features less irregular. But it isn't that alone, no, I'm sure it isn't. By the way, you'll see him yourself on Sunday, you're coming to dinner at Mortefontaine, aren't you?"

Upper-class Parisians have a house in the country, and writers a garden to which they can retire. Since Joseph sees himself as an upper-class Parisian as well as a writer he bought the charming Villa Mortefontaine with the large park belonging to it, about an hour's drive from Paris. Next Sunday we were to dine there in the company of Napoleon and Josephine.

To-day's events would never have come to pass had Jean-Baptiste still been Minister of War on Napoleon's return. But a short time before that he had had another of his violent arguments with Director Sieyès, and in a fit of anger he offered his resignation. Pondering over it and remembering that Sieyès assisted Napoleon with his *coup d'état*, I think it highly probable that Sieyès had an inkling of Napoleon's intention of returning and deliberately brought about the argument in order to force Jean-Baptiste's resignation. Jean-Baptiste's successor did not dare to court-martial Napoleon, because some Generals and the circle of Deputies round Joseph and Lucien were too openly on Napoleon's side.

In those autumn days Jean-Baptiste received many visitors. One of them, General Moreau, came almost every day, and suggested that the Army ought to intervene if Napoleon really ' dared '. A group of Jacobin members of Paris City Council turned up to inquire whether, in case of riots, General Bernadotte would take over command of the National Guard. Jean-Baptiste answered that he would gladly take it over, provided the Government, that is the Minister of War, appointed him in due and proper manner. At that the Councillors departed in dismay.

On the morning of the Sunday on which we were to go to Mortefontaine I suddenly heard a well-known voice downstairs. " Eugenie," it shouted, " I want to see my godchild ! "

I ran down the stairs, and there he was, tanned, his hair cut short.

" We wanted to surprise you and Bernadotte," he said. " You are going to Mortefontaine, aren't you? So Josephine and I thought we could fetch you. Besides, I want to meet your son and admire your new house and say hallo to Colleague Bernadotte, whom I have not yet seen since my return."

" You are looking very well, my dear," Josephine, leaning gracefully against the verandah door, interposed.

Jean-Baptiste appeared on the scene now, and I ran into the kitchen to tell Marie to make coffee and serve liqueurs. On returning I saw that Jean-Baptiste had fetched Oscar and Napoleon was bending over the little bundle, tickling his chin and clucking at him.

Oscar didn't like it, and started to scream.

" Well, Colleague Bernadotte," said Napoleon laughingly to Jean-Baptiste, and amiably patted his back, " more recruits for the Army, eh? "

I rescued our son from the arms of his father, who stiffly held him away from himself and insisted that the bundle felt damp.

Enjoying Marie's bitter-sweet coffee, Josephine involved me in a conversation on roses. Roses are her passion, and I had already been told that she was planning a costly rose garden at Malmaison. She had seen a few rather miserable rose trees outside our verandah, and she wanted to know how I tended them. Therefore we didn't hear what Jean-Baptiste and Napoleon were talking about, but both Josephine and I were silenced abruptly on hearing Napoleon say:

"I am told, Friend Bernadotte, that you, had you been in office on my return, would have had me court-martialled and shot. What is it you are blaming me for?"

"I believe you know our Service Regulations as well as I do," Jean-Baptiste answered, and added, "perhaps even better, for you had the advantage of having been trained at an officers' training establishment, and of starting your active service as an officer, whereas I served for many years in the ranks, as you may have heard."

Napoleon bent forward and tried to catch Jean-Baptiste's eyes. At this moment I realised why he looked different now. His short hair made his head appear round and his lean face ampler; moreover, I had never noticed before the severely jutting, almost angular chin. However, all this emphasised the change only, it had not brought it about. What was decisive in this change was his smile, the smile which once up a time I loved so much and later I hated so much, the smile which once upon a time had played so rarely and so fleetingly round his intense face. Now it never left his face, had become winning, had become at once begging and demanding.

But what did this uninterrupted smile demand? And for whom was it meant? For Jean-Baptiste, of course! He was to be won over, to be turned into a friend, a confidant, an enthusiastic follower.

"I have returned from Egypt," he was now saying, "in order to put myself once more at the disposal of our country, as I consider my mission in Africa to have come to an end. You are telling me now that France's frontiers are secure and that you during your term as Minister of War had tried to put 100,000 infantry and 40,000 cavalry into the field. The few thousand men whom I left behind in Africa can therefore be of no importance to the French Army, whose strength you increased by 140,000 men, whereas a man like me in the present desperate position of the Republic——"

"The position is not at all desperate," said Jean-Baptiste calmly.

Napoleon smiled. "Isn't it? Since the moment of my return I have been told by all and sundry that the Government is no longer in control of the situation. The Royalists are on the move again in the Vendée region, and certain people in Paris are quite openly in contact with the Bourbons in England. The Manège Club, on the other hand, is preparing for a Jacobin revolution. I suppose you know that the Manège Club intends to overthrow the Directory, Colleague Bernadotte?"

" As for the Manège Club," Jean-Baptiste said slowly, " you are certainly much better informed about its aims and intentions than I. Your brothers Joseph and Lucien founded it and preside over its meetings."

" In my opinion it is the duty of the Army and its leaders to gather together all the positive forces, to guarantee law and order and to contrive a form of government worthy of the Revolution and all it stands for," said Napoleon imploringly.

I found the conversation boring and therefore turned back to Josephine. But to my amazement her eyes were riveted firmly on Jean-Baptiste, as if his reply were of decisive importance.

" Any intervention of the Army or its leaders in order to secure a change in the Constitution I am bound to consider as high treason," was his answer.

The winning smile did not wane on Napoleon's face. But Josephine, at the words, ' high treason ', raised her thin brows. I poured out fresh coffee.

Napoleon continued : " If I were, let us say, being approached universally—and I emphasise : universally !—and if it were suggested to me to bring about a concentration of all positive forces and, with the help of sincere patriots, to work out a new Constitution which would give expression to the true desires of the people, if that happened, Friend Bernadotte, would you stand by me? Could the circle of men who intend to realise the ideals of the Revolution count on you? Jean-Baptiste Bernadotte, may France rely on your help?"

Napoleon's grey eyes, charged with emotion, drilled like gimlets into Jean-Baptiste.

" Listen, Bonaparte," said Jean-Baptiste, and put his cup down firmly, " listen, if you've come to persuade me to commit high treason over a cup of coffee I must ask you to leave my house."

Napoleon's eyes went dull and his eternal smile looked uncannily like a mechanical trick. " Am I to take it, then, that you would oppose by force of arms those of your colleagues to whose hands the country entrusted the rescue of the Republic?"

Jean-Baptiste suddenly broke out into laughter, deep, cordial, uncontrollable laughter, which made the tension snap : " My dear Bonaparte, when you were sunning yourself in Egypt it was suggested to me not once but three or four times that I should play the strong man, and, backed by the Army, bring about something like—what do you and your brother Joseph call it?—ah, yes, a ' concentration of all the positive forces '. But I refused. We have two Chambers of Deputies full of people's representatives, and if they and those whom they represent are dissatisfied they can bring in all the acts they want to change the Constitution. As far as I am concerned, I am of the opinion that the existing Constitution is quite sufficient to keep law and order and to defend our frontiers. But if the Deputies think fit to adopt a different form of government without having been forced into it at the point of a gun, then that is no business of mine or of the Army's."

"But if the Deputies were forced to a change of the Constitution at the point of the gun, Colleague Bernadotte, what attitude would you adopt then?"

Jean-Baptiste got up, went to the door of the verandah and looked into the greyish autumn sky outside. Napoleon's eyes followed him, and there was silence in the room as we waited for the answer.

Abruptly Jean-Baptiste came back into the room towards Napoleon and put his hand heavily on his shoulder. "Bonaparte," he said, "I fought under your command in Italy, I know something of your generalship, and I realise that France has no better commander than you. But the things the politicians suggest to you are unworthy of a General of the Republican Army. Don't do it, Bonaparte, don't do it!"

Napoleon looked attentively at the embroidered tablecloth and not a muscle of his face moved.

Jean-Baptiste took his hand from Napoleon's shoulder and went back to his chair. "If, however, you do attempt it after all, I shall oppose you by force, provided——"

Napoleon looked up: "Provided what?"

"Provided that the lawful Government orders me to do so!"

"How obstinate you are!" murmured Napoleon. Then Josephine thought it time to set off for Mortefontaine.

Julie's house was full of visitors. Talleyrand was there, and Fouché, and of course Napoleon's personal friends, Generals Junot, Murat, Leclerc and Marmont. They showed themselves agreeably surprised at seeing Jean-Baptiste arrive with Napoleon.

After dinner Fouché remarked to Jean-Baptiste: "I didn't know you and Napoleon were friends."

"Friends? At any rate we are relatives."

Fouché smiled: "Some people are very careful in the choice of their relatives."

"Choice? God knows, these relatives are not of my choosing," Jean-Baptiste answered good-humouredly.

In the days that followed this Sunday the whole of Paris talked of nothing else but whether Napoleon would dare or not.

Once I drove by chance through the Rue de la Victoire and saw a whole crowd of adolescents shouting in chorus "*Vive Bonaparte!*" up towards the closed windows. Fernand had it that these fellows were paid for their services. Jean-Baptiste, however, said that many of them found it difficult to forget the immense sums of money which Napoleon squeezed out of the defeated Italian States and sent to Paris.

Yesterday morning, on entering our dining-room, I knew at once: to-day is the day! Joseph was there, button-holing Jean-Baptiste and talking at him for all he was worth. He wanted to persuade him to go to Napoleon with him that very moment.

"At least you ought to hear him," Joseph said, "so that you can see for yourself that all he wants is to save the Republic."

"I know his plans," said Jean-Baptiste, "and I know that they have nothing to do with saving the Republic."

"For the last time, do you refuse to help my brother?"

"For the last time, I refuse to participate in any kind of high treason."

Joseph turned to me: "Désirée, can't you make him see reason?"

"Can I get you a cup of coffee, Joseph? You are so excited," I said.

Joseph said no and left, and Jean-Baptiste went to the verandah door to stare into the garden.

An hour later General Moreau, Monsieur Sazzarin, the former secretary of Jean-Baptiste, and other members of the War Office staff swept into the house like an avalanche. They demanded that Jean-Baptiste should put himself at the head of the National Guard and bar Napoleon's way to the Council of the Five Hundred.

But Jean-Baptiste insisted: "I can't do it without the Government's order."

Some City Councillors, the ones who had been before, arrived in the middle of it and made the same demand. To them Jean-Baptiste explained that he couldn't act on the City Council's orders. He needed the authorisation of the Government, or, if the Directors were no longer in office, that of the Council of the Five Hundred.

Late that afternoon I saw Jean-Baptiste for the first time in civilian clothes. He wore a dark red jacket which looked a bit on the tight as well as on the short side, a funny big hat and a very elaborately knotted yellow scarf. My General looked like someone who had disguised himself.

" Where are you going?" I asked.

" Oh, just for a stroll," he said.

His stroll took him a good few hours, and when in the evening Moreau and his friends turned up again they had to wait for him. It was pitch-dark when he came back at last. Naturally we were curious to know where he had been all this time.

" At the Tuileries and the Luxembourg," he said. " There are troops everywhere, but all is quiet. I think the soldiers were mostly from the former Army in Italy. I recognised some faces."

" Napoleon is sure to make them plenty of promises," said Moreau.

Jean-Baptiste smiled wryly. " He's done so already, through their officers. They're all back again in Paris, Junot, Masséna, Marmont, Leclerc, the whole Bonaparte circus."

" Do you think these troops are ready to oppose the National Guard?" wondered Moreau.

" They wouldn't dream of it," said Jean-Baptiste. " I talked for a long time to an old sergeant and some of his men who took me for an inquisitive civilian. They believe that Bonaparte would be given command of the National Guard. Their officers told them that."

" That's the dirtiest lie I've ever come across," exploded Moreau. But Jean-Baptiste said calmly:

" I think it very likely that Napoleon will demand the command of the National Guard from the Deputies to-morrow."

" And we insist that you share this command with him," Moreau shouted. " Are you prepared to do that?"

Jean-Baptiste nodded: " Yes. What you could do is to put it to the War Minister that if Bonaparte is entrusted with the command of the National Guard, Bernadotte is to share it with him as the representative of the Minister of War."

For the whole of the night I could find no sleep. All the time the voices from downstairs drifted up into the bedroom, the voices of Moreau, Sazzarin and all the rest of them.

That was yesterday. Heavens, to think that it was only yesterday.

During the course of to-day messengers kept coming all the time. Mostly they were officers. But finally a young soldier rode up, bathed in sweat. He jumped from his horse and shouted: " Bonaparte is First Consul! First Consul!"

" Sit down, man," said Jean-Baptiste, without showing any excitement. " Désirée, give him a glass of wine."

Even before the young man had had time to collect himself

to tell the tale a young captain rushed into the room, shouting: "General Bernadotte, Consular Government has just been proclaimed. Bonaparte is First Consul."

And now we heard the whole story. During the morning Napoleon had first gone to the Council of Ancients and asked for a hearing. The Ancients, mainly venerable and somnolent lawyers, had listened to him in the semi-coma of boredom, as, excitably and confusedly, he talked about a plot against the Government and demanded unlimited powers to cope with the emergency. The chairman of the Council then told him in a tortuous speech that he should talk to the Government about it, and so, accompanied by Joseph, Napoleon had set off for the Council of Deputies. There the mood had been a very different one. Although every single Deputy knew what the appearance of Napoleon meant, they had at first gone on with the agenda in a spirit of forced equanimity. Suddenly, however, the President of the Council, the young Jacobin Lucien Bonaparte, had pushed his brother on to the rostrum, announcing that General Bonaparte had something to say of decisive importance to the Republic. Napoleon at once had started to speak amidst the 'Hear, hear!' of his friends and the whistles and catcalls of his enemies, and all witnesses agreed in saying that he had stumbled and fumbled through his speech, in which he talked about a plot against the Republic and against his own life, that the agitation had grown louder and louder till he became inaudible and that at last he had had to stop altogether.

By now the agitation had become an indescribable tumult. The followers of Bonaparte forced their way to the rostrum, their opponents, belonging to all parties, made for the doors, which they found barred by troops. No one knows as yet how the troops had got there 'to protect' the Deputies. At any rate, Polette's husband, General Leclerc, was there at their head, and the National Guard, whose task it is to ensure the safety of the Deputies, made common cause with Leclerc's troops. The whole place looked like a witches' cauldron. Lucien and Napoleon stood side by side on the rostrum, and then a voice had shouted "*Vive Bonaparte!*", a dozen others chimed in, then thirty, then eighty, and the gallery, where Murat, Masséna, and Marmont had appeared among the journalists, roared it too. In the end the rest of the Deputies, seeing nothing but rifles and uniforms, had screamed in desperation "*Vive Bonaparte, vive . . . vive . . .!*"

After that the last act had begun. The soldiers had withdrawn into the corners of the hall, the Minister of Police,

Fouché, had appeared, accompanied by a few gentlemen in civilian clothes, and discreetly invited those Deputies who might disturb the new dispensation of law and order to follow him. The Council, reassembling to debate a new Constitution, showed considerable gaps. The President moved the proposals for the formation of a new Government to be headed by three Consuls, General Bonaparte was unanimously elected First Consul and the Tuileries, at his desire, put at his disposal as his official residence.

In the evening Fernand brought us the special editions of the papers. The name of Bonaparte stood out in enormous letters in each of them.

"You remember, Marie," I said to her in the kitchen, "you remember the special paper at home, in Marseilles, the one you brought me out on the terrace, 'Bonaparte appointed Military Governor of Paris'?"

Marie went on filling the feeding-bottle for Oscar.

"And to-night," I continued, "he'll move into the Tuileries. Perhaps he'll even sleep in the King's former bedroom."

"Shouldn't wonder," growled Marie. "It would be like him."

I went to the bedroom and fed Oscar, and Jean-Baptiste came up and sat with us. A moment later Fernand entered and handed him a slip of paper.

"Sir," he reported, "a strange woman left this a moment ago."

Bernadotte looked at it and then showed it to me. On it was written in a trembling hand: 'General Moreau has just been arrested'.

"A message from Madame Moreau which she sent by her kitchen maid."

Oscar fell asleep, we went downstairs, and ever since then we have been waiting for the police.

I started writing in my diary.

Some nights are long, so long that they never seem to end.

Suddenly there was the noise of a carriage stopping in front of our house. Now they're coming for him, I thought, got up quickly and went into the drawing-room. Jean-Baptiste was standing there, rigid, in the middle of the room, listening tensely. I went up to him and put my arm round his shoulders. Never before in my life had I felt so close to him.

The door knocker banged, once, twice, three times. " I'll go and see," said Jean-Baptiste, and freed himself from my arm. At the same time we heard voices, a man's voice first and then a woman's laughter. My knees went weak, I fell into the nearest chair and wiped the tears from my eyes: it was Julie, thank God, it was only Julie!

They came into the salon, Joseph, Lucien and Julie. My hands shook as I put new candles into the candelabrum. A bright light filled the room.

Julie was wearing her red evening gown. Obviously she had had too much champagne. Small feverish spots were burning on her cheeks and she giggled so much that she could hardly speak.

They had all come from the Tuileries. Napoleon had been in conference all night, had worked out the details of the new Constitution and drafted a provisional list of ministers. In the end Josephine, who, meanwhile, had unpacked her trunks in the former Royal apartments, had insisted on a celebration, had sent the State equipages to fetch Madame Letitia, Julie and Napoleon's sisters, and had one of the great ballrooms in the Tuileries festively illuminated.

" We drank such a lot," babbled Julie, " but it is such a great day, isn't it? Napoleon will govern France, Lucien is Minister of the Interior, and Joseph is going to be Minister of Foreign Affairs—at any rate he is down on the list, and, and—you must excuse our waking you. But as we were driving past your house I said, why not say good morning to Désirée and Jean-Baptiste——"

" You didn't wake us up, we haven't been to sleep yet," I said.

"——and the three Consuls," I heard Joseph say, " will be assisted by a Council of State composed mainly of experts. I suppose that you, Bernadotte, will be one of the Councillors."

" Josephine is going to refurnish the Tuileries," Julie babbled on. " I don't blame her, I don't. Everything's so full of dust and so old-fashioned. She wants her bedroom all white. And imagine, Napoleon wants her to have a real court like a Queen, with ladies-in-waiting and all. Just imagine! He wants other countries to see that the wife of our new Head of State knows how to represent——"

" I insist that General Moreau be set free," Jean-Baptiste's voice broke through Julie's patter, followed by Lucien's, who declared that Moreau's arrest was only a protective custody, a protection against mob excesses. "One never knows what the people of Paris in their enthusiasm for Napoleon and the new Constitution——"

At that moment a clock struck six.

"Good God, we must be off," exclaimed Julie. "She is waiting for us in the carriage outside. We only wanted to say good morning."

"Who's waiting in the carriage?" I asked.

"Madame Letitia. She was too tired to get out. We promised to take her home."

I felt the need to speak to Madame Letitia and ran out of the house. It was misty outside, and a few shadows slipped away into the mist when they saw me. Apparently some people had waited in front of our house all night.

Opening the door of the carriage I peered into the dark interior. "Madame Letitia," I called out, "it's me, Désirée. I want to congratulate you."

The figure in the corner shifted. But it was so dark inside that I couldn't see the face. "Congratulations? On what, my child?"

"On Napoleon becoming First Consul and Lucien Minister of the Interior and Joseph——"

"The boys shouldn't meddle so much with politics," her voice came out of the dark.

'Madame Bonaparte will never speak French properly,' I thought. 'She speaks to-day exactly as she did when I first met her in Marseilles. And what an awful-smelling cellar they lived in then! And now they are having the Tuileries refurnished.' "I thought you'd be very pleased, Madame," I said awkwardly.

"No. The Tuileries are no place for Napoleone. It is not proper," the voice in the dark carriage said firmly.

"But we live in a Republic," I said.

"Call Julie and the two boys. I am tired. You will see, he will get into mischief in the Tuileries, into very great mischief."

At last Julie, Joseph and Lucien came out of the house. Julie embraced me and pressed her hot cheek against my face. "It's so marvellous," she whispered, "so marvellous. Come to lunch with me. I must talk to you."

Jean-Baptiste joined us in the street to see our visitors off. On his appearance the strange shadows I had seen slipping away before emerged again out of the mist and a trembling voice shouted: "*Vive Bernadotte!*" It was taken up by three or four other voices: "*Vive Bernadotte, vive Bernadotte!*" and it seemed a bit ridiculous to me that they made Joseph start.

The morning is grey and rainy. A moment ago an officer of the National Guard arrived with the message: "By order of the First Consul, General Bernadotte will report to him at the Tuileries at eleven o'clock."

I close my book and lock it. Later on I shall take it to Julie.

PARIS, March 21st, 1804. (Only the Authorities keep to the Republican calendar now and call it 1st Germinal of the Year XII.)

I was crazy to drive in the dead of night to the Tuileries to see Napoleon. I knew I was crazy, have known it from the very beginning, and yet I got into Madame Letitia's carriage, trying to think what I was going to say to him.

Somewhere a clock struck eleven. The carriage was rolling along by the banks of the Seine, and in my imagination I saw myself passing along the vast empty corridors of the Tuileries, entering his room, going up to his desk and starting my explanation.

Down there was the river. In the course of the years I have come to know most of the bridges. There is one particular bridge, however, which, every time I pass it, makes my heart beat faster. I was passing it now, and I stopped the carriage, and got out and went to the bridge. *My* bridge!

It was a night in early spring, a bit chilly still, but the air felt sweet and balmy. After a day's rain the clouds were breaking up and stars appeared in the gaps.

'He couldn't have him shot,' I thought as I leaned over the edge of the bridge and saw the lights of Paris dancing on the waves, 'he couldn't.'

Couldn't he? Of course he could. He could do anything. Slowly I began to walk the length of the bridge, backwards and forwards.

My thoughts went back to all the past years through which I have lived in a whirl of events, big and small. There were the weddings I danced at, the receptions at the Tuileries I attended, the victories I celebrated, the dresses I wore and the champagne I drank: they were the small things. And there was Oscar's first tooth and Oscar's first 'Mummy' and Oscar's first toddle, holding my hand, from the piano to the chest-of-drawers: they were the big ones. All these memories flooded through my mind, and they seemed to persuade me to delay the moment when I should continue on my way to the First Consul.

Only a few days ago Julie gave me back my diary.

"I cleared out that old chest-of-drawers, you know, the big one from our house in Marseilles, to make room for the children's things. They are growing, they need a bit of extra space. So I put it in the nursery, cleared it out and found your diary. I needn't keep it for you any longer now, need I?"

"No, you needn't," I said, "or, at any rate, not at the moment."

"There are lots of things for you to write down now," said Julie and smiled. "I'm sure you haven't even entered that I have two daughters."

"No, how could I? I handed the book over to you the night after the *coup d'état*. But now I shall record that you went to Plombières Spa regularly every year with Joseph, and that Zenaïde Charlotte Julie was born two and a half years ago and Charlotte Napoléone thirteen months later. And I shall also record that you read fiction as enthusiastically as ever and that a story about a harem so entranced you that you called your poor elder daughter Zenaïde."

"I hope she'll forgive me for it," said Julie remorsefully.

I took the book home. 'Above all,' I thought, 'I must note down Mama's death.' Last summer, when Julie was sitting with us in our garden, Joseph came with a letter from Etienne. He wrote that Mama had died after a heart attack in Genoa.

"Now we are quite alone," said Julie.

"But you have me," said Joseph.

He didn't understand what Julie meant. Julie belongs to him and I to Jean-Baptiste, but after Papa's death only Mama could tell us what things had been like when we were children.

On the evening of that day Jean-Baptiste told me: "You know that we are all subject to the laws of nature. They determine that we should survive our parents. It would be unnatural if it were the other way round. All we can do is to obey the laws of nature."

That was his way of consoling me. Every woman who in childbirth suffers almost unbearable pain is told that she is only sharing the fate of all mothers. But that, I think, is small consolation.

From my bridge I could see Madame Letitia's carriage standing there, dark in the darkness, like a threatening monster. Meanwhile on Napoleon's desk there was a death sentence waiting to be signed, and I was going to say to him—well, what was I going to say to him? One could no longer talk to him as one talks to ordinary people, one couldn't even sit down if he didn't allow it. . . .

The floodtide of my memories was not diverted by the sight of that monstrous black carriage. There was the morning after that endless night during which we were expecting Jean-Baptiste's arrest, when Napoleon had ordered Bernadotte to appear in the Tuileries.

"You have been called into the Council of State, Bernadotte," said Napoleon to him. "You will represent the Ministry of War."

"Do you believe that I have changed my convictions in the course of one night?" answered Jean-Baptiste.

"No. But in the course of this one night I have become responsible for the fate of the Republic, and I cannot afford to do without one of its ablest men. Will you accept, Bernadotte?"

A long silence fell, so Jean-Baptiste told me later, a silence in which he looked attentively round the room, at the ceiling, at the desk, through the windows: a silence in which he watched the soldiers of the National Guard below in the courtyard; a silence in which he pondered the legal position of the Consular Government which had been recognised by the Directors before their resignation; a silence in which he came to the conclusion that the Republic had delivered itself into this man's hand to avoid a civil war.

"You are right, Consul Bonaparte," he said at last, "the Republic needs every one of its citizens. I accept."

On the very next day Moreau and all arrested Deputies were set free, and Moreau was given a new command. Napoleon prepared for a new Italian campaign and appointed Jean-Baptiste Supreme Commander of the Western Army. In this capacity Jean-Baptiste guarded the Channel coast against British attacks; his command stretched all the way to the Gironde. He had set up his headquarters in Rennes and was not at home at the time that Oscar had whooping cough. Later Napoleon won the battle of Marengo and Paris nearly convulsed itself with victory celebrations. Our troops occupied half Europe now, because of the many territories ceded to France in Napoleon's peace treaties, and these territories all needed garrisoning.

There are more lights dancing on the waves of the Seine now than at that time long ago, I thought. Then I believed that nothing in the world could be more magnificent and exciting than Paris. But Jean-Baptiste maintained that our present-day Paris is a hundred times more splendid than the Paris of that time and that I had no real basis of comparison.

One thing Napoleon did was to allow the fugitive aristocrats to return. And so once more plots and intrigues abounded in the mansions of the Faubourg St. Germain, confiscated property was handed back to its former owners and torchbearers ran alongside the calashes of the Noailles, the Radziwills, the Montesquieus and the Montmorencys. These former ornaments of the Court of Versailles themselves, however, moved once more with measured, graceful steps through the great state rooms of the Tuileries, bowing to the Head of State of the Republic and bending low over the hand of the ex-widow Comtesse de Beauharnais, who had never fled abroad and never gone hungry but had her bills paid by Monsieur Barras and danced with the ex-lackey Tallien at the ball of the ' Association of Guillotine Victims '. Once more, too, the royal courts from all the quarters of the globe sent their most distinguished diplomats to Paris. Sometimes my poor head buzzed in confusion when I wanted to remember the names of all these princes, counts and lords who were introduced to me.

Memories, memories, there was no end to them!

" I'm afraid of him, he has no heart. . . ." That was Christine's voice calling to me in the early spring night on my bridge, Christine, the peasant girl from St. Maximin, the wife of Lucien Bonaparte. Innumerable witnesses saw Lucien push his brother on to the rostrum and heard him force the first " *Vive Bonaparte!*" from their reluctant lips. A few weeks later the walls of the Tuileries resounded with the furious arguments of the two brothers and told just as many witnesses what Lucien Bonaparte, Minister of the Interior, and Napoleon Bonaparte, First Consul, were shouting at each other. First they argued about the press censorship introduced by Napoleon, then about the exiling of authors, and every now and then about Christine, the innkeeper's daughter who was never received in the Tuileries.

Lucien did not remain Minister for long, nor did Christine cause family strife for any length of time. The well-set-up girl from the country with the apple cheeks and the dimples began to cough blood after a damp winter.

One afternoon I was sitting with her and we talked about spring and looked at fashion magazines. Christine wanted a gold-embroidered dress she saw illustrated.

" In a dress like that," I said, " you'll go to the Tuileries and be introduced to the First Consul, and you'll be so beautiful that he'll envy Lucien."

Christine's dimples disappeared. "I'm afraid of him, he has no heart," she said.

In the end Madame Letitia succeeded in persuading Napoleon to receive Christine, and a week later he said casually to his brother:

"Don't forget to bring your wife along to the opera tomorrow night and introduce her to me."

"I am afraid," answered Lucien, "my wife is not in a position to accept your most flattering invitation."

Napoleon's lips at once tightened: "This is not an invitation, Lucien, but an order from the First Consul."

Lucien shook his head: "My wife cannot even obey an order from the First Consul. My wife is dying."

At Christine's burial everybody noticed the inscription on the most expensive of the wreaths: 'To my dear sister-in-law Christine—N. Bonaparte.'

After Christine the widow Jourberthon!

The widow Jourberthon had red hair, a full bosom and dimpled cheeks which reminded one a bit of Christine. She had been married to a petty bank clerk. Napoleon demanded that Lucien should marry a daughter of one of the returned great noblemen. Instead one day Lucien arrived at the registry office with Madame Jourberthon, whereupon Napoleon at once signed a decree banishing the French citizen Lucien Bonaparte, former member of the Council of Five Hundred, ex-Minister of the Interior of the French Republic, from the country.

Before Lucien left for Italy he came to us to say good-bye.

"On that day in Brumaire," he said, "I only wanted everything to be for the best for the Republic. You know that, Bernadotte, don't you?"

"I know," said Jean-Baptiste, "I know. But you made a great mistake, on that day in Brumaire!"

Then there was Hortense.

Two years ago Hortense broke out into such weeping and screaming that the sentries in the courtyard of the Tuileries looked up to her windows in fright. Napoleon had ordered the engagement of his stepdaughter to his brother Louis, fat, flat-footed Louis who cared nothing for the colourless Hortense and preferred the actresses from the Comédie Française. But Napoleon was not going to tolerate another *mésalliance* in his family and so ordered his engagement to Hortense. As a result Hortense had locked herself in her bedroom and screamed the house down. When she refused to let her mother in, Julie was sent for.

Julie hammered on Hortense's door till the girl opened.

" Can I help you?" Julie asked.

Hortense shook her head.

" You love someone else, don't you?"

Hortense's sobbing ceased and her face became rigid.

" You love someone else," repeated Julie.

This time Hortense nodded almost imperceptibly.

" I shall speak to your stepfather," said Julie. But Hortense stared hopelessly at the floor.

" Does this other man belong to the First Consul's circle? Could your stepfather consider him a suitable candidate?"

Hortense did not move. Only her tears continued to stream down her cheeks.

" Or perhaps this other man is married already?"

Hortense's lips opened, she tried to smile, instead of which she suddenly burst into laughter, loud, shrill, uncontrollable laughter which made her shake like someone possessed by demons.

Julie grabbed her by the shoulders: " Stop it! Control yourself! If you don't I'll fetch the doctor."

But Hortense couldn't stop. She went on laughing crazily till my patient sister Julie lost her patience and slapped her face. That made her stop.

Hortense shut her wide-open mouth and breathed deeply a few times. Then she said very quietly and almost inaudibly: " But I love—him!"

" Him? Napoleon?" This possibility had never entered Julie's mind. " Does he know?"

Hortense nodded. " There are few things he does not know. And those few the Minister of Police Fouché ferrets out for him."

How bitter it sounded!

" Marry Louis," said Julie, " marry him. It's the best thing to do. After all, Louis is his favourite brother. . . ."

A few weeks later they got married. Polette had been held up as an example to Hortense. How she had fought against her marriage to General Leclerc! Napoleon had almost had to force her into the match. And how she had wept because Napoleon ordered her to accompany Leclerc on his journey to San Domingo! In San Domingo Leclerc died of yellow fever, and then Polette had been so inconsolable that she cut off her honey-coloured hair and put it in his coffin. This the First

Consul kept citing as conclusive proof of Polette's great love for the dead man. But I told him:

"Just the opposite! It proves that she never loved him. Because she never loved him she wanted to do something special for him once he was dead!"

Polette's hair grew again; it grew in curls down to her shoulder, and now Napoleon insisted that she should put them up with the help of the most precious combs in the world: the pearl-studded combs of the Borghese family. The Borghese family belongs to the oldest families of Italy and is related to almost all the royal houses of Europe. The then head was the knock-kneed, shaky Prince Camillo Borghese, and into the arms of this elderly prince Napoleon put his favourite sister Polette. Her Highness, the Princess Polette Borghese! Yes, Her Highness Polette, little Polette with the patched dress who had street corner *affaires* with men. . . .

Yes, how they have changed, all of them!

For the last time I looked down to the water where the lights of Paris were dancing up and down as before. Why, I thought, why do they say that I am the only one who could succeed in this task?

I went back to the carriage. "To the Tuileries!"

On the way I sorted out one by one the points of this desperate task. The Duc d'Enghien, a Bourbon who has been said to be in the pay of the British and who for a long time threatened to reconquer the Republic for the Bourbons, had been captured. But this capture took place not on French soil but in a little town in Germany called Ettenheim, outside the French frontiers. Four days ago Napoleon all unexpectedly ordered three hundred dragoons to attack this little town. They crossed the Rhine, kidnapped the Duc in Ettenheim and dragged him away into France. Now he was a prisoner in the Fortress of Vincennes, awaiting the verdict. To-day a military tribunal condemned him to death for high treason and an attempt on the life of the First Consul.

The death sentence has been put before the First Consul for confirmation or commutation. The aristocrats who are now daily guests at Josephine's implored her, naturally enough, to ask Napoleon for mercy on the prisoner's behalf. They went to the Tuileries in force and the foreign diplomats laid siege to Talleyrand. Napoleon, however, saw no one. At table Josephine tried to take up the matter, only to be cut short by Napoleon's "Please, Madame, the matter is closed." Towards evening Joseph tried his hand and asked his brother for an interview. Napoleon inquired through his secretary what Joseph wanted to see him about, and when Joseph told the secretary it was about 'a matter of justice' the First Consul refused to see him.

During dinner that evening Jean-Baptiste was unusually quiet. But suddenly he banged the table with his fist: "Do you realise," he said, "what Napoleon's been doing? With 500 dragoons he's kidnapped a political adversary on foreign territory, brought him to France and put him before a military tribunal! For anyone with the slightest sense of justice that is a blow in the face."

"And what is going to happen to the prisoner? He couldn't have him—shot!" I said in horror.

Jean-Baptiste shrugged his shoulders. "And to think that he took the oath to the Republic, to defend the Rights of Man!"

We dropped the subject. But I couldn't help thinking all the time of the death sentence which, we had heard, was waiting on Napoleon's desk for his signature.

The silence at table grew oppressive. Finally, in order to break it I said: "Julie told me that Jerome Bonaparte has agreed to divorce his American wife."

Jerome, that dreadful boy of the days in Marseilles, had become a naval officer and on one occasion had very nearly been captured by the British. He only escaped by landing in a North American port, where he met and married a Miss Elisabeth Patterson. It caused Napoleon another fit of fury, and so Jerome, now on his way home, had given way to his great brother and agreed to divorce the former Miss Patterson. The only objection he dared to raise in his letter was: 'But she has a lot of money.'

"The First Consul's family affairs," remarked Jean-Baptiste, "are of no interest to me."

Outside we heard a carriage draw up. "It's gone ten o'clock," I said, "a bit late for calls."

Fernand came in and announced Madame Letitia Bonaparte.

That was a surprise indeed. Madame Letitia as a rule did not visit without a previous appointment. And there she was already heaving herself into the room behind Fernand with a "Good evening, General Bernadotte, good evening, Madame."

Madame Letitia has grown younger rather than older during recent years. Her former hard and careworn face looked fuller, the wrinkles round her mouth seemed smoothed away. But there were a few grey strands in her dark hair, which she still wears in the Corsican peasant women's manner, tied in a knot on her neck; a few fashionable curls falling down over her forehead seem rather out of harmony with her whole personality.

We took her into the drawing-room, where she sat down and slowly stripped off her pearl-grey gloves. Looking at her hands with the big cameo ring—a present from Napoleon from Italy— I remembered the red, chapped skin of her fingers in that cellar dwelling, the fingers which had to wash clothes all day long.

"General Bernadotte, do you think it possible that my son will condemn this Duc d'Enghien to death?" she asked without any further preliminaries.

Jean-Baptiste answered cautiously: "It was not the First Consul but a military tribunal that condemned him."

"The military tribunal judges according to my son's wishes. Do you think it possible that he will have the sentence carried out?"

"Not only possible but probable. Otherwise, why should he have given the order to seize the Duc on foreign territory and put him before a court-martial?"

"I thank you, General Bernadotte." Madame Letitia looked at her cameo ring. "Do you know my son's reasons for this step?"

"No, Madame."

"Have you any ideas about them?"

"I should not like to put them into words."

She fell silent again. Sitting on the sofa bent forward and with knees slightly apart, she had the air of a very tired peasant woman who wanted a moment's rest.

"General Bernadotte, do you realise what the carrying out of this sentence means?"

Jean-Baptiste did not answer. I could see how embarrassing the conversation was for him.

Madame Letitia raised her eyes to meet his and said: "Murder, that is what it means, foul murder!"

"You should not excite yourself, Madame——"

She raised both her hands and cut him short: "Not excite myself, you say? General Bernadotte, my son is about to commit a foul murder, and I, his mother, I am not to excite myself?"

I went and sat down by her side and took her hand. It trembled. "Napoleon may have political reasons," I murmured.

"Hold your tongue," she said, and turned back to Jean-Baptiste. "There is no excuse for murder, General! Political reasons are——"

"Madame," said Jean-Baptiste, "many years ago you sent

your son to a military academy and made him an officer. Perhaps, Madame, as an officer he may judge the value of an individual human life different from you."

She shook her head. "General, this is not the question of the value of an individual human life in battle. This is a question of a man who has been dragged by force into France, there to be killed. With this killing France will lose her greatness. I will not have my Napoleone turning into a murderer, you understand, I will not have it!"

"You should go and talk to him, Madame."

"No, no, Signor——" Her voice became uncertain and her lips twitched. "It would be no use. He'd just say 'Mama, you don't understand these things. Go to bed. You want me to raise your allowance?' No, Signor, *she* must go, she, Eugenie!"

My heart stopped beating. I shook my head in desperation.

"Signor General, you don't know, but at that time when my Napoleone had been arrested and we were afraid that they might shoot him, she, little Eugenie, went to the Authorities and helped him. Now she must go to him, must remind him of it and ask him——"

"I don't believe that that would make any impression on the First Consul."

"Eugenie—I am sorry, Signora Bernadotte, Madame—you do not want your country to be called a murderous Republic by the rest of the world? You do not, do you? I have been told—oh, many people came to me to-day on behalf of this Duc —I have been told that he has an old mother and a fiancée and—oh, Madame, have pity on me, help me, I will not have my Napoleone——"

Jean-Baptiste had got up and paced restlessly up and down the room. Madame Letitia kept on:

"General, if your boy, your little Oscar, were about to sign this death sentence——"

"Désirée"—Jean-Baptiste said it gently but very firmly— "Désirée, get ready and go to the Tuileries!"

"You are coming with me, Jean-Baptiste, aren't you?"

"You know quite well, my girl, that that would destroy the Duc's last chance." Jean-Baptiste smiled wryly and took me in his arms: "No, you will have to go alone. I fear it will be useless, but, darling, you must try." His voice was full of pity.

Still I did not give in: "It looks bad if I go to the Tuileries by myself at night. Too many women——" I hesitated a moment, but then went on regardless of whether Madame

Letitia heard it or not—"too many women come late at night to the First Consul by themselves."

"Put on a hat, take a cape and go," was all Jean-Baptiste answered.

"Take my carriage, Madame. And if you don't object I should like to wait here for your return." I nodded and then heard her add: "I shall not disturb you, General. I shall sit here by the window and wait."

Since on Christmas Eve four years ago a bomb exploded behind the First Consul's equipage, and almost every month a new plot on the First Consul's life is being discovered by Fouché, it is impossible to enter the Tuileries without being stopped every ten yards or so by guards wanting to know your business. In spite of that everything was far simpler than I had thought. Whenever I was stopped I simply said "I want to see the First Consul," and was allowed to pass on. Nobody asked either my name or the purpose of my visit. The National Guards suppressed a smile and stared at me impertinently. I felt dreadfully embarrassed.

At last I reached the door which is supposed to lead to the First Consul's offices. I had never been here before. The few family parties to which I had gone in the Tuileries had taken place in Josephine's apartments.

The two guards in front of this door did not ask me any questions at all. So I just entered. Inside, a young man in civilian clothes was sitting at a desk, writing. I had to clear my throat twice before he heard me. He shot up from his seat in surprise: "Mademoiselle?"

"I should like to see the First Consul."

"I am afraid, Mademoiselle, you have mistaken the room. This is his office."

I didn't know what the young man was driving at. "He hasn't gone to bed yet?" I asked.

"The First Consul is still working."

"Why, then, take me to him."

"Mademoiselle——" The young man, who, in his dilemma, had not dared to take his eyes from his boots, now looked up and faced me for the first time: "Mademoiselle," he said, blushing, "Constant, the valet, surely must have told you that he would expect you at the back door. These rooms here are—are the offices."

"But I want to speak to the First Consul, not to his valet. Go to him and ask him if I may disturb him for a moment. It is very important."

"Mademoiselle!" the young man said imploringly.

"Don't call me Mademoiselle but Madame. I am Madame Jean-Baptiste Bernadotte."

"Mademoi—I am so sorry—Madame—so sorry——" He looked at me as if I were a ghost. "So sorry," he murmured.

"All right. But would you mind announcing me now?"

The young man disappeared and returned almost immediately. "Madame, may I ask you to follow me? Some gentlemen are with the First Consul at the moment, and he asks you to wait just one second."

He took me into a small waiting-room where dark-red velvet chairs were grouped round a marble table. But I didn't have to wait long.

A door opened. Three or four men carrying piles of documents under their arms appeared, bending low and saying good night to someone invisible to me, and went out towards the ante-room, whilst the secretary darted past them and into the First Consul's room. Next moment he shot out again and announced solemnly:

"Madame Jean-Baptiste Bernadotte, the First Consul will see you now."

"This is the most charming surprise for years," said Napoleon as I entered. He was standing close by the door, and he took my hands and put them to his lips, kissing first my right and then my left. I withdrew them quickly and didn't know what to say.

"Sit down, my dear, sit down. And tell me how you are. You are getting younger, younger every time I see you."

"Oh no," I said, "time flies. Next year we'll have to look round for a tutor for Oscar."

He pressed me into the easy-chair next to his desk. He himself, however, didn't sit down. Instead, he kept wandering round the room, and I had to crane my neck not to lose sight of him.

It was a very big room with a number of small tables standing about in it, all loaded with books and documents. But on the big writing desk the documents were arranged in two neat piles resting on wooden boards. Between the two piles, directly in front of the desk chair, lay a single sheet with a dark red seal affixed to it. A big fire roared in the fireplace. The room was hot to suffocation.

"You must see this," he said, and held out a few sheets closely printed in tiny letters with paragraph signs standing out in the margin, "the first copies fresh from the printers! It

is the new Civil Law, the *Code Civil* of the French Republic!
The laws for which the Revolution strove, here they are: worked
out, written down and printed. And in force, for all time! I
have given France its new Civil Law!"

Year after year, I knew, he had closeted himself with France's
greatest lawyers and worked out the new code of law. And
now, here it was, in print and in force.

"The most humane laws in history!" he said. "Just look
here, for instance, concerning children: the first-born has no
more rights than his younger brothers and sisters. And here:
all parents are compelled to look after their children. And see
here——" He fetched some more sheets from one of the small
tables and began to explain their contents: "See here, the new
marriage laws. They make possible not only divorce but
separation. And here——" He fished out another sheet.
"This concerns the nobility. Hereditary titles are abolished."

"The man in the street already calls your *Code Civil* the
Code Napoléon," I said. This was perfectly true, but besides,
I wanted to keep him in good humour.

He threw the sheets back on the mantelpiece and came up to
me. "I am sorry," he said, "this must be very boring for you.
Do take off your hat, Madame!"

"No, no," I said, "I am only going to stay for one moment,
I only wanted——"

"But it doesn't suit you, Madame, really. May I take it off?"

"No. Besides, it is a new hat, and Jean-Baptiste said it
suited me excellently."

He drew back at once. "Of course, if General Bernadotte
says so——" He began pacing up and down again behind my
back.

'Now I've annoyed him,' I thought, and quickly undid the
ribbon holding my hat.

"May I ask," he said somewhat sharply, "how I came to
have the honour of your visit at this hour?"

"I've taken the hat off," I said.

He stopped at once, and then came back to my chair touching
my hair very lightly with his hand. "Eugenie," he said, "little
Eugenie." It was the voice of that rainy night, the night when
he and I got engaged.

I bent my head quickly to escape his hand. "I wanted to
ask you a favour," I said in a trembling voice.

He went away across the width of the room and leaned
against the mantelpiece. The flames from the fire were mirrored
in his polished boots. "Of course," was all he said.

"Why ' of course '?" I said.

"I realise that you would not have come to see me without some ulterior motive," he said pointedly. Stooping to throw a log into the fire he continued: "Almost everybody who comes to me asks for some favour or other. One gets used to that in my position. Well now, Madame Jean-Baptiste Bernadotte, what can I do for you?"

His jeering was more than I could bear: "Do you imagine," I said in a fury, "that I'd have come to you in the middle of the night if it had not been for something particularly urgent?"

He seemed to enjoy my anger. Amusedly he rocked from his heels to his toes and back again. It struck me that apart from his short hair and his immaculately cut uniform he looked hardly different from the man who came to us in our garden in Marseilles.

"No," he said, "I should hardly think so, Madame Bernadotte, though perhaps, at the bottom of my heart, I may have hoped so. There is always room for hope, Madame, is there not?"

'That's the wrong way,' I thought in despair, 'I can't even get him to take me seriously.' My fingers started to play nervously with the silken rose on my hat.

"You are ruining your new hat, Madame," he said.

I didn't look up. A lump came into my throat, and I felt a hot tear running down my cheek. I tried to lick it up with the tip of my tongue.

"What do you want me to do, Eugenie?"

There he was again, the Napoleon of the old days, the gentle and candid one.

"You say that many people come to you to ask you favours. Do you usually do what they ask of you?"

"If it can be done, of course."

"'Can be done'? But surely you are the most powerful man in France, aren't you?"

"I must be able to do it with a good conscience, Eugenie. What is your wish?"

"I am asking you to spare his life."

He did not answer at once, and the roar of the fire was the only sound.

"You are talking about the Duc d'Enghien?"

I nodded.

Tensely I waited for his answer, but he took his time. Meanwhile I tore the silken rose on my hat to pieces.

186

"Who has sent you with this request, Eugenie?"

"What does that matter? Many people are making this request, and I am one of them."

"I want to know who sent you," he said sharply.

I only shook my head.

"Madame, I am used to having my questions answered." I looked up. He had pushed his head forward, his mouth was twisted and little flecks of foam appeared at the corners of his mouth. "You needn't shout," I said, "I am not afraid of you." And it was quite true, I wasn't afraid of him any longer.

"Yes, I know. You are very fond of acting the courageous young lady. I remember the scene at the house of Madame Tallien," he said between his teeth.

"I am not courageous at all, I am really rather a coward. But when there is much at stake I try to pluck up my courage."

"And," he said, "at that time, at Madame Tallien's, there was a lot at stake for you?"

"Everything," I said, and waited for some cynical remark from him. It did not come. I looked up and tried to catch his eye. "But there had been one occasion before that when I had had to pluck up my courage. That was at the time when my fiancé—you know, I was engaged once, long before I met General Bernadotte—when my fiancé had been arrested after the fall of Robespierre. We were afraid that he might be shot. His brothers thought it very dangerous, but I went with a parcel of underwear and a cake to the Military Commandant of Marseilles and——"

"Yes. And that is why I must know who it was that sent you to-night."

"What has that got to do with it?"

"Let me explain, Eugenie. The person or persons who sent you obviously know me very well. They really have found the one chance to save Enghien's life. Mind you, I am only saying 'chance'. But I am interested to find out who it is who possesses such exact knowledge of me, who uses this chance so cleverly and at the same time tries to oppose me politically. Well?"

I couldn't help smiling. The complications he saw in everything, the political problems!

"Do try, Madame, to see the situation for once through my eyes. The Jacobins blame me for allowing the *emigrés* to return and even for favouring them socially. At the same time they are busy spreading the rumour that I am selling the Republic to the Bourbons. Selling our France, this France which I created, France of the *Code Napoléon*, doesn't that sound crazy?"

As he was speaking he went up to the desk and took up the sheet with the dark red seal. He stared at the few words on it, threw it down on to the desk and turned back to me.

"By having this man Enghien executed I shall prove to the whole world that I consider the Bourbons as nothing but a gang of traitors. Do you understand, Madame? When I've finished with Enghien, however," here he started swaying backwards and forwards on his heels again, heel to toe, heel to toe, and an air of triumph appeared on his face—"the turn of the others will come, the rioters, the malcontents, the pamphleteers and those confused dreamers who call me a tyrant. I shall eliminate them from the ranks of the French people and protect France against its internal enemies."

Internal enemies . . . where had I heard that before? Yes, Barras had said it once, a long time ago, and he had looked at Napoleon as he said it.

The golden clock on the mantelpiece showed the time: one o'clock. I rose. "It's getting very late," I said.

But he made me sit down again. "Don't go yet, Eugenie," he said. "I am so glad that you came to see me. And the night is long yet."

"You'll be tired yourself."

"I am a bad sleeper, I——" A hidden door which I hadn't noticed opened a few inches on the far side of the room. Napoleon didn't notice it.

"Someone's opened the door over there," I said.

Napoleon turned round. "What is it, Constant?"

A lackey, small and gesticulating ridiculously, appeared. Napoleon went over to him. The little man whispered agitatedly "——doesn't want to wait any longer." "Tell her to get dressed and go home," I heard Napoleon say. The lackey disappeared.

That was probably Mademoiselle George from the Théâtre Français, I thought. All Paris knows that Napoleon had had an affaire with the singer Grassini, and that she was succeeded by 'Georgina', this sixteen-year-old actress Mademoiselle George.

"I won't keep you any longer," I said, and got up.

"Now that I have sent her away you can't leave me to myself," he answered, and again I had to resume my seat. His voice grew tender: "You have asked me a favour, Eugenie. For the first time you have asked me for something."

I shut my eyes, weary. His constant change of mood exhausted me, and the heat in the room was stifling. Also, the man radiated a feverish restlessness which made me feel dizzy. Strange, strange, that after all these years I could still echo every mood and every sentiment of this man. I knew without a doubt that, at this moment, he was trying to come to a decision, he was at odds with himself. No, this was not the moment to go; if I stayed he might give way, he might, he might.

"But, Eugenie, you don't know what you are asking. It is not the person of this Enghien that matters, no, what matters is to show all these Bourbons, to show the whole world what France feels. The French people itself will choose its ruler——" Here I pricked up my ears, as Napoleon continued: "Free citizens of a free Republic will go to the poll."

Was he reciting poetry, rehearsing a speech?

He went to the desk once more and took up the document. The dark red seal hung down from it like a gigantic drop of blood.

"You asked me," I said very loudly, "who had sent me to you to-night. I will answer that question before you make your decision."

"Well? I am listening," he said without looking at me.

"Your mother."

Slowly he put the document down, went to the fireplace and put on another log. "I did not know," he said in low tones, "that my mother occupied herself with politics. Most likely she has been pestered and plagued——"

"Your mother does not consider the death sentence as a political matter."

"But as?"

"Murder."

"Eugenie! You have gone too far now!"

"Your mother asked me so very urgently to speak to you. God knows, it's no easy matter!"

The ghost of a smile flitted over his face, and he began to rummage among the piles of documents and files on the small tables. At last he had found what he wanted, a big sheet of drawing paper which he unrolled and held out to me. "How do you like this? I have not shown it to anybody yet."

The top of the sheet showed the sketch of a big bee, and

a square in the middle showed a number of small bees at regular intervals from each other. " Bees?" I asked in amazement.

" Yes, bees." He nodded, gratified. " So you know what they stand for?"

I shook my head.

" It is an emblem."

" An emblem? Where are you going to use it?"

He made a sweeping gesture. " Where? Everywhere. On walls, carpets, curtains, liveries, court equipages, the coronation robe of the Emperor——"

I sat up, startled. It made him stop and look at me. His eyes held mine as he said slowly: " Do you understand— Eugenie, little fiancée?"

I felt nothing but my heart racing in my body. Already he was unrolling another sheet. It contained lions, lions in all sorts of positions, lions rampant, lions puissant, lions couchant. Across the top of the sheet Napoleon's hand had written: ' An eagle with outspread wings.'

" I commissioned the painter David to design the coat of arms." He dropped the lions to the floor and handed me the sketch of an eagle with wings spread. " This is my choice. Do you like it?"

It was so hot in the room, I could hardly breathe. The outlines of the eagle blurred before my eyes. It seemed to grow to alarming proportions.

" My coat of arms. The arms of the Emperor of the French."

Had I dreamed these words or had I really heard them? I pulled myself together. The sketch trembled in my hands. I hadn't noticed that he had given it to me.

Napoleon was back at his desk, standing there rigidly, his mouth a thin hard line, his chin jutting out, staring at the document with the red seal. Beads of perspiration ran down my forehead, but my eyes were as if riveted to his face.

He bent forward now. He seized the pen. He wrote a single word on the paper and sanded it. Then he rang the handbell, a bell on the top of which was fixed the brass figure of an eagle with outspread wings.

The secretary arrived within a second. Napoleon folded the document carefully and gave it to him. " Seal it!" he said and watched the secretary do so. " Go at once to Vincennes," he ordered, " and hand it to the Commanding Officer himself. I'll hold you responsible for placing it in the Commanding Officer's hands."

The secretary bowed himself out of the room. In a hoarse

voice I asked: "I should like to know what you have decided."

Napoleon stooped down to collect from the floor the leaves of the silk rose from my hat. "You have ruined your hat, Madame," he said, and passed me the handful of bits.

I rose, put the sketch of the eagle on one of the tables and threw the bits into the fire.

"Don't take it to heart," he said. "The hat did not suit you anyway."

Napoleon accompanied me through the empty corridors. Bees, I thought, as we went along, bees will be on all the walls here.

He took me right down to the carriage.

"Your mother is waiting for the answer. What am I to tell her?"

He bent over my hand but did not kiss it. "Give her my best wishes. And many thanks to you, Madame, for your visit."

I found Madame Letitia where I had left her, in the arm-chair by the window. The light of dawn was spreading over the sky and the first birds twittered in the garden. Jean-Baptiste was working at his desk.

"I am sorry that I have been so long," I said. "He would not let me go. He talked about all sorts of things." My head felt like bursting.

"Has he made his decision?" Madame Letitia asked.

"Oh yes. But he didn't tell me what it was. And I am to give you his best wishes, Madame."

"Thank you, my child." Madame Letitia got up and went to the door. There she turned round again and said: "Thank you, thank you—whatever happens."

Jean-Baptiste carried me up to the bedroom. He undressed me. I was too tired to do anything at all. "Do you know," I said, "that Napoleon wants to be Emperor?"

"I have heard the rumour, probably spread by his enemies. Who told you?"

"Napoleon himself."

Jean-Baptiste stared at me, then turned away abruptly and went into the dressing-room. I heard him walking up and down there for hours, and I could only fall asleep after he, at last, had come to bed and I could put my head on his shoulder.

I slept very late next morning and had awful dreams of a white sheet of paper over which blood-red bees kept crawling. Marie brought me my breakfast and a late morning edition of the *Moniteur*. There, on the front page, it said that at five o'clock this morning at the Fortress of Vincennes the Duc d'Enghien had been executed by a firing squad.

A few hours later Madame Letitia left to join her exiled son Lucien in Italy.

PARIS, May 20th, 1804.
(1st Prairial of the Year XII.)

" Her Imperial Highness, the Princess Joseph!" Fernand announced. And my sister Julie swept into the room.

" *Madame la Maréchale*, and how are you this morning?" said Julie, and the corners of her mouth twitched, with laughter or with tears?

" Thank you, Your Imperial Highness," I said, and bowed low, exactly as Monsieur Montel had taught me in days gone by.

" I've come a bit earlier, so that we can have a few moments in the garden," said my sister, Her Imperial Highness, Princess of France.

Our garden is small, and in spite of Josephine's advice the rose trees haven't done too well, and there is no tree to equal the beautiful chestnut tree in Sceaux. But when the lilac and the two little apple trees, which Jean-Baptiste planted on Oscar's first birthday, are in bloom there is no lovelier place for me anywhere on earth than this garden in the Rue Cisalpine.

Julie dusted the garden seat carefully before sitting down in her light blue satin frock. Marie brought us some lemonade and looked critically at Julie. " Imperial Highness ought to put a bit of rouge on," she said. " *Madame la Maréchale* looks much prettier."

Julie threw back her head angrily: " *Madame la Maréchale* hasn't got my troubles. I am so bothered, Marie. We are moving into the Luxembourg Palace."

" The beautiful house in the Rue du Rocher doesn't seem to be good enough for Princess Julie," said Marie acidly.

" Marie, you are unfair. I hate castles, I hate them. But we must move there because the Heir to the Throne of France and his wife must live in the Luxembourg Palace."

Julie, wife of the Heir to the Throne of France, looked very miserable. But Marie did not change her tune. " The late Monsieur Clary would not have approved of it, indeed he wouldn't," she said, putting her hands on her hips. " Your late papa was a Republican, you know!"

192

Julie made a despairing gesture. "It isn't my fault," she moaned.

"Leave us alone for a bit, Marie," I asked. When Marie had gone I said to Julie: "Don't listen to that old dragon."

"But really, it isn't my fault," she wailed. "Moving is no fun, God knows, and all these ceremonies make me ill. Yesterday, during the parade for the Marshals, we had to stand for three whole hours, and to-day, in the Dôme des Invalides——"

"To-day we're going to sit down," I assured her. "Drink your lemonade."

The lemonade had exactly the same kind of taste as the one that these last days had left on my tongue, bitter-sweet. They had been sweet because we had been inundated with congratulations on Jean-Baptiste's promotion to Marshal of France.

The Marshal's rank is every soldier's dream whether he is a private or a General. And now this dream has come true for my husband, but so differently, so very differently from the way we had imagined.

Shortly after my visit to the Tuileries the leader of the Royalists, George Cadoudal, had been captured. After the Duc d'Enghien's execution no one had any doubts as to what was going to happen to him. But I grew nearly sick with anxiety for Jean-Baptiste when suddenly General Moreau, General Pichegru and other officers were arrested as Cadoudal's accomplices. At any moment we expected the police. Instead of that, however, Jean-Baptiste, as once before, was called to the Tuileries to the First Consul.

"The French people has decided for me. Are you going to oppose the will of the people?"

"I have never opposed the will of the people, and I cannot imagine myself ever doing it," Jean-Baptiste answered calmly.

"We shall promote you to the rank of Marshal."

"We?" asked Jean-Baptiste.

"Yes, We, Napoleon the First, Emperor of the French."

Jean-Baptiste was speechless, and Napoleon, seeing his speechless stupor, slapped his knee and danced about the room in merriment.

General Moreau was found guilty of high treason but not condemned to death, only banished. He went to America in the uniform of a French General and with his sword, on which were engraved all the names of the victorious battles he had fought, dangling from his belt.

After that things happened in quick succession. The day before yesterday the First Consul went hunting near St. Cloud.

There he allowed himself to be surprised by the decision of the Senate to elect him Emperor of the French. Yesterday, during an elaborate military parade he handed the Marshal's baton to eighteen of the most famous Generals of the French Army. A week before that Jean-Baptiste had been told in strict confidence to order a Marshal's uniform according to a drawing which reached him from the Tuileries. After they had received their batons each of the new Marshals made a short speech. All eighteen of them addressed Napoleon as 'Your Majesty'. During Murat's and Masséna's speeches Napoleon kept his eyes half shut; one could tell how these last days had exhausted him. When Jean-Baptiste started his speech, however, a tense expression came into Napoleon's face, which finally changed into a smile, that winning spell-binding smile of his. He walked up to Jean-Baptiste, shook his hand and told him to consider him 'not only his Emperor but also his friend'. Jean-Baptiste stood to attention and did not let an eyelid flicker.

I witnessed all this from a stand erected for the wives of the eighteen Marshals. Oscar was with me, although it had been hinted that this would not be desirable. "Just imagine, *Madame la Maréchale,*" some master of ceremonies had moaned, "just imagine how awful it would be if your infant interrupted His Majesty's speech by his crying!" But I wanted Oscar to be present when his papa was made a Marshal of France. When the many thousands of spectators cheered Napoleon because he was shaking Jean-Baptiste by the hand, Oscar in excitement waved the little flag which I had bought for him.

Julie was in a different stand, that of the Imperial family. Since an Emperor has to have an Imperial family Napoleon made his brothers—with the exception of Lucien, of course—Imperial Princes and their wives Imperial Princesses. Joseph is regarded as the heir apparent so long as Napoleon himself has no son. Madame Letitia's title caused Napoleon a lot of headaches. He could not well call her 'Empress Mother', since she had never been an Empress, only the wife of the modest Corsican lawyer Carlo Buonaparte. But he and his brothers and sisters usually talk about her as '*Madame Mère*', and so he hit on the idea of introducing her to the nation as just that: *Madame Mère. Madame Mère,* by the way, is still in Italy with Lucien. As for Hortense, wife of the flat-footed Prince Louis, and Eugene her brother, they too were promoted to Imperial rank.

Napoleon's sisters had very rashly got themselves gowns embroidered all over with bees. Yet the *Moniteur* had nothing to say about any promotion of theirs to Princess. Caroline, who had married General Murat shortly after the *coup d'état* in Brumaire, became a *Madame la Maréchale* like me. According to the *Moniteur* a Marshal of France has a right to be addressed as ' Monseigneur ', and Caroline, having taken her place next to me in the stand, asked me seriously whether I was going to address my husband in future as ' Monseigneur ' in public. Such a stupid question, I thought, merited a very stupid answer, and so I said: " No. I call him Jean-Baptiste when there are other people about. Only in our bedroom do I call him Monseigneur."

After the ceremony we, the eighteen Marshals and their wives, dined with the Imperial family in the Tuileries. The walls, the carpets, the curtains were covered with embroidered bees. Many hundreds of women must have been working day and night to get them all embroidered in time.

At first I couldn't think of what this bee design reminded me. But as the evening went on and I had more and more champagne the bees seemed to be standing on their heads. And suddenly I knew: the lily! Napoleon's bee was the Bourbon lily upside down! ' That can't be an accident,' I thought, and I wanted to ask Napoleon about it. But he was sitting too far away from me. I sometimes heard him laugh loudly, and once, when there was a moment's silence, I heard him address his youngest sister Caroline as ' *Madame la Maréchale* '.

" I don't know how it is all going to end," I said to Julie as we were sitting now on our garden seat.

" But it has only just started," said Julie in low tones, and held a smelling-bottle to her nose.

" Aren't you feeling well?" I asked her, frightened.

" I can't sleep at all now," she said. " Imagine, if the Emperor really has no son and Joseph does succeed him and I——" She began to tremble violently and threw her arms round my neck. " Désirée, you are the only one who understands me. Désirée, I am only the daughter of the silk merchant Clary, how can I——"

Gently I took her arms from my neck. " You must pull yourself together, Julie. Show them who you are, show Paris, show the whole country."

" But who am I, Désirée, who am I?" She trembled more violently than ever.

" You are the daughter of the silk merchant François Clary," I said with great emphasis. " Don't you forget that, Julie Clary! Aren't you ashamed of yourself?"

195

Julie got up and I took her to my bedroom. Her hair was disarranged and her nose red from tears. I helped her to put herself straight again. In the middle of it I couldn't help laughing out loud. " No wonder, Julie, that you feel tired and worn. Ladies belonging to a noble house are always most delicate, and Princess Julie of the noble family of the Bonapartes is therefore bound to be less robust than *Citoyenne* Bernadotte."

" You are making a great mistake, Désirée, if you don't take Napoleon seriously," said Julie.

" You forget that I was the very first person ever to take him seriously," I told Julie. " But let's hurry up now. I want to see the procession of the Senators on our way to the Dôme."

In Julie's carriage we reached the Luxembourg Palace and there heard Napoleon proclaimed Emperor of the French. The proclamation procession arrived with a battalion of dragoons at its head, followed, on foot, by twelve perspiring City Councillors. Obviously it could have been no fun for these pouchy gentlemen to march in slow procession right across Paris. Behind them appeared the two Prefects in dress uniform, and, announced by the roaring laughter of the crowd, old Fontanes, the President of the Senate, on horseback. The horse, a very gentle bay, was led along by a groom. In spite of that the President looked most precarious in his saddle. In his left hand he held a parchment roll, whereas his right clung to the horse's neck for dear life. All the members of the Senate followed their President, and then a band came in sight playing a vigorous march which frightened Fontanes on his horse even more. The highest officers of the Paris garrison and four cavalry squadrons brought up the rear.

The procession stopped in front of the Luxembourg Palace. A trumpeter sounded a signal in all four directions, old Fontanes drew himself up solemnly and read from his parchment something which—as I read later in the papers—said that the Senate had resolved to elect the First Consul General Napoleon Bonaparte to be Emperor of the French. The crowd listened in silence to the trembling voice of the old man, and when he had finished a few voices shouted " *Vive l'Empereur!*" The band played the Marseillaise and the procession went on its way to repeat the proclamation at other places.

Julie and I went on from there to the Dôme des Invalides. We were taken to the gallery which was reserved for the Empress, the Imperial ladies and the wives of the Marshals. We only just arrived in time.

Below there was a sea of uniforms. Seven hundred pensioned officers and two hundred pupils of the Polytechnic filled the seats. In front of them, on eighteen gilded chairs, sat the Marshals in blue and gold uniforms. They were conversing eagerly and were not, like the ex-officers and the future technicians, overpowered by the solemnity of the occasion.

Now the cardinal approached the altar, and as he knelt down in silent prayer the Marshals, too, fell silent. At the same time trumpets outside and the sound of innumerable voices shouting "*Vive l'Empereur, vive l'Empereur*" announced the arrival of Napoleon.

The cardinal rose and, followed by ten priests of high rank, went slowly towards the entrance. Here he received the Emperor of the French.

The Emperor entered accompanied by Joseph, Louis and his ministers. The two Princes wore peculiar uniforms which made them look like flunkeys on the stage of the Théâtre Français. The column of great secular and clerical dignitaries shimmered in all the colours of the rainbow as it moved up towards the altar with Napoleon and the cardinal at its head. But Napoleon's uniform, alone amidst all the glitter of the rest, was of an inconspicuous dark green and showed no medals at all.

"He's mad," whispered Caroline, "he's only put on a colonel's uniform without any medals."

Hortense, her neighbour, dug her elbows into Caroline's ribs and hushed her.

Slowly Napoleon ascended the three steps leading up to the throne on the left of the altar. At any rate, I thought that it was a throne, never having seen one before. And there he sat, a small lonely figure in a colonel's field uniform.

I strained my eyes in order to make out the emblem on the high back of the throne. It was an N, a big N surrounded by a laurel wreath.

The rustle of satin gowns around me made me realise that Mass had begun and that I had to kneel. Napoleon had got up meanwhile and descended two steps. I heard Caroline whisper into Polette's ear that he had refused to make his confession, although Uncle Fesch had tried hard to get him to change his mind. Hortense hissed at her and Caroline grew silent. Josephine had put her folded hands in front of her face and she looked as if she were deep in prayer.

Uncle Fesch, yes, Uncle Fesch! The rotund abbot who during the Revolution had preferred to become a commercial traveller, and had asked Etienne for a job with the firm of Clary, had long ago returned to his clerical garb. From the day on which French troops had entered Rome and General Bonaparte had dictated the terms of peace to the Vatican, there had never been any doubt that a cardinal's hat was waiting for Uncle Fesch. And there he was now down below in a cardinal's crimson robe, holding aloft the monstrance.

Everybody was kneeling: the Marshals, the ex-officers who in the hour of the Republic's need had defended its frontiers at the head of peasants, workmen, fishermen, clerks and raw recruits, the young pupils of the Polytechnic, Josephine, the first Empress of the French, and the whole Bonaparte family by her side, and all the priests, high or low. Only Napoleon was on his feet, standing on the first step to the throne and politely inclining his head.

The last tone of the organ died away. Absolute silence reigned, as if the thousand people filling the Cathedral had stopped breathing.

Napoleon had taken a paper from his tunic and started speaking. But he never looked at his notes; he spoke freely and effortlessly. His voice floated through the nave with a metallic hardness and purity.

" He's taken lessons from an actor," whispered Caroline again.

" No, an actress, Mademoiselle George," giggled Polette under her breath.

" Hush ! " said Hortense.

As Napoleon came to the end of his speech he descended from the last step of his throne, went before the altar and raised his hand, saying: " And lastly you swear that, with all the strength at your disposal, you will guard liberty and equality, the principles on which all our institutions are based. Swear ! "

All hands flew up, and mine with them. In unison the congregation shouted, " We swear ! " The mighty shout rose up to the cupola and ebbed away.

The organ intoned the ' Te Deum '. Napoleon returned to his throne with measured steps, sat down and looked at the assembly. The sound of the organ filled the Cathedral.

Accompanied by his eighteen Marshals in their resplendent uniforms, Napoleon, an inconspicuous spot of green among the golden glitter, left the Dôme. Outside he mounted a white horse and rode back to the Tuileries at the head of the officers of his Guard regiments. The crowd went delirious with joy; one woman held up her baby to him and shouted : " Bless my son, bless him ! "

Jean-Baptiste was waiting for me by our carriage. On the journey home I asked him, "You've been sitting right in front close to him. Did his face show any signs of emotion as he sat there on his throne?"

"He smiled. But only his face, not his eyes."

He didn't say any more, and stared silently in front of him.

"What are you thinking of?" I asked.

"Of the collar of my uniform. The regulation height is awful, I can't stand it. Besides, the collar is too tight."

I studied his get-up more closely: a white satin waistcoat, a dark blue tunic embroidered with oak leaves in gold thread. The blue velvet greatcoat was lined with white satin and bordered with gold, and gigantic golden oak leaves were strewn along the edges.

"Your one-time fiancé is making it easy for himself. He squeezes us into this strangulating outfit, yet he himself puts on the comfortable field officer's uniform," Jean-Baptiste said, disgruntled.

Leaving the carriage in front of our house we found ourselves surrounded by some shabbily dressed young men. "*Vive Bernadotte!*" they shouted, "*Vive Bernadotte!*"

Jean-Baptiste eyed them for a fraction of a second and answered: "*Vive l'Empereur!*"

Later on, as we faced each other at table, he remarked casually: "You'll be interested to know that the Emperor has given his Chief of Police the order to keep watch not only over the private life of his Marshals but also over their private correspondence."

I thought this over and said after a little while: "Julie told me that he is having himself crowned properly in the winter."

Jean-Baptiste laughed. "Crowned by whom? By his Uncle Fesch in Notre-Dame perhaps?"

"No, he wants the Pope to crown him."

He put the glass of wine which he had just taken up back on the table with such vehemence that the wine spilled out all over the tablecloth. "That is, that is——" He shook his head. "No, Désirée, I think that that is out of the question. Do you think that he'd go on a pilgrimage to Rome to have himself crowned there?"

"Oh no. He wants the Pope to come here for the coronation."

Jean-Baptiste found this unbelievable. He explained to me that the Pope to the best of his knowledge had never yet left the Vatican for coronations abroad.

I put salt on the wine stains so that they could be more easily removed in the laundry, and said: "Joseph thinks that Napoleon is going to force the Pope to come."

"God knows, I hold no brief for the Holy Church of Rome— you wouldn't expect it of an old sergeant in the Army of the Revolution, anyway—but I don't think it right to force the old gentleman to a journey from Rome to Paris over these miserable roads."

"They've dug up an old crown somewhere, a sceptre and an orb, and everybody is going to have a part in the ceremony," I said. "Joseph and Louis are having costumes made in the Spanish court manner. Louis in particular, with his corporation and his flat feet, will look smart."

Jean-Baptiste pondered and then said: "I shall ask him to give me some administrative job somewhere as far as possible away from Paris. A really responsible job for some territory, not only just a military one but one that involves civil authority as well. I have thought out a new licensing system and Customs law, and I think I could do something to raise the prosperity of the country of which I should be put in charge."

"But then you would have to go away again!"

"I should have to do that in any case. Bonaparte will never give us permanent peace, you know. We Marshals shall be for ever crossing Europe till——" He paused for a moment, then continued, "till we have ruined ourselves with our victories."

During these words Jean-Baptiste had started to undo his collar. "This Marshal's uniform is too tight for you," I said.

"True, my little girl. The Marshal's uniform is too tight for me. And that's why Sergeant Bernadotte is going to leave Paris soon. Come, drink up, let's go to bed."

PARIS, 9th Frimaire of the Year XII.
(November 30th, 1804, according to the Church calendar.)

The Pope did come to Paris after all to crown Napoleon and Josephine!

And Jean-Baptiste made a dreadful scene because he had suddenly turned jealous—of Napoleon, not of the Pope.

This afternoon in the Tuileries we rehearsed the coronation procession of the Empress. My head is still heavy from it. Besides, I am feeling desperate because of Jean-Baptiste's jealousy. So, what with one thing and another, I can't go to sleep and I'm sitting at Jean-Baptiste's writing desk with his many books and maps on it and writing in my diary. Jean-Baptiste himself has gone out, I don't know where.

In two days' time the coronation will take place, and for months past Paris has been talking of nothing else. It will be the most magnificent spectacle of all time, Napoleon said. He forced the Pope to come to Paris to let the whole world, and in particular the adherents of the Bourbons, see for themselves that the coronation in Notre-Dame is the real thing.

Most of the former grandees of the Court of Versailles—all of them pious Roman Catholics—had secretly laid bets against the Pope's coming. Hardly one of them thought he would. And lo and behold, who arrived a few days ago with a suite of six cardinals, four archbishops, six prelates and a whole host of physicians, secretaries, Swiss bodyguards and lackeys? His Holiness Pope Pius VII!

Josephine gave a banquet in his honour in the Tuileries, from which the Pope retired and in high dudgeon because she wanted to amuse him with a ballet performance afterwards. Oh yes, she had meant well. " Seeing that he is in Paris anyway. . . ." she tried to explain to Uncle Fesch. But Uncle Fesch, every inch a cardinal now, was much annoyed and cut her short.

The members of the Imperial family have been rehearsing the coronation ritual for weeks, alternately at Fontainebleau and in the Tuileries. This afternoon we too, the wives of the eighteen Marshals, were ordered to the Tuileries to rehearse the Empress's coronation procession. I went there with Laura Junot and Madame Berthier, and we were taken to Josephine's white room. We arrived there in the middle of a furious argument between various members of the Bonaparte family.

The responsibility for the conduct of the ceremony falls on Joseph, but all the details are in the hands of the Master of Ceremonies, Monsieur Despreaux, who is to receive a fee of 2400 francs for his work. He therefore is actually in charge, assisted by this dreadful Monsieur Montel who, years ago, gave me lessons in deportment.

We Marshals' wives huddled together in a corner and tried to find out what the argument was about.

" But it is His Majesty's explicit wish!" shouted Despreaux at this moment, in despair.

" And even if he throws me out of France as he did poor Lucien, I'm not going to do it," vituperated Eliza Bacciochi.

" Carry the train? Me carry the train?" shouted Polette indignantly.

Joseph tried to calm them down: " But Julie and Hortense

have to do it too, and they don't refuse although they are Imperial Highnesses."

"Imperial Highnesses indeed!" hissed Caroline. "Why haven't we, the Emperor's sisters, been made Highnesses, may I ask? Are we less than Julie, the silk merchant's daughter, and——"

I felt my face grow red with rage.

"—and Hortense, the daughter of this—of this——." Caroline fumbled for a suitable word of abuse for Her Majesty Empress Josephine.

"Ladies, ladies, please!" implored Despreaux.

"It's about the coronation robe with that enormous train," whispered Laura Junot into my ear. "The Emperor wants his sisters and the Princesses Julie and Hortense to carry it."

"Well, can we start the rehearsal?" It was Josephine who had entered by a side door. She looked very peculiar in two sheets sewn together over her shoulder to represent the coronation gown, which apparently was not ready yet. We sank into a deep curtsey.

"Please take your places for Her Majesty's procession," Joseph called out.

"And if she stands on her head, I am not going to carry her train," said Eliza Bacciochi once more.

Despreaux came over to us. "Hm," he said, "the eighteen Marshals' ladies are only seventeen, I see. *Madame la Maréchale* Murat as the Emperor's sister is carrying the train."

"She wouldn't dream of it," shouted Caroline across the room.

"I don't quite see," meditated Despreaux, "how seventeen ladies, two by two—— Montel, can you tell me how to group seventeen ladies in nine couples to proceed ahead of Her Majesty?"

Montel danced towards us and frowned heavily. "Seventeen ladies—in couples—not one must go by herself——"

"May I assist you in the solution of this strategic problem?" asked a voice close to us. Startled we spun round, and immediately sank into another curtsey.

"I suggest that only sixteen of these ladies open the procession of Her Majesty. Then Securier, as arranged, with the ring of the Empress, Murat with her crown and finally one of these ladies with a—with a cushion with one of Her Majesty's lace handkerchiefs on it. It will give it a very poetic flavour."

"Magnificent, Your Majesty," murmured Despreaux, and bowed deeply, as did Montel by his side.

"And this lady carrying the lace handkerchief——" Napoleon paused and with apparent thoughtfulness his eyes glanced round us, from Madame Berthier to Laura Junot, from Laura Junot to the ugly Madame Lefébvre.

But I knew his decision. Firmly I avoided looking at him. I wanted to be one of the sixteen, just the wife of Marshal Bernadotte, neither more or less. I certainly didn't want an exceptional position, I certainly didn't want——

But Napoleon spoke: "We ask Madame Jean-Baptiste Bernadotte to take over this task. Madame Bernadotte will look charming. In sky-blue, don't you think so?"

"Sky-blue doesn't suit me," I jerked out, remembering the pale blue silk frock I had worn in Madame Tallien's salon.

"Yes, sky-blue, I think," the Emperor, who no doubt remembered that frock too, repeated, and turned away.

As he went over towards his sisters, Polette opened her mouth and said: "Sire, we don't want——"

"Madame, you are forgetting yourself!" Napoleon's voice came cuttingly across the room. Of course, no one may speak to the Emperor without permission.

Napoleon turned to Joseph: "More difficulties?"

"The girls don't want to carry the Empress's train."

"Why not?"

"Sire, the Ladies Bacciochi and Murat and the Princess Borghese are of the opinion that——"

"In that case the Princesses Joseph and Louis Bonaparte will carry the train by themselves," Napoleon decided.

Here Josephine intervened.

"The train is far too heavy for two," she said.

"If we don't get the same rights as Julie and Hortense," said Eliza, "we shall do without the same duties."

"Hold your tongue!" Napoleon turned to Polette, of whom he is quite fond. "Well, what exactly do you want?"

"We have the same claim to Imperial rank as those two," said Polette, pointing with her chin in Julie's and Hortense's direction.

He raised his eyebrows. "Indeed! One would think that I had inherited our father's Imperial crown and was cheating my brothers and sisters out of their rightful inheritance! They seem to forget that every distinction conferred is nothing but a proof of goodwill on my part, a goodwill so far entirely unearned, surely?"

In the silence following his words Josephine's voice came sweetly: "Sire, I beg of you that you, in your gracious kindness, may see fit to raise your sisters to the rank of Imperial Highness."

She is looking for allies, it occurred to me, she is afraid. Perhaps it was true what people were saying, that he was thinking of divorce. . . .

Napoleon laughed. He seemed to find it all very amusing, and I saw now that the whole thing had been amusing him from the very beginning. "All right," he said, "if you promise to behave I shall confer on you——"

"Sire!" shouted Eliza and Caroline in joyous surprise, and Polette said breathlessly: "*Grazie tante*, Napoleone!"

"I should like to see the rehearsal of the coronation procession," said Napoleon, turning to Despreaux. "Please start!"

Someone played a solemn hymn on a piano. It was meant to indicate the organ. Despreaux divided up the Marshals' ladies into eight couples, and Montel showed them how to walk gracefully and at the same time solemnly. But the ladies were quite unable to do it because of the presence of the Emperor, who with a stony face kept staring at their feet. Dreadfully embarrassed and awkward, they stumbled through the room, and Polette put her hand to her mouth to prevent a fit of laughter. At last Securier and Murat were called in. They joined the parade of ladies, gravely carrying a cushion from a divan on their outspread palms. After them I had to do the walking by myself, likewise carrying an ordinary cushion. Finally it was Josephine's turn, and the freshly promoted Imperial Highnesses, with Julie and Hortense, carried her dragging bed-sheets without the slightest objection.

Four times we walked up and down the room. We stopped only when Napoleon turned to go. We curtsied as he left. But Joseph ran after him shouting, "Sire, I implore you, Sire!"

Impatiently Napoleon said, "I have no more time to spare."

"Sire, it concerns the virgins," Joseph explained, and beckoned Despreaux to come.

Despreaux came and repeated, "The virgins, Sire. They are a difficult problem. We cannot find any."

Napoleon suppressed a smile. "For what do you need virgins, gentlemen?"

"It may have escaped Your Majesty's memory, but the chronicle about the medieval coronation ritual in Rheims, according to which we are to proceed, states that, after the anointing of Your Majesty, twelve pure virgins have to go up to the altar, a candle in each hand. We thought of a cousin

of Marshal Berthier's and one of my mother's sisters, but——"
Despreaux stammered, "but, but both ladies are—are not——"

"They are virgins but too old," Murat's voice trumpeted across the room. Murat, the cavalry officer, had momentarily forgotten his courtier's dignity.

"I have repeatedly stressed my desire to allow France's traditional nobility to take part in the coronation ceremonies, which are the concern of the whole of France. I am convinced, gentlemen, that among the families of the Faubourg St. Germain you will find some suitable young ladies." With that he finally disappeared.

Refreshments were handed round, and Josephine sent one of her ladies-in-waiting to ask me to join her on the sofa. She wanted to show her pleasure at the distinction Napoleon had conferred on me. She sat between Julie and myself and emptied a glass of champagne in hasty gulps. The delicate face seemed to have shrunk during the last few months, the eyes under their make-up looked unnaturally big, and the magnificent layer of paint on her cheeks showed tiny cracks. Two fine lines ran from her nostrils down to the corners of her mouth, and her forced smile made them show up considerably. But her babyish curls, brushed upwards as usual, still had their old spell of touching youthfulness about them.

"Le Roy won't be able," I remarked, "to let me have a sky-blue gown within two days."

Josephine, exhausted by hours and hours of rehearsal, forgot that she must no longer bring up her past and said: "Paul Barras once gave me some sapphire ear-rings. If I can find them I shall gladly lend them to you to go with your blue gown."

"Madame, you are too kind, but I believe——"

Here I was interrupted by a very agitated-looking Joseph.

"What is it now?" Josephine asked.

"His Majesty asks Your Majesty to see him at once in his study."

Josephine arched her eyebrows. "New difficulties about the coronation, my dear brother-in-law?"

Joseph could no longer contain his malicious joy and, bending forward, he said: "The Pope has just told the Emperor that he refuses to crown Your Majesty."

An ironical smile curled round Josephine's lips. "And what reason does the Holy Father give for his refusal?"

Joseph looked round the room with affected discretion.

"You may speak. Except for Princess Julie and Madame

205

Bernadotte nobody can hear us, and these two ladies are members of the family, are they not?"

Putting on an impressive air Joseph said: "The Pope has learnt that His Majesty and Your Majesty did not contract their marriage in church, and he has stated that he could not—I apologise, but these are the words of the Holy Father—that he could not crown the concubine of the Emperor of the French."

"And where did the Holy Father learn so suddenly that Bonaparte and I were married in a registry office only?" Josephine inquired calmly.

"We do not know yet," Joseph answered.

"And how, do you think, is His Majesty going to answer the Holy Father?" Josephine looked thoughtfully at the empty glass in her hand.

"His Majesty will naturally enter into negotiations with the Holy Father."

"There is a very simple way out." Josephine smiled, rising to her feet and pressing the champagne glass into Joseph's hand. "I shall talk to Bona—, to the Emperor about it at once. We shall get married in church, and everything will be all right."

Joseph passed the glass on to one of the lackeys and ran after her to be present at the interview if possible. Julie meditated and said: "I shouldn't be surprised if she has drawn the Pope's attention to it herself."

"Yes, otherwise she would have shown some genuine surprise," I admitted.

Julie studied her hands. "You know, I am sorry for her. She is so afraid of a divorce. And it would be so mean if he kicked her out now, simply because she can't have any more children. Don't you think so too?"

I shrugged my shoulders. "Here he is, staging this elaborate coronation farce in the style of Charlemagne and the ritual of Rheims and Heaven knows what, in order to impress on the world that he has founded a dynasty. And all that simply to make Joseph Emperor, if he survives him, or the small son of Louis and Hortense."

"But he can't just throw her into the street!" Tears came into Julie's eyes. "She got engaged to him when he was too poor to buy himself a pair of trousers. She accompanied him in his career step by step, she helped him make his way, and now that her crown has been delivered and everybody regards her as the Empress——"

"No," I said, "he can't play at Charlemagne and have himself crowned by the Pope, and at the same time, like any Tom, Dick and Harry, be involved in a divorce action. If even *I* see that, Josephine, who is a hundred times cleverer than I, sees it most certainly too. No, Napoleon is sure to insist on her coronation and therefore will hastily arrange a church marriage ceremony."

"And once their marriage has the Church's sanction a divorce will be far more difficult, won't it? And Josephine counts on that, doesn't she?"

"I'm sure she does."

"Besides," continued Julie, "he loves her, in his own way, of course, but he loves her and wouldn't just abandon her like that."

"Wouldn't he? Wouldn't he? Believe me, Napoleon would."

At that moment the Empress returned. Passing a lackey, she took a glass of champagne from him, called to Despreaux, "One more rehearsal, please," and came to us.

"Uncle Fesch is going to marry us secretly to-night in the Imperial Chapel," she said, drinking with nervous haste. "Is it not funny? After having been man and wife for nine years! Well, *Madame la Maréchale*, have you thought it over, and would you like to borrow my sapphires?"

On the way home I decided that I would not let myself be forced by Napoleon to wear pale blue. To-morrow morning Le Roy would deliver my shell-pink robe—all the Marshals' wives are to be dressed in shell-pink—and I should carry Josephine's handkerchief across Notre-Dame in shell-pink.

Jean-Baptiste was waiting for me in the dining-room, apparently in a very bad temper. "What were you doing all this time in the Tuileries?"

"I listened to the Bonapartes arguing among themselves and then took part in the rehearsal. By the way, they've given me a special part to play. I am not to walk with the other Marshals' ladies but by myself behind Murat and I am to carry a handkerchief for Josephine on a cushion. What do you say to this distinction?"

Jean-Baptiste flew out: "But I don't want you to have a special position. Joseph and this monkey, Despreaux, thought it out because you are Julie's sister. But I forbid it, you understand?"

I sighed. "That won't be any use. It's nothing to do with Joseph and Despreaux. The Emperor wants it."

I should never have thought it possible that anything could upset Jean-Baptiste as badly as this did. In a hoarse voice he brought out: "What was that you said?"

"The Emperor wants it. It isn't my fault."

"I will not have it! I will not have my wife compromised before the whole of France!" Jean-Baptiste roared so violently that the glasses on the table tinkled.

I didn't know what to make of his rage. "Why are you so furious?" I asked.

"They will point at you. His fiancée, they will say, Madame Jean-Baptiste Bernadotte, the great love of his youth whom he cannot forget, they will say, his little Eugenie to whom he wants to show special favour on the day of his coronation, now as ever his little Eugenie, that's what they will say! And I shall be the laughing-stock of all Paris, do you see?"

Disconcerted, I stared at Jean-Baptiste. Nobody knows as well as I do how his strained relationship with Napoleon tortures him, how he is haunted constantly by the thought of having betrayed the ideals of his youth, and how agonisingly he is waiting for the independent command as far away from Paris as possible, for which he has applied and for which Napoleon keeps him waiting, waiting, waiting. But that this painful waiting should have led to this scene of jealousy came to me as a shock.

I went up to him and put my hands on his chest. "Jean-Baptiste," I said, "it really isn't worth your while to get angry at one of Napoleon's whims."

He pushed my hands away. "You know quite well what he is about," he gasped, "you know it. He wants to make people believe that he is only showing favour to his little fiancée of old. But let me tell you, let me tell you as a man that he is not interested in this 'old old', he is interested in you now, at this moment, he is in love with you and wants to do something special for you so that——"

"Jean-Baptiste!"

He brushed his hand across his forehead. "I am sorry. It is not your fault," he said under his breath.

Fernand appeared and put the soup tureen on the table. We sat down, facing each other in silence. Jean-Baptiste's hand which held the spoon shook.

"I shall not take part in the ceremony at all," I said, "but go to bed and be ill."

Jean-Baptiste did not answer. After the meal he left the house.

And so I am sitting now at his desk, writing, and trying to make clear to myself whether Napoleon really loves me again or not.

That endless night in his office before the execution of the Duc d'Enghien he spoke to me in the tones of the young lover. " Do take off your hat, Madame . . ." and a little later " Eugenie, little Eugenie . . ." He sent Mademoiselle George away. Perhaps because he remembered that night by the hedge in our garden in Marseilles, perhaps because he remembered the fields and the stars of that night? Isn't it strange that the little Buonaparte of that night in two days' time will be crowned Emperor of the French? Isn't it quite unimaginable that there was a time in my life when I did not belong to my Bernadotte?

The clock in the dining-room strikes midnight. Perhaps Jean-Baptiste has gone to see Madame Récamier. He speaks about her so often, Juliette Récamier, the wife of an old and wealthy banker, who reads all the books that are published and even some that are not, and lies on a sofa all day long. She fancies herself as the muse of all the famous men but will have herself touched by none, least of all, according to Polette, by her own husband. Jean-Baptiste often talks to this muse about books and music, and sometimes she sends me boring novels, ' masterpieces ' which she asks me to read. I hate her, and I admire her.

It's half-past twelve now. Napoleon and Josephine are at this moment most likely on their knees in the chapel of the Tuileries, and Uncle Fesch is marrying them according to the canon of the Church. How easy it would be for me to explain to Jean-Baptiste why Napoleon does not forget me, but it would only annoy him. I am a part of Napoleon's youth, that is the explanation, and no man ever forgets his youth even if he thinks of it only rarely. If I turn up in blue at the coronation I shall be for Napoleon no more than a memory come to life. Of course, it is possible that Jean-Baptiste is right and that Napoleon wants to revive his old feelings. A declaration of love from Napoleon would be like balm on a wound that doesn't need balm any longer because it healed long ago. To-morrow I shall stay in bed with a heavy cold, and the day after to-morrow as well. His Majesty's Memory in Blue has a cold and sends her apologies. . . .

I fell asleep over my diary and woke up when someone took me gently in his arms and carried me to the bedroom. The metal braids of his epaulettes scratched my cheeks as they so often do. Sleepily I murmured: "You've been to see your muse. I'm very offended."

"I have been to the opera, my little girl, and on my own. To hear some decent music. I sent the carriage away and walked home."

"I love you very much, Jean-Baptiste. And I'm very ill, I've a cold and a sore throat and I can't go to the coronation."

"I shall apologise to the Emperor for Madame Bernadotte." After a little while he added: "You must never forget, my little girl, that I love you very much. Do you hear me, or are you asleep again?"

"I am dreaming, Jean-Baptiste, I'm dreaming. What do you do if suddenly someone wants to pour balm on a wound that healed long ago?"

"You laugh at him, Désirée."

"Yes, let's laugh at him, the great Emperor of the French. . . ."

PARIS, on the evening after Napoleon's coronation (December 2nd, 1804.)

It was very solemn, the coronation of my ex-fiancé as Emperor of the French, and once or twice it was funny too. Yes, I was there, it turned out very differently from what I expected.

The day before yesterday Jean-Baptiste explained to the Master of Ceremonies, Monsieur Despreaux, that, to my infinite distress, a high temperature and a heavy cold were making it impossible for me to attend the coronation. Despreaux couldn't understand it; the other ladies, he thought, would willingly rise from their death-bed to get to Notre-Dame. Couldn't I make it possible to attend after all? But Jean-Baptiste pointed out that my sneezing would drown the organ music.

I did stay in bed all next day. Julie, who had heard about my illness, came about lunch time and made me drink hot milk and honey. I dared not tell her that I wasn't ill at all.

However, yesterday morning I was so bored lying in bed that I got up, dressed and went into the nursery. We played merrily, but always careful not to make a mess for fear of Marie, who gets more severe with us every day.

In the middle of our playing Fernand appeared and announced Napoleon's physician. Before I had a chance of telling him that I would be ready to see Dr. Corvisart in my bedroom within five minutes this fool of a Fernand had shown him into the nursery. Dr. Corvisart put his black bag on the saddle of Oscar's rocking-horse and bowed politely.

"His Majesty," he said, "has commissioned me to inquire after *Madame la Maréchale's* health. I am glad to be able to report to his Majesty that you have quite recovered."

"But, Doctor, I am still feeling very weak," I said, in despair.

Dr. Corvisart raised his funny triangular eyebrows and said: "I believe I can say, with a good conscience as a doctor, that you will be sufficiently strong to carry Her Majesty's handkerchief in the coronation." Without the ghost of a smile he bowed once more, saying: "His Majesty's instructions have left no doubt in my mind."

I had a lump in my throat. It occurred to me that Napoleon could demote Jean-Baptiste with a stroke of his pen, that in fact we were completely in his power.

"If you really advise me to, Doctor——" I said.

Dr. Corvisart bent over my hand. "I advise you most urgently, Madame, to attend the coronation." He took his black bag and left.

In the afternoon Le Roy sent my shell-pink robe and the white ostrich feathers for my hair. Round about six o'clock I was terrified by a sudden volley of artillery which shook the windows. I ran into the kitchen and asked Fernand what was going on.

"From now till midnight there will be a salvo every hour," he said, polishing Jean-Baptiste's gilded sword with great zeal. "At the same time there will be fireworks in all the public squares. We ought to take Oscar to see them."

"It's snowing too hard," I said, "and Oscar was coughing this morning."

I went up to the nursery, sat down by the window and took Oscar on my knee. It was quite dark in the room but I didn't put on the light. Oscar and I watched the snowflakes dancing through the light of the big street-lamp in front of our house.

"There is a town where every winter the snow stays lying in the streets for many months, not just for a few days as here," I said.

"And then?" Oscar asked.

"Then? Nothing."

Oscar was disappointed. "I thought you were going to tell me another story."

"It isn't a story. It's true."

"What town is that?"

"Stockholm."

"Where is Stockholm?"

"Far, far away. Near the North Pole, I believe."

"Does Stockholm belong to the Emperor?"

"No, Oscar, Stockholm has a King of its own."

"What is his name?"

"I don't know, darling."

The guns thundered again and made Oscar jump. Frightened, he pressed his face against my neck.

"You mustn't be afraid," I said, "they are only shots in honour of the Emperor."

Oscar raised his head. "I am not afraid of guns, Mama. I want to be a Marshal of France some day, like Papa."

The snowflakes continued to dance. I didn't know why, but out of the past the rhythm of the falling snow brought the horse-face of Persson back to my mind.

"Perhaps you will be a good silk merchant like your grandfather," I said.

"But I want to be a Marshal. . Or a sergeant. Papa told me that he had been a sergeant. And so was Fernand." Something important seemed to have occurred to him. "Fernand told me that I may go to the coronation with him to-morrow."

"Oh no, Oscar. Children must not be taken into the church. Papa and Mama did not get a ticket for you."

"But Fernand wants to be outside the church with me. Fernand says we can see the whole procession from there. The Empress and Aunt Julie and—and, Mama, the Emperor with his crown. Fernand promised me that."

"It's far too cold, Oscar. You can't stand outside Notre-Dame for hours. And there will be such a crowd that a little man like you would be trampled under foot."

"Please, Mama, please, please!"

"I shall tell you later exactly what it was like, Oscar."

He put his little arms round me and gave me a sweet and rather wet kiss. "Please, Mama, if I promise to drink all my milk every night?"

"No, really, Oscar, it's impossible. It's so cold and you've got a cough. Be sensible, darling."

"But, Mama, if I drink the whole bottle of nasty cough cure, Mama, may I go?"

"In this town of Stockholm," I began, "close to the North Pole there is a big lake with green ice-floes——" But he was no longer interested in Stockholm.

"Mama, Mama, I want to see the coronation, please, please, Mama!" He was sobbing now.

"When you are grown up, then you may go and see the coronation."

Sceptically Oscar asked: "Is the Emperor going to be crowned again later?"

"No—o—o. We shall go to see another coronation, Oscar, you and I, I promise you that. And it'll be a much more beautiful coronation than the one to-morrow."

"*Madame la Maréchale* is not to talk nonsense to the boy!" came Marie's voice out of the dark behind us. "Come on, Oscar, drink up your milk and cough medicine." She lit the lamp, and the snowflakes became invisible in the dark outside.

Later on, when Jean-Baptiste came up to say good night to Oscar, he started complaining again. "Mama won't let me go with Fernand to-morrow to see the Emperor with his crown."

"Nor will I," said Jean-Baptiste.

"Mama says that she'll take me to another coronation later on when I'm grown up. Are you coming too, Papa?"

"Whose coronation is that?" asked Jean-Baptiste.

"Mama, whose coronation is that?"

I didn't know how to extricate myself. So I put on a very mysterious air and said: "I'm not telling now. It'll be a surprise. Good night, darling, sweet dreams."

Jean-Baptiste carefully tucked him up and extinguished the light.

For the first time for I don't know how long I prepared our evening meal myself. Marie, Fernand and the kitchen maid had gone out, probably to one of the free shows that were running in all the theatres of Paris. Yvette, my new personal maid, had disappeared long before the others. I had had to engage Yvette because Julie insisted that the wife of a Marshal of France must neither do her hair nor her sewing herself. Before the Revolution Yvette had been lady's maid to some duchess or other and so, naturally, she thought herself several rungs above me in the social ladder.

After the meal we did the washing up and Jean-Baptiste put on Marie's pinafore and helped me dry. "I always used to help my mother," he said with a smile.

Turning serious he went on: "I heard from Joseph that you had a visit from the Emperor's physician."

I sighed. "In this town everybody knows everything about everybody else."

"No, not everybody. But the Emperor knows a lot about a lot of people. That's the way he governs."

Falling asleep I heard the guns thunder once more. Dreamily it went through my head that I would have been very happy in a country cottage near Marseilles raising chickens. But neither Napoleon, Emperor of the French, nor Bernadotte, Marshal of France, would have been interested in chicken-farming.

I woke up to find Jean-Baptiste shaking me by the shoulders. It was still quite dark. "What is it? Is it time to get up?"

"No," said my husband, "but you were crying so bitterly in your sleep that I had to wake you up. Did you have a bad dream?"

I tried to recall my dream, and slowly in the telling it came back to me. "I went to a coronation with Oscar, and we had to get into the church at all costs. But there were so many people outside that we couldn't get to the doors and were pushed and shoved and jostled. The crowd grew bigger and bigger, I held Oscar by the hand and all of a sudden the thousands of people turned into chickens which got under our feet and cackled for all they were worth."

"And that was so dreadful?" he asked soothingly, tenderly.

"Yes, dreadful," I said, snuggling up to him, "dreadful. The chickens cackled like—like—yes, like people when they are curious and agitated. But that wasn't the worst. The worst was the crowns."

"The crowns."

"Yes. Oscar and I were wearing crowns, and they were awfully heavy. I could hardly keep my head up; I knew all the time that my crown would fall down the moment I bent my head the slightest little bit. And Oscar too had a crown which was much too heavy for him. I could see how he stiffened his neck to keep his head straight, and I was so afraid the child might collapse under the weight of the crown. And then, thank God, you woke me up. It was such an awful dream."

He put his arm under my head and kept me close to him. "It is quite natural that you should have dreamt of a coronation. In two hours' time we shall have to get up and get ready for the ceremony in Notre-Dame. But however did the chickens get into your dreams?"

I didn't try to answer that, I tried to forget the nasty dream and go to sleep again——

It had stopped snowing. But it was much colder than last night. Yet in spite of that the people of Paris had started collecting outside Notre-Dame and lining the streets through which the gilded equipages of the Imperial family were to pass from five o'clock onwards.

Jean-Baptiste and I were to go to the Archbishop's palace, where the procession would be formed. While Fernand was helping Jean-Baptiste with his uniform Yvette arranged the white ostrich feathers in my hair. I thought I looked dreadful in this headgear, like a circus horse.

Every two seconds Jean-Baptiste called from his corner, "Are you ready, Désirée?" But the ostrich feathers refused to stay put on my head.

Marie burst into the middle of my dressing difficulties with a little parcel which, she said, had just been delivered by a lackey of the Imperial Household. Yvette placed it before me on the dressing-table. Under Marie's watchful eyes I stripped off the paper cover and a casket made of red leather appeared. Jean-Baptiste came up and stood behind me, and our eyes met in the mirror over my dressing-table. Without a doubt, I thought, Napoleon has thought of some more terrible things and Jean-Baptiste will be furious. My hands shook so badly that I couldn't open the casket. At last Jean-Baptiste said, "Let me do it," pressed a little lock and the casket opened.

"Oh!" sighed Yvette, and Marie muttered admiringly "Mhm!" The casket showed a box of gold, glittering gold with an eagle with outspread wings engraved on its top. Uncomprehendingly I stared at it.

"Open it," said Jean-Baptiste.

I fumbled awkwardly with the top of the box. At last it came off. The box was lined with red velvet, and what shone out at me from among the velvet folds? Gold coins!

I turned round to Jean-Baptiste. "Do you understand?"

Jean-Baptiste didn't answer. He stared indignantly at the coins. His face had turned pale.

"They are gold francs," I said, and absent-mindedly I took out the top layer of coins and spread them on my dressing-table, around and between hair brushes, pieces of jewellery and my powder bowl. In doing so I heard a slight rustle and discovered a folded piece of paper among the coins. I pulled it out and opened it and recognised at once Napoleon's writing, his big untidy letters.

'Madame la Maréchale,' it said, 'in Marseilles you were so very kind as to lend me your personal savings to make the journey to Paris possible for me. This journey turns out to have been a journey into good fortune. On this day I feel the need to pay my debt and to thank you. N.' A postscript added 'The sum involved at that time was 98 francs.'

"Ninety-eight francs in gold, Jean-Baptiste," I said, "but I only lent him paper money at the time, *assignats.*" I noticed to my relief that Jean-Baptiste was smiling. " I had saved up my pocket money to buy a decent uniform for the Emperor; his field uniform was too shabby. But then he needed the money to pay debts, and the bills for Marshals Junot and Marmont which they had run up in their hotels. Otherwise they couldn't have got away."

Shortly before nine o'clock we arrived at the Archbishop's palace. In an upper room we met the other Marshals and their wives. We drank hot coffee and watched from the windows the exciting scenes outside before the portal of Notre-Dame. There six battalions of grenadiers supported by hussars of the Guards were trying to keep order. Inside the Cathedral feverish hammering was still going on. A double row of soldiers of the National Guard kept the curious crowds at bay. Jean-Baptiste had been told by Murat, who, as Governor of Paris, was in command of these troops, that 80,000 men had been mobilised to guard the Emperor's coronation procession.

At about this time the Prefect of Police closed all streets leading to the Cathedral to vehicular traffic. Thus it came about that the ladies and gentlemen invited to attend had to walk the last stretch to Notre-Dame. What was worse, whereas we, the participants in the procession, were allowed to leave our coats in the Archbishop's palace, these other guests had to leave theirs in their coaches, and had to arrive at Notre-Dame without any overcoats. It made me shiver to see the ladies trip through the cold weather in the thinnest of silk robes.

Something funny happened. One group of these unfortunate ladies ran into a knot of red-robed High Court judges. These gentlemen gallantly opened their wide robes to grant the freezing ladies some protection in their folds. We could hear the screaming laughter of the spectators through the closed windows.

A few carriages were allowed through, however, those of the foreign Princes who were considered guests of honour. " Third-raters," said Jean-Baptiste to me, and pointed out to me the Margrave of Baden and the Prince of Hesse-Darmstadt, and immediately behind him the Prince of Hesse-Homburg, for all of whom Napoleon pays travelling and hotel expenses.

How good Jean-Baptiste is at pronouncing those impossible Teutonic names, I thought, leaving the window for another cup of coffee. Meanwhile some dispute had arisen by the door. But I became attentive only when Madame Lannes came and told me: "I believe, dear Madame Bernadotte, that the argument by the door concerns you."

True enough, it did! A gentleman in a brown jacket and a somewhat disarranged scarf was trying in vain to slip through the guards by the door. "I must see my little sister, Madame Bernadotte, I must, I must."

It was Etienne. When he caught sight of me he shouted like someone drowning: "Help, Eugenie, help!"

"Why don't you allow my brother in?" I asked one of the guards.

He mumbled something about "Strict order to admit only participants in the procession."

I pulled Etienne into the room and called Jean-Baptiste. Between us we sat Etienne, who was perspiring with agitation, in an arm-chair.

He had been travelling day and night to get here for the coronation. "You know, Eugenie," he said, "how close the Emperor is to me. He is the friend of my youth, the man on whom I had staked all my hopes——" he panted, a picture of misery.

"In that case, why are you so miserable?" I asked. "Your friend of your young days will be crowned Emperor any moment now, what else do you want?"

"To see it," he implored me, "to see the ceremony."

Jean-Baptiste said soberly: "You ought to have come earlier to Paris, brother-in-law. There are no tickets left now."

Etienne, who has grown very stout these last years, wiped the sweat from his forehead. "The bad weather," he said, "it held up my coach every few hours."

"Perhaps Joseph might help," I said to Jean-Baptiste in an undertone, "we can't do anything now."

"Joseph is with His Majesty in the Tuileries and can't see anybody," wailed Etienne. "I've been there."

I tried to soothe him, and said: "Listen, Etienne, you never liked Napoleon very much, you can't really be all that keen on seeing his coronation."

At that Etienne exploded. "How can you say such a thing! Don't you know that in Marseilles I was his most intimate, his best friend, his——"

"I only know that you were disgusted because I wanted to get engaged to him."

"Really?" said Jean-Baptiste, and slapped my brother's shoulder, "were you really? Did you want to forbid Désirée's engagement? Etienne, brother-in-law, you are my friend indeed, and if the church were so crowded that I had to sit you on my knee I'd take you, I'd get you in." Laughingly he turned round and shouted: " Junot, Berthier, we must smuggle Monsieur Etienne Clary into the Cathedral. Come on, we've done more difficult things than that."

From the window I watched brother Etienne, under cover of three Marshals' uniforms, disappear inside Notre-Dame. After a little while the uniforms reappeared. Etienne, I was told, had been found a seat among the members of the Diplomatic Corps, next to the green-turbaned Turkish Minister in fact.

At this moment the Papal procession came into view, headed by a battalion of dragoons and followed by Swiss Guards. Behind him came a monk on a donkey, holding aloft a cross. We heard Berthier murmur, " That donkey costs 67 francs per day to hire," and Jean-Baptiste laughed. The monk was followed by the Pope's coach drawn by eight grey horses. We recognised the coach at once as the state equipage of the Empress, which had been put at the Pope's disposal.

The Pope entered the Archbishop's palace, but we did not see him. In one of the ground-floor rooms he put on his insignia, and, leading a group of the highest Church dignitaries, he left the palace and walked slowly towards the portal of Notre-Dame. We heard someone open a window. The crowd was silent; only some women knelt down, whereas most men did not even uncover their heads. Once the Pope stopped, said a few words and made the sign of the cross over a young man who was standing, with head lifted high, in the front rank. We were told later that the Pope had let his eyes rest smilingly on this young man and those around him and said, " I don't think that an old man's blessing can do any harm." Twice more he made the sign of the cross in the air, before he disappeared inside the Cathedral. The robes of the cardinals floated after him like a red wave.

" What is happening in Notre-Dame now?" I wanted to know.

Somebody explained to me that on the Pope's entry the choir of the Imperial Church intoned ' Tu es Petrus ' and that the Pope was going to take his seat on a throne to the left of the altar. " And now the Emperor ought to be here," my informant added. But the Emperor kept them waiting for another hour yet, the people of Paris, the regiments on duty, the illustrious guests and the head of the Holy Roman Catholic Church.

At last gun salvoes announced the approach of the Emperor. I don't know why, but suddenly everybody fell silent. In silence we prepared to leave the palace, and when I put a last dab of powder on my face I noticed to my surprise that my hands shook.

" *Vive l'Empereur! Vive l'Empereur!* " At first it sounded like the rushing sound of wind carried over a great distance: it grew louder and louder, and finally it came roaring round the next corner.

Murat appeared first, on horseback in the gold-braided uniform of the Governor of Paris: behind him came dragoons, and heralds in purple tunics with gold bees painted on their batons. I stared, mesmerised by this purple splendour. 'That,' I thought, ' is all for the man for whom I once wanted to buy a uniform because his old one was too shabby. . . .'

Then came one gilded equipage after another, each drawn by six horses, unloading first Despreaux, then the Emperor's adjutants, then the ministers, and finally the Imperial Princesses all in white and with tiny crowns in their hair. Julie came to me and pressed my hand with her ice-cold fingers. " I hope everything will be all right," she said.

" Yes," I answered in a whisper, " but look after your crown. It's sitting on one side."

When the Emperor's carriage turned the corner it was like the sun suddenly rising over a grey winter scene, such was the splendour of its colour and its ornaments. Eight horses with white plumes drew it majestically. It came to a stop. We had gone out of the palace to form a guard of honour.

The Emperor sat in the right-hand corner of the carriage. Dressed in purple velvet, wide Spanish knee-breeches and white stockings strewn with diamonds, he gave the effect of a stranger, a man in disguise, an operatic hero with short legs as he descended. The Empress on his left, however, looked more beautiful than ever. The biggest diamonds I had ever seen shone from her babyish curls. She smiled, a radiating, youthful, oh so youthful smile, and I could see in spite of her heavy make-up that her smile was genuine. The Emperor had married her in church, he was having her crowned. What had she to fear now?

When Joseph and Louis went past me I couldn't believe my eyes. The way they had got themselves up! All in white from top to toe! But Joseph, who, I noticed, had grown fat, strode into the palace grinning from ear to ear, whereas Louis waddled along gloomily and on flat feet.

In the palace Napoleon and Josephine put on their coronation robes. Josephine's almost bore her down, but she managed to steady herself till the Princesses had seized the train and taken the weight off her. Napoleon looked us over for the first time, as he tried to force his hands into a pair of stiff gloves. " Let us start ! " he said.

Despreaux had divided the different insignia among us, and we were only waiting for his sign. But the sign didn't come. Instead, we saw Despreaux whisper something to Joseph and saw Joseph shrug his shoulders. Napoleon meanwhile had turned away and was gravely examining his image in a mirror. What would the mirror show him? Only an undersized man in splendid robes, the ermine collar of which nearly reached up to his ears. It would show a man who had fished a crown out of the gutter. . . .

Our embarrassed whispering and awkward standing about reminded me of a funeral. I looked round to find Jean-Baptiste and saw him standing with the other Marshals, holding the velvet cushion with the chain of the Emperor's Legion of Honour, and gnawing his lips thoughtfully.

" What are we waiting for, Despreaux? " Napoleon sounded impatient.

" Sire, it was agreed that *Madame Mère* was to open the coronation procession and *Madame Mère* is——"

" Mama has not come," Louis said, and there was a trace of glee in his voice.

We knew that Napoleon had sent many couriers to Italy to ask his mother to be in Paris in good time for the coronation. When she could no longer resist the pressure she had said good-bye to her exiled son Lucien and set out for Paris.

" We regret it very much," said Napoleon without any expression in his voice. " We will proceed."

The fanfares trumpeted and the procession began to move slowly and solemnly. First came the heralds, then pages in green, Despreaux, the sixteen Marshals' wives stiff as marionettes, Securier and Murat. Then it was my turn. An icy current of air met me as I came out of the door carrying the cushion with the handkerchief in front of me like a sacrificial gift. From the crowd restrained by an impenetrable cordon of soldiers there came a few isolated shouts as I passed : " *Vive Bernadotte—Bernadotte!*" I kept my eyes fixed on Murat's gold-braided back and never let them stray.

I entered Notre-Dame, which was full of the roll of the organ and incense, carried the cushion the length of the nave, and came to a halt at the very end, where Murat stepped aside and the altar and the two golden thrones appeared. On the throne to the left, rigid as a statue, sat a little old gentleman in white, Pope Pius VII. He had been kept waiting here by Napoleon for almost two hours.

I took my place beside Murat and watched Josephine walk up towards the altar, her eyes wide open, a smile on her lips. She stopped in front of the first step to the double throne to the right of the altar, so that the Princesses who carried her train came to a halt immediately in front of me. Then Napoleon appeared with the paladins carrying his insignia, Jean-Baptiste among them.

The organ played the Marseillaise, as Napoleon slowly made his way to the altar till he reached the side of Josephine. Behind him stood his brothers and his Marshals.

The Pope rose and said Mass. When he had finished Despreaux gave a sign to Marshal Kellermann. Kellermann advanced and held the crown up to the Pope, whose delicate hands could hardly bear its weight. Napoleon let his purple gown slide from his shoulders; his brothers caught it and handed it to Talleyrand. Here the organ ceased.

In a clear and solemn voice the Pope pronounced the words of the blessing. He raised the heavy crown, waiting for Napoleon to incline his head. But Napoleon did not incline his head. His hands in his gold-embroidered gloves reached up and snatched the crown away from the Pope, holding it high in the air for a fraction of a second. Then he placed it slowly on his head.

A movement of startled surprise went through the ranks of the spectators. Napoleon had broken the pre-arranged crowning ritual and had crowned himself! The rest of the ceremony, the handing over by the paladins of the different insignia, went smoothly, and Napoleon ascended the steps to his throne once more. Joseph and Louis took up positions on either side of the throne. "*Vivat Imperator in æternum!*" came the voice of the Pope.

The Pope now turned to Josephine, making the sign of the cross over her and kissing her on the cheek. Murat was to hand him her crown. But Napoleon intervened, coming down from his throne and stretching out his hand, whereupon Murat handed the crown to him instead of to the Pope.

For the first time to-day I saw a smile on the Emperor's face. Very, very carefully, so as not to disarrange her coiffure, he placed the crown on her babyish curls and then put his hand lightly under her elbow to conduct her up the steps to their throne. Josephine took a step forward, swayed and very nearly fell back: Eliza, Polette and Caroline quite deliberately had let go of the train in order to make Josephine fall, to make her ridiculous in the moment of her greatest triumph. Julie and Hortense, however, held on with all their strength, and Napoleon gripped her arm and supported her. Thus she escaped the indignity of falling, she only stumbled on the first step to the throne.

Young girls of the old French nobility—the pure virgins whom Despreaux had had such difficulty in finding—approached the altar with wax candles in their hands, as the Pope and high clergy retired to the chapter house. Napoleon sat rigidly and with eyes half closed. What, I wondered, was he thinking of now?

I couldn't take my eyes off his face. Now a muscle moved in it and, believe it or not, he stifled a yawn! At the same time his eyes chanced on me, he opened them wide and for the second time to-day he smiled, a good-tempered, lighthearted smile, that seemed to have come right out of the past, out of our garden in Marseilles when we raced each other and he let me win. 'Didn't I tell you,' his eyes asked, 'that time by the hedge, and you wouldn't believe me? Didn't you want me to be thrown out of the Army to make a silk merchant of me?' Yes, there he sat with crown and ermine, and yet for one moment he was the Napoleon from the garden in Marseilles. The next moment I remembered the Duc d'Enghien, and Lucien the first of the exiles, and Moreau and all the others, great and humble, who followed them. I turned my eyes away and only looked towards the throne again when I heard the voice of the President of the Senate.

He stood in front of Napoleon unrolling a parchment. One hand on the Bible, the other raised high, the Emperor repeated the words of the oath after the President. In a voice clear and cool Napoleon vowed to preserve and guard the religious, political and civil liberties of the French people.

The clergy returned to accompany the Imperial couple out of the Cathedral. Cardinal Fesch found himself next to Napoleon, and the Emperor with boyish pleasure dug his uncle in the ribs with the sceptre. The cardinal's face expressed such horror at his nephew's spontaneous gesture that Napoleon turned away with a shrug of his shoulders. Within a few seconds of this the Emperor turned round to Joseph and called out to him: "What would our father have said if he had seen us here!"

Following Murat out of the Cathedral I managed to catch a glimpse of Etienne. He was sitting next to the green-turbaned

Turkish Minister, staring open-mouthed in rapture after his Emperor long after he had disappeared from his sight.

"Does the Emperor keep on his crown in bed?" asked Oscar, when I put him to bed that night.

"No, I don't think so," I said.

"Perhaps it's too heavy for him?" he pondered.

I laughed. "Too heavy? No, darling, not in the least. On the contrary!"

"Marie says that the police pay people to shout 'Vive l'Empereur!' in the street. Is that true, Mama?"

"I don't know. But you must never say such a thing."

"Why not?"

"Because it is——" I wanted to say 'dangerous', but I suppressed it. We want Oscar to say what is in his mind, but on the other hand the Minister of Police banishes from Paris people who say what is in their minds, for instance Madame de Staël, the authoress and great friend of Madame Récamier. "Because your grandfather Clary was a convinced Republican," I said.

"I thought he was a silk merchant," said Oscar.

Two hours later, for the first time in my life, I danced the waltz. It was at a great ball which His Imperial Highness, brother-in-law Joseph, gave for all the foreign Princes and diplomats and Marshals—and Etienne, as Julie's brother, he had graciously invited too. Marie Antoinette at one time had tried to introduce the Viennese waltz at Versailles; but only those received at court ever saw it danced, and after the Revolution anything that reminded people of the Queen from Austria was taboo. But now these sweet rhythms from an enemy country have infiltrated into Paris life once more.

I remembered that Monsieur Montel had shown me some waltz steps, but I had no idea how to dance them. Jean-Baptiste, however, who had been Ambassador in Vienna, showed me how to do it. He counted 'one two three, one two three' the way a sergeant does on the barrack square, and I felt like a recruit. But gradually his voice became gentler and gentler, he held me quite close to him, his mouth was in my hair, and we pirouetted and pirouetted till the illuminations of the ballroom in the Luxembourg had coalesced into a sea of lights.

"I saw the Emperor flirt with you—one two three, one two three—during the coronation," Jean-Baptiste murmured. "I saw it, I saw it."

"I had the feeling his heart wasn't in it," I said.

"In what? In the flirting?"

"Don't be horrid! In the coronation, I mean."

"Don't forget the rhythm, my girl!"

I insisted. "A coronation ought to be something which you feel very deeply."

"Not Napoleon, my girl, not Napoleon. To him it is only a formality. He crowns himself Emperor and at the same time swears loyalty to the Republic, one two three, one two three."

Somebody shouted: "To the Emperor!" and glasses clinked.

"That was your brother Etienne."

"Let's dance on, let's dance on," I whispered. His mouth was in my hair again, the cut-glass lustres glittered with all the colours of the rainbow, the whole room seemed to pirouette and sway with us. The voices of the many guests came as from a great distance. . . .

On the way home we drove past the Tuileries. They shone in splendid illumination. Pages with torches flickering red through the night stood guard. Somebody had told us that the Emperor and Josephine had dined alone and that Josephine had to keep on her crown because he liked her so much with it. After their meal the Emperor had retired to his study to pore over maps. "He is preparing his next campaign," explained Jean-Baptiste to me as we passed. Snow had started to fall and many torches went out.

PARIS, two weeks after the coronation.

A few days ago the Emperor handed over the eagle standards to his regiments. We all had to put in an appearance on the Champs de Mars, and Napoleon had again put on his coronation robes and his crown.

Each regiment was given a standard with a gilded eagle and a tricolour underneath. The eagles must never be allowed to fall into the enemy's hands, the Emperor said, and promised new victories to his troops. For many hours we had to stand on a platform and let the regiments march past. Etienne, who was up there with me, shouted himself hoarse with enthusiasm.

It has started snowing again. The parade never seemed to be coming to an end and we all had wet feet. But it gave me time to think out the preparations for the ball of the Marshals in the Opéra. The Master of Ceremonies had hinted to the Marshals that they ought to give a ball in honour of the Emperor. It was to be the most magnificent ball imaginable, and therefore we had rented the Opéra.

We Marshals' wives held innumerable sessions and checked over and over again the list of people to be invited. We could not afford to forget or insult anybody. Monsieur Montel taught us how to receive the Imperial couple and how to escort Napoleon and Josephine into the hall. From Despreaux we heard that the Emperor would offer his arm to one of us whilst one of the Marshals would have to conduct the Empress to her throne. This information caused long and grave discussions as to which Marshal and which Marshal's wife were to be chosen. At last we agreed on Murat, husband of an Imperial Princess, as the suitable man to receive the Empress. As for the lady, the choice lay between Madame Berthier, the senior in age, and myself, sister to Her Imperial Highness the Princess Julie. However, I succeeded in convincing the others that fat Madame Berthier was ideally suited to welcoming the Emperor. I didn't want to do it, I was too furious with him, because he kept Jean-Baptiste waiting and waiting for the independent command which he so longed for, as far away as possible from Paris.

On the morning of the great ball I had an unexpected visit from Polette, who turned up accompanied by an Italian violin virtuoso and a French captain of dragoons. She left them both in the drawing-room and retired with me to my bedroom.

" Guess," she said, and laughed, " which of the two is my lover?" She looked charming in her glittering attire and her skilful make-up, with priceless emeralds from the jewellery of the Borghese family in her tiny ears. Her eyes reminded me of Napoleon.

" Well," she repeated, " which of the two is it?"

I said I couldn't guess it.

" Both!" she exclaimed triumphantly, sitting down before my dressing-table, on which the golden casket was still standing.

" Whoever," she asked, " was so tasteless as to make you a present of a casket with such dreadful Imperial eagles on its lid?"

" It's your turn to guess now," I said.

She thought strenuously. Suddenly she looked up: " Was it—tell me—was it——"

I didn't move an eyelid. " I owe this casket to the infinite goodness of our Imperial lord and master."

Polette whistled like a street urchin. " I don't understand it," she said, "I don't. I thought Madame Duchâtel, the court lady with the long nose, was his mistress of the moment."

I blushed. "On the day of his coronation he repaid an old debt to me from his Marseilles days. That's all."

"Of course," said Polette protestingly, "of course, my dear child, that is all." She paused, meditating on something. Then she came out with it: "I want to talk to you about Mama. She arrived here, secretly, yesterday. I don't think even Fouché knows that she's in Paris. She's staying with me and you must help them."

"Help whom?" I asked.

"*Madame Mère*, and him, Napoleone, the boy with the crown." She laughed, a rather forced laugh. "I feel rather bothered. Napoleone insists that Mama has to obey the court ceremonial and to be received in formal audience by him in the Tuileries with curtsies and all the trimmings." She stopped, and I tried to imagine Madame Letitia curtseying formally before Napoleon. "He is furious," Polette continued, "because she deliberately travelled very slowly in order to miss the coronation. And he is angry because Mama didn't want to see his triumph. Yet he is longing for her, badly, and—Eugenie, Désirée, *Madame la Maréchale*, couldn't you bring the two together? Manage a kind of accidental meeting, you know, and leave them alone at the moment of their reunion so that the court ritual doesn't matter two sticks? Couldn't you arrange that somehow?"

I sighed. "You really are a dreadful family."

Polette didn't mind my saying that. "You've always known that, haven't you? You know, by the way, don't you, that I'm the only one of us whom Napoleon really likes?"

"I'd guessed that," I said, and remembered a morning in Marseilles when Polette went with me to the Town Commandant.

"The others," said Polette, beginning to polish her nails, "the others only want to get as much as possible out of him. Incidentally, Joseph no longer seems to be considered the successor since Napoleon adopted the two little sons of Louis and Hortense. Josephine is on at him day and night to make one of her grandsons his successor. And, do you know," here Polette waxed indignant, "what is the vilest thing of all? She tries to convince him that it is his fault that they have no children! His fault, I ask you!"

"I shall bring Madame Letitia and the Emperor together," I put in quickly. "I shall arrange it at the Marshals' ball. I shall send you word through Marie, and all you have to do is to see to it that your mother comes to the private box which I shall indicate to you."

"You are a treasure, Eugenie! Heavens, I feel better now." Earnestly she started making up her face and lips. "The other day an English paper published a scandalous article about me. My violin virtuoso translated it for me. The writer of the article calls me a 'Napoleon of love'. Such nonsense! We have completely different methods, Napoleon and I: he wins his offensive wars and I—I lose my defensive battles." A wan smile flitted over her face, as she went on: "Why does he marry me to men who don't interest me in the least? First Leclerc, now Borghese. My two sisters have an easier time of it, they, at any rate, have ambitions. They're not interested in people, only in influential connections. Eliza can't forget that dreadful cellar dwelling in Marseilles, she is obsessed by fear that one day she may be a pauper again, and so she snatches possessions where she can. Caroline was so young at the time that she doesn't remember it at all, but she'd be ready for any foul deed if it could help her towards a real royal or imperial crown. I on the other hand——"

"I fear your two knights are going to be impatient," I interrupted her flow.

Polette jumped up. "You're right. I must fly. Well then, I shall expect to hear from you, and I will send our *madre* to the Opéra. Agreed?"

"Agreed."

> "*Allons, enfants de la patrie,*
> *Le jour de gloire est arrivé. . . .*"

On Jean-Baptiste's arm I slowly descended the steps to the strains of the orchestra, to welcome the Emperor of the French as the guest of his Marshals.

> "*Aux armes, citoyens!*
> *Formez vos bataillons!*"

The Marseillaise, the song of my early girlhood! Once upon a time I stood in my nightgown on the balcony and threw down roses to our volunteers, the tailor Franchon, and the bandy-legged son of our cobbler, and the Levi brothers, who went out in their Sunday suits to defend the Republic which had given them full citizenship against the whole world, that Republic which did not even have money enough to provide its soldiers with boots.

> "*Formez vos bataillons!*
> *Marchons, marchons. . . .*"

227

Silken trains rustled, state swords clattered, and we bowed deeply to Napoleon.

When I met Napoleon for the first time I couldn't understand that the Army accepted officers as short as he is. Now he even emphasised his short stature by surrounding himself with the tallest adjutants possible, and dressed in a plain General's uniform.

"How are you, Madame?" the Emperor addressed fat Madame Berthier and, without giving her time to reply, turned to the next Marshal's lady: "I am delighted to see you, Madame. You should always dress in Nile green, it suits you. By the way, the Nile is not really green at all but yellow. I remember it as ochre."

Feverish spots appeared on the faces of the ladies thus addressed. "Your Majesty is too kind," they breathed. 'Do all crowned heads talk like Napoleon,' I thought, 'or has he prepared these short, hammered-out phrases because he supposes that that is how monarchs converse with their subjects?'

Meanwhile Josephine bestowed her highly polished smile on the ladies. "How are you?" she inquired. "I heard your little girl had whooping cough. I was so sorry to hear it. . . ." Each one of them had the feeling that the Empress for days past had wanted nothing so much as to have a few words with her.

The Imperial Princesses followed in Josephine's wake, Eliza and Caroline with arrogance, Polette obviously a bit under the weather after a lively meal, Hortense awkward and anxious to appear friendly, and my Julie, pale and trying hard to overcome her shyness.

Murat and Josephine proceeded slowly along the ballroom with Napoleon and Madame Berthier behind them. We others followed. Here and there Josephine stopped to say a few kind words. Napoleon talked mainly to men. Among them were numerous officers as representatives of provincial regiments, and Napoleon inquired after their garrisons. He seemed to know each military barracks in France inside out. Meanwhile I tried to think how to lure him to Box 17, and decided that the first thing necessary was to get him to drink a few glasses of champagne. After that I'd risk it. . . .

Champagne was handed round. Napoleon declined. He stood on the stage by his dais, with Talleyrand and Joseph talking to him. Josephine called me to her and said: "I am so sorry, I could not find the sapphire ear-rings the other day."

"Your Majesty is too kind, but I was unable to dress in blue in any case."

"Are you satisfied with Le Roy's dresses, Madame?"

I forgot to answer, because suddenly, in the crowd at the farther end of the ballroom, I discovered a ruddy squarish face which I thought I knew, a face over a colonel's uniform.

"With Le Roy's dresses, Madame?" repeated the Empress.

"Yes, yes, very," I said, and looked for that squarish face again. A woman, impossibly provincial in dress and looks, was with him. 'I don't know her,' I thought, 'but I do know him, some colonel from some provincial garrison, but where?'

A little later I managed to cross the ballroom towards that face. It annoyed me that I couldn't remember who he was, and so I tried to get near him without attracting attention. But everybody gave way politely, my name was whispered, officers bowed low and ladies smiled. I smiled back, I smiled till my mouth hurt me. But at last I got near my colonel, and I heard the provincial lady hiss into his ear: "So that's the little Clary girl!"

And then I knew him! The Commanding Officer of the Fortress of Marseilles! Without a wig now, but otherwise unchanged. The unimportant little General whom he had arrested ten years ago has meanwhile become the Emperor of the French.

"Do you remember me, Colonel Lefabre?" I asked. The provincial woman bowed awkwardly. "*Madame la Maréchale!*" she said. "François Clary's daughter," said Square Face. Both waited for what I would say next.

"I haven't been in Marseilles for many years," I said.

"It would bore Madame dreadfully, such a dull backwater!" said the lady.

"If you ever wish to be moved, Colonel Lefabre," I said.

"Could you put in a word with the Emperor for us?" Madame Lefabre asked, excited.

"No, but with Marshal Bernadotte."

"I used to know your father very well," the colonel was beginning when the orchestra struck up the polonaise.

I left the Lefabres and in the most undignified manner ran back. Murat was to open the polonaise with Julie, the Emperor with Madame Berthier and I with Prince Joseph. The dance had begun when I reached Joseph, who was standing alone on the stage waiting for me.

He was indignant. "I could not find you anywhere, Désirée."

"I am so sorry," I said, and we started off. But his indignation took a long time to disappear.

After two more dances everybody made for the buffet.

Napoleon had withdrawn towards the back of the stage, talking to Duroc. I beckoned a servant to follow me with champagne and approached the Emperor, who immediately interrupted his conversation.

"I have something to say to you, Madame," he said.

"May I offer some refreshment to Your Majesty?"

Both Napoleon and Duroc took a glass of champagne. "Your health, Madame!" he said politely: he drank only the tiniest little drop and put the glass back. "Well, Madame, what I wanted to say——" Napoleon stopped and looked me over from head to foot. "By the way, *Madame la Maréchale*, have I ever told you how pretty you are?"

Duroc smiled broadly, clicked his heels and asked permission to withdraw.

"Certainly, certainly, Duroc, go and entertain the ladies!" Then his eyes returned to me, measuring me in silence. Slowly a smile began to play round his mouth.

"Your Majesty wanted to say something to me," I said, and added quickly: "If I may be so bold as to make a request I should be most grateful to Your Majesty if we could go to Box 17."

He did not trust his ears. Bending forward he raised his eyebrows and repeated: "Box 17?"

I nodded.

Napoleon looked round the stage. Josephine was making conversation with a number of ladies, Joseph appeared to be haranguing Talleyrand and his bad-tempered-looking brother Louis, and the Marshals were distributed on the dancing floor. His eyes narrowed and began to flutter. "Is it—proper, little Eugénie?"

"Sire, please do not misinterpret me!"

"'Box 17,' there is nothing to be misinterpreted, is there?" Quickly he added: "Murat will accompany us, it looks better."

Murat, as well as all the rest of the Emperor's entourage, had watched us all the time out of the corner of his eyes. A sign from Napoleon brought him across post-haste.

"Madame Bernadotte and I are going to a box. Show us the way."

The three of us left the stage and passed along the lane of overawed people which forms at once wherever the Emperor goes. On the narrow stairs leading up to the boxes we disturbed a few couples. Young officers sprang to attention out of the arms of their ladies. I found it funny, but Napoleon remarked: "The manners of these young people are too free and easy. I shall have a word with Despreaux about it. I want unexceptionable morals in my entourage."

We found ourselves before Box 17, the door of which was closed. "Thank you, Murat!" said the Emperor, and Murat left.

"Your Majesty wanted to say something to me. Is it good news?"

"Yes. We have approved the application of Marshal Bernadotte for an independent command with extensive civil administration. To-morrow your husband will be appointed Governor of Hanover. I congratulate you, Madame. It is a great and responsible position."

"Hanover!" I murmured, without having the slightest idea where Hanover was.

"When you go to visit your husband you will reside in royal castles and you will be the First Lady of the country. Here we are, Madame. Please enter and make sure that the curtains are properly drawn."

I opened the door to the box and closed it quickly behind me. I knew quite well that the curtains were drawn.

"Well, my child?" said Madame Letitia.

"He is outside. And he doesn't know you are here."

"Don't be so nervous, child. He won't bite off your head."

'No,' I thought, 'my head is all right, but what about Jean-Baptiste's position as Governor?' "I am calling him in now," I said.

Outside I said: "The curtains are drawn." I wanted to let the Emperor go in first and then simply disappear. But without any more ado he pushed me into the little room.

Madame Letitia had risen from her chair. Napoleon stood by the door rooted to the spot. The strains of a Viennese waltz filtered through the heavy curtains.

"My boy, will you not say good evening to your mother?" She took a step towards him. 'If only she made a bow, the tiniest bow of her head, everything would be all right,' I thought. The Emperor did not move. Madame Letitia took another step.

"*Madame Mère*, what a beautiful surprise," said Napoleon, motionless.

A last step brought Madame Letitia right up to him. She inclined her head, not to bow but to kiss him on the cheek! Without thinking of court ceremonial I pressed past him to the door, thus giving him a little push which made him land in his mother's arms.

When I reappeared down below, Murat came to me at once, his flat nose sniffing like a dog hot on the scent.

" You are back quickly, Madame!"

I looked at him in astonishment.

He grinned. " I told the Empress that Bernadotte would be glad if she had a few words with him, and I hinted to Bernadotte to be near the Empress. In that way they could neither of them pay attention to what is happening in the boxes."

" Happening in the boxes? What are you talking about, Marshal Murat?"

Murat was so hot on the scent that he completely missed the gasp of surprise that, all of a sudden, filled the ballroom.

" I mean one particular box, Madame, the one to which you conducted His Majesty."

" Oh, you mean Box 17!" I laughed. "Why must Jean-Baptiste and the Empress not know what's happening in Box 17, since the whole room knows it already?"

His face was a picture. He looked up, followed the direction of the glances from the eyes of the assembly and was just in time to see the Emperor pulling aside the curtains in Box 17. Madame Letitia was standing by the Emperor's side.

Despreaux gave a sign to the orchestra, which saluted with a mighty flourish, followed by a storm of applause.

" Caroline did not know her mother was back in Paris," said Murat, and regarded me suspiciously.

" *Madame Mère*, I believe, will always want to be with the son who needs her most. First she lived with Lucien, the exile, and now she is here with Napoleon, the Emperor."

The dance went on till morning dawned. During the last waltz I asked Jean-Baptiste: " Where is Hanover?"

" In Germany. It's the country where the British royal family comes from. The population had a very bad time during the war."

" Who, do you think, is going to govern Hanover as French Governor?"

" No idea," he said. " And for all I care——" He stopped in the middle of the sentence, in the middle of the waltz, and looked at me: " Is it true?" was all he asked.

I nodded.

" Now I am going to show them," he said, and continued the dance.

" Whom are you going to show what?"

" How to administer a country. I am going to show the

Emperor and the Generals. Particularly the Generals. I shall make Hanover a contented place."

He spoke quickly, and for the first time in many years I felt that he was happy, really happy. Strange that at this moment he never thought of France, only of Hanover, a State in Germany.

" You'll have to live there in a royal castle," I said.

" I suppose so. It will probably be the best accommodation," he said, with no indication of being thrilled at all. It was then that I realised that Jean-Baptiste only thought the very best quarters just good enough for him. The English King's castle in Hanover was just good enough for the one-time Sergeant Bernadotte. Why does it all seem so monstrous to me, I wondered.

" Jean-Baptiste, I'm dizzy, I'm dizzy."

But he only stopped dancing when the orchestra started packing up their instruments and the Marshals' ball had come to an end.

Before Jean-Baptiste went to Hanover he fulfilled my wish and had Colonel Lefabre moved to Paris. The story of Napoleon's underclothing gave him the idea of appointing him to the Quartermaster-General's department where he had to deal exclusively with the troops' uniforms, boots and underclothes.

The colonel and his wife came to thank me.

" I knew your father very well, very decent chap, your father," he said.

My eyes felt watery, but I smiled. " You were right, Colonel, you remember? ' A Bonaparte is no husband for—for François Clary's daughter '."

His wife was shocked. I had committed *lèse-majesté*. The colonel, too, looked embarrassed, but he did not flinch.

" You are right, *Madame la Maréchale*. I am certain your late father, too, would have preferred Bernadotte."

The transfers of all senior officers are regularly reported to Napoleon, and when he saw the name of Colonel Lefabre in a list, he thought hard for a moment and then laughted out loud: " My colonel of the underwear! Now Bernadotte has put him in charge of all the underwear of the Army to do his wife a favour!"

Murat saw to it that Napoleon's comment became known, and to this day everybody calls poor Lefabre ' colonel of the underwear '.

In a coach between HANOVER in GERMANY and PARIS, September 1805. (The Emperor has forbidden the use of the Republican calendar. Mama, who is dead now, would have been glad, because she could never get used to it.)

We were very happy in Hanover, Jean-Baptiste, Oscar and I. The only arguments we had there were on account of the valuable parquet floors of the royal castle. More than once Jean-Baptiste would shake his head and say: "I can understand Oscar when he thinks that the polished ballroom floor has been made specially for him so that he can slide on it. After all, he is only a little brat of six. But you . . .!" And every time he said that there would be anger as well as amusement in his voice, and I would promise by all that was holy that I would never again slide in Oscar's company across the ballroom of the castle of the former Kings of Hanover, Marshal Bernadotte's residence as the Governor of Hanover. But however often I promised I could never resist the temptation to slide across the parquet floor. Which is really too bad of me, seeing that I am the First Lady of Hanover with a small suite of my own consisting of a reader, a lady-in-waiting and the wives of the officers of my husband's staff. But I am apt to forget that sometimes. . . .

Yes, we were very happy in Hanover. And Hanover was very happy with us. That, I feel sure, sounds strange, for Hanover was occupied country and Jean-Baptiste the commander of an Army of Occupation.

Jean-Baptiste worked from six in the morning till six in the evening and sometimes after dinner till deep into the night, and the documents on his desk never seemed to grow less in number. He began his 'government' of this Teutonic country with the introduction of the Rights of Man. In France plenty of people had shed their blood in order to bring about the equality of all people before the law. But in Hanover, conquered land, the stroke of Bernadotte's pen was enough. He abolished flogging. He abolished the ghettoes and allowed the Jews to follow whatever professions or trades they liked. The Levis of Marseilles did not march into battle in their Sunday suits in vain, after all!

An ex-sergeant, naturally, knows well what is necessary for the provisioning of troops, and the levies exacted from the citizens of Hanover for the upkeep of our Army do not hurt them very much. All the contributions they have to make are laid down in writing by Bernadotte, and no officer is allowed to collect taxes on his own authority.

The citizens of Hanover are better off than they ever were before, because Jean-Baptiste did away with the Customs frontiers. In the midst of war-ravaged Germany Hanover is now like an island of prosperity trading in all directions. As the State grew wealthier and wealthier Jean-Baptiste raised the taxes a bit and with the extra money he bought flour and sent it to North Germany, where there was a famine. The Hanoverians shooks their heads about it, our officers thought him crazy, but you can't really blame someone simply because he acts unselfishly. On top of it all Jean-Baptiste advised the merchants to make friends with the towns of the Hanseatic League and earn even more money that way. This advice left the Hanoverians speechless. It's an open secret, of course, that the Hanseatic towns do not observe the Emperor's Continental Blockade very strictly, and still trade with Britain. That, however, is one thing, whereas this advice by a Marshal of France to his poor miserable enemies is quite another. . . . Once trade with the Hanseatic towns had got under way properly the exchequer of the State of Hanover flourished enormously, and Jean-Baptiste could even send big sums of money to support the University of Göttingen, where some of the greatest scholars of the day are teaching. Jean-Baptiste is very proud of ' his ' university. And he is very glad when he can pore over his documents.

Sometimes I found him studying enormous tomes. " The things an uneducated ex-sergeant has to learn! " he would say then, and stretch out his hand to me without looking up. And I would go up to him and stand by his side, and he would put his hand on my cheek. " You do an awful lot of governing," I'd say then awkwardly, and he would only shake his head: " I'm trying to learn, my girl, and to do my best. It is not too difficult as long as he leaves me alone. . . ." We knew, both of us, whom he meant.

I gained weight during my time in Hanover. We didn't dance for nights on end, and didn't watch never-ending parades, at any rate never for more than two hours. For my sake Jean-Baptiste reduced the number and length of parades.

After dinner our officers and their ladies would very often sit with us in my drawing-room, where we talked over the latest news from Paris. We heard that the Emperor still had his headquarters near the Channel coast, preparing his attack on Britain, and we talked in whispers about Josephine's debts.

Sometimes professors from Göttingen would be present who tried to acquaint us, in their dreadful French, with their various theories. Once one of them read a play to us in German written by a man called Goethe, the author of the bedside novel *The Sorrows of Werther* which we used to devour as girls. During the reading I tried to signal to Jean-Baptiste to cut the torture short. Our German was too bad for this sort of thing.

Another one told us about a great doctor at Göttingen who was said to be able to make the deaf hear again. At that Jean-Baptiste pricked up his ears, for many of our soldiers have become hard of hearing because of the thunder of our own cannon, and he called out:

" I have a friend who ought to go and see this doctor. He lives in Vienna, and I shall write him and tell him that he should go to Göttingen. Désirée, you must meet him. He is a musician whom I got to know during my time in Vienna. He is a friend of Kreutzer's, you know."

This announcement frightened me. I didn't want to play to this musician. I had managed to wriggle out of my lessons in deportment and music; what I had learnt from Monsieur Montel years ago was sufficient for all my purposes, and as for music, I had very little use for that.

Well, in the end I never did play to that musician. The evening he came to see us became unforgettable to me. It began very beautifully, though. . . .

Oscar's eyes shine when he can listen to music, and that day he pestered me so much that I had to let him stay up. He knew far more about the concert than I. The musician's name was—oh, I had the name down somewhere, a very outlandish name, Teutonic I should say—yes, that was it, Beethoven!

Jean-Baptiste had ordered all the players of the former Royal Court Orchestra to hold themselves at the disposal of this Beethoven from Vienna, and to rehearse with him for three mornings in the great ballroom. During these days Oscar was tremendously excited: " How long may I stay up, Mama? Till after midnight? How can a deaf man write music? Do you think that he won't even be able to hear his own music? Has Monsieur Beethoven really an ear trumpet? Does he blow it sometimes?"

Oscar fired all these questions at me when I took him for a drive, which I often did in the afternoon, along the avenue of linden trees which leads from the castle to the village of Herrenhausen.

"Papa says that he is one of the biggest men he knows. How big could he be? Bigger than a grenadier of the Emperor's bodyguard?"

"Papa doesn't mean physical bigness but intellectual. This musician is probably a genius. That's what Papa means."

Oscar pondered. "Is he bigger than Papa?" he asked at last.

I took Oscar's sticky little fist, which concealed a sweet, in my hand. "That I don't know, darling."

"Bigger than the Emperor, Mama?"

The valet, who was sitting next to the coachman in front of us, turned round and looked at me curiously.

I didn't move an eyelid as I said: "No man is bigger than the Emperor, Oscar."

"Perhaps he can't hear his own music," Oscar continued his pondering.

"Perhaps," I answered, and felt sad. 'I had wanted to bring up my son differently,' I thought, 'to be a free human being in my father's sense.' The new tutor, whom the Emperor himself had recommended to us for Oscar and who arrived here a month ago, tried to teach the child the addition to the Catechism which must now be taught in all French schools and which runs: 'We owe our Emperor Napoleon the First, the image of God on earth, respect, obedience, loyalty, military service. . . .'

I happened the other day to come into Oscar's schoolroom just as he was being taught that, and I didn't believe my ears. But the narrow-chested, rather unsympathetic young teacher, former pride of the officers' training academy at Briennes, repeated the words to me and left no doubt: "Emperor Napoleon the First, image of God on earth. . . ."

"I shouldn't like my son to learn that. Leave out the addition," I said.

"It is taught in all the schools of the Empire, by law," the young man answered, adding with a blank face: "His Majesty is very interested in the education of his godchild, and he has ordered me to report regularly about his progress. After all, the pupil is the son of a Marshal of France."

I looked at Oscar, who was bending over a copybook, drawing little men, bored. 'At first nuns taught me,' I thought, 'then the nuns were jailed or driven away, and we were told that there was no God, only Pure Reason which we were to worship. Then there came a time when no one bothered about our faith and everybody could worship exactly what he wanted. Napoleon became First Consul, and the priests returned, sworn not to the Republic, but to the Church of Rome. Finally Napoleon forced the Pope to come to Paris to crown him, and made Roman Catholicism the official religion. And now he has made this addition to the Catechism. . . .'

'They fetch the peasants' sons from the fields,' I continued my train of thought, ' so that they may march in Napoleon's armies. Not many peasants have the 8,000 francs needed to buy a son off military service, and so they simply hide their sons and the gendarmes take wives, sisters and fiancées as hostages instead, whilst no one bothers about the many deserters. France has enough troops, since the defeated Princes have to put their soldiers at the Emperor's disposal to prove their loyalty to him. Jean-Baptiste complains so often that his soldiers have to be commanded by his officers with the help of interpreters. Why then does Napoleon make the young men march, march to new wars and to new victories, since France's frontiers no longer need defending? France no longer has any frontiers. Or do these new wars and victories no longer concern France but only him, Napoleon, the Emperor?'

I don't know how long I had been standing there facing the young teacher. At last I turned away and went to the door, repeating: "Leave that addition out. Oscar is too small for it yet, he doesn't know what it means."

Outside, in the empty corridor, I leaned helplessly against the wall and began to cry. 'Napoleon,' I thought, 'you pied piper of souls, because they are too small, because they don't know what it means, you make the children learn that. A whole country bled itself white for the sake of the Rights of Man, and after they had at last been established you went and put yourself at the country's head. . . .'

I don't know how I got to my bedroom. I only remember that I was lying on my bed, sobbing. These proclamations! We know them so well, they always fill the front page of the *Moniteur*, always in the same words, the words he used once by the Pyramids, the words which he read to us once during a Sunday dinner. "The Rights of Man are the guiding principles of this Order-of-the-Day," someone said to him during that meal—Joseph, the eldest Bonaparte, who hates his brother, and he had added: "They did not come from your brain." No, Napoleon, you only use them to be able to tell the peoples that you have come to liberate them, whereas in reality you subject them, you only use the words of the Rights of Man in order to shed blood in their name. . . .

Someone put his arms around me. "What is the matter, Désirée?"

"Do you know the new addition to the Catechism which Oscar is supposed to learn?" I sobbed. "But I've forbidden it. You do agree, Jean-Baptiste, don't you?"

"If you had not forbidden it, *I* should," was all he said, holding me tight.

"Can you imagine, Jean-Baptiste, that I very nearly married that man?"

He laughed, and it relieved me immeasurably to hear him laugh. "There are things, my little girl, which I just will not imagine!"

That was a few days before Oscar asked me all those questions about Beethoven on one of our afternoon drives. When the musician arrived he turned out to be a well-set-up man of medium height with the untidiest hair I've ever seen at our table. He had a round, bronzed, pock-marked face, a flat nose and sleepy eyes. But when you talked to him his eyes became keen and seemed to concentrate on the lips of the speaker.

I knew he was rather hard of hearing and therefore shouted at him how glad I was that he had come to see us. Jean-Baptiste slapped his shoulder and asked how things were in Vienna. It was merely a polite question, but the musician took it seriously.

"We prepare for war," he said. "We expect the Emperor's armies will march against Austria."

Jean-Baptiste frowned and shook his head. He hadn't wanted that answer. He diverted the conversation at once and asked: "What do you think of my orchestra?"

The stout musician shook his head and Jean-Baptiste repeated the question in as loud a voice as possible.

The musician raised his heavy eyelids, his eyes winked roguishly. "I heard you the first time, Mr. Ambassador— sorry, Mr. Marshal, that's your title now, is it not? Your orchestra plays very badly, sir."

"But you will conduct your new symphony all the same, won't you?" Jean-Baptiste shouted.

Monsieur Beethoven chuckled: "Yes, I will, because I want to know what you think of it, Mr. Ambassador!"

"Monseigneur!" shouted my husband's adjutant into the visitor's ear.

"You may call me Monsieur van Beethoven. I am no seigneur."

The adjutant was in despair: "You must address *Monsieur le Maréchal* as Monseigneur!" he shouted whilst I put a handkerchief to my mouth to suppress my laughter.

Our guest turned his eyes gravely on Jean-Baptiste: "It is so difficult to know your way with all these titles," he said. "I am grateful to you, Monseigneur, for wanting to send me to this doctor in Göttingen."

"Can you hear your own music?" a child's high-pitched voice asked behind the composer. He had heard the voice, turned round and saw Oscar. Before I had time to say something to make him forget the cruel question he had bent down to Oscar and said: "Did you ask me something, my boy?"

"Can you hear your own music?" Oscar crowed as loudly as he could.

Monsieur van Beethoven nodded solemnly. "Oh yes, very well indeed. In here," he said putting his hand on his chest. "And here!" and he put his hand on his mighty forehead, adding with a broad grin: "But the musicians who play my music I can't always hear clearly. And that is sometimes a good thing, particularly when they are as bad as those of your Papa."

After dinner we all went into the ballroom. The players were tuning their instruments and turned timid eyes in our direction.

"They are not used to playing Beethoven symphonies," said Jean-Baptiste. "Ballet music is easier."

Three red silk chairs embossed with the gilded crown of the House of Hanover had been put in front of the rows of seats. Here Jean-Baptiste and I sat down, Oscar, who almost disappeared in his deep chair, between us. Monsieur van Beethoven stood in the midst of the orchestra giving them directions in German which he emphasised with quiet movements of his hands.

"What is he going to conduct?" I asked Jean-Baptiste.

"A symphony which he wrote last year."

Monsieur van Beethoven came to us now and said thoughtfully: "At first I had intended to dedicate this symphony to General Bernadotte. But on second thoughts I found it better to dedicate it to the Emperor of the French. But——" He paused and stared in front of him and seemed to forget all about us and his audience. At last he remembered where he was, pushed a thick strand of hair back from his forehead and murmured: "We shall see. May we begin, General?"

"Monseigneur!" hissed Jean-Baptiste's adjutant, who was sitting immediately behind us.

Jean-Baptiste smiled. "Please begin, my dear Beethoven."

The heavy figure ascended the conductor's rostrum awkwardly. We only saw his back and the broad hand with the oddly small fingers holding the baton. He knocked on the rostrum, silence fell and he began.

I had no idea whether our orchestra played well or badly. I only knew that this stout man with the wide movements of his arms spurred it on and made it make music as I had never heard it make music before. Sometimes it sounded like an organ and then again like the sweet song of violins, jubilant yet despondent. I pressed my hand to my mouth because my lips trembled. This music had nothing to do with the Marseillaise. But the Marseillaise must have sounded like this when they went into battle for the Rights of Man and the frontiers of France, at once like a prayer and a shout of joy.

I bent forward to look at Jean-Baptiste. His face was like a face of stone, his mouth had become thin, his nose jutted out boldy and his eyes showed a strange fire. His right hand gripped the arm of his chair and held it so hard that his veins stood out.

Nobody had noticed the appearance of a courier by the door, or had seen Adjutant-Colonel Villatte get up noiselessly and take a letter from the courier. When Villatte touched my husband lightly on his arm, he looked round, startled, before he met the adjutant's eyes. He took the letter, gave him a sign, and Villatte remained behind his chair. The concert went on and the music carried me away again into other realms.

In the silence between two movements I heard the rustle of paper. Jean-Baptiste broke the seal and undid the letter. Monsieur van Beethoven had turned round towards Jean-Baptiste, who gave him a sign to continue.

Jean-Baptiste read. Once he looked up and seemed to listen to this heavenly music with a deep nostalgic longing in his eyes. But then he took a pen from his adjutant, scribbled a few words on a pad and handed them to the officer, who left at once. Another officer took up his position next to Jean-Baptiste. He left in his turn with a message, and a third one appeared, this time with a clicking of heels which broke through the sound of the Beethoven music and caused Jean-Baptiste's lips to twitch in irritation for one short moment, before he went on with yet another of his messages. Only when that had been handed over did he listen again, no longer with complete abandonment and enthusiasm as before but biting his lower lip. Only during the very last passage, the choral hymn to liberty, equality and fraternity, he once more raised his head. But I felt that this was not on account of the voice from the orchestra but on account of the voice which was speaking inside himself. I couldn't tell what this voice that spoke to the accompaniment of Beethoven's music said to him, I only saw that Jean-Baptiste smiled a bitter smile.

The end came, and great applause. I took off my gloves to be able to clap more loudly. The maestro bowed gauchely and pointed to the musicians with whom he had been so dissatisfied before.

All three adjutants had now collected behind Jean-Baptiste, where they were waiting with tense faces. Jean-Baptiste, however, went towards the rostrum and helped Monsieur van Beethoven down as if he were an exalted dignitary. " Thank you, Beethoven," he said, " from the bottom of my heart, thank you."

The pock marked face of the musician suddenly had an air of smoothness and restfulness about it, and even of amusement. " Do you remember, General, how, one evening in Vienna, you played the Marseillaise to me?"

" With one finger on the piano," laughed Jean-Baptiste, " that is all the playing I do."

" That was the first time I heard your hymn, the hymn of a free people." Jean-Baptiste towered about him, and Beethoven had to raise his head to be able to see into Jean-Baptiste's eyes. " I have often thought of that evening during the writing of this symphony. That was why I wanted to dedicate it to you, a young General of the French people."

" I am no longer a young General, Beethoven."

Beethoven didn't answer that. He kept staring at Jean-Baptiste so that he thought he hadn't heard him, and shouted once more: " I was saying I am no longer a young General."

Still Beethoven didn't answer. The three adjutants behind Jean-Baptiste started to make gestures of impatience.

" Somebody else came," Beethoven at last said heavily, " somebody else, and carried the message of your people across all frontiers. That is why I thought that I should dedicate the symphony to him. What do you think, General Bernadotte?"

" Monseigneur!" the three adjutants shouted almost in unison. Jean-Baptiste, angrily, motioned them to stop.

"Across all frontiers, Bernadotte," Beethoven repeated with an artless, almost childlike smile. "That night in Vienna you told me about the Rights of Man. I had known very little about them before, I am not interested in politics. But that, that, you see, had nothing to do with politics." He smiled again. "You played the Marseillaise to me with one finger, Bernadotte."

"And that is what you made of it, Beethoven," said Jean-Baptiste, deeply moved. A pause followed. One of the adjutants whispered, "Monseigneur!"

Jean-Baptiste collected himself, his hand went over his face as if to wipe away old memories. "Monsieur van Beethoven, I thank you for your concert. I wish you a happy journey to Göttingen and I do hope that the doctor there will not disappoint you."

Then Jean-Baptiste turned round to our guests, the garrison officers and their ladies and the cream of Hanover's society. "I should like to bid you good-bye. To-morrow morning I am joining the Army in the field." Smilingly he bowed. "On the Emperor's order! Ladies and gentlemen, good night."

Then he offered me his arm.

Yes, we were very happy in Hanover.

In the grey of a dawn eerily shot through with yellow streaks of candlelight Jean-Baptiste said good-bye to me. "You and Oscar are going back to Paris to-day," he said.

Fernand had prepared Jean-Baptiste's luggage. The gold-embroidered Marshal's uniform had been packed away carefully in the travelling bag together with table silver for twelve persons and a narrow camp bed. Jean-Baptiste wore the plain field uniform with the General's epaulettes.

I took his hand and pressed it against my face.

"My little girl, don't forget to write often! The War Ministry will——"

"Forward my letters, I know. Jean-Baptiste, will there never be an end to it? Will it always be like this, always and always?"

"Give Oscar a big kiss from me, little girl."

"I asked you, Jean-Baptiste, will it always be like this?"

"The Emperor's order: to conquer and occupy Bavaria. You are married to a Marshal of France. This should not be a surprise to you," he said in a voice which had lost all expression.

"Bavaria? And when you've conquered Bavaria, are you

243

coming back to me in Paris or are we going to return to Hanover?"

"From Bavaria we shall march against Austria."

"And then? But there are no more frontiers to defend. France has no more frontiers, France——"

"France is Europe. And France's Marshals have to march, my child. Orders of the Emperor!"

"To think how often you have been asked in the past to assume power! If only you had at that time——"

"Désirée!" His voice broke in sharply. And in a gentler tone he continued: "My little girl, I started as an ordinary private soldier and I never went to an officers' training academy, but I would never dream of picking up a crown out of the gutter. I do not pick up things out of the gutter. Do not forget that! Do not forget that, ever!"

He extinguished the candle. The grey farewell dawn broke through the curtains.

Shortly before I got into the coach Monsieur van Beethoven appeared once more. I had just put on my hat and Oscar was proudly holding his own little travelling bag when he came in, slowly, awkwardly and with a stiff bow.

"I should like you," he fumbled for words, then went on: "I should like you to tell General Bernadotte that I cannot dedicate the new symphony to the Emperor either. Least of all to him." He paused, then said: "I shall simply call it 'Eroica', to commemorate a hope which did not find fulfilment. General Bernadotte will know what I mean," he sighed.

"I shall give him your message and I'm sure he will understand, Monsieur," I said, and gave him my hand.

"Do you know, Mama, what I want to be?" asked Oscar as our coach was rolling along the endless roads. "I want to be a musician."

"I thought you wanted to be a sergeant or a Marshal like your Papa. Or a silk merchant," I said absent-mindedly. I had my diary on my knee and was writing.

"I thought it over. I want to be a composer like Monsieur Beethoven. Or—a King."

"Why a King?"

"Because as a King one can do good to so many people. A servant told me so in the castle. Hanover used to have a King, before the Emperor sent Papa there. Did you know that?"

Now even my six-year-old son had found out how uneducated I am!

He insisted: "Composer or King!"

"Then you'd better be a King," I said. "That's easier."

PARIS, June 4th, 1806.

If only I knew where Ponte Corvo is! But I shall read about it to-morrow morning in the paper. So why bother about it now? I'd rather write down what has happened since my return from Germany.

Oscar had the whooping cough and was not allowed to go out. My friends avoided our house like the plague because they were afraid their chldiren would catch it. I had wanted to start my piano and deportment lessons again, but even Monsieur Montel, that ballerina in trousers, was mortally afraid of infection. Anyway, I was really rather glad not to have to go to the lessons, as I was always so tired. Oscar coughed and was sick, mostly at night, and therefore I had his bed put in my room to be near him.

At Christmas time the three of us, Oscar, Marie and I, were quite alone. I gave him a violin for his present and promised him violin lessons as soon as he was well again.

Now and then Julie came to see us. During her visits she made Marie massage her feet, which were quite swollen owing to the long spells of standing about at the great receptions which she and Joseph had to give during the Emperor's absence. I kept away from her and sat in the dining-room so as not to infect her, whilst she had her massage in the drawing-room. Through the open door Julie shouted out all the news to me.

"Your husband has conquered Bavaria," she shouted one day in late autumn. "You'll read it to-morrow in the *Moniteur*. He met an Austrian army there and beat it. Marie, massage a bit harder, otherwise it's no good. Your husband is a great General, Désirée!"

In October she mentioned casually: "We've lost our whole navy. But Joseph says it doesn't really matter. The Emperor will show our enemies who is the master of Europe."

In December she appeared one day quite out of breath: "Désirée, we've won a tremendous battle, and to-morrow Joseph and I are going to give a ball for a thousand guests. Le Roy has his people working all night to get a dress ready for me. Wine-coloured, Désirée. How d'you like that?"

"But, Julie, red doesn't suit you, don't you know? What news of Jean-Baptiste? Is he all right?"

"All right? More than all right, darling! Joseph says that the Emperor is, so to speak, in his debt because he prepared everything so well. You know, five Army Corps marched into the battle at Austerlitz——"

"Austerlitz? Where is Austerlitz?"

"No idea. Does it matter? Somewhere in Germany, I think. Listen, five Army Corps, one each under Lannes, Murat, Soult, Davout and your husband. Jean-Baptiste and Soult held the centre."

"What centre?"

"How do I know? The centre of the line, I suppose, I'm no strategist. Napoleon with the five Marshals stood on a hill, and all the enemies of France are now beaten for good. Now we shall really have peace, Désirée!"

"Peace," I said, and tried to imagine Jean-Baptiste's return. "Then he's coming home at last," I shouted across the dining-room.

"They say he's on his way at this moment. We have to manage all Europe now and he'll have to think it all out," Julie called back.

"Never mind Europe, he's got to come home because Oscar keeps asking for him."

"I see, you're talking about Jean-Baptiste, but I mean the Emperor. He's on his way back, and Joseph says Jean-Baptiste can't come yet. The Emperor has ordered him to administer not only Hanover but Ansbach as well. Alternately he's to be there and in Hanover. You ought to go to him in Ansbach and have a look at things there."

"I can't," I said, somewhat subdued, "not with Oscar's whooping cough."

Julie didn't hear me. "Do you really think wine-red is wrong for me? Joseph likes me in it, he says it's a regal colour. Ow, Marie, not too hard, please. Why don't you answer, Désirée?"

"I'm unhappy," I said, "I so want to see Jean-Baptiste. Why can't he have leave?"

"Don't be childish, Désirée! How is the Emperor to hold the conquered territories if he doesn't put his Marshals in command there?"

'Yes, how is he to hold them?' I thought bitterly. 'With this new victory he's won the whole of Europe, with this and the help of eighteen Marshals. And I, I of all people, am married to a Marshal. There are millions of Frenchmen, but only eighteen Marshals. Why, why did I have to marry one of these eighteen? And I love him and want him so badly, oh so badly!'

"Drink a cup of chocolate and lie down, Eugenie," said Marie. "You never slept a wink last night, you know."

I looked up. "Where is Julie?"

"You fell asleep and she left to try on dresses, I suppose, and make arrangements for her ball and dust the Elysée Palace before a thousand guests arrive."

"Marie, is it ever coming to an end, this war-making, this taking over of other countries which have nothing to do with us?"

"Oh yes, but to a dreadful end," said Marie gloomily. She hates wars because she fears that one day her son will be called up too. And she hates all the royal castles we live in because she is a Republican. So were we all, once upon a time.

I lay down and fell into a fitful sleep from which I was awakened very soon by the sound of Oscar's coughing and panting for breath. . . .

Many weeks passed. Spring came, and still Jean-Baptiste hadn't returned. His letters were short and uninformative. He was residing in Ansbach and trying to introduce there the same reforms as in Hanover. I should come to him, he wrote, as soon as Oscar was better.

But Oscar recovered very slowly. We gave him lots of milk to drink and put him outside in the garden in the spring sun. Josephine came once and said that I don't look after my roses properly. So she sent me her gardener. The gardener was awfully expensive and made such a mess of my roses that hardly anything was left of them.

People at last stopped being afraid of catching infection from Oscar, and Hortense invited him to play with her two boys. After Napoleon's adoption of their two sons Hortense and Louis Bonaparte imagine that their eldest boy will one day inherit his throne. On the other hand there is Joseph who thinks that the throne will be his. (Why Joseph should take it for granted that he would survive his younger brother, or why no one thinks it possible that Napoleon might nominate a son of his own to be his heir I don't understand. After all, there is little Leon, the son of Josephine's reader Eleonore Revel, who was born last December, and there is just a chance that the Empress may repeat her performance of her first marriage. . . . Thank God, the whole thing is no concern of mine!) As I was saying, Oscar had been invited to play with Hortense's sons, and a few days later he had a temperature and a sore throat and wouldn't eat. Now, of course, it was worse than ever before and nobody would come anywhere near our house: Oscar had got German measles.

Dr. Corvisart called and prescribed cold compresses to get Oscar's temperature down. But the compresses were no good. Oscar raved in his fever and called desperately for his father. At night he wouldn't sleep anywhere but in my bed, and I would clasp him tightly to me. There was a risk of infection, but Marie said that one rarely got this kind of illness twice. Oscar's thin body was full of little red blisters which, Dr. Corvisart said, he must not scratch.

I never saw my reader these days. Heaven knows to whom she read, certainly not to me, she was so afraid of measles. It annoyed me, though, that I had to pay her her salary all the same. Since Jean-Baptiste's promotion to Marshal we've had so many unnecessary expenses.

The days passed, one very much like the other. Then, one spring afternoon, Julie turned up surprisingly, because since Oscar's measles she had stopped coming completely and only sent her maid regularly to inquire how he was. She appeared in the drawing-room full of excitement, and when I entered the house from the garden she shouted: "Don't come near me, you'll infect me. But I want to be the first to tell you the great news. It's inconceivable——"

Her hat sat askew, little trickles of perspiration ran down her face and she was pale.

I was terrified. "For heaven's sake, what is the matter?" I asked.

"I've become a Queen, Queen of Naples," she said in a toneless voice; her eyes were wide with terror.

At first I thought she had fallen ill and was raving, that she had caught measles somewhere, though certainly not from us, and I shouted: "Marie, come quickly, Julie isn't well."

Marie appeared, but Julie declined her help. "Leave me alone, I am all right, only I can't get used to the idea yet. A Queen, me a Queen! The Queen of Naples. Naples is in Italy, isn't it? My husband, His Majesty King Joseph! And I am Her Majesty Queen Julie. Oh, Désirée, the whole thing is terrible. We shall have to go to Italy again and live in those dreadful marble palaces. . . ."

"Your father wouldn't have liked it, Mademoiselle Julie," put in Marie.

"Hold your tongue!" said Julie harshly. I had never heard

her speak like that to Marie before. Marie's mouth set in a thin hard line and she left the room, slamming the door behind her. But no sooner had she gone than my companion, Madame La Flotte, appeared in her very best gown and sank into a deep curtsey before Julie as if she were the Empress. "Your Majesty, may I congratulate you?" she lisped.

Julie, whom Marie's furious exit had left in a state of near-collapse, gave a nervous start at the sight of Madame La Flotte and the corners of her mouth twitched. She collected herself quickly and her face was that of a bad acrtess who wants to play a Queen. "Thank you. How do you know what has happened?" she asked in a new, strange voice.

My companion was still in her deep curtsey on the carpet before Julie. "The whole town talks of nothing else, Your Majesty." Somewhat absurdly she added: "Your Majesty is too gracious!"

"Leave me alone with my sister," said Julie in her new voice. At that my companion tried to remove herself with her back to the door, an effort which I watched with great interest. When at last she had managed to get out through the door I said: "She seems to think that she is at court."

"In my presence," said Julie, "from now on one has to behave as at court. Joseph is busy this afternoon collecting a real regal suite." She shuddered, as if she were cold. "Désirée, I'm so afraid of everything."

I tried to encourage her. "Nonsense, you'll always be yourself."

But Julie shook her head and hid her face in her hands. "No, it's no good. You can't talk it away, I am a Queen now."

She began to weep, and without thinking I went up to her. She screamed at once: "Don't touch me, go away. Measles!"

I went back to the door to the garden. "Yvette!" I called.

Yvette, my maid, came, and on seeing Julie she, too, curtsied deeply.

"Bring a bottle of champagne, Yvette."

"I can't do it," said Julie, "I can't do it. More receptions, more court balls in a strange country. Away from Paris. . . ."

Yvette returned with the bottle and two glasses, and I poured out for us. Julie took her glass and at once began to drink hurriedly, thirstily.

"Your health, darling," I said, "I suppose it's an occasion for congratulations."

"It's all your doing," she smiled, "you brought Joseph into our house."

I remembered the whispers that were going round about Joseph being unfaithful to Julie. Small *affaires*, though, nothing really serious. He realised a long time ago that his talent as an author didn't amount to much but that his political talent was something to be proud of. And now brother-in-law Joseph had become a King.

" I hope," I said, " you are happy with Joseph."

" I have him so rarely to myself," she said, and stared past me into the garden. " I suppose I am happy, really. I have the children, Zenaïde and little Charlotte Napoleone."

" Your daughters will all be Princesses now, and everything will be all right," I said, and smiled. At the same time I tried to get it all into focus: Julie was a Queen, her daughters were Princesses, and Joseph, the little secretary of the *Maison Commune* who married Julie on account of her dowry, was King Joseph I of Naples.

" The Emperor, let me tell you, has decided to turn the conquered territories into independent States to be governed by the Imperial Princes and Princesses. And, of course, these States are to be linked to France by pacts of friendship. We, Joseph and I, are going to govern Naples and Sicily, Eliza has become Duchess of Lucca, Louis King of Holland and Murat Duke of Cleves."

" Good heavens, do you mean to say that the Marshals too will have to take their turn?" I asked, startled.

" No, it's because Murat is married to Caroline, and Caroline would be mortally insulted if she didn't have the revenues of a country to dispose of like the others."

I felt relieved.

" In any case," Julie went on, " someone will have to reign over the countries which we have conquered."

" Which who conquered?" I asked pointedly.

Julie made no answer but poured herself another glass, drank it hastily and said: " I wanted to be the first to tell you all that. And now I must go. Le Roy is going to do my robes of state. So much purple!"

" No," I said firmly. " You must object to that. Red just doesn't suit you, it doesn't. Have the coronation robe green, not purple."

" And all the packing I have to do!" wailed Julie. " And the ceremonial entry into Naples! You are coming with us, aren't you?"

I shook my head. " No. I have to nurse my boy, and besides,

well, I am waiting for my husband. Jean-Baptiste is bound to come home some time or other, isn't he?"

From that day till this morning I heard no more from Julie. I only read in the *Moniteur* about her, about Their Majesties the King and Queen of Naples and their balls, receptions and preparations for their journey.

To-day Oscar was allowed out of bed for the first time and he sat by the open window. It has been an enchanting June day, the air was filled with the scent of lilac and roses, and the sweetness everywhere made me long more than ever for my Jean Baptiste.

A carriage stopped outside our door. Every time a carriage draws up unexpectedly at our house there is a breathless moment when my heart waits for a miracle to happen. There was a breathless moment now, but it was only Julie who got out of the carriage. I heard her ask for me, and the next moment she came into the room. My companion and Yvette curtsied deeply, Marie, however, who had just been dusting, strode away into the garden with a stony face. She didn't want to see Julie.

Julie's regal gestures, which I am sure she owes to Monsieur Montel's tuition, swept everybody out of the room. Oscar got up and ran towards her.

"Aunt Julie," he cried, "I am well again." She took him in her arms and pressed him to her. Looking at me over his curly head she said:

"I wanted to tell you before you read it to-morrow morning in the *Moniteur* that Jean-Baptiste has become Prince of Ponte Corvo. Your Serene Highness, I offer you my congratulations!" She laughed and kissed Oscar, adding: "Congratulations, my little heir to the Principality of Ponte Corvo!"

At first I didn't know what to say, but at last I managed to bring out: "I don't understand that. Jean-Baptiste isn't a brother of the Emperor, is he?"

"But he governs Hanover and Ansbach so well that the Emperor wants to confer a distinction on him," she said in a jubilant voice, letting go of Oscar and coming close to me. "Aren't you pleased, Your Highness? Aren't you pleased, Princess?"

"I suppose——" I interrupted myself: "Yvette, champagne!" then turned back to Julie: "Champagne in the morning makes me drunk, I know. But Marie won't serve us chocolate any more since you made her furious that time. Well, now tell me: where is Ponte Corvo?"

Julie shrugged her shoulders. " How stupid of me! I should have asked Joseph. I don't know, darling. But does it matter?"

" Perhaps, if we have to go there and reign there. But wouldn't it be dreadful!"

" The name sounds Italian. Perhaps it's near Rome," Julie said. " In that case you might be quite close to us. But that," her face clouded over, " that would be too good to be true. Your Jean-Baptiste is a Marshal, and the Emperor needs him for his campaigns. No, I'm sure you'll be able to stay on here and I'll have to go to Naples without you."

" These wars must end some time, mustn't they?"

' Ruin ourselves with our victories,' who said that to me once? Jean-Baptiste did. France has no more frontiers to defend, France is Europe, and Napoleon and Joseph and Louis and Caroline and Eliza reign over it all, and now the Marshals are to take a hand too. . . .

" Your health, Your Serene Highness!" Julie raised her glass.

" To yours, Your Majesty!"

' And to-morrow we'll read it in the *Moniteur*,' I thought, as the champagne trickled sweetly down my throat. Ponte Corvo, where was Ponte Corvo? And when would my Jean-Baptiste come home?

Summer 1807, in a coach somewhere in EUROPE.

Marienburg, that was the name of the place I was making for. I had no idea where it lay, but a colonel was sitting by my side whom the Emperor had given me as my escort, and the colonel held a map on his knees from which he now and then shouted directions to the coachman. I took it therefore that we should get to Marienburg in due course. . . .

Marie, who was sitting opposite me, kept grumbling about the bad roads in which we got bogged so often. From the language which I heard people use when we stopped to change horses I guessed that we were passing through a stretch of Poland. It didn't sound Germanic to me. The colonel explained to me that we were taking a shorter route.

" We could have gone through Northern Germany," he said. " But it would have meant a detour, and Your Highness is in a hurry."

Yes, I was in a great hurry.

" Marienburg is not very far from Danzig," said the colonel.

That didn't mean anything to me either, as the whereabouts of Danzig were as unknown to me as those of Marienburg.

"A few weeks ago there was still fighting along these roads," the colonel went on. "But now we are at peace."

Yes, Napoleon had concluded another treaty of peace, this time at Tilsit. The Germans, under the leadership of the Prussians, had risen, and with the help of the Russians had tried to chase our troops out of the country. In the *Moniteur* we read all about our glorious victory at Jena. At home, however, in the secrecy of our four walls, Joseph told me that Jean-Baptiste had refused to obey an order from the Emperor, 'for strategical reasons', and that he had told the Emperor plainly that he could court-martial him if he liked. But before that could come to pass Jean-Baptiste had surrounded General Blücher and his army in Lübeck (another place I wouldn't know where to look for on the map!) and taken the town by assault.

There followed an endless winter during which I hardly got news at all. Berlin had been taken and the enemy troops were pursued across Poland. Jean-Baptiste was in command of the left wing of our Army. Near Mohrungen he won a victory over an enemy far superior in numbers. On that occasion he not only won a decisive success against the advancing foe but even managed to save the Emperor himself. This personal act of bravery made such a profound impression on the Prussian High Command that they sent his travelling bag with the Marshal's uniform in it, and the camp bed, which had already fallen into their hands, back to him.

All that, however, happened many months ago. Meanwhile Jean-Baptiste's regiments beat back all attacks on the flank of our army, the Emperor won the battles of Eylau and Jena, and dictated the conditions of peace to a Europe united in subjection to him. And one day, to everybody's surprise, Napoleon arrived back in Paris, and his lackeys in their green uniform— green is the colour of Corsica—rode from house to house to distribute invitations to a great victory ball in the Tuileries.

For this ball I put on my new robe of pale pink satin with dark roses on the bodice, and on my head I wore the diadem made of rubies and pearls which Jean-Baptiste had sent me through a courier on the last anniversary of our wedding day in August.

"Your Serene Highness is going to have a good time," said my companion jealously, staring at the golden casket with the engraved eagle in which I keep my jewellery, the casket which was given me on the day of the coronation.

I shook my head. "I shall be very lonely in the Tuileries. Not even Queen Julie will be there." No, she wouldn't be there because she was in Naples enduring in the southern heat an infinite loneliness.

The ball in the Tuileries took a course very different from the one I had expected. We forgathered in the great ballroom and waited there till the doors opened and the Marseillaise rang out. The Emperor and the Empress appeared and we curtsied deeply. They made a slow round of the guests, talking to some and making others miserable by overlooking them.

I couldn't see Napoleon properly at first because of the tall adjutants who surrounded him. Suddenly he stopped, quite close to me, in front of a Dutch dignitary, I thought, and he began:

"I am told that malicious tongues maintain of my officers that they only send their troops to the fighting line, whereas they themselves keep out. Well, is not that what they say in your country, in Holland?" he thundered all at once.

I knew that the Dutch were very dissatisfied with French overlordship in general and with their awkward King Louis and their melancholy Queen Hortense in particular. I was not surprised, therefore, about the Emperor's displeasure towards them, and didn't listen to what he said but studied his face instead. The sharp features under the short-cut hair had become ampler, the smile of his colourless mouth had changed from the winning and challenging smile of years ago to one of superiority. Besides, he had grown fatter, he looked as if he were going to burst out of his plain General's uniform, which bears no medals except that of the Legion of Honour which he himself had founded. He had a pronounced look of rotundity about him, and this rotund image of God on earth harangued with wide gestures and only now and then controlled himself and clasped his hands behind his back, as formerly in moments of great tension. He had clasped them behind his back now as if he were trying to keep a grip on those far too restless fingers of his.

His superior smile turned sneering: "Gentlemen, I believe that our great Army has proved the bravery of its officers in unique style. Not even the highest officers refrain from exposing themselves to danger. In Tilsit I received news that one of the Marshals of France has been wounded."

There was deep silence. Could the whole ballroom hear my heart beat?

"The Marshal in question is the Prince of Ponte Corvo," he added after an artificial pause.

"Is—that—true?" My voice cut through the circle of etiquette which surrounds the Emperor. At once a frown appeared on his face. One doesn't shout in the presence of His Imperial Majesty. . . . The frown disappeared from his face, and at that moment I knew that he had seen me before he spoke. So that was the way in which he wanted to inform me, in front of thousands of strangers, as if he wanted to punish me. Punish me for what?

"My dear Princess," he said, and I curtsied deeply. He took my hand and pulled me up. "I regret to have to tell you this," he said, at the same time looking indifferently away from me. "The Prince of Ponte Corvo, who has gained great distinction in this campaign and whose conquest of Lübeck we greatly admired, has been slightly wounded in the neck, near Spandau. I am told that the Prince is already on the road to recovery. I beg you not to alarm yourself, dear Princess."

"And I beg you to make it possible for me to go to my husband, Sire," I said in a toneless voice. Only now the Emperor turned his eyes on me fully. Marshals' wives do not usually follow their husbands to their headquarters.

"The Prince has gone to Marienburg to have himself looked after properly. I advise you against this journey, Princess. The roads through Northern Germany, and above all in the region round Danzig, are very bad. Moreover, these districts were battlefields only a short while ago. They are no sight for the eyes of beautiful women," he said coldly. But he examined my face with great interest.

'That's his revenge,' I thought, 'for my visit to him the night before the execution of the Duc d'Enghien, his revenge for my escape from his hands that night, his revenge for my love of Jean-Baptiste, the General whom he had not wanted me to marry.'

"Sire, I ask you from the bottom of my heart to enable me to get to my husband. I have not seen him for nearly two years."

His eyes still rested on my face. He nodded. "Almost two years. You see, gentlemen, how the Marshals of France sacrifice themselves for their country! If you want to risk it, dear Princess, you will be given a passport. For how many persons?"

"For two. I am only taking Marie."

"I beg your pardon, Princess—whom?"

255

"Marie. Our faithful old Marie from Marseilles. Your Majesty will perhaps remember her," I said defiantly.

At last! His face stopped being a marble mask and a smile of amusement appeared on it. "Of course, faithful Marie! Marie of the marzipan tarts!" He turned to one of the adjutants: "A passport for the Princess of Ponte Corvo and one accompanying person."

His eyes glanced round his circle and stopped at a tall colonel in the uniform of the grenadiers. "Colonel Moulin, you will go with the Princess, and you are responsible to me for her safety." Turning back to me, "When do you want to depart?"

"To-morrow morning, Sire."

"I should like you to convey my kind regards to the Prince and to take him a present from me. In recognition of his services for this victorious campaign I am presenting him with——" I saw his eyes change colour, his smile turn to a jeer; now, I felt, he was going to strike—"I am presenting him with the house of the former General Moreau in Rue d'Anjou. I bought it from his wife a short time ago. I am told the General has gone into exile in America. A pity, an able soldier but unfortunately a traitor to France, a great pity. . . ."

Curtseying deeply again, I only saw his back and his hands stiffly clasping each other behind it. General Moreau's house! That Moreau who, together with Jean-Baptiste, wanted to stand by the Republic on that 18th Brumaire and whom, five years later, in connection with a Royalist plot, they arrested and condemned to prison for two years. The ludicrousness of it, to arrest this most loyal General of the Republic as a Royalist. The First Consul subsequently commuted the sentence to exile for life. And now, as Emperor, he bought his house and gave it as a present to Moreau's best friend, the man whom he hates but can't do without. . . .

And that was how I came to travel along highways through battlefields, past dead horses with inflated bellies stretching their limbs to the sky, past little mounds surmounted by slanting crosses hastily put together. And all the time it was raining, raining, raining.

"And all of them had mothers," I said, apparently apropos of nothing.

The colonel, who had fallen asleep by my side, started. "I beg your pardon? Mothers?"

I pointed to the small mounds of earth outside in the rain. "Those dead soldiers. Are they not all mothers' sons?"

Marie pulled the curtains across the carriage windows. Puzzled, the colonel looked from one to the other. We said nothing. He shrugged his shoulders and closed his eyes once more.

"I am longing for Oscar," I said to Marie. It was the first time since he was born that I had left him. In the early hours of the morning before my departure I had taken him to Madame Letitia at Versailles, where the Emperor's mother lives in the Trianon Palace. She had just returned from early Mass when we arrived, and she promised me to look well after Oscar. "After all, I have brought up five sons," she said.

'Brought up, yes, but badly,' I thought. But one couldn't say such things to the mother of Napoleon.

"You go to your Bernadotte, Eugenie, I'll look after him," she repeated, and stroked his hair with her horny hand.

"Should we not stop at an inn?" the colonel asked.

I shook my head.

At nightfall Marie pushed a hot-water-bottle, which we had filled at a coaching inn, under my feet. The rain drummed on the roof of the coach, and the soldiers' graves and their pitiful crosses were drowned in the downpour. And on we went on our way to Marienburg.

"This really is too awful!" I said involuntarily when our coach came at last to a halt outside Jean-Baptiste's headquarters. I had slowly got used to mansions and palaces, but the Marienburg is neither one nor the other but a medieval, grey, desolate, decayed, eerie castle.

There were crowds of soldiers outside by the gate, and great was the excitement and clicking of heels when Colonel Moulin showed my passport. Fancy, the Marshal's wife herself!

Getting out of the carriage I said: "Please do not announce me. I want to surprise the Prince."

Two officers took me through the portal into a miserably paved courtyard. The mighty ruined walls around it shocked me deeply. Any moment I expected to see knightly damsels and minnesingers. Instead I saw only soldiers of a number of different regiments.

"Monseigneur has very nearly recovered. About this time Monseigneur works and does not generally wish to be disturbed. What a surprise!" said the younger of the two officers, and smiled.

"Was it impossible to find a better headquarters than this minnesinger castle?" I couldn't help saying.

"In the field it is a matter of indifference to the Prince where he resides. And at any rate there is plenty of room here for our offices. In here, Your Highness, if you please."

He opened an inconspicuous door and we passed along a corridor. It was cold in here and the air smelt stale. At last we reached a little ante-chamber and there Fernand rushed up to me. "Madame!" he shouted.

He was so elegantly dressed that I hardly recognised him.

"Dear me, you *have* become elegant, Fernand!" I laughed.

"We are now the Prince of Ponte Corvo," he said solemnly. "Please to look at the buttons, Madame!" He pushed out his stomach to show me the gold buttons on his wine-red livery. They showed a strange armorial design. "The arms of Ponte Corvo, the arms of Madame!" he said proudly.

"At long last I am setting eyes on them," I said, and regarded the complicated engraving with interest.

"We are really quite well again. Only the new skin over the wound still itches," said Fernand. I put my finger over my mouth. Fernand understood and very quietly opened a door.

Jean-Baptiste didn't hear me. He was sitting by a desk, his chin in his hand, studying a folio. The candle near the book threw its light on his forehead, a clear and serene forehead.

I looked round. Jean-Baptiste had put a strange mixture of things into the room. The desk covered with documents and leather-bound folios stood against the fireplace, in which a big fire roared. A map of enormous size hung by the mantelpiece and the flickering flames threw a red glare over it. In the background I saw his narrow camp bed and a table with a silver washing bowl and some bandaging material. Apart from that the vast room was empty.

I went nearer to him. The logs in the fire crackled and Jean-Baptiste didn't hear me. The collar of his dark blue field uniform stood open and showed a white scarf. It was loosened under the chin and I saw a white bandage. Now he turned a page of the heavy tome and wrote something in the margin.

I took off my hat. It was warm by the fireplace, and for the first time for days I felt warm and sheltered, but tired too, dreadfully tired. Yet tiredness didn't matter now, I had arrived.

"Your Highness," I said, "dear Prince of Ponte Corvo——"

He jumped to his feet. "My God, Désirée!" And the next moment he stood by my side.

"Does the wound still hurt?" I asked between two kisses.

"Yes, particularly when you put your arm on it as firmly as now," he said.

I dropped my arms at once. "I shall kiss you without putting my arms round you," I said.

"Marvellous!"

I sat on his lap and pointed to the big tome on his desk. "What is that you are reading?"

"Law. An uneducated sergeant has to learn a lot if he is to administer the whole of Northern Germany and the Hanse towns."

"Hanse towns? What are they?"

"Hamburg, Lübeck and Bremen. And don't forget that we are still responsible for Hanover and Ansbach besides."

I shut the book and clung tightly to him. "Oscar was ill," I whispered, "and you have been away from us for so long. You were wounded and you were far away from me. . . ."

I felt his mouth on mine. "My little girl, my little girl," he said, and held me tightly.

Suddenly the door was flung open, which was rather embarrassing. I jumped down from his lap and tidied my hair. But it was only Marie and Fernand.

"Marie wants to know where the Princess is going to sleep. She wants to unpack," Fernand said in a doleful voice. I realised, of course, that he was furious because I had brought Marie.

"My Eugenie can't sleep in this place full of bugs," said Marie.

"Bugs?" Fernand shouted. "There aren't any here. It's far too cold and damp for them."

"When these two are arguing I feel I am back home in Rue Cisalpine," said Jean-Baptiste, and laughed. As he spoke I remembered the Emperor's present, Moreau's house. 'After supper I shall have to tell him,' I thought. 'But first let's eat, and drink some wine, and then we'll see.'

"Fernand, you'll see to it that within an hour you'll have a bedroom and a drawing-room ready for the Princess," ordered Jean-Baptiste. "And don't take any of the damp furniture from the depot. Tell the Adjutant on Duty to requisition some decent furniture from the big houses in the district."

"And without bugs!" hissed Marie.

"The Princess and I want to dine alone here, in my room, in an hour."

We heard them continue their argument outside, and we

laughed a lot, remembering our bridal bed full of roses and thorns. I climbed back on to his knees and talked to him about everything that came into my mind, about Julie's difficulties as a Queen, Oscar's whooping cough, his measles, and Monsieur Beethoven's message to him about the new symphony, which he could not, after all, dedicate to the Emperor but would simply call ' Eroica ' to commemorate a hope which he had nourished once upon a time. . . .

Fernand laid a small table and we sat down to a delicious chicken and marvellous Burgundy.

" You have bought new cutlery, Jean-Baptiste! With the initials of the Prince of Ponte Corvo! At home I am still using our old cutlery with the simple ' B ' on it."

" Have the ' B ' erased and the new arms put in its place, darling. You need not economise, we are very rich," said Jean-Baptiste.

Fernand, having finished waiting on us, disappeared, and I braced myself to deliver the blow. " We are richer than you think," I said. " The Emperor has given us a house as a present."

Jean-Baptiste looked up at me. " House? What house?"

" The house of General Moreau in the Rue d'Anjou. He bought it from Madame Moreau."

" I know, for 400,000 francs. He bought it some months ago, and it caused a lot of talk among officers."

Jean-Baptiste slowly divided an orange into segments and I drank a glass of liqueur. He looked suddenly very tired.

" Moreau's house," he murmured. " Friend Moreau went into exile whilst I have become the recipient of great Imperial presents. I had a letter from the Emperor to-day in which he tells me that he is going to hand over to me estates in Poland and Westphalia which guarantee me a yearly income of another 300,000 francs. But he doesn't say a word about Moreau's house and your visit. It is not easy to spoil a man's joy at reunion with his wife. But the Emperor of the French manages it all right."

" He said that he admired your assault on Lübeck very much," I said.

Jean-Baptiste did not answer. A deep frown had appeared on his forehead.

" I shall furnish the new house very comfortably," I went on, feeling helpless. " You must come home. The child keeps asking about you."

Jean-Baptiste shook his head. " Moreau's house will never

be my home, only a *pied-à-terre* where I shall call to see you and Oscar sometimes." He stared into the fire and a smile came into his face: " I shall write to Moreau."

" But how can you communicate with him across the Continental Blockade?"

" The Emperor wants me to administer the Hanseatic towns. From Lübeck it is easy to write to Sweden, still a neutral country from which letters go to England and America. And I have friends in Sweden."

A memory came back to me, half forgotten and yet very clear: Stockholm near the North Pole, a white sky. . . . " What do you know of Sweden?" I asked.

" When I took Lübeck," said Jean-Baptiste, returning to his livelier mood, " I found some Swedish troops, a squadron of dragoons, in the town."

" How was that? Are we at war with Sweden, too?"

" With whom are we not at war? That is to say, since Tilsit we are allegedly at peace again. Anyway, at that time Sweden had made common cause with our enemies. Its crazy young King imagined himself to be the tool of God to bring about Napoleon's destruction. Apparently some kind of religious mania."

" What's his name?"

" Gustavus. The fourth of that name, I believe. The Swedish Kings are all called Carl or Gustavus. His father, the third Gustavus, was so unpopular that he was murdered during a masked ball by a member of the Swedish aristocracy."

" How awful, how barbarous—during a masked ball!"

" When we were young," said Jean-Baptiste ironically, " the guillotine used to do that kind of job. Do you think that less barbarous? It is difficult enough to judge, but more difficult still to condemn." He stared into the fire for a moment, then his good temper came back to him once more. " Well, the son of this murdered Gustavus, the fourth Gustavus, sent his dragoons into the war against France, and that was how I came to capture a Swedish squadron in Lübeck. I happen to be interested in Sweden for a particular reason, and having at last the opportunity of meeting some Swedes I asked the captured officers for a meal. And so I met Mr. Mörner——" He stopped. " Wait, I have the names somewhere." He got up and went to his desk.

" It's unimportant," I said. " Go on."

" No, it is not unimportant. I want to remember the names." He rummaged in a drawer, found a piece of paper and came back to me. "So I met Mr. Gustavus Mörner, Mr. Flach, Mr. de la Grange and the Barons Leijonhjelm, Banér and Friesendorff."

"What unpronounceable names!" I said.

"These officers explained the situation to me. Their King had entered the war against the will of the people. He thought that in this way he would curry favour with the Tsar. The Swedes have always been afraid that Russia might take Finland from them."

"Finland?" I shook my head. "Where is Finland?"

"Come, I'll show you on the map," said Jean-Baptiste, and I had to go with him to the big map by the fireplace.

Here he explained to me in great detail the merits of the geographical situation of Denmark, Sweden and Norway, the madness of King Gustavus' policy towards Russia and France, and his firm belief that the only thing to do for the Swedes was to cede Finland to Russia and try for a union with Norway, at present under the unpopular sovereignty of the King of Denmark.

"Did you explain that to the Swedish officers in Lübeck?"

"I certainly did. I also told them that we are going to despatch French troops to Denmark very soon. 'Save your country through armed neutrality, gentlemen,' I said to them, 'and, if you needs must have a federation, forget about Finland and look to Norway for your partner'."

"And what did the Swedes answer?"

"They stared at me as if I were a seven days' wonder. Don't look at me, look at the map, I told them." Jean-Baptiste paused, smiling. "And next morning I sent them home, since when I have friends in Sweden."

"Why do you want friends in Sweden?"

"It is always useful to have friends in all sorts of places. But I wish the Swedes would stop being bellicose to Russia and France at the same time. Otherwise I shall have to occupy their country. We expect the British to attack Denmark to use it as a base against us, and that is why Napoleon wants to station French troops in Denmark. As I am to be the Governor of the Hanseatic towns I expect to be Commander-in-Chief of the troops in Denmark, and if the Swedish Gustavus does not see reason some day the Emperor will give me the order to occupy Sweden. Getting there will be easy: I shall simply cross the Öre Sound from Denmark into the southern tip of Sweden. Come, have another look at the map." And I had to take up my position in front of the map again. But this time

I didn't look. I had travelled for days and nights without interruption to nurse my husband, not to listen to lectures on geography.

"The Swedes can't defend the southern part of their country; it is strategically impossible." He pointed to somewhere on the map. "I suppose they would stand and try to hold a line here."

"Tell me, did you say to these Swedish officers that you may possibly conquer their country? And that they could not hope to defend their southernmost region but would have to try to defend themselves farther north?"

"I did. And you cannot imagine how they were taken aback when I told them. Especially this man Mörner. He kept exclaiming 'Monseigneur, you are giving your secret plans away. How can you take us into your confidence?' And you know what I answered?"

"No," I said, and moved slowly across to the camp bed. I was so tired that I could hardly keep my eyes open. "What did you answer, Jean-Baptiste?"

"'Gentlemen,' I said, 'I cannot imagine that Sweden would be able to hold out if it is attacked by a French Marshal.' That was my answer. Little girl, are you asleep?"

"Almost," I said, and tried to make myself comfortable on that miserable camp bed.

"Come," said Jean-Baptiste, "I have made them get a bedroom ready for you. Everybody has gone to bed. I shall carry you across and nobody will see it," he whispered.

"I don't want to get up any more. I am so tired."

Jean-Baptiste bent down to me. "If you want to sleep here I can sit at the desk. I have so much reading to do yet."

"No-o. You are wounded. You must lie down."

Undecided, Jean-Baptiste sat down on the edge of the bed.

"You must take my shoes off and my dress. I am so tired."

"I think the Swedish officers will talk to their ministers and give them no rest till they force their King to abdicate. His successor would be an uncle of his."

"Another Gustavus?"

"No, a Charles, Charles the Thirteenth. Unfortunately this uncle has no children, and he is said to be very senile. Why, darling, did you put three petticoats on?"

"Because of the cold and the rain. Poor Mörner, senile and childless."

"No, not Mörner, the thirteenth Charles of Sweden."

"If I made myself very small and moved over as far as

possible we would both have room in your camp bed. We could try."

"Yes, we could try, my little girl."

I woke up some time during the night lying on Jean-Baptiste's arm.

"Are you uncomfortable, little girl?"

"No, I am very comfortable. Why aren't you asleep, Jean-Baptiste?"

"I am not tired. So many things are going through my head. You go to sleep again, darling."

"Stockholm is on Lake Mälar," I murmured, "and green ice-floes float on the Lake."

"How do you know that?"

"I just know it. I used to know a man called Persson. . . ."

I didn't return to Paris till autumn. Jean-Baptiste and his staff went to Hamburg, where Jean-Baptiste started his administration. From there he wanted to visit Denmark and inspect the coastal fortifications opposite Sweden.

The weather was good on my return journey, hot-water-bottles were superfluous. A tired-looking autumn sun shone into the carriage, on the highway and the fields which had seen no harvest this year. We saw no dead horses and only a few war graves. The rain water seemed to have levelled the little mounds and the wind had pushed over the wooden crosses. One could also forget that one was travelling across recent battlefields, or that thousands of men lay buried here. One could, but I didn't.

Somewhere Colonel Moulin succeeded in finding an old issue of the *Moniteur*. In it we read that the Emperor's youngest brother Jerome, that naughty boy Jerome who at Julie's wedding had eaten too much and been sick, had become a King. King Jerome the First of Westphalia, a kingdom made up of some German principalities. In addition Napoleon had managed to marry the twenty-three-year-old King to Princess Catherine of Württemberg, the descendant of one of the oldest German princely families. I wondered whether Jerome still remembered Miss Patterson from America whom he so willingly divorced on Napoleon's orders.

I told Marie the news.

"Now nobody can keep him under control and he'll overeat himself every day," she said.

Colonel Moulin was shocked. It was by no means the first *lèse-majesté* he had heard from her.

I threw the old *Moniteur* out of the carriage window and the wind carried it across the battlefields.

In our new home in the Rue d'Anjou in PARIS. July 1809.

The church bells woke me up. It was hot already although it was still very early. I pushed the blanket back, folded my arms under my head and mused. The bells of Paris. . . .

'Perhaps,' I thought, 'it's the birthday of one of the many Kings of the Bonaparte family.' Napoleon had turned every member of it into Kings and Princes. Joseph, by the way, was no longer King of Naples but of Spain, and for months, literally months, Julie had been on her way to Madrid. The Spaniards, it turned out, didn't want Joseph as their King, ambushed his troops, surrounded and defeated them, and finally the rebels instead of King Joseph entered Madrid in triumph. So the Emperor had to send more troops to Spain to deliver Joseph's people from these misguided patriots.

In Naples Murat and Caroline had taken the place of Joseph and Julie. Murat, being a Marshal of France as well as King of Naples, had to be away most of the time on some front or other, leaving Caroline to represent the royal family. But Caroline didn't bother much about her kingdom and her son but stayed mostly with her eldest sister Eliza, who reigned in Toscana, getting fatter year by year and having an *affaire* with her court musician, a man called Paganini.

Julie told me all about that. She had been in Paris for a few weeks before setting out for Spain, to have her new robes of state made here. They had to be purple, of course, at Joseph's wish.

Oh those bells! Which Bonaparte's birthday could it be to-day? It wouldn't be Jerome nor Eugene de Beauharnais, now the Viceroy of Italy. This timid young man had changed a lot since he had married a daughter of the King of Bavaria. 'Some of his timidity has disappeared,' I thought, 'and he, at any rate, seems happier.'

The bells went on. I could distinguish the deep chime of Notre-Dame from the rest. When was King Louis' birthday? That boy was going to reach a good old age in spite of his many imaginary ailments, of which only his flat feet were real. What, by the way, was the name of the Dutch rebels who repeatedly attempted to rise against Louis? Saboteurs, that was it, saboteurs, because of their sabots, the wooden shoes which they wear like our fishermen at home in Marseilles. They hate Louis because Napoleon made him their King. If only they knew how Louis dislikes his brother! Every time a merchant ship secretly left one of his ports to sail for England Louis turned a blind eye. Louis was the Dutch saboteur-in-chief to annoy his brother. He seemed to think that the least Napoleon could have done was to allow him to choose his own wife.

Who was it who talked to me about Louis only the other day? Ah, Polette of course, the only Bonaparte who has never meddled in politics but only lived for her pleasure and her lovers. No church bells would ring for her birthday, or for Lucien's for that matter. Napoleon offered the still exiled Lucien the crown of Spain on condition that he divorced his red-haired Madame Jourberthon. Lucien, the blue-eyed idealist, refused, and tried to make his way to America. His boat was intercepted by the British, who took him as an 'enemy alien' to England. The other day he succeeded in getting a letter smuggled through to his mother in France, in which he wrote that he lived under observation—yet free! To think that it was Lucien who helped Napoleon to the Consulate in order to save the French Republic! No, there wouldn't be any church bells for Lucien either. . . .

The door opened a bit. "I thought that the bells had wakened you," said Marie. "I'll get you your breakfast."

"What's all this bell-ringing for, Marie?"

"What for? The Emperor has gained a great victory."

"Where? When? Anything in the paper?"

"I'll send you your breakfast and your reader." She bethought herself a moment. "No, your breakfast first, then the young madame who reads to you."

It's a continual source of fun to Marie that I, like the other ladies at court, have to engage a young girl of the old impoverished nobility to read the *Moniteur* to me, and novels. But I'd much rather read by myself and in bed. The Emperor insists that we Marshals' wives be attended as if we were eighty and not, as in my case, twenty-eight.

Yvette brought my morning chocolate and opened the window. Immediately sunshine and the scent of roses streamed into my bedroom. The garden—there are only three rose trees in it—is very small, which is no wonder as the house is right in the middle of the town. Most of Moreau's furniture which

I found here I gave away, and bought new and very expensive furniture instead. In the drawing-room I discovered a bust of the former owner. I didn't know at first what to do with it. Certainly I couldn't leave it where I found it, as Moreau is in disgrace. But I didn't want to throw it away either. So I put it in the hall, and the obligatory portrait of the Emperor into the drawing-room.

I was fortunate in obtaining a copy of Napoleon's portrait painted when he was First Consul by Adolphe Yvon. In this painting the face of the image of God on earth is as lean and straight as it was in the days at Marseilles. The hair is shown as untidy and as long as it was at that time, and the eyes have not yet acquired their present steeliness and eerie iridescence but look dreamily yet sensibly into the distance. His mouth in the portrait is still that of the fledgling Napoleone who one summer night leaned against a hedge and spoke of men chosen to make history. . . .

Meanwhile the bells went on and on. My head felt like starting to ache any moment, although by now we ought to have got used to victory bells.

"Yvette," I asked, "where and when did we win this victory?"

"At Wagram, Your Highness, on July 4th and 5th."

"Send Mademoiselle in and Oscar."

They came in at the same time. I pulled Oscar to me on to the bed, and Mademoiselle started reading. And so we learnt that at Wagram, near Vienna, an Austrian army of 70,000 men had been completely destroyed. Only 1,500 Frenchmen had fallen, three thousand had been wounded. Among the details were the names of the Marshals present at that battle. Yet there was no mention of Jean-Baptiste, although I knew that he was in Austria with his troops, the Saxon regiments fighting with the Emperor's Army.

"I hope nothing has happened to him," I couldn't help saying.

"Is there nothing about Papa in the paper?" Oscar wanted to know.

Mademoiselle went once more through the report. "No, nothing," she said in the end.

There was a knock on the door and Madame La Flotte put her charmingly made-up face into the room. "Your Highness, His Excellency, Monsieur Fouché, the Minister of Police, asks you to see him."

The church bells stopped. Fouché, did she say? He had never been before. Perhaps I had misheard the name. "Who did you say?"

"Monsieur Fouché, the Minister of Police," Madame La Flotte repeated, full of agitation in spite of her obvious attempt to appear unconcerned.

"Out with you, Oscar. I must get ready quickly. Yvette, Yvette!"

Thank God, there was Yvette, holding the lilac-coloured dressing-gown ready for me. "Madame La Flotte, take His Excellency to the small drawing-room."

"I have taken him there already, Madame."

"Mademoiselle, go down and ask His Excellency to be patient a second. Tell him I'm just dressing. Or rather, don't tell him that. Hand him the *Moniteur* to read."

A smile flitted across the pretty face of Madame La Flotte. "Your Highness, His Excellency reads the *Moniteur* before it is printed. It is one of his duties."

"Yvette, there's no time to do my hair, give me the pink muslin scarf, put it round my head turban fashion."

Madame La Flotte and Mademoiselle disappeared. But I called Madame back: "Tell me, don't I look like Madame de Staël in this turban? Madame de Staël, the banished authoress?"

"Your Highness, Madame de Staël has a face like a dachshund and Your Highness could never——"

"Thank you, Madame. Yvette, where is my rouge?"

"In a drawer in the dressing-table. Your Highness uses it so rarely——"

"Yes, I know, my cheeks are too red anyway. Princesses ought to be pale-cheeked by nature. But at this moment I'm a bit too pale myself. Is it really hot outside or is it only me?"

"It is very hot, Your Highness," said Yvette.

I went slowly downstairs. Someone once called Fouché everybody's bad conscience. People are afraid of him because he knows too much. During the Revolution they called him ' bloody Fouché ' because no one signed so many death sentences as Deputy Fouché. He was too bloodthirsty even for Robespierre. But before Robespierre could remove him Fouché exploded his plot against Robespierre, and Robespierre went to the guillotine, not Fouché. Under the Directory Fouché disappeared from sight. The Directors wanted to prove to the world that France was no republic of murderers. Fouché, however, knew all their secrets and they couldn't get rid of him.

He attended at Madame Tallien's every day and he knew everything and everybody. When someone suggested firing at the hungry mob of Paris to quell a riot, he said: "Bernadotte will never do it. But what about that little wretch who keeps hanging round Josephine these days?"

How did it come about that bloodthirsty Fouché got a job again after all? Director Barras used him first, sending him abroad as a French secret agent. Shortly before the overthrow of the Directors he became their most trusted support and they made him Minister of Police. The first thing he did as the new Minister was that he, the former president of the Jacobin Club, went to the clubhouse of his old comrades of the extreme Left in the Rue du Bac and closed it down for good, thus setting the official seal on the end of the Revolution. From then on he kept all ministries and offices, ministers and officials, officers and civilians of any importance under observation, an easy enough job when you have plenty of money to pay your spies. Who was his spy? Or rather, who was not his spy?

On the day the Directors feared was the one chosen by Napoleon for his *coup d'état*, they relied completely on their Minister of Police. But that very day the Minister of Police had to spend in bed with a cold. And during the night following the *coup d'état* the warrant for the arrest which Jean-Baptiste and I expected to arrive any minute would have been signed not by the First Consul but by the Minister of Police he had just appointed, by Monsieur Fouché.

'What does he want of me?' I wondered again and again before entering the small drawing-room. 'What did the mass murderer of Lyons want?' That's what people called him during the Revolution when they talked about the death sentences he imposed in Lyons. 'Stupid to remember that just now,' I thought. 'He doesn't look like a murderer, anyway,' I told myself, ' he is a very neatly dressed gentleman, strikingly pale probably because he is anæmic, and he speaks most politely and gently with half-closed eyes. . . .' The communiqué this morning did not mention Jean-Baptiste with so much as a syllable, and I felt that I knew what had happened. ' But, Monsieur Fouché, I have nothing to hide, only my fear.'

He jumped to his feet when I entered. "I have come to congratulate you, Princess. We have gained a great victory, and I read that the Prince of Ponte Corvo and his Saxon regiments were the first to get into Wagram. With seven to eight thousand soldiers your husband crushed the resistance of 40,000 men and took Wagram."

"Yes, but," I stammered as I asked him to keep his seat, "but that's not in the paper."

"I only said that *I* read it, my dear Princess, but not where I read it. No, you would not find it in the papers, only in the Order-of-the-Day from your husband to the Saxon troops in which he praised their bravery."

He paused and took a little Dresden bonbon dish from the table between us and examined it with great interest. "Moreover, I also read the copy of a letter from His Majesty to the Prince of Ponte Corvo. In that the Emperor expresses outspoken displeasure at the Prince's Order-of-the-Day and even goes so far as to state that this Order contains a number of inaccuracies. His Majesty states for instance that Oudinot had taken Wagram and that it would therefore have been impossible for the Prince of Ponte Corvo to have taken it first. Furthermore the Saxons could not have gained any distinction under your husband's leadership simply because they never fired a single shot. For the rest, His Majesty wanted the Prince of Ponte Corvo to know that he, the Prince, had not distinguished himself in any way during the campaign."

"You, you mean that—the Emperor—wrote that to Jean-Baptiste?" I asked, completely confounded.

Fouché replaced the china bowl carefully on the table. "There is no doubt about that. A copy of the Imperial letter was added to a letter to me. I have been ordered——" he looked me full in the eyes, but with an amiable expression—"I have been ordered to supervise the person of the Prince of Ponte Corvo and his correspondence."

"But, Monsieur Fouché, that is going to be difficult. My husband is in Austria with his troops."

"You are mistaken, Your Highness. The Prince of Ponte Corvo is due to arrive in Paris at any moment. After the correspondence with His Majesty he has resigned his command and asked for leave for reasons of health. This leave has been granted him for an indefinite period. I congratulate you, Princess. You have not seen your husband for such a long time, there will be a reunion for you very soon."

"May I think for a moment?"

A smile of amusement flitted over his face. "Of what, Your Highness?"

I put my hand to my forehead. "Of everything. I am not very clever, Monsieur Fouché; please don't contradict me, I must try and make clear to myself what has happened. You say that my husband wrote that his Saxon troops had distinguished themselves, didn't you?"

"They stood like a rock. That at any rate is what the Prince wrote."

"Why then is the Emperor annoyed about the rock-like stand of my husband's regiments?"

"In a secret circular to all his Marshals the Emperor laid down that His Majesty is in personal command of all his troops and that it is solely up to him to single out some formations for special praise. Besides, he wants them to be quite clear about the fact that the French Army owes its victories to French and not to foreign soldiers. Any other version the Emperor declares to be incompatible with our honour as well as with our policy."

"Someone told me only the other day that my husband had complained to the Emperor about allotting him nothing but foreign troops. Jean-Baptiste really did all he could to command French troops and to get rid of those poor Saxons."

"Why poor Saxons?"

"Because the King of Saxony sends his subjects into battles which are no concern of theirs. Why did the Saxons fight at Wagram at all?"

"They are France's allies, Your Highness. But don't you see yourself how wisely the Emperor acted in putting the Saxon regiments under the command of the Prince of Ponte Corvo?"

I gave no answer.

"They stood like a rock, Your Highness, under your husband's leadership."

"But the Emperor says it isn't true."

"No, all the Emperor said was that he alone had the right to praise individual army contingents, and that it was impolitic and incompatible with our national honour to praise foreign troops. You did not listen to what I said, Princess."

'I have to get his room ready, he's coming home,' I thought. I got up. "You'll excuse me, Your Excellency, I want to get everything ready for his reception. And thank you very much for your visit, though I don't know——"

He was standing right in front of me, a man of medium height, narrow-shouldered, a bit stooping. His long nose with its slightly distended nostrils seemed to sniff. "What is it you don't know, Your Highness?"

"What you've really come for. Did you want to tell me that you are putting my husband under observation? I can't prevent you from doing that and it is a matter of complete indifference to me, but—why did you tell me?"

" Can't you guess, my dear Princess?"

An idea occurred to me which at once made me choke with rage. But I collected my wits and said very emphatically and clearly: " If you, Monsieur Fouché, thought that I would help you to spy on my husband, you are mistaken." I wanted to raise my hand with a grand gesture and shout ' Out with you ', only I am not very good at that kind of thing.

He said calmly: " If I had thought that, I should have been mistaken. Perhaps I did think it, perhaps I did not. I really do not know myself now."

' Why all this,' I asked myself, ' why? If the Emperor wants to banish us he'll banish us. If he wants to court-martial Jean-Baptiste he'll court-martial him. And if he wants reasons his Minister of Police will supply them for him. After all, France is no longer a country where justice is done. . . .'

" Most ladies owe money to their dressmaker," he said in an undertone.

" Monsieur, you have gone too far now."

" Our beloved Empress, for example. She is always in debt to Le Roy. Naturally I am at Her Majesty's service whenever she wishes."

What did he mean? What was he hinting at? That he pays the Empress? For spying? ' But that's crazy,' I thought. And yet I knew instantly that it was true.

" Sometimes it is quite entertaining to control the correspondence of a man. One experiences surprises, surprises which are, shall we say, of less interest to me than to the man's wife."

" Don't trouble," I said, disgusted. " You will find that Jean-Baptiste has been writing to Madame Récamier for years and that he receives tender letters from her. Madame Récamier is a very intelligent and cultured woman, and it is a great pleasure for a man like my Jean-Baptiste to correspond with her. And now you really must excuse me, I shall have to get his room in order," I added, thinking that, all the same, I would give a lot if I could really have a look at those clever love letters from Jean-Baptiste to Madame Récamier.

" One moment, please, my dear Princess. Would you kindly give the Prince a message from me?"

" Yes. What is it?"

" The Emperor is at Schönbrunn Castle in Vienna. It is therefore impossible for me to get news through to him in time about the massing of English troops intended for landing at

Dunkirk and Antwerp. My information is that they will march straight from the Channel coast to Paris. Therefore, on my own responsibility and for the safety of the country I shall call up the National Guard. I am asking Marshal Bernadotte to take over the command of these troops for the defence of France immediately on his arrival. That, Madame, is all."

I was stunned. I tried to visualise it all: invasion by the British, attack by the British, march on Paris by the British. All the Marshals were away with the armies abroad. We had hardly any troops in the country, and at that very moment Britain attacked France.

Fouché was playing with the bonbon dish again.

" The Emperor mistrusts him," I said, " and you—you want to give him the command of the National Guard to defend our frontiers?"

" I myself am no commander of troops, Princess. I used to be only a teacher of mathematics, not a—sergeant. Heaven sends me a Marshal to Paris, so I say thank Heaven for the Marshal! Will you give my message to the Prince?"

I nodded and accompanied him to the door. Then I thought of something. Perhaps it was all a trap? This Fouché was such a cunning man.

" But I don't know," I said, " if my husband will really take on the command if His Majesty does not know anything about it."

Fouché was standing quite close to me. " You may rest assured, Madame, if it is a question of defending the frontiers of France Marshal Bernadotte will take on the command." And, after a moment he added, almost inaudibly: " As long as he is still Marshal of France."

He kissed my hand and left.

The very same evening Jean-Baptiste arrived, accompanied only by Fernand. He had left even his personal adjutants behind.

Two days later he set out again. For the Channel coast.

Villa La Grange near PARIS.
Autumn 1809.

I have not enough time now to write anything in my diary. I have to be round Jean-Baptiste all day long now to try and cheer him up.

Fouché had not exaggerated the danger on that day in July.

The British really did land on the Channel coast and took Vlissingen. Within a few days Jean-Baptiste achieved the miracle of fortifying Antwerp and Dunkirk so strongly that not only were all British attacks thrown back but many prisoners and an enormous booty were captured from them. The British managed to reach their ships near Dunkirk by the skin of their teeth, and fled.

These events agitated the Emperor at Schönbrunn dreadfully. In his absence a minister had dared to call up the National Guard and appoint as Commander-in-Chief precisely the one Marshal whom he, the Emperor, had put under police supervision. Publicly Napoleon could not but acknowledge that Fouché with the help of Jean-Baptiste had saved France. Without the mobilisation of the National Guard and the energy of a Marshal who turned untrained peasants whose hands hadn't held a rifle for more than ten years into an army, France would have been lost. He made Fouché Duke of Otranto.

Duke of Otranto, as romantic a name as Ponte Corvo! Fouché knows his duchy as little as I our Italian principality. The Emperor himself designed Fouché's arms, a golden pillar round which a serpent is twisted.

The golden pillar caused general amusement. The former president of the Jacobin Club, who used to confiscate fortunes indiscriminately by classing their owners as anti-Republican, is now one of the richest men in the country. One of his best friends is Ouvrard, the former lover of Theresa Tallien, arms contractor and, at the same time, banker who carries out Fouché's deals on the Stock Exchange. Nobody, however, talks about the serpent round the pillar, though everybody seems to interpret it in one way only: Napoleon is indebted to his Minister of Police and uses the opportunity to tell him what he thinks of him. . . .

Everybody expected the Emperor to confer a distinction on Jean-Baptiste and entrust a new command to him. But he didn't even write him so much as a letter of thanks. When I spoke to Jean-Baptiste about it he said: "Why should he? I don't defend France for his sake."

We moved out from Paris to La Grange, where Jean-Baptiste had bought an attractive big house. As to the house in the Rue d'Anjou, Jean-Baptiste never felt at home in it. Although I had all the rooms beautifully decorated he found too many 'ghosts' lurking in all the corners.

"You agree, don't you, to my placing Moreau's bust in the

hall?" I asked him when he entered the house for the first time.

Jean-Baptiste looked at me: "You couldn't have found a better place for it. There it will tell every visitor at once that we do not forget whose house this used to be. Strange, my little girl, how you always guess my unspoken thoughts."

"Why strange? I love you," I said.

I enjoyed every day of Jean-Baptiste's disgrace, which made it possible for us to live quietly in the country. Julie kept me informed about events in the Imperial family. She and Joseph came back to Paris. The Emperor had sent Junot's army to Spain to enable Joseph to enter Madrid at last. But Junot's army was almost annihilated by the Spanish patriots, who had the assistance of the British. According to Junot this defeat was due to no one but Joseph, because Joseph had insisted that he, as King of Spain, would take over the command himself, and had not listened to Junot. Imagine Joseph as a commander in the field! Of course, he only did it to prove to Napoleon that he could conduct campaigns as well as 'my little brother, the General'. I wondered whether Julie still had any illusions left about her Joseph.

If Napoleon's luck suddenly deserted him as it did that time in Marseilles, would they all desert him too? No, not all. Josephine would stand by him. And yet she is the one he wants to get rid of. He wants to divorce her, they say. I have been told that he intends to found a dynasty at last with the help of an Austrian Archduchess, a daughter of Emperor Francis. Poor Josephine, it is true she deceived him, but she would never leave him to his fate.

We had a very surprising visit yesterday. Count Talleyrand, the Prince of Benevento, called. It was a 'neighbourly' visit, said the Prince, laughing, because the Duchy of Benevento adjoins the principality of Ponte Corvo, and he was given it at the same time as we were given our present.

Talleyrand is, with Fouché, the most powerful man in the service of Napoleon, although he resigned his post as Minister of Foreign Affairs last year, after a row with Napoleon in which he warned him against new wars. But apparently Napoleon couldn't do without his diplomatic services. He appointed him 'Vice-Grand Elector' of the Empire and demanded that Talleyrand should continue to be consulted in all important foreign affairs. I've always liked this lame dignitary, a witty and charming man, who never talks about politics and wars to women, and I find it difficult to believe that he used to be a bishop. But he was, he was even the first bishop to take the oath to the Republic. That didn't help him much with Robespierre, though, because of his aristocratic descent, and he had to flee to America.

A few years ago Napoleon forced the Pope to absolve Talleyrand from his clerical vows. His intention in doing so was to force his Foreign Minister to marry and thus to stop him having so many mistresses. (Yes, Napoleon had become very virtuous, particularly where the ladies and gentlemen of his court were concerned.) But Talleyrand kept excusing himself, saying that he really couldn't get married and that he had to live in celibacy. In the long run, however, he couldn't escape and had to marry his last mistress. As soon as he had married her he was never seen with her in public again. . . .

Well, however that may be, this powerful man came to see us yesterday and asked: "How is it that I never see you in Paris now, my dear Prince?"

Jean-Baptiste answered politely: "That cannot have surprised you, Excellency, as you may perhaps have heard that I am on sick leave."

Talleyrand nodded gravely and inquired whether Jean-Baptiste wasn't feeling any better yet. As Jean-Baptiste goes out for a ride every day for hours and looks very bronzed, he had to admit that he was feeling a bit better.

"Have you had any interesting news from abroad lately?" asked Talleyrand. 'A stupid question,' I thought, 'because he knows very much better than everybody else what goes on abroad.'

"Ask Fouché," said Jean-Baptiste calmly. "He reads all the letters I get before I read them. Anyway, I have heard nothing of importance from abroad."

"Not even greetings from your Swedish friends?"

This question didn't strike me as anything out of the ordinary. Everybody knows that Jean-Baptiste had been very magnanimous in Lübeck towards some Swedish officers by sending them home instead of keeping them prisoners, and it is only natural that these people with unpronounceable names should sometimes write to him. Yet this question seemed to have a certain significance, for Jean-Baptiste looked up at Talleyrand and tried to catch his eye.

He nodded. "Oh yes, a few greetings. Did Fouché not show you the letter?"

"Monsieur Fouché has a very great sense of duty, and naturally he showed me the letter. But I should not call these greetings quite unimportant. Neither unimportant nor, as yet, important."

"The Swedes deposed their mad King in March and made his uncle, Charles the Thirteenth, their King," said Jean-Baptiste.

Here I pricked up my ears. "Really? This Gustavus who thought that he had been selected by Providence to defeat the Emperor has been deposed?"

They didn't answer me but continued to look into each other's eyes. The silence became oppressive to me. "Don't you think, Excellency," I said, to break this silence, "that this Gustavus is really mad?"

"It is difficult for me to judge from here," said Talleyrand, and smiled at me. "But I am convinced that his uncle is of the highest importance for the future of Sweden. This uncle is rather senile and ailing and has no children either, if I am not mistaken, Prince?"

"He has adopted a young relative and made him his successor, Prince Christian Augustus of Holstein-Sonderburg-Augustenburg."

"How well you pronounce these foreign names," said Talleyrand admiringly.

"I lived in Northern Germany long enough, one got used to these names there."

"You did not take an interest in the Swedish language, my friend?"

"No, Excellency, I had no cause to do that."

"You surprise me. A year ago, when you were in Denmark with your troops, the Emperor left it to your judgment whether to attack Sweden or not. I remember writing to you about it. But you confined yourself to looking from Denmark across to Sweden and did nothing. Why not? I have always wanted to ask you about it."

"You say yourself that the Emperor left it to me. He wanted to help the Tsar to take Finland. Our help was not needed. It was enough, as you remarked correctly, to look from Denmark across to Sweden."

"And the view? How did you like the view of Sweden, my friend?"

Jean-Baptiste shrugged his shoulders. "On clear nights one can see the lights of the Swedish coast from Denmark. But the nights were mostly foggy. I rarely saw the lights."

Talleyrand bent forward and tapped the golden knob of his walking cane, which he always carries with him on account of his lameness, gently against his chin. I couldn't understand what pleasure he got out of this conversation. " Are there many lights in Sweden, my friend?" he asked.

Jean-Baptiste put his head on one side and smiled. He, too, seemed to get a lot of pleasure out of this talk. "No, only a few. Sweden is a poor country, a great power of the day before yesterday."

" Perhaps also a great power of—to-morrow?"

Jean-Baptiste shook his head. "No, not politically, but perhaps in other ways. I don't know. Every nation has possibilities once it is ready to forget its great past."

Talleyrand smiled. " Every individual human being, too, has possibilities once he is ready to forget—his little past! We know examples, my dear Prince."

" It is easy for you to talk, Excellency. You are descended from a noble family and you had a good education. Everything was easier, far easier for you than for those to whom you allude."

The blow went home. Talleyrand's smile disappeared. Calmly he said : " I have deserved this reprimand, Prince. The former bishop apologises to the former sergeant." Was he waiting for a smile from Jean-Baptiste? Probably.

But Jean-Baptiste sat bent forward, his chin in his hands, and did not look up. At last he said: "I am tired, Your Excellency, I am tired of your questions, tired of the Police Minister's supervision, tired of distrust. I am tired, Prince of Benevento, very tired."

Talleyrand rose at once. " Then I shall hasten to put my request to you and go at once."

Jean-Baptiste, too, got to his feet. "A request? I can't imagine how a Marshal in disgrace could do a service to the Minister of Foreign Affairs."

" You see, my dear Ponte Corvo, it concerns Sweden. I heard yesterday that the Swedish Council of State have sent some gentlemen to Paris to negotiate about the resumption of diplomatic relations between our two countries, which resumption I take to be the main reason for their change of sovereign. These gentlemen—I don't know whether their names mean anything to you, a Monsieur von Essen and a Count Peyron— asked after you in Paris immediately on their arrival."

A deep frown appeared on Jean-Baptiste's forehead. " These names mean nothing to me. Nor do I know why they should have asked after me."

" The young officers who were your guests after the capture

of Lübeck talk a lot about you. You, my dear Ponte Corvo, are considered a friend of—hm—of the European North. And these gentlemen who have come as Swedish negotiators probably hope that you will put in a good word with the Emperor for their country."

"You can see how badly informed they are in Stockholm," said Jean-Baptiste.

"I should like to ask you to receive these gentlemen," said Talleyrand in an expressionless voice.

Jean-Baptiste's frown deepened. "Why? Could I be of any use to them with the Emperor? No. Or is it your intention to tell the Emperor that I meddle in foreign affairs which are no concern of mine? I should be very grateful to you, Excellency, if you could tell me in so many words exactly what it is you want."

"It is so simple. I should like you to receive these gentlemen and say a few kind words to them. What words you are going to use I leave entirely to you, of course. Is that asking too much?"

"I believe you don't know what you are asking," said Jean-Baptiste tonelessly. Never before had I heard him speak like that.

"I do not want the Swedes to get the impression that the Emperor has, let us say, temporarily dispensed with the services of one of his most famous Marshals. It would create the impression abroad of dissension within the circles close to the Emperor. You see, the reason for my request is a very simple one."

"Too simple. Far too simple for a diplomatist such as you. And far too complicated for a sergeant such as me." He shook his head. "I don't understand you, Excellency, really I don't." He put his hand heavily on Talleyrand's shoulder. "Are you going to tell me that a former bishop's sense of duty is not as great as that of a former teacher of mathematics?"

With a graceful movement of his cane Talleyrand pointed to his lame foot. "That is a lame comparison, Ponte Corvo. As lame as my foot. The question is, you see, to whom one feels one owes his duty."

At that Jean-Baptiste laughed, relieved, laughed far too loudly for a Prince, laughed as he must have laughed as a recruit in the Army. "Whatever you do, don't you say that you owe anything to me. I should never believe that."

"Of course not. Allow me to arrange my thoughts in a somewhat wider context. You know, we former bishops had no easy time during the Revolution, and I withdrew from this perilous period by going to America. My stay there taught me to think not in terms of individual countries but of continents. I feel a duty towards a continent generally, a duty to our continent, dear Ponte Corvo. To Europe in general. And, of course, to France in particular. Good-bye, my beautiful Princess, farewell, dear friend—it was a most stimulating conversation!"

Jean-Baptiste spent the whole afternoon riding. In the evening he did sums with Oscar and made the poor boy add and multiply till he nearly fell asleep over it and I tried to drag my tired son to bed. He has become far too big now to be carried to bed.

We did not mention Talleyrand's visit any more because of a dispute we had over Fernand just before we went to bed. Jean-Baptiste said:

" Fernand complains that you are too generous with your money. Every moment you put a franc or two in his hand."

" But you told me yourself that we are rich now and that I needn't economise any more. And if I wanted to please Fernand, this old school friend of yours, this most loyal of all loyal servants, there was no need for him to complain to you behind my back and say that I am too open-handed."

" Stop your tipping! Fernand gets a monthly salary from Fouché now and earns more than he knows what to do with."

" What?" I was disconcerted. " Is Fernand stooping so low as to spy——"

" My little girl, Fouché offered to pay him for spying on me, and he accepted because he thought that it would be a pity to forgo all that nice money. But, immediately after, he came to me and told me how much Fouché was paying him and suggested that I should deduct it from his salary. Fernand is the most decent fellow under the sun."

" And what does he tell the Minister of Police about you?"

" Oh, there is something to tell every day. To-day, for instance, I did sums with Oscar, which ought to be very interesting to the former teacher of mathematics. Yesterday——"

" Yesterday you wrote to Madame Récamier, and that annoys me very much," I broke in. Now we had reached a familiar subject, and we forgot all about Talleyrand.

It was terrible, it was terrible and embarrassing for all those who had to be present. The Emperor had ordered all the members of his family, of his Government, of his court and all his Marshals to attend, and in their presence he divorced Josephine.

For the first time after a long interval Jean-Baptiste and I had been requested to appear in the Tuileries. We were to be there at eleven o'clock in the morning. But I was still in bed at half-past ten. I had decided that whatever happened I wasn't going to get up. The day was cold and grey, and I closed my eyes.

" Whatever does this mean? You are still in bed?" said Jean-Baptiste.

I opened my eyes and saw Jean-Baptiste in his gala uniform covered with gold braid and medals.

" I've got a cold. Please excuse me to the Lord Chamberlain," I said.

" Like that day before the coronation. You know the Emperor will send you his physician. Get up at once and get ready. Otherwise we shall be late."

" I don't think that this time the Emperor will send me his physician," I said calmly. " It might happen, might it not, that Josephine at the moment when she reads out her consent to the divorce looks round and catches sight of me. I expect that the Emperor wants to spare her that." I looked imploringly at Jean-Baptiste. " Don't you understand me? I just couldn't bear this ugly, this awful triumph."

Jean-Baptiste nodded. " Stay in bed, my girl. You have got a very bad cold. And take it easy."

He left and I closed my eyes once more. When the clock struck eleven I pulled the blanket right up to my chin. ' I too am getting older,' I thought, ' I too shall have wrinkles round my eyes and no longer be able to bear children. . . .' In spite of my eiderdown I suddenly felt chilly. I called Marie and asked her for some hot milk. After all, hadn't I got a cold?

She brought the milk, sat down on my bed and held my hand. Before the clock struck twelve Jean-Baptiste returned and brought Julie with him.

Jean-Baptiste undid his high embroidered collar and said: " That was the most embarrassing scene I have ever witnessed. The Emperor asks a bit too much of his Marshals." With that he left my bedroom. Marie left with him on account of Julie, whom she still has not forgiven although Julie is now a Queen without a country. How so? Because the Spaniards finally drove Joseph away. But no one in Paris may say so.

Julie started talking at once. " We all had to take our places in the Throne Room, each according to his rank. We, I mean the Imperial family, stood quite close to the throne. Then the Emperor and the Empress entered at the same time, behind them the Lord Chamberlain and Count Regnaud. Count Regnaud kept close to the Empress, who was in white, as always. And powdered pale, you know. To look the martyr ! "

" Julie, don't be so nasty about her. It must have been frightful for her."

" Of course it was frightful for her. But I've never liked her, I've never forgiven her for what she did to you at that time—— "

" She didn't know anything about me then, and it wasn't her fault," I said. " What happened then? "

" There was a deathly silence. The Emperor started to read out a document, something about only God knowing how difficult a step this was for him and no sacrifice being too great for him where the well-being of France was concerned. There was also something in it about Josephine having been the sunshine of his life, of his having crowned her with his own hands and of Josephine's right to the title of Empress of France for the rest of her life."

" What did he look like when he read that? "

" You know what he looks like now on all public occasions : stony. Talleyrand calls it his mask of Cæsar. He put his mask of Cæsar on and read so fast that one had difficulty in following him. He wanted to get it over as quickly as possible."

" And then? "

" Yes, then it all turned so terribly embarrassing. The Empress was given her document and she began to read out. At first her voice was so quiet that I couldn't understand a word. Then, all of a sudden, she broke into tears and passed the paper to Regnaud, who had to read on for her. It was a dreadful sight."

" What did it say in her document? "

" That she herewith stated, with the permission of her beloved husband, that she was no longer able to have children. And therefore the well-being of France demanded of her the greatest sacrifice ever to have been asked of a woman. And she thanked the Emperor for his kindness and was firmly convinced that this divorce was necessary so that a direct descendant of the Emperor could reign over France in years to come. But not even the dissolution of her marriage could alter her feelings in any way. . . . All this Regnaud droned out as if it were some regulation, whilst the Empress kept sobbing most pitifully all the time."

" And then?"

" Then we, the members of the family, went to the Emperor's big study, where Napoleon and Josephine signed the document of divorce, and we signed after them as witnesses. Hortense and Eugene took their weeping mother away and Jerome said, ' I am hungry,' which earned him a vicious look from Napoleon. The Emperor turned away, saying ' I believe there will be a bite for the family in the Great Hall. Please excuse me,' and left. Everybody rushed to the buffet, and then I saw Jean-Baptiste ready to leave. I asked after you and he said you were ill and so I have come along with him." She paused for a moment.

" Your crown isn't straight, Julie!" As at all official functions, she was wearing a diadem shaped like a crown, and as always it wasn't straight.

She sat down at my dressing-table to put it right, powdered her nose and continued her chatting: " She's leaving the Tuileries to-morrow to go to Malmaison, which the Emperor has given her. He has also paid all her debts, and she is going to have an annuity of three million francs, two million from the Exchequer and one from the Emperor. On top of that the Emperor has given her another 200,000 francs for the plants she had bought for Malmaison and 400,000 francs for the ruby necklace which a jeweller is making for her."

" And Hortense and Eugene, what's going to happen to them?"

" Hortense will stay on in the Tuileries, and Eugene remains Viceroy of Italy. After all, Napoleon adopted them, didn't he? Imagine that Hortense still thinks her eldest son will be heir to the throne! She must be crazy! The Princess whom Napoleon is going to marry is a Hapsburg and that means that there will be plenty of offspring." She got up. " I must be off."

" Where?"

" Back to the Tuileries. The Bonapartes will be annoyed with me if I don't take part in their celebration. Good-bye, Désirée, get better soon."

After she had gone I lay for a long time with eyes closed. ' Julie's got used to the Bonapartes and their crowns,' I thought, ' she's changed, oh how she has changed! Wasn't it my fault?

I brought the Bonapartes to our father's simple, clean and unpretentious middle-class house. But I never intended all this, Father, I didn't. . . .

I had to stay in bed all day, and fell asleep early in the evening. But I woke up with a start in the middle of the night to find Marie and Madame La Flotte by the side of my bed. " Queen Hortense asks you to see her."

" Now? What is the time?"

" Two o'clock in the morning."

" What does she want? Didn't you tell her I was ill, Madame La Flotte?"

Madame La Flotte's voice squeaked with excitement. " Of course I did. But she won't go. She wants to see you all the same."

" Hush, don't shout," I said, and rubbed the sleep from my eyes, " you're waking the whole house."

" The Queen of Holland is very agitated and is crying," said Madame La Flotte. I noticed that she wore an expensive dressing-gown with ermine trimmings on the sleeves and it struck me that Fouché was probably paying her dressmaker's bills.

" Marie," I said, " give the Queen of Holland a cup of hot chocolate, that'll soothe her. And you, Madame La Flotte, tell her that I am not well enough to receive her."

" Yvette is making the chocolate for the Queen at this moment," said Marie, " and you are getting up now. I've told the Queen that you'll see her at once. Come, I'll help you. Don't keep her waiting, she's—crying!"

" Tell Her Majesty I shall be with her in a few moments," I said to La Flotte.

Marie brought me a plain dress. " Better dress properly," she said. " She'll ask you to go along with her."

" Where?"

" Get dressed. I think you'll be needed in the Tuileries."

" Princess," said Hortense, sobbing when I went out to her, " my mother has sent me. She asks you to come to her at once, for pity's sake." Tears were streaming down her face, her nose was red and some of her mousy hair fell over her forehead.

" But I can't do anything for your mother," I said, and sat down by her side.

" That's what I said to Mama. But she insisted that I should ask you."

" Why me?"

" I don't know why. But it's you she wants."

" And now, in the middle of the night? "

Hortense groaned. " The Empress can't sleep anyway. And she won't see anybody but you."

" I suppose I'd better go with you, Madame," I said, and sighed. Marie, standing by the door, had everything ready, hat, coat and muff.

The rooms of the Empress were only dimly lit. But her bedroom was full of light. There were candelabra everywhere, in all the corners, on all the tables, on the mantelpiece, even on the floor. Trunks stood about, wide open and half-packed. Garments were lying on every inch of floor and over the furniture, hats, gloves, robes of state, underwear, in an impossible confusion. A jewellery box stood open, its contents disarranged, and under an arm-chair glittered a diadem of brilliants.

The Empress was alone. She was lying on her bed, her arms stretched wide, her slim back shaking with desperate sobs as she cried wildly into the pillow. From the adjoining room came subdued female voices. They were probably packing there. But Josephine was alone, quite alone.

" Mama, here is the Princess of Ponte Corvo," said Hortense.

Josephine did not move. She went on crying even more desperately.

" Mama," said Hortense again, " the Princess of Ponte Corvo."

I decided to act and went up to her bed, took her by her shoulders and turned her round. Now she was lying on her back and staring at me out of her swollen eyes. I took fright. ' She is an old woman,' I thought, ' she has become an old woman in this one night.'

" Désirée," she said painfully. Then the tears started flowing again. I sat down and took her hands, and at once her fingers closed round mine.

I saw her now at close quarters, without any make-up, and the many candles revealed mercilessly the ravages wrought by time and the destruction brought on by the last twenty-four hours. ' Has Napoleon ever seen her without make-up?' I wondered.

Josephine spoke. " I have tried to pack," she said through her tears.

" Above all, Your Majesty must get some sleep," I said. I turned to Hortense: " Do put out all those candles, Madame!"

Hortense obeyed. Like a shadow she glided from candelabrum to candelabrum till only one tiny night-light remained.

Josephine's tears had dried up at last. In their place came

short hard sobs which shook her whole body and seemed to be worse than tears.

"Your Majesty must sleep now," I repeated, and tried to rise. But her fingers would not let me go.

"You must stay with me to-night, Désirée," said her trembling voice. "You know how he loves me. He loves me, better than anybody else in the world. You know that, don't you? Don't you? Better than anybody else——"

So that's why she wanted to see me to-night. Because I knew how much he loved her! If only I could help her!

"Yes, Madame, he loves you, only you. When he met you, he forgot everything and everybody else. Me, for instance. You remember, Madame?"

An amused smile flitted round her mouth. "You threw a glass of champagne at me. They couldn't get the stains out of my frock afterwards. . . . I made you so unhappy then, little Désirée. Forgive me, I didn't mean to."

I stroked her head and let her go on talking about the past. How old had she been then? About as old as I was now.

"Mama, you will be all right at Malmaison. You always looked upon it as your real home, didn't you?"

Josephine started, torn from her reminiscences into the present. "Hortense is staying on in the Tuileries," she said, trying to catch my eyes. The smile had gone, she looked aged and tired once more. "She is still hoping that Bonaparte will make one of her sons his successor. I should never have allowed her marriage to his brother. She has had so little out of life, a husband whom she hates and a stepfather whom she——"

—whom she loves, Josephine had wanted to say. But before she could say it Hortense rushed up to the bed. Did she want to hit her mother? I held her back. At that she began to sob helplessly.

'We can't go on like this,' I thought; 'now Hortense is having hysterics and will set the Empress off again at any moment.' "Get up, Hortense, and pull yourself together," I said. Who was I to give orders to the Queen of Holland? All the same, the Queen of Holland obeyed at once. "Your mother needs rest now, and so do you. When is Her Majesty going to Malmaison?"

"Bonaparte wishes me to leave to-morrow morning," whispered Josephine. "He's already ordered the workmen to get my rooms in——"

The rest of the sentence was drowned in renewed floods of tears. I turned to Hortense.

" Did Dr. Corvisart not leave any sleeping draught for Her Majesty?"

" He did. But Mama will not take it. She thinks they want to poison her."

I looked at the crying Josephine. " He has known all along," she stammered, " all along that I could not have any more children. I told him once because I expected one and Barras ——" She broke off and then, suddenly, screamed: " And this bungler, this blunderer, this oaf to whom I was dragged by Barras ruined me completely, ruined me, ruined me!"

" Hortense, ask one of the ladies-in-waiting to bring a cup of hot tea, and then go and rest. I shall stay here till Her Majesty is asleep. Where is the sleeping draught?"

Hortense found a small bottle among the heap of bottles, flagons and tins on the dressing-table, and handed it to me. " Five drops, Dr. Corvisart said."

" Thank you. Good night, Madame."

I undressed Josephine and put her to bed. When the tea came I emptied the whole contents of the little bottle into the cup, six drops. ' So much the better,' I thought.

Jossephine sat up obediently and hastily drank the tea. " It tastes like everything in my life," she said, and smiled, bringing back in that smile a likeness of the former Josephine, " it tastes very sweet with a bitter after-taste."

She dropped back on the pillows. " You were not at the— at the ceremony this morning," she said in a tired voice.

" No, I thought you'd prefer it."

" I did." There was a little pause. I heard her breathe more regularly now. " You and Lucien were the only Bonapartes not present."

" But I am not a Bonaparte at all," I said. " My sister Julie is married to a Bonaparte, and that is as far as the relationship goes."

" Don't leave him, Désirée."

" Whom?"

" Bonaparte."

The draught seemed to have set her mind adrift and soothed her at the same time. I stroked her hand evenly and without much thought, a hand with prominent veins, the hand of a frail, ageing woman.

" When he loses his power," she went on, "—and why should he not? All men I have known lost their power and some even their head like the late Beauharnais. When he loses his power——" Her lids fell and I let go of her hand. "Stay with me. I am afraid."

"I shall go and sit down in the next room and wait till Your Majesty has had a good night's rest. Then I shall accompany you to Malmaison," I said.

"Yes, to Malmai——" she said and fell asleep.

I put out the candle and went into the other room, which was in complete darkness. I felt my way to the window, drew the curtains aside and looked into a grey, gloomy winter dawn. Near the window I found a deep arm-chair. I took off my shoes and settled myself in the chair with my legs tucked under my body. My head ached furiously and I was tired. Utter silence reigned everywhere.

Suddenly I started. Someone had come into the room and the flicker of a candle moved along the walls towards the fireplace. I heard the subdued clanking of spurs.

I craned my neck round to try to look over the high back of the chair towards the fireplace. Who dared to enter without knocking the lounge adjoining the bedroom of the Empress?

Who? He, of course.

He was standing in front of the fireplace gazing attentively round the room. I made an instinctive movement. At once he turned his face towards the chair. "Is anybody here?"

"It is only I, Sire."

"Who is 'I'?" His voice sounded furious.

"The Princess of Ponte Corvo," I said, and tried to get my legs from under me to sit up properly and put on my shoes. But my feet had got numb and were full of pins and needles.

"The Princess of Ponte Corvo?" Incredulous, he came over to me.

"I am sorry, Your Majesty, my feet are numb and I can't find my shoes. One moment, please," I stammered. At last I found my shoes, got up and made my formal curtsey.

"Tell me, Princess, what are you doing here at this time of night?"

"That's what I'm asking myself, Sire," I said, rubbing my eyes. He took my hand. "Her Majesty has asked me to keep her company to-night. She is sleeping, at last." He said nothing, and as I had the feeling that he was annoyed I added: "I should like to withdraw so as not to disturb Your Majesty. But I don't know where one can withdraw to from this room, and I don't want to wake the Empress."

"You don't disturb me, Eugenie. Keep your seat."

Meanwhile the morning had grown lighter. I sat down again, desperately fighting my tiredness.

"I could not sleep," he said abruptly. "I wanted to say good-bye to this place. The workmen are coming to-morrow, no, this morning."

I nodded. But I found it embarrassing to have to be present at this leave-taking.

"See here, Eugenie. That is she. Do you not think that she is beautiful?"

He held a snuff-box out to me, which had a portrait painted on its lid. Before I could look at it he went across to the mantelpiece, fetched a candlestick and held the box against its light. It showed a round girlish face with blue eyes and very pink cheeks. The whole face gave an impression of pinkness.

"It's so difficult for me to judge from these snuff-box miniatures," I said. "They all look alike to me."

"I am told that Marie-Louise of Austria is very beautiful." He opened the box, took snuff and pressed his handkerchief against his face, a very elegant and well-trained way of taking snuff.

He put portrait and handkerchief away and looked at me penetratingly. "I still don't understand how you got here, Princess."

As he gave no sign of sitting down I wanted to get up again. He pushed me back into the chair. "You must be dead-tired, Eugenie. I can tell by your face. Tell me, what are you doing here at all?"

"The Empress wanted to see me. I remind Her Majesty——" I swallowed, it was such a difficult thing to say—"I remind Her Majesty of the afternoon when she got engaged to General Bonaparte. It was a very happy time in the life of Her Majesty."

He nodded. Then, without more ado, he sat on the arm of my chair. "Yes, it was a very happy time in the life of Her Majesty. And in yours, Princess?"

"I was very unhappy, Sire. But it is so long ago and the wound is no longer there," I said in a low voice. I was so tired and so cold that I forgot who was sitting next to me. Only when my head dropped sideways and on to his arm did I realise what had happened and was overcome with fright. "Do excuse me, Your Majesty."

"Leave your head where it is. I shall not be quite so alone then." He tried to put his arms around my shoulders and to pull me towards him. But I made myself stiff and leaned my head against the back of the chair.

" I was very happy in this room, Eugenie."

I didn't move.

" The Hapsburgs are one of the oldest dynasties in the world, do you know that?" he said without any preliminaries. "An Archduchess of Austria is worthy of the Emperor of the French."

I sat up, trying to see his face. Did he really mean that? A Hapsburg Princess just about good enough for the son of the Corsican lawyer Buonaparte?

He stared in front of him and then, unexpectedly, shot a question at me: " Can you dance the waltz?"

I nodded.

" Can you show me how to do it? They told me in Vienna that all the Austrian girls dance it. But at that time in Schönbrunn I had no time for it. Show me how to dance it."

I shook my head. " Not now, not here."

His face became distorted and he shouted: " Now! And here!"

I pointed to the door to Josephine's bedroom. " Sire, you will wake her up."

He only lowered his voice. " Show it me! At once. This is an order, Princess."

I got to my feet. " It is difficult without music," I said. Then I started turning slowly, counting " One two three and one two three, that's how you dance the waltz, Your Majesty."

But he didn't look at me at all. He was still sitting on the arm of my chair staring into space.

I raised my voice a bit. " And one two three and one two three."

He looked up now. The grey morning light made his face heavy and bloated. " I was so happy with her, Eugenie."

I stopped dead and looked at him, not knowing what to do. At last I brought out: " Is it—necessary, Your Majesty?"

" I can't wage a three-front war. There are revolts in the south, there is the Channel coast, and Austria——" He chewed his lower lip. " Austria will leave me in peace once the Austrian Emperor's daughter is my wife. My friend, the Tsar of Russia, is arming, my dear Princess, and I shall only manage to cope with my friend, the Tsar of Russia, if Austria keeps out for good." He pulled out the snuff-box and regarded the portrait once more. " She will be my hostage, my sweet young hostage."

He got up with a jerk and looked round the room very intently. "That is what it was like here," he murmured as if he wanted to commit to memory once and for all the details of the room. When he turned towards the door I curtsied deeply. With an abrupt movement he put his hand on my hair and stroked it absent-mindedly. "Can I do anything for you, my dear Princess?"

"Yes, if Your Majesty would be kind enough to send me some breakfast. Strong coffee, if possible."

He laughed out loud, a young, carefree laugh, and left the room.

At nine o'clock in the morning I accompanied the Empress out of the Tuileries through a back door. There her carriage was waiting for us.

She wore one of the three priceless sable coats which the Russian Tsar had given the Emperor as a present when they met in Erfurt. The second he had put round Polette's shoulders. What happened to the third nobody knows. Josephine was made up very carefully, her face looked almost as sweet as ever, betraying only the slightest signs of age.

Hortense was waiting for us in the carriage. "I had hoped," said Josephine in a low voice, "that Bonaparte would come to say good-bye to me." She bent forward to see the rows of windows in the Tuileries. There were curious faces behind every one of them. The carriage moved off.

"The Emperor rode to Versailles early this morning," said Hortense. "He intends to spend a few days with his mother."

Not another word was spoken during the whole of the journey to Malmaison.

PARIS.
The end of June 1810.

She really looks like a sausage. Our new Empress, I mean.

The wedding festivities are over, and it is said that the Emperor spent about five million francs in furnishing Marie-Louise's room in the Tuileries.

It began in March when Marshal Berthier was sent to Vienna to ask formally for the hand of the Emperor's daughter. The wedding took place there by proxy. Afterwards Caroline was sent to the frontier to receive the Emperor's wife. On the way to Paris, near Courcelles, two disguised men on horseback stopped the coach and forced themselves inside. It was the Emperor and Murat. They broke the journey at Compiègne Castle, and next morning Napoleon had his breakfast by Marie-Louise's bedside. They had had their wedding night before Uncle Fesch repeated the wedding ceremony in Paris.

During the first few months the Empress was not allowed to hold receptions on any scale. For some reason or other Napoleon imagined that women conceived more easily if they don't overtax their strength. But at last he could delay it no longer, and yesterday all of us, Marshals, Generals, Ambassadors, Princes and dignitaries of all kinds, were asked to the Tuileries to be presented to the new Empress.

It was exactly as it had been once before. The great ballroom, the lights, the brilliant robes and uniforms, the Marseillaise, the opening of the great doors, the appearance of the Emperor and the Empress: it was a precise repetition of the coronation ball. Marie-Louise, dressed in pink satin and scented with jasmine, was far taller than the Emperor and had a full bosom in spite of her youth. She kept on smiling the entire evening. As she was the daughter of a real Emperor, who had been trained to smile graciously at two thousand people at once, it didn't seem to be any strain on her at all. When I was presented to her I noticed that she wore hardly any make-up, which gave her an air of great naturalness compared with all those highly artificial creatures at her court. Her pale blue eyes looked as if they were made of china, and they had no expression at all.

The Imperial couple took their seats on their thrones and the orchestra played a Viennese waltz. Julie joined me at this point. She was dressed in purple velvet and the crown jewels of Spain glittered all over her. But again her crown wasn't straight.

" My feet hurt," she complained. " Come, let's go and sit in the next room."

At the entrance to that room we met Hortense, dressed in white as her mother used to be, and flirting with Count Flahault, her equerry. We sat down on a sofa and drank champagne.

" I wonder whether she remembers that her aunt used to live here in the Tuileries," I said, apropos of nothing.

Julie looked at me in surprise. " What are you talking about? At this Imperial court you will find no one who ever had an aunt living in the Tuileries."

" Oh yes, you will. The new Empress! She is the grand-niece of Queen Marie Antoinette."

"Queen Marie Antoinette!" repeated Julie, her eyes suddenly wide with fear.

"Yes, Julie Clary, she too was a Queen. Your health, darling, and forget about her." I drank, and remembered how many reasons Marie-Louise had for hating us. . . . "Tell me," I asked Julie, who had been with her several times already, "does the new Empress smile all the time?"

Julie nodded gravely. "All the time. And I shall bring up my daughters to do the same. It seems to be the right thing for Princesses."

I smelled the bitter-sweet scent of an exotic perfume around us and knew: Polette! Here she was, putting her arm around my shoulders.

"The Emperor thinks Marie-Louise is pregnant," she said, bursting with laughter.

"Since when?" Julie wanted to know, excited.

"Since yesterday!" said Polette, and passed on in her exotic aura.

Julie got up. "I must get back to the ballroom. The Emperor likes to have the members of his family near his throne."

I looked round for Jean-Baptiste, and saw him leaning against one of the windows glancing round at the crowd with utter indifference. I went up to him. "Can't we go home?" I said.

He nodded and took my arm. Turning to go we found our way barred by Talleyrand.

"I have been looking for you, Prince," he said. "These gentlemen have asked to be introduced to you." Behind him I saw some tall officers in foreign uniform, dark blue with yellow sashes. "This is Count Brahe, a member of the staff of the Swedish Embassy. Colonel Wrede, who, as the personal representative of the King of Sweden, has brought his sovereign's good wishes to the Emperor on his marriage. And Lieutenant Baron Charles Otto Mörner, who arrived this morning from Stockholm as a special courier with some very bad news. Baron Mörner, by the way, is a cousin of that Mörner whom you, my dear Prince, once took prisoner in Lübeck. You remember him, don't you?"

"We write to each other," said Jean-Baptiste calmly, and cast his eyes over the Swedes. "You are one of the leaders of the Union Party in Sweden, Colonel Wrede, are you not?"

The tall man bowed, whilst Talleyrand explained to me that the Union Party stood for the union of Sweden and Norway. Jean-Baptiste, meanwhile, smiled politely and, still holding my arm, turned his eyes on Mörner, a dark, thick-set man with short hair. This man looked very intently at Jean-Baptiste and said in fluent, somewhat harsh French:

"I have brought the news that the Swedish Heir to the Throne, His Royal Highness Prince Christian Augustus of Augustenburg, has lost his life in an accident."

Jean-Baptiste suddenly gripped my arm so hard that I very nearly screamed. It lasted only the tiniest fraction of a second. Then Jean-Baptiste said most calmly: "How dreadful! I should like to express to you, gentlemen, my deepest sympathy."

There was a pause, filled only by the tune of a waltz. 'Why don't we go?' I wondered. 'Surely all this is no concern of ours? What of it if the childless Swedish King has to find a new heir to his throne? Let's go,' I thought, 'let's go.'

"Has a successor to the deceased heir been designated?" asked Talleyrand casually, with polite interest. Just then I happened to look at Mörner, and it struck me as curious that he was still staring at Jean-Baptiste as if he wanted to convey something to him.

'For God's sake,' I thought, 'what do they want of my husband? He can't bring their dead Prince back to life, the accident can't possibly be of any interest to him. We have our hands full enough here in Paris, we have to be careful, we are in disgrace.'

But now I realised that this tall Colonel Wrede or something was staring at Jean-Baptiste in exactly the same way. At last Baron Mörner said:

"The Swedish Parliament will be convened for August 21st to decide the question of the succession to the Throne."

Another incomprehensible pause followed. Then I spoke up and said: "I am afraid, Jean-Baptiste, we shall have to say good-bye to these Swedish gentlemen." The officers understood and bowed.

"I ask you once again," said Jean-Baptiste, "to convey to His Majesty the King of Sweden my sympathy and add how greatly I share his and his people's sorrow."

"Is that all I am to tell him?" Mörner ejaculated.

Half turning to go, Jean-Baptiste once more let his eyes go from one Swedish face to another. They came to rest on young Count Brahe, who couldn't have been more than nineteen years of age. Jean-Baptiste said: "Count Brahe, you belong, I believe, to one of the oldest Swedish noble families. Therefore I ask you to remind your friends and your brother officers that I have not always been Prince of Ponte Corvo or Marshal of

France. I am what in your circles is called a former Jacobin General, and I began my career as a sergeant. In a word, I am—a *parvenu*. I should like you to remember that, so that you do not——" he took a deep breath and once more his fingers gripped my arm hard—"that you do not hold it against me later." And quickly he added: "Good-bye to you, gentlemen."

Strangely enough, we met Talleyrand once more before we left. His carriage was standing next to ours outside the Tuileries. We were just about to get into ours when I saw him limp towards us. "My dear Prince," he said to Jean-Baptiste, "man has been given the gift of language to conceal his thoughts. But you, my friend, use this gift in the opposite direction. No one could say of you that you concealed your thoughts towards the Swedes."

"Do I have to remind you, a former bishop, that it says in the Bible 'Let your speech be Yea yea, nay nay: and whatsoever is more than these is of the evil one'? That is how the Bible quotation runs, does it not, my Lord Bishop?"

Talleyrand bit his lips. "I had never realised that you could be witty, Prince," he murmured. "You surprise me."

Jean-Baptiste laughed heartily.

"Do not over-rate the modest jokes of a sergeant who is used to a bit of fun with his comrades round the camp fires!" He turned serious. "Did the Swedish officers tell you whom the Swedish royal house is going to propose as heir to the Throne?"

"The brother-in-law of the late heir, the King of Denmark, is going to be a candidate," Talleyrand answered.

Jean-Baptiste nodded. "Anybody else?"

"Yes, the dead man's younger brother, the Duke of Augustenburg. Besides these there is a son of the deposed King who now lives in Switzerland in exile. But as his father is considered insane the son is not held in very high esteem. Well, we shall see. The Parliament of Sweden is going to be convened and the Swedish people themselves can make their choice. Good night, dear friend."

"Good night, Excellency."

At home Jean-Baptiste went at once to his dressing-room and tore open his high, richly embroidered collar.

"I have been telling you for years," I said, "that you should have your collar let out. The Marshal's uniform is too tight for you."

"Too tight," he murmured, " my dear little stupid girl never realises what she is saying. Yes, far too tight." Without paying any further attention to me he went into his bedroom.

I am writing this now because I can't go to sleep. And I can't go to sleep because I am afraid of something, something that seems to loom over me, inescapably. I am very much afraid. . . .

PART III

NOTRE-DAME DE LA PAIX

PARIS.
September 1810.

A light shone straight into my face. "Get up at once, Désirée. Get up and dress quickly."

It was Jean-Baptiste holding a candelabrum over my bed and buttoning up the jacket of his Marshal's uniform.

"Are you mad, Jean-Baptiste? It's the middle of the night!"

"Hurry up. I told them to wake Oscar as well. I want the boy to be present."

I heard voices and steps on the ground floor. Yvette slipped into the room. She had hurriedly thrown a maid's uniform over her nightdress.

"Hurry up," said Jean-Baptiste impatiently, and to Yvette: "Do help the Princess, won't you?"

"For God's sake, has anything happened?" I asked in terror.

"Yes—and no. You will hear it all yourself. But do get dressed quickly."

"What am I to put on?" I asked in confusion.

"The most beautiful dress you have, the most elegant, the most precious, you understand?"

I was furious now. "No, I understand nothing at all. Yvette, bring me the yellow silk dress, the one I wore at court the other day. Jean-Baptiste, won't you tell me—"

But he had gone already. I did my hair with shaking hands.

"The diadem, Princess?" asked Yvette.

"Yes, the diadem. Bring me my jewellery box. I am going to put on everything I have. If I'm not told what's happened I can't know what to dress for. And to wake the child, in the middle of the night!"

"Désirée, are you ready?"

"If you don't tell me, Jean-Baptiste——"

"A spot of rouge on the lips, Princess," said Yvette. I saw my sleep-drenched face in the mirror. "Yes, Yvette, rouge and powder, quickly."

"Do come, Désirée, we cannot keep them waiting any longer!"

"Whom can't we keep waiting any longer? As far as I know it's the middle of the night. As far as I'm concerned I want to go back to bed."

Jean-Baptiste took my arm. "You must keep a grip on yourself now, little girl."

"What is the matter? Won't you kindly tell me what is happening?" I said furiously.

"The greatest moment of my life, Désirée."

I wanted to stop and stare at him, but he held me firmly by the arm and led me downstairs. Outside the door of the big reception-room Fernand and Marie pushed an excited Oscar towards us. His eyes shone with excitement.

"Papa, is it war? Papa, is the Emperor coming to see us? How beautifully Mama is dressed. . . ."

They had put the boy into his best suit and brushed his unruly curls close to his head. Jean-Baptiste took him by the hand.

The reception-room was brightly lit. All our candelabra had been collected and put here. Some gentlemen were waiting for us.

Jean-Baptiste took my arm again, and with the boy on one side and me on the other walked slowly towards the group of visitors.

They wore foreign uniforms embellished with blue-and-yellow sashes and glittering medals. One of them, a young man, however, was clad in a grimy tunic, his high boots were splashed all over with mud and his fair hair hung untidily down over his face. In his hand he was holding a very big sealed envelope.

They all bowed deeply as we entered, and there was a sudden silence. Then the young man with the sealed envelope stepped forward. He had the look of a man who had been riding for days and nights without interruption. Dark circles surrounded his eyes.

"Gustavus Frederik Mörner of the Uppland Dragoons, my prisoner of Lübeck," said Jean-Baptiste slowly, "I am glad to see you again. I am very glad."

So that was that man Mörner with whom Jean-Baptiste had talked one night about the future of the North. His trembling hands held out the envelope to Jean-Baptiste. "Your Royal Highness——" he said.

My heart stopped beating.

Jean-Baptiste released my arm and calmly accepted the letter.

"Your Royal Highness," the young man continued, "as Chief Chamberlain of His Majesty King Charles XIII of Sweden I beg to report that the Parliament of Sweden has unanimously elected the Prince of Ponte Corvo to be Heir to the Throne. His Majesty King Charles XIII wishes to adopt the Prince of Ponte Corvo and to welcome him in Sweden as his beloved son."

Gustavus Frederik Mörner swayed on his feet. An elderly man, his chest full of medals and stars, quickly put his hand under Mörner's arm. "I am sorry," Mörner said in a low voice, "I have not been out of the saddle for days." Then, louder: "May I introduce these gentlemen to Your Royal Highness?"

Jean-Baptiste nodded almost imperceptibly.

"Our Ambassador Extraordinary to France, Field-Marshal Count Hans Henrik von Essen."

The elderly man clicked his heels, his face was rigid.

Jean-Baptiste nodded again. "You were Governor-General in Pomerania, Field-Marshal. You defended it excellently against me at that time."

Mörner continued. "Colonel Wrede."

"We know each other." Jean-Baptiste's eyes fell on the sheet of paper which Wrede had suddenly produced.

"Count Brahe, a member of the staff of the Swedish Embassy in Paris." The young man whom I had met at the court ball bowed.

"Baron Friesendorff, adjutant to Field-Marshal Count von Essen."

Friesendorff smiled. "Another of your prisoners at Lübeck."

Mörner, Friesendorff and young Brahe gazed at Jean-Baptiste with a fervent glow in their eyes. Wrede waited with a deep frown on his brow, and the face of Field-Marshal von Essen bore no expression whatever; only his taut lips had an air of bitterness.

It was so still that we could hear the guttering of the candles.

Jean-Baptiste took a deep breath and said: "I accept the nomination of the Parliament of Sweden." He looked across at von Essen, the man whom he had once conquered, the ageing servant of an ageing childless King, and, deeply moved, he added: "I want to thank His Majesty King Charles XIII and the Swedish people for the trust they are placing in me. I vow to do everything in my power to justify this trust."

Count von Essen bent his head, bent it deeply and bowed, and all the other Swedes bowed with him.

At this moment something strange happened. Oscar, who

up till now had not moved at all, stepped forward and went over to the Swedes. There he turned round and his child's hand gripped the hand of young Brahe, who was not ten years his senior. There he stood, among the Swedes, and like the Swedes he bowed his head deeply, bowed it before his Papa and his Mama.

Jean-Baptiste felt for my hand. Protectively his fingers closed over mine. " The Crown Princess and I wish to thank you for bringing this message."

After that a lot of things happened simultaneously. Jean-Baptiste said: " Fernand, the bottles which have been in the cellar since Oscar's birth!" I turned round and my eyes searched for Marie. All our servants were standing by the door. Madame La Flotte in an expensive evening gown, no doubt paid for by Fouché, curtsied deeply, and so did my reader. Yvette was sobbing for all she was worth. Only Marie did not move at all. She was wearing her woollen dressing-gown over her old-fashioned linen nightdress. She had had to dress Oscar and therefore found no time to dress herself.

" Marie," I whispered, " did you hear? The Swedish people offer us their crown. It's different from Julie and Joseph. It is quite different. I am afraid, Marie, I'm afraid."

" Eugenie!" Marie's voice sounded hoarse, choked with emotion, a tear rolled down her cheek, and then Marie, my old Marie, sank into a curtsey before me.

Jean-Baptiste, meanwhile, was leaning against the mantelpiece studying the letter which Mörner had given him. That severe man, Field-Marshal Count von Essen, went up to him.

" Those are the conditions, Your Royal Highness," he said.

Jean-Baptiste looked up and said: " I presume that you yourself were informed of my selection only an hour ago. You have been in Paris during all this time. I am very sorry——"

Field-Marshal von Essen raised his brows: " Why are you sorry, Your Royal Highness?"

" That you had no time to get used to the idea. I am very sorry indeed. You defended with great loyalty and fortitude whatever policy the House of Vasa chose to adopt. That cannot always have been easy for you, Count von Essen."

" It was very difficult at times. The campaign which I had to conduct against you I lost, unfortunately."

" Together we shall rebuild the Swedish Army," said Jean-Baptiste.

" Before I forward the answer of the Prince of Ponte Corvo to Stockholm to-morrow morning," said the Field-Marshal in a tone which sounded almost menacing, " I should like to draw your attention to one point in this letter. It concerns your citizenship. It is a condition of the adoption that the Prince of Ponte Corvo becomes a Swedish citizen."

Jean-Baptiste smiled. " Did you think that I would assume the Swedish succession as a French citizen?"

An expression of incredulous surprise spread over the Count's face. But I thought I must have misheard him.

" To-morrow," Jean-Baptiste went on, " I shall address an application to the Emperor of France in which I shall ask him to allow me to renounce French citizenship for myself as well as for my family. Ah, here comes the wine. Fernand, open all the bottles!"

Triumphantly Fernand placed the dusty bottles on a table. These bottles had come with us all the way from Sceaux via the Rue du Rocher to the Rue d'Anjou.

" When I bought the wine," said Jean-Baptiste, " I was Minister of War. Oscar was born then and I told my wife ' We shall open these bottles the day the boy enters the French Army '."

" I shall be a musician, Monsieur," I heard Oscar's high-pitched voice. He was still holding young Brahe's hand. " But Mama wanted me to be a silk merchant like Grandfather Clary." Everybody laughed, even the tired Mörner. Only Count von Essen did not move an eyelid.

Fernand poured out the dark wine.

" Your Royal Highness is going to learn the first word of Swedish now," said Count Brahe. " It is ' Skål ' and means ' Your health '. I should like to drink to His Royal——"

Jean-Baptiste interrupted him. " Gentlemen, I ask you to drink with me to the health of His Majesty the King of Sweden, my gracious adoptive father!"

They drank slowly and solemnly. Someone shouted: " To the health of His Royal Highness, the Crown Prince Charles John!"

" Han skål leve, han skål leve." It sounded from all sides.

What did that mean? Could that possibly be Swedish? I was sitting on the little sofa next to the fireplace. ' They've woken me up,' I thought, ' in the middle of the night, they've told me that the Swedish King wants to adopt my husband so that he becomes Crown Prince of Sweden.' But I'd always thought that only small children could be adopted. ' Sweden, Sweden,' I mused, ' next-door to the North Pole, Stockholm, the town with the whitewashed sky. Persson will read it all in

301

the papers to-morrow and will never guess that the Princess of Ponte Corvo, the wife of the new Heir to the Throne, is the little Clary girl of his Marseilles days. . . .'

"Mama, these gentlemen say that my name is now Duke of Södermanland," said Oscar. His cheeks were red with excitement.

"Why Duke of Södermanland, darling?"

Young Baron Friesendorff explained eagerly that it was usual in Sweden for the brother of the Crown Prince to be known by this title. "But as in this case——" He broke off, blushing.

Jean-Baptiste calmly completed the sentence for him: "But as in this case the Crown Prince does not intend to take his brother along with him to Sweden his son will take this title. My brother lives in Pau. I do not want him to change his residence."

"I thought Your Royal Highness had no brother," said Count Brahe involuntarily.

"I have. I made it possible for him to study law so that he need not be a clerk in a lawyer's office for the rest of his life like my late father. So, gentlemen, my brother is a lawyer."

At the same moment Oscar asked: "Are you looking forward to Sweden, Mama?"

Deep silence fell. Everybody wanted to hear my answer. 'What can they expect me to say?' I thought. 'After all, I'm at home here, I'm French.' Then it came back to me what Jean-Baptiste had said about renouncing our French citizenship, it came back to me that I was now Crown Princess of a country which I had never seen, a country with a nobility as old as the hills, and not a new one like ours in France. I saw how they smiled at Oscar when he said that my father had been a silk merchant, all of them but the Count von Essen, who had felt nothing but shame. . . .

"Say it, Mama, that you are looking forward to it," urged Oscar.

"I don't know Sweden yet," I said, "but I shall do my best to enjoy it."

"The people of Sweden cannot ask more than that," Count von Essen said gravely.

His harsh French reminded me of Persson. I very much wanted to be friendly and so I said: "I have an acquaintance in Stockholm, a man called Persson, a silk merchant. Perhaps you know him, Field-Marshal?"

"I regret I do not, Your Royal Highness," came the brief answer.

"Perhaps you do, Baron Friesendorff?"

"I am very sorry, Your Highness."

I tried Count Brahe. "Perhaps you know a silk merchant Persson in Stockholm, by chance?"

Count Brahe smiled: "Really, I don't, Your Royal Highness."

"And you, Baron Mörner?"

Mörner, Jean-Baptiste's oldest friend in Sweden, wanted to be helpful. "There are many Perssons in Sweden, Your Royal Highness. It is a very common middle-class name."

Someone extinguished the candles and drew back the curtains. It was day and the sun glittered over Jean-Baptiste's uniform. "I do not want to sign any party manifesto, Colonel Wrede," he was saying, "not even that of the Union Party."

Mörner, still dusty and exhausted, standing by Wrede's side, put in: "But at that time in Lübeck Your Royal Highness said——"

"I said that Norway and Sweden form a geographical unit, and we shall do our best to bring about the union. But that is the concern of the Swedish Government, not just of one individual party. And, by the way, the Crown Prince must stand above all parties. Good night, gentlemen, or rather good morning."

I don't remember how I got up to my bedroom. Perhaps Jean-Baptiste carried me, or Marie with the help of Fernand.

Lying on my bed with eyes closed I felt Jean-Baptiste's presence. "You must not shout at your new subjects like that," I said.

"Try to say Charles John," he said.

"Why?"

"That is going to be my name. Charles, after my adoptive father, and John for Jean, of course." He played with the words. "Charles John, Charles XIV John. 'Carolus Johannes' it will be on the coins. Desideria, Crown Princess Desideria."

I sat up with a jerk. "That's going too far. I won't have myself called Desideria. Under no circumstances, you understand!"

"It is the wish of the Queen of Sweden, your adoptive mother-in-law. Désirée is too French for her. Besides Desideria sounds more impressive. You must admit that."

I fell back on the pillows. "D'you think I can do away with my own self? Can I forget who I am, what I am, where I belong? Can I go to Sweden and play at being a Crown Princess? Jean-Baptiste, I fear I'm going to be very unhappy."

But he wasn't listening, he was still playing with the new

names. "Crown Princess Desideria. Desideria is Latin and means the longed-for one. Is there a more fitting name for a Crown Princess whom a people itself has chosen?"

"No, Jean-Baptiste, the Swedes don't want me. They want a strong man, yes. But they certainly don't want a weak woman who, moreover, is the daughter of a silk merchant and whose only acquaintance is a Monsieur Persson."

Jean-Baptiste got up. "I am going to have a cold bath now, and then dictate my application to the Emperor."

I made no move.

"Pay attention, Désirée, please. I am applying on behalf of my wife, my son and myself for permission to relinquish French citizenship in order to acquire Swedish citizenship. You agree, don't you?"

I gave no answer and didn't look at him either.

"Désirée, I shall not apply if you object. Don't you hear me?"

Still I gave no answer.

"Désirée, don't you see what is at stake?"

At last I looked up at him, and I felt as if I saw him for the first time properly: the high forehead with the dark, curly hair fringing it, the bold nose jutting out, the deep-set eyes, at once inquiring and reassuring, the small yet passionate mouth. Then I remembered the leather-bound tomes in which the former sergeant studied law, and the Customs regulations in Hanover which revived that country's prosperity. . . . 'Napoleon picked a crown out of the gutter, but you, Jean-Baptiste,' I thought, 'were offered it by a whole people with the King at its head.' And as I thought it out I was filled with the miracle of it all.

"Yes, Jean-Baptiste, I know what is at stake."

"And you are coming to Sweden with Oscar and me?"

"If I am really Desideria, the longed-for one. And if you promise never to call me that?" At last I had found his hand and pressed my cheek against it. I loved him, my God, how I loved him!

"I promise I shall never call you Desideria."

"I'll come," I said.

I slept long and fitfully and woke with the feeling that something dreadful had happened. I looked at the clock on the bedside table. Two o'clock. Two o'clock in the morning or in the afternoon?

I heard Oscar's voice from the garden and a man's voice I

didn't recognise. Daylight filtered through the closed shutters. How did it come about that I had slept so late? Uncomfortably I felt that something had happened. But I couldn't think what.

I rang the bell. Madame La Flotte and my reader came in together and curtsied. " Your Royal Highness desires?"

Then I remembered and I felt unhappy, desperate.

" The Queen of Spain and the Queen of Holland have asked when Your Royal Highness can see them," said Madame La Flotte.

" Where is my husband?"

" His Royal Highness and the Swedish gentlemen are in conference in his study."

" With whom is Oscar playing in the garden?"

" He is playing ball with Count Brahe."

" Count Brahe?"

" The young Swedish count," said Madame La Flotte with an ecstatic smile on her face.

" Oscar has smashed a window-pane in the dining-room," my reader added, and Madame La Flotte commented, " That means good luck."

" I am awfully hungry," I said. My reader curtsied and left at once.

" What message can I give to Their Majesties of Holland and Spain?" asked La Flotte.

" I've got a headache, and I want to eat, and I don't want to see anybody but my sister. Tell the Queen of Holland that— oh well, invent something you can tell her. And now I'd like to be alone."

La Flotte curtsied and disappeared. '.This curtseying business is going to drive me mad,' I thought. ' I'm going to forbid it."

After the meal I got up. Yvette came in curtseying and I told her to get out. I put on my plainest gown and sat down at the dressing-table.

Desideria, Crown Princess of Sweden, I mused. Former silk merchant's daughter from Marseilles, wife of a former French General, everything I loved and was familiar with seemed to be ' former ' now. In two months' time I should be thirty-one years of age. Could people tell by my face? It was still smooth and round, too round even, I would have to eat less whipped cream. There were a few wrinkles round the eyes, barely visible, perhaps only caused by smiling. When I tested them by trying to laugh they deepened.

I had never known my mother-in-law. Mothers-in-law are

supposed to be a difficult problem. Would adoptive mothers-in-law be easier to deal with? I realised I didn't even know the Swedish Queen's name. And why, I wondered, why did the Swedes pick on Jean-Baptiste, of all men, for their Crown Prince?

I got up, opened the shutters and looked down into the garden.

"You are aiming at Mama's roses, Count," Oscar was shouting.

"You Highness must catch the ball. Look out, I am going to throw," shouted young Brahe. He threw hard and made Oscar sway as he caught the ball. But—he caught it!

"Do you think I could ever win battles like Papa?"

"Throw the ball back, hard!" commanded Brahe.

Oscar threw and Brahe caught it. "A good shot," he said, and as he threw the ball back once more it landed among my yellow roses, my big yellow fading roses which I love so much.

"Mama will be very annoyed," said Oscar, and looked up to my windows. He saw me. "Mama, did you sleep well?"

Count Brahe bowed.

"I should like to speak to you, Count Brahe. Can you spare me a minute? I shall come down into the garden."

I went down and sat between the young Count and Oscar on the small bench by the espalier fruit. The gentle September sunshine flowed gently over me, and I felt very much better now.

"Could you not talk to the Count later on, Mama? We have been playing so beautifully."

I shook my head. "I want you to listen carefully." I heard voices coming from the house, and Jean-Baptiste's among them sounded determined and loud.

"Field-Marshal Count von Essen and the members of his mission are going back to Sweden to-day to convey His Royal Highness's answer," said Count Brahe. "Mörner is staying here. His Royal Highness has appointed him his aide-de-camp. A special courier has gone on ahead to Stockholm."

I nodded whilst I searched hard in my mind for a suitable starting point for my questioning. I didn't find one and therefore said straight out: "Please tell me candidly, my dear Count, how it is that Sweden should offer the crown to my husband, of all men."

"His Majesty King Charles XIII has no children, and for years now we have admired the magnificent administration, the great abilities of His Royal Highness, and——"

I cut him short. "I am told that one King has been deposed because he was believed to be insane. Is he really insane?"

Count Brahe looked away towards the espalier peaches and said: "That is what we suppose."

"Why?"

"His father, King Gustavus III, before him had been rather—rather strange. He wanted to restore Sweden's old position as a great power, and attacked Russia. The aristocracy and all the officers were against it. And in order to show his noblemen that the King alone and no one else decides on peace or war he turned to the, well—to the lower classes and——"

"To whom?"

"To the business men, the craftsmen, the farmers."

"I see. What happened then?"

"Parliament, in which only the lower classes were represented at that time, conferred wide powers on him and the King marched once more against Russia. But the country was on the verge of bankruptcy and could not pay for this continuous arming. Therefore the nobility decided to take a hand and the King was murdered during a masked ball by some men in black masks. He died in the arms of his faithful von Essen. After his death our present King, his brother, took over the regency till the murdered King's young son, Gustavus IV, came of age. Unfortunately it soon became obvious that he was of unsound mind."

"This is the King who imagines himself to be God's chosen instrument for the destruction of the Emperor of the French, isn't it?"

Count Brahe nodded and continued to look towards the espalier peaches.

"Do go on with your murder story, Count Brahe," I said.

"Murder story?" He looked at me as if I had been joking. But I did not smile, and he hesitated to go on. I repeated my request and he continued.

"So we fought first against France, and when Russia and France came to terms, against Russia as well. You know what happened. We lost Finland to the Tsar and Pomerania to your husband—I am sorry, to His Royal Highness—and if the Prince of Ponte Corvo at that time when he was in Denmark with his troops had marched across the frozen Sound there would have been no Sweden left. Your Royal Highness, we are a very old nation, we are tired and bled white in wars, but we do want to —to go on living." He gnawed his lips, then went on. "That was why our officers decided to put an end to this mad policy.

So they imprisoned Gustavus IV in his castle in Stockholm, deposed him and crowned his uncle, the former Regent and now adoptive father of Your Royal Highnesses."

"And where is he now, this mad Gustavus?"

"In Switzerland, I believe."

"He has a son, hasn't he?"

"Yes, another Gustavus. He has been declared by Parliament incapable of succession."

"How old is he?"

"About as old as Oscar, Prince Oscar." Count Brahe got up absent-mindedly and picked a withered leaf from the espalier peaches.

"Come back and tell me what are the objections to this little Gustavus."

Count Brahe shrugged his shoulders. "Nothing in particular. But there is nothing in his favour either. Sweden is afraid of a diseased strain in the Vasa family. It is a very old family, Your Highness, with too much inbreeding."

"Has the present King always been childless?"

Brahe came to life again. "Charles XIII and Queen Hedvig Elizabeth Charlotte had a son, but he died many years ago. At his accession the King had to adopt a successor and he chose the Prince of Augustenburg, brother-in-law to the King of Denmark and Governor of Norway. He was very popular with the Norwegians, and we had hopes of a union between Sweden and Norway through him. After his fatal accident Parliament was convened and you know the result, Your Highness."

"I know the result, yes. But I don't know how it came about. Please tell me about that."

"Your Highness knows that the Prince—I mean His Royal Highness—at the time of the Pomerian campaign took some Swedish officers prisoner in Lübeck?"

"Of course I do. Aren't there two of them with Jean-Baptiste at this very moment? This dusty Mörner—I hope they've given him a bath meanwhile—and Baron Frie——"

"Yes, Mörner and Friesendorff. The Prince of Ponte Corvo invited these young officers, when they were his prisoners, to dinner, and during the course of the conversation told them, realistically with maps and figures, how he sees the future of Scandinavia. When our officers returned home they reported their conversation and ever since then it has been said more and more loudly in Army circles that we need a man like the Prince to save Sweden. And that, Your Highness, is all there is to it."

But it wasn't all. When I pressed him for details Count Brahe painted a frightening picture of cliques, intrigues and murder, of poverty and decay. Between the younger officers who were enthusiastic about Jean-Baptiste's ideas, and those represented by men like Count Fersen—at one time lover of Queen Marie Antoinette, whom he had tried unsuccessfully to get out of France with King Louis XVI and her family—a man abhorrent of anything the French Revolution and men like Jean-Baptiste stood for, there was a furious tug-of-war. It was complicated by the general economic deterioration of the country, and it ended on the day of the funeral of the Prince in the murder of Count Fersen of Augustenburg, by the mob outside the Royal Castle, with Army detachments passively looking on. After his disappearance the whole of Sweden agreed to the younger officers' choice of Jean-Baptiste as successor to the King, the aristocracy because they realised that a strong man was needed, the middle and lower classes because they thought that a man who was on good terms with Napoleon might manage to keep Sweden out of Napoleon's Continental Blockade and put trade and industry on their feet again. Besides, said Brahe, the traders and peasants disliked the Vasas because they were so poor that they could hardly pay their gardeners, and when they were told that the Prince of Ponte Corvo was rich their last hesitations vanished.

Murder, intrigue, poverty, and on top of that life in a castle inside which the nobility had murdered an unpopular count: no no, it was too much. 'No, Jean-Baptiste,' I thought, 'not that,' and covering my face with my hands I cried helplessly.

"Mama, dear Mama!" Oscar pressed his arms round my neck and clung to me.

I wiped away my tears and turned to see Brahe's grave face. Did this young man understand at all why I was weeping?

"Perhaps I should not have told you all that," he said, "but I thought, Your Highness, that it would be better if you knew."

"So the whole Swedish people chose my husband. And what about His Majesty the King?"

"The King, Your Highness, is a Vasa and a man of over sixty who has had several strokes already, is plagued by gout and not very lucid in his brain. He put up opposition to the very last, suggested one North German cousin after the other and all the Danish Princes. In the end he had to give in."

'So in the end he had to give in and adopt Jean-Baptiste as his beloved son,' I thought. "The Queen is younger than His Majesty, isn't she?"

" Her Majesty is slightly over fifty years of age now, a very energetic and intelligent woman."

" How she will hate me ! "

" Her Majesty is looking forward very much to seeing the little Duke of Södermanland," said Count Brahe, unperturbed.

At the door of the house Mörner appeared, freshly washed, beaming and wearing a gala uniform. Oscar ran up to him to admire the armorial insignia on the buttons on his uniform. " Look, Mama, look ! " he shouted.

Mörner paid no attention to Oscar but, noting the traces of tears on my face and the young count's gravity, looked thoughtfully from one to the other.

" Her Royal Highness wanted me to tell her about developments in Sweden and the history of our royal family during recent years," said Brahe, embarrassed.

" Are we now members of the Vasa family too ? " asked Oscar eagerly.

" Nonsense, Oscar, you stay what you are, a Bernadotte," I said sharply, and got up. " Did you want me, Baron Mörner ? "

" His Royal Highness asks Your Royal Highness to come to his study."

Jean-Baptiste's study was a strange sight. Next to his desk, where as usual documents were piled high, someone had placed the big mirror from my dressing-room. In front of it Jean-Baptiste was trying on a new uniform. Three tailors were kneeling around him, their mouths full of pins. Very attentively the Swedes followed the fitting manœuvres.

I glanced at the new dark blue tunic. Its high collar did not have the heavy gold braid of the Marshal's uniform, only a plain gold trimming. Jean-Baptiste examined himself very closely in the mirror. " It pinches," he said, as grave as a judge, " it pinches under the right arm."

The three tailors shot up in a bunch, undid the seam under the armpit and did it up again.

" Can you find a fault anywhere, Count von Essen ? " asked Jean-Baptiste.

Essen shook his head, but Friesendorff put his hand on Jean-Baptiste's shoulders—" Pardon me, Your Highness," he said—moved it along his back and then declared that there was a crease under the collar.

All the three tailors felt for the crease but could not spot it. Fernand finally settled the matter : " Sir, the uniform fits."

" Your sash, Count von Essen ! " And before the sour-looking

Count had realised what he wanted Jean-Baptiste had taken the Count's blue-and-yellow sash from him and tied it round himself. "You will have to go back to Sweden without your sash, Count. I need it for to-morrow's audience. There are none to be had in Paris. Send me three Swedish Marshal's sashes as soon as you arrive in Stockholm."

Only now he noticed my presence. "The Swedish uniform. Do you like it?"

I nodded.

"We are to go to the Emperor to-morrow morning at eleven o'clock. I asked for the audience, and I want you to accompany me. Essen, is the sash meant to be worn about the belt or to cover the belt?"

"To cover the belt, Your Royal Highness."

"Good. Then I need not borrow your belt as well. I shall wear the belt of my French Marshal's uniform. No one will notice it. Désirée, do you really think the uniform fits properly?"

At that moment Madame La Flotte announced Julie. Leaving the room I heard Jean-Baptiste say: "I shall also need a Swedish ceremonial sword."

Julie, standing by the window and gazing pensively down into the garden, looked sad and lost in the heavy folds of her purple velvet coat. "I am sorry, Julie, to have kept you waiting," I said.

Julie started. Then, stretching her neck forward and widening her eyes as if she had never seen me before, she made a solemn curtsey.

"Don't poke fun at me," I shouted furiously, "I've got enough to put up with as it is."

But Julie remained solemn: "Your Royal Highness, I am not poking fun at you."

"Get up, get up and don't annoy me. Since when does a Queen bow to a Crown Princess?"

Julie got up. "If it is a Queen without a country, whose subjects rose against her and her husband from the very first day onwards, and if it is a Crown Princess whose husband was unanimously elected by the representatives of their future subjects, then it is the right thing for that Queen to bow to that Crown Princess. I congratulate you, my dear, I congratulate you from my heart."

"But how did you get to know it all? We only learnt about it last night." I sat down with her on the little sofa.

"All Paris talks about nothing else. People like us were

simply placed by the Emperor on the thrones he had conquered, as his representatives, so to speak. But in Sweden Parliament meets and voluntarily—no, Désirée, it's beyond me." She laughed. "I had lunch in the Tuileries to-day. Napoleon talked about it a lot and chaffed me dreadfully."

"Chaffed you?"

"Yes. Imagine him wanting to make me believe that Jean-Baptiste would now ask to be discharged from the French Army and to become Swedish! Oh, how we laughed!"

I stared at her in amazement. "Laughed? What is there to laugh at? I could cry when I think of it."

"But, darling, for heaven's sake, it isn't true, is it?"

I said nothing.

"But none of us has ever heard of such a thing," she stammered. "Joseph is King of Spain, but he is a Frenchman all the same. And Louis is King of Holland, but he wouldn't thank you for calling him a Dutchman. And Jerome and Eliza and——"

"That is just the difference," I said. "You yourself pointed out a moment ago the great difference there was between your case and ours."

"Tell me, are you really going to settle in Sweden?"

"Jean-Baptiste says so. As far as I'm concerned it depends."

"Depends on what?"

"I shall go, of course. But, you know," I said, dropping my voice, "they want me to call myself Desideria. That's Latin and means 'The longed-for one', 'the wanted one'. I shall stay there only if they really want me in Stockholm."

"The nonsense you talk! Of course you're wanted."

"I am not so certain of that. The old aristocratic families and my new mother-in-law——"

"Don't be stupid. Mothers-in-law only hate you because you take their son from them," Julie argued, thinking probably of Madame Letitia. "But Jean-Baptiste is not the real son of the Swedish Queen. Besides, there is Persson in Stockholm. He won't have forgotten how good Mama and Papa were to him, and all you need do is to raise him to the peerage and then at once you have a friend at court."

"You have the wrong idea of it." I sighed, realising that Julie did not really understand what had happened.

And, to be sure, her thoughts were off on another tack once more. "Listen, something incredible has happened. The Empress is pregnant! What do you think of that! The Emperor is beside himself with joy. The son is going to be known as the King of Rome. Napoleon, you know, has no doubt whatever that it will be a boy."

"How long has the Empress been pregnant? For the last twenty-four hours again or what?"

"No, for the last three months, and——"

There came a knock on the door. Madame La Flotte announced that the Swedish gentlemen who were leaving for Stockholm to-night asked to be allowed to take their leave of Her Royal Highness.

"Show the gentlemen in."

I don't suppose any of them could tell by my face how afraid I was of the future. I shook hands with Field-Marshal Count von Essen, the most loyal subject of the House of Vasa, and he said: "We shall meet again in Stockholm, Your Highness."

Seeing Julie out to the hall I was amazed to meet young Brahe there. "Aren't you going back to Stockholm to-night?"

"I have asked to be appointed provisionally Your Royal Highness's gentleman-in-waiting. My request has been granted. I am reporting for duty, Your Royal Highness."

Tall, slim, nineteen years of age, dark eyes shining with enthusiasm, curly hair like my Oscar, that was Count Magnus Brahe, scion of one of the oldest and proudest families of Sweden, gentleman-in-waiting now to former Mademoiselle Clary, daughter of a silk merchant from Marseilles.

"I should like Your Royal Highness to grant me the honour of accompanying you to Stockholm." I dare them to look down their noses at our new Crown Princess with a Count Brahe by her side, was the thought written all over his face.

I smiled. "Thank you, Count Brahe. But, you see, I've never before had a gentleman-in-waiting, and I really don't know what I could give him to do."

"Your Royal Highness will think of something. And meanwhile I could play ball with Oscar—I am sorry, the Duke of Södermanland."

"Provided you don't smash any more windows!" I laughed. For the first time my anxiety about the future weakened a bit. Perhaps it wouldn't be quite so bad after all.

We were ordered to appear before the Emperor at eleven o'clock in the morning.

At five minutes to eleven we entered the ante-chamber where Napoleon keeps diplomats, Generals, foreign Princes and French ministers waiting for hours. When we entered a hush fell on the assembly. Everybody stared at Jean-Baptiste's

Swedish uniform and shrank back from us, shrank back literally. Jean-Baptiste requested one of the adjutants of the Emperor to announce " the Prince of Ponte Corvo, Marshal of France, with wife and son ".

Among these people we felt as if we were sitting on an island. Nobody spoke to us, nobody congratulated us. Oscar clung to me tightly. They all knew what was going on. A foreign people had, of its own accord, without any compulsion, offered its crown to Jean-Baptiste. And now in there, on the Emperor's desk, lay his application for permission to relinquish French citizenship, to be discharged from the Army. Jean-Baptiste Bernadotte no longer wanted to be a French citizen. They looked as if we were an apparition, something weird and uncanny.

Everybody at court knew that we were in for a dreadful scene in the Emperor's room, one of those scenes of Imperial hysterics which make the walls shake and everybody tremble. ' Thank God,' I thought, ' that he gives you a good long waiting time outside to collect yourself.' Giving Jean-Baptiste a sidelong glance, I saw him staring at one of the two sentries by the door to the Emperor's apartments. It was the bear-skin cap which attracted his attention. He studied it as if he were seeing it for the first time, or for the last time.

The clock struck eleven. Meneval, the Emperor's private secretary, appeared and called us.

The Emperor's study is almost as big as a ballroom. His desk is at the very end of this huge room, and the way from the door to the desk seems endless. For that reason the Emperor receives his friends mostly in the middle of the room. We, however, had to cross the whole of it.

Like a statue, immovable, Napoleon sat behind his desk, stooping forward a bit as if he were lying in wait for us. Talleyrand, Prince of Benevento, and the present Foreign Minister, the Duke of Cadore, stood behind him whilst we, I in front with Oscar's hand in mine and Jean-Baptiste behind me followed by Meneval, walked up to him. When I came near enough I saw that the Emperor had affected the stony Cæsarean pose. Only his eyes seemed alive.

The three of us, Oscar in the middle, ranged ourselves before his desk. I curtsied.

The Emperor did not move but kept staring viciously at Jean-Baptiste. All of a sudden he jumped up, pushed back his chair and came out from behind the desk, yelling: " In what

314

kind of attire dare you appear before your Emperor and Commander-in-Chief, Marshal?"

Jean-Baptiste answered in a low, rather jerky voice: "This uniform is a copy of the Swedish Marshal's uniform, Sire."

"And you dare appear here in a Swedish uniform? You, a Marshal of France?" He screamed like a madman.

"I thought it was a matter of indifference to Your Majesty what uniforms the Marshals wore," said Jean-Baptiste quietly. "I have repeatedly seen Marshal Murat, the King of Naples, appear at court in some very curious uniforms."

That went home. Napoleon's childish brother-in-law Murat loves flamboyant uniforms and the Emperor laughs at them without ever calling him to order.

"As far as I am informed my royal brother-in-law's uniforms are—his own inventions." A fugitive smile played round the corners of his mouth and vanished at once, as he stamped the floor and started screaming again: "But you dare to appear before your Emperor in a Swedish uniform!" Oscar almost crept behind me in fear. "Well, Marshal, what have you to say to that?"

"I thought it right to appear at this audience in Swedish uniform. It was not my intention to insult Your Majesty. Part of the uniform, by the way, is my own invention, too. If Your Majesty would like to see——"

He pulled up the sash to show the belt. "I am wearing the belt of my old Marshal's uniform, Sire."

"Stop these disrobing scenes, Prince! Let us get down to business!"

His voice sounded different, as if he were in a hurry now. The introductory scene which was meant to intimidate us was over. 'He acts like a prima donna,' I thought, and felt quite exhausted. Wasn't he going to offer us a chair?

He certainly wasn't. He remained standing behind his desk looking down at a document, Jean-Baptiste's application.

"You sent me a very strange application, Prince. In it you express your intention to let yourself be adopted by the King of Sweden, and request permission to resign your French nationality. A strange document. An almost incomprehensible document if one thinks back— But you probably do not think back, Marshal of France?"

Jean-Baptiste compressed his lips in order to keep silent.

"Don't you really think back? For example to the time when you went out as a young recruit to defend the frontiers of France? Or to the battlefields where this young soldier fought first as a sergeant, then as a lieutenant, then as a colonel and finally as a General of the French Army? Or to the day when the Emperor of the French made you a Marshal of France?"

Still Jean-Baptiste was silent.

"It is not so very long ago that you defended the frontiers of your fatherland without my knowledge." His old winning smile appeared unexpectedly. "Perhaps at that time you saved France. I told you once before—it is a very long time ago, and as unfortunately you do not remember the past you will probably have forgotten that too—yes, I told you once before that I cannot do without the services of a man like you. It was during those days in Brumaire. Perhaps you remember it after all? If at that time the Government had given you the authority, you and Moreau would have had me shot. The Government of the Republic did not give you the authority. Bernadotte, I repeat, I cannot do without you."

He sat down and pushed the application a bit to one side. Then he looked up and remarked with forced casualness: "Since the people of Sweden have chosen you——" he shrugged his shoulders and smiled ironically, "you of all men, to be heir to their throne, I as your Emperor and Supreme Commander herewith give you permission to accept their offer, but as a Frenchman and a Marshal of France. That is all!"

"In that case I shall have to inform the King of Sweden that I cannot assume the succession to his throne. The people of Sweden want a Swedish Crown Prince, Sire."

Napoleon jumped to his feet. "But that is nonsense, Bernadotte! Look at my brothers, Joseph, Louis, Jerome. Has any one of them resigned his citizenship? Or my stepson Eugene in Italy?"

Jean-Baptiste didn't answer. Napoleon came out from behind his desk and began to pace the floor backwards and forwards like a madman. I caught Talleyrand's eye and he winked at me almost imperceptibly. What did he mean? That Jean-Baptiste would win through in the end? It certainly didn't look like it now.

Abruptly the Emperor stopped in front of me. "Princess," he said, "I believe you do not know that the Swedish royal family is insane. The present King is incapable of enunciating clearly a single sentence, and his nephew had to be deposed because he is a lunatic. Because he is really—cuckoo!" He tapped his forehead. "Princess, tell me, is your husband crazy too? I mean, is he so crazy that he wants to stop being a Frenchman for the sake of the Swedish succession?"

"I must ask you not to insult His Majesty King Charles XIII in my presence," Jean-Baptiste said sharply.

"Talleyrand, are the Vasas cuckoo or not?"

"It is a very old dynasty, Sire. Old dynasties are often not very healthy," Talleyrand answered.

"And you, Princess, what do you think of it? Bernadotte's request for relinquishing French citizenship applies to you and the child as well."

"It is a matter of form, Sire. Otherwise we cannot accept the Swedish succession," I heard myself say. Did I say the right thing? I looked at Jean-Baptiste, but he stared past me. I glanced across to Talleyrand, and he nodded gently.

"Next: your discharge from the Army. That is out of the question, Bernadotte, really, that is out of the question." The Emperor went back behind his desk and studied the application, perhaps for the hundredth time. "I would not dream of doing without one of my Marshals. If war breaks out again——" He stopped, then added quickly: "If Britain does not give in, war is bound to break out again and in that case I shall need you. You will be as usual in command of one of my Armies. And it will not make any difference to me whether you are Crown Prince of Sweden or not. Your Swedish regiments will simply form part of your Army. Or do you believe——" here he broke into a smile which made him look ten years younger— "or do you believe I could put anybody else in command of the Saxons?"

"Since it stated in Your Majesty's Order-of-the-Day after the battle of Wagram that the Saxons did not fire a single shot, I do not think it matters much who will command them. Why not hand the command over to Ney, Sire? Ney is ambitious and has served under me."

"The Saxons took Wagram and I most certainly will not hand over your command to Ney. I will allow you to become Swedish if you remain Marshal of France. I have much sympathy for the ambitions of my Marshals. Moreover, you are a brilliant administrator, as you have shown in Hanover and the Hanse towns. You are an excellent Governor, Bernadotte."

"I asked to be discharged from the French Army."

Napoleon's fist crashed down on the table at that. It sounded like a thunderclap.

"My feet hurt, may I sit down, Sire?" I said involuntarily.

317

The Emperor gazed at me. His wavering eyes became quieter, grey. Did he, I wonder, remember at this point a little girl in a garden over which evening was falling, a little girl who raced him to the hedge and whom he allowed to win? . . .

"You will have to stand for many hours when you receive your subjects as the Crown Princess of Sweden, Eugenie," he said calmly. "Please, sit down. Gentlemen, let us all sit down."

And thus we found ourselves comfortably seated round the table.

"Where were we? Oh yes, you wish to be dismissed from the Army, Prince of Ponte Corvo. Do I understand correctly that you want to join our Armies not as a Marshal of France but as an ally?"

An expression of intent interest became visible in Talleyrand's face. So that was what Napoleon was driving at, had been driving at the whole time, at the alliance with Sweden.

"If I accede to the requests which for formal reasons you consider to be necessary I shall do it because I do not want to put obstacles in the way of one of my Marshals whom an old and not very healthy dynasty wishes to adopt. I should even go further and call it an excellent idea on the part of the Swedes to express their friendship for France by the choice of one of my Marshals. If I had been asked before the selection was made I should have suggested one of my own brothers, to show clearly how much store I set by that alliance and how highly I esteem the House of Vasa. However, I have not been asked, and as I have to say what I think about this selection, such a surprising one to me, after it has been made, let me say, then, that—that I congratulate you, Prince."

"Mama, he really isn't so bad," said Oscar.

Talleyrand bit his lips to stifle a laugh, and so did the Duke of Cadore. Napoleon looked thoughtfully at Oscar and then said: "What a coincidence that I should have picked on a Nordic name for this godson of mine! And on the hot sands of Egypt at that!" He laughed as if he were going to burst and slapped Jean-Baptiste's thigh: "Is not life crazy, Bernadotte?"

He turned to me: "You have heard, Princess, that Her Majesty is expecting a son?"

I nodded: "I am very glad about it, Sire."

Napoleon looked once more at Oscar. "I understand that you have to become Swedish, Bernadotte, if only for the child's sake. I am told that the deposed lunatic has a son, too. You must never lose sight of this exiled son, Bernadotte, you understand?"

'Now he's mapping out our future,' I thought, 'now everything's going fine. He's accepting things now.'

"Meneval, the map of Scandinavia!"

The maps were brought. "Sit here, Bernadotte."

Bernadotte went and sat on the arm of Napoleon's chair. The Emperor unrolled the map and spread it on his knee. 'How often these two must have sat like that in their headquarters,' I thought.

"Sweden, Bernadotte, breaks the Continental Blockade. There, at Gothenburg, British goods are unloaded and secretly taken to Germany."

"And to Russia," remarked Talleyrand casually.

"My ally, the Tsar of Russia, unfortunately does not devote sufficient attention to this question. There are British goods even in my ally's country. However that may be, Bernadotte, Sweden is at the bottom of it all. You will clean up in Sweden and, if necessary, declare war on the British."

Meneval had started writing down the salient points of the conversation, and Talleyrand looked curiously at Jean-Baptiste. The Duke of Cadore nodded contentedly and said: "Sweden will complete the Continental Blockade. I believe we can rely on the Prince of Ponte Corvo."

Jean-Baptiste was silent.

"Have you any objections to raise, Prince?" the Emperor asked sharply.

Jean-Baptiste looked up from the map. "I shall serve the interests of Sweden with all the means at my disposal."

"And the interests of France?" the Emperor said pointedly.

Jean-Baptiste rose, folded up the map of Scandinavia carefully and handed it to Meneval. "As far as I know, Your Majesty's Government and the Government of Sweden are at this moment negotiating a non-aggression pact which could be extended into a pact of friendship. I believe that I am therefore in a position to serve not only Sweden but at the same time my former motherland as well."

Former motherland, how that expression hurt! Jean-Baptiste looked tired and weary.

"You are the ruler of a small territory under French suzerainty," said the Emperor coldly. "I have no option but to withdraw from you the Principality of Ponte Corvo and its not considerable revenues."

Jean-Baptiste nodded. "Certainly, Sire. I made a point of asking for just that in my application."

"Do you intend to arrive in Sweden as plain Monsieur Jean-Baptiste Bernadotte, Marshal of France, retired? If it is your wish you might, in view of your services, be allowed to retain the title of Prince."

"I prefer," said Jean-Baptiste, "to renounce the Principality as well as the title. Should Your Majesty, however, be so gracious as to grant me a wish, I should like to ask that a barony be conferred on my brother in Pau."

Napoleon was astonished. "But are you not taking your brother along with you to Sweden? You could make him a count or a duke there."

"I do not intend to take my brother or any other member of my family along with me to Sweden. The King of Sweden desires to adopt only me and not all my relatives as well. Believe me, Sir, I know what I am doing."

We all looked at the Emperor, probably thinking the same thing: the man who showers crowns, titles and dignities on his stupid brothers.

"I believe you are right, Bernadotte," the Emperor said slowly. He rose, and we did the same. Looking at the application for the last time, he asked, with his thoughts apparently elsewhere: "And what about your estates in France, in Lithuania, in Westphalia?"

"I am about to sell them, Sire."

"To pay the debts of the Vasas?"

"Yes, and to pay for the court expenses of the Bernadotte dynasty."

Napoleon took up a pen and looked from Jean-Baptiste to me and back to Jean-Baptiste again. "With this signature you, your wife and your son will cease to be French citizens, Bernadotte. Do you want me to sign?"

Jean-Baptiste, his eyes half-closed, his mouth a thin hard line, nodded.

"This signature also retires you from the French Army, Marshal. Do you really want me to sign?"

Again Jean-Baptiste nodded. I felt for his hand.

At that moment a trumpet signal sounded in the yard for the Changing of the Guard. Its noise drowned the scratching of Napoleon's pen.

This time Napoleon accompanied us on the long way from his desk to the door, his hand on Oscar's shoulder. In the ante-chamber diplomats, Generals, Princes and ministers bowed deeply as Meneval opened the door for his master.

"Gentlemen," the Emperor said, "I should like you to join me in congratulating Their Royal Highnesses the Crown Prince and the Crown Princess of Sweden, and my godson——"

"I am the Duke of Södermanland," cried Oscar's bright voice.

"And my godson, the Duke of Södermanland," Napoleon added.

On the drive home Jean-Baptiste sat silently in his corner. I didn't disturb him.

A small crowd had assembled in the Rue d'Anjou, and some-one shouted, "*Vive Bernadotte, vive Bernadotte!*" exactly as on the day of Napoleon's *coup d'état* when some people thought that Jean-Baptiste could defend the Republic against him.

Count Brahe, Baron Mörner and some Swedish gentlemen who had just arrived from Stockholm with important messages were waiting for us at the house door.

"I must ask you to excuse us," Jean-Baptiste told them. "Her Royal Highness and I wish to be alone."

We went past them into the small drawing-room. But there was another visitor waiting for us, Fouché, the Duke of Otranto. He had fallen into disgrace recently because of his secret negotiations with the British, which had come to Napoleon's ears.

He held out to me a bunch of very deep red, almost black roses. "May I congratulate you?" he lisped. "France is very proud of her great son."

"Stop it, Fouché," said Jean-Baptiste wearily. "I have just renounced my French citizenship."

"I know, Your Highness, I know."

"Then please excuse us. We cannot see anybody just now," I said, taking the roses.

When we were alone at last we sat down side by side on the sofa, tired, very tired, as if we had come home from an endless walk. After a little while Jean-Baptiste got up, went to the piano and listlessly picked out a tune on it with one finger, the only tune he can play, the Marseillaise. Suddenly he said: "To-day I have seen Napoleon for the last time in my life." Then he continued playing, the same tune, always the same tune. . . .

At lunch time to-day Jean-Baptiste departed for Sweden.

He had been so busy during these last days that we had seen very little of each other. The French Foreign Ministry at his request made him a list of those Swedish personalities whom it considers important. Mörner and Count Brahe told him afterwards who the people on the list were.

One afternoon Baron Alquier was announced, a man in the gold-embroidered gala uniform of an Ambassador and with an eternal court smile. " His Majesty has appointed me Ambassador in Stockholm," he said, " and I should like to call on Your Royal Highness before your departure."

" You need not introduce yourself," said Jean-Baptiste, " we have known each other for years. Let me see, you were His Majesty's Ambassador in Naples when the Neapolitan Government was overthrown and a Cabinet after His Majesty's wishes put in its place."

Baron Alquier nodded smilingly. " Magnificent country round Naples——"

" And you were His Majesty's Ambassador in Madrid and the Spanish Government was forced to resign in order to make way for a Government acceptable to His Majesty," Jean-Baptiste continued.

" A beautiful city, Madrid," remarked Alquier, " only a bit too hot."

" And now you are going to Stockholm," concluded Jean-Baptiste.

" A fine town, but very cold, I hear."

Jean-Baptiste shrugged his shoulders. " Perhaps it depends on the kind of welcome one receives. There are warm ones, and cold ones ! "

" His Majesty the Emperor assured me that Your Royal Highness would welcome me very warmly. As an ex-fellow countryman, so to speak."

" When are you leaving, Excellency?"

" On September 30th, Your Highness."

" Then we shall probably get to Stockholm at the same time."

" What a fortunate coincidence, Your Highness ! "

" Generals rarely leave things to chance and coincidence, Excellency. And the Emperor is first and foremost a General," said Jean-Baptiste. He rose, and Alquier had to take his leave.

Couriers from Stockholm brought news about the preparations for a magnificent reception. Danish diplomats called to report that Copenhagen was getting ready for a great welcome to the Swedish Crown Prince. And every morning the pastor of the Protestant community in Paris came to instruct Jean-Baptiste in the tenets of Protestantism, which is the State religion in Sweden. Before Jean-Baptiste reaches Sweden, at the Danish port of Elsinore, he is to be received into the Protestant faith and has to sign the Augsburg Confession in the presence of the Archbishop of Sweden.

One day I asked Jean-Baptiste: " Have you ever been to a Protestant church?"

" Yes, in Germany, twice. It looks the same as a Catholic church, but without the pictures of the saints."

" Must I become a Protestant too?"

He pondered. " I do not think it necessary. You can do as you wish. But at the moment I have no time for this nice young pastor. He can instruct Oscar instead. I want him to learn the Augsburg Confession by heart, in Swedish as well if possible. Count Brahe could help him with it."

So Oscar learnt the Confession in French and Swedish.

I've also taken an interest in those lists of important Swedes. Among the many Löwenhjelms on the list is one, Charles Axel Löwenhjelm, whose name is underlined on the list. He is to meet Jean-Baptiste in Elsinore and accompany him to Stockholm as his lord-in-waiting and to inform him on questions of Swedish court etiquette.

" I leave you the lists," said Jean-Baptiste. " Learn them by heart."

" But I can't pronounce them," I said. " How, for instance, do you pronounce ' Löwenhjelm '?"

Jean-Baptiste couldn't do it either. " But I shall learn to do it. One can learn anything if one wants to." He added: " Hurry with your preparations for the journey. I do not want you and Oscar to stay here longer than is absolutely necessary. As soon as your rooms in the castle in Stockholm are ready you must set off at once. Promise me that!"

He sounded most serious about it, and I nodded.

" By the way," he added, " I have thought of selling this house."

" No, no, Jean-Baptiste, you can't do that to me."

He looked at me in amazement. " But if you want to come to Paris later on you can always stay with Julie. It is an entirely superfluous luxury to keep up a big house like this."

"It is my home, and you can't take my home away just like that. If we still had Father's villa in Marseilles, yes. But we haven't got it any more. Please, Jean-Baptiste, please, leave me this house!" And I added: "You too are sure to come to Paris again, and then you'll be glad of this house. Or are you going to stay at a hotel or the Swedish Embassy from now on?"

It was late at night. We were sitting on the edge of the bed, his bags packed ready around us.

"If I ever return," he murmured, "it will be a sad business, it will hurt me." He stared into the candlelight. "You are right, my girl. It will be better to stay here, if ever I do come here again. We will keep the house."

At lunch time to-day the big coach drew up at the gate. Fernand, still wearing his purple livery, but with the buttons showing the insignia of Sweden, put the luggage inside and waited by the carriage door.

Baron Mörner was waiting in the hall as we came downstairs, Jean-Baptiste, Oscar and I, Jean-Baptiste with his arm round my shoulders. It was all very much as it had been so often before when he left me to go to the front or to go somewhere as Governor.

Jean-Baptiste stopped in front of General Moreau's bust and stared at it. "Send the bust to Stockholm together with my other things," he said. He embraced Oscar and me and turned to Count Brahe: "It is your responsibility to see to it that my wife and Oscar follow me as soon as possible," he said in a hoarse voice. "It may even be of the utmost importance that my family leaves France very quickly. Do you understand?"

"I do, Your Highness."

Jean-Baptiste and Mörner got into the coach, Fernand took his seat beside the coachman. A few passers-by stopped, and an invalided soldier with the medals of all the campaigns on his chest shouted, "*Vive Bernadotte!*" Jean-Baptiste closed the curtains and the coach moved off.

ELSINORE IN DENMARK.
During the night of the 21st to the 22nd of December 1810.

I never knew how long and how cold nights could be. Marie brought me four hot-water-bottles. But in spite of them I am still freezing. Perhaps the night will pass more quickly if I go on with my diary.

To-morrow I shall board the Swedish man-of-war that will carry us across the Sound to the Swedish port of Hälsingborg, me, the Crown Princess Desideria, and my dear little son, Oscar, the future Heir to the Throne.

I would so much like to get up and go into Oscar's room and sit quietly down by his bed and hold his hand and feel the warmth of his young life. I used to do it so often in the past when I felt lonely and his father was away at some war or other. I never thought that there might be a time when I could no longer go into his room as I please. But that time has come now. You, my son, are no longer alone in your room, for at your father's order Colonel Villatte, for many years his faithful adjutant, shares it with you till we get to Stockholm. Why? In order to protect you, my darling, from assassins, from those people who are ashamed of Sweden's choice of plain Monsieur Bernadotte and his son Oscar to be their future Kings. That is why your father demanded that Villatte should sleep in your room and Count Brahe in the one adjoining it. Yes, my darling, we are afraid of murderers now.

Marie sleeps in the room next to mine. How she snores, my God, how she snores!

We have come a long way, and for the last two days we have been held up here in Elsinore by the fog which makes it impossible to cross the Sound. And it is so cold here. But people say, "That's nothing. You wait till you are in Sweden, Highness!"

We left our house in the Rue d'Anjou at the end of October, shut it up and moved to Julie in Mortefontaine to spend the last days with her. Young Brahe and the gentlemen of the Swedish Embassy seemed hardly able to wait for my departure from France. I only learnt yesterday why they were so impatient for me to leave. But I couldn't very well go without my new court robes which Le Roy was making for me. Some of them were to be white, the colour which I never wanted to wear in Paris because Josephine always wore it. But in Stockholm where nothing would remind me of her it would be different. At last, on the first of November, they were ready and delivered, and on the third we left.

We travelled in three coaches, myself, Colonel Villatte, the physician whom Jean-Baptiste engaged for the journey, and Madame La Flotte in the first, Oscar, Count Brahe and Marie in the second and our luggage in the third. I had left my reader behind. She couldn't face leaving Paris, and in any case, as Count Brahe told me, there was a complete staff waiting for me in Stockholm which the Queen had appointed for me. But I took Madame La Flotte, who very much wanted to come because she had fallen in love with Count Brahe.

That day of departure seems to be a long way back in the past. But in reality it is only six weeks since we left. In these six weeks, however, we have been on the road from morning till night, and wherever we arrived there would be an official reception ceremony, in Amsterdam, in Hamburg and in places with such strange-sounding names as Apenrade and Itzehoe. We did not stop for any length of time till we reached Nyborg in Denmark, where we were to cross from the Isle of Fünen to the Isle of Zealand on which lies the capital, Copenhagen. Here a courier of Napoleon caught up with us, a young cavalry officer carrying a big parcel.

We were just going to board our boat when he arrived, tied his horse to a stanchion on the quay and ran after us with his big parcel. " From His Majesty the Emperor, with his kindest regards!"

Count Brahe took the shapeless parcel and Villatte asked him: " Any letters for Her Highness?"

The young officer shook his head. " No, only this verbal message. When the Emperor was told of Her Highness's departure he said, ' A dreadful time of the year to travel to Sweden!' He looked round, saw me and gave me the order to ride after Your Highness and deliver this parcel. ' Hurry up! Her Highness will need it very badly!' he said." The officer clicked his heels.

I gave him my hand. " Thank His Majesty for me and remember me to Paris." The cold wind made my eyes water.

In the ship's cabin we unpacked the parcel. My heart stopped beating when I saw what was in it: a sable coat. The most beautiful fur I had ever seen!

" One of the Tsar's three furs!" said La Flotte, visibly shaken. We had all heard about the three furs which the Tsar gave the Emperor. The first Napoleon presented to Josephine, the second to his favourite sister Polette, and the third—the third was here, on my knee!

A marvellous fur! But I still went on feeling cold to the marrow. The Generals' greatcoats in the days of old warmed me better than even this fur coat, Napoleon's greatcoat during the night of the thunderstorm in Marseilles, Jean-Baptiste's during the rainy night in Paris. They were not as gold-embroidered, the Generals' greatcoats of those days, as they are to-day, they were coarse and badly cut, but they were the coats of the brave young Republic.

The crossing from Nyborg to Korsör took us three hours, and some of us, such as Madame La Flotte and the doctor, were much the worse for it. We only spent a few hours in Korsör and then continued our journey, as we had to be in Copenhagen on December 17th. The King and Queen of Denmark were preparing a great reception for us, and we had to keep to the timetable. So we crept, all of us, into one coach to keep warm, and passed our time talking about Denmark, its history and its royal family. It seemed that not only the Vasas but the Kings of Denmark as well belonged to a family which was not too healthy mentally, and I shuddered at the thought that Oscar would have to marry a Princess of old royal blood some day.

Madame La Flotte noticed my shuddering and suggested that we should stop and get some hot water for our bottles. I shook my head. My shudders didn't come from the cold alone, they came from anxiety for the future, a future which was full of the shadows caused by the twilight over the Royal Houses of the North.

The evening in Copenhagen passed like a confused dream. I saw the Royal Castle by the glare of torches, a charming small building in the rococo style, friendly and inviting. But I was stiff with cold and exhaustion. Marie massaged my feet and Yvette did my hair in preparation for the reception, and I put on one of my new white robes.

I asked after Oscar. Marie said that he could hardly keep his eyes open, and so I ordered him to bed. But a moment later Count Brahe appeared and insisted that the young Prince had to take part in the gala dinner at all costs. I was furious but had to give in, and Oscar, instead of going to bed, had to appear in the uniform of a Swedish officer cadet which Bernadotte had had made for him.

Marie gave me a glass of champagne to cheer me up. But I didn't feel much cheered when I went to the banquet. The Danish royal couple were very kind to me. They both spoke French very well and emphasised how much they admired the Emperor of France. The King urged me to go next morning and see the devastation wrought by the bombardment of Copenhagen by the British Navy. I promised I would. During the meal the King repeated how much he sympathised with Napoleon. Britain, he said, was the common enemy.

" And yet your mother was an English Princess," I said involuntarily.

I had had no intention of being tactless, but I was so tired that I said anything that came into my mind. The mention of his mother created a painful impression on the King. All the same, catching sight of Oscar, who was almost falling asleep over his ice-cream, I added, " One should never deny one's mother, Your Majesty." Thereupon His Majesty rose very soon to end the banquet and we all went into the ballroom. . . .

And so we've been in this little town of Elsinore for almost three days. But for the fog one could see Sweden from here. And the sea was so rough that Count Brahe kept postponing the crossing time and time again. " Your Highness cannot arrive in Sweden in a state of seasickness," he said. " There will be an enormous crowd on the other side of the Sound wanting to catch a first glimpse of the new Crown Princess."

And so we wait and wait.

The Swedish commercial agent Glörfelt, who lives here, asked me to be godfather to his son and find a nice name for him. I agreed and called the baby Jules Désiré Oscar, Jules because I was longing for Julie so badly. Oscar and I went to Kronborg Castle, and as we crossed the moat the guns roared out a salvo in salute. La Flotte, who never loses an opportunity to show off her knowledge, told me the story of a prince called Hamlet, his murdered father, his uncle and his mother, all of whom were supposed to have lived here.

" How long ago was that?" I asked La Flotte.

She didn't know. She only knew that an English author had written a tragedy about it. It certainly was an eerie castle and I was glad that we were not going to live there. . . .

At last it has been decided: we are crossing to-morrow. The fog is still there, but the sea is calmer. Once more I am going through the list of the names of the ladies and gentlemen who will receive me to-morrow in Hälsingborg: my new ladies-in-waiting Countess Caroline Lewenhaupt and Miss Mariana Koskull, my equerry Baron Reinhold Adelswärd, my lords-in-waiting Count Erik Piper and Sixten Sparre and finally my physician Pontin.

My candles are burnt low, it is four o'clock in the morning and I want to try and get some sleep.

Jean-Baptiste is not coming to meet me. It is only here that I learnt of Napoleon's ultimatum to the Swedish Government of November 12th. Either, Napoleon demanded, Sweden declares war on Britain within the next five days, or Sweden will be at war with France, Denmark and Russia. The Council of State was convened in Stockholm and everybody's eye was on the new Crown Prince. Jean-Baptiste, at this meeting, said: " Gentlemen, I ask you to forget that I was born in France and that the Emperor holds hostage what is dearest to me in this life. Gentlemen, I do not wish to take part in this conference in order not to exercise any influence whatever on your decisions." I understand now why the gentlemen of the Swedish Embassy in Paris demanded that Oscar and I should hurry our departure.

The Swedish Council of State decided for war with Britain and handed their declaration of war to the British Ambassador on November 17th. But Count Brahe told me that he knew the Crown Prince had sent a secret message to Britain to consider this declaration of war as a mere formality. ' Sweden ', this message said, ' wishes to continue the trade in British goods and proposes that British ships bound for Gothenburg from now onwards should sail under the American flag.'

I can't make head or tail of all this. Napoleon could have kept Oscar and me in France as hostages. But he let us go and sent me a sable fur because I needed it so badly here. Jean-Baptiste, however, asked the Council of State not to take his family into account at all. Sweden was far more important than his family, it was the most important thing on earth for him. . . .

Everybody tells me how the Swedes are looking forward to our boy. Ruthlessly I have been driven through the fog and the cold to hand over my child into their keeping, and I do not know whether it will be for the best.

Are heirs to a throne meant to be happy, I wonder?

HALSINGBORG, 22nd December, 1810. (To-day I arrived in SWEDEN.)

The guns of Kronborg Castle thundered as we went on board the Swedish man-of-war. The crew stood to attention, Oscar put his little hand to his three-cornered hat, and I tried to smile. It was still very foggy and the wind was as icy as ever. So I went down into the cabin. But Oscar stayed on desk to have a good look at the cannon.

" My husband hasn't come, really? " I had asked Count Brahe again and again whenever another message came from Hälsingborg about details of the reception arrangements.

" Important political decisions make His Royal Highness's

329

presence in Stockholm necessary. New demands by Napoleon are expected." With that answer I had to be satisfied.

I had put on a green velvet hat with a red silk rose on it, a green tight-fitting velvet coat which made me look a bit taller, and a green velvet muff. Inside the muff I crumpled up the slip of paper with the names of the members of my Swedish suite. I had tried to learn them, but it seemed hopeless.

"Your Highness is not afraid, is she?" asked Count Brahe.

"Who is looking after Oscar? I don't want him to fall into the water."

"Your own Colonel Villatte is looking after him," said Count Brahe, and I thought that his 'your own' sounded a bit sarcastic.

"Is it true Your Highness has put on woollen underwear?" Madame La Flotte asked in horror. She was fighting seasickness again and her face looked greenish under her make-up.

"Yes. Marie bought them in Elsinore when she saw them in a shop window. I think you want warm underwear in this climate, particularly when we shall probably have to stand by the quayside for hours over there and listen to speeches. Why not, anyway? No one can see what you are wearing under your skirt!"

As soon as I said it I regretted it. It's not what you expect a Crown Princess to say. My new Swedish lady-in-waiting would be horrified if she had heard it.

"The Swedish coast can be seen quite clearly now. Perhaps Your Highness would like to come on deck?" Clearly he wanted me to rush out of the cabin at once.

"I'm so cold and tired," I said, and snuggled deeper into Napoleon's sable fur.

"Of course, I am sorry," murmured the young Swede, and withdrew.

The thunder of guns made me start up. They were the guns of our ship and were answered at once by the batteries on the coast. I got ready and repaired my make-up. But there were deep shadows under my eyes, the result of sleepless nights.

"Your Highness looks very beautiful," said Count Brahe reassuringly.

But it didn't reassure me. 'I shall disappoint them,' I thought. 'Everybody expects a Crown Princess to be like a princess from a fairy-tale, and I am no fairy-tale princess, I am only the former citizeness Eugenie Désirée Clary.'

I went on deck and joined Oscar.

"Look, Mama, that is our country!" the boy shouted.

"Not ours, Oscar. It's the country of the Swedish people. Don't forget that, ever!"

The strains of military music were carried across to us from the quayside. Colourful dresses and golden epaulettes shone through the fog. I saw a bouquet of pink flowers, roses or carnations. Flowers like that would cost a fortune here in winter, I felt sure.

Count Brahe gave us his last directions. "As soon as the ship ties up at the quay I shall run down the gangway and then hold out my hand to you and help you down. I should like the Prince to keep close to Your Royal Highness and, once you are on land, to take up his position to the left of Your Royal Highness. I myself shall be immediately behind you."

'Yes,' I thought, 'my young knight will be quite close behind me to protect the daughter of the Middle Class from the derisive laughter of the Swedish nobles.'

"Have you understood, Oscar?"

"Look, Mama, all the Swedish uniforms, a whole regiment, look!"

"And where am I to stand, Count Brahe?" asked La Flotte.

I turned to her. "You keep with Colonel Villatte in the background. I fear that this reception has not been arranged for your benefit."

"Do you know," asked Oscar, as the guns were firing around us, "what Count Brahe was called in Elsinore, Mama? Admiral Brahe."

"Why that, Oscar? He isn't in the Navy, he is a cavalry officer."

"But they did call him Admiral of the Navy.* Do you understand that, Mama?"

I burst out laughing, and I was still laughing when the boat landed in Hälsingborg.

"Kronprinsessan skål leve! Kronprinsessan, Arveprinsen!" Many voices shouted rhythmically out of the fog from behind the cordon of soldiers. But I could only see the faces of the Swedish courtiers in front of the cordon, faces rigid and frigid that stared at us without a smile. The laughter froze on my face.

The gangway was put in position and the band played the Swedish anthem, not an inspiring battle song like the Marseillaise but rather a hymn, devout, hard and solemn.

* Translator's note: This is a play on the German meaning of the French name La Flotte, 'the navy'.

Count Brahe ran past me on to the quay and held out his hand to me. I walked towards it quickly, not feeling very secure. But then I felt his hand under my elbow, felt the land under my feet and Oscar by my side. The bouquet of glowing roses moved towards me, and a gaunt old man in the uniform of a Swedish Marshal handed them to me.

"This is the Governor General of the Province of Skåne, Count John Christopher Toll," Count Brahe introduced him.

I saw the pale eyes of an old man examining me without any sign of friendliness in them. I took the roses, and the old man bent over my right hand, and then bowed deeply to Oscar. Ladies in silk fur-trimmed cloaks curtsied, and uniformed backs bowed.

It started to snow. I shook hands with the ladies and gentlemen, who forced themselves to an artificial smile. The smile became more natural, however, as Oscar went round to shake hands with them. Count Toll, in harsh French, made a speech of welcome.

Suddenly snowflakes danced round us in thick swirls. Oscar stared at them enraptured. The anthem sounded again in its strange solemnity. The moment it stopped Oscar's voice rang out through the silence: "We shall be very happy here, Mama. Look, it's snowing!"

How is it that my son always manages to say the right thing at the right moment, exactly like his father?

The old man offered me his arm to conduct me to the waiting equipages. Count Brahe kept close behind me. I looked at the forbidding face of the old man beside me, the strange faces behind me, the bright hard eyes, the critical glances, and I said in a toneless voice: "I ask you always to be kind to my son."

These words were not in the programme, they came out on the spur of the moment, and perhaps they were tactless and contrary to etiquette. An expression of great astonishment came over their faces, at once arrogant and touched. I felt the snowflakes on my eyelids and on my lips, and nobody saw that I was crying.

That evening, as I was undressing, Marie said: "Wasn't I right? I mean about the woollen knickers? Otherwise this ceremony in the harbour might have been your death!"

In the Royal Castle in STOCKHOLM, during that endless winter of 1810-11.

The journey from Hälsingborg to Stockholm seemed endless. We travelled by day and danced the quadrille by night. I don't know why, but the aristocracy here dance nothing but the quadrille and behave as if they were at the Court of Versailles. They asked me, didn't that make me feel at home? and I could only smile and shrug my shoulders. I know nothing about the Court of Versailles, all that happened before I was born, and we never had any contact with the court.

By day we broke our journey in different towns, and we got out each time. The schoolchildren sang each time, and all the mayors made speeches in a language totally incomprehensible to me. On one occasion I sighed, " If only I could understand Swedish!"

"But," Count Brahe whispered, "the mayor is speaking in French, Your Highness!"

Maybe, I thought, but this French sounded like a very foreign language to me.

It snowed and snowed and never stopped snowing, and the temperature fell to below zero. Most of the time my new lady-in-waiting, Countess Lewenhaupt, was sitting with me, and this Countess, slim and no longer young, was intent on discussing with me all the French novels of the last twenty years. Sometimes I let my other lady, Miss Koskull, travel in my coach. She is about my age, tall and broad-shouldered like most Swedish women, with healthy red cheeks, thick hair done in an impossible manner and strong healthy teeth. I don't like her because she always looks at me in such a curious and calculating way.

I was told all the details of Jean-Baptiste's arrival in Stockholm. He had won over the King and the Queen immediately. The ailing King had got up from his arm-chair with a great effort when Jean-Baptiste entered and stretched out his trembling hand to him. Jean-Baptiste had bent down and kissed it as tears rolled down the cheeks of the old man. Afterwards Jean-Baptiste had called on Queen Hedvig Elizabeth Charlotte, who had dressed up for his reception. But on her breast she had worn, as usual, the brooch with the portrait of the exiled Gustavus IV. As Jean-Baptiste bent down over her hand I was told that he said quietly, ' Madame, I understand your feelings. All I ask you is to remember that Sweden's first

333

King was a soldier too, a soldier who wanted nothing but to serve his people.'

Jean-Baptiste apparently spends every evening in the Queen's drawing-room, and the old King shows himself in public only with the Crown Prince by his side. During audiences, during the sessions of the Council of State, everywhere Jean-Baptiste has to be by his side and support him, a tender son to a loving father. . . .

I tried to visualise the new family idyll. What part was I to play in it? Everybody called the Queen a very intelligent and ambitious woman whom Fate had married to a prematurely senile man and deprived of her only son while still a child. She is in her early fifties, and Jean-Baptiste was to take her son's place and—no, it was all too difficult for me.

Someone said: " No one but Miss Koskull has managed up till now to make His Majesty listen and even laugh. But now this is no longer the privilege of the beautiful Mariana alone, she has to share it with His Royal Highness." Hearing that, I reflected that perhaps His Majesty was not quite so senile after all, perhaps this Miss Koskull was his mistress. I looked at her and she laughed and showed her strong healthy teeth.

On the afternoon of January 6th we drew near to Stockholm at long last. The roads were so ice-bound that at the slightest rise of the road the horses could not draw us up the incline at all. I had to get out with the others and trot along after our carriages. The icy wind whipped me with such fury that I had to bite my lips in order to stifle a scream. Oscar, however, was not in the least disturbed by the cold. He ran alongside the coachmen leading a horse and talking to the poor creature.

The landscape around us was all white, like a winding-sheet, I thought, like a winding-sheet, Persson, and not a freshly laundered bed-sheet. Suddenly I remembered Duphot. I hadn't thought for years of the dead General who had wanted to marry me. He was the first corpse I had ever seen, his the first winding-sheet. How warm it had been in Rome at that time, how warm!

" How long does winter last with you, Baron Adelswärd?" I asked. The gale drowned my words and I had to repeat my question several times.

" Till April," he said.

In April the mimosas are in flower in Marseilles.

We got back into our carriage at last. Oscar insisted on riding outside beside the coachman on his box. " I can see Stockholm better when we arrive, Mama," he said.

"But it's getting dark, darling," I said.

It was snowing so hard that nothing could be distinguished at all through the curtain of white, and at last dusk and darkness submerged everything. Now and then one of the horses stumbled on the icy road.

Then, quite unexpectedly, our coach stopped amid the red glare of torches, and the door was torn open.

"Désirée!"

It was Jean-Baptiste, who had come in a sledge to meet me. "We are only a mile from Stockholm now," he said. "Only another few moments and you are at home, my little girl."

"Papa, may I ride in a sledge? I have never ridden in a sledge before."

Count Brahe and Countess Lewenhaupt went into another sledge and Jean-Baptiste joined me. In the dark of the coach I sat pressed tightly against him. But we were not alone. Miss Koskull sat opposite us.

I felt his hand in my muff. "What cold hands you have, my girl!"

I wanted to laugh, but all I brought out was a sob. The temperature was below zero, and this climate Jean-Baptiste already called—home!

"Their Majesties expect you for tea in the Queen's drawing-room. No need to change your dress, they only want to welcome you and Oscar without formalities. To-morrow Her Majesty will give a ball in your honour."

He spoke quickly, as if hard pressed by something or somebody.

"Aren't you well, Jean-Baptiste?"

"Of course I am well. Only a bit of a cold and too much work."

"Any trouble?"

"Mm."

"Great trouble?"

Jean-Baptiste said nothing for a moment and then broke out: "Alquier, you know, the French Ambassador in Stockholm, has handed us a new note from the Emperor. He demands that we put two thousand sailors at his disposal. Just like that, two thousand Swedish seamen to prove Sweden's friendly feelings for France!"

"And your answer?"

"Please, try to see the situation correctly: it is the question of the answer of the Government of His Majesty the King of Sweden, and not that of the Crown Prince. We refused. We told him that we cannot spare these men if France forces us at the same time to declare war on Britain."

" Perhaps that'll make Napoleon desist?"

" He desist, when he at the same time concentrates troops in Swedish Pomerania? They are ready to invade Pomerania any moment. Davout is in command of them."

Lights were appearing at intervals along both sides of the road. "We are almost there, Your Highness," said Miss Koskull out of the dark.

" Aren't you longing for the lights of Paris, Jean-Baptiste?"

His hand pressed mine inside my muff. I understood: with Swedes present I was not to speak any more about our longing for Paris.

" Are you going to defend Pomerania?" I asked.

Jean-Baptiste laughed. "Defend? With what? Do you really think that the Swedish Army in its present shape could stand up to our—— I mean to a French attack? To an attack by a Marshal of France? Never, never! I myself told the Swedes in Pomerania——" He interrupted himself, then continued: "I have started the reorganisation of the Swedish Army. Every month a different regiment is coming to Stockholm, where I myself take its training in hand. If I had two years, only two years . . .!"

The lights along the road grew more frequent. I bent towards the window and tried to look out, but I could see nothing but whirling snowflakes.

" Is that not a new fur you are wearing, Désirée?"

" Yes, just imagine, a farewell present from the Emperor sent after me by courier to Nyborg in Denmark. Strange, isn't it?"

" I suppose it was difficult to refuse it."

" Jean-Baptiste, the woman isn't born yet who would refuse a sable. It's one of the three furs which the Tsar gave to the Emperor."

" I don't know whether you have been made familiar with the court etiquette here. Have you discussed it with my wife, Miss Koskull?"

She said she had, but I couldn't remember.

" It is still a bit like——" Jean-Baptiste cleared his throat, " as it was in—in the old days, you know."

I put my head against his shoulder. "As in the old days? I wasn't born then, so I don't know."

" Darling, I mean as it was at Versailles."

" I wasn't at Versailles either," I sighed. " But I'll manage it somehow, I'll pull myself together."

Flares appeared on either side, and we drove up a ramp. The coach came to a stop. I was stiff with cold when Jean-Baptiste lifted me down to the ground. Long rows of high, brightly illuminated windows looked down at me. " The Mälar Lake, can one see the Mälar Lake from here?" I asked.

" You will see it to-morrow morning," said Jean-Baptiste. " The castle is situated on Lake Mälar."

The next moment the ground around us was full of people, gentlemen in short jackets and knee-breeches, all in black and red, appeared from nowhere. " For God's sake," I said, " this isn't a masked ball, is it?" Black masks once murdered a King, I remembered. But then I heard a woman laugh stridently.

" Darling," explained Jean-Baptiste to me, " these are no fancy-dress costumes but the uniform worn here at court. Come along, Their Majesties are waiting for you."

No, Jean-Baptiste didn't want to keep his dear adoptive parents waiting. Oscar and I were chased up the marble stair-cases and hardly had time to take off our coats. I looked awful, I thought, with my white face, red nose, squashed hat and untidy hair, and there was no Yvette anywhere near to help me. But at any rate I could rely on La Flotte, who gave me a comb to tidy my hair. My feet were wet in my shoes from walking behind our coaches on the snow and ice-bound roads, but that couldn't be helped now. A door opened before me, a blinding brightness crushed down on me and I found myself in a white salon.

" My wife Desideria, who wishes to be a good daughter to Your Majesty. And my son Oscar!"

At first I didn't believe my eyes, for the Queen wore her hair powdered as they did many years ago in France. ' I must tell Julie,' I thought. She had a black velvet ribbon round her neck and her light-coloured eyes were screwed up as if she were short-sighted. I bowed to her.

The stare of her eyes drilled into me like gimlets. She smiled, but it was not a smile of gladness. She was far taller than I, and in her old-fashioned pale blue velvet robes she had a royal air about her. Holding out her hand to me, probably for me to kiss, she said in measured tones: " My dear daughter Desideria, I welcome you."

I touched her hand with the tip of my nose, I didn't feel like kissing it. Then I found myself in front of an old man with watery eyes and a few strands of thin white hair on a pink skull. " Dear daughter, dear daughter . . ." this old man whimpered. Jean-Baptiste stood by his side supporting him.

The Queen came to me a moment later and said: "I should like to introduce you to the Dowager Queen." She took me to a pale thin woman in black. The theatrical black widow's hood on her powdered hair seemed to float above a completely lifeless face. "Her Majesty Queen Sophia Magdalena," said the cold measured voice.

'For heaven's sake,' I thought, 'who is that? How many Queens are there at this court? The Dowager Queen, that must be the wife of the murdered Gustavus III, the mother of the exiled Gustavus IV, the grandmother of the boy whose place Oscar is taking . . .' I bowed deeply to her, deeper even than to the Queen.

"I hope you will be happy at our court, Your Highness," the old woman said in a very low voice, hardly opening her mouth as she spoke. Perhaps she didn't think it worth her while.

"And this is Her Royal Highness, Princess Sofia Albertina, His Majesty's sister."

I saw a woman with the face of a goat, a face of quite indeterminable age, her long teeth bared in a sweetish smile. I bowed again and then made my way towards the big white china stove, the kind of stove they have here, high and round, against which I loved to lean during the breaks in my journey. My hands and feet were still like ice. It was marvellous to lean against the hot stove. A lackey served me a glass of mulled wine. I folded my hands round the warm glass and felt a bit better. Count Brahe was standing near me, but where was Jean-Baptiste? There he was, bending down towards the trembling King, who was sitting in his arm-chair now, patting Oscar's cheek with a hand twisted by gout.

Suddenly I felt everybody's eyes turned on me. What did they expect of me? Through the whole of my being I felt a wave of disappointment lapping up at me. I didn't look a Queen, I was no striking beauty, no *grande dame*. No, I was propping myself against the stove, I felt and looked cold, I had a turned-up nose and my short hair stuck to my head in wet curls.

"Will you not take a seat, Madame?" The Queen sat down in an arm-chair in a beautifully trained, beautifully studied rustle of clothes and pointed to an empty chair by her side.

"I am sorry, but my feet are so wet. Jean-Baptiste, couldn't you take my shoes off? Or ask Villatte to do it?"

At that everybody looked horrified.

Did I say something wrong? As I was holding the warm glass in my hands I couldn't very well at the same time take off my shoes. Jean-Baptiste or Villatte have done it hundreds of times for——

I looked round the faces in the room. Silence had closed round me like an iron band. It was broken by a loud unrestrained giggle which came from Mariana Koskull. The Queen turned to her sharply, and at once the giggle changed into a cough.

Jean-Baptiste came and offered me his arm. " May I ask Your Majesties to excuse my wife? She is wet and tired out from the journey and would like to retire."

The Queen nodded. The King's mouth gaped half open as if he were still pondering on what he had heard.

I kept my eyes fixed on the floor. When I looked up again I met the bitter, sarcastic smile of the Dowager Queen. Later I was told that this was the first time she had smiled for years. Her smile seemed to say, ' How have the Vasas fallen!'

By the door I turned round to call Oscar. But he was busy examining the buttons on His Majesty's tunic. The old gentleman looked very happy. Seeing that, I said no more and left on Jean-Baptiste's arm.

Jean-Baptiste kept silent till we reached my bedroom. " I have had your suite done up completely, with Parisian wallpapers and Parisian carpets. Do you like it?"

" I want a bath, a hot bath, Jean-Baptiste."

" That is impossible. It is the only wish I cannot grant you yet."

" How do you mean? Don't people have baths in Stockhome?"

He shook his head. " No. I am the only one, I believe."

" What? The Queens, the lords and ladies, no one has a bath here?"

" No one. I told you, everything is here still as it was at Versailles in the time of the Bourbons. One does not have a bath here. I had an idea that it would be like that and therefore took my bath tub along with me, but it is only during the last week that I have managed to get hot water. The kitchen is too far away from my rooms. Now they have put up a stove somewhere near my bedroom where Fernand can heat water for my bath. I shall get you a stove like that too and try and find a tub. But you must be patient for a bit, patient in every respect."

" Couldn't I have a bath in your tub to-night?"

"Are you mad? Have a bath and then run in your dressing-gown from my rooms to yours! The whole court would talk of nothing else for weeks."

"Does that mean that I could never go in my dressing-gown —I mean that I could never go into your bedroom, that I——" Stupefied, I added: "Jean-Baptiste, does etiquette at the Swedish court forbid us——" I faltered again. "You know what I mean."

Jean-Baptiste broke into a burst of laughter. "Come here, my girl, come here. You are marvellous, you are unique! I have not laughed like this since I left Paris." He threw himself into an arm-chair and roared with laughter. "Listen," he said. "Next to my bedroom there is another room occupied day and night by a gentleman-in-waiting. That is part of the etiquette. Naturally I have Fernand in this room as well. We are careful, darling. We receive no men in black masks and tolerate no plots among the colonnades like Gustavus IV. So, as there is always someone in the adjoining room, I prefer, shall we say, for certain conversations of a more intimate kind with my little girl, to visit the rooms of Her Royal Highness. Do you understand?"

I nodded. "Jean-Baptiste, tell me, did I behave very badly? Was it a real crime against etiquette that I wanted Villatte to take off my shoes?"

He stopped laughing and looked at me gravely, almost sadly. "It was bad, my little girl, really bad. But," he said, getting to his feet, "how were you to know that? And the court ought to have prepared against something like that. I warned the emissaries of the King that night when they offered us the crown."

"Offered *you* the crown, Jean-Baptiste, not us."

Marie took me to bed. She put hot-water-bottles under my feet and the Emperor's sable fur over my blanket. "All wives maintain that their mothers-in-law are terrible. But, Marie, mine really is."

The next evening we danced in the ballroom of the King and Queen till late into the night, and two days later the citizens of Stockholm gave a ball in my honour in the ballroom of the Exchange. I wore my white robes and a golden veil over my hair and shoulders. The Swedish court ladies possessed marvellous jewellery, big diamonds and dark blue sapphires and magnificent diadems. Never before had I seen such precious gems.

On the day after the ball in the Exchange Countess Lewenhaupt brought me a pair of ear-rings made of diamonds and emeralds.

"A present from the Queen?" Perhaps she thought I had looked too poverty-stricken?

"No, a present from the Dowager Queen," said Countess Lewenhaupt imperturbably. "She used to wear them often. Now she wears mourning only and never any jewellery."

I wore these ear-rings on January 26th, Jean-Baptiste's birthday. The Queen gave a party in his honour, during which a kind of pageant was acted, but unfortunately not by proper actors and actresses but by Sweden's young aristocrats. They danced a quadrille in the different regional costumes of the country, and ended up by forming a circle into which tripped so-called Valkyries, Nordic goddesses of the battlefield or whatever they are. The ladies acting them wore a kind of nightgown made of tiny pieces of metal which jingled and clanked as they moved, and they each carried a shield and a spear. Miss Koskull in golden armour was the central figure, and she smiled victoriously. The others danced around her singing, "Oh Brynhild, oh Brynhild!" Miss Koskull inclined her shield and her head and looked deeply into Jean-Baptiste's eyes. During the last figure of the dance all the Valkyries danced towards us with dainty steps in minuet rhythm, bowed before Oscar, and before we realised what was happening they had lifted him into the air and amidst the applause of the spectators carried him out of the ballroom.

All that had been an idea of beautiful Koskull, and nobody could imagine a more pleasant birthday party.

Jean-Baptiste was sitting between the Queen and myself. His eyes seemed to lie deep in their sockets and he chewed his lower lip restlessly.

"Is Davout going to attack Pomerania?" I asked him, whispering. He gave a faintly perceptible nod.

"Great anxieties?"

Again he nodded. After a pause he added: "I sent a courier to the Russian Tsar."

"But he is Napoleon's ally. Do you think anything will come of that?"

Jean-Baptiste shrugged his shoulders, then said: "Perhaps. The Tsar is arming." Then a very urgent tone came into his voice: "Désirée, when you talk to Swedes never mention Finland, never. You understand?"

"I know nothing about Finland. Is it so important to them?"

"Yes, it is a matter of national emotion. They hope they'll get the Tsar to give the country back to Sweden."

"Is he likely to?"

"No, never. Just look at the map and you will see why not."

This was the moment the Valkyries danced their minuet. It was dreadful, and I applauded enthusiastically.

The next day but one was the birthday of King Charles XIII. It was our turn now to give a party to Their Majesties. Everything had been settled before my arrival. *The Barber of Seville* was performed, and Miss Koskull sang the leading part. The childish King devoured her with his eyes and again and again raised his shaky hands to applaud. At the opening of the ball Jean-Baptiste danced the first dance with Miss Koskull. They looked a well-matched couple. She is the first woman I have seen who is almost as tall as Jean-Baptiste himself. As to me, I had the honour of being asked for the first dance by a little man in a brand-new court uniform. "May I ask you for this dance, Mama?" said the little man. It was Oscar's first court ball.

A few days later the old King had a stroke. I heard about it when I was in my new bath tub, which at one time had been nothing but a laundry tub. This tub was put at the far end of my very large bedroom behind a screen made of magnificent tapestries and from there I heard Madame La Flotte talking to Miss Koskull, but not very loudly. Marie bent over me rubbing my back.

A door opened, and I gave Marie a sign to stop. The voice of Countess Lewenhaupt said: "I have just come from the rooms of Her Majesty. His Majesty the King has had a slight stroke."

"Oh!" said Miss Koskull.

"It cannot have been the first," said Madame La Flotte indifferently. "How is the King?"

"His Majesty must have complete rest for the time being. There is no danger, the doctors say, but he must be careful and may not do any work for the next few weeks. Where is Her Royal Highness?"

I moved my legs and made some splashing noises.

"The Crown Princess is having a bath and cannot see anybody at the moment."

"Of course, having a bath! She will never get rid of her cough that way."

I continued my splashing.

" Is the Crown Prince going to take over the regency?"

Hearing that I stopped splashing.

" The Chancellor suggested it to Her Majesty, because of our difficult situation. There are the secret negotiations with Russia and the threatening notes from France to take care of, and so the Chancellor wishes the Crown Prince to take over the Government as soon as possible."

" And?" asked Koskull. The breath-taking tension in her voice was quite obvious to me.

" The Queen refuses to suggest that to the King. And the King does only what she wants him to do."

" Really?" said Miss Koskull sarcastically.

" Yes, really. Even if you imagine yourself to be his favourite. Your reading to him and your laughing do no more than keep him awake, which at any rate is something. . . . By the way, you read very rarely to him now. You do not seem to set so much store by being His Majesty's ray of sunshine. Am I mistaken?"

" It is more amusing," put in Madame La Flotte, " to dance with the Prince of Ponte Corvo, oh, I am sorry, I mean it is far more amusing to dance with your Crown Prince."

" *Our* Crown Prince, Madame La Flotte," corrected Miss Koskull.

" Why? He is not *my* Crown Prince, I am not Swedish, and as a French woman I owe allegiance to the Emperor Napoleon, if it is of any interest to the ladies."

" It is not," said the Countess.

Marie was leaning against the tapestries in complete silence. We looked at each other, I moved my legs in the warm water and then slipped deeper into the tub.

" And why, if I may ask, does one not, in these weeks which are of such decisive importance to Sweden, transfer the regency to the Crown Prince?" inquired Madame La Flotte.

" Because she will never allow it as long as she is alive," whispered Countess Lewenhaupt. But she whispered it so loudly that I realised this conversation was for my benefit.

" Of course not," said Madame Koskull. " She is playing first fiddle now."

" But she was Queen before the arrival of the Crown Prince," said La Flotte.

" Yes. But the King had no power at all. That was in the hands of his ministers," was Miss Koskull's friendly explanation.

Madame La Flotte laughed. " Do you imagine perhaps that

343

the King has any power now? He invariably goes to sleep in all the meetings of the Council of State. Do you know what happened the day before yesterday? I know because Count Brahe, who, as the Cabinet Secretary of His Royal Highness, has to be present, told me. The King was dozing away sweetly and in the intervals between the reports of the different ministers he murmured mechanically, ' I agree to the suggestion of the Council of State'. They were just discussing some death sentence or other, the Minister of Justice proposed that the King should sign it, and the King murmured his automatic ' I agree to the suggestion.' Suddenly the Crown Prince gripped the King's arm, shook him hard and waking him shouted—yes, shouted, your King is half-deaf too on top of everything else! —' Your Majesty, wake up, a man's life is at stake!' So you see how it is, and yet the Queen will not make him Regent."

"And yet the Queen will not make him Regent," said Countess Lewenhaupt clearly. "She will suggest to the King to hand over the chairmanship of the Council of State to the Crown Prince. But he is not going to be Regent, at least not as long as——"

"As long as what?" asked Madame La Flotte.

I didn't stir, and Marie stood like a statue.

"If the Crown Prince is made Regent the Crown Princess will be the Regent's Consort," Countess Lewenhaupt said cuttingly.

There was a pause, and then the Countess said casually: "The Crown Prince will preside over the Council of State and the Queen, during His Majesty's illness, will act as Regent and represent the King."

Miss Koskull laughed. "And on the arm of the Crown Prince Her Majesty his Mama, his dearly beloved Mama, will show herself to the people to show them who governs Sweden. That would suit her!"

"The Queen has told the Chancellor in so many words that that would be the only possible solution," the Countess concluded.

"What reason did she give for it?" asked Miss Koskull.

"That the Crown Princess did not possess sufficient experience to fulfil the duties of representation which fall on a Regent's wife. It would be injurious, the Queen maintained, to the prestige of the Crown Prince, if Her Royal Highness let herself be seen in public too often."

"I wonder whether she will tell that to the Crown Prince," said Madame La Flotte.

" She has told him. The Crown Prince was present during this interview, as well as the Chancellor and myself."

" You were present? How is that?" asked Madame La Flotte. " As far as I am informed you are lady-in-waiting to Her Royal Highness, are you not?"

" Your information is quite correct. But I also happen to have the honour of being a friend of the Queen's."

' And so the whole thing is a message of the Queen to me,' I thought. " The towel, Marie!"

Marie gave me the towel and with her strong and loving arms rubbed me dry. " Don't put up with that, Eugenie," she said, " don't stand for it." She passed me a dressing-gown.

I came out from behind the screen. My three ladies had put their heads together and were whispering. " I should like to rest. Please leave me alone," I said.

Countess Lewenhaupt bowed. " I have come with sad news, Your Highness. His Majesty has had a slight stroke, the left arm seems paralysed to some extent. His Majesty is to take a rest——"

" Thank you, Countess. I have heard it all during my bath. I should like to be left alone now."

I wrapped myself more tightly into my dressing-gown and went to the window. It was five o'clock in the afternoon and already quite dark. Masses of snow had been shovelled away and piled high against the walls of the castle. ' They are burying me here, burying me in snow,' I thought. But that was a stupid thing to think, and it occurred to me that I had not yet done my Swedish lesson for the day. Jean-Baptiste engaged a Councillor Wallmark to teach him Swedish, and this gentleman turned up every afternoon at Jean-Baptiste's rooms in vain. Jean-Baptiste was always in some conference or other and never had time for him, and as I thought it was a pity to waste all that money on lessons which Jean-Baptiste never took, I decided to have a lesson with Councillor Wallmark every day. Oscar knows quite a lot of Swedish already, but then he has three Swedish teachers and goes skating with Swedish children of his own age.

Jag er, du er, han er, I learn, *Jag var, du var, han var . . . Jag er* I am, *du er* you are, *han er* he is . . . " Marie!"

" Did you call me, Eugenie?"

" You could do me a favour, Marie. There is a street here in Stockholm called Västerlånggatan or something like that. Persson's father had his shop there. You remember Persson, don't you? Perhaps you could make your way there and find

345

out whether Persson's silk shop still exists. If it does, ask for young Persson."

" He won't be quite so young any longer."

" Tell him that I am here. Perhaps he doesn't know that the new Crown Princess is the former Eugenie Clary. And if he remembers me, tell him to come and see me."

" I don't know whether that is very wise, Eugenie."

" Wise! I don't care whether it is or not. Imagine if Persson came to see me and I had someone here who knew our house in Marseilles and our garden and our summer-house where Julie got engaged, and Mama and Papa and—Marie, someone who knows exactly what it was like once upon a time! You must try and find him!"

Marie promised she would, and at last I had something to look forward to.

On the evening of that day the Queen took the King's heavy signet-ring and put it on Jean-Baptiste's hand. That meant that the King had entrusted Jean-Baptiste with the conduct of the Government. But it did not mean that he was to be Regent.

Slowly, very slowly, with roaring floods heaving under green ice-floes, spring approached. On one of the very first spring afternoons Countess Lewenhaupt appeared with an invitation from the Queen to have tea with her in her drawing-room. Every evening after Jean-Baptiste, Oscar and I had our dinner we spent at least an hour with the Queen, whose husband's health, by the way, had considerably recovered from the effects of the stroke. But I had never been to see the Queen by herself. What was the use of it, anyway? We had nothing to say to each other.

" Tell Her Majesty that I am coming," I said to Countess Lewenhaupt, tidied myself up a bit and went across to Her Majesty's rooms over miles of cold marble staircases.

They were seated round a small table, the three of them: Queen Hedvig Elizabeth Charlotte, my adoptive mother-in-law, who ought to love me, Queen Sophia Magdalena, who had every reason to hate me, and Princess Sofia Albertina, an old flat-chested spinster with a childish ribbon in her hair and a tasteless string of amber beads round her scraggy neck, to whom I could mean nothing and who could mean nothing to me. All three were busy embroidering.

" Sit down, Madame," said the Queen.

They continued their embroidering till tea was served. Then

they dropped their frames and stirred their tea. I swallowed a few drops hastily, burning my tongue.

The Queen motioned to the servants. They withdrew. Not a single lady-in-waiting was present either. "I should like to have a few words with you, dear daughter," said the Queen.

Princess Sofia Albertina showed her long teeth in a smile full of glee, but the Dowager Queen stared indifferently down into her cup.

"I should like to ask you, my dear daughter, whether you yourself feel that you are fulfilling all the obligations resting on you as the Crown Princess of Sweden?"

Her pale short-sighted eyes drilled into my face and I knew I was blushing. "I don't know, Madame," I managed to say at last.

The Queen arched her dark, boldly curving eyebrows. "You don't know?"

"No," I said. "I can't judge about that. It's the first time I have been a Crown Princess, and I'm only just starting, too."

Princess Sofia Albertina started bleating. She really bleated like a goat.

Irritated, the Queen raised her hand. In a silky voice she said: "The Swedish people, and the Crown Prince chosen by the Swedish people, are much to be pitied that you do not know how to conduct yourself as Crown Princess." Very slowly the Queen raised her cup to her lips and, drinking, looked at me fixedly over the top of her cup. "Therefore I should like to tell you, my dear daughter, how a Crown Princess has to behave."

'So everything was in vain,' I thought, 'the lessons in deportment from Monsieur Montel and the piano lessons and my keeping quietly in the background at all the court receptions in order not to embarrass Jean-Baptiste, all was in vain."

"A Crown Princess never goes for a drive in the company of one of her husband's adjutants without being escorted by a lady-in-waiting."

Whom did she mean, Villatte? "I—I have known Colonel Villatte for many years. He's been with us since Sceaux and we like talking about old times," I said with difficulty.

"At court receptions the Crown Princess has to speak graciously to everyone present. You, however, stand about awkwardly and almost as if you were deaf and dumb, Madame."

"Man has been given the gift of language to conceal his thoughts," I exclaimed.

347

The Princess bleated loudly and the pale eyes of the Queen widened in surprise. I added quickly: "That isn't my own phrase but comes from one of our—from a French diplomatist, Count Talleyrand, Prince of Benevento. Perhaps Your Majesty has heard——"

"Of course I know who Talleyrand is," the Queen said sharply.

"Madame, if one isn't very clever and very educated, but has to conceal one's thoughts, one is forced to—keep silent."

A teacup clattered. The Dowager Queen had put her cup down with a hand that trembled suddenly.

"You have to force yourself to make conversation, Madame," said the Queen. "Besides, I do not know why you should conceal your thoughts from your Swedish friends and future subjects."

I folded my hands in my lap and let her talk. 'Everything must come to an end,' I thought, 'even this tea party.'

"One of my servants reported to me that your old maid asked him about the shop of a certain Persson. I should like to draw your attention to the fact that you will not be able to make purchases in this shop."

I looked up. "Why not?"

"This Persson is not appointed as Purveyor to the Court and will never be so. On account of your inquiry I asked for information about him. He is considered to be—well, let us say to be in favour of certain revolutionary ideas."

My eyes grew wide. "Persson?"

"This Persson was in France at the time of the French Revolution, allegedly to learn the silk trade. Since his return he has frequently surrounded himself with students, writers and other muddle-headed persons and he spreads those ideas which years ago became responsible for the misery of the French nation."

What could she mean? "I don't quite understand, Madame. Persson lived with us in Marseilles, he worked in Father's shop, in the evenings I often gave him French lessons, together we learnt the Rights of Man by heart——"

"Madame!" It sounded like a slap in the face. "I implore you to forget this. It is quite out of the question that this Persson has ever taken lessons from you or—or ever had anything to do with your father."

"Madame, Papa was a greatly respected silk merchant, and the firm of Clary is still a very solid business even to-day."

"I must ask you to forget all that, Madame. You are Crown Princess of Sweden."

A very long silence followed. I looked down at my hands and tried to think. But my thoughts got all mixed up, only my feelings remained clear. "*Jag er Kronprinsessan*," I murmured in Swedish and said awkwardly, "I have started to learn Swedish. I wanted to make a special effort. But apparently it isn't enough."

There was no answer.

I looked up. "Madame, would you have persuaded His Majesty to appoint Jean-Baptiste Regent if that had not meant that I should become the Regent's Consort?"

"Possibly."

"Another cup of tea, Madame?" asked the bleating spinster. I shook my head.

"I should like to feel that you are going to ponder my words and act accordingly, dear daughter," said the frigid voice of the Queen.

"I am pondering them at this very moment."

"You must never for a moment forget the position of our dear son, the Crown Prince, Madame," concluded the Queen.

At that my patience gave out. "Your Majesty has just reproached me for not forgetting who and what my dead father was. Now you admonish me not to forget my husband's position. I should like you to know once and for all that I never forget anything or anybody!"

Without waiting for a sign from the Queen I got up. To the devil with etiquette! I bowed whilst the three ladies sat more stiffly than ever. "Madame, in my home town of Marseilles the mimosas are in blossom now. As soon as it is a little warmer I shall go back to France."

That went home. All three of them were startled. The Queen stared at me in fright, the goat with incredulity, and even the Dowager Queen's face registered surprise.

"You are going—back?" the Queen brought out at last. "When did you decide on that step, dear daughter?"

"At this moment, Your Majesty."

"It is politically unwise, very unwise, surely. You must speak to the Crown Prince about it," she said hastily.

"I never do anything without my husband's consent."

"And where are you going to reside in Paris, Madame?" asked the goat in agitation. "You have no palace there, have you?"

349

" I've never had a palace there. We kept our home in the Rue
d'Anjou, an ordinary house, certainly not a castle, but very
prettily furnished. I don't need a castle, I'm not used to living
in castles, and, Madame, I even hate castles!"

The Queen had regained her composure. " Your country
house near Paris would perhaps be a more adequate residence
for the Crown Princess of Sweden."

" You mean La Grange? But we sold La Grange and all our
other estates to pay Sweden's foreign debts. They were considerable, Madame."

She bit her lips, then said quickly: " Crown Princess
Desideria of Sweden in an ordinary Parisian dwelling house?
No, impossible. Moreover——"

" I shall discuss it with my husband. By the way, I don't
intend to travel under the name of Desideria of Sweden." I felt
tears coming into my eyes. ' Oh, no tears now,' I said to
myself, ' don't give them that pleasure.' Throwing back my
head I said: " Desideria, the longed-for one! I should like to
ask Your Majesty to find an incognito for me. May I retire
now?" And I banged the door behind me so that it resounded
through the marble halls, as it did once in Rome, in the first
castle to which the winds of Fate had carried me. . . .

From the Queen's drawing-room I went straight to Jean-
Baptiste's study. In the ante-chamber one of the lords-in-
waiting barred my way. " May I announce Your Royal
Highness?"

" No, thank you. I am used to entering my husband's room
without previous announcement."

" But I am compelled to announce Your Highness," he
insisted.

" Who compels you? His Royal Highness perhaps?"

" Etiquette, Your Highness. For centuries——"

I pushed him aside, and my touch made him start as if he
had been stung. I laughed. " Never mind, Baron, I shall not
prevent you from upholding etiquette much longer." I entered
Jean-Baptiste's study.

He was sitting at his desk, studying documents and listening
to the Chancellor Wetterstedt and two other gentlemen at the
same time. A green eyeshade covered the upper half of his face.
I had learnt from Fernand that his eyes had suffered because
the early darkness here forces him to work most of the time in
artificial light. His usual working hours were from half-past
nine in the morning to three o'clock the next morning, and his
eyes always looked badly inflamed. But only the gentlemen

of his immediate surroundings knew of this eyeshade. It had been kept a secret from me so that I shouldn't worry. I wasn't surprised, therefore, that he took it off as soon as I came in.

"Has anything happened, Désirée?"

"No. I only wanted to speak to you."

"Are you in a hurry?"

"No. I shall sit down somewhere and wait till you've finished."

I pulled an arm-chair towards the big round stove and warmed myself. At first I heard snatches of what Jean-Baptiste said. "We must realise that the Swedish currency is at the present moment the weakest in Europe." And: "I will not spend our few English pounds, which we earn with such difficulty through our secret trade with Britain, on unnecessary imports." Or: "But I *am* forced to intervene, I am sacrificing my whole private fortune to stabilise the rate of exchange, I am to mobilise and yet cannot take men away from our steel mills and saw mills, and I must provide artillery, or do you believe that one can win battles with sword and shield nowadays?"

Later I began to bring order into my own thoughts, then felt quite certain that I was right and grew calm. But it made me sad, very sad.

Jean-Baptiste had forgotten my presence and put his eyeshade on again, peering at a document. It concerned an incident, I heard Jean-Baptiste point out, which he considered very important. We had arrested some British sailors in Hälsingborg and the British had arrested three Swedes just to show Napoleon that we were at war with each other, and now a British diplomatist, a Mr. Thornton, had been sent to us to settle the exchange of the prisoners with the man in charge of this affair on our side, a Mr. Engström. But Jean-Baptiste also wanted the Russian Ambassador in Stockholm, Suchtelen, to take part in these negotiations. Why that? I wondered. Did Jean-Baptiste want to bring about secretly an understanding between the Russians and the British, the enemies of France? Nominally the Tsar was still Napoleon's ally, but he had started to prepare for war, and Napoleon was massing troops in Pomerania and Poland.

"Perhaps one could use this opportunity to talk about Finland with Suchtelen," one of the gentlemen was saying now.

Jean-Baptiste sighed, irritated. "You always hark back to that. You bore the Tsar and——" He interrupted himself. "I am sorry, gentlemen. I know what Finland means to you.

I shall take it up with Suchtelen and I shall mention it in my next letter to the Tsar. We shall continue to-morrow. Good night, gentlemen."

The gentlemen bowed themselves out backwards to the door. Jean-Baptiste took off the eyeshade and closed his eyes. His face reminded me of Oscar's when he was asleep: tired and contented. He loves governing, I thought. Most likely he governs well, too.

"Well, little girl, what is it?"

"I am going, Jean-Baptiste. In summer, when the roads are better I am going home, dearest," I said very gently.

He opened his eyes. "Have you gone crazy? Here is your home, here in the Royal Castle of Stockholm. In summer we are moving to Drottningholm, a beautiful country residence with a big park. You will like it there very much."

"But I must go," I insisted. "It's the best thing to do." I repeated my conversation with the Queen word for word, and he listened in silence. The frown on his forehead grew deeper and deeper till he exploded: "What I have to listen to! Her Majesty and Her Royal Highness do not get on well with each other! Incidentally, the Queen is right, you do not always behave like a—as the Swedish court expects you to. You will learn that all right, why shouldn't you? But, God knows, I cannot possibly concern myself with these things now. Have you any idea at all what is happening in the world? And what is going to happen in the next few years?"

He rose to his feet and came towards me. "Our existence is at stake," he said in a voice hoarse with agitation, "the existence of the whole of Europe. Napoleon's European bloc is tottering, the South doesn't give him a minute's rest, in Germany his opponents have established secret alliances, while his soldiers are being ambushed almost every day, and in the North——" He broke off chewing his lower lip. "As the Emperor can no longer rely on the Tsar he is going to invade Russia. Do you understand what that means?"

I shrugged my shoulders. "He's invaded and subjugated so many countries. We know him."

Jean-Baptiste nodded. "Yes, we know him. The Swedish Crown Prince knows him better than anybody else. And for that reason the Tsar of all the Russias will come to the Crown Prince of Sweden for advice in his hour of need. And when the conquered countries unite in a new coalition under the leadership of Russia and Britain, they will come to Sweden and

352

demand a decision from us, are we for Napoleon or against him?"

"Against him? That would mean that you——" I didn't finish the sentence.

"No, it would not. Napoleon and France are not the same thing. Have not been the same thing since the days of Brumaire, the days which neither he nor I have forgotten. That is why he concentrates troops on the frontiers of Swedish Pomerania too. If he wins the war against Russia he will simply trample Sweden under foot and put one of his brothers on the throne. But as long as the Russian campaign lasts he wants to have my support. At the moment he is bidding for it, offers me Finland and wants to put in a good word with the Tsar on our behalf. As far as appearances go the Tsar is still his ally after all."

"But you said that the Tsar will never part with Finland?"

"Of course not. But the Swedes cannot get used to that idea. However, I shall compensate them for the loss of Finland." Quite unexpectedly a smile appeared on his face. "Once Napoleon is beaten and the great cleaning up in Europe begins, Napoleon's most loyal ally, Denmark, will have to pay a price. The Tsar will suggest to Denmark the cession of Norway to Sweden. And that, my little girl, is written not only in the stars but right across the map of Europe."

"Napoleon isn't beaten yet. Besides, you are saying all the time that the fate of Sweden is at stake, and you don't want to see that for that very reason I must go back to Paris."

He sighed. "If you knew how tired I am you would not be so obstinate about this. I cannot let you go. You are the Crown Princess here, and that is the end of it."

"Here I can only do harm, but in Paris I can do a lot of good. I've thought it all out."

"Don't be childish! What can you do? Spying on the Emperor for me? I have my own spies in Paris, you can be sure of that. I could tell you, for instance, that Talleyrand corresponds secretly not only with the Bourbons but also with me."

"I don't want to do any spying. But, when the great cleaning up, as you call it, comes, all Napoleon's brothers will be chased from their thrones. France was a Republic before Napoleon made himself Emperor, and even if Talleyrand corresponds with the Bourbons, they can't force France to recall them."

Jean-Baptiste shrugged his shoulders. "You can be sure that

the old royal families stick together, and they will certainly try it. But what has it to do with us, with you and me?"

"If that is so, the old royal families will also try to exclude the former Jacobin General Bernadotte from the Swedish succession. And who is going to stand by you then?"

"I cannot do more than serve the interests of Sweden with all my strength. Every penny I have saved I am putting into this country to get it on its feet, and I am thinking of nothing but of ways and means of preserving Sweden's independence. If I succeed, Désirée, then the Swedish-Norwegian union will materialise as a matter of course." He was leaning against the stove and covering his inflamed eyes with his hand. "Nobody can ask more than that of any human being. As long as Europe needs me to fight Napoleon, Europe will protect me. But does one know who is going to stand by me afterwards, Désirée?"

"The people of Sweden, Jean-Baptiste, the people only, but they are what matters. Hold on to the Swedes who called you in."

"And you?"

"I am only the wife of a man who is probably a genius and not that Desideria for whom the Swedish nobility longed. I am doing harm to your prestige. The aristocracy pokes fun at me, and the ordinary Swedes when it comes to taking sides prefer their aristocracy to a foreigner. Let me go, Jean-Baptiste. It will make your position stronger." I felt a sad smile creep over my face. "After the King's next stroke you'll be made Regent. You can pursue your policy better once you take over the Regency. It'll be easier for you without me, darling."

"It sounds very reasonable, my girl, but no, no! To begin with, I cannot send the Swedish Crown Princess to Paris to be Napoleon's convenient hostage. My decisions would be influenced if I knew you to be in danger all the time and——"

"Really? But didn't you ask the Council of State shortly after your arrival here not to be influenced in any way by consideration of what is dearest to you in this life? At that time Oscar and I were still on French territory. No, Jean-Baptiste, you must not take us into consideration. If you want the Swedes to stand by you, you must stand by them." I took his hand, pulled him down to the arm of my chair and sat close to him. "Besides, do you really believe that Napoleon would ever arrest his brother Joseph's sister-in-law? Very unlikely, isn't it? He knows you, and he knows therefore that that would lead to nothing. Didn't he give me a sable fur at the same time that he received an unaccommodating letter from the Swedish Government? No, dearest, no one takes me seriously. Let me go."

He shook his head impatiently. "I am working day and night, I am doing an endless number of jobs, and I cannot go on with them if I know that you are not near me. I need you, Désirée."

"Others may need me more. A day may come when my house is perhaps the only one to offer shelter for my sister and her children. Do let me go, Jean-Baptiste, I implore you!"

"You must not profane Swedish authority in order to help your family. I shall never tolerate that."

"I shall always profane Swedish authority if it helps someone in distress. Sweden is only a small country, Jean-Baptiste, with at most a couple of million inhabitants. Magnanimity alone can make it great."

At that Jean-Baptiste smiled. "I almost believe you take the time to read books."

"I shall take the time in Paris, dearest, when I have nothing else to do. I shall try to educate myself so that you and Oscar need not be ashamed of me later on."

"Désirée, the child needs you. Can you really envisage a separation from him for any length of time? No one knows how the situation is going to develop. It may be that you could not return here easily once you are in Paris. Europe is going to be turned into a battlefield and you and I——"

"Darling, I shouldn't be allowed to accompany you to the front in any case. And the child——" Yes, the child. All the time I had tried to push the thought of him away from me. The idea of a separation from him was like an open wound, it hurt. "The child is now Heir to the Throne, surrounded by an adjutant and three teachers. Since we came here he's had very little time for me. At first he'll miss me, but then he'll realise that an heir to a throne cannot indulge his sentiments, only his sense of duty. In this way our boy will be brought up like a Prince by birth, and nobody could ever call him later on a *parvenu* King." I put my head on his shoulder and cried. At last I pulled myself together and got up. "I think it's time to eat."

Jean-Baptiste sat on the arm of the chair without moving. Away from the stove I felt at once the icy cold of the room. "D'you know that in Marseilles the mimosas are in bloom at this time?" I said.

" The Chancellor told me spring would be here in four weeks'
time, and he is a reliable man," said Jean-Baptiste in a low
voice.

I walked towards the door, slowly, waiting feverishly for a
word from him, for his decision. I would take it as a judgment.
When I arrived by the door I stopped. Whatever his decision
was, it would break me, I felt.

" And how am I to explain your departure to Their Majesties
and the court?" It sounded casual, as if the whole thing were
of almost no importance.

" Say that I have to go to Plombières for reasons of health to
take the waters there, and that I shall spend autumn and winter
in Paris because I cannot stand the raw climate here."

I left the room quickly.

DROTTNINGHOLM CASTLE in SWEDEN. The
beginning of June 1811.

The night sky spreads like pale green silk over the park. It is
midnight, but still not dark. I had dark blinds put at the
windows to help me to sleep, but I didn't sleep well in spite of
that. I don't know whether the green twilight or my impending
departure for France to-morrow morning is responsible for my
sleeplessness.

Three days ago the court moved to Drottningholm, the
summer residence with an endless park. The light nights are
full of sweet scents, the eerie light makes everything look unreal.
One doesn't sleep, one only stares into the green space. Unreal
too in this light are all the last talks and farewells, painful and
yet easy to bear because I am allowed to go back home. I am
turning over the pages of my diary, and I remember Papa.

On June the first the Swedish court left Stockholm for this
place. Perhaps I am dreaming, I tell myself this last night in
which I still call myself the Crown Princess of Sweden. To-
morrow morning I shall start my journey incognito under the
name of Countess of Gothland. Perhaps it's all been nothing
but a dream and I shall wake up in my bedroom in Sceaux, and
the next moment Marie will come in and give me Oscar. But
the outlines of my trunks in the room here are very real indeed.
Oscar, my boy, your mother is going away to France, but not
just for health reasons, and I shall not see you again for a very
long time. And when I do see you again you won't be a child
any more, at least not *my* child. You'll be a real Prince instead,

bred to occupy a throne. Jean-Baptiste was born to reign, you are being bred to reign. But your mother was neither born nor bred to it, and that is why in a few hours I shall leave. . . .

For weeks the court found it impossible to understand that I was really going away. They whispered and threw curiously furtive glances at me. I thought they'd be annoyed with me for it. But strangely enough they were annoyed with the Queen instead. It was said that the Queen had not been a good mother-in-law to me and, so to speak, had forced me to leave. But if they had expected feuds between Her Majesty and Her Royal Highness they were disappointed. I am leaving the scene to-morrow morning as the unknown Countess of Gothland.

I only went along to Drottningholm to see the famous summer seat of the Vasas where Oscar is going to spend his summers from now onwards.

The evening after our arrival we were given an entertainment in the little theatre built by the mad King Gustavus III at enormous expense. Miss Koskull, in her blissful amateurishness, sang a few arias which the King applauded enthusiastically, but she had no response whatever from Jean-Baptiste. Yet there was one moment during that dark winter when I thought that . . . Now the tall Miss Koskull, the Valkyrie, the goddess of the battlefield, had lost all attraction for Jean-Baptiste, now that I was going. All the same, my darling, I am going whatever happens. . . .

In my honour Their Majesties gave a farewell banquet. After the meal we even danced a little. The King and Queen sat in gilded arm-chairs and smiled graciously, that is to say, as far as the King with his drooping mouth and uncomprehending face can smile at all.

I danced with Baron Mörner, Chancellor Wetterstedt and Foreign Minister Engström, and finally with Jean-Baptiste's youngest Cabinet Secretary, our Count Brahe. After the dance I said to him: "It is hot in here. I should like a breath of fresh air." We went outside.

"I should like to thank you, Count Brahe," I told him. "You stood by my side chivalrously when I arrived, and I know that you will see me just as chivalrously to my carriage to say good-bye. You did everything in your power to give me an easy beginning here. Forgive me for having disappointed you. This is the end of the beginning."

He hung his dark head and chewed the little moustache which he had been growing. "If Your Highness wishes——"

I shook my head energetically. "No, Count, no! Believe me,

my husband is a good judge of men, and if he's made you a Cabinet Secretary in spite of your youth, then it is because he needs your services, needs them here in Sweden."

He didn't thank me for this compliment but continued chewing his moustache. But then he raised his head abruptly. "I ask Your Royal Highness not to go. I implore Your Highness!"

"The matter was settled weeks ago, Count Brahe. And I believe I am doing right."

"But no, Your Highness. I implore you once more to postpone your departure. The time does not seem to me——" He stopped, ran his fingers through his hair and then jerked out: "I am certain that the time you have chosen is wrong."

"The time is wrong? I don't understand you."

He turned his head away. "A letter came from the Tsar. More than that I cannot say."

"Then don't say it. As His Highness's Secretary you must not mention his correspondence. But I'm glad that the Tsar has written. The Crown Prince greatly values a good understanding with him, and I hope that it was a friendly letter."

"Too friendly."

I could make nothing of young Brahe's behaviour. What did my departure have to do with the Tsar?

"The Tsar has offered the Crown Prince a token of his friendship," said Brahe in despair, and he continued without looking at me: "The Tsar began his letter with the words 'My dear Cousin,' great sign of friendship, that."

Yes, a very great sign indeed, the Tsar addressing the former Sergeant Bernadotte as his cousin. I smiled and said: "That means a lot for Sweden."

"It is a question of the alliance, and we have to decide now either for Napoleon or for Russia. Both proposed an alliance to us. And that is why the Tsar wrote 'My dear Cousin, if it can be of any assistance in strengthening your personal position in Sweden I offer you——'"

"Finland, isn't it?"

"No, he says nothing about Finland. 'If it can be of any assistance in strengthening your personal position I offer you entry into my family'." Count Brahe's shoulders seemed to sag as if under a heavy burden.

I stared at him uncomprehending. "What does it mean? Does the Tsar, too, want to adopt us?"

"The Tsar speaks only about—His Highness." At last he turned his face back to me. It had a tortured look about it.

"There are other possibilities, Your Highness, for bringing about an entry into a family." Then I understood what he meant.

Oh, yes, there were other possibilities. Napoleon married his stepson to a Bavarian Princess and he himself is the son-in-law of the Emperor of Austria, and therefore related to the Hapsburgs. All one had to do was to marry a Princess. It was very simple indeed. A Government measure, a document of State such as the one that Josephine had had to read out. . . . And before my mind's eye I saw Josephine screaming, Josephine moaning with pain on her bed.

"That would indeed secure the position of His Highness," I said in a toneless voice.

"It would not, not with us in Sweden. The Tsar has taken Finland away from us, and we cannot get over this loss so quickly. But, Your Highness, with the rest of Europe it would greatly enhance his position."

Josephine came back to my mind. But Josephine had not given him a son, had she?

"And therefore," Count Brahe concluded, "I should like to point out that this is not a favourable time for Your Highness's departure."

"Yes, it is, Count Brahe. Now even more so. One day you will understand." I gave him my hand. "I ask you very sincerely to stand loyally by my husband. We have the feeling that here they grudge us our French friends and servants. For that reason Colonel Villatte, my husband's oldest and most faithful adjutant, is returning with me to Paris. Try to take his place, Count, my husband will be very lonely. I shall see you to-morrow."

I didn't return to the ballroom immediately. Instead I walked slowly down the endless park as if in a daze. It was to this palace, to this park, that Gustavus IV had been brought as a captive after his enforced resignation. Here, in the alleys and avenues, he ran up and down with his warders running behind him, talking to himself and the lime trees in his despair and madness. And there, by the Chinese pavilion, where in his young days he used to compose his elegies, his mother would wait for him every day, the mother of a madman, the widow of a murdered man, Sophia Magdalena.

The wind of summer soughed gently in the leaves. I noticed a shadow, and then I saw that the shadow was moving towards me. I screamed, I wanted to run away but stood rooted to the spot. Immediately in front of me on the pebble path in the pale light of the moon stood the Dowager Queen in her black dress.

"I am sorry if I frightened you," she said.

"You—you were waiting here for me, Madame?" I felt ashamed because the wild beating of my heart hardly allowed me to speak.

"No, I could not know that you prefer a walk to dancing, Madame," said the flat voice. "I myself always go for a walk on fine summer nights. I do not sleep well, Madame. And this park brings back many memories."

I could hardly find an answer to that. Her son and grandson had been banished, my husband and my son had been called to their place. "I am saying good-bye to these avenues which I hardly know. I am returning to France to-morrow morning." I was glad to have found something to say.

"I did not expect ever to be able to speak to you alone. I am glad of this opportunity."

We walked along side by side. I had lost my fear of her, an old lady in black clothes. The air was full of the scent of the limes.

"I ponder often over your departure. I believe I am the only one who knows your reasons," she said.

"It's better not to talk about it," I said, and walked a bit faster. At that she reached for my arm, and the unexpected touch frightened me so much that I shrank back.

"But, my child, are you afraid of me?" Her voice had gained an unsuspected depth and sounded full of an irredeemable sadness. We stopped.

"Of course not, that—yes. I am afraid of you, Madame."

"Of me, a sick, lonely woman?"

I nodded. "Because you hate me like all the other ladies of your family. I disturb you, I don't belong here—there's no sense in talking about it. It doesn't alter the facts. I do understand you very well, Madame. You and I attempt to do exactly the same thing."

"Do please explain what you mean by that."

I felt tears rising in my throat. This last evening with all its misery made me cry. But only one short sob came out, then I had myself under control again. "You are staying in Sweden, Madame, in order to remind everybody by your presence of your son and grandson. As long as you are here it will be impossible to forget the last Vasas. Perhaps you would have preferred to live in Switzerland with your son, who is said to live in very modest circumstances. Perhaps you would prefer to keep house for him and darn his socks instead of doing

360

embroidery in Her Majesty's drawing-room." I lowered my voice. "But you're staying, Madame, because you are the mother of an exiled King and serve his interests by staying here. Am I right, Madame?"

She didn't stir, but stood there, gaunt and upright, a black shadow in the green twilight. "You are right," she said. "And you, Madame, why are you leaving?"

"Because by leaving I best serve the interests of the future King."

A long silence followed. At last she said: "That was exactly what I thought." A few bars of guitar music floated through the park, and the voice of Miss Koskull singing came to us for a moment. "Are you sure that your leaving would also serve your own interests?" she asked.

"Quite sure, Madame. I am thinking of the distant future and of King Oscar I," I said. Then I bowed deeply to her and went back to the castle.

It is two o'clock in the morning. The birds have just begun to twitter in the park. Somewhere here in this castle there lives an old woman who can't find sleep. Perhaps she is still wandering about in the park. She is staying, I am leaving. . . .

I have described the last evening. There's nothing more to add to it. But still, I can't escape my thoughts. Has the Tsar any daughters? Or sisters? For heaven's sake, I am seeing ghosts again.

My door opens very, very gently. Are there any ghosts walking about the castle? I could shout for help, but perhaps I am wrong. No, the door is really opening, I force myself to go on writing——

Jean-Baptiste!

In the coach during the journey from SWEDEN to FRANCE.
The end of June 1811.

My passport is made out in the name of Countess of Gothland. Gothland is a big Swedish island. I don't know it at all. The Queen thought of it for my title. Under no circumstances was she going to allow her dear daughter, the Crown Princess, to travel through Europe in too modest a style. But on the other hand no attention was to be drawn to the fact that Desideria, the allegedly longed-for one, after a few months in her new home was already on her way back. Hence the disguise.

The Queen came to see me off. Oscar cried inconsolably but tried to hide his tears. The Queen put her hand on his shoulder; the boy, however, shook it off.

"Promise me, Madame, that you will see to it that the boy goes to bed every evening at nine o'clock," I asked her.

"I had a letter the other day from Madame de Staël. She makes some very sensible and progressive suggestions for the Prince's education," said Jean-Baptiste.

"Oh, that woman!" I murmured, and repeated, "At any rate, bed at nine o'clock!" I looked at Jean-Baptiste for the last time for nobody knows how many weeks to come. So many intelligent and educated women around him, perhaps even a Russian Grand Duchess. . . .

Jean-Baptiste put my hands to his lips. "Count Rosen will be at your side whatever happens."

Count Rosen, Count Brahe's best friend, clicked his heels. He is my new adjutant, a young man with gleaming fair hair and the adjutant's sash around his waist. Count Brahe came, but we didn't have any more conversation with each other.

"I wish you a very good journey, Madame," said the Queen, who all at once looked old. She seemed not to have slept well. The pouches under her pale eyes were swollen. Was there anybody at all who had slept well last night?

Oh yes, the Countess Lewenhaupt had! She was positively beaming now that she no longer had to be lady-in-waiting to a silk merchant's daughter. Miss Koskull, too, looked fresh and blooming, well made-up and very sure of triumph. No doubt, she saw possibilities. . . .

At the last minute everybody crowded round me so eagerly that they pushed Oscar aside. But he elbowed his way back to me. He is almost as tall as I am now, which is not saying very much. All the same, he really is tall for his age.

I took him into my arms. "May God protect you, darling!" His hair gave out a fresh fragrance, the fragrance of sun and lime blossom. He must have been out riding this morning.

"Mama, can't you stay? It is so beautiful here!"

How good that he found it beautiful here, how good!

I entered the carriage. Jean-Baptiste propped a cushion up behind my back, and Madame La Flotte took her seat next to me. Villatte and Count Rosen joined us in our coach, Marie and Yvette travelled in a second one. As the carriage started to move I bent forward and looked at the row of windows. I felt sure that at one of the windows on the first floor there would be a black figure standing. And there was! She stayed, I left.

"When we arrive in Plombières we won't have a single summer dress of the latest fashion," said Madame La Flotte. "We should go to Paris first and do some shopping there."

Fair-haired children were standing by the roadside, waving, and I waved back at them. Already I was longing for Oscar, already. . . .

PARIS. January 1st, 1812.

When all the church bells of Paris were ringing in the New Year we were facing each other alone, Napoleon and I.

That surprising invitation came to me through Julie. "Their Majesties receive after midnight. But the family is asked for ten o'clock, and you are to come along with us at all costs, the Empress said."

When Julie told me this we were sitting as usual in the small drawing-room in the Rue d'Anjou where she tells me all her cares and worries. She seems contented with her life as the Queen of Spain whose husband has never managed to sit on his throne, contented with her life at the court in Paris where she finds the Empress a really majestic figure and the Empress's son, the blue-eyed and fair-haired King of Rome, a really adorable little baby. She couldn't understand at first why I didn't call at the Tuileries after my return. I didn't call, and I have been leading a very quiet life ever since, seeing only Julie and a few friends. That was why this invitation came as a surprise, and I couldn't rid myself of the feeling that it was an invitation for a purpose. But what purpose?

And so for the third time in my life I rode to the Tuileries with fear in my heart. The first time was the night I asked Napoleon in vain to spare the life of the Duc d'Enghien. The second time I went with Jean-Baptiste and Oscar before we went to Sweden.

Last night I wore my white and gold robe and the ear-rings from the Dowager Queen, and though I didn't feel cold, I had thrown Napoleon's sable round my shoulders. 'In Stockholm,' I thought, 'the temperature will be down to thirty degrees below freezing point.' I breathed deeply when I entered the palace. I felt at home among the dark-green liveries of the servants, the tapestries and the carpets with the bee pattern, bees, bees everywhere, exactly as he had told me that night. And there were bright lights everywhere, no half-darkness and no ghosts.

The whole family had foregathered in the Empress's salon. When I came in everybody rushed to greet me, a genuine Crown Princess now. Even Marie-Louise rose and came to meet me. She still wore pink, her eyes still looked as if they were made of china, but her smile was more effusive than ever. Her first question was about her 'dear cousin' the Queen of Sweden. Naturally a member of the Vasa family is nearer to the heart of a Hapsburg than all the Bonapartes of the world together.

I had to sit beside her on a very fragile sofa. Madame Letitia was there, too, and I was pleased to meet the old lady again, *Madame Mère* with Parisian curls and carefully manicured finger-nails. Polette, the Princess Borghese, more beautiful than ever, drank a lot, and I remembered that Julie had recently hinted at a mysterious illness Polette had contracted, a quite unmentionable illness. Of course I hadn't been able to imagine what kind of illness that might be. Then there was Joseph, too, smiling disagreeably when talking of the 'Bernadotte dynasty'.

It was past eleven o'clock and the Emperor had not yet appeared. "His Majesty is still working," Marie-Louise explained. The champagne glasses were filled and Julie inquired when we would be shown the baby.

"At the beginning of the New Year," said Marie-Louise. "The Emperor wants to see it in with the boy in his arms."

At that moment Meneval, the Emperor's secretary, came. "His Majesty wants to speak to Your Royal Highness."

"Do you mean me?"

His face remained grave. "Your Royal Highness, the Crown Princess of Sweden."

Marie-Louise, talking to Julie, didn't seem to be surprised. I realised that she had invited me on the Emperor's order. The Bonapartes, however, fell silent.

Meneval took me to Napoleon's small study. The two former interviews had taken place in his big one. Napoleon looked up for a moment as we entered, said: "Take a seat, Madame," and then, very impolitely, continued with what he was doing. Meneval disappeared, I sat down and waited.

A file with many closely written sheets was lying in front of him. I thought I recognised the writing. Probably Alquier's despatches from Stockholm, I reflected. The clock on the mantelpiece kept ticking towards the New Year, and I sat and waited.

Suddenly I heard myself say: "There is no need, Sire, to intimidate me by keeping me waiting. I am timid by nature, and where you are concerned I am not very brave."

He still didn't look up but said: "Eugenie, Eugenie, one waits till the Emperor opens the conversation. Did Monsieur Montel not manage to teach you even that much etiquette?" Then he continued to read.

I studied his face. The mask of Cæsar was running to flesh now, the hair had thinned out. 'Strange,' I thought, 'this is the face I once loved.' It was a long time ago, but I remembered how I loved him. It was only the face I had forgotten.

My patience gave way. "Sire, you called me to examine me on questions of etiquette?"

"Among others things. I should like to know why you came back to France."

"On account of the cold climate, Sire."

He leant back, folding his arms across his chest, screwing up his mouth ironically. "Well, well, the cold climate. You were cold in spite of my sable fur?"

"In spite of your sable fur, Sire."

"And why did you not call at court? The wives of my Marshals are in the habit of calling on Her Majesty regularly."

"I am no longer the wife of one of your Marshals, Sire."

"Quite right. I very nearly forgot. We have to deal now with Her Royal Highness the Crown Princess Desideria of Sweden. But in that case, Madame, you should know that members of foreign royal families when they are visiting my capital usually ask for an audience. If only for politeness' sake, Madame!"

"I am not visiting here. I am here at home."

"Oh, I see, you are here at home." He rose slowly, came out from behind his desk and suddenly yelled at me: "And you think I accept that, do you? You are here at home, and your sister and the other ladies tell you every day what is going on at court. And you sit down and write it all to your husband. Do they think you so clever in Sweden that they sent you here as a spy?"

"No, on the contrary, I am so stupid that I had to return here."

He hadn't expected this answer. He had even held his breath to continue his yelling. Now he said in an ordinary voice: "What does that mean?"

"I am stupid, Sire, stupid, unpolitical, uneducated, and unfortunately I have not made a good impression on the Swedish court. And as it is very important that we, Jean-Baptiste, Oscar and I, become popular in Sweden I came back. It's all very simple."

"So simple that I do not believe you, Madame!" It sounded like the crack of a whip. He began pacing the room. "Perhaps I am mistaken, perhaps you are not here at Bernadotte's direction after all. In any case, Madame, the political situation is so precariously balanced that I must ask you to leave France."

I stared at him, disconcerted. Was he throwing me out? "I should like to stay here," I said in a low voice. "If I can't remain in Paris I should like to go to Marseilles."

"Tell me, Madame, has Bernadotte gone mad?" He threw this question at me out of the blue. Rummaging among the papers on his desk he pulled out a letter. The writing on it I recognised as Jean-Baptiste's. "I offered Bernadotte an alliance and his answer is that he is not one of my vassals!"

"I don't meddle in politics, Sire. And I don't know what that has to do with my staying here."

"Then let me tell you, Madame!" He banged his fist on the table, and I heard plaster drop from the ceiling. Now he was really infuriated. "Your Bernadotte dares to refuse an alliance with France! Why, do you think, did I offer him this alliance? Well, tell me!"

I kept silent.

"Not even you can be as stupid as all that, Madame. You are bound to know what everybody knows in all the drawing-rooms. The Tsar has raised the Continental Blockade and his Empire will soon cease to exist. The biggest army of all time will occupy Russia. The biggest army of all time . . ." The words seemed to intoxicate him. "On our side Sweden could reap immortal glory. It could regain its position as a great power. I offered Finland to Bernadotte, if he marches with us, Finland and the Hanseatic towns. Imagine that, Madame, Finland! And Bernadotte refuses! Bernadotte is not going to march! A French Marshal who is not taking part in this campaign!"

I looked at the clock. In a quarter of an hour the New Year would begin. "Sire, it will be midnight soon."

He didn't hear me. He was standing in front of the mirror by the fireplace staring at his own face. "Two hundred thousand Frenchmen, one hundred and fifty thousand Germans, eighty thousand Italians, sixty thousand Poles, apart from one hundred and ten thousand volunteers of other nations," he murmured. "The Grand Army of Napoleon I. The greatest army of all time. I am marching again."

Ten minutes to midnight. "Sire——" I began.

He swung round, his face distorted with fury: " And Bernadotte slights this army!"

I shook my head. " Sire, Jean-Baptiste is responsible for the
well-being of Sweden. His measures serve the interests of
Sweden and nothing else."

" Who is not for me is against me! Madame, if you do not
leave France voluntarily I could have you arrested as a hostage."

I did not stir.

" It is rather late," he said suddenly, went quickly up to his
desk and rang the bell. Meneval appeared at once. " Here,
Meneval, despatch this at once by express messenger." Turning
to me he said: " Do you know, Madame, what that was? An
order to Marshal Davout. Davout and his troops will cross the
frontiers and occupy Swedish Pomerania. What do you say
now, Madame?"

" That you are trying to cover the left flank of your great
army, Sire."

He laughed out loud. " Who taught you that sentence?
Have you talked to any of my officers lately?"

" No, Jean-Baptiste told me that a long time ago."

His eyes grew narrow. " Is he thinking of defending Swedish
Pomerania? It would be amusing to see him fighting Davout."

" Amusing?" I remembered the battlefields, the long rows
of miserable little mounds with their wooden crosses blown
over by the wind. And that he thought amusing. . . .

" You realise, Madame, don't you, that I could have you
arrested as a hostage in order to force the Swedish Government
into an alliance?"

I smiled. " My fate would not influence in the least the
decisions of the Swedish Government. But my arrest would
prove to the Swedes that I am ready to suffer for my new
country. Are you really going to make a martyr out of me,
Sire?"

The Emperor bit his lips. ' Even a fool can stumble on to
the right answer at times,' I thought. ' Napoleon was certainly
not going to turn Madame Bernadotte into a Swedish national
heroine. . . .'

He shrugged his shoulders. " We shall force our friendship
on nobody. We are accustomed to be wooed for it."

It was three minutes to midnight.

" I expect you to persuade your husband to ask for our
friendship." Putting his hand on the door handle he added:
" If only for your own sake, Madame!"

He had an air of malice about him and I looked at him questioningly. At this moment the church bells rang out. Their chimes drowned my question and his answer. He let go of the handle and stared in front of him, listening to the bells like someone mesmerised. When they had finished he murmured: "An important year in the history of France has opened." I turned the handle and we went out.

In the big study adjutants and lords-in-waiting were assembled. "We must hurry. Her Majesty is expecting us," the Emperor said, and broke into a run. His gentlemen ran after him with clanking spurs. I followed slowly with Meneval, through the empty rooms.

"Did you send off the order?" I asked him.

He nodded.

"The Emperor violates the neutrality of a country. The first action of the New Year," I said.

"No, Your Highness," he corrected, "the last one of the old."

When I got back to the salon of the Empress I saw the little King of Rome for the first time. The Emperor was holding him and he cried enough to move a heart of stone. He was dressed in a lace shirt and the broad sash of an order. "Sashes instead of nappies, I must say!" lamented Madame Letitia. The Emperor with the Empress at his side tried to soothe his screaming son and tickled him tenderly. But the crush of foreign diplomats and giggling ladies round him made him more frightened than ever. Catching sight of me, Napoleon came over to me with his fleshy face beaming down on his yelling son. Without thinking what I was doing I held out my arms and took the baby from him. Madame de Montesquieu, the child's aristocratic nanny, was on the scene at once, but I held on to the child. He was wet under the shirt. I tickled his fair hair on the nape of his neck, he stopped crying and looked at me timidly. I pressed him to me, and my thoughts strayed across Europe to Oscar. 'Oscar,' I thought, 'my Oscar. . . .' I kissed the fair silky hair of the little boy and handed him back to his nurse. Someone shouted "To the health of His Majesty the King of Rome!" His Little Majesty was at this moment carried out of the room.

The Emperor and the Empress were in excellent mood and conversed—what did the Swedish Queen call it? 'graciously'—and conversed most graciously with their guests.

"Your Highness will see, the Crown Prince is going to link up with Russia. And the Crown Prince is right!" Did I dream these words or did someone whisper them into my ear? I looked round and saw Talleyrand limping away from me.

I wanted to go home, I was tired. But now the Emperor came towards me, the Empress on his arm. 'If only she didn't wear pink, with those pink cheeks of hers,' I thought.

"And here is my hostage, my beautiful little hostage," he said amiably. The groups around us broke into cultured laughter. "But, ladies and gentlemen," he said in irritation, because he sometimes dislikes people to laugh prematurely at his jokes, "you don't know what the point is. Besides, I fear Her Royal Highness will not feel like laughing. Marshal Davout has regrettably been forced to occupy a part of the Nordic motherland of Her Highness."

There was dead silence everywhere.

"I suppose the Tsar has more to offer than I have, Madame. I am told he is even offering the hand of a Grand Duchess. Can you imagine that this would attract our former Marshal?"

"Marriage to a member of an old princely family is always attractive to a man of middle-class origin," I said slowly. The faces around me grew icy with terror.

"No doubt," the Emperor smiled. "But an attraction like that could endanger your own position in Sweden, Madame. Therefore I advise you as an old friend to write to Bernadotte and persuade him to an alliance with France. In the interests of your own future, Madame!"

"My future is assured, Sire." I bowed deeply. "At least— as mother of the future King."

Astonishment covered his face. When he had recovered he thundered at me: "Madame, I do not want to see you at court again before the Swedish-French alliance has been concluded." He passed on with Marie-Louise.

Marie was waiting for me at home. Yvette and the other girls had the evening off to celebrate New Year's Eve. Marie undid the ear-rings and opened the gold clasps of the robe on my shoulders.

We had a glass of wine. "Your health, Marie. The Emperor told me he has massed the biggest army of all time and he also told me I am to write to Jean-Baptiste about an alliance. Could you tell me, Marie, how I managed to get all mixed up with world history?"

"Look, if you hadn't fallen asleep in the *Maison Commune* in your young days, that gentleman Joseph Bonaparte would not have had to wake you. If you hadn't taken it into your head that he and Julie——"

" Yes, and if I hadn't been burning with curiosity about his brother, the little General! How shabby he looked in his worn-out uniform!"

I propped my elbows on the dressing-table and closed my eyes. ' Curiosity,' I thought, ' pure unadulterated curiosity got me into all this.' But the way over Napoleon led to Jean-Baptiste. And I had been very happy with Jean-Baptiste.

" Eugenie," Marie said cautiously, " when are you travelling to Stockholm again?"

' If I hurry,' I thought, ' I might just be in time to celebrate my husband's engagement to a Russian Grand Duchess.' I felt desperate and didn't say anything.

" A happy New Year!" Marie said at last.

A happy New Year? It had only just begun, but I had an idea that it would be anything but happy.

PARIS. April 1812.

Pierre, my Marie's son, arrived as a complete surprise to everybody. He had volunteered to join the biggest army of all time. Up till now I had gladly paid the 8,000 francs every year necessary to exempt him from conscription—gladly, because I've always had a bad conscience about him, as Marie had had him brought up away from her so that she could come as a nurse to our house. Pierre, a sinewy, tall fellow with a sun-tanned, cheerful face and Marie's dark eyes, was in a brand-new uniform.

Marie was stunned by his arrival. Her bony hands kept stroking his arms. " But why?" she kept asking, " why? You were so satisfied with the bailiff's job Her Highness got you."

Pierre showed his gleaming teeth. " Mama, one's got to be in on it, march with the Grand Army, overthrow Russia, occupy Moscow! The Emperor's called us to arms to unite Europe. Just think of all the chances, Mama! You can——"

" You can what?" Marie asked bitterly.

" Become a General, a Marshal, a Prince, a King and God knows what!" The words tumbled out of him, the enthusiastic volunteer about to march with the Grand Army, and, like all the enthusiasts of all the grand armies of all time, he wanted his rifle garlanded with roses. So Marie picked our roses, and we put roses in all the buttonholes of his tunic, wound them round the hilt of his bayonet and stuck one red bud into his rifle barrel.

He stood to attention and saluted as he left. " Come back safely, Pierre!" I said.

Marie took him to the door. When she came back the furrows in her face had deepened even more. She took a rag and began to polish the silver candlesticks with passionate intensity.

A regiment with drums beating was marching past just then. Villatte had joined us in the room. Since the Grand Army had begun to march a strange restlessness had come over him.

I listened to the regimental music down in the street, and thought how empty it sounded, how tinny, all drums and trumpets and nothing else. How long ago it was that I had last heard the Marseillaise without any musical accompaniment, just sung, by dock workers, bank clerks and tradesmen! Now a thousand trumpets blare out the tune whenever Napoleon shows himself. . . .

Count Rosen entered holding a despatch in his hand and saying something. I couldn't hear him because of the noise of the trumpets outside. We turned away from the window.

" I have very important news for Your Highness. On April 5th Sweden concluded an alliance with Russia."

" Colonel Villatte!" My voice went completely flat as I called Jean-Baptiste's old colleague, his loyal friend, his most trusted collaborator, our friend Villatte. . . .

" Your Highness?"

" We have just been told that Sweden and Russia have made an alliance." I couldn't turn to face him but I had to go on. " You are a French citizen and a French officer, and I suppose that this agreement with the enemies of France will make your stay in my house impossible. When we left you asked your regiment to grant you leave to make it possible for you to accompany us and to assist me. I am asking you now to consider yourself free from all obligations towards me."

It hurt, it hurt badly to have to say that.

" But, Your Highness, I—I cannot possibly leave you now," said Villatte. I bit my lips, then looked towards the fair-haired Count Rosen. " I shall not be alone."

The Count stared past me into a corner. Did he realise that I was saying good-bye to our best friend? " Count Rosen has been appointed my personal adjutant. He will protect me if necessary." I didn't mind Villatte seeing the tears running down my cheeks. I gave him both my hands. " Good-bye, Colonel Villatte."

"Has there been no letter from the Marshal, I mean from His Highness?"

"No. I received the news through the Swedish Embassy."

He looked helpless. "I don't really know——"

"But I know what you feel. You must either ask for your discharge from the French Army like Jean-Baptiste or——" I pointed towards the window through which came the sound of marching boots—" or march, Colonel Villatte."

"Oh no, not march," Villatte said indignantly, "ride!"

I smiled through my tears. "Ride, Villatte, ride with God! And come back safely."

PARIS.
The middle of September 1812.

Thank God for my diary! I should go mad if I hadn't that to write in. In all this big city I have no one now to whom to confide my thoughts, not even Julie, the wife of a Bonaparte. Nobody is left, strangely enough, but Count Rosen, who, Swedish to the core, cannot understand how the new Crown Prince could have made an alliance with the old arch-enemy of his country, Russia.

Count Talleyrand, Prince of Benevento and adviser to the Ministry of Foreign Affairs, and Fouché, Duke of Otranto and former Minister of Police, were here and only left a few hours ago. They came separately, and met by chance in my drawing-room. Talleyrand arrived first. I am not used to having visitors now. My friends are intoxicated by the Emperor's victories in Russia and avoid my house.

Talleyrand was waiting in the drawing-room, studying the portrait of Napoleon as First Consul through half-closed eyes. Before I could introduce Count Rosen to him the Duke of Otranto was announced.

"I don't understand it!" I exclaimed.

Talleyrand arched his eyebrows. "I beg your pardon?"

"It's such a long time since I had any visitors at all," I said, confused. "Show the Duke in."

Fouché was disagreeably surprised to find Talleyrand there. He lisped, "I am glad to see Your Highness in company. I was afraid Your Highness would be very lonely."

"I was very lonely till this moment." I sat down under the portrait of the First Consul, the gentlemen took their seats opposite me. Yvette brought in tea, and as Count Rosen handed the teacups round I explained to him that the second visitor was France's famous Minister of Police who had retired to his estates for reasons of health.

We talked about the Russian campaign and I remarked that the church bells had been ringing almost continuously since the capture of Smolensk.

" Oh yes, Smolensk," said Talleyrand, opening his eyes fully at last to examine Napoleon's picture more closely still, " oh yes, Smolensk. By the way, the bells are going to ring again in half an hour's time, Your Highness."

" You don't say so, Your Excellency!" Fouché exclaimed.

Talleyrand smiled. " Does that surprise you? After all, the Emperor is leading the greatest army of all time against the Tsar. So, as a matter of course, the bells are going to ring again soon. Does it upset you, Your Highness?"

" Of course not. On the contrary, I am, after all——" I broke off. I was going to say ' I am a Frenchwoman after all ', but I am not a Frenchwoman any longer and my husband had concluded a pact of friendship with Russia.

" Do you believe the Emperor will win the war?" Talleyrand asked.

" He has never lost a war yet," I answered.

There was a curious pause, Fouché regarding me intently whilst Talleyrand drank the really excellent tea slowly and with great enjoyment. " The Tsar has asked for advice," he said at last, putting down his cup.

" The Tsar will sue for peace," I said, bored.

Talleyrand smiled. " That was what the Emperor expected after the victory of Smolensk. But the courier who arrived in Paris an hour ago with the news of the victory at Borodino knows nothing about peace negotiations. And that in spite of the fact that this latest victory opens the road to Moscow."

" I suppose that means the end of the Russian campaign, doesn't it? Have a piece of marzipan, Excellency."

" Has Your Highness heard from His Royal Highness the Crown Prince lately?" asked Fouché.

I laughed. " Oh yes, I forgot, you no longer supervise my correspondence. Your successor would be able to tell you that I haven't heard from Jean-Baptiste for a fortnight. But Oscar has written. He is well, he——" I stopped. It would bore the gentlemen to be told about my son.

" The Swedish Crown Prince has been away from home," said Fouché, never taking his eyes off me.

Away from home? I looked at them in astonishment, and so did Count Rosen.

"His Royal Highness was in Abo," Fouché continued.

Count Rosen gave a start. "Abo? Where is Abo?" I asked him.

"In Finland, Your Highness." His voice was hoarse.

Finland again! "Finland is occupied by the Russians, isn't it?"

Talleyrand drank his second cup, and Fouché said with obvious enjoyment of the situation: "The Tsar had asked the Swedish Crown Prince to meet him in Abo."

"Say that again, very slowly," I asked.

"The Tsar had asked the Swedish Crown Prince to meet him in Abo."

"But what does the Tsar want of Jean-Baptiste?"

"Advice," said Talleyrand in a bored voice. "A former Marshal of France who knows the Emperor's tactics thoroughly is an excellent counsellor in a situation like the present one."

"And as a result of the advice of the Crown Prince of Sweden the Tsar is not sending negotiators to the Emperor but letting our army continued to advance," said Fouché. The note of enjoyment had gone out of his voice. It sounded quite flat now.

Talleyrand looked at his watch. "The church bells will start ringing at any moment to proclaim the victory at Borodino. Our troops will be in Moscow in a few days."

"Has he promised him Finland?" Count Rosen burst out.

"Who was to promise Finland to whom?" asked Fouché.

"Finland? What makes you say that, Count?" Talleyrand said.

I tried to explain. "Sweden is still hoping to get Finland back. Finland is very dear to the hearts of the—I mean to the hearts of my compatriots."

"Is it also dear to the heart of your husband, Your Highness?" Talleyrand pursued.

"Jean-Baptiste thinks that the Tsar would on no account renounce Finland. But he very much wants to unite Sweden and Norway."

Talleyrand nodded slowly. "My informant hinted at a promise made by the Tsar to the Swedish Crown Prince to support the union of Sweden and Norway. Of course, after the end of the war."

"But isn't the war finished once the Emperor has entered Moscow?"

Talleyrand shrugged his shoulders. "I do not know what kind of advice your husband gave to the Tsar."

There was another curiously heavy pause. Fouché took another piece of marzipan and smacked his lips.

"But that advice which His Royal Highness is supposed to have given to the Tsar——" Count Rosen began.

Fouché grinned. "The French Army enters villages burned by their inhabitants. The French Army finds nothing but burnt-out stores. The French Army marches from victory to victory and—starves. The Emperor is forced to bring up supplies from his base, and he had not bargained for that. Nor had he bargained for the flank attacks of the Cossacks, who never come out into the open for a pitched battle. But the Emperor hopes to find all the supplies he needs in Moscow, a rich and well-provisioned town where he is going into winter quarters with his Army. You see, everything depends on the capture of Moscow."

"Do you doubt its capture?" asked Count Rosen.

"The Prince of Benevento said a moment ago that the church bells are going to ring at any moment for the victory of Borodino. The road to Moscow is clear. The Emperor will most likely be in the Kremlin the day after to-morrow, dear Count," Fouché said, still grinning.

A great fear began to rise in me and choke me. In despair I looked at the two gentlemen. "Please will you tell me candidly what you have come for?"

"I have been wanting to call on Your Highness for a long time," said Fouché. "And since I have learnt about the important part the Crown Prince of Sweden is playing in this gigantic conflict it is my heartfelt need to assure Your Highness of my sympathy. A sympathy of many years' standing, if I may say so."

'Oh yes, of many years' standing as Napoleon's spy,' I thought.

"I don't understand you," I said, and looked at Talleyrand.

"Is it so difficult to see through a former teacher of mathematics?" said Talleyrand. "Wars are like equations. Even in wars one has to calculate with unknown quantities, and in this war the unknown quantity is a person who, since the meeting with the Tsar, is no longer—unknown. The Swedish Crown Prince has intervened, Madame!"

"And what advantage does this intervention hold for Sweden? Instead of armed neutrality there is a pact with Russia!" Count Rosen exclaimed passionately.

"I am afraid Sweden's armed neutrality does not impress the Emperor greatly. He has occupied Swedish Pomerania. You are not dissatisfied with the policy of your Crown Prince, young man, are you?" Talleyrand said amiably.

But my blond young Count didn't give in so easily. "The Russians have one hundred and forty thousand men under arms, and Napoleon——"

"Nearly half a million," Talleyrand confirmed. "But a Russian winter without proper quarters will defeat the biggest and the best army, young man."

Now I understood. No proper quarters! I certainly understood. Oh my God. . . .

At this moment Madame La Flotte flung the door open and shouted: "A new victory! We have won the bottle of Borodino!"

None of us moved. The sea of chimes seemed to drown me. 'Napoleon wants to winter in Moscow,' I thought. 'What kind of advice did Jean-Baptiste give to the Tsar? Fouché and Talleyrand have spies in all the camps, they'll always be on the right side at the right moment. Their visit to-day meant that Napoleon was going to lose the war, would lose it somehow sometime whilst the victory bells were still ringing out over Paris. Jean-Baptiste had intervened and assured its freedom to a small country in the North. But meanwhile Marie's Pierre might freeze and Colonel Villatte bleed to death.'

Talleyrand was the first to take his leave. Fouché, however, sat on, eating marzipan, smacking his lips and looking very self-satisfied. With the latest victory? Or with himself for having fallen into disgrace at a convenient juncture?

He stayed till the bells had fallen silent. "The welfare of the French people is at stake," he announced, "and the people want peace. The Swedish Crown Prince and I have the same aim—peace!" He bent over my hand, but his lips were sticky and I withdrew my hand quickly.

I went out into the garden and sat on the bench. All the fear I had felt inside the house came back, redoubled. In my restlessness and anxiety I asked for my carriage, and when I went out to it I found Count Rosen waiting to open the carriage door for me. I keep forgetting that I have a lord-in-waiting around me all the time. I should have preferred to be alone now.

We drove along the banks of the Seine. Rosen was talking to me. I didn't pay any attention till he asked me about Fouché's title. He went on to tell me details Fouché had related to him about Jean-Baptiste's meeting with the Tsar in Abo. A British emissary had taken part in it at one time, and it was rumoured that His Royal Highness was trying to engineer an alliance of decisive importance between Britain and Russia to which even Austria might secretly——

"But the Austrian Emperor is Napoleon's father-in-law," I argued.

"That means nothing, Your Highness. Napoleon forced him into this relationship. No Hapsburg would ever have voluntarily accepted this *parvenu* into his family."

The carriage rolled slowly past the towers of Notre-Dame, black against the deep blue of the evening. I told the Count about my part in the coronation of Napoleon and that I had carried a velvet cushion with a lace handkerchief on it for the beautiful Josephine. "I shall introduce you to the Empress Josephine, Count," I said. The idea had come to me suddenly. I would show this little Count the most beautiful woman in Paris, who, having cried for two days and two nights after the divorce, had become her old self again, the best-made-up woman in Paris. I would show her to him and ask her at the same time how to use make-up. If the Swedes were meant to have a *parvenu* Crown Princess they should at any rate have a beautiful one. . . .

As soon as we got home I started writing my diary. Then Marie came and asked if Colonel Villatte had written and said anything about Pierre.

I shook my head.

"After this last victory the Tsar will sue for peace," said Marie contentedly, "and Pierre will be back here before winter comes." She knelt down before me and took off my shoes. There are many white strands in her hair, her hands are coarse from the work she has had to do all through her life, and every penny she has earned she has sent to Pierre. And now Pierre was marching towards Moscow. Jean-Baptiste, what was going to happen to Pierre in Moscow?

"Sleep well, Eugenie, sweet dreams!"

"Thank you, Marie. Good night!" Exactly as it was in my childhood days.

And who was putting Oscar to bed at this moment? One, two or even three adjutants or lords-in-waiting?

Once again I was the black sheep of the family!

Julie and Joseph came back from Mortefontaine to Paris and gave a banquet to celebrate the entry of Napoleon into Moscow. They asked me too, but I didn't want to go and wrote to Julie that I had a cold. The very next day she was on my doorstep.

" I very much want you to come," she said. " People talk so much about you and Jean-Baptiste. Of course, your husband ought to have marched with the Emperor to Russia. Then they would have had to stop spreading rumours about Jean-Baptiste being allied to the Tsar. I want this malicious talk——"

" Julie, Jean-Baptiste *is* allied to the Tsar."

Flabbergasted, Julie stared at me. " Do you mean to say that it is all true, what people say?"

" I don't know what people say. Jean-Baptiste had a meeting with the Tsar and gave him advice."

Julie moaned and shook her head in despair. "Désirée, you really are the black sheep of the family!"

I had been called something like that before, when I asked Joseph and Napoleon Bonaparte to visit us in Marseilles. That was how it all began . . . " Tell me, Julie, which family do you mean?"

" The Bonapartes, of course."

" But I'm no Bonaparte."

" You are the sister-in-law of the Emperor's eldest brother."

" Among other things, my dear, among other things. Above all, I am a Bernadotte, the first Bernadotte, if you consider us as a dynasty."

" If you don't come they'll talk even more about you and they'll know that Jean-Baptiste Bernadotte allied himself secretly to the Tsar."

" But, Julie, it's no secret at all. Only the French papers mustn't mention it."

" But Joseph has expressly demanded your presence. Don't make trouble for me, Désirée."

I hadn't seen Julie all through last summer. Her face looked aged and miserable. A tenderness arose in me for my old Julie, now a careworn, deeply disappointed woman. Perhaps she had heard about Joseph's amorous *affaires*, perhaps he treated her badly because he himself gets more and more embittered, knowing that he owes everything to Napoleon. Perhaps she felt that

Joseph had never really loved her and only married her for her dowry, a dowry which means nothing now to Joseph, who, through the money he made in property speculations and crown estates, is a very rich man. 'Why then,' I thought, 'does she not leave him? Out of love? Sense of duty? Obstinacy?'

"If I can do you a service in that way I shall come," I said.

She pressed her hand against her forehead. "I've got these dreadful headaches again. Yes, please come. Joseph wants to prove, through your presence, to the whole of Paris that Sweden is still neutral. The Empress is coming too and all the diplomatic corps."

"I shall bring Count Rosen, my Swedish adjutant."

"Your what? Oh, of course. Yes, do bring him, we're always short of men, with everybody in the Army. I am so anxious about this banquet. I only hope everything will go all right." Then she left.

The tall bronze candelabra in the Elysée Palace shone brightly. I heard people talking behind my back and felt their eyes following me as I passed. But the presence of young Count Rosen reassured me and made me ignore whispers and glances. At the entry of the Empress the orchestra played the Marseillaise. Everybody present bowed deeply. I, however, as the member of a resigning house, bowed less deeply than the rest.

The Empress—in pink, as ever—stopped and talked to me in her vague impersonal manner about the new Austrian Ambassador to Stockholm, a Count Neipperg, with whom she said she had danced the waltz at her one and only court ball before she married. I could only say that Count Neipperg must have arrived after my departure from Stockholm. Marie-Louise went on to talk graciously to someone else.

At midnight the trumpets once more blared out the Marseillaise. Joseph stepped to the place beside the Empress and holding up his champagne glass he said: "On the 15th of September His Majesty the Emperor entered Moscow at the head of the most glorious army of all time and took up residence in the Kremlin, the palace of the Tsar. Our victorious Army will spend the winter in the capital of our conquered enemy. *Vive l'Empereur!*"

I was emptying my glass slowly when Talleyrand appeared before me. "Has Your Highness been forced to attend?" he inquired, pointing in Joseph's direction.

I shrugged my shoulders. "Whether I'm here or not is of no importance, Excellency. I know nothing of politics."

"It is strange that Fate should choose you of all people to play such a significant part, Your Highness."

"What do you mean by that?" I asked, terrified.

"Perhaps one of these days I shall turn to you with a request of the greatest importance, Your Highness. Perhaps you will grant it. I shall address this request to you in the name of France."

"Would you mind telling me what you are talking about?"

"Your Highness, I am very much in love. Don't misunderstand me, please, I am in love with France, Your Highness, with—our France." He took a sip from his glass of champagne and continued. "I mentioned to Your Highness a short time ago that the Emperor is battling no longer against an unknown quantity but a very well-known one, a very well-known friend of ours. You remember, Highness, don't you? Well, to-night we are celebrating the Emperor's entry into Moscow, where the Grand Army is taking up its winter quarters. Do you think, Your Highness, that that is a surprise to our well-known friend?"

My hand clutched the stem of the glass I was holding.

"My brother should be very comfortable in the Kremlin. The Tsar's residence is supposed to be furnished with oriental luxury," someone said close by. It was Joseph. "Magnificent," he continued, "that my brother managed to finish the campaign so quickly. Now our troops can stay the winter in Moscow."

But Talleyrand shook his head. "I am afraid I cannot share Your Majesty's optimism. A courier arrived half an hour ago with the news that Moscow is burning, has been burning for the last fortnight, including the Kremlin."

In the flickering candlelight Joseph's face looked green, his eyes were wide open, his mouth gaped with dread. Talleyrand, on the other hand, had his eyes half closed, unconcerned and unmoved as if he had been expecting for a long time this news which only arrived half an hour ago.

Moscow was burning, had been burning for a fortnight!

"How did it happen?" Joseph asked in a hoarse voice.

"Arson, no doubt. It broke out in different parts of the town at the same time. Our troops have been trying to cope with it in vain. Every time they thought they had the fire under control it started again in a different part of the city. The population is suffering terribly."

"And our troops?"

"Will have to retreat."

"But the Emperor told me that under no circumstances whatever could he march his troops through the Russian steppe during the winter months. He counts on Moscow for his winter quarters."

"I am only reporting the courier's message. The Emperor cannot billet his troops in Moscow because Moscow has been burning for the last fortnight." Talleyrand raised his glass towards Joseph. "Please act as if nothing had happened, Your Majesty. The Emperor does not want the news to become known for the time being. *Vive l'Empereur!*"

"*Vive l'Empereur!*" Joseph repeated in a voice which had lost all colour.

"Your Highness?" Talleyrand raised his glass towards me, too. But I stood paralysed. I saw the Empress dancing with a gouty old gentleman, saw Joseph wiping beads of perspiration from his forehead, and said: "Good night, Joseph. Give my love to Julie. Good night, Excellency." And then I left, entirely against all etiquette, before the Empress had left herself. But what did I care about etiquette? I was dreadfully tired, and dreadfully troubled.

"It was an unforgettable, a splendid ball," said the young Swedish Count on the way home.

Quite! Unforgettable. . . . "Do you know Moscow, Count Rosen?"

"No, Highness. Why?"

"Because Moscow is burning, Count."

"The advice His Royal Highness in Abo——"

"Don't let's talk any more, please. I am very tired."

And Talleyrand's 'request of the greatest importance', what could it be? When would it be?

PARIS. December 16th, 1812.

Josephine at Malmaison showed me how to use make-up and powder in her own way and how to pluck my eyebrows in order to make my eyes appear much bigger. In the intervals of beauty treatment we made bandages for the wounded in the Russian campaign. Then, quite by chance, as Josephine was doing my eyebrows, I caught sight of this morning's issue of the *Moniteur*, and in it I read Napoleon's 29th Bulletin, the 29th Bulletin which told the world that the Grand Army was frozen, starved to death and buried in the snow wastes of Russia, that the Grand Army had ceased to exist.

"Have you seen that, Madame?" I asked Josephine, holding the paper out to her.

"Of course. Bonaparte's first communiqué for weeks. It only confirms what we feared: he has lost the war with Russia. I suppose he'll soon be back in Paris. Have you ever tried to use henna when you wash your hair? Your dark hair would have an auburn glint in candlelight. It would suit you, Désirée."

"'This Army'," I read, "'which was still such a splendid body on the sixth, was quite different on the fourteenth. It had no longer any cavalry, any artillery, any transport. The enemy realised the calamity that had befallen the French Army and tried to put it to good account. He surrounded the columns with his Cossacks . . .'" And the bulletin went on to describe in detail and in sober language how the greatest army of all time had marched to its doom. Of hundreds of thousands of cavalrymen only six hundred were left, it said. The words 'exhaustion' and 'starvation' kept cropping up, and it ended with the words: 'The health of His Majesty has never been better.'

Looking up into the mirror my face was strange to me, so unfamiliar, so beautiful. I could look beautiful, after all. Returning to the bulletin I asked: "What's going to happen now, Madame?"

She shrugged her shoulders. "Life is full of possibilities, Désirée. He could make peace. Or he could continue to make war——"

"And France, Madame?" I shouted at her so that I made her start, but I couldn't help it.

Before my mind's eye I saw men marching through the snowy wastes in their thousands, saw them fall, saw them keeping wolves at bay till the men could move no longer, saw them torn to pieces by the beasts, shot by the Cossacks, drowning among the ice-floes of the Beresina, death, death in all its terror. . . . But His Majesty's health had never been better, never. "And France, Madame?" I repeated dully.

"Why? Bonaparte is not France, is he?" Josephine smiled down at her gleaming nails which she was polishing. "Napoleon the First, by the grace of God Emperor of the French. . . ." She winked at me. "By the grace of God! You and I know exactly how he got there, don't we? Barras needed someone to suppress hunger riots and Bonaparte was ready to do it. After that, Bonaparte the Military Governor of Paris, Bonaparte the Commander-in-Chief in the South, Bonaparte the Conqueror

of Italy, Bonaparte in Egypt, Bonaparte the First Consul——"
She stopped, then said with pleasure in her voice: "Perhaps
Marie-Louise will leave him now that his luck has turned."

"But she is the mother of his son!"

"That means little, very little. Whatever happens you must
not forget what I told you about looks, Désirée. Promise me!"

Looks, Moscow, make-up, death in the Beresina, I felt so
confused I could say nothing.

"Between ourselves," Josephine continued, "there are
prouder dynasties than the Bernadotte family, Désirée. But the
Swedes chose Bernadotte and he will not disappoint them. He
knows how to govern, Bonaparte said so often enough. But
you, my girl, you can neither govern nor do anything else. In
that case you must do the Swedes at least the favour of looking
pretty."

"But my turned-up nose?"

"You can't do anything about that. But it suits you, in your
young face. You will always look younger than you are. . . .
Well now, let's go down and make Theresa read the cards for
us. Pity it's raining, I should have liked to show the garden to
your Swedish Count."

Going downstairs Josephine stopped suddenly. "Désirée,
why is it that you are not in Stockholm?"

I avoided her eyes. "Stockholm has a Queen and a Dowager
Queen. Isn't that enough?"

"You are not afraid of your predecessors, are you? Predecessors are never dangerous, only successors. Frankly, I was
afraid you had come because you were still in love with him—
with Bonaparte, I mean."

Down in her white and yellow drawing-room Josephine's
ladies and Polette were still busy with their bandages, Queen
Hortense lay on a divan reading letters, and a very fat lady
with an oriental scarf round her neck, which made her look like
a gaudily coloured ball, was playing patience. My young Count
Rosen gazed unhappily at the rain.

When we entered all the ladies except Polette got up. The
gaudily coloured ball sank into a deep curtsey before me.

"Your Highness remembers Princess Chimay?" asked Josephine. It's Désirée when we are alone, it's 'Your Highness'
in public, I noticed. Chimay? It was the name of one of the
oldest aristocratic French families. I was certain never to have
met one of its members before.

But Josephine laughed. "It's Notre-Dame de Thermidor!
My friend Theresa!"

Oh, Josephine's friend Theresa, the ex-Marquise de Fontenay who married the ex-valet and later Deputy Tallien! I invaded her house to look for my fiancé. But I had lost him there and found Jean-Baptiste instead. . . . Her reputation was worse even than Josephine's, and Napoleon, who as Emperor had become very strict, had forbidden her the court. Theresa, fat and mother of seven children, got her own back on Napoleon by marrying Prince Chimay, whom the Emperor would have liked to see at court because of his very aristocratic descent. The Prince, however, did not go because of Theresa's continued banishment from the Tuileries.

" I am glad to see you again, Princess," I said.

" See me again?" Theresa's eyes grew wide with astonishment. " I have not yet had the honour of being presented to Your Highness."

Polette interrupted us from the fireplace. " Désirée, the Empress has put her gold paint on your eyelids. It suits you. But tell me, is your adjutant there deaf and dumb?"

" No, only dumb," Count Rosen said furiously.

I realised it had been a mistake to bring the young Swede into this house. Josephine tried to mollify him by putting her hand on his arm, and at her touch I saw him give an almost imperceptible start. " When it stops raining I shall show you the garden," she said, smiling at him without showing him her bad teeth, and looking deep into his eyes. Then she turned to Hortense, whom she asked about Count Flahault, Hortense's official lover since her separation from her husband.

" He writes," said Hortense, " that from Smolensk onwards he has been marching by the side of the Emperor. The Emperor no longer has a horse because almost all the horses have been frozen to death or killed and eaten by the starving troops. The Emperor wears the fur coat which the Tsar gave him once, and a cap made of Persian lamb. He walks with a stick, accompanied by the Generals who have lost their regiments. He walks between Murat and Count Flahault."

" Nonsense, he walks with his faithful Meneval," said Josephine.

Hortense turned over the sheets of the long letter she was reading and said: " No. Meneval collapsed of exhaustion and was loaded on to a cart together with other casualties."

A great silence fell on the room. The logs on the fire crackled, yet we felt very cold.

" I shall arrange for a Service of Intercession to-morrow," Josephine said in a much subdued voice, and asked Theresa to read the cards for Bonaparte. Notre-Dame de Thermidor collected her cards gravely, remarking that Bonaparte was King of Hearts as usual, divided them in two piles, made Josephine cut them, and began to lay the cards in the form of a big star. Josephine and Hortense looked on, breathless with excitement, Polette nestled close to me and tried to catch Count Rosen's eye. But his eyes avoided our group, he probably thought us crazy.

Theresa, having laid out her star and contemplated it in solemn silence for a long time, said at last: " It looks bad. I see a journey. A journey across water, a journey by boat." After another silence she repeated: " No, unfortunately, it does not look good."

" And I?" Josephine wanted to know.

" You? I see the usual thing, money trouble, nothing else."

" I am in debt again with Le Roy," Josephine admitted.

Theresa suddenly raised her hand importantly: " I see a separation from the Queen of Diamonds."

" That's Marie-Louise," whispered Polette.

" But I see nothing but calamity. By the way, what could the Knave of Hearts mean? He lies between him and the Knave of Clubs. The Knave of Clubs is Talleyrand——"

" The other day it was Fouché," said Hortense.

" Perhaps the Knave of Hearts is the little King of Rome," suggested Josephine. " Bonaparte returns to his child."

Theresa collected the cards and shuffled them once more to lay out a new star. " No," she said, " same thing again, the sea journey, financial troubles, desertion by——"

" By the Queen of Diamonds?" Josephine asked breathlessly. Theresa nodded.

" And I?" Josephine repeated.

" I don't understand. There is nothing between the Queen of Spades and the Emperor. All the same, he is not joining her, I don't really know why not, Josephine. And there, you see, is the Knave of Hearts again, by the Emperor's side, always by the Emperor's side. Seven of Clubs and Ace of Clubs cannot get a him because of the Knave of Hearts in between. It can't be the little King of Rome, it must be a grown-up. But who?"

She looked round helplessly. We couldn't give her any clue. She turned back to the cards, pondering. " It might be a female, a girl perhaps whom the Emperor does not treat as a woman, someone who has known the Emperor all his life and does not desert him in the hour of his need, perhaps——"

" Désirée, it's Désirée!" Polette shouted.

Theresa stared, uncomprehending. Josephine, however, nodded emphatically. " It could be," she said, " the little friend, a young girl of his early days. I really believe it is Her Royal Highness."

" Please leave me out of it," I said, and felt ashamed of all this in the presence of the young Count.

Josephine understood and stopped the game. " I think it has stopped raining," she said to the Count. " Let me show you my roses and the greenhouses."

In the evening we returned to Paris. It was raining again.

" I am afraid," I said, " you must have been very bored at Malmaison. But I wanted to introduce you to the most beautiful woman in France."

He answered politely : " The Empress Josephine must have been very beautiful—once."

' She lost her beauty in one night,' I thought. ' So shall I, with or without gold paint on my eyelids. But I hope I shall not lose it in one night. That, however, depends on Jean-Baptiste. . . .'

" The ladies at Malmaison are quite different from our ladies in Stockholm," said Count Rosen out of the blue. " They talk about their prayers and their *affaires*."

" One prays and loves in Stockholm just the same."

" Oh yes. But one does not talk about it."

PARIS. 19th December, 1812.

Since my visit to Malmaison it has been raining without interruption. But the rain has not stopped people standing about in the streets talking about the fate of their dear ones in Russia, has not stopped them from going to the churches to attend the services of intercession.

Last night I couldn't sleep. I wandered about the lonely, big, cold house till in the end I put on Napoleon's sable fur and sat down in the small drawing-room to write a letter to Oscar. Marie and Count Rosen kept me company, Marie knitting a grey scarf for Pierre, of whose fate we know nothing, and Count Rosen reading Danish papers, as Swedish papers cannot be bought any more. Madame La Flotte and the servants had gone to bed.

I heard a carriage stop in front of my house, and the next

moment loud knocks resounded on the door. Then voices came from the hall.

"I am not at home to anybody," I said, "I have gone to bed."

Count Rosen left the room and a moment later his harsh French could be heard outside.

A door opened. He escorted someone into the big drawing-room adjoining the small one.

'Is he out of his senses?' I thought. 'I told him I wouldn't receive anybody.' "Go in there at once, Marie, and tell him that I've gone to bed."

Marie immediately went into the other drawing-room. I heard her start a sentence and break off abruptly. Not a sound came from the next room. It was inconceivable to me whom they could possibly have allowed in at this time of night against my wishes. I heard the rustling of paper and the sound of logs being put in the fireplace. Quite obviously someone was making a fire. That was the only noise, otherwise there was complete silence out there.

At last the door opened and Count Rosen came in. His movements were strangely stiff and formal.

"His Majesty the Emperor!"

I started. "Who?" I thought I hadn't understood him properly.

"His Majesty has just arrived in the company of a gentleman, and wishes to speak to Your Royal Highness."

"But the Emperor is at the front," I said, confused.

"His Majesty has just returned." The young Swede was pale with agitation.

Meanwhile I had calmed down. 'Nonsense,' I thought, 'he can't intimidate me, I don't want to be forced into this awful situation, I don't want to see him again, at least not now, not alone.' "Tell His Majesty that I've gone to bed."

"I have told His Majesty that already. His Majesty insists on speaking to Your Highness."

I didn't stir. There was the Emperor, he'd lost his Army. And the first person he came to was me.

I got up slowly and smoothed my hair away from my forehead. I realised that I was wearing my old velvet dressing-gown and my sable fur over it, and probably looked a ridiculous sight. Reluctantly I went towards the door. "I am frightened, Count Rosen," I confessed.

The young Swede shook his head. "I don't think Your Highness need be frightened."

The big drawing-room was brightly lit. Marie was just placing candles in the last of the big candelabra. In the fireplace the fire flickered merrily.

On the sofa under the portrait of the First Consul sat Count Caulaincourt, the Emperor's Grand Equerry. He wore a sheep-skin coat and a woollen cap which he had pulled down over his ears. His eyes were shut and he seemed to be asleep.

The Emperor was standing in front of the fire with his arms propped on the mantelpiece. His shoulders stooped. He seemed so tired that he had to prop himself up in order to be able to stand at all. A cap of grey Persian lamb sat aslant on his head. The man standing there looked a complete stranger to me.

Neither of the two had heard me come. "Sire," I said, stepping to the side of the Emperor.

Caulaincourt shot up, tore his cap off his head and stood to attention. The Emperor slowly raised his head.

I forgot to bow. Completely put out, I looked at his face. For the first time in my life I saw an unshaven Napoleon. Reddish stubble spread over his face, the bloated cheeks were slack and grey. Under a thin mouth his chin, which had lost its flesh, jutted out like a promontory. All the life had gone out of the eyes which were now turned on me.

"Count Rosen," I said sharply, "nobody has taken His Majesty's cap and coat."

"I am cold," Napoleon murmured, taking off his cap with a tired gesture.

Count Rosen took Caulaincourt's sheepskin out of the room. "Come back at once, Count," I told him. "Marie, cognac and glasses!" I wanted Count Rosen to be present during the conversation.

"Please sit down, Sire," I said, and took my seat on the sofa. The Emperor didn't move, and Caulincourt stood irresolute in the middle of the room.

Count Rosen returned and Marie brought cognac and glasses. "A glass of cognac, Sire?"

The Emperor didn't hear.

I looked questioningly at Caulaincourt.

"We have been travelling for thirteen days and nights with-out a break," he said. "No one at the Tuileries knows that we are back. His Majesty wanted to talk to Your Highness first."

A fantastic situation! The Emperor had travelled thirteen days and nights to arrive at my house weary to death, and no one knew that he was in Paris! I filled a glass with cognac and went to him.

" Sire, drink that. It'll warm you," I said loudly.

He raised his head and stared at me, at my old dressing-gown, the sable fur which he himself had given me, and poured down the drink at one gulp. " Does one always wear a fur coat over one's dressing-gown in Sweden?" he asked.

" Of course not. I am cold, that's all. Did Count Rosen not tell you that I was in bed?"

" Who?"

" My adjutant, Count Rosen. Come here, Count, be presented to His Majesty."

Count Rosen clicked his heels. The Emperor held his glass out to him. " Give me another glass. And give Caulaincourt one too. We have made a long journey."

Again he poured down the cognac in one go. " You are surprised to see me here, Highness?"

" Naturally, Sire."

" Naturally? We are old friends, Highness, are we not? Very old friends, if I remember aright. Why, then, are you surprised?"

" Because of the time of your call. And because you have come unshaven."

Napoleon felt his beard with his hand, and a trace of the young, uncaring laughter of his Marseilles days played for a fleeting moment over his grey face. " I am sorry, Highness, I forgot to shave recently. I wanted to reach Paris as quickly as possible. Tell me, what was the effect of my last bulletin?"

" Wouldn't you like to take a seat, Sire?"

" Thank you, I prefer to stand by the fire. But do not inconvenience yourself, Madame. Sit down, gentlemen."

We all sat down, Marie, myself, Count Rosen and Count Caulaincourt, who, I remember now, bore the title of Duke of Vicenza.

" May I ask, Sire——" I began.

" No, Madame, you may not ask! You may not ask, Madame Jean-Baptiste Bernadotte!" he screamed at me at the top of his voice. Count Rosen started on his chair.

Calmly I said: " But I should like to know to what I owe the honour of this unexpected visit."

" My visit is not an honour for you but an ignominy. If you had not been such a childish thoughtless creature all your life, you would realise what an ignominy this visit is to you, Madame Jean-Baptiste Bernadotte!"

" Keep your seat, Count Rosen. His Majesty is too tired to find the right tone," I said soothingly to the Count, who had jumped up, his hand on his sword. That would have been the last straw indeed.

The Emperor paid no attention to us. He came nearer to stare at the portrait of the First Consul, the portrait of the young Napoleon with the lean face, the radiant eyes, the long untidy hair. "Do you know at all where I have just come from?" he said in a monotonous yet hurried voice. "I have come from the steppes where my soldiers are buried. I have come from the wastes where my hussars are dragging themselves through the blinding snow. I have come from the bridge which collapsed under Davout's grenadiers, the bridge across the Beresina. I have come from the camps where men crawl between the corpses of their comrades at night to keep warm, I have——"

"How can I get the scarf to him, how?" It was Marie screaming. She had jumped up and fallen on her knees in front of the Emperor. "Majesty, help a mother, send a courier with the scarf——"

Repelled, Napoleon shrank back. I bent down to her quickly. "It is Marie, Sire, Marie from Marseilles. Her son Pierre is in Russia."

Marie had dug her finger-nails into his sleeve. Napoleon freed himself, his face distorted with rage.

"I have the number of his regiment," whimpered Marie. "This scarf, only this warm scarf——"

"Are you mad, woman?" Foam appeared at the corners of Napoleon's mouth. "I am to send a scarf to Russia, one scarf! Doesn't it make you laugh?" And he began to laugh, louder and louder and louder. "One scarf for my hundred thousand dead, for my frozen grenadiers, one beautiful warm scarf for my Grand Army!"

I took Marie to the door. "Go to bed, dearest, go."

Napoleon had fallen silent. Helplessly he stood in the middle of the room. Then he went with strangely stiff movements to the nearest chair and collapsed into it. "Forgive me, Madame. I am very tired."

Endless minutes passed, not one of us spoke. This is the end, I felt, the end. My thoughts went across land and sea to Jean-Baptiste.

Suddenly Napoleon spoke up in a clear hard voice. "I have come to dictate to you a letter to Marshal Bernadotte, Madame."

"I ask you to dictate this letter to one of Your Majesty's secretaries."

"I wish you to write this letter, Madame. It is a very personal letter and not at all long. Tell the Swedish Crown Prince that we have returned to Paris to prepare the final defeat of the enemies of France." The Emperor got up and began to pace the floor. "Tell him that we remind the Swedish Crown Prince of the young General Bernadotte who with his regiments came in spring, 1797, to the assistance of General Bonaparte in Italy. That crossing of the Alps in an incredibly short time, a masterpiece of organisation, decided the issue of the Italian campaign in our favour. Will you remember that, Madame?"

I nodded.

"Then remind Bernadotte of the battles in which he defended the young Republic and of the song:

Le Régiment de Sambre et Meuse
Marche toujours aux cris de la liberté
Suivant la route glorieuse. . . .

"Tell him that I heard the song a fortnight ago in the Russian snow from two grenadiers who could go no further and sang the song as they dug themselves into the snow to wait for the wolves. Perhaps they were former soldiers of your husband's Rhine Army. Do not forget to mention this incident to him."

My finger-nails dug into the palms of my hands.

"Marshal Bernadotte advised the Tsar to safeguard the peace of Europe by capturing me during the retreat. You can tell him, Madame, that he very nearly succeeded, but only very nearly. I am here, in your drawing-room, and I shall safeguard the peace of Europe myself. In order to assure the final destruction of my enemies I propose an alliance to Sweden. Have you understood me, Madame?"

"Yes, Sire. You propose an alliance to Sweden."

"To put it plainly, I want Bernadotte to march with me once more. Tell your husband that, word for word."

I nodded.

"To defray the cost of rearming, Sweden will be paid one million francs a month besides goods to the value of six million francs." His eyes fastened on the young Count. "At the conclusion of peace Sweden will receive Finland, and of course Pomerania. Tell Bernadotte: Finland, Pomerania and," with a wide sweep of his arm, "the whole of the Baltic coast from Danzig to Mecklenburg."

"Count Rosen, get a piece of paper and note it down."

"Not necessary," said Caulaincourt, "I have a memorandum

here dictated by His Majesty this morning." He handed Rosen a closely covered sheet.

"Finland?" the young Swede said incredulously.

Napoleon smiled at him, the winning smile of his young days. "We shall restore to Sweden her position as a great power. By the way, young man, you will be interested to hear that the archives of the Kremlin yielded me a description of the Russian campaign of your heroic King Charles XII. I wanted to learn from him. But I have the feeling," he said, smiling wryly, "that someone else, someone in Stockholm, has read these descriptions as well and seems to have learnt a lot from them, your—what do you call him? Charles John, my old Bernadotte!" He shrugged his shoulders, breathed deeply and looked at me. "Madame, you will write to Bernadotte tomorrow. I must know where I stand."

So that was why he came. "You haven't told me what would happen if Sweden refused to enter the alliance, Sire."

He did not answer, but returned to his portrait. "A good picture. Did I really look like that, so—thin?"

I nodded. "And in Marseilles you were thinner still, you looked really starved then."

"In Marseilles?" His face registered keen surprise. "How do you know? Oh, of course, I had forgotten, quite forgotten. Yes, we have known each other for a long time, Madame."

I got up.

"I am so tired, so terribly tired," he said, almost inaudibly.

"Go to the Tuileries, Sire, and rest."

"No, dearest, I cannot. The Cossacks are on the move, and the coalition which Bernadotte has got together, Russia, Sweden, Britain. Do you know, Eugenie, what that means?"

He was back to calling me Eugenie now, and he even seemed to have forgotten that I was Bernadotte's wife. His head was too full. "What's the good of writing," I asked, "if the coalition is a fact?"

At that he screamed at me: "Because I shall wipe Sweden off the map if Bernadotte does not march with me." Abruptly he turned to the door. "You yourself, Madame, will bring me your husband's answer. If it is a rejection you can then take your leave at the same time. It would no longer be possible for me to receive you at court."

I curtsied. "I should no longer come to court, Sire."

Count Rosen saw the Emperor and Caulaincourt out. Slowly I went from candelabrum to candelabrum and put out the candles.

392

Rosen returned. "Is Your Highness going to write to the Crown Prince to-morrow?"

"Yes. And you'll help me with the letter, Count."

"Do you think, Your Highness, that the Crown Prince will answer the Emperor?"

"I am sure of it. And it will be the last letter my husband will write to the Emperor." I looked into the dying embers.

"I should prefer not to leave Your Highness alone just now," the young man said hesitantly.

"That's very kind of you. But I am going to Marie to console her."

I spent the rest of the night by Marie's bedside. I promised her to write to Murat, to Marshal Ney and to Colonel Villatte, of whom I had heard nothing for many weeks. I promised to travel with her to the Russian steppes in spring to find Pierre. I promised and promised and promised, and in her fright she was like a child and really thought I could help her.

This morning, special editions of the papers shout it out to the rest of the world that the Emperor had unexpectedly returned from Russia. His Majesty's health, they say, has never been better.

PARIS.
The end of January 1813.

At long last a courier arrived with letters from Stockholm.

'My dear Mama,' wrote Oscar in his neat and very adult-looking handwriting—yes, in six months' time he'll be fourteen!—'My dear Mama, on the sixth of January we saw a marvellous play in the Gustavus III Theatre. Imagine, a famous French actress, Mademoiselle George, who used to be at the Théâtre Français in Paris, played the leading part. Afterwards Papa gave a dinner for Mademoiselle George, and the Queen didn't like it at all that Papa and the actress talked of Paris and the old days all the time. She kept interrupting them and calling him "Our dear Son Charles John," which made Mademoiselle George laugh a lot, and at last she exclaimed: "General Bernadotte, that I'd find you here in Stockholm and as the son of the Swedish Queen at that is the last thing I'd have imagined." That annoyed the Queen so much that she sent me to bed and withdrew with all her ladies. The actress stayed for coffee and liqueur with Papa and Count Brahe, and Miss Koskull took to her bed for a week with a cold in anger and jealousy. Papa works sixteen hours a day as a rule and doesn't look at all well. . . .'

I laughed, and cried a bit too, and felt like going to bed for a week exactly like Mariana Koskull.

That was the letter Oscar had written without his governor's supervision. In his second letter my son expressed himself somewhat more stylishly about the visit to Stockholm of Madame de Staël, the authoress whom Napoleon had banished and whom Papa received very often. He'd signed the letter ' Your ever loving son Oscar, Duke of Södermanland ', whereas the other letter was signed simply ' Your Oscar '.

I looked in vain for a letter from Jean-Baptiste. He must have had my letter about Napoleon's visit and offer of alliance long ago. But all I found was a few hastily scribbled lines. ' My beloved little girl,' it read, ' I am badly overworked, I shall write at greater length next time. Thank you for your report about the Emperor's visit. I shall answer him, but I need time. My answer will be meant not only for him but also for the French nation and for posterity. I don't know why he wishes to have it handed over to him by you. However, I shall send it to you and I only regret that in doing so I shall have to make you suffer once more. I embrace you—Your J.B.'

Besides the letters the big envelope contained a sheet of music. In the margin Jean-Baptiste had scribbled : ' Oscar's first composition, a Swedish folk dance. Try to play the tune. J.B.' At once I sat down at the piano and played it, again and again. And I remembered Oscar saying in the coach that took us back from Hanover to Paris that he wanted to be a composer or a King. And thinking of Jean-Baptiste's scribbled lines about the answer to Napoleon that would be meant for the French nation and posterity as well, I also remembered Monsieur van Beethoven. ' I shall simply call my symphony " Eroica " to commemorate a hope which did not find fulfilment. . . .'

I rang the bell for Count Rosen. He, too, had had letters from Sweden. " Good news from home, Count?"

" I can read between the lines of the letters—they have to be careful, of course, because of the French Secret Police—that the allies, Russia, Sweden, Britain, intend to entrust the plans for the coming campaign to His Royal Highness. And Austria's attitude is most benevolent towards them."

So even his father-in-law, the Austrian Emperor Francis, would take the field against Napoleon.

" The occupied German territories, the Prussians above all, are preparing for an uprising. All the preparations for this greatest campaign in history are being made secretly in Sweden." The Count's voice, hoarse with excitement, had dropped to a whisper. "We shall be a great power again, and Your Highness's son, the little Duke of Södermanland——"

"Oscar's just sent me his first composition, a Swedish folk dance. I shall practise it and play it you to-night. Why do you look at me in such a strange manner? Are you disappointed in my son?"

"Of course not, Your Highness. I am surprised, that's what it is, I did not know——"

"You didn't know that the Prince is very musical? And yet you talk about Sweden regaining her great position?"

"I thought of the country that the Crown Prince will leave to his son when the time comes." The words came tumbling out of him now. "Sweden elected one of the greatest Generals of all time to be the heir to its throne. The Bernadotte dynasty will rebuild Sweden's traditional position as a great power."

"Count, you talk like an elementary reader for school-children," I said, repelled. "In the coming campaign your Crown Prince will do nothing but fight for the Rights of Man which we call Liberty, Equality and Fraternity. He has fought for them for fifteen years, Count Rosen. That was why all the old royal courts secretly called him the Jacobin General. And later, when everything is over and Jean-Baptiste has won this dreadful war on behalf of all Europe, they'll call him that again. Then——" I broke off, because I could tell that Rosen didn't understand a word I was saying. Finally I said in a very low voice: "A musician who never knew anything about politics once told me about a hope which never found fulfilment. Perhaps it will find fulfilment after all, at least in Sweden, and your small country will really be a great power again, Count, but in a way very different from the one you are thinking of. It will be a great power whose Kings no longer make war but have time to write poetry and make music. Aren't you glad that Oscar is musical?"

"Your Royal Highness is the strangest woman I have ever met."

Suddenly I felt very tired. "You only think so because I am the first middle-class woman you have come to know better. All your life you have known nothing but the court and the castles of the nobility. Now you are the adjutant of a silk merchant's daughter. Try to get used to that, will you?"

One evening about seven o'clock the letter I had been expecting for so long arrived. I ordered my carriage immediately and went with Count Rosen to the Hôtel Dieu Hospital opposite Notre-Dame. The wet pavement reflected the rainbow colours of the lights of Paris.

" I have just a had a letter from Colonel Villatte," I explained to Rosen. " He succeeded in getting Marie's son into a transport of wounded for the Hôtel Dieu Hospital. I am told the hospital is overcrowded, and I should like to take Pierre home."

" How is Colonel Villatte?"

" He couldn't come to Paris, he's been sent to the Rhineland, where they are trying to collect the remnants of his regiment."

" I am glad he is well," Rosen said politely.

" He isn't well, he's suffering from the effects of a wound in the shoulder. But he hopes to see us again."

" When?"

" Some time, when it is all over."

" A strange name for a hospital—Hôtel Dieu."

" Our Lord's Hostel, a beautiful name for a hospital. The only transport of wounded to reach Paris has been accommodated there, and Villatte managed to get Pierre into it."

" What is the matter with Pierre?"

" Villatte doesn't say. That's why I haven't told Marie yet. Here we are."

The gate was locked. Count Rosen rang the bell and after a while the gate opened just enough to show the doorkeeper, a one-armed invalid from the Italian campaigns, to judge by his medals. " No visitors allowed!" he said.

" But it is Her Royal Highness——"

" No visitors allowed!" The door was banged to.

" Knock again, Count."

He knocked, loud and long. At last the gate opened once more, I pushed Rosen aside and said quickly: " I have permission to visit the hospital."

" Have you got a pass?" the man asked suspiciously.

" Yes," I said, and we were allowed in. In a dark gateway the invalid looked us over by the light of a candle and asked for the pass.

" I haven't got it with me," I said. " I am the sister-in-law of King Joseph. You understand that I could have a pass at any time. But I am in such a hurry that I could not wait to ask for one. I wanted to fetch someone."

He didn't answer, so I repeated: "I am really King Joseph's sister-in-law."

"I know you, Madame. You are the wife of Marshal Bernadotte."

'Thank God,' I thought, and smiled. "Did you perhaps serve under my husband?"

Not a muscle in his face moved and he kept silent.

"Please call someone to take us to the wards," I said in the end.

Still he did not move. The man became alarming to me. "Lend us the candle. We shall find our own way," I said, feeling rather helpless.

He gave me the candle, stepped back and disappeared in the dark. But we heard him say in a sneering, croaking voice, "The wife of Marshal Bernadotte indeed!" and he spat resoundingly on the floor.

Count Rosen took the candle out of my hand, as it trembled badly. With painful difficulty I said: "Don't pay any attention to that man. We must search for Pierre."

We felt our way up a wide flight of stairs and came to a corridor with many doors. The doors were not properly shut, and groaning and whimpering could be heard from inside.

Quickly I pushed the first door open, and an indescribable odour of blood, sweat and excrement hit me in the face. I summoned all my strength.

The whimpering came from quite close by, close by my feet in fact. I took Rosen's candle and held it high to see. Both sides of the room were occupied by rows of beds, and down the centre of the room straw palliasses covered the floor. The other end of the room seemed a long way away. There I could see a candle on a table and a red sanctuary light. A nun was seated at the table.

"Sister!"

But my voice didn't carry far enough through the moaning of the wounded men to reach her. Cautiously I took a few paces forward and shouted again: "Sister!"

At last she heard me, took the candle and came. I saw a thin, expressionless face under a big white bonnet.

"Sister, I am looking for a wounded man by the name of Pierre Dubois."

"There are too many here," she said in a low voice, indifferently, "we do not know their names."

"But I have permission to look for Pierre Dubois. How am I to find him?" I couldn't help sobbing as I said it.

"I do not know," the nun answered politely. "If you have permission to look for him, then you must look for him. Go from bed to bed, perhaps you will find him." She turned round and went to her table.

For a moment the stench almost overwhelmed me. But I pulled myself together. "Let's go along the beds," I said to the Count.

Thus we went along from bed to bed, from palliasse to palliasse, saw men dying, men dead, men asking for water, men asking for their wives, men stammering requests to which I had no time to listen. But we didn't find Pierre.

It was the same in the next ward, with the only difference that here the nun was young and gentle and full of pity. She thought I was looking for my husband, but I shook my head silently and continued my fruitless search.

When we had left the next ward Rosen suddenly couldn't go on. He leant against the wall, and when I raised the candle to look at him I noticed beads of perspiration on his forehead. He turned away quickly, staggered a few paces and was sick. I felt sorry for him, but could do nothing but wait till he felt better.

In the distance I saw a red votive candle under a statue of the Madonna. I went up to it. It was a very naïve statue of the Mother of Our Lord in a blue and white robe, with healthy red cheeks, sad eyes and a laughing pink baby in her arms. I put my candle down on the floor, and for the first time in many years I clasped my hands in prayer, here under the flickering light with misery seeping out of all the doors around me.

I heard steps behind me and took up the candle.

"I apologise, Your Highness," said my young Swede, ashamed.

Before we went into the next ward I told him he had better stay outside.

He hesitated, then said: "I should like to see this through to the end with you, Highness."

"You shall, Count, you shall!" I answered, and went in, leaving him outside.

At the end of the ward sat an old nun reading in a small black book. She looked up at me without showing any surprise. "I am looking for a certain Pierre Dubois," I said, and could hear the hopelessness in my voice.

"Dubois? I think we have two of that name."

She took me by the hand and led me towards a palliasse in the middle of the room. I knelt down and by the light of the candle saw an emaciated face surrounded by untidy strands of white hair. It wasn't Pierre's face. Then the nun took me to the last bed on the left wall.

Yes, it was Pierre. His dark, wide-open eyes stared at me indifferently. The lips were swollen and had blood on them.

" Good evening, Pierre! " I said.

He kept on staring.

" Pierre, don't you recognise me? "

" Of course, " he murmured, " *Madame la Maréchale.* "

I bent over him. " I've come to take you home, Pierre, to your mother, now. "

His face remained without expression.

" Pierre, aren't you glad? "

Still no answer.

Utterly at a loss, I turned to the nun. " This is the man I am looking for. I should like to take him home to his mother. I have a carriage downstairs. Have you got anybody here to help me? "

" The porters have gone home, Madame. You must wait till to-morrow. "

But I didn't want Pierre to stay here a minute longer. " Is he very seriously wounded? My adju— a gentleman is waiting outside, and he and I could support him, if Pierre could walk down the stairs and—— "

The sister seized my hand and lifted it so that the light fell full on the blanket. Where Pierre's legs ought to have been the blanket was flat, quite flat.

My breath left me. At last I managed to say with difficulty: " I have a coachman downstairs who can give me a hand. I shall be back in a minute, sister. "

I told Count Rosen to fetch the coachman to carry Pierre to the carriage. " Take my candle and bring all the blankets we have with us, " I added.

I waited, and thought of Pierre who had lost his legs and would never be able to walk again. Yes, this was the Hôtel Dieu, Our Lord's Hostel where one person learnt to pray and another to be sick, where one began to understand that the whole world was one big Hôtel Dieu.

They came, Rosen and the coachman Johansson.

" Please help us, sister, to wrap him up in the blankets. Johansson will carry him downstairs. "

The sister pulled Pierre up by the shoulders. He couldn't

resist, but his eyes sparkled with hatred. "Leave me alone, Madame, leave me——" he shouted.

The nun pulled back the bed cover and I shut my eyes. When I opened them Pierre Dubois lay before me like a well-tied-up parcel.

Somebody tugged at my coat. I turned and saw the man in the next bed trying to sit up. But he fell helplessly. I bent down to him.

"*Madame la Maréchale* he called you, didn't he? Which Marshal?" the man asked.

"Bernadotte."

He motioned me to go nearer to him. A bewildered smile distorted his mouth, his feverish lips nearly touched my ear. "I thought so," he whispered, fighting for breath, "give your husband . . . in his castle in Stockholm . . . the regards of one of his men . . . who crossed the Alps with him. . . . Tell him, if we had known . . . Tell him, he would never have got over the Alps . . . alive . . . if we had known. . . ." Small bubbles of blood and saliva trembled on his lips as he continued with increasing difficulty: "If we had known . . . that he . . . would let us die in Russia. . . . My regards . . . to him, Madame . . . from . . . an old comrade."

A protective hand, that of the nun, took my arm. "His will be done on earth and in Heaven. Let us go, Madame."

Johansson lifted the parcel which had once been Pierre, a young man who went to war with a rose-bud in his rifle, and carried it through the door. Count Rosen took the candle and showed the way. But I clung to the old woman and she led me down the stairs. "But you are no longer the wife of Marshal Bernadotte," she said unexpectedly, "but the Crown Princess of Sweden, are you not?"

I lost control of myself and sobbed loudly.

"Go with God, my child, and strive for peace with your people."

She let go my arm. The one-armed doorkeeper opened the gate in silence. When I turned round to kiss the old nun's hand she had disappeared into the dark.

Count Rosen sat on the back seat. The parcel that had been Pierre Dubois lay by my side. I felt over the blankets for his hand. When I found it it was cold and limp.

And that was how I brought Marie's son back to her.

PARIS.
The beginning of April 1813.

'In half an hour I shall see him for the last time in my life,'
I thought, as I put some gold paint on my eyelids. 'After that
the long acquaintance which began as my first love will be over
and done with.' I finished my make-up and put on a new hat
tied under the chin with a pink ribbon. A Crown Princess with
gold-painted eyelids, a purple velvet costume, a bunch of pale
violets on the low-cut neck of the blouse and new model hat
with a pink ribbon, that is how he will remember me, I reflected.

Last night a courier brought Jean-Baptiste's answer to
Napoleon. It was sealed. But Count Brahe had sent a copy of
it for my information and added that the text of this letter from
the Swedish Crown Prince to Napoleon had been transmitted
to all papers for publication.

I got up and read my copy for the last time:

'*The sufferings of the Continent cry out for peace, and
Your Majesty cannot reject this demand without multiply-
ing ten-fold the sum total of crimes you have committed
up till now. What did France receive as compensation for
its gigantic sacrifices? Nothing but military glory, super-
ficial splendour and deep misery within her own
frontiers. . . .*'

And this letter I was to take to Napoleon! Things like that
could happen only to me. I grew hot with fear as I read on:

'*I was born in that beautiful France over which you reign,
and her honour and well-being can never be a matter of
indifference to me. But without ever ceasing to pray for its
happiness I shall always defend with all the means at my
disposal the rights of the nation which called me and the
honour of the monarch who accepted me to be his son. In
the fight between tyranny and freedom I shall say to the
Swedes: I shall fight with you and for you, and all peoples
who love their freedom will bless our arms.*

*As far as my personal ambition goes, let me say this: I
am ambitious, very ambitious, but only in order to serve
the interests of mankind and to gain and guarantee the
independence of the Scandinavian peninsula.*'

The letter addressed to Napoleon, France and the world ended on a personal note:

> '*Independent of any decision you may come to, Sire, whether peace or war, I shall always cherish for Your Majesty the devotion of an old comrade of many wars.*'

I put the copy back on the bedside table and went out. We were to be at the Tuileries at five o'clock. Within the next few days the Emperor would take the field again with his new armies, to face the advancing Russians and the Prussians who had joined them.

Count Rosen was wearing the full-dress uniform of the Swedish dragoons and the adjutant's sash.

"You accompany me on many difficult missions, Count," I said as we passed over the Pont Royal. Since that night in the Hôtel Dieu a strange kind of affinity connected us, probably because I had been present when he was sick. These things bring people together more than one thinks.

We drove in an open carriage through the sweet-smelling dusk of an early spring day. 'A pity,' I thought, 'to have to go for an interview with the Emperor of the French instead of going for a sweet and secret rendezvous. . . .'

We were shown in at once to the Emperor's big study. Caulaincourt and Meneval were present as well as Count Talleyrand, who was leaning against the window.

Napoleon, in the green uniform of the Chasseurs, his arms folded over his chest, refused to meet us half-way but waited for us standing behind his desk at the far end of the room, a supercilious smile on his face. I bowed and handed him the letter. He broke open the seal, read it without a muscle in his face moving and then handed it to Meneval. "Have a copy made for the archives of the Ministry of Foreign Affairs and put the original with my private papers," he ordered. Turning to me he said: "You have dressed up nicely, Your Highness. Purple suits you. By the way, you are wearing a strange hat. Are tall hats the latest fashion?"

This sneering was worse than the violent eruption I had anticipated. I said nothing.

Napoleon turned to Talleyrand: "You know something about beautiful women's fashions, don't you, Excellency? How do you like the new hat of the Crown Princess of Sweden?"

Talleyrand kept his eyes half shut. He seemed to be infinitely bored. Napoleon turned to me. "Did you dress up for my sake, Highness?"

"Yes, Sire."

"And adorned yourself with violets"—his tone became jeering—"to bring me this scribble by the former Marshal Bernadotte? Violets, Madame, flower in quiet places and their scent is sweet. But this treason, at which all Russian and English papers exult, stinks to high Heaven!"

I bowed. "I ask to be allowed to leave, Sire."

"You are not only allowed to leave, Madame," he yelled, "I shall force you to leave. Or did you think that you could come and go here at court when Bernadotte marches into battle against me? He is going to train his guns on the regiments which he himself commanded in innumerable battles, and you, Madame, dare to appear here adorned with violets!"

"Sire, that night when you returned from Russia you urged me to write to my husband and bring you his answer. I read a copy of his letter, and I realise that I am seeing you for the last time, Sire. I put on the violets because they suit me. Perhaps they'll induce you to remember me more agreeably. May I now say good-bye to you, for the last time?"

Silence fell on us, a dreadful awkward silence. Meneval and Caulaincourt stared at the Emperor in amazement, and Talleyrand, interested, opened his eyes, because Napoleon quite unexpectedly became embarrassed and looked restlessly round the room. At last he said in a totally different voice: "Please wait here, gentlemen, I should like to have a few words with Her Royal Highness in private." He pointed to a door in the wall: "Please follow me, Your Highness. Meneval, offer the gentlemen a glass of brandy."

I entered the room where years ago I had pleaded for the life of the Duc d'Enghien. Nothing much had changed here, the same small tables, the same piles of documents and files. On the carpet in front of the fireplace I saw a number of small wooden blocks, in different colours, with prongs sticking out of them.

Involuntarily I picked up a red one. "What are these? Toys of the King of Rome?"

"Yes—and no. I use these blocks to plan out my campaign. Each black represents an army corps, and the prongs mean the number of divisions of that particular corps. The red one you have picked up is the Third Corps of Marshal Ney. It has five prongs. So Ney's corps has five divisions. The blue one is the Corps Marmont with three divisions, and so on. If I put them up on the floor I can see the order of battle quite clearly on the map. I know the map by heart."

"But do you chew these blocks?" I asked, and looked at the red one in surprise.

"No, that is the little King of Rome. When he is brought in here he gets them out to play with and chews them too."

I put the red block back on the floor. "You wanted to have a word with me, Sire? I am afraid I cannot discuss my husband with you."

He made a deprecatory gesture. "Who wants to talk about Bernadotte? No, it was not that, Eugenie, it was only——" He came close to me and stared into my face as if he wanted to commit to memory every feature of it. "No, when you said good-bye for the last time I thought——" He turned away brusquely and went to the window. "We cannot say good-bye like that when we have known each other for so long, can we?"

I stood in front of the fireplace and with the tip of my foot played with the small wooden blocks representing armies. I gave no answer.

"I said," came Napoleon's voice from the window, "one cannot leave just like that."

"Why not, Sire?"

He turned back to me. "Why not? Eugenie, have you forgotten the days of Marseilles? The hedge? The field? Our talks on Goethe's novel *Werther*? Our youth, Eugenie, our whole youth? You never realised why I came to you that night, after my return from Russia. I was cold, I was tired, I was lonely."

"When you dictated to me the letter to Jean-Baptiste you had quite forgotten that you knew me when I was still Eugenie Clary. Your visit was meant for the Crown Princess of Sweden, Sire." I felt sad. 'Even when we see each other for the last time he must lie,' I thought.

He shook his head vigorously. "Of course I had pondered over the alliance with Bernadotte on the morning of that day. But when I came to Paris I only wanted to see you, you alone. And then, I don't know how it all happened, I was so tired that night, as soon as we mentioned Bernadotte I forgot about Marseilles. Can't you understand?"

It grew dark. Nobody came to light the candles. I could no longer see his face. What in the world did he want of me?

"I brought together a new army of two hundred thousand men. By the way, did you know that Britain is paying Sweden one million pounds to equip Bernadotte's troops?"

No, I didn't know. But I made no reply to Napoleon.

" Madame de Staël is with him in Stockholm. Did you know that, Madame?"

Of course I did. It doesn't matter, why talk about it?

" Bernadotte does not seem able to get hold of more pleasant company in Stockholm."

I laughed. " Oh yes, Sire, he does. Mademoiselle George was in Stockholm a short time ago and enjoyed the benevolent patronage of His Royal Highness. Did you know that, Sire?"

" My God, Georgina, sweet little Georgina!"

" His Royal Highness will soon be united with his old friend Moreau. Moreau is returning to Europe and is going to fight under Jean-Baptiste. Did you know that, Sire?"

It was a good thing that darkness stood between us like a wall.

" It is being said that the Tsar offered Bernadotte the French crown." Napoleon's voice came slowly through the dark.

' That sounds crazy,' I thought, ' but possible.'

" Well, Madame? If Bernadotte ever as much as toyed with the idea it would be the blackest treason ever committed by a Frenchman."

" It would. Treason against his own ideals! May I go now, Sire?"

" If ever you yourself feel unsafe in Paris, Madame, I mean if the mob should ever inconvenience you, you must take refuge at once with your sister Julie. Will you promise me that?"

" Gladly. And the other way round, too."

" What do you mean, ' the other way round '?"

" That my house will always be open for Julie. That's why I am staying here."

" So you are counting on my defeat, Eugenie?" He came quite close to me. " The scent of your violets is intoxicating. I should really banish you from the country. You probably tell everybody that the Emperor is going to be beaten. Besides, I don't like it that you go for drives with that tall Swede of yours."

" But he is my adjutant. I have to take him with me."

" All the same, your Mama would not have liked it. And your very strict brother Etienne . . ." He felt for my hand and laid it against his cheek.

" At least you have shaved to-day, Sire," I said, and withdrew my hand.

" A pity you are married to Bernadotte," he said.

Quickly I felt my way back to the door.

He called out " Eugenie!"

But I had reached his brightly lit big study. The gentlemen were sitting round Napoleon's desk drinking brandy. Talleyrand seemed to have made a joke, for Meneval, Caulaincourt and my Swede were holding their sides with laughter.

"Let us share the joke, gentlemen," the Emperor demanded.

"We were just saying that the Senate had passed the measure for the conscription of another 250,000 recruits for the Army," recounted Meneval still laughing. Caulaincourt continued: "We found that this measure concerns youngsters far too young for the Army yet, children almost. It was then that the Prince of Benevento declared that there would have to be one day's armistice at least next year so that Your Majesty's new Army could go to church to be confirmed."

The Emperor laughed. But it didn't sound quite genuine. The recruits, I gathered, were of Oscar's age. "That is not funny," I said, "but sad."

Once more I bowed. This time the Emperor saw me to the door. We didn't exchange another word.

On the return journey I asked Rosen if it was true that the Tsar had offered Jean-Baptiste the French crown.

"That is an open secret in Sweden. Does the Emperor know?"

I nodded.

"What else did he talk about?" he asked rather timidly.

I tried to think what else he had talked about. Suddenly I tore my bunch of violets from my decolletage and threw it out of the carriage window. "About violets, Count, about nothing but violets."

That same evening a little package came from the Tuileries for me. The servant who brought it said it was a present for the Crown Prince of Sweden. I undid it and found a chewed wooden block with five prongs. When I see Jean-Baptiste again I shall give it to him.

PARIS.
In summer 1813.

Johansson the coachman had carried Pierre into the garden. I was sitting by the window watching Marie bringing her son a glass of lemonade. When he had emptied it Marie put it down on the lawn and sat down with him, supporting his back with her arm.

His left leg had been amputated at the top of the thigh. But of the right leg a stump was left above the knee, and the doctor hoped that a wooden leg could be fastened on to it once the wound had healed. But so far the wound had refused to heal. Whenever Marie had to change the bandage Pierre screamed with pain like a child.

I gave him Oscar's room, and Marie had put her bed alongside his. 'But,' I thought, 'I must find him a room on the ground floor, it is so difficult to have to carry him up and downstairs all the time.'

Talleyrand came to visit me in the evening, supposedly to inquire whether I didn't feel too lonely.

"I should have been lonely this summer in any case," I told him. "I am used to having my husband away from me at the front."

He nodded agreement. "Yes, at the front. Which means that, in different circumstances, Your Highness would be alone but not—lonely!"

I shrugged my shoulders. We sat in the garden, and Madame La Flotte poured out iced champagne. Talleyrand told me that Fouché had been given a post, that of Governor of Illyria. Illyria is an Italian state which the Emperor created for the sole purpose of sending Fouché there.

"The Emperor cannot afford to have someone intriguing against him in Paris. And Fouché is sure to start a plot."

"And you," I said, "is the Emperor not afraid of you, Excellency?"

"Fouché plots to gain power or keep it. I, however, my dear Highness, desire nothing but the well-being of France."

I gazed up at the sky where the first stars had appeared.

"How quickly our allies left us!" remarked Talleyrand between two sips. "First of all the Prussians, who are now under your husband's supreme command. He has set up his headquarters in Stralsund."

I nodded. Count Rosen had told me all about it. "The *Moniteur* says the Emperor of Austria is trying to bring about an armistice between France and Russia," I said at last.

Talleyrand passed his empty glass to Madame La Flotte. "He is doing that to gain time for Austria's mobilisation."

"But the Austrian Emperor is the father of our Empress," Madame La Flotte said sharply.

Talleyrand paid no attention to her but looked at his glass.

"Once France is beaten all the members of the coalition will try to enrich themselves at our expense. Austria wants to stake its claim to a share and therefore will join the coalition."

"But," I objected—my mouth was so dry that I could hardly speak—"surely the Austrian Emperor cannot go to war against his own daughter and grandson?"

"No? But he is doing it already." He smiled. "Only, you would not find it published in the *Moniteur*, Madame. The armies allied against us have 800,000 men under arms, the Emperor hardly half that number."

"But His Majesty is a genius," La Flotte said with trembling lips. It sounded like something learnt by heart.

"Quite, Madame. His Majesty is a genius. By the way, the Emperor has forced the Danes to declare war on the Swedes. Now the Crown Prince of Sweden has the Danes threatening him from the rear."

"I suppose he can cope with the situation," I said impatiently, and thought, 'I'll have to find an occupation for Pierre, that is the most important thing, a regular job for Pierre.' "Did you say anything, Excellency?"

"Only that the day is not far off now when I shall put my request to you," said Talleyrand, and rose to his feet.

"Give my love to my sister, when you see her, Excellency. King Joseph has forbidden her my house."

Talleyrand raised his narrow eyebrows. "And where, Highness, are your two faithful adjutants?"

"Colonel Villatte joined the Army a long time ago. He went with the Army to Russia. And Count Rosen told me a few days ago that as a Swedish nobleman he felt obliged to fight by the side of his Crown Prince."

"Nonsense, he is only jealous of Count Brahe," put in Madame La Flotte.

"No, he meant it. The Swedes are a very serious-minded people, Madame. 'Ride, ride with God and come back safely!' I told him, exactly what I had told Villatte before. You are right, Excellency, I *am* lonely."

I stared after him as he limped away. He limps so gracefully, so elegantly. At the same time I decided to entrust the administration of my money and my household to Pierre. I thought that a good idea.

Every time I fall asleep now I have the same dream. I dream I see Jean-Baptiste riding alone across a battlefield, a battlefield a fortnight after a battle, the kind of battlefield I saw once on the journey to Marienburg, full of small mounds of earth and dead horses with inflated bellies. Jean-Baptiste is on his white horse which I know from so many parades, leaning forward in the saddle. I can't see his face, but I know he's crying. The white horse stumbles over the mounds and Jean-Baptiste falls forward even more and doesn't sit up again. . . .

For more than a week a rumour has been going round Paris about a decisive battle near Leipzig, but nobody knows anything for certain. . . .

I had been dreaming again of Jean-Baptiste on his white horse when I heard it whinny. It woke me up. It was the first time that I had heard it whinny in my dream.

I opened my eyes. The night-light had burned down, the hand of the clock seemed to point to half-past four. Suddenly I heard the whinnying of a horse, outside the house. I sat up in bed and listened. Then a very gentle knock came at the door, so gentle that nobody else could have heard it.

"Who's there?" I asked.

"Villatte," one voice said, and another, "Rosen."

I pushed back the heavy bolt. "For God's sake," I said, "where have you come from?"

"From Leipzig," said Villatte.

"With the kind regards of His Royal Highness," added Rosen.

I went back into the hall and, feeling cold, pulled the dressing-gown tightly round my shoulders. Count Rosen lit one of the candelabra, whilst Villatte had disappeared, probably to put the horses into the stable. I noticed that Rosen wore the coat and bearskin cap of a French grenadier. "A strange uniform for a Swedish dragoon," I said.

"Our troops are not on French soil yet. So His Highness sent me here in this ridiculous disguise, in order to avoid difficulties for me."

Villatte returned. "We rode night and day," he said. His face was emaciated and he looked exhausted. "By the way," he said quite inconsequentially, "we lost the decisive battle."

"We won it," exclaimed Rosen passionately, "and His

409

Highness himself took Leipzig. The moment that he entered Leipzig at one end Napoleon fled from the other. His Highness was at the head of his troops from beginning to end."

"And why aren't you with the French Army, Colonel Villatte?"

"I am a prisoner of war, Your Highness."

"Rosen's prisoner?"

The ghost of a smile went over Villatte's face. "Yes, so to speak. His Highness did not send me to a prisoner-of-war camp but sent me here to be at your side till——"

"Till?"

"Till the enemy troops enter Paris."

So that was it, that was why the lonely rider across the battlefield was crying in my dream. "Come, gentlemen, I will make some coffee."

Villatte and Rosen between them managed to make a fire and I put the kettle on. Then we sat round the kitchen table and waited. The boots, hands and faces of both men were caked with mud.

"How is Jean-Baptiste? Have you seen him, Villatte? Is he well?"

"Very well! I saw him myself, before the gates of Leipzig, in the midst of the hardest fighting, and he was very well indeed!"

"Did you speak to him, Villatte?"

"Yes, afterwards. After the defeat, Madame."

"Victory, Colonel Villatte, victory! I shall not tolerate——" Count Rosen's high-pitched voice piped.

"What did he look like, Villatte, afterwards?"

Villatte shrugged his shoulders and stared in front of him. The water boiled, I made the coffee and poured it into the inelegant cups of the servants.

"Well, Villatte, what did he look like?"

"He has gone grey, Madame."

The coffee tasted bitter, I had forgotten the sugar. I fetched it and put it on the table. It took me some time to find it, and I felt ashamed that I didn't know where things were in my own house.

"Your Highness makes wonderful coffee," said Rosen.

"That's what my husband says, too. Well now, Count, tell me all you know."

"If I only knew where to start! There is so much, so much!"

Yes indeed, there was so much! Rosen began by describing

how he arrived at Jean-Baptiste's headquarters at Trachtenberg Castle, where Jean-Baptiste in the presence of the Tsar and the Emperor of Austria drafted the plans for the campaign and, incidentally, overawed Their Majesties by his phenomenal memory and precision, which neither they nor their Generals could match.

"What," I wanted to know, "did His Highness say when you turned up out of the blue?"

Rosen looked uncomfortable. "To be frank, he was furious and shouted at me that he could very well win the war without my help. And—yes, I ought to have stayed in Paris to be with Your Highness."

"Of course you ought to have stayed here," Villatte agreed.

"And you? You went away too to be in it."

"No, no, not to be 'in it' but to defend France. Besides, Her Royal Highness is your Crown Princess, not mine. But that is of no importance now, is it?"

Count Rosen went on to describe Jean-Baptiste's first big battle against the French at Grossbeeren, where he stood firm against the most vicious assaults. The French Army contained the Dupas Division, the regiments of which had served for many years under Bernadotte. 'How could you bear it,' I thought, 'how could you bear it, Jean-Baptiste?'

"In the evening," Rosen went on, "His Highness rode along from regiment to regiment to thank the men. Count Brahe and I accompanied him. Near the tent of the Prussian General Bülow we saw some French prisoners. When His Highness saw them he hesitated at first but then rode slowly towards them and alone their line and looked closely at each man. Once he stopped and told the nearest man that he would see to it that they lacked nothing. But the man did not answer. So His Highness rode on and suddenly seemed dead tired and he leaned forward in the saddle. He only recovered when he saw the captured French flags. The Prussians had planted them in neat rows in front of their General's tent—mind you, without having any permission to do so from His Highness, the Commander-in-Chief, and His Highness dismounted, went to the Eagle Standards, saluted them and stood to attention in front of them for a few minutes. Then he turned abruptly and went back to his headquarters. There he shut himself into his tent and gave orders that he would see nobody, not even Brahe, his Personal Adjutant. Only Fernand brought him some soup."

We were silent and I poured out some more coffee. After a little while Count Rosen continued. "At the Battle of Leipzig, on October 18th, His Highness attacked Schönefeld, just outside Leipzig. Schönefeld was defended by French and Saxon regiments under Ney."

At that I looked at Villatte, and Villatte, the tired Villatte, smiled and said: "As you see, Madame, Napoleon put his best troops against Bernadotte, the Saxons among them, of course. The Emperor had never forgotten that Bernadotte maintained the Saxons always stand like rocks. Count Rosen, how did the Saxons stand in the Battle of Leipzig?"

"If I hadn't seen it with my own eyes, Highness, I should never have believed it. It was fantastic! Before the battle began His Highness changed, for the first time during the campaign, from his field uniform into his gala uniform which everyone can see miles away, asked for his white horse, gave the order to attack and then rode straight towards the enemy lines where the Saxon regiments were drawn up. And the Saxon regiments——"

"Stood like rocks!" laughed Villatte, "not a shot was fired!"

"Exactly, not a shot was fired! Brahe and I rode after His Highness. He halted quite close to the Saxons and they—presented arms! 'Vive Bernadotte!' shouted one of them, and the whole line took it up: 'Vive Bernadotte!' His Highness raised his baton, turned his horse round and rode back; the Saxons followed in perfect order, the regimental music at their head, twelve thousand of them with forty guns. His Highness told them where to take up their positions in the firing-line. Then, during the battle, he sat on his horse for hours and hours, never moving, never having to refer to maps or to use field-glasses, yet always knowing exactly what was going on. At night, when the firing had died down, he quite unexpectedly demanded the dark-blue greatcoat of his field uniform, a hat without any badges and a fresh horse, not a white one. He and Fernand rode away and only returned at dawn next morning. A sentry saw them ride past in the night and saw His Highness dismount and walk on while Fernand stayed behind to hold the horses. Another sentry saw him sit down by a fallen soldier and heard him talk. Perhaps His Highness had not realised that the man was dead. It was a French soldier, by the way."

Another silence. "And then?" I asked at last.

"Then His Highness began the attack on Leipzig. He took it and entered it at the so-called Grimma Gate the moment that Napoleon fled through the West Gate at the other end of the town. His Highness rode to the Market Place of Leipzig and waited there for his allies, the Tsar, the Emperor of Austria and the King of Prussia. At Trachtenberg Castle he had told them he would meet them on Leipzig Market Place, and so he sat there and waited. As it so happened French prisoners were led past at that moment. His Highness had his eyes half closed; I thought he wasn't looking at the prisoners at all. But all of a sudden he raised his baton and pointed to a colonel. 'Villatte,' he said, 'come here, Villatte!'"

Here Villatte took up the story. "I stepped forward. 'What are you doing here, Villatte?' he asked. 'I am defending France,' I said. 'Are you? Then I must tell you you are defending it very badly, Villatte. Besides, I expected you to stay with my wife in Paris.' 'Your wife herself sent me to join the Army,' I said. He made no answer to that. I stood next to his horse and saw my captured comrades march past. In the end I thought he had forgotten I was there and wanted to go and join the other prisoners. But as soon as I stirred Bernadotte bent down from his horse and held me by the shoulder. 'Colonel Villatte, you are a prisoner of war. I order you herewith to return immediately to Paris to my wife's house. Give me your word of honour as a French officer that you will not leave her till I come myself.' Those were his words. I gave him my word of honour."

Villatte's part of the story ended, Rosen took over again and reported the strange arrangement Jean-Baptiste made for them. Villatte was the prisoner, but on French soil, beyond the reach of the allied armies, he was to guarantee Rosen's safety and to procure him the right of asylum in my house from the authorities in Paris. To get Rosen through the French lines Villatte got him a French bearskin cap and uniform. It sounded a complicated arrangement to me. I daresay they themselves didn't know who was in charge of whom. In any case, the arrangement worked, they rode and rode day and night, and they had arrived here safely.

I heard a clock strike half-past six. "And the Emperor?" I asked.

"He hopes to defend the Rhine frontier somehow," answered Villatte, "and, if that fails, to defend at least Paris."

'The Rhine frontier,' I thought, 'the front where Jean-Batpiste became a General. . . .'

Someone came into the kitchen and said: "Damnation, who's gone into the kitchen without my permission?—oh, I am sorry, Your Highness!"

It was my fat cook. A kitchen maid opened the windows, and the cold morning air made me shudder.

"A cup of hot chocolate, Your Highness?" suggested the cook.

I shook my head, "No, thank you," and then told Villatte and Rosen to go to their old rooms. "You'll find everything as you left it."

I asked for a duster, instead of which the maid brought me a beautiful white napkin. She probably thought that that was the right kind of duster for a Crown Princess. However, I took it and went to Jean-Baptiste's room to give it a good dusting. The room looked very inhospitable. All the things that Jean-Baptiste valued went with him to Stockholm, so there was nothing much left here to make it friendly.

I opened the window to let some fresh air in. Marie came in. "Don't stand by the open window in your dressing-gown," she said. "You'll catch a cold. What are you doing here, anyway?"

"I'm preparing the room for Jean-Baptiste. His troops are marching on Paris, he's coming home, Marie!"

"He ought to be ashamed of himself!" she hissed, not very loudly but loud enough for me to hear, and I remembered the rider of my dream, my poor, lonely rider. . . .

PARIS.
The last week of March 1814.

Marie had just come home from the baker's, where the women shoppers were telling each other dreadful tales about the things the Cossacks had in store for the female sex, when we heard for the first time the distant thunder of the guns. That was two days ago. Since then they have never been silent.

We knew the Austrians, the Cossacks and the Prussians were in France, but that was all we knew. Now they are here on our doorstep.

I am waiting for Jean-Baptiste, but I don't know where he is. I don't get any more letters, either from him or from Oscar. Now and then a message is smuggled through to us, and that is how I know that Jean-Baptiste has refused to pursue the beaten French across the Rhine, that he gave up his command of all troops bar his 30,000 Swedes, that he was marching northwards through Hanover against the Danes and that he had written a letter to the Tsar demanding that France's frontiers should remain inviolate because Napoleon was not

France and Napoleon had been beaten already anyway. . . . But the Prussians, the Russians and the Austrians invaded France all the same, whilst Jean-Baptiste continued his private war against Denmark, Napoleon's ally whom he had forced into war against Sweden.

Marshal Marmont is in charge of the defence of Paris, Marmont who once wanted to marry me. But the thunder of the guns is coming nearer and nearer hourly.

Meanwhile we had news that Jean-Baptiste had reached Kiel and sent an ultimatum to the King of Denmark from there. He demanded the cession of Norway to Sweden and offered a million *thaler* in exchange. Denmark accepted the demand for the cession of Norway but rejected indignantly the offer of money. " So you are Crown Princess of Sweden and Norway," said Count Rosen when he received the message, the last message we had had from him, about three weeks ago. Since then we have heard nothing except that he gave in to the demands of his allies and marched towards the Rhine, towards Belgium, and that he got into a carriage there—it was said together with Count Brahe—and disappeared, just disappeared.

I am writing in my diary, writing feverishly to run away from my anxiety, writing down everything. Nobody knows where Jean-Baptiste is. Some say that Napoleon secretly in his despair asked Jean-Baptiste for help. Others that he had a disagreement with the Tsar because of the Tsar's refusal to recognise France's frontiers of 1794. Meanwhile the papers in Paris write that he has gone mad, that his father had died as a lunatic and that his brother, too, was out of his mind and—no, I can't repeat that, now that Jean-Baptiste is wandering about somewhere. Marie and Yvette try to keep from me the papers which write this kind of stuff, but Madame La Flotte takes jolly good care to leave them lying about in the drawing-room.

His chamberlain Count Löwenstein managed to get two messages through to me from Liége recently. In both of them he wanted to know whether I had any idea of the whereabouts of His Royal Highness. I hadn't, I haven't now, but I can guess, and my guess is that he has come home and is somewhere in France. Perhaps, my dear chamberlain Count Löwenstein, it is better to leave him alone for the time being now that he is looking round the ruins. . . .

Yesterday, March the 29th, at half-past six in the morning, Marie came into my bedroom. " You are to go to the Tuileries at once."

" To the Tuileries? " I asked incredulously.

"King Joseph has sent a carriage for you. You must go to Julie at once."

I got up and dressed quickly. Julie, obedient to her husband, had not been to see me for months. And now this unexpected request!

"Shall I wake one of the adjutants?" asked Marie.

"No," I said. Surely I could go to Julie without either my 'allied' or my 'prisoner-of-war' adjutant.

Shuddering with cold, I rode through empty streets where only the street cleaners were busy. I saw them sweeping together posters printed in big letters. The lackey got me one which read:

'Parisians, surrender! Do as your fellow countrymen did in Bordeaux, call Louis XVIII to the throne and safeguard peace!'

It was signed by Prince Schwarzenberg, the Austrian Commander-in-Chief.

A whole regiment of cuirassiers sitting immovably on their horses was lined up outside the Tuileries. Inside, the yard was filled with coaches, carriages, ten green State equipages and wagons of all kinds. Lackeys were carrying innumerable heavy iron chests to the wagons. 'The crown jewels and treasures of the Imperial family and its money,' I thought. The sentries looked on with expressionless faces.

I was surprised to be taken to the private rooms of the Empress. When I got there I found Joseph standing in front of the fireplace and trying very hard to look like Napoleon. He had clasped his hands behind him and spoke in a hurried voice with his head thrown back. The Empress, whom Napoleon had made Regent during his absence, sat on a sofa with Madame Letitia. Madame Letitia had thrown a scarf round her shoulders peasant fashion, and the Empress wore a travelling coat and a hat and had the air of a visitor who could hardly spare a minute to sit down. Meneval was there, some members of the Senate and King Jerome of Westphalia, now a tall slim man in immaculate uniform. Many candles lit the room brightly, their light mingled with the grey light of dawn and made the whole scene look unreal.

Joseph was just reading a letter from Napoleon. "Here it is," he said, "here: 'Do not leave my son, and remember that I would rather have him dead in the Seine than alive in the hands of enemies of France' and so on and so on."

416

"But we know that. You read the letter to us before, last night in the Council of State. What possibilities are there of preventing the child from falling into the river or into the hands of the enemy?" asked Jerome in the deliberate nasal drawl which he had acquired in America.

Joseph pulled another letter from Napoleon out of his breast pocket and read it aloud. It contained exact instructions as to how many men were to be posted at each gateway and how they were to be armed: fifty men with rifles and shot-guns and a hundred men with lances. Besides the troops at the gates they were to form a mobile reserve of three thousand men, armed in the same way.

"That is all very clear, Joseph," remarked Madame Letitia. "Have you carried out the orders?"

Joseph, who was responsible for the defence of the city proper, answered that he couldn't because there were neither rifles nor shot-guns left in the depots.

He, Jerome and Meneval argued for a while as to what could or could not be done with lances against guns. When they had ended Marie-Louise asked calmly and as if it were a matter of no importance: "Well? What is the decision? Am I to leave with the King of Rome or am I to stay?"

"Madame," said Jerome, planting himself in front of her, "the officers of the Guards have sworn never to surrender Paris as long as you and the King of Rome are in it. Every man capable of bearing arms will, to the last drop of blood——"

Joseph interrupted him: "Jerome, we have nothing but lances for the men capable of bearing arms."

"But the Guards are still fully armed, Joseph!"

"Yes, but there are only a few hundred of them. However, I realise that the presence of the Regent and her son will spur on the Guards as well as the people of Paris to fanatical resistance, whereas their departure would have an unfortunate influence on the populace. I fear that in that case——" He broke off in the middle of the sentence.

"Well?" the Empress asked once more.

"I leave the decision to the Regent," said Joseph, tired. He had lost his well-studied resemblance to Napoleon; nothing was left of him but a fat, elderly, helpless man.

Marie-Louise said: "I want to do my duty and don't want to be blamed for anything afterwards." She sounded very bored.

"Madame," urged Jerome, "if you leave the Tuileries now you may lose any claim to the French crown, you and your son.

Stay, Madame, let the Guards defend you, entrust your fate to the people of Paris."

"Well, let's stay, then," she said amiably, and began to undo the ribbons of her hat.

"But, Madame, think of His Majesty's instructions!" moaned Joseph. "You know he wants his son dead in the Seine rather than——"

"Don't repeat that dreadful sentence!" I exclaimed. Everybody turned round to me. It was very embarrassing. I was still standing in the doorway and, bowing in the direction of the Empress, I said: "I am sorry, I didn't want to intrude."

"The Crown Princess of Sweden in the Regent's rooms? Madame, this is a challenge which cannot be left unanswered!" shouted Jerome, and rushed at me like a madman.

"Jerome, I myself asked for Her Royal Highness because of—because of Julie," Joseph said awkwardly, pointing to my sister. I followed his movement and discovered Julie with her daughters on a sofa at the far end of the room. Their outlines were blurred by the uncertain morning light.

"Please take a seat, Highness," said Marie-Louise kindly.

Quickly I went over to Julie and sat down by her side. She had put her arm round the shoulders of her daughter Zenaïde. "Don't get agitated, Julie," I whispered, "you shall come to me with your children."

Meanwhile the discussion near the fireplace raged on, till Joseph came away from the group there to us.

"If the Regent and her son go to Rambouillet I shall have to accompany her," he said to Julie.

"But how can you if you are to defend the city?"

"The Emperor has told me that I am not to let his son out of my sight. The whole family is coming along. Julie, I am asking you for the last time——"

Julie, tears streaming down her face, shook her head. "No, no, please. We'll be chased from castle to castle till the Cossacks catch up with us. Please, let me go to Désirée, Joseph, her house is safe. Isn't it, Désirée?"

Joseph and I looked at each other for a long time. "You too could come to me, Joseph," I said at last.

He shook his head and forced himself to smile. "Perhaps Napoleon will be here in time to hold Paris, and in that case I shall be back with Julie in a few days' time. If not——" he bent to kiss my hand, "let me thank you for all you are doing for Julie and my children, you and your husband."

At this moment the chamberlain announced that the Prince of Benevento requested an audience. Smilingly the Empress asked him in.

Talleyrand, tired and worn, but with his hair carefully powdered and wearing the uniform of the Vice-Grand Elector of the Empire, limped quickly towards the Empress. "Your Majesty, I have just come from the Minister of War, who is in touch with Marshal Marmont. The Marshal requests Your Majesty to leave Paris immediately with the King of Rome. He does not know how much longer he will be able to keep open the road to Rambouillet. I am disconsolate to have to be the bringer of this dreadful message."

A deep silence fell. It was broken only by the rustling of the silk ribbons of Marie-Louise's hat, which she started tying up again under her chin. "Shall I be able to meet His Majesty in Rambouillet?"

"But His Majesty is on the way to Fontainebleau and from there will go on straight to Paris," said Joseph.

"But I mean His Majesty the Emperor of Austria—my papa."

Joseph grew deathly pale, Jerome clenched his teeth, and I saw a vein on his forehead swell. Only Talleyrand smiled. He didn't seem at all surprised. Madame Letitia, however, gripped the arm of her daughter-in-law fiercely: "Come on, Madame, come on!"

By the door Marie-Louise turned round and surveyed the room. Her eyes met those of the still smiling Talleyrand. "I hope no one is going to blame me for anything afterwards!" she sighed, and went out.

But her son, the little King of Rome, didn't feel like going. He screamed and screamed and shouted: "Don't want to! Don't want to!" At long last Hortense appeared. She knew how to deal with the boy, and a moment later Napoleon's son went obediently down the stairs between his two governesses.

"Exit Napoleon II," murmured Talleyrand close to me.

"I am very uneducated," I said. "What does 'exit' mean?"

"Exit is a Latin word and means 'goes out', 'leaves', 'disappears'. Exit Napoleon II, therefore, stands for Napoleon II disappears from—the Tuileries? The pages of world history?" He looked at his watch. "I am afraid I have to say good-bye, my carriage is waiting."

He, like the Empress, surveyed the room thoughtfully. Looking at the curtains with the bees, he said: "A pretty pattern! Pity that they will soon be removed!"

"If you hang them upside down the bees look like lilies. Like the Bourbon lilies!"

He raised his lorgnette to his eyes. "Indeed! How strange! But really, I must go now, Highness."

"No one is keeping you, Prince. Is it true you are going to follow the Empress?"

"I am. But first I shall be taken prisoner by the Russians outside the gate. That's why I must not be late. The Russian patrol is waiting for me now. *Au revoir*, Highness!"

"Perhaps Marshal Marmont will rescue you," I hissed. "You deserve it."

"Do I? But I fear I must disappoint you. Marshal Marmont is far too busy to bother about me at the moment: he is conducting the negotiations for the surrender of Paris. But keep this piece of news to yourself, Highness. We want to avoid unnecessary bloodshed and confusion." He bowed gracefully and limped away.

I drove home with Julie and her daughters. For the first time since the day Julie had become Queen, Marie spoke to her again. Like a mother she laid her arm round Julie's narrow shoulders and led her up the stairs.

"Marie, give Oscar's room to Queen Julie and Madame La Flotte's to her children. Madame La Flotte will have to move into the spare room."

"And General Clary, the son of Monsieur Etienne?" asked Marie.

"What do you mean?"

"The General arrived an hour ago and would like to stay here for the time being."

General Clary was Etienne's son Marius, who had become an officer instead of going into Papa's firm, and with the help of God and Napoleon had reached General's rank. I decided that the two adjutants could share Rosen's room and that he should have Villatte's.

"And what about Countess Tascher?"

This question only made sense to me when I entered the drawing-room. There Etienne's daughter Marceline, who is married to a Count Tascher, threw herself into my arms, crying.

"I am so frightened, Aunt, in my house. The Cossacks might come at any moment," she sobbed.

"And your husband?"

"He is somewhere at the front. Marius stayed at my house

last night and we decided to come here to you for the time being——"

I let her have the spare room and thought of putting Madame La Flotte on the divan in my boudoir.

"And my children's governess?" Julie wailed. "You must give her a room of her own. Otherwise she'll give me notice. Who is having Jean-Baptiste's bed?"

'Not the governess,' I thought in fury, and fled into Jean-Baptiste's empty bedroom. There I sat down on the wide empty bed and listened into the night. . . .

At about five o'clock in the afternoon the guns had ceased firing. Villatte and Rosen, returning from a walk, reported that Blücher had taken Montmartre by storm and that the Austrians were in Menilmontant. The allies, they said, demanded unconditional surrender.

PARIS.
March 30th, 1814.

At two o'clock this morning the capitulation was signed. When I looked out of the window I saw the Swedish flag flying over my house. Count Rosen had put it up with the help of Johansson, the Swedish coachman. A dense crowd was waiting outside. Its voice rose dully to my window.

"What do they want, Villatte?"

"There is a rumour that His Royal Highness is coming to-day."

"But what do they want of Jean-Baptiste?"

The sounds from outside grew louder and more menacing, and I stopped asking.

A carriage arrived at the gate. Gendarmes pushed back the crowd and I saw Hortense with her two sons, the nine-year-old Napoleon Louis and the six-year-old Charles Louis Napoleon, get out. The murmur of the crowd ceased. One of the boys pointed to the Swedish flag and asked a question. But Hortense quickly pulled her boys into the house.

Madame La Flotte came. "Queen Hortense asks Your Highness if the Emperor's nephews could live under the protection of Your Highness for the time being. The Queen herself is going to join her mother at Malmaison."

'Two little boys in the house,' I thought, 'there may even be some toys of Oscar's left in the attic.' "Tell Her Majesty I shall look after the boys."

Their arrival needed another rearrangement of bedrooms. I saw their mother drive away. "*Vive l'Empereur!*" the crowd shouted. Then it closed its ranks once more, and the ominous sound of its low murmur was with me all day long.

PARIS.
April 1814.

On the 31st of March the allies entered Paris. The Parisians didn't have much time to bother about their conquerors, they were too busy queueing at the bakers' and grocers'. The store-houses round Paris had been destroyed and the roads to the southern provinces blocked, and the result was starvation.

On April 1st a provisional Government headed by Talleyrand was formed, and negotiations started with the allied powers. Talleyrand gave a brilliant banquet in honour of the Tsar, who was staying at his palace, and the members of the old aristocratic families whom Napoleon had allowed to return took part in it.

Napoleon himself was at Fontainebleau with 5,000 men of his Guards regiments. Caulaincourt negotiated for him with the victors. On April 4th he signed his declaration of abdication. It said that since, in the view of the allied powers, his person formed the only obstacle to the restoration of peace in Europe, he was willing to renounce his throne and to leave France for the sake of his country's well-being, which was inseparable from the rights of his son, the rights of the Empress's regency and the continued validity of the Imperial laws.

Two days later, however, the Senate declared that a regency on behalf of Napoleon II was out of the question. Everywhere in Paris I suddenly saw the white flags of the Bourbons which no one bothered to remove and no one bothered to hail. In the *Moniteur* I read that only the reinstatement of the Bourbons could guarantee lasting peace. . . .

Most members of the Bonaparte family had fled to Blois with the Empress. Marie-Louise was seeing nobody. She had asked her father for protection for herself and her son, and her father, the Austrian Emperor, discarded his grandson's name Napoleon and called him Francis.

Julie had several letters from Joseph written at Blois. They were smuggled through the allied lines by young peasants who liked doing it because it was a chance for them of seeing Paris. Julie and the children were to stay with me, wrote Joseph, till the new Government and the allies had decided what to do about the Bonapartes and their property. Meanwhile Julie had run out of money and I had to lend her some to pay the governess. Joseph had taken everything, even her jewellery, she said. My nephew Marius was in the same position, and I told Pierre to advance him what he needed. Then Marceline bought two new hats and had the bill sent to me. So it went on, till Pierre told me that I had no money left at all. I went to see him in his little office—I had given him the former caretaker's flat on the ground floor—and he accounted to me for all the money we had spent.

"Could Your Highness count on money from Sweden within the next few days?" he asked.

I shrugged my shoulders.

"Perhaps you could ask His Highness the Crown Prince?"

"But I don't know where he is."

"I could borrow all the money we need, of course, if Your Highness would sign a promissory note. The Crown Princess of Sweden has an unlimited credit these days. Do you want to sign?"

"No, I can't. How can I borrow money? Certainly not as the Crown Princess of Sweden. It would make a very bad impression and my husband wouldn't like it. No, really, it's impossible."

Marie came in. "You could sell some of your silver, Eugenie."

"Yes, I could do that. No, Marie, I can't do that either! All our silver has our initials on it. All Paris would know soon that we have no money and that would injure the reputation of Sweden badly."

"I could pawn some of Your Highness's jewellery," suggested Pierre. "No one would know whose it is."

"No, I have so little valuable jewellery, and what little I have I need if I have to receive the Tsar or the Austrian Emperor."

"Julie has plenty," said Marie.

"Joseph has taken all hers with him."

"But how are you going to feed all the people under your roof?"

I stared at the empty cash-box. "Let me think."

They let me think.

"Marie, the firm of Clary has always had a warehouse in Paris, at least in Papa's days, hasn't it?"

"Oh yes. It's still there. Every time Monsieur Etienne

comes to Paris he goes there. Has he never told you about it?"

"No. There's never been any reason for mentioning it."

Marie raised her eyebrows. "Hasn't there? Who's inherited that half of the firm which belonged to your Mama, then?"

"I don't know——"

"According to the law you, Queen Julie and your brother Etienne own one third each of that half," explained Pierre.

"But Julie and I had our dowries."

"Yes," Marie said, "that was your share of the estate left by your father. When he died Etienne inherited one half of the firm and your mother the other. So since your mother's death you own——"

"One sixth of the firm of Clary, Your Highness," said Pierre.

'I ought to talk it over with Julie,' I thought. But Julie was in bed with migraine. How could I go to her and say that I had no money for our lunch? "Marie," I said, "let cook fetch some veal. The butcher will get his money to-night. Please get me a *fiacre* as quickly as possible."

The big drawing-room was full of life. Marius and Villatte were poring over maps and fighting the battles of the last months all over again. Julie's daughters were having a noisy argument with Hortense's sons about the contents of a *bon-bonnière* made of magnificent Sèvres, and Madame La Flotte, translating an article to Count Rosen, was in tears because this article called Napoleon a bloodhound.

I went up to Marius. "Where," I asked him, "is the ware-house of the firm of Clary?"

He blushed. "But, Aunt, you know I have nothing to do with the silk trade. I have been an officer all my life." Obviously it was embarrassing to him to talk about it in Villatte's presence.

I persisted. "But your father is a silk merchant and, surely, you remember where his warehouse is. He went there every time he came to Paris."

"But I never went with him, I——"

I watched him closely and that made him break off. Then, quickly, he said: "In a cellar in the Palais Royal, if I remember right." And he gave me the address.

The cab took me to a very spacious and elegant basement shop in the Palais Royal. Entering I found myself in a very neatly furnished office and opposite an elderly man in formal clothes who was sitting behind a writing-desk. He wore the white rosette of the Bourbons in his buttonhole. The shelves seemed nearly empty.

"What can I do for you, Madame?"

"Are you the manager of the firm of Clary in Paris?"

"I am, Madame. White satin is unfortunately sold out, but——"

"That isn't what I have come for."

"Oh, I understand, Madame wishes to purchase some dress material? Till yesterday I had some brocade with the lily pattern left, but it is all sold out now, unfortunately. But velvet or——"

"Business is flourishing, Monsieur——"

"Legrand, Madame," he introduced himself, "Legrand."

"Tell me, Monsieur Legrand, these white materials, brocade with the Bourbon lily, white satin and muslin to put over the curtains, when did they arrive here? As far as I know all the roads to Paris are blocked."

He laughed heartily and loudly so that the two double chins whipped merrily up and down over his high collar. "Monsieur Clary sent all these materials months ago from Genoa. The first consignments arrived shortly after the Battle of Leipzig. Monsieur Clary, the head of the firm, is very well informed. As Madame may know, Monsieur Clary is——" he cleared his throat, smirking, "Monsieur Clary is the brother-in-law of the victor of Leipzig, the brother-in-law of the Swedish Crown Prince. Madame will realise that——"

"And so you've been selling white silk for weeks to the ladies of the old nobility?" I interrupted him.

He nodded proudly.

I gazed at the white rosette on his lapel. "I could never understand where all the white rosettes sprang from overnight. So these noble ladies whom the Emperor received at his court have all been sitting down secretly sewing white rosettes?"

"But, Madame——"

But I was furious, dreadfully furious. I understood now why the shelves were nearly empty. "And you sold white silk, one roll after the other. Whilst the French troops were still fighting to throw back the enemy you have been sitting here making money, haven't you?"

"But, Madame, I am only an employee of the firm. Besides, most of the stuff has not been paid for yet. The ladies will only be able to pay when the Bourbons have returned and when the husbands of these ladies get their big jobs——" He stopped and looked at me with suspicion. "Madame, what can I do for you?"

"I need money. How much have you got in your till?"

" Madame, I don't understand——"

" I own one sixth of the firm of Clary, I am a daughter of the founder of the firm, and I need money urgently. How much have you got in your till, Monsieur Legrand?"

" Madame, I don't quite understand. Monsieur Etienne has only two sisters, Madame Joseph Bonaparte and Her Highness the Crown Princess of Sweden."

" Quite right. And I am the Crown Princess of Sweden. How much money have you got in your till?"

Monsieur Legrand felt for his waistcoat pocket with a trembling hand, pulled out his spectacles and looked at me. After this examination he bowed as deeply as his stomach would allow. When I shook hands with him he was nearly overcome with emotion.

" I was an apprentice in your father's shop in Marseilles when Your Highness was still a child, a dear child, and so naughty!"

" You wouldn't have recognised me, would you? Not even with your glasses?" I felt like crying myself. " I am not quite so naughty now, I'm doing my best——"

Legrand rushed to the door and locked it. " We don't need any customers now, Your Highness," he said.

" I've thought and thought how to manage without making debts," I said. " A Clary can't make debts, can she? I am only waiting for my husband——"

" The whole of Paris is waiting for the triumphant entry of the victor of Leipzig," said Legrand. " The Tsar is here already, the Prussian King too, it can't be long now."

" In all these years I've not drawn out my share in the profits of the firm," I said. " Therefore I should like to take anything you have in cash."

" I have very little cash. The day before he left King Joseph asked me for an enormous sum." I opened my eyes in amazement. He went on talking without noticing my surprise. " King Joseph drew out his wife's share in our takings twice a year. What we took to the end of March by the secret sale of the white materials has been drawn out by King Joseph. There are only the outstanding debts left."

So even Joseph Bonaparte made money on the white rosettes. Whether he knew about it or not, what does it matter now?

" Here," said Legrand, and gave me a bundle of notes. " That is all we have at the moment."

" Better than nothing," I said, and put them into my bag. An idea occurred to me, and I said: " Legrand, we must at

426

once collect all outstanding debts. People say that the franc is going to fall. My cab is waiting outside. Take it and go round all the customers. If they refuse to pay, ask for the material back. Will you?"

"But I can't leave the shop. I sent the only apprentice we have left with some samples to an old customer of ours who urgently needs some new clothes, the wife of Marshal Marmont, in fact. And Le Roy's buyer—they are working day and night for the ladies of the new court—may call at any moment."

I took off my coat. "Whilst you're going round collecting I shall see to the customers here."

"But, Your Highness——"

"What are you 'butting' about? I helped often enough in the shop in Marseilles. Don't be afraid. I know how to handle silk. Hurry up, Monsieur!"

Legrand, completely put out, stumbled towards the door.

"One moment, Monsieur. Please take off the white rosette if you call on behalf of the firm of Clary."

"But, Your Highness, most people——"

"Yes, most people, but not my papa's former apprentices. I'll see you later."

When he had gone, I sat down behind the desk and once more felt like crying. That was because of the memory of Marseilles. A naughty child with not a care in the world whom Papa had taken in hand and taught the Rights of Man. That was a long time ago, a very long time ago.

The door-bell rang, and a man in a light blue, beautifully embroidered tail-coat and with a white rosette came in, Le Roy's buyer. He didn't know me, I had always dealt with the manageress.

"You are Le Roy's buyer, aren't you? I am deputising for Monsieur Legrand. What can we do for you?"

"I should have liked to see Monsieur Legrand himself."

"I am sorry," I said, and pulled a heavy roll of velvet from the shelf. A label affixed to it said '*Madame Mère's* order. Returned.' It was dark green, the colour of Corsica, with the bee pattern woven into it. "Here," I said, "dark green velvet with the Bourbon lily pattern," and turned the roll round so that the bees lay upside down.

The buyer held up his lorgnette and examined the velvet sceptically. "The lilies remind me of the bee," he criticised.

"That's not my fault," I said.

"Besides, dark green is out of fashion now. We saw too much of that colour during the Empire. In any case, velvet is too heavy for spring weather. Have you any pale lilac-coloured muslin?"

I looked along the shelves which had some shades of muslin. The one he wanted was on the top shelf. It would be! I found a ladder and climbed up.

Meanwhile he went on: "The Empress Josephine desires a pale lilac dress. It is a subtle indication of mourning. She needs the dress for her reception of the Tsar."

I nearly fell off the ladder. "She—she wants to receive the Tsar?"

"Yes. She very much wants to see him to talk with him about her allowances. They are still negotiating about the annuities for the Bonaparte family. It looks as if they are going to be generous to these successful nobodies. Well, have you the muslin I want or not?"

I climbed down the ladder with the material and unrolled it before him.

"Too dark," he said.

"Lilac, the new fashion," I said.

He regarded me with contempt. "What makes you say that?"

"It looks well and a bit melancholy. Just right for Josephine. By the way, we can only sell for cash at the moment."

"Out of the question just now. Our customers do not pay on delivery, either. Of course, as soon as the situation is cleared up, Mademoiselle——"

"It is cleared up. The franc is falling. We can only sell for cash on the spot."

I took the roll of cloth from the desk and carried it back to the shelf.

"Where is Monsieur Legrand?"

"I told you, not here."

His eyes scanned the half-empty shelves. "You have hardly any stock left."

I nodded. "Almost sold out. And all for cash."

He stared, mesmerised, at a few rolls of satin. "Madame Ney," he murmured.

"Shall we say light blue satin for *Madame la Maréchale* Ney?" I suggested. "It would go with her rubies and she likes light blue."

"You seem to be well informed, Mademoiselle——"

"Désirée," I said amiably. "Well? How shall we dress Marshal Ney's wife for the occasion of her presentation to the Bourbons in the Tuileries?"

" You sound so bitter, Mademoiselle Désirée. You are not by any chance a partisan of the Bonapartes at heart, are you?"

" Take light blue for Madame Ney. I'll let you have the satin at the pre-war price." The price was on a tag in Etienne's thin writing. I named it.

" I shall give you a bill of exchange," he said.

" You'll pay cash or you'll leave the material here. I have other customers."

He paid.

" And the lilac muslin?" I asked, measuring and cutting the satin as I had seen Papa and Etienne do it at home.

" But the Empress never pays promptly," he lamented.

I paid no attention to that. At last he sighed and said: " Seven and a half yards of muslin, then."

" Make it nine. She'll be wanting a scarf of the same material."

Reluctantly he paid for Josephine's melancholy dress. When he went he said: " Ask Legrand to reserve the green velvet with the gold lilies for us till to-night." I promised I would.

I attended to three more customers before Legrand returned. " Did you get it all?" I asked.

" Not all, but a part. Here it is." He gave me a leather bag full of banknotes.

" Make a note of everything and I shall give you a receipt."

He began to write out a receipt and pushed it towards me for my signature. I thought for a moment and then signed as ' Désirée, Crown Princess of Sweden, *née* Clary.'

" From now onwards I shall settle the accounts regularly with my brother Etienne. And, by the way, get as much of the lilac-coloured muslin in as you can, it's the new fashion, you'll see. And reserve the green velvet which *Madame Mère* sent back for Le Roy. No, I'm not joking, he really wants it. Good-bye, Monsieur Legrand."

I got back into the cab and told the driver to take me to the Rue d'Anjou. He gave me a newspaper. It was a special edition containing Napoleon's declaration of abdication. ' Yes,' I thought, ' yes, and we'll have veal to-night, and I must keep an eye on my bag with all the money in it, and the air is full of spring already. . . .' Women were still queueing up in front of bakers' and butchers' shops, and copies of the abdication edition disintegrated on the wet pavements.

Suddenly the cab stopped. A chain of gendarmes barred the entrance to the Rue d'Anjou. The driver dismounted and opened the door. " Can't drive on," he said, " the Rue d'Anjou is cordoned off; they expect the Tsar."

" But I must get into the Rue d'Anjou, I live there."

The driver explained that to a gendarme, and I was allowed to pass, but only on foot. So I got out and paid the driver.

Gendarmes drawn up on both sides of the street formed a lane, the carriage-way was empty and made my steps resound. Just before I reached my house I was stopped by a sergeant-major of the gendarmerie on horseback. " No entry here!"

I looked up at him. His face seemed familiar. Yes, it was the man who for years had been standing guard over our house by order of the Minister of Police. I never knew what it meant, whether honour or supervision. Napoleon had the houses of all his Marshals guarded. This sergeant-major was an elderly man in a shabby uniform and a shabby hat. His tricorn showed a darker patch, the patch where up till two days ago he had worn the blue-white-red rosette of the Empire. It was obvious that he had left that patch free by design. The white rosette of the new Government was loosely fastened alongside it.

" Let me pass, you know I live in that house over there." I nodded in the direction of my house, in front of which gendarmes were standing in a bunch.

" In half an hour's time His Majesty the Emperor of Russia is going to pay a call on Her Royal Highness the Crown Princess of Sweden. My orders are not to let anybody walk past the house," he rattled off without looking at me.

' My God,' I thought, ' that's the last straw, the Tsar visiting me!' " In that case let me pass at once," I shouted furiously. " I must change my dress!"

But the shabby sergeant-major was still looking over my head into space.

I stamped my foot. " Look at me, will you? You have known me for years. You know very well that I live in that house there."

" Sorry, my mistake! I mistook Your Highness for the wife of Marshal Bernadotte." At last he turned his eyes on me, eyes full of a malicious glint. " I apologise for the mistake. I realise now, Your Highness is the lady who receives the Tsar's call." He roared: " Clear the way for the Crown Princess of Sweden!"

I ran the gauntlet of the gendarmes. My feet were as heavy as lead, but I kept running.

They were waiting for me at home. The front door opened

from inside when I reached it and Marie hauled me in. "Quick, quick," she said, "the Tsar will be here in half an hour's time."

I threw the bag with the money to Pierre and ran up to my boudoir. Marie undressed me quickly, Yvette started brushing my hair, and I shut my eyes, exhausted. Marie forced a glass of cognac on me, which I drank in one gulp. It made my throat burn.

"What will you wear?" asked Marie, and I decided on the purple velvet dress which I had worn at the last interview with Napoleon.

Just as I was putting on my gold paint and rouge I saw in the mirror that Julie had come in, dressed in one of her purple gowns and holding one of her small crowns in her hand. "Shall I wear the crown or not, Désirée?"

I turned round and looked at her, uncomprehending. She had gone so thin that the purple dress, which doesn't suit her anyway, hung round her body in loose folds. "For Heaven's sake, what do you want the crown for?"

"I thought—I mean when you present me to the Tsar you would probably introduce me by my old title and——"

I turned away and spoke to her reflection in the mirror. "Your really want to be presented to the Tsar, Julie?"

She nodded energetically. "Of course I do. I shall ask him to protect my interests and those of my children. The Emperor of Russia——"

"Aren't you ashamed of yourself, Julie Clary? Napoleon has only just abdicated, his family shared in his success, you accepted two crowns from him, now you must wait for what is going to be decided about you. Your interests——" I swallowed. My mouth felt dry. "Julie, you are no longer a Queen but only Julie Bonaparte née Clary. No more. But no less either."

The little crown fell clattering to the floor. The next moment Julie had banged the door behind her.

Yvette placed the ear-rings of the Swedish Dowager Queen in my ears, and Marie said that all day long people had been asking for me.

"What did you tell them?"

"Nothing. You've been away a long time."

"Yes. I sent the manager round to collect debts, and I had to attend to the customers while he was away."

"Five minutes to go," said Marie. "How is business?"

"Flourishing. They are selling satin and muslin for the new

431

court dresses for the wives of Napoleon's old Marshals. Give me another glass of cognac."

Marie poured out another glass without a word, and without a word I gulped it down. It burnt my throat, but now it was rather an agreeable burning.

I looked at myself in the mirror. The last time I had worn this dress I had had a bunch of violets on my decolletage. 'A pity,' I thought, 'I haven't any to-day.'

"By the way, Eugenie, some flowers have come for you, violets. I put them on the mantelpiece in the drawing-room. You must go down now."

I don't know whether it was my tiredness or the cognac, at any rate I floated down the stairs as if in a dream. In the hall everybody had lined up, Marceline, General Clary, Madame La Flotte, Julie's daughters, Hortense's sons, Count Rosen in a Swedish full-dress uniform, and, in the background, Colonel Villatte. As soon as I got down Villatte asked to be excused from attending, and I let him go.

"I should like you all to go into the big drawing-room and stay there. I shall receive the Tsar in the small drawing-room." I saw astonishment on all their faces. "I notice, Count Rosen, that you have found yourself a Swedish adjutant's uniform."

"His Royal Highness sent it me through a Russian adjutant."

'Jean-Baptiste,' I thought, 'never forgets the tiniest detail.' "You will accompany me into the small drawing-room, Count."

"And we?" exclaimed Marceline.

From the door to the drawing-room I said: "I shouldn't like to ask anybody French to be introduced to the ruler of a hostile power before peace has been concluded between France and the members of the coalition. To the best of my knowledge the Emperor has only just abdicated."

Marius blushed, Marceline uncomprehendingly shook her head, Madame La Flotte bit her lips and the children asked whether they might be allowed to peep through the keyhole. The small drawing-room was in perfect order. Champagne, glasses and sweetmeats were arranged on the small table by the mirror, and on the mantelpiece stood a silver basket with violets in it, puny-looking and past their best, and against it a sealed envelope.

The sound of trumpets and horses' hooves filled the room as a carriage drew up outside. I stood, rigid, in the middle of the room.

The door opened and the Tsar strode in, a giant with a

round boyish face, fair hair and a carefree smile, a giant in a brilliantly white uniform with glittering white epaulettes. Immediately behind him came Talleyrand and a host of people in foreign uniforms. I bowed and held out my hand to the young giant, who put it to his lips.

"Your Highness, it is my deeply felt need to pay my respects to the wife of the man who has contributed so largely to the liberation of Europe," said the Tsar.

My two servants crept round, offering champagne. The Tsar sat down with me on the small sofa, and Talleyrand took the chair opposite. "The Prince of Benevento was kind enough to put his house at my disposal," said the Tsar, and smiled.

'Does he always wear uniforms of brilliant white,' I wondered, 'even in battle? Nonsense, the Tsar was no leader of armies, he was a monarch waiting for news of victory from his Generals. Only Jean-Baptiste was Prince and General at the same time,' I thought, and smiled into my glass of champagne.

"It was a matter of infinite regret to me that Your Highness's husband did not enter Paris by my side," he continued with eyes suddenly narrowing. "It was something I had counted on. We exchanged a number of letters during the advance across the Rhine, a small difference of opinion concerning the future frontiers of France. . . ."

I drank and smiled into my glass of champagne.

"I should have been glad if His Royal Highness could have taken part in the discussions on the shaping of the new France. After all, Your Highness's husband is better informed about the wishes of the French people than I or our dear cousins, the Emperor of Austria and the King of Prussia. Moreover, they and their advisers are apt to pursue quite different and particular interests." The Emperor emptied his glass and an adjutant refilled it. Neither of my servants was allowed near him.

I kept smiling.

"I am awaiting with impatience the arrival of your husband, Highness. Perhaps Your Highness knows when I may expect him?"

I shook my head and drank my champagne.

"The provisional Government of France under the leadership of our friend, the Prince of Benevento "—he raised his glass to Talleyrand and Talleyrand bowed—" has informed us that France longs for the return of the Bourbons and that only their restoration can guarantee internal peace. This has surprised me. What does Your Highness think of it?"

"I know nothing about politics, Sire."

"During my frequent conversations with Your Highness's husband I had rather gained the impression that the Bourbon dynasty is not—hm, well, is not at all acceptable to the French people. Therefore I suggested to His Royal Highness——" he held his empty glass up to the adjutant without taking his eyes off me, "Madame, I have therefore proposed to your husband to persuade the French people to elect its great Marshal Jean-Baptiste Bernadotte, Prince of Sweden, as its King."

"And what did my husband answer, Your Majesty?"

"Nothing, Your Highness, quite incomprehensibly, nothing. Our dear cousin, the Crown Prince of Sweden, has not answered our letter, he has not arrived in Paris at the appointed time, my couriers can no longer establish contact with him. His Highness has—disappeared." He emptied the freshly filled glass and looked at me sadly. "The Emperor of Austria and the King of Prussia support the return of the Bourbons, and Britain is putting a man-of-war at our disposal to convey Louis XVIII across. As the Crown Prince of Sweden has not answered me I shall conform to the wishes of the French Government and of my allies." He stared thoughtfully into his glass. "Pity," he said, "pity." And abruptly he added: "You have a charming salon, Madame."

We rose, and the Emperor went to the window and looked out into the garden. I was standing quite close to him and hardly reached to his shoulders.

"This is Moreau's old house," I said.

The Tsar, overcome by sudden painful memories, closed his eyes. "A shell smashed both his legs when he was serving as a member of my General Staff. He died at the beginning of September. Did Your Highness not know?"

I pressed my head against the cool glass of the window. "Moreau is an old friend of ours from the days when my husband still hoped to be able to preserve the Republic for the people of France." I spoke in a very low tone, and not even Talleyrand was near enough to hear us.

"And is it for the sake of this Republic that your husband will not accept my suggestion?"

I made no answer.

"No answer is answer enough," he smiled.

Then I remember something and became very angry. "Sire," I said.

He bent down. "My dear cousin?"

"You offered my husband not only the French crown but also the hand of a Grand Duchess!"

He laughed. "It is said that walls have ears. But that even the thick walls of Abo should possess them! . . . Do you know what your husband answered, Highness? 'But I am married already,' he said, and the subject has never been touched on again. Does that reassure you, Highness?"

"I never needed a reassurance, Sire, at least in that respect. Will you have another drink, my dear—cousin?"

Talleyrand joined us, bringing glasses, and he didn't leave us alone for another second.

"If I could do anything for you, dear cousin, you would make me very happy."

"You are very kind, Sire. But I need nothing."

"Perhaps you would like a guard of honour of Russian Guards officers?"

"For Heaven's sake, no!" I exclaimed. Talleyrand smiled ironically.

"I understand," the Tsar said gravely, "of course I understand, my dearest cousin." He bent over my hand. "Had I had the honour of knowing you before I should never have made that suggestion to the Crown Prince. I mean the Abo suggestion."

"But you meant well, Sire."

"The ladies of my family who might have been considered are very ugly. You, however, my dear, my very dear cousin . . ."

The rest of his sentence was drowned by the clicking of his spurred heels. Then he left with his entourage.

After he had gone my thoughts wandered back to Moreau who had come back from America to fight for France's liberty. He had not lived to see the return of the Bourbons and the white rosettes. . . . I caught sight of the faded violets. "Count Rosen, where did the flowers come from?"

"Caulaincourt brought them. He was on his way from Fontainebleau to Talleyrand to hand over the instrument of abdication."

I went to the mantelpiece. There was no address on the sealed envelope. I tore it open and found a sheet of notepaper with nothing on it but a scribbled 'N'. I took out a bunch of the violets. They smelled beautifully as if they were still fresh, still quite alive, yet they were half dead already.

I felt very tired. Selling satin and muslin for the firm of Clary, reading Napoleon's abdication, entertaining the Tsar of

Russia, learning the news of Moreau's death, and now the violets from Fontainebleau, it was enough to make me reel with tiredness. So I told Rosen to apologise for me at table and went straight to my room.

At the bottom of the stairs Marie was waiting for me. She took me to bed, undressed me and tucked me in as if I were a child.

I woke in the middle of the night and sat up in bed with a jerk. Everything was black around me and perfectly still. I pressed my hands against my temples to remember what it was that had woken me. What had it been? A thought? A dream? No, the knowledge that something was going to happen during the night, perhaps at this hour, something that I had felt coming all through the evening, something—— Suddenly I knew. It was something to do with abdication and the violets.

I lit the candle and went into my boudoir. The special edition with the announcement of the abdication was still lying on my dressing-table. I read it through very very carefully: '. . . the Emperor declares that he renounces the thrones of France and Italy and that there is no sacrifice, not even that of his life, which he is not willing to make . . .' ran the Emperor's proclamation.

That was it, ' no sacrifice, not even that of his life. . . .' They were the words that had woken me. I knew, I knew for certain that he was going to commit suicide. That was why he had sent the violets: a man alone at the end of his life looked back to his youth, to the beginning of his journey where he found the young girl leaning against the hedge in a dreamy garden and, since she was still within reach, he sent her the last greeting, her, who had been the first.

The violets were all the proof I needed that he was going to take his life. ' I shall order Villatte,' I thought, ' to ride to Fontainebleau at once and to force his way into his bedroom. Perhaps he will be too late, but I must try it, I must.

' Why must I, why? Was there any obligation on me? Must I really?'

I slipped from the chair down to the floor, fighting hard not to lose my self-control, not to scream, not to wake anybody, fighting hard the sense of doom. It was an endless night. Not till dawn broke did I get back to my bed. My limbs ached and I felt terribly cold.

After breakfast I sent for Colonel Villatte: "Go to Talley-rand's office in the course of the morning and inquire on my behalf after the state of the Emperor Napoleon's health!"

Later I took a cab and drove with Count Rosen to the shop of the firm of Clary. I had been told that the Prussians were 'shopping' in Paris without paying for the goods. When we arrived Monsieur Legrand was just trying unsuccessfully to prevent Prussian soldiers from carrying off our last rolls of silk. I told Rosen, whose Swedish uniform commanded respect, to deal with them, and he managed to persuade the Prussians to pay up.

When we returned an enormous crowd had assembled in front of my house. Two Russian Guardsmen were solemnly pacing up and down the length of the house. As I got out, these men, who wore enormous beards and looked altogether frightening, presented arms. "It is a guard of honour," said Count Rosen.

"But what are these people waiting for? Why are they staring up at the windows?"

"Perhaps there has been a rumour that His Royal Highness is returning to-day. After all, to-morrow is the day for the official entry of the victorious rulers and their Marshals. It seems hardly possible that His Royal Highness should not take part in the victory parade at the head of the Swedish troops."

Hardly possible, yes, hardly possible. . . .

Before the mid-day meal Colonel Villatte reported to me on his visit to Talleyrand. "At first," he said, "they hedged. But when I said that you had sent me, Talleyrand told me in strictest confidence that——" Villatte recounted what Talleyrand had told him and finished up by saying: "It is inconceivable."

The meal took place in a most depressing silence. Even the children didn't say a word. And what was the reason for it? Firstly, said Julie, because I hadn't presented any of them to the Tsar, and secondly, I had been so strange, so unapproachable to them lately that the children, who very much wanted to see the victory parade, dared not ask me to lend them my carriage with the Swedish colours on it. I told Julie that I had plenty of problems and cares, and that I slept badly and that these were sad days. But they could gladly have my carriage if they wanted to see the parade. They would be safe in it and I didn't need it. I would stay at home to-morrow. When I had said that the horizon brightened considerably. . . .

During the night, the night from the 12th to the 13th of April, I kept the candle on my bedside table burning all night. About eleven o'clock the murmur from the crowd outside died down. The Rue d'Anjou became very quiet and the steps of the two Russian sentries rang out through the lonely night. The clock struck midnight. The clock struck one, the first hour of the day of the victory parade. I listened to every inexplicable forlorn creaking of the world with all the muscles of my body tensed, I listened, I listened, I listened. The clock struck two.

Suddenly the silence of the night was shattered by the sound of wheels rolling along the street, wheels grating to a standstill outside my house. I heard the sentries spring to attention and present arms, heard a loud knock on the front door, heard voices, three or four voices, but not the one I was waiting for. I lay quite still, with eyes closed.

Someone came running up the stairs. Someone tore open the door of my bedroom, kissed my mouth, my eyes, my forehead, my cheeks: Jean-Baptiste, my Jean-Baptiste!

"You must eat something, you've had a long journey," I said awkwardly, and opened my eyes. Jean-Baptiste was kneeling by my bed, his face lying on my hand.

"A long journey, a dreadfully long journey," he said tonelessly.

I stroked his hair with my free hand. It had gone quite grey, I could see it by the light of the candle, quite grey.

I sat up in bed. "Come, Jean-Baptiste, go into your bedroom and have a rest. I'll got into the kitchen meanwhile and make you an omelette, shall I?"

But he didn't move. He pressed his head against the edge of my bed and didn't move.

"Jean-Baptiste, you're at home, you're at home at last!"

Slowly he lifted his head.

"Jean-Baptiste, get up. Your room is waiting and——"

He smoothed his forehead with his hand as if he wanted to smooth away old memories. "Yes yes, of course. Can you find beds for them all?" he asked.

"All?"

"I am not alone, you know. There are Brahe and Löwenhjelm, besides Admiral Stedingk and——"

"That's out of the question. The house is overcrowded as it is. With the exception of your bedroom and your study there isn't a single free room."

"Overcrowded?"

"Yes, Julie, her children, Hortense's sons and——"

He jumped to his feet. "Do you mean to say that you offered shelter to all the Bonapartes and are feeding them at the expense of the Swedish court?"

" Only to Julie and the children and a few Clarys. The two adjutants you sent me yourself. As to feeding, the cost of the household as well as all the salaries I am paying out of my own money."

" Out of your own money?"

" Yes, money I earned by selling silk for the firm of Clary." I went into my boudoir and slipped into my pretty green dressing-gown with the mink collar. " And now I'm going to get you and your gentlemen something to eat."

Then the miracle happened: Jean-Baptiste laughed, laughed as if he were going to burst, sat on my bed and laughed and opened his arms. " My little girl, my priceless little girl, come, come to me! The Crown Princess of Sweden and Norway sells silk! Come, my girl!"

I went to him. " I don't know what there is to laugh at. I had no money left, and everything is so dreadfully expensive. You'll see!"

" A fortnight ago I sent you a courier with money."

" Unfortunately he never arrived. Listen, when your gentlemen have had something to eat we'll have to find hotel rooms for them."

He became serious again. " They can stay at the Swedish headquarters in the Rue St. Honoré." He opened the door from my bedroom into his. I held up the light.

" Everything's ready for you," I said.

But he stared round his old familiar room with the old familiar furniture as if he had never seen it before. " I think, I too shall stay in the Rue St. Honoré." Once more his voice had become toneless. " You see, I shall have to receive very many people. And I can't do that here, I can't. Don't you understand, Désirée?"

" You don't want to stay here?"

He put his arm round my shoulder. " I have only come to Paris to let the Swedish troops take part in the victory parade and to see the Tsar. But one thing I can tell you, Désirée: I shall never again return to this room, never."

" But five minutes ago you wanted to stay here with the whole of your staff!"

" That was before I had set eyes on my room again. Forgive my mistake. But there is no return to where I came from." He held me close to him. " Well, let's go down now. My staff hope that you will welcome them. I am sure that Fernand has prepared something to eat."

Mention of Fernand brought me back to reality. I put on

some rouge and powder, and Jean-Baptiste and I went arm-in-arm down to the dining-room. Young Brahe was there—I should have liked to kiss him but didn't dare because of Löwenhjelm—Löwenhjelm, Admiral Stedingk, a much-bemedalled man, and Fernand in a brand-new livery with gold buttons. "How is Oscar?" I asked him.

Jean-Baptiste took some letters out of his breast-pocket and said proudly: "The Prince has composed a regimental march!"

My heart gave a little leap of joy when I heard that Oscar composed music.

Fernand's coffee was bitter and sweet at the same time. 'Exactly like this homecoming,' I thought.

We sat in front of the fireplace in the big drawing-room. I noticed Jean-Baptiste gazing towards the portrait of the First Consul in the far half-dark end of the room. One by one we fell silent till at last Jean-Baptiste turned to me and asked in a sharp voice: "And—he?"

"The Emperor is at Fontainebleau waiting to learn what is decided about him. By the way," I added, "he tried to commit suicide the night before last."

"What?" they exclaimed with one voice. Only Jean-Baptiste said nothing.

"Since the Russian campaign the Emperor's always carried poison about with him," I said, not looking at the men but into the fire. "The night before last he swallowed it. But his valet had seen him and he took the necessary measures at once. Napoleon has completely recovered now."

"That is grotesque," said Stedingk, "tragic and ridiculous at the same time. If he wanted to make an end why didn't he shoot himself?"

Again there was silence, silence as heavy as lead. At last Count Brahe cleared his throat and said: "Your Highness, concerning to-morrow's victory parade——"

Jean-Baptiste started, then recovered himself and began in his usual precise manner: "Above all, I shall have to clear away every actual and possible misunderstanding between myself and the Tsar. He expected me, as you know, to advance with the allies into France. I did not, and I did not take part in any battle on French soil. If my allies take it amiss——" He broke off.

I looked at Brahe, who, hesitantly, answered my unspoken question: "We drove about in Belgium and France for weeks, aimlessly, Your Highness. His Highness wanted to see the battlefields."

"The villages where fighting took place are completely destroyed. That is not the way to make war," said Jean-Baptiste between his teeth.

Löwenhjelm, deciding that this was the moment, opened the briefcase he had with him and produced a bundle of letters. "Your Highness, I have here all the letters from the Tsar to you which have not been answered. They chiefly concern——"

"Don't say it!" shouted Jean-Baptiste at him. I had never before seen him lose his self-control to such an extent. He bent forward and stared into the fire. The eyes of the Swedes, I noticed, were directed to me. I seemed to be their last hope.

"Jean-Baptiste," I began. But he gave no sign of having heard me. I got up, knelt by his side and put my head against his arm. "Jean-Baptiste, you must listen to these gentlemen. The Tsar offered you the crown of France, didn't he?"

I felt his body stiffen, but I didn't give up. "You didn't answer the Tsar. And that is what has made it possible for the Count of Artois, Louis XVIII's brother, to come to Paris to-morrow and prepare everything for the return of the Bourbons. The Tsar had no option but to conform to the wishes of the other allies and the suggestions of Talleyrand."

"But the Tsar will never understand why I kept aloof from the French campaign and why I did not answer his proposal. Sweden cannot afford a disagreement with the Tsar, don't you understand?"

"Jean-Baptiste, the Emperor is very proud to be your friend. And he realises that you cannot accept the French crown. I explained it all to him."

"You what?" Jean-Baptiste gripped my shoulders and stared at me.

"Yes, he was here to pay his respects to the wife of the victor of Leipzig."

I could hear them all, Jean-Baptiste and his Swedes, breathe a sigh of relief.

I got up. "And now, gentlemen, you will want to rest a few hours before the big parade. I hope that everything will be ready for you at the Rue St. Honoré."

I left the drawing-room quickly. I didn't want to see Jean-Baptiste leave his home to stay in some palace or other. But he came after me and caught up with me on the staircase, leaning on me heavily. In my bedroom he dropped on my bed, and I had to undress him as if he were a child. I put out the candle, but already the morning was creeping through the chinks of the shutters and there was little sleep for us.

"This confounded victory parade," Jean-Baptiste said. "How can I march with bands playing across the Champs Elysées at the head of the Northern Army?"

"Of course you can. Why not? The Swedes have fought bravely for European freedom, and now they want to enter Paris in triumph with their Crown Prince at their head. How long will it all take, after all? One hour, perhaps two at most. It will be much easier than—Leipzig, Jean-Baptiste."

"Tell me, Désirée, what exactly did you tell the Tsar?"

"That in France you are a Republican and in Sweden the Crown Prince. Not perhaps in those words, but the Tsar understood me all right."

"What else did you talk about, my girl?"

"About Grand Duchesses. The Tsar thought you'd better stay with me. His Grand Duchesses are not at all pretty."

"Mhm," Jean-Baptiste said.

At last he fell asleep, a short and restless sleep like that of a traveller in the bed of some indifferent hotel room.

An argument between Fernand and Marie about the big clothes-iron put an end to Jean-Baptiste's sleep. He went into his dressing-room, where Fernand helped him to dress. Meanwhile Marie brought our breakfast and grumbled: "The Marshal might have left Fernand at home."

"Where do you call home?"

"Stockholm, of course."

The door between my boudoir and Jean-Baptiste's dressing-room was not closed, and after a while I heard the voices of Brahe and Löwenhjelm. They reported that Wetterstedt, the Prime Minister of Sweden, had arrived, and that our own headquarters was being stormed.

"By the Parisians?" asked Jean-Baptiste.

"Oh no, the street has been cordoned off and the Tsar has put a Russian regiment at our disposal," said Brahe.

Jean-Baptiste's answer was given so quickly that I only caught a few words: "Swedish dragoons . . . under no circumstances Russian sentries. . . ."

Then I heard Löwenhjelm say who it was who had stormed our headquarters. Apparently Talleyrand had called in the name of the French Government, followed by the Marshals Ney and Marmont, the Personal Adjutant of the King of Prussia, the British Ambassador, a deputation of the citizens of Paris, and so on.

In the middle of this enumeration Colonel Villatte was announced. Jean-Baptiste asked him in at once. I went to join him. Fernand was just sprinkling him with eau de Cologne and handing him the Grand Cross of the Legion of Honour. Jean-Baptiste took it as usual without thinking, when suddenly he seemed to notice it and froze in the act of putting it round his neck. Löwenhjelm warned him that the time was getting short. Slowly Jean-Baptiste came to life again and put it on. "On parade, Marshal Bernadotte!" he whispered to the hollow-cheeked face that stared back at him from the mirror.

At that moment Villatte came in. Jean-Baptiste turned to him quickly, went to meet him and slapped his shoulder. "Villatte, how glad I am to see you again!"

Villatte stood to attention.

Jean-Baptiste shook him by the shoulder. "Well, old friend?"

Villatte remained immobile, his face rigid.

Jean-Baptiste's hand slipped from his friend's shoulder. "Can I do anything for you, Colonel?"

"I am told that the allied powers yesterday ordered the discharge of all French prisoners of war. I therefore request my—release."

I laughed. But Villatte did not smile. His face became very sad instead.

"Of course, Colonel, you are free to go," said Jean-Baptiste. "I should be very glad if you could stay with us as our guest for the time being."

"I thank Your Highness for the very kind offer. I regret that I cannot accept it and I ask Your Highnesses to excuse me now."

"Villatte," I said, "you have gone such a long way with us. Won't you stay with us?"

"The Emperor has released his Army from the oath of loyalty to him," Jean-Baptiste added hoarsely. "Even his Marshals are calling on me. Why will you of all people——"

"That is just why. The Marshals have not thought it necessary to say good-bye to their Supreme Commander. I am only a colonel, Your Highness, but I know what I have to do. I shall go to Fontainebleau first and then join my regiment."

He turned and the next moment he was gone. Jean-Baptiste looked very grey in the face.

Before he left I took him into my boudoir, sat him down on the stool before the dressing-table, and began to rub his grey cheeks carefully with rouge. He protested vigorously.

"You can't ride across the Champs Elysées at the head of your victorious troops liiking like death itself. If you enter like a victor you must look like a victor." I examined my handiwork and noticed with satisfaction that his cheeks looked a very natural red.

But Jean-Baptiste shook his head in revulsion. "I can't. Really, I can't." It sounded almost like sobbing.

I put my hands on his shoulders. "After the parade you'll show yourself at the command performance in the Théâtre Français. You owe that to Sweden. And now, dearest, I fear you must go."

He buried his head on my breast. All the colour had gone out of his lips, they were sore and full of cracks. "I believe that during the victory parade there will be only one other man as lonely as I and that is—he!"

"Nonsense! You are not lonely. After all, I am with you and not with him! Go now, your staff is waiting."

He got up and put my hand to his lips. "Promise me not to go and see the parade."

I promised him that.

When the bells began to ring for the beginning of the parade I went and sat in the garden. Everybody had gone in my coach to be there too, and I had given the servants the day off. Hence no one was there to announce the unexpected visitor. This unexpected visitor had found the front door open, entered and wandered through the empty house into the garden. I didn't notice him because I had my eyes closed and was thinking of Jean-Baptiste at the victory parade. "Your Highness!" I heard someone shout through the ringing of the bells, and when I, startled out of my thoughts, opened my eyes, I saw Fouché with his pointed nose and small eyes, and a very big white rosette on the lapel of a rather modest tail-coat. He made a deep bow.

Rather overcome, I pointed to the bench. He sat down with alacrity and at once began to talk. I couldn't hear him because of the bells. He stopped talking, smiled and waited. Then the bell-ringing came to an end.

"I am sorry to disturb Your Highness, I have come on Talleyrand's behalf to see Madame Julie Bonaparte. Talleyrand is very busy these days, whilst I unfortunately have very much time. I had in any case intended to call on you, and so I offered to take the document along. It concerns the future of the members of the Bonaparte family."

He handed me the copy of a very lengthy document.

"I shall pass it on to my sister."

" Do have a look at the list, Your Highness."

I looked and read: the mother of the Emperor—300,000 francs; King Joseph—500,000 francs; King Louis—200,000 francs; Queen Hortense and her children—400,000 francs; King Jerome and his wife—500,000 francs; Princess Eliza—300,000 francs; Princess Polette—300,000 francs.

" These are annuities, Your Highness, annuities! Our new Government is really generous."

" Where may the members of the Bonaparte family live?"

" Only abroad, Your Highness!"

So Julie, who always feels miserable away from France, will be an exile, an exile for the rest of her life! And why? Because I, once upon a time, had brought Joseph into our house in Marseilles. ' I must try to help her,' I thought, ' I must do all I can to keep her here.'

" Perhaps you could ask His Royal Highness to intervene on behalf of Madame Julie Bonaparte? Or go and see His Majesty King Louis XVIII and put in a good word for her with him?"

" King Louis. . . ." I repeated, and tried to get used to the name.

" His Majesty is expected to arrive at the Tuileries in the next few days."

" What did this King Louis do during his exile?" I wanted to have an idea what the brothers Bonaparte might do with their time in their future asylums.

" His Majesty engaged in studies. He translated a famous book into French, Gibbon's *Decline and Fall of the Roman Empire*."

' Translated history, not made it,' I thought. " Is he bringing his own court with him?"

" Yes," he said, and went on to make the astonishing request that I should mention his name to His Majesty King Louis to help him obtain a post.

" I'm sure you have not been forgotten, Monsieur Fouché," I said. " Even I, who was only a child at the time, remember clearly the many thousand death sentences you signed."

He fumbled with his white rosette. " That, Your Highness, is no longer remembered. What I should like to be remembered, however, is the fact that several times during the last few years I tried secretly to come to an arrangement with Britain. General Bonaparte called me a traitor, Your Highness, I risked my life."

I cast another glance at the document in my hand. " What are the conditions for—General Bonaparte?"

"Very favourable ones. He may go where he likes outside France. He can take with him four hundred of his men, whom he can pick himself. Besides, he may retain the title of Emperor. Very magnanimous, is it not?"

"What has he decided on?"

"I heard the Island of Elba mentioned, a charming place much like Corsica in character."

"And the Empress?"

"She will be made Duchess of Parma provided she renounces the claims of her son to the French throne. All these details are to be thrashed out at a big congress in Vienna. Reconstruction of Europe, return of the dynasties driven out by Bonaparte, and so on. I expect His Royal Highness will want to go to Vienna to maintain his rights to the Swedish throne. I am told that Austria and Prussia insist that His Highness has no legitimate claim. I shall gladly put myself at His Highness's disposal at any time to sound opinion in Vienna and——"

I got to my feet. "I don't know what you are talking about. I shall hand the document to my sister."

If he had stayed another minute I should have screamed for help!

A little later the children came back from the victory parade and told me excitedly how marvellous Uncle Jean-Baptiste had looked in his resplendent uniform and that he had sat on his horse like a marble statue without once moving. The Tsar of Russia had kept smiling, the old Emperor of Austria waving his hand, the King of Prussia made a very angry face, but Jean-Baptiste had just sat on his horse, they said.

"And what did the spectators say?" I asked.

"All sorts of things. There was so much to see, the many foreign uniforms, and the beautiful horses, and the Cossacks with their whips and the Prussians with their goose-step which made everybody laugh."

"And what did they say while Uncle Jean-Baptiste rode past?"

The children looked at each other. Finally Louis Napoleon said hesitantly: "Everybody was suddenly quiet. It was as quiet as the grave."

I sent them into the house to have something to eat and went to Julie with the document Fouché had brought.

"I won't go," Julie sobbed in despair, "I won't go. They can't take Mortefontaine, they mustn't take Mortefontaine from me. Oh, Désirée, you must try and get them to let me stay on at Mortefontaine, me and the children."

I stroked her thin lustreless hair. "For the time being you'll stay here with me. Later on we can try to get Mortefontaine back. But what about Joseph? If he doesn't get permission to stay, what then?"

"He's written to me from Blois. He wants to go to Switzerland and buy an estate there, and I am to follow him as soon as possible. But I'm not going, I'm not going!" Julie sat up. "Désirée, you won't leave me, will you, you'll stay with me till everything is settled, you'll stay with me here in your house, won't you?"

I nodded. 'I brought her into the Bonaparte crowd,' I thought, 'it's my fault that she is without a home now, I must help her.'

"Will you promise me?"

"I promise I'll stay with you, Julie."

On the evening of King Louis XVIII's first court ball in the Tuileries I had a cold, not a real one, of course, only the kind of cold I had at Napoleon's coronation. I stayed in bed, Marie brought me milk and honey, and I read the papers. The *Moniteur* described the departure of Napoleon for Elba. He left on April 20th. Not a single one of his Marshals had been present. General Petit paraded a regiment of Guards, the Emperor kissed the regimental colours and climbed into a coach in which General Bertrand waited for him, and that, according to the *Moniteur*, had been all. In the *Journal des Débats*, however, I found an interesting article on the Crown Prince of Sweden. There I read that the Crown Prince intended to divorce his wife Désirée Clary, sister of Madame Julie Bonaparte. After the divorce the former Crown Princess would continue to live in her home in the Rue d'Anjou in Paris under the name of the Countess of Gothland. The Crown Prince, I read, would have the choice between a Russian and a Prussian Princess. The entry of the former Marshal J.-B. Bernadotte into one of the legitimate dynasties of Europe would be of the greatest importance for his future position in Sweden.

After that, milk and honey had lost their taste for me, and I didn't want to read any more papers either. I remembered that it was the night of the first court reception of the Bourbons, and I wondered whether Jean-Baptiste had accepted the invitation.

Since the night of his arrival we have hardly been alone together. I have visited him in the Swedish headquarters in the Rue St. Honoré often enough, and in his ante-chamber I

447

found Fouché waiting every time I called, Talleyrand on three occasions, and even Marshal Ney was sitting patiently there once or twice. In Jean-Baptiste's office there seemed to be eternal conferences between Wetterstedt, the Prime Minister, and his Generals and Admirals, whilst Jean-Baptiste either pored over documents or dictated letters.

This afternoon we had a reception in the Rue St. Honoré in honour of the Tsar. To my horror the Tsar brought along the Count of Artois, brother of the new King of France. This Count, a man with a coarse and embittered face, wears a wig. The Bourbons are trying to persuade themselves that the Revolution has changed nothing. Yet Louis XVIII had to promise to take the oath of obedience to the laws of France, which meant to the *Code Napoléon*.

The Count of Artois dashed forward towards Jean-Baptiste. "Dear cousin, France will be eternally in your debt." Jean-Batpiste grew pale, but before he could say anything the Bourbon had turned to me and said: "Your Highness, you will come to-night to the reception in the Tuileries, will you not?"

Pressing my handkerchief to my nose I answered that I was suffering from a spring cold. The Tsar was very concerned when he heard that and hoped that I would soon recover.

Lying in bed I tried to imagine what was going on in the Tuileries. All the soft furnishings would have lilies instead of bees, there would be no Marseillaise, of course, Louis XVIII, an old gentleman suffering from dropsy, would stare with tired eyes at the ballroom from which they dragged his brother to his doom many years ago, and perhaps he would embrace a certain J.-B. Bernadotte, a fanatical Republican and Crown Prince of Sweden, and call him 'our meritorious cousin', perhaps . . .

My thoughts were interrupted by the sound of steps coming quickly up the staircase. Who could it be? Everybody was in bed, as far as I knew.

"I hope I did not wake you, my girl."

It was Jean-Baptiste, not in full court dress but in his blue field uniform.

"You are not really ill, Désirée?"

"Of course not. And you, Jean-Baptiste? Why aren't you at the Tuileries?"

"Because of the strange fact that a former sergeant seems to have more sense of what is fitting than a Bourbon King." There was a pause. "A pity you are in bed, I wanted to say good-bye," he went on. "I am leaving to-morrow morning."

I thought everybody in the house would hear the hammering of my heart. He was going to-morrow, to-morrow. . . .

"I have done what I came to do here. Nobody could ask for more than that. Besides, the allies have agreed to my treaty with Denmark. But imagine, Désirée, the Norwegians don't want the union with Sweden."

'So that is our farewell,' I thought. 'I am in bed, a candle flickers, he talks of Norway.' "Why don't they?"

"Because they want to be independent."

"Then let them," I said.

Jean-Baptiste pointed out to me that that was out of the question for a variety of reasons. Above all, he had promised the Swedes this union and his position depended to a great extent on the fulfilment of his promise. If he disappointed them the Swedish Parliament that had elected him to the Succession could also exclude him from it.

After he had said that he caught sight of the papers on my bedside table. Absent-mindedly he turned the pages of the *Journal des Débats*. An article, I knew well which, attracted his attention and he began to read.

"If you married a Princess, you could become a member of one of the old dynasties," I said, and my heart felt as heavy as a stone. He kept on reading the *Journal*. "Haven't you seen this article before?"

"No. I really have no time for scandal stories. Disgusting court cackle!" He threw the paper back on the table. "Pity, I have a carriage waiting downstairs and wanted to suggest— no, let's leave it, you are probably too tired."

"You wanted to say good-bye and to suggest something," I said, pulling myself together. But I couldn't prevent my voice from sounding flat and toneless. "Say it quickly, or I'll go crazy."

He stared at me in surprise. "It is not as important as all that. I only wanted to drive with you once more through the streets of Paris. For the last time, Désirée."

"For—the last time?"

"Yes, because I shall never come to Paris again."

At first I thought I hadn't heard aright. When I knew that he had said just that, I started crying, crying with relief.

"What is the matter, Désirée? Are you not feeling well?"

"I thought you were going to tell me that you wanted a divorce," I sobbed, and pushed back the bed-cover. "I'll dress quickly and we'll drive through Paris, shall we?"

The carriage, an open one, rolled along the Seine quays.

I put my head against his shoulder and felt his arm holding me. When we got to 'our' bridge the carriage stopped, and we went arm-in-arm and looked over the side of the bridge into the water where the lights of Paris shone back at us. The words of our first conversation there came into my mind and without thinking I asked them again: "Do you know General Bonaparte?"

"Yes," he answered, "and I don't like him."

I went on speaking, addressing my words to the lights of Paris dancing on the waters of the Seine: "I had to work my way up. I joined the Army when I was fifteen, was nothing but a sergeant for many years. I am a Divisional General now, Mademoiselle! My name is Jean-Baptiste Bernadotte. For years I have saved up part of my salary. I could buy a little house for you and the child. . . . That's what you said at the time, you remember?"

"Of course. But I should rather like to know how you envisage your future, Désirée."

"If you think that it is necessary, for you and Oscar, to marry a Princess, then let us have a divorce," I said fumblingly at first. But the last part came out all right. "On one condition," I added.

"And that is?"

"That you make me your mistress."

"Out of the question! I don't want to start this mistress business at the Swedish court. Besides, I couldn't afford a mistress, my girl. No, you will have to remain my wife, Désirée, whatever happens."

The murmuring of the water from below the bridge came up to me like sweet music. "Even if the worst happens and you are King?"

"Yes, darling, even if I am King."

Slowly we made our way back to the carriage.

"You could do me a favour and stop selling silk yourself," he remarked a bit later.

"I shall ask Pierre to draw my share of the profits regularly. He'll be my steward, Marius Clary my chamberlain and Marceline Tascher my lady-in-waiting. I want to dismiss Madame La Flotte."

Driving past Notre-Dame, Jean-Baptiste told the coachman to stop, and he looked at the Cathedral for a long time, as if he wanted to commit to his memory every stone and every line of it. Then we went on to have a look at our first house in Sceaux. The stars were out, lilac trees blossomed behind garden walls.

"I went this way twice daily when I was Minister of War," he said, and most unexpectedly he added: "When, do you think, may I expect Your Royal Highness in Stockholm?"

"Not yet," I said, nestling to his shoulder, "the next years will be difficult enough for you. I don't want to make them any more so. You know how unsuited I am for the life of the Swedish court."

He looked at me sharply. "Do you mean to say that you are never going to accept the Swedish court ceremonial?"

"When I come," I said with emphasis, "I shall be in a position to determine all questions of etiquette myself."

The carriage stopped in front of No. 3 Rue de la Lune in Sceaux. Strangers lived in it now. 'Up there,' I thought, 'behind those first-floor windows, Oscar was born.'

At that very moment Jean-Baptiste said: "Imagine, Oscar has to shave already. Twice a week!"

On the way back we were so close to each other that we did not speak at all. Only when the carriage was rounding the corner into the Rue d'Anjou Jean-Baptiste said sharply: "You have no other reasons for wanting to stay here? Really not?"

"Yes, Jean-Baptiste, I have. Here I am wanted, and there I am superfluous. I must help Julie."

"I have beaten Napoleon at Leipzig. Yet I can't get rid of these Bonapartes all the same!"

"It's not the Bonapartes, it's the Clarys. Don't forget that, please!"

For the last time the carriage stopped. It all happened very suddenly. Jean-Baptiste got out with me and gazed at the house, attentively, in silence. I gave Jean-Baptiste my hand, which he put to his lips. "Whatever rumours the papers spread, don't believe them, you understand?"

"A pity. I should have liked to be your mistress. Ow!" I said, because Jean-Baptiste had bitten my finger.

Unfortunately, the two sentries were watching all the time.

PARIS.
Whit-Monday, May 30th, 1814.
Late in the evening.

Nothing is more disagreeable to me than having to make visits of condolence, particularly when it is a beautiful Whit-Sunday!

Last night a tear-stained ex-lady-in-waiting from Malmaison appeared to tell me that Josephine had died at mid-day the day –

before. She had died of a heavy cold which she had contracted a few days before during an evening stroll in the Park at Malmaison on the arm of the Tsar. "The evening was very cool," the lady reported, "but Her Majesty would not under any circumstances put on a coat. She wore her new muslin frock with a very low decolletage and only a very thin and transparent scarf round her shoulders."

'Josephine, I know that muslin,' I thought, 'not substantial enough for a May evening. Purple it was, wasn't it? A bit melancholy and so becoming. . . .'

The former lady-in-waiting gave me a letter from Hortense. 'Bring the children along, my sole comfort,' wrote Hortense with many dashes and exclamation marks. And so I went to Malmaison with Julie and the two sons of the former Queen Hortense.

I tried to make the boys understand that their grandmother had died.

"Perhaps she isn't dead at all, perhaps she is only feigning it and is secretly going to join the Emperor at Elba," said Charles Napoleon.

In the Bois de Boulogne lime blossoms floated into our carriage. It seemed impossible to realise that Josephine was no longer alive.

At Malmaison we found Hortense and Eugene Beauharnais. Eugene was sitting in front of a minute writing desk rummaging among piles of bills. Pointing to them the gauche young man, former Viceroy of Italy and husband of a Bavarian princess, sighed. "It is inconceivable to me. Nothing but unpaid bills. For dresses, hats, rose trees!"

"Mama could never manage on her allowance," said Hortense.

"The State and the Emperor between them paid her three million francs a year! And yet——" He ran his fingers through his hair, obviously at his wits' end. "I should like to know who is going to pay these debts, which go into millions."

"That will not interest the ladies," said Hortense, and asked us to sit down. We sat down stiffly, and through the open french windows the scent of Josephine's roses came in from the garden.

"The Tsar of Russia called on Mama, and Mama asked him to dinner," Hortense said. "I suppose she wanted to ask him to take an interest in my children. You know that I am divorced now, don't you?"

We nodded politely. Hortense's lover, Count Flahault,

appeared, and Eugene continued to exasperate himself about his mother's unpaid bills.

"Do you want to see her?" Hortense asked in the midst of her brother's laments.

Julie shook her head, but I said "Yes" instinctively.

Count Flahault took me up to Josephine's bedroom where she lay. Tall candles burned steadily. The shutters were closed and there was an overpowering odour of incense, roses, and the heavy perfume which Josephine used. The whole room was shrouded in half-darkness. When my eyes were used to it I saw nuns like giant black birds kneeling at the end of the bed, and I heard them murmur their requiem in a monotonous undertone.

At first I was afraid to look at the dead woman. But then I pulled myself together and went to the bed. Her coronation cloak was spread over the bed in soft folds like a good warm blanket. Her ermine collar had been placed over her breast and shoulders. It shone yellow in the light of the candles, yellow like the face of the dead Josephine.

No, Josephine didn't look horrifying, nor did she make one want to cry. She was too beautiful for that, even now. Only her small nose had an air of sharpness and strangeness about it, which emphasised the smile that was still hovering round her closed mouth, and her babyish curls held the aura of youthful attraction in their strands as they had done in life.

"How charming she looks!" said someone by my side. It was an old gentleman with a bloated face and beautiful silvery hair. He seemed to have come out of some dark corner.

"My name is Barras," he introduced himself, and raised a lorgnette to his eyes. "Have I the pleasure of knowing Madame?"

"It's a long time ago," I said. "We met at General Bonaparte's house and you were Director of the Republic at the time."

He dropped his lorgnette. "This coronation robe, Madame, this coronation robe is Josephine's debt to me. 'You marry this little Bonaparte,' I told her at the time, 'I shall make him Military Governor of Paris and all the rest will take care of itself, my dearest Josephine!' And, as you know, Madame, everything else has taken care of itself." He laughed softly. "Was she a close friend of yours, Madame?"

'No, Monsieur, she only broke my heart once,' I thought, and began to cry.

"A fool, this Bonaparte, a fool!" the old man said, and

smoothed out with a tender hand a fold of the purple cloak. " A fool to divorce the only woman with whom, even on a lonely island, he would never have known a moment's boredom ! "

Red roses were lying on the ermine collar of the Empress of the French. The heat of the candles had made them fade and their scent was almost painful. It seemed to choke me, to make me gasp for breath, I felt my knees grow weak, and suddenly I fell down by the side of Josephine's bed and buried my face in the velvet depths of her coronation robe.

" Don't cry for her, Madame. Josephine died as she lived: on the arm of a very powerful man, who, on an evening in the month of May among the rose trees of Malmaison, promised to pay all her debts. Are you listening, dear, dear Josephine? "

When I got to my feet again the old gentleman had disappeared into his dark corner. Nothing was heard but the monotonous flow of the requiem from the lips of the big black birds. I bent my head to Josephine once more and her long eyelashes seemed to flutter lightly.

I went downstairs and straight into the garden. The sun was so strong that the air shimmered and everywhere there were roses of every colour. I came to a little pond. On the low wall enclosing it sat a small girl watching the funny little ducklings and their fat mother on the water. I sat close to her. She had brown curly hair which fell to her shoulders in corkscrew fashion, and wore a white frock with a black scarf. When she turned her head to look at me my heart almost stopped beating: a sweet oval face with long lids over almond-shaped eyes. The child began to smile. She smiled with closed mouth.

" What's your name? " I asked.

" Josephine, Madame. "

She had blue eyes and beautiful pearly teeth, and golden lights sparkled from her hair. ' Like Josephine,' I thought, ' like Josephine.'

" Are you one of the ladies-in-waiting, Madame? " the child asked politely.

" No. Why? "

" Because Aunt Hortense said that the Crown Princess of Sweden was coming, and Crown Princesses always bring ladies-in-waiting along. Of course only when they are grown-up Princesses. "

" And little Princesses? "

" Little Princesses have governesses. "

454

The child turned her attention back to the ducks. "The ducklings are so small. I think they can't have come out of their mother's stomach earlier than yesterday."

"Nonsense, ducklings come out of eggs."

The child smiled in a very superior manner. "You need not tell me fairy-tales, Madame."

"But ducklings do come out of eggs!" I insisted.

The child nodded, bored. "As you wish, Madame."

"Are you the daughter of Prince Eugene?"

"Yes. But I don't think Papa is still a Prince. If we are lucky the allies will give us a duchy in Bavaria. My grandfather, that is my mama's father, is the King of Bavaria."

"Then you at any rate are a Princess," I said. "Where is your governess?"

"I have run away from her." She put her hand into the water. Then an idea seemed to cross her mind. "If you are not a lady-in-waiting you are perhaps a governess?"

"Why?"

"Because you must be something."

"Perhaps I am a Princess too?"

"Impossible. You don't look like a Princess. I should like to know who you are."

"Would you?"

"I like you. In spite of this stupid duckling story you have been telling me. Have you any children?"

"Yes, a son. But he isn't here."

"What a pity. I would much rather play with boys than with girls. Where is he?"

"In Sweden. But you wouldn't know where that is."

"I know exactly where it is, I am having geography lessons, you know. And Papa says——"

"Josephine, Josephine!" someone shouted.

The child sighed. "My governess!" She winked at me and pulled a real street Arab's face. "A horrid woman, but don't tell anybody, Madame!"

I made my way back to the house. Only Hortense, Eugene, Julie and I were there for dinner.

"Do you know when we shall be allowed to send a courier to Elba?" he asked Julie before we left. "I should like to inform the Emperor as quickly as possible about Mama's death. And also I want to let him have the unpaid bills."

On the way back through a blue evening it occurred to me that if one had to start a dynasty it might as well be a

455

charming one. A shooting star fell at that moment and I wished very hard on it. "The Swedes would call her Josephina," I said aloud.

"Whom are you talking about?" Julie asked, surprised.

"Oh, no one. I was only thinking of the shooting star."

PARIS.
In the late autumn 1814.

Behind his steward's back Oscar wrote to me from Norway. I will paste his letter into my diary so as not to lose it.

Christiania, November 10th 1814

MY DEAR MAMA,

Count Brahe is sending a courier from here to Paris and I hasten to write to you. A special reason for writing now is that my steward, Baron Cederström, is in bed with a cold. He always wants to read my letters to you to see whether they are properly styled. The old idiot!

My dear Mama, my heartiest congratulations! You have just become Crown Princess of Norway. Norway and Sweden have been linked in a union, and the Swedish King is now also King of Norway. We have just been through a campaign in which we conquered Norway. Last night I arrived with Papa here in Christiania, the capital of Norway. But I had better tell you all in proper order.

Papa's entry into Stockholm was magnificent. The whole population lined the streets through which Papa drove, and shouted with joy. His Majesty embraced Papa and cried for happiness, and Her Majesty cried too, only a bit more discreetly. The Swedes feel like a heroic nation once again as in the day of Charles XII. But Papa was tired and rather sad. Can you imagine why, Mama?

And then although the Danes had ceded Norway to us the Parliament of Norway wanted their country to be independent and just to annoy us made a Danish Prince Regent and declared they would defend their independence.

Our Swedish officers were enthusiastic about the campaign, and the old King asked Papa for a warship with which to go into battle. Papa said Sweden could not afford a war longer than three months and he bought the warship out of his own pocket. The old King doesn't know that.

I said that if the old King could come along I wanted to be there too and Papa did not mind. He said these Norwegians were marvellous. They had an army only half the size of ours and had hardly any ammunition at all, and yet they risked war. He was very touched and said he would give them the most liberal constitution in Europe.

But these marvellous Norwegians insisted on their independence. So Papa and his General Staff went off to the campaign and the King and Queen and the whole Royal household and I myself followed him on board the man-of-war. When we took the fortress of Kongsten there was such a lot of shooting and firing that I said to Papa, who was standing next to me: " Papa, send an officer to the Norwegians and tell him that they could be independent for all you cared. Don't keep on shooting at them with your guns." And Papa said: " Of course not, Oscar, we are only shooting at them with dummy shells." " But in that case, Papa, it is not a real campaign, it it?" " No, Oscar, only an excursion." Papa said the Norwegians would retire behind their mountains, and when I asked him if he could cross the mountains Papa said he had crossed the Alps once with an army, and when he said that he looked very sad. " In those days," he said, " I defended a young Republic's independence. To-day I am taking it away from a small freedom-loving people. That shows you, Oscar, how one outlives oneself."

The whole campaign lasted only a fortnight, and we returned to Stockholm and Papa let the old King drive in triumph through the streets. Four days later Papa and I went back to Norway, because Papa had to appear in Christiania in person to confirm the union of Sweden and Norway. We rode there on horseback and had to sleep in tents because Papa did not want to inconvenience the peasants. I enclose a little song which I call ' Song of the Rain ' and which I composed during this endless ride to Christiania.

We passed through the Fortress of Frederiksten, where the Norwegians defended themselves once against the Swedish King Charles XII, the famous Swedish King who made war against the Russians and lost it and then tried to conquer Norway. As we were riding through rain and mist we suddenly came to a big wooden cross on which was written 'This is the spot on which Charles XII fell.' The Marshals Essen and Adlercreutz at once started to say the Lord's Prayer, but Papa did not join in their prayer (he never prays!), and when we went on he said to Essen and Adlercreutz: "You had better forget that man, he was Sweden's misfortune!" Adlercreutz was offended and said: "Opinions differ on that, Your Highness!" From that you can see, Mama, that you have to be very careful when talking about Charles XII, whom Papa calls 'the greatest amateur in military matters' and whom the Swedes revere as a hero.

Last night at long last we reached Christiania in an equipage which had followed us from Stockholm. The streets were pitch-black and deserted, and there was only the guard of honour to receive us outside the palace of the former Danish Governor, and the Speaker of the Norwegian Parliament and the members of the Government inside.

The Speaker addressed Papa in excellent French. Papa smiled his winning smile, shook the solemn gentlemen by the hand and said he brought the good wishes of His Majesty the King of Sweden and Norway. I had the impression that these solemn men found it difficult not to burst out laughing at that. After all, what has the old gentleman in Stockholm to do with this union? This union is exclusively Papa's work. Papa at once started a weighty speech. "Norway's new constitution defends the Rights of Man for which I have been campaigning in France ever since I was fifteen. This union is more than just a geographical necessity, it has been a deeply felt desire of my heart for a long time!"

I don't think it made any impression on the Norwegians. And I don't think either that they will ever forget that Papa beat them with dummy shells. . . .

I went with Papa to his bedroom and saw him take off all his medals and throw them on the dressing-table with a gesture of disgust. He said: "Yesterday was Mama's birthday. I hope our letters reached her in time," and then he went to bed.

Dear Mama, I am very sorry for Papa. But you cannot be a Crown Prince and a Republican at the same time. Do please write him a nice cheerful letter. We shall be home in

Stockholm at the end of the month. And now I can hardly keep my eyes open and the courier is waiting. I embrace you and kiss you.

Your son

OSCAR.

PS.: Do you think you could manage to find Monsieur Beethoven's Seventh Symphony in Paris and send it to me?

The courier who brought Oscar's letter also brought a letter from Count Brahe to Count Rosen. It said that on all official occasions the Norwegian flag has to be flown alongside the Swedish on my house. And on the door of my coach the arms of Norway have to be painted by the side of the Swedish arms. I asked for a map of Europe and looked for the second country of which I am now Crown Princess.

PARIS.
March 5th, 1815.

The afternoon began to-day like so many afternoons. With the help of my nephew Marius I drafted an application to Louis XVIII to get an extension of Julie's permit to stay on as my guest. Julie sat in the small drawing-room and wrote a long and dull letter to Joseph in Switzerland. Then Count Rosen entered and announced Monsieur Fouché, the Duke of Otranto.

This type of man is quite incomprehensible to me. When in the days of the Revolution the members of the National Assembly were asked to cast their votes about the fate of Louis XVI, Deputy Fouché cast his vote for death. And now he is moving heaven and earth in order to be received graciously by the brother of the executed King and to be given a job. The man was odious to me, but I let him come in.

He was in cheerful mood. His face, the colour of parchment, had red spots. Tea was served and he stirred his tea with an expression of great pleasure.

" I hope I did not disturb Your Highness in any important occupation?"

I didn't answer. But Julie said: " My sister has just drafted an application for me to His Majesty."

" Which Majesty?" asked Fouché.

I thought that the most stupid question possible. "King Louis, of course," said Julie, irritated. "As far as I know there is no other Majesty in France."

"This morning I might have had the chance of supporting your application, Madame. You see, His Majesty has offered me the job of—Minister of Police."

"Impossible!" I said.

"And?" asked Julie anxiously.

"I refused." Fouché took several well-bred sips of tea.

"If the King offers you the position of Minister of Police it is a sign that he feels insecure. And there is really no reason for that," put in Marius.

"Why not?" Fouché was surprised.

"The list, the secret list on which he puts not only all Republicans but also all adherents of the Emperor, is enough to give him unlimited power," said Marius. "It is said that your name is at the top of the list, Duke!"

Fouché put his cup on the table. "The King has interrupted the compiling of the list. If I were in his place I too should feel insecure. After all, he is advancing irresistibly."

"Would you mind telling me whom you are talking about?" I asked.

"Of the Emperor, of course."

The whole room began to spin round, shadows moved before my eyes and I felt dizzy, the kind of feeling I have not experienced since the days before Oscar's birth. Fouché's voice came to me as from a distance: "The Emperor embarked eleven days ago with his troops in Elba and arrived at Cannes on March 1st."

I heard Marius say: "But that is fantastic. He only has 400 men with him," and part of Fouché's answer: ". . . have gone over to him with flags flying and are marching with him in triumph to Paris."

"And the foreign powers, Duke?"

Count Rosen's harsh French rang out for a moment: "The foreign powers——"

"But, Désirée, you are pale, aren't you feeling well?" said Julie, and Fouché added: "Quick, a glass of water for Her Highness!"

They gave me some water and the room stopped spinning round and everything became clear again, clearer even than before.

I saw the glowing face of my nephew Marius. "He has the

460

whole Army behind him," he said. "You cannot with impunity halve the salaries of the officers of France who made this nation great. We are marching, we are marching once more!"

"Against the whole of Europe?" Marceline asked pointedly. (Her husband has not returned to her. He fell in the battles around Paris, but, to be exact, he fell into the arms of a young girl who hid him. . . .)

A servant announced another visitor, the wife of Marshal Ney. She, a very big woman, came in like a whirlwind, pressed me to her mighty bosom and shouted: "Well, what do you say to that? But he will show him, he will! He banged his fist on the table and said he would show him once and for all!"

"Sit down, *Madame la Maréchale*, and tell me who is going to show whom."

"My husband is going to show the Emperor!" Madame Ney thundered, and fell into the nearest chair. "He has just received the order to stop the Emperor at Besançon and take him prisoner. And do you know what my old Ney answered? He'll lasso him like a mad bull and put him in a cage and exhibit him round the country, that's what he said."

"Pray forgive me, Madame," lisped Fouché, "why is Marshal Ney so annoyed with his former Supreme Commander and Emperor?"

Madame Ney hadn't noticed him before she spoke, and now became strangely embarrassed. "So you are here too?" she said. "How is that? Are you not in disgrace at court? Are you not supposed to be on your estates?"

Fouché smiled and shrugged his shoulders.

At that she lost her assurance. "You don't think, do you, that the Emperor—will manage it?" she brought out in a voice that trailed away into a whisper.

"Yes," said Marius with great certainty, "yes, Madame, he will manage it."

Julie rose. "I must write that to my husband. It will interest him greatly."

Fouché shook his head. "Don't do that, Madame. The King's Secret Police will certainly intercept the letter. Besides, I feel sure that the Emperor is in contact with your husband and has informed his brothers about his plans in advance."

"You don't think, Duke, that it is a pre-arranged plan, do you?" asked Madame Ney. "Surely my husband would know that!"

Marius thundered at her: "It cannot have escaped the attention of Marshal Ney that the Army is dissatisfied because officers and men have been put on half-pay and the pensions of the veterans and invalids have been reduced."

"Nor that of the Emperor in Elba," Fouché added amiably, and took his leave.

When he had gone there was a long silence. With a jerk Madame Ney turned to me and her deep voice growled: "Madame, as a Marshal's wife you will agree——"

"You are mistaken, I am no longer the wife of a Marshal but the Crown Princess of Sweden and Norway. I must ask you to excuse me. I have a headache."

Yes, I had a headache as never before in my life. My head was full of hammering, ringing, banging noises. I lay down and said that I wasn't at home to anybody. I felt I wasn't even at home to myself, least of all myself. . . .

You can escape your servants, you can escape your family. But whatever happens you cannot escape Hortense. At eight o'clock in the evening Marie announced "the Duchess of Saint Leu, former Queen of Holland". I pulled the blanket over my head.

Five minutes later Marceline wailed outside my door: "You must come, Aunt. Hortense is in the small drawing-room and says she'll wait for you if she has to sit up all night. She has brought her sons along, too."

I gave in. "Let her come in, but only for a moment!"

Hortense came in, pushing her sons before her. "Don't refuse your protection to my children," she cried. "Take them in till everything is decided." Hortense has gone thin during the last year, her mourning dress makes her look very pale, and her hair is untidy and uncared for.

"Your children are in no danger," I said.

"But of course they are. The King may have them arrested at any moment as hostages against the Emperor. My children are the heirs to the throne, Madame!"

"The heir to the throne is called Napoleon like his father, and lives in Vienna at the moment."

"And if anything happens to this child in his captivity in Vienna? What then, Madame?" Her eyes rested lovingly on her two gangling boys. "Napoleon III," she murmured with a strangely aimless smile, and smoothed the hair of the younger one back from his forehead. "The King will not dare to pursue my children into the house of the Swedish Crown Princess. I implore you——"

"Of course," I said, "the children can stay here."

Later—I was just on the point of falling asleep—candlelight

462

and rustling noises woke me. I sat up in bed and saw Julie rummaging in my chest. "Julie, what are you looking for?"

"My crown, Désirée, the one I dropped on the floor in your boudoir the day the Tsar called."

"It's in the bottom drawer. What do you want with it in the middle of the night, Julie?"

"Just to try it on, and perhaps polish it up again."

PARIS.
March 20th, 1815.

Last night Louis XVIII crept out of the Tuileries by a back door and went into exile once more, this time only as far as Ghent. This morning the tricolour went up over the Tuileries, pamphlets containing a proclamation by Napoleon were distributed in the streets, and all the buttonholes and lapels, latent but gradually getting worn, showed the blue-white-red ribbon instead of the white rosette.

In the Tuileries a great scrubbing and washing started, with Hortense in command; the new curtains disappeared and the dark green ones with the bee pattern came out of the obscurity of the storehouses. All Napoleon's gilded eagles were fetched out of the vaults, dusted by Hortense herself and placed in their old positions.

My house, too, had been turned upside down. A message from the Emperor to Julie announced that he would arrive at the Tuileries at nine o'clock in the evening, and Julie prepared herself, complete with purple and crown, to receive him. She was in a dreadful state of agitation. "Imagine Hortense and and me having to receive him alone! I'm so afraid of him!"

"Nonsense, Julie, it's the same Buonaparte as in Marseilles! Your brother-in-law, Julie."

"Is he really the same man? After his triumphal march from Cannes via Grenoble to Paris, with everyone going over to him, including Marshal Ney?"

Yes, it was quite true, the Army literally fell on its knees before him, including the brave Marshal Ney. "Julie," I said, "the Army may be shouting hurrah, but everyone else is silent!"

She looked blank when I said that, then borrowed the earrings of the Swedish Dowager Queen and left. 'I only hope,' I thought, 'that Joseph brings her jewellery back with him.'

Meanwhile Marie and I bathed Hortense's boys and, at

Hortense's special wish, curled their hair with a pair of curling tongs. They were to go to the Tuileries later with Julie. Louis Napoleon, whom his mother had called Napoleon III, wondered whether the little King of Rome was coming back too. But I didn't answer him.

At night.

At eight o'clock in the evening a state equipage, still with the Bourbon lily on its doors, fetched Julie and the children. My house felt very quiet when they had gone.

Count Rosen, leaning out of a window, said that he would have liked to see the Emperor's arrival. I told him to change into civilian clothes and put on a tricoloured ribbon. I would come along with him, I said, and slipped into a plain coat and put on a hat.

It was difficult to get to the Tuileries. We were caught up in an almost impenetrable crowd and slowly pushed along. I hung on to my young Count's arm like grim death.

The Tuileries were brilliantly illuminated as in the days of the great receptions. But I knew that upstairs in the ballroom there would be only a handful of people, Julie, Hortense, a few children, the Duke of Vicenza, Marshal Davout and perhaps a few more Generals.

Soldiers on horseback cleared a lane, and from the distance we heard a noise, first like the soughing of wind, then growing to a gale, a typhoon, and then it was all over and around us, the one mighty roar "*Vive l'Empereur, Vive l'Empereur!*" A carriage came into view driving madly towards the Tuileries, with officers of all ranks and all regiments riding after it in a wild gallop.

Servants holding torches appeared on the steps in front of the palace, the door of the carriage opened and the Emperor stepped out followed by Marshal Ney. The crowd broke through the line of soldiers, seized the Emperor and carried him shoulder-high into the Tuileries. I saw his face illuminated by the glare of torches. It smiled with eyes closed, the face of a man who had been dying of thirst and was now at last given a drink.

Another carriage drove up. But it was only Fouché who emerged from it, wanting to welcome the Emperor and offer him his services.

I had had enough. We managed to force our way through the dense crowd and wandered home through empty streets. But from every house the tricolour was flying.

Marie was just bringing me my breakfast in bed when the guns began to fire and the church bells rang out.

" Heavens!" said Marie, " he's won!"

As she said it I realised that we hadn't really expected that, neither we nor the others. But there were the guns and the bells! Now everything was all right again!

Julie and Joseph went back to the Elysée Palace; Madame Letitia and all her sons came back. Only, in the Tuileries Hortense was mistress now in the absence of Marie-Louise, who still hung back, in spite of all Napoleon's letters.

As soon as he came back Napoleon ordered a general election, to prove to the world how unpopular the Bourbons were. This was the first free election since the days of the Republic, and old names reappeared in the new National Assembly, Carnot, for instance, and—Lafayette! Lafayette, who first proclaimed the Rights of Man, who had fought for the freedom of the United States, who had founded the National Guard to defend our young Republic—Lafayette, of whom Papa had spoken with such enthusiasm, was back again!

But others were absent: Jean-Baptiste's Ambassador, and the Ambassadors of all the powers, had been recalled; no country would enter into diplomatic relations with Napoleon, no Prince answered his letters. They sent not Ambassadors but armies! Inexorably 800,000 men moved towards France, without any declaration of war. And Napoleon had none to send against them but one hundred thousand men of his own. He could get no more: the young men went into hiding, the officers, including my nephew Marius, sent medical certificates instead of reporting for duty, and the Marshals with the exception of Ney and Devout, retired to their country estates.

Three days ago Napoleon crossed the frontier at the head of his army, to face the allies. His Order-of-the-Day ran: ' For every brave Frenchman the time has come to win or die.' When that was published all Paris was in the utmost gloom. And then, after all, the miracle happened: the church bells rang out for victory!

I dressed and went into the garden. Then I was startled to find that the bells had stopped ringing.

The deathly silence was so oppressive that I was glad to see a stranger coming into the garden. I went to meet him: it was

Lucien Bonaparte! How strange that he should return at this of all moments, after his many years of exile in England!

"You remember me, Désirée? I was present at the two betrothals, yours and Julie's."

We sat down on a bench.

"Why have you come back, Lucien?"

"Yes, why?" Lucien leaned back and looked round the garden. "How lovely, and how peaceful!"

"The victory bells have stopped ringing."

"Yes, Désirée, it was a mistake. Old Davout, whom Napoleon had left in Paris, had them rung prematurely. Napoleon had only won a little skirmish at Charleroi; the decisive battle was fought at Ligny and Waterloo, and Napoleon was beaten. Look at that beautiful blue butterfly!"

"And the Emperor?"

"He will arrive to-night, very quietly. He'll stay with Joseph and Julie, not in the Tuileries. 'For every brave Frenchman the time has come to win or die!' You read his fine phrase, didn't you? No doubt he finds it embarrassing to have done neither."

"And the Army, Lucien?"

"What army?"

"His army, the French Army!"

"There is no army left! Of his 100,000 men, sixty thousand have died. But I haven't come to tell you that. I only wanted to ask you to remember me to Jean-Baptiste Bernadotte when you write to him. I often think of him."

"Lucien, why have you chosen this moment to come back?"

"To find somewhere to spend ten minutes in peace. The Government is fully informed, and the National Assembly is in permanent session as in the days of the Revolution."

He got up. "I must go now. I am expecting further messages."

I went to the gate with Lucien, and he took my arm familiarly. "I have often regretted," he said, with his head bent, "that day in Brumaire when I spoke for him in the Council of the Five Hundred. But I still had faith in him then."

"And now?"

"Désirée, shall we wager that he is going to send me once more to the Deputies? They are going to demand his abdication, and he will ask me to defend him. Do you know what I am going to do?"

I smiled. "You are going to defend him. And that is why you came back, isn't it?"

After he had gone I thought for one moment that the whole thing wasn't true, that Lucien had been mistaken, not Marshal Davout, about the bells. But then I heard a carriage draw up, and Hortense came in. She begged me, with tears in her eyes, to give shelter to her defenceless children.

PARIS.
June 23rd, 1815.

I had just begun to read the *Moniteur* with Lafayette's speech in that decisive session of the National Assembly—"If after all these years I raise my voice again"—when the door of my boudoir was flung open, and Julie stumbled in and dropped in front of me, putting her head in my lap.

"He has abdicated!" she sobbed. "The Prussians will be here at any moment."

Bit by bit I gathered the story of last night's events. Napoleon had come back at dead of night in an old stage coach. He had lost everything, even his personal baggage. He called all his brothers and his ministers to him immediately after his arrival, but the ministers only stayed for five minutes and then went back to the Assembly. The Emperor demanded another 100,000 men and then sent poor Lucien to face the Deputies on his behalf and reproach the nation for deserting him.

"And did Lucien actually go?" I asked.

"Yes, he went—and was back in twenty minutes! He hardly managed to get a hearing, and when at last they did listen to him and he told them that the nation had deserted his brother, Lafayette jumped to his feet and shouted: 'France has sacrificed three millions of her sons to your brother. Does he want yet more?' And Lucien left the Assembly without another word."

Fouché had told her that, said Julie; Lucien himself had told her nothing.

Later Joseph and Lucien were closeted with the Emperor throughout the night. The Emperor shouted and banged the table, but his brothers could not persuade him to abdicate till Fouché brought the news of Lafayette's motion in the National Assembly that the throne should be declared forfeited if General Bonaparte did not resign it voluntarily within the next hour. When the Emperor heard that, he signed at last, but he abdicated in favour of his son. Of course the Government would take no notice of that.

" I'm not going back to the Elysée," said Julie. " I want to stay here with the children. They can't arrest me here, can they?"

" The allied troops aren't even here yet," I said. " Perhaps they won't come at all."

" The allied troops? No, no—our Government! They've sent a General Becker to Napoleon to keep an eye on him. The Directory——"

" Directory?"

" Yes, the new Government calls itself the Directory. They are in touch with the allies. Carnot and Fouché are two of them." She began sobbing again.

Then Joseph arrived.

" Julie, you must get ready at once," he said. " The Emperor wants to leave Paris and go to Malmaison. The whole family are going with him. Come along, Julie."

Julie clung to me more than ever.

" The whole family are going to Malmaison, Julie," Joseph repeated. His face was grey. He could not have had any sleep for the last two nights.

I took Julie's in mine. " Julie, you must go with your husband."

But she shook her head. " The crowds are shouting ' Down with the Bonapartes '."

" That's why you must go with your husband," I said, and pulled her to her feet.

" Désirée, may we go to Malmaison in your carriage?" Joseph asked, without looking at me.

" I was going to lend it to Madame Letitia," I said. " But perhaps you can all find room in it."

" You'll help me, Désirée, you'll help me, won't you?" cried Julie. Joseph gently led her to the door.

It is now about a year since Josephine died, and when they reach Malmaison they'll find the roses in bloom.

PARIS.
The night of June 29th, 1815.

His sword lies on my bedside table, his fate is sealed, and I was the one to seal it! Everyone is talking of my great mission, but I am full of grief.

Early this morning—it sounds crazy, but it's true!—I learned that the nation wanted to speak to me.

I had been lying awake for hours. The last guns we have were rolling past my house, to attempt the hopeless defence of Paris against the Austrians, Russians, Prussians, Saxons, and English. Suddenly Yvette came to say that Count Rosen wanted urgently to speak to me. The Count rushed in after her, and said that the representatives of the nation wanted to speak to me as soon as I could see them.

"Which nation?" I asked, as the Count buttoned up the jacket of his full-dress uniform.

"The French nation," he said, finishing his buttons and standing to attention.

"Yvette, some strong coffee, please. Until I've had some coffee, Count, you'll have to speak slowly. The French nation, you say? What does it want of me?"

"They are asking for an audience. It was of immense importance, their spokesman said. That is why I have put on my full-dress uniform."

Yvette brought some very hot coffee.

"What shall I tell them?" asked the Count.

"I'll see them in half an hour."

I found that the nation was represented by MM. Fouché and Talleyrand and by a third person whom I didn't know. He was small and very thin, and was wearing an old-fashioned white wig and a faded foreign uniform. His face was wrinkled, but he was a very bright-eyed old man.

"Your Highness, may we present to you General Lafayette?" said Talleyrand.

My heart stood still. The nation had indeed come to me! I curtsied like an awkward schoolgirl.

Lafayette began to smile with such genuineness that I plucked up courage and said:

"My father always treasured the first broadsheet of the Rights of Man. I never dreamed that one day I should have the honour of welcoming its author under my own roof."

"Your Highness," began Fouché, "in the name of the French Government, represented by the Minister of Foreign Affairs and myself, and in the name of the French nation, represented by Deputy General Lafayette, we turn to you in this grave hour."

I looked at them all. Fouché, one of the five Directors now ruling France, and Talleyrand, who only returned a few days ago from the Congress of Vienna where he had represented the

Bourbons, were both ex-Ministers of Napoleon, both in gold-embroidered tail-coats, much bemedalled. Between them sat Lafayette in his faded uniform, without a single medal.

" What can I do for you, gentlemen? " I asked.

" Your Highness, I anticipated a situation like this long ago," said Talleyrand, speaking very fast and in a low voice. " Perhaps Your Highness will remember that I indicated to you once that the day might come when the nation would turn to you with a very important request. Do you remember, Your Highness? "

I nodded.

" That situation has arisen now. The French nation is putting to the Crown Princess of Sweden its great petition."

" I should like to give Your Highness a picture of the situation," said Fouché. " Through the Prince of Benevento we have offered unconditional surrender to Wellington and Blücher, in order to prevent needless destruction and bloodshed."

" They have told us that they will enter into negotiations only on one condition," put in Talleyrand, " and that is——."

" That General Bonapartes leaves France immediately! " shouted Fouché.

' What do they want of me? ' I thought, looking at Talleyrand. But it was Fouché who continued:

" Although we communicated to Napoleon the wish of the French Government and nation that he should leave, he has not done so. On the contrary "—Fouché's voice trembled with rage—" on the contrary, he has approached us with a monstrous proposal. He sent his A.D.C., Count Flahault, with the suggestion of a defence of Paris by the remnants of the Army under his command. In other words, he wants a general massacre. This, of course, we rejected, and repeated our demand for his departure, whereupon he transmitted to us what one can only call another challenge. He demands—demands, Your Highness!—to be given the command of the last available regiments in order to defend Paris. He takes his success for granted and assumes that it will enable us to secure better terms of peace. Only then will General Bonaparte consent to go abroad."

Fouché breathed hard and mopped his brow.

" The irony of it, Your Highness! "

I said nothing.

" We cannot capitulate and preserve Paris from destruction until General Bonaparte has left France. The allies are at

Versailles. We cannot delay another moment, Your Highness. General Bonaparte must leave Malmaison to-day and go to Rochefort."

"Why Rochefort?"

"I am afraid the allies are going to insist that we shall hand over General Bonaparte to them," said Talleyrand, yawning furtively. "But on abdicating General Bonaparte demanded that two frigates of the French Navy should be put at his disposal. These frigates have been waiting for him in vain in the harbour at Rochefort."

"The British Navy has blockaded every port. I am told that the cruiser *Bellerophon* is lying at anchor alongside the frigates at Rochefort," said Fouché.

"What have I to do with it?" I asked.

Talleyrand smiled.

"You, my dear Crown Princess, as a member of the Swedish royal family, are in a position to speak to General Bonaparte in the name of the allies."

"At the same time," said Fouché, hastily pulling a sealed envelope out of his breast pocket, "Your Highness could hand the answer of the French Government to General Bonaparte."

"I am afraid the French Government will have to send one of its couriers to Malmaison with the document."

Suddenly Fouché was furious again. "And the demand to go abroad?" he shouted. "Or to put himself at the disposal of the allies, so that France may at last have peace?"

I shook my head slowly. "You are mistaken, gentlemen. I am here only as a private person."

"My child, you have not been told the whole truth." It was Lafayette who spoke now for the first time, in a deep, calm, kindly voice. "This General Bonaparte has assembled a few battalions of young men, daredevils ready for anything. Our fear is that the General will be carried away and do something that cannot possibly change the course of events but may cost yet more lives. And lives are precious, my child."

I bent my head.

The calm voice continued:

"The wars of General Bonaparte have cost Europe more than ten million lives already."

I looked up, and over the shoulders of the three men I saw the portrait of Napoleon as First Consul. "I shall try, gentlemen," I heard myself say. Then Fouché pushed the sealed envelope into my hand, and offered General Becker as escort and a whole battalion of the Guards for my protection. I refused both. I would only take my Swedish A.D.C.; I certainly needed no protection.

Yvette gave me my hat and gloves. Talleyrand said something about being grateful and 'perhaps' granting 'special concessions to Madame Julie'. But I paid no attention to him.

"My child, if you permit I shall go and sit in your garden and there await your return," said General Lafayette.

"Even if it takes all day?"

"Even if it takes all day, and my thoughts will accompany you!"

Close behind us, as I drove with Count Rosen to Malmaison, rode a man on horseback. It was General Becker, who by order of the French Government had to keep watch on the former Emperor of the French.

Close to Malmaison the road was barricaded. The soldiers manning the barricade let us pass as soon as they saw General Becker. The entrance into the park was heavily guarded too. Becker dismounted and opened the gates for us. I was full of apprehension, and tried to tell myself that this was just another little trip to Malmaison, where I knew every garden seat and every rose tree.

Meneval and the Duke of Vicenza received me on the steps, and a moment later I was surrounded by familiar faces— Hortense, Julie, Joseph, Lucien. From the open window of the drawing-room Madame Letitia beckoned to me.

"Joseph," I said, nervously, "I should like to speak to your brother, immediately."

"How kind of you, Désirée! But you must wait a few minutes. The Emperor is expecting an important communication from the Government, and he wishes to be alone meanwhile."

"I have it with me," I said. "And I want to speak to General Bonaparte."

I saw Joseph's face pale when I said 'General Bonaparte'.

"His Majesty is sitting on the bench in the maze. You know the maze, don't you?"

"I know the park very well indeed," I answered, and turning to Rosen I said: "Wait for me. I must see this through alone."

I knew how to find my way through the maze so as to come up to the bench unobserved—that little white bench with just room for two.

There I found Napoleon. He wore the green uniform of the Chasseurs. He was sitting with his chin in his hand, staring unseeing into the flowering hedge in front of him.

When I saw him all my fear fell away, and with it every tender memory. Before I could call to him he turned a little and caught sight of my white frock.

" Josephine," he said, " lunch time already?"

Only my silence brought him back to reality. He recognised me and said in surprise, and with evident pleasure: " Eugenie, you have come after all!"

No one heard him call me Eugenie, no one saw him move to make room for me. When I sat down he looked at me with a smile.

" It is many years," he said, " since you and I looked at a flowering hedge side by side."

I still said nothing.

" You remember, don't you?"

He smoothed an imaginary strand of hair back from his forehead.

" I am waiting for a very important message from the Government. And I am not used to waiting!"

" You need wait no longer, General Bonaparte. Here is the Government's answer," I said, handing him the letter. I did not look at him as he read it.

" How is it that you, Madame, bring the letter? Does the Government not even think it worthwhile to send me its answer through a minister or an officer? Why is a lady who is paying me a chance visit charged with the message?"

" I am not a chance visitor, General Bonaparte," I said, bracing myself. " I am the Crown Princess of Sweden."

" And what do you mean by that?" he said between his teeth.

" The French Government has asked me to tell you that the allies will only enter into negotiation for the surrender of Paris, and so save Paris from destruction, on condition that you leave before to-night."

" I offer the Government to beat back the enemy before the gates of Paris, and the Government refuses," he roared.

" The allied advance guards have reached Versailles," I said. " Are you going to allow yourself to be captured at Malmaison?"

" Don't trouble, Madame. I know how to defend myself."

" That's just it! The Government wants to avoid unnecessary bloodshed."

His eyes narrowed to two slits. " Indeed? What if it is necessary for the honour of a nation?"

' I could tell him of all the millions who fell for the honour of the county,' I thought. ' But he would be better at figures

473

than I, it wouldn't be much good. No, I must just sit here and not give in.'

Napoleon had risen and wanted to pace up and down. But there wasn't room enough. "Madame," he said, standing so close in front of me that I had to throw back my head to see his face. "You say the French Government wants me to leave. And the allies?" His face was distorted.

"The allies insist on your imprisonment, General."

He looked at me for one more second. Then he turned his back on me and leaned against the hedge. "This piece of paper which you have brought me from the self-styled French Government directs my attention for the second time to the frigates at Rochefort. I am free to go where I like, apparently. Why, Madame, does the Government not hand me over?"

"Probably the gentlemen hesitate to do that."

He turned back to me. "All I need do, then, is to go on board one of these ships and tell the captain where to go, and——"

"The port of Rochefort, like all other ports, is being blockaded by the British Navy. You wouldn't get far, General."

He didn't roar, he didn't rage, he sat down quietly on the bench next to me, breathing hard.

"When I saw you just now, Madame, and recognised you, I thought for one short moment that my youth had come back. I was mistaken, Your Royal Highness!"

"Why? I remember the evenings very well when we raced each other. You were a General then, a very young and handsome General. Sometimes you even let me win. But you've probably forgotten that."

"No, Eugenie."

"And once—it was late in the evening and the field beyond our garden was quite dark—you told me that you knew your destiny. Your face was as pale as the moonlight. That was the first time I was afraid of you."

"And that was the first time I kissed you, Eugenie."

I smiled. "You were thinking of the dowry, General."

"Not only, Eugenie. Really, not only——"

After that neither of us said anything. I realised that he was giving me sidelong glances, that he had had an idea connected with me. 'Lives are precious,' I thought. 'If only I could pray!'

"And if I did not let myself be taken prisoner but surrendered voluntarily, what then?"

474

"I don't know."

"An island? Another island? Perhaps that rock in the sea, St. Helena, of which they talked at the Congress in Vienna?"

I could see terror in his eyes.

"Is it St. Helena?"

"I really don't know. Where is St. Helena?"

"Beyond the Cape of Good Hope, Eugenie, beyond!"

"Whatever happened, General, in your place I should never let myself be taken prisoner, I would rather surrender of my own free will."

He sat, bent, with his hand over his terrified eyes. I got up, but he didn't move.

"I'm going now," I said, and waited.

He lifted his head. "Where are you going, Eugenie?"

"Back to Paris. You have given no answer either to the Crown Princess of Sweden or to the French Government. But there is time yet, till to-night."

He laughed loudly, and so unexpectedly that I shrank back. "Shall I prevent them from capturing me? Here or in Rochefort? Shall I?" He fumbled with his sword. "Shall I spoil the fun for Messrs. Blücher and Wellington?" He pulled the sword out of its scabbard. "Here, Eugenie, take it! Take the sword of Waterloo!"

The sun glinted on the steel blade. Hesitantly I put out my hand to it.

"Careful, Eugenie, don't touch the blade!"

Clumsily I took the sword and stared at it, overcome. Napoleon had risen to his feet. "At this moment," he said, "I am surrendering to the allies. I consider myself a prisoner of war. It is customary to hand your sword to the officer who captures you. Let Bernadotte explain to you all about that."

"And your answer to the Government, General?"

"Show them my sword, and tell them that I have put myself in the hands of the allies as their prisoner. I shall leave in one —no, let us say two hours for Rochefort. From there I shall write a letter to my oldest and best enemy, the Prince Regent of Britain. What happens to me after that depends on the allies." He paused, and then added hastily: "I want the frigates to wait for me whatever happens."

"They lie alongside the British cruiser *Bellerophon*," I said. I waited for a word of farewell, but none came. I turned to go.

"Madame!"

I quickly turned back to him.

"They say that the climate of St. Helena is very unhealthy.

475

Is it possible to hope that the British, if asked, might conceivably change my place of residence?"

"You said yourself that St. Helena is beyond the Cape of Good Hope."

He stared at the ground. "After my first abdication I tried to commit suicide, but I was saved. Have you ever been between life and death?"

"Once. On the night you were betrothed to Viscountess Beauharnais, I wanted to throw myself into the Seine."

His eyes returned to me. "You wanted to——? And how were you saved?"

"Bernadotte prevented it."

He shook his head, baffled. "Strange, Bernadotte prevented you from throwing yourself into the river, you are going to be Queen of Sweden, I hand you the sword of Waterloo! You believe in destiny, don't you?"

"No, only in curious coincidences." I gave him my hand.

"Can you find your way back through the maze by yourself, Eugenie?"

I nodded.

"Tell my brothers to have everything ready for my departure, above all a civilian suit. I want to stay here by myself for a short time. And, Eugenie, our betrothal, in Marseilles, it was not only because of the dowry . . . Go now, Eugenie, go quickly, before I regret——"

I went. The paths of the labyrinth seemed endless, the sun shone down mercilessly, there was not a breath of air, not a leaf stirred, not a bird sang. 'I'm carrying his sword,' I thought, 'all is over, I'm carrying his sword.' My gown stuck to my skin, the air was palpitating. At last I heard a window open, and Julie called out: "That's taken a long time!"

They were waiting on the steps—his brothers, Count Rosen, and General Becker. They stood there rooted to the ground, and stared at the sword, which I was carefully holding away from me.

I stopped. Count Rosen put out his hand to take the sword, but I shook my head. None of the others moved.

"General Becker," I said, "General Bonaparte has decided to surrender to the allies, and has handed his sword to me as Crown Princess of Sweden. In two hours he will leave for Rochefort."

Julie and Madame Letitia came out of the house. "Napoleone——" whispered Madame Letitia and began to cry softly. "In two hours?"

476

"I shall accompany my brother to Rochefort, General Becker," said Joseph calmly. 'He still hates him,' I thought, ' otherwise he would not go with him now.'

I heard one of the officers say softly to Joseph, "Two regiments are ready under His Majesty's order to——"

"That," I shouted, "is what General Bonaparte wants to spare France—civil war. Spare him that!"

"Has Napoleone had anything to eat?" wailed Madame Letitia. "Is he going a long journey?" I heard Julie sob close to me.

I managed to say that the General had asked for civilian clothes and wanted to be left alone for a little while. Then, somehow, I must have got into my carriage. I saw the open road, and the fields, and trees and bushes. A slight fragrant breeze played round us.

Count Rosen took the sword from my cramped fingers and put it in a corner of the carriage. Just then something made me throw my head back, and at that moment a very sharp stone crashed painfully on my knee.

Rosen shouted something in Swedish to Johansson, the coachman, and Johansson whipped up the horses to a gallop. The next stone only hit the back wheel. My Count's face was deathly pale.

"I swear," he said, "that the attackers shall be tracked down."

"Why? It's of no importance."

"Of no importance? An attack on the Crown Princess of Sweden?"

"But it wasn't an attack on the Crown Princess of Sweden. It was meant for *Madame la Maréchale* Bernadotte, and she no longer exists!"

Darkness was beginning to fall as we reached the suburbs. Everywhere there were clusters of people talking in murmurs. 'By now,' I thought, 'Napoleon must be on his way to the coast, on the first stage of his long voyage. And Paris is saved.'

Near the Rue d'Anjou we encountered a large crowd making its way slowly toward my street. We had to stop, someone recognised me, and a shout went up, "*La Princess Royale de Suède!*" In a moment the whole town seemed to be shouting it. Gendarmes appeared and made a way for me, and at last I reached my house. Torches were burning in front of it, the gate stood open, and we drove straight in. Behind us the gate was shut immediately.

As I was getting out of the coach I felt a violent pain in my knee. I clenched my teeth, reached for the sword, and limped into the house. The hall was brightly lit and filled with strange people.

Lafayette came forward to meet me. "In the name of France I thank you—Citizeness!" He put his hand under my elbow to support me.

"But who are all these strange people?" I asked.

"The representatives of the nation," said Lafayette, smiling.

"And *la grande nation* has many representatives, Your Highness." It was Talleyrand speaking. He came toward me followed by Fouché, who had two white rosettes in his buttonhole. The many representatives of the nation bowed low amid deep silence.

"And," I asked, "the thousands of people outside, what are they waiting for?"

"It has become known that Your Highness has tried to mediate," said Fouché. "The people of Paris have been awaiting Your Highness's return for hours."

"Tell the people that General Bonaparte has surrendered to the allies and has left Malmaison. That will make them go home."

"They want to see you, Citizeness," said Lafayette.

"See me?"

Lafayette nodded. "You are bringing us peace, capitulation without civil war. You have fulfilled your mission, Citizeness."

I shook my head. No, I didn't want to show myself. But Lafayette insisted. "Show yourself to your people, Citizeness. You have saved many lives. May I conduct you to a window?"

He took me to a window in the dining-room. The noise of the crowd rushed in from the street the moment the window was opened, and it ebbed away the moment Lafayette stepped up to it and showed himself to the people. He began to speak, and his voice sounded like a flourish of trumpets:

"Citizens and Citizenesses, peace is assured. General Bonaparte has given himself up into captivity and a woman from your midst, a simple woman whom a freedom-loving nation in the North has made its Crown Princess, has received his sword from him, the sword of Waterloo!"

The roar of the crowd redoubled as Lafayette made room for me. Remembering Josephine's advice, I had asked for a footstool so as not to be too small for a Crown Princess, and I mounted it now. With both hands I held the sword out of the window into the torch-lit darkness below. A few words were

being shouted over and over again; in the end I caught them—
"*Notre-Dame de la Paix! Notre-Dame de la Paix!*"

"Our Lady of Peace," they were calling me, "Our Lady of Peace!" I wept—I could not but weep.

Lafayette pushed Count Rosen toward the window, seized a candelabrum, and let its light fall on Rosen's Swedish uniform and blue and yellow sash. "Sweden, long live Sweden!" was shouted up from the street, and again "*Notre-Dame de la Paix!*"

The window was closed as I went back into the room, feeling suddenly strange and forlorn among the excited groups of Deputies. Unfortunately they showed no sign of leaving. I put the sword on the table under the portrait of the First Consul, and decided that I must offer the Deputies something to eat and drink. But all I had apart from wine were the cherries we had meant to bottle. So Marie and I gave them to the representatives of the nation, who fairly fell on them. I remembered the people outside in the street who had had to form queues for every bit of food in recent days, and I told Marie and the chef to let them have all the flour we had stored away in the cellar.

Talleyrand was the first to notice that something was wrong with my knee. "Is Your Highness hurt?" he asked as I limped toward the door.

"No, only—a bit tired."

He raised his lorgnette to his eyes. "Our Republican friend the Marquis de Lafayette seems to be an old favourite of Your Highness!"

The tone in which he said it made me furious. "He's the only man with clean hands in this room," I said.

"Naturally, Your Highness! He has spent all these years planting cabbages in the country and so has kept his hands clean!"

"Philosophers," I said, "in quiet backwaters——"

"——Are always a dictator's best subjects!"

He listened to the noise of the flour distribution outside.

Lafayette came. "How kind you are, my child! First you secure peace, and now food!"

"How kind, and how clever!" said Talleyrand, and smiled, taking at the same time a glass of wine from a servant. "The small country of the North and its great future: to secure peace —and food! To Sweden, Your Highness!"

Just then I saw that Fouché was about to take the sword. "Oh no," I called out, and limped quickly toward him.

"But the French Government——" he urged.

For the first time I noticed the greedy glint in his eyes. "Oh no," I said, "the sword has been handed to the allies and not to the French Government. I shall keep it till General Blücher and Wellington decide what to do with it." I took it from him and, as my knee hurt badly, went up with it to my bedroom, leaving the Deputies to argue together for I don't know how long.

Marie undressed me. She shook her head at my blue and swollen knee.

The street outside had become quiet, and I started writing my diary. And over the writing of it morning has dawned.

Papa, Lafayette has grown old. And your pamphlet with the declaration of the Rights of Man is probably in Sweden now.

Only ninety days—no, about a hundred, have passed since Napoleon's return from Elba, a hundred days like so many eternities.

In the Battle of Leipzig my old Jean-Baptiste died, and young Désirée breathed her last in the maze at Malmaison. How shall these twain ever come together again?

Papa, I don't think I shall ever again write in my diary.

PART IV

QUEEN OF SWEDEN

I was at the piano, trying to play a new piece Oscar has composed, when the Swedish Ambassador was announced. I was pleased at his visit, for this dark, rainy afternoon was just right for a cup of tea in company.

But on entering he closed the door and remained standing there, with the whole room between us. As he didn't stir from the door I got up to go to meet him. Then he bowed very low, very ceremoniously, and I noticed the black band round his arm.

" Your Majesty! "

He straightened up slowly. " Your Majesty, I have come with sad news. King Charles died on February the 5th."

I stood paralysed. I hardly knew the small shaky King. But his death meant——

" His Majesty has commissioned me to inform Your Majesty of the circumstances of the King's death and to hand to you this letter."

I made no move. The Ambassador came up to me and held out a sealed letter.

Hesitantly I took the letter. " Sit down, Baron," I said, and sank into the nearest chair. My hands trembled as I opened the letter. It was a big sheet on which Jean-Baptiste had scribbled in haste: ' Dearest, You are now the Queen of Sweden. Please conduct yourself accordingly. In haste—Your J.-B.

' P.S. Don't forget to destroy this letter at once.'

I dropped the sheet and smiled—and remembered that the Ambassador was watching me. Quickly I tried to put on a face full of sad dignity. " My husband writes that I am now the Queen of Sweden and Norway," I said gravely. The Ambassador smiled, I should have liked to know why.

" His Majesty," said the Ambassador, " was proclaimed King Charles John IV of Sweden and Norway by the heralds on February 6th, and his wife Her Majesty Queen Desideria."

" Jean-Baptiste ought never to have allowed me to be called Desideria. How did His Majesty die?"

" His Majesty had a very easy death. He had a stroke on the first of February. Two days later it was known that the end was near. His Majesty and His Highness the Crown Prince kept vigil in the sick-room."

I tried to visualise the scene: the castle in Stockholm, the crowded sick-room, Jean-Baptiste, Oscar—Crown Prince Oscar!—the Queen, Princess Sofia Albertina—and who else? The Ambassador told me who else had been there and in the adjoining room, and he also told me how the King never took his eyes from Jean-Baptiste and how gradually his breath grew slower and fainter, till it was all over.

The Ambassador went on to tell me of Jean-Baptiste's first acts as the new ruler! he told me that the coronation was to take place on May 11th.

" Really?" I said. " May 11th?"

" Did His Majesty have a special reason for the choice of that particular day?" asked the Ambassador.

" On the 11th of May it will be exactly twenty-five years since Jean-Baptiste Bernadotte was promoted sergeant in the French Army. It was a great day in my husband's life."

" Yes, quite, Your Majesty!"

I rang for tea, which we took with Marceline, who, of course, knew nothing. When she learned the news she was so startled that she dropped her teacup.

The Ambassador left. Marceline, since dropping her cup, had stared steadily at me in awe. " Her Majesty the Queen of Sweden and Norway!" she said slowly, and continued to stare at me.

" I'll have to get some mourning dresses to-morrow," I said, and went back to the piano. Once more I looked at the music composed by Oscar, Crown Prince of Sweden and Norway, once more I touched the keys, and then I closed the lid.

" I shall never play the piano again, Marceline," I said.

" Why not, Aunt?"

" Because I play too badly for a Queen."

" Now we shall not be able to go and see Aunt Julie. You will have to go to Stockholm, I suppose. Aunt Julie was looking forward so much on your visit."

" She can still count on it," I said, and went to my bedroom to lie down.

' Julie Bonaparte,' I thought, ' away in Brussels, exiled like all those who bear the name of Bonaparte.' Ever since the Hundred Days I had been writing to ask Louis XVIII to grant Julie permission to return, and again and again I had received a very courteous refusal. And after every refusal I had gone to Brussels to console my inconsolable Julie. Joseph? He went to America under the name of Count Survillier, bought a farm near New York, and wrote contented letters in which he fondly imagined that Julie would soon be well enough to follow him. In her state of health, how could she?

And Hortense? Accompanied by Count Flahault she had managed to escape to Switzerland, darkly hinting at her departure that one of them would come back and be the Third. And when I asked who and as what, she said, " One of my sons, Madame, Napoleon—the Third! "

Not all had been lucky enough to escape like Hortense. Marshal Ney was caught, sentenced to death and executed. Many others who were on the lists of proscribed Republicans and Bonapartists suffered exile at the hands of Louis XVIII, or prison, or death. And the man who had handed the lists of proscriptions to King Louis, Fouché, what had happened to him? The King made him his Minister of Police in recognition of his services as a traitor. But when the lists of the proscribed had come to an end King Louis thought it time to exile his Minister of Police. And the rest of the Bonapartes? They lived in Italy.

But I was still here, and now I might even have to endure a visit of condolence from King Louis.

Marie came in and lit the candles. ' She'll grumble at me,' I thought, ' for lying on my bed with my shoes on.' But she only held up the light to see my face—and she looked at me in much the same way as Marceline had done.

" Don't be annoyed," I said, " I'll take my shoes off."

" Your niece has told me everything. You might have told me yourself."

" I know what you are thinking," I said. " You think that Papa wouldn't have liked it. I know that myself, without your telling me."

She undressed me.

" If you have to be a Queen, be at least a good one. When are we leaving for Stockholm? "

I took the letter. Scribbled in such haste, I noticed, full of fear that I might be unworthy of him. I held it to the candle and burned it.

" Well, when are we leaving, Eugenie? "

" In three days. That means I shan't have any time left to receive King Louis. By the way, we're going to Brussels. Julie needs me and in Stockholm I'm quite superfluous."

" But they can't have a coronation without us! "

I looked for my book, and for the first time for years I started writing my diary again.

It really has happened to me: I am Queen of Sweden!

PARIS.
June 1821.

Among the letters on my breakfast table to-day was one with a dark-green seal that showed clearly a coat-of-arms forbidden the world over—the Emperor's coat-of-arms. It was addressed to Her Majesty Queen Desideria of Sweden and Norway. At last I opened it, and read:

'Madame, I have been informed that my son, the Emperor of the French, died on the 5th of May this year on the Island of St. Helena. He was buried with the military honours due to a General. The British Government forbade the inscription " Napoleon " on the tombstone, and would only allow " General N. Bonaparte." I therefore gave instructions that the grave should remain without any inscription whatever.

' I am dictating this letter to my son Lucien, who often comes to see me in Rome. I am blind now.

' Lucien has begun to read me my son's memoirs, which Napoleone dictated to Count de Montholon on St. Helena. In the memoirs this sentence occurs: " Désirée Clary was Napoleon's first love." You will see from that my son never ceased to remember his first love.

' I am told that the manuscript will soon be published, and I ask you to let us know if you wish this sentence to be left out. We realise that you in your position will have to be particularly careful, and we shall be glad to do whatever you wish.

' My son Lucien wishes to be remembered to you.

                    ' I remain
                    ' Yours always——'

The blind old woman had signed the letter herself. Her signature, in Italian and barely legible, ran:

'Letitia
madre di Napoleone'
(Letitia, mother of Napoleon.)

During the day I asked my nephew Marius, whom I had made my Lord Chamberlain, how the letter with the forbidden seal arrived here.

"An attaché brought it from the Swedish Embassy, where it had been sent from the Swedish Chargé d'Affairs in Rome. Why, was it an important letter?"

"It was the last letter with the Emperor's coat-of-arms on it. I should like to ask you to send some money to the British Ambassador and ask him to use it for a wreath to be laid on my behalf on the grave in St. Helena. On the grave without a name, you will have to say."

"I am afraid, Aunt, it cannot be done. There are no flowers on St. Helena. The dreadful climate of the islands kills all flowers."

"Do you think, Auntie," said Marceline, "that Marie-Louise will now marry that Count Neipperg, by whom she has three children already, or so they say?"

"She married him a long time ago. Talleyrand told me so. The Pope probably declared her first marriage invalid."

"And what about the King of Rome?" said Marius hotly. "After the Emperor's second abdication he was called Napoleon II officially for a few days."

"His name is now Francis Joseph Charles, Duke of Reichstadt, son of Marie-Louise, Duchess of Parma. His father isn't even mentioned in his ducal patent. Anyone would suppose that the father was—unknown!"

"If Napoleon had had any idea of what was to happen to him!" began Marceline.

"He had," I said, as I went to my writing desk.

'An island without flowers,' I thought. The pictures of our garden in Marseilles, the field, and the flowering hedge came into my mind as I began writing to Madame Letitia.

"Aunt Julie once said something about you, or perhaps him," said Marceline hesitantly, some time later.

"You'll read all that in his memoirs," I said, as I sealed the letter. "Nothing will be left out of them."

This morning, sitting at my dressing-table in the hotel, getting ready, I thought how strange it is that at forty-two I should be experiencing once more all the sweetness, the anxiety, the impatience of a first rendezvous.

" And when am I to see him?" I asked for the twentieth time.

" At half-past twelve, Auntie, in your drawing-room," Marceline answered patiently.

" But he'll be here early in the morning, won't he?"

" It was difficult to give the exact time of his arrival. That's why the visit was fixed for half-past twelve."

" And then he'll have a meal with me?"

" Yes, together with his lord-in-waiting, Charles Gustavus Löwenhjelm."

He is the uncle of my Gustavus Löwenhjelm whom they sent me a short time ago to take the place of Count Rosen, who went home. My Löwenhjelm is so pompous and formal that I hardly dare speak to him.

" The only others will be Marius and myself, Auntie, so that you can talk to him freely."

Two Löwenhjelms, Marius and Marceline? No, I said to myself, no! I sent for Löwenhjelm and told him to instruct his uncle to withdraw immediately he saw me. I felt sure that after his arrival at his hotel Oscar would go straight to the Cathedral like any other tourist. I decided to meet him there.

Of course, my Löwenhjelm was terribly upset. " The advantage of ceremonial preparations lies in the avoidance of surprises," he explained to me. But I didn't give in and in the end he agreed.

I put on my hat and a veil that covered my face, and went out by myself to the Cathedral. ' This is the last great surprise of my life,' I thought on the way; ' the first meeting with a man can mean everything or nothing. In half an hour we should know.'

I went into the Cathedral and sat down in a choir stall. Instinctively I folded my hands.

Eleven years is a long time, I reflected. Perhaps meanwhile, without noticing it, I've turned into a middle-aged lady. He, at all events, had grown up into a young man who was being sent round the European courts to look for a wife.

This morning innumerable tourists visited the Cathedral and

crowded round the stone slab over the alleged tomb of Charlemagne. I looked at every single one of them. Was it that one? Or that other one? Or the little flat-footed fellow over there?

I don't know what a mother feels when she sees her son growing up, and notices the first faint growth of beard and the signs of his first falling in love. All that I have never known. I was waiting for a man who was to be like the one I had dreamt of all my life and had never met, my stranger son!

I recognised him at once, not because of Löwenhjelm, who had hardly changed since my Stockholm days, but because of his bearing, his walk, the movements of his head. He wore dark civilian clothes and seemed almost as tall as his father, only much thinner.

I left my seat and went toward him, without thinking how to address him. He was standing over the slab of Charlemagne's alleged tomb and bending down to read the inscription. I touched Löwenhjelm's arm. He looked up and, seeing me, withdrew without a word.

"Is that Charlemagne's tomb?" I asked in French. It was the most stupid question possible because the inscription said quite plainly that it was.

"As you see, Madame," he said without turning round.

"I know that my conduct is very unseemly, but I—I should like to make the acquaintance of Your Highness."

This time he looked up. "So you know who I am, Madame?" I saw the dark, forceful eyes of long ago and the thick curls, my curls! But he had a small ridiculously waxed moustache.

"Your Highness is the Crown Prince of Sweden," I said. "And I am a compatriot of yours. My husband lives in Stockholm, you see."

I stopped. He was looking steadily at me.

"I wanted to ask Your Highness a favour, but—but it will take a little time."

"I see," he said. Looking round for his escort he murmured, "I don't know where my companion has gone. But I have an hour to spare. If you will permit me, Madame, I should like to accompany you." Smiling, he added: "Is it permitted?"

I nodded, and I felt a lump rising in my throat. Making our way toward the door, I saw Oscar's Löwenhjelm lurking behind a pillar. Fortunately Oscar didn't notice him.

Without speaking we went out, crossed the fish market outside the Cathedral, and finally entered a narrow street. I pulled

487

the veil more tightly round my face, as I felt that Oscar was giving me sidelong glances now and then. At last we stopped at a small café with a few miserable tables outside and two dusty palm trees.

"May I invite my charming compatriot to a glass of wine?" he asked.

I looked at the dreadful shrubs with horror. 'But that won't do,' I thought, and I felt that I was blushing. 'Doesn't he see that I am a middle-aged lady? Or does he give these invitations to every chance acquaintance?' But I calmed myself with the thought that he had probably invited me because he was glad to be rid of Löwenhjelm.

"It is not very elegant here, Madame," he said, "but at least we can talk undisturbed."

To my horror he ordered champagne.

"Not now, in the morning," I said.

"Why not? Why not at any time when there is something to celebrate?"

"But there is nothing to celebrate."

"There is. Your acquaintance, Madame. Could you not put your veil aside a bit so that I could see your face? I can see nothing but the tip of your nose."

"My nose is a very unfortunate one. When I was young it used to offend me a good deal. Strange that no woman ever seems to have the nose she wants."

"My father has a really fantastic nose. Like an eagle's beak! His face is nothing but nose and eyes."

The waiter brought the champagne and poured it out.

"Skål, ma compatriote inconnue. French and Swedish at the same time—is that not so?"

"Like Your Highness," I said. The champagne was far too sweet.

"No, Madame, I am only a Swede now—and, of course, a Norwegian. The champagne is awful, don't you think so?"

"Too sweet, Your Highness."

"I am glad, Madame, that we seem to have the same taste. Most women prefer their wine very sweet. Our Madame Koskull, for instance."

I sat up sharply. "What does that mean—our Madame Koskull?"

"That is our lady-in-waiting, Mariana Koskull. First she was the late King's ray of sunshine, then Papa's favourite and, if Papa had had his way, my—mistress! What is there so surprising in it, Madame?"

"That you tell these things to a stranger," I said angrily.

"A compatriot! Mariana used to read to the old King, and he was so happy to be allowed to stroke her arm. Papa has simply taken over the Swedish court ceremonial as it was, perhaps in order not to offend anybody, and so he has taken over Madame Koskull as well."

I stared at him, completely put out. "Do you mean that?"

"Madame, my father is the loneliest man I know. My mother has not been to see him for many years, he works sixteen hours a day, and what spare time he has he spends in the company of a few friends from the days before his accession, such as Count Brahe, if the name means anything to you, or Madame Koskull. She brings her guitar and sings Swedish drinking songs to Papa. They are quite amusing songs, but Papa unfortunately does not understand them."

"And court balls and receptions? You can't have a court without its court functions?"

"Oh yes, Papa can. Don't forget, Madame, we are a court without a Queen!"

I emptied my glass slowly, and he filled it again. "It will all be different once you get married."

"Do you think that any young Princess will feel at ease in a huge cold castle where the King refuses to see anybody but his ministers and old friends? My father has altered strangely, Madame. A King who does not speak the language of his people is easily obsessed by the fear that he may be deposed. Do you know how far things have gone? They have gone so far that my father has prohibited journals that have published articles disagreeable to him personally. Yet the Swedish Constitution guarantees freedom of the press!"

Oscar's face had gone white with agitation. Tonelessly I asked: "You are not hostile to your father, are you?"

"No, if I were, all this would not upset me so much. Madame, my father has made Sweden great again, and prosperous; Sweden owes its liberty to him alone. Yet this same man fights every liberal tendency Parliament shows. Why? Because he imagines that liberalism leads to revolution and revolution will cost him his crown. But there is not the ghost of a chance of any kind of revolution in Scandinavia, only healthy evolution. A former Jacobin just can't see that. Do I weary you, Madame?"

I shook my head, and he went on: "It has come to this, that some people, individuals, Madame, not parties, talk of suggesting abdication to him—in my favour!"

"You must never even think of that," I said in a low tone, trembling.

Oscar bent forward. "I am tired, Madame. I wanted to be a composer, and what has come of it? A few songs, a few military marches, that's all. I have begun an opera and cannot find time to finish it, not only because of my duties at court and in the Army but especially because I have to spend so much time trying to convince my father of the necessities for changes, changes, incidentally, which the French Revolution ought to have taught him. He ought to receive the middle-class at court instead of only the old nobility; and he should stop talking at every prorogation of Parliament about his deserts as a General and the sacrifice of his private fortune to pay Sweden's external debts. Papa ought to——"

I couldn't contain myself any longer, I had to interrupt him and ask: "And what about this Madame Koskull?"

"I don't think she has ever done more for him than sing songs. As for me, he seemed to have the old-fashioned idea that Crown Princes ought to be introduced to the amatory arts by ladies who were experienced campaigners. Not long ago, Madame, he sent Mistress Koskull to my room at midnight armed with her guitar!"

"Your Papa meant well, Your Highness."

"He locks himself up in his study and loses all contact with reality. What he lacks——" He broke off to pour out more champagne. A frown appeared on his forehead, reminiscent of Jean-Baptiste. "When I was a child, Madame, I badly wanted to see Napoleon's coronation. I was not allowed to, I don't know why. But I do remember my mother sitting in my room and saying that we should both go to another coronation; she promised me that, and it was to be a far more beautiful one than Napoleon's. Yes, Madame, I did go to another one, but my mother wasn't there. But, Madame, you are crying!"

"Your mother's name is Desideria, the longed-for one, the wanted one. Perhaps she wasn't wanted at the time."

"Not wanted? My father has her proclaimed Queen and she, she does not even come for that! Do you believe that a man like my father can bring himself to ask her on his knees?"

"Perhaps being a Queen is not a very congenial occupation for your mother?"

"Madame, my mother is a marvellous woman. But she is at least as obstinate as my father. I tell you that the presence of the Queen in Sweden is not only desirable but necessary!"

490

" If that is so, perhaps the Queen had better come," I said very softly.

" Thank God, Mama! Thank God! And now take off your veil so that I can have a real look at you. Yes, you have changed. You have become more beautiful, your eyes are bigger, and your face and— Why are you crying, Mama?"

" When did you recognise me, Oscar?"

" Recognise you? I only went to look at Charlemagne's tomb to wait there for you. I was quite curious, I must say, to know how you were going to address a strange man."

" I thought your Löwenhjelm would keep quiet about it."

" It was not his fault. I intended all along to meet you without witnesses. He noticed how I racked my brains about it and so he confessed that you had anticipated me."

" Oscar, is what you told me about Papa true?"

" It is. Only I painted it very black so that you couldn't but decide to come home. When are you coming?"

He took my hand and put it against his cheek.

" Oscar, you have a beard like a man. Come home? You don't know how they vexed me at that time in Stockholm."

" But, dear Mama, they are all dead, except Princess Sofia Albertina! Who could vex you now? Don't forget you are the Queen!"

No, I thought, how could I forget that? I'm so afraid of it.

" Mama, in the Cathedral you said something about asking me a favour. Did you say that only to start the conversation with me?"

" No, I really have a favour to ask you. It concerns my daughter-in-law."

" But there is no daughter-in-law yet. Papa has compiled a whole list of Princesses I am to look at, all horribly ugly. Papa got their portraits for me."

" I should like you to marry for love, Oscar."

" Believe me, so should I. When you get home I shall show you my little daughter, secretly. Her name is Oscara, Mama."

Heavens, I am a grandmother!

" Mama, Oscara has inherited your dimples!"

" And who is Oscara's mother?"

" Jaquette Gyldenstolpe, a charming mother!"

" Does Papa know?"

" Of course not, Mama! Promise me never to tell him!"

" But shouldn't you——"

" Marry her? Mama, you forget who I am."

For some reason it irritated me to hear him say that. Oscar continued:

"Papa thought at first of a connection with the house of Hanover. But the Bernadotte dynasty is not good enough yet for the English, and I shall have to marry a Prussian Princess."

"Listen, Oscar. The arrangements were that we were going together from here to Brussels for the marriage of Aunt Julie's daughter Zenaïde to a son of Lucien Bonaparte. We expect Joseph Bonaparte back from America for the wedding. He may even stay on in Europe afterwards."

"I am sorry, Mama, but I don't like the Bonapartes. Well, the wedding. And then?"

"From Brussels I'm going on to Switzerland to Hortense— you know, Josephine's daughter. I should like you to come along too."

"Mama, I really should not like that. All these Bonapartes——"

"I want you to meet Hortense's niece."

"Who is she?"

"The daughter of Eugene de Beauharnais, former Viceroy of Italy, now Duke of Leuchtenberg. His wife is a daughter of the King of Bavaria. And the daughter is the most beautiful girl you can imagine."

"Even if she is, I still couldn't marry her. The daughter of a Duke of Leuchtenberg is no match for the Crown Prince of Sweden, Mama—for a Bernadotte!"

"No? Then let me tell you, Oscar—but give me a little more champagne first, I am beginning to like it—let me tell you: her grandfather on her father's side was the Viscount Beauharnais, a General in the French Army. Her grandmother was the Viscountess Beauharnais, the most beautiful woman of her time, the most charming and expensive of cocottes. On her second marriage she became Empress of the French. Your paternal grandfather, however, was a lawyer's clerk in Pau, and nothing at all is known about his wife, your father's mother."

"But, Mama——"

"Let me finish. Her grandfather on her mother's side is the king of Bavaria, and the Bavarian royal family is one of the oldest reigning families in Europe. Your grandfather on your mother's side was the Marseilles silk merchant François Clary."

He clapped his hands to his head. " The grand-daughter of a cocotte!"

" Yes, and an enchanting one at that! I've only seen the little Josephine once, when she was a child, but she has the same smile, the same charm as the big one had."

Oscar sighed. " Mama, simply for dynastic reasons——"

" Exactly, for dynastic reasons! I want to be the ancestress of a beautiful dynasty."

" Papa will never give his consent."

" Imagine anybody asking him to marry an ugly woman! I shall handle Papa. You go and have a look at Josephine."

We left the café arm-in-arm and went to our hotel. My heart was beating with happiness and bad champagne.

" How old is she, Mama?"

" Only fifteen. But at that age I had my first kisses."

" You were a precocious child, Mama."

We came in sight of the hotel. Oscar, suddenly very serious, took my hand.

" Mama, you'll promise me, won't you, to accompany my fiancée to Stockholm?"

" Yes, I promise."

" And that you will stay on?"

I hesitated. " That depends."

" On what?"

" On myself, Oscar. I shall only stay on if I succeed in becoming a good Queen. I shall take it very seriously indeed."

" All you need, Mama, is practice. Look! There they are, your Löwenhjelm and mine, both looking anxious."

" I shall introduce some reforms at the Swedish court," I whispered into his ear. " We shall send Miss Koskull to her well-earned retirement." We looked at each other and laughed heartily.

" Mama, we are both a little drunk," said Oscar.

Well, well, is that really becoming for an illegitimate grandmother, I mean the grandmother of an illegitimate child?

At the ROYAL CASTLE *in* STOCKHOLM.
Spring 1823.

" How beautiful our country is!" said my daughter-in-law, the Crown Princess Josefina of Sweden, in an awed voice.

We were standing near the bows of the impressive warship that had met us at Lübeck and was now nearing Stockholm.

Oscar and Josephine had been married in Munich. As she is a Roman Catholic and Oscar a Protestant, she insisted on being married in a Roman Catholic church, by proxy as Oscar couldn't be there. The proper ceremonies for the wedding are to take place in Stockholm after our arrival.

We passed countless rocky islets covered with black fir trees, with green shoots showing on every branch, or birches veiled with yellow blossom.

"Our beautiful country," repeated Josephine's granddaughter, and her shining eyes drank in the sight of the marvellous birch forests.

Marceline, Marius, and Marie and Pierre were with me, and Yvette, of course, the only one who could do my hair properly besides Julie. They were the little bit of France I had brought with me. I had appointed Marceline my chief stewardess and Marius my financial adviser, to their intense satisfaction and that of their father. I had left Julie behind in Brussels; she was far more reconciled to her exile than I had ever known her to be, and talked of joining her daughter Zenaïde, who was married and living in Florence. Joseph had come over from America, and his main topic of conversation was cattle breeding. He too talked vaguely of going to live in Italy when he was old. "And so," said Julie, linking her arm in his, "everything has turned out for the best." But she said it without conviction.

"I am so happy, Mama," whispered Josefina into my ear. "From the moment we set eyes on each other, Oscar and I knew that we were meant for each other. But I was sure that neither you nor His Majesty would allow it."

"But why not, Josephine?"

"Because, Mama, I am only the daughter of the Duke of Leuchtenberg, and I am sure you counted on a Princess from a royal family, did you not?"

"Counted? You don't count on anything where your children's happiness is concerned, you only hope for the best."

A salvo came from the coastal fortress of Vaxholm, which we were passing, and I noticed a small boat approaching our ship.

"And that is my advice to you, Josefina," I continued. "Never stand in the way of your children if they want to marry for love."

"But, Mama, what about the succession?"

"Leave that to fate and the future. But teach all Bernadottes that love is the only honourable reason for marrying."

494

Josefina looked horrified. "But, Mama, what if it is a commoner?"

"What of it? Aren't we commoners, we Bernadottes?"

Another salvo thundered. I put the field-glasses to my eyes and studied the little boat making for us. "Josefina, Oscar's coming on board!"

We entered the port of Djurgården. The air was reverberating with the thunder of the guns, great crowds were lining quays and streets as far as we could see, and lots of small garlanded boats danced round our ship. Oscar and Josefina were standing beside me, waving. Josefina wore a blue dress and an ermine stole that had begun to go yellow with age. Once upon a time Napoleon had given that stole to Josephine, and Hortense made a present of it to Josefina to remind her of her beautiful grandmother.

I felt my hands turn clammy as I clenched them in growing excitement. Marie touched them reassuringly with her hard hand and put the heavy mink stole over my shoulders.

"This is the end of your journey, Eugenie," she said.

"No, Marie, this is only the beginning."

The guns had stopped firing, and a band began to play.

"I composed that music for you," said Oscar to Josefina. Meanwhile I looked round through the field-glasses and found what I was looking for: a purple velvet cloak and white plumes on a hat.

The gangway was brought out and I found myself facing it alone. Everybody, even Oscar and Josefina, had gone back a few paces. The band on the quayside struck up the Swedish national anthem, and everybody froze into immobility. Then two gentlemen who had been waiting close to the purple velvet cloak rushed toward the gangway to escort me down. They were Counts Brahe and Rosen, the one smiling, the other pale with excitement. But the purple cloak came between them and me at the end of the narrow shaky gangway and I felt a familiar grip on my arm.

The crowd cheered, the guns thundered, the band played, as we walked on to the quay followed by Oscar and his Crown Princess. Under a triumphal arch made of birch branches a little girl in white handed me a giant bouquet of blue lilies and yellow tulips and recited a poem of welcome. Then, to the obvious surprise of all present, I opened my mouth to say something in return. A great hush fell on the quayside. I was almost paralysed with fear, but my voice was loud and calm as I began with the words:

"*Jag har varit länge borte——*"

I could see them holding their breath! Swedish, the Queen was speaking Swedish! I had composed the little address, Count Löwenhjelm had translated it for me, and I had learnt it by heart. It was dreadfully difficult, and I felt relieved when I reached the last words: "*Länge leve Sverig!*"

We drove through the streets in an open equipage, Josefina nodding graciously left and right next to me, Jean-Baptiste and Oscar facing us. I sat stiffly upright, smiling to the crowds till my face ached. But even then I continued to smile.

"I was amazed," said Oscar, "at your speaking in Swedish, Mama. I am very proud of you."

I felt Jean-Baptiste's eyes on me, but I couldn't bring myself to look at him. Why not? Because I realised how much I was still in love with him, still or again, I don't know which.

And all the time I was chuckling a little at the thought that he was a grandfather already, without knowing it!

DROTTNINGHOLM CASTLE.
August 15th-16th, 1823.

At midnight to-night I was a ghost for the first time in my life. In my white dressing-gown I 'walked' the corridors of the castle as the 'white lady'.

We came here to Drottningholm for a rest after a strenuous summer in which Oscar and Josefina and I danced every night at some ball or other, in some castle or other, in South Sweden as well as here. And we had made Jean-Baptiste attend and dance too, in spite of all his excuses. Everything at court is new and fresh, new lords and ladies-in-waiting, new liveries, new furniture, new wallpaper and paint, and so is this régime of cheerfulness and new life and new contact with the people. But it has been strenuous! And so we have come here.

Last night I went early to bed, but I couldn't sleep. The summer nights here are so disturbingly light.

The clock struck midnight. It's the 16th of August, I remembered. I slipped into my dressing-gown and started 'walking'. I wanted to go to Jean-Baptiste. It was completely silent everywhere, only the parquet floor creaked under my steps. How I hate castles!

In Jean-Baptiste's study I very nearly collided with Moreau's white marble bust, but in the end I managed to feel my way to

Jean-Baptiste's dressing-room door. I opened it and—stared straight at the barrel of a pistol! Someone hissed at me in French.

"Who goes there?"

I laughed. "A ghost, Fernand, that's all!"

"Your Majesty has given me a fright," said Fernand, offended. He was in a long nightshirt, and he still held the pistol as he bowed to me. His camp bed was pulled across Jean-Baptiste's door.

"Do you always sleep in front of His Majesty's door?"

"Yes. The Marshal is afraid."

The door was flung open, and Jean-Baptiste, his green shade pushed up on to his forehead, bellowed:

"What does this mean?"

I curtsied. "Your Majesty, a ghost requests an audience."

Fernand pushed the camp-bed aside, and for the first time since our arrival in Drottningholm I stood in Jean-Baptiste's bedroom. Even there every inch of space seemed to be filled with leather tomes and files of papers. 'He's still studying,' I thought, 'as in Hanover, as in Marienburg.'

Jean-Baptiste stretched himself wearily, and asked with a smile:

"And what does the ghost want?"

"It only wants to announce its presence," I said, and sat down comfortably in an arm-chair. "It's the ghost of a young girl who, once upon a time, married a General and went into a bridal bed full of roses and thorns."

Jean-Baptiste sat down on the arm of my chair and put his arm round me.

"And why does this ghost announce its presence on this particular night?"

"Because it was twenty-five years ago to-night."

"Heavens!" he exclaimed, "it is our silver wedding day, is it?"

"Yes," I said, nestling close to him, "and in the whole of Sweden no one besides ourselves will think of it. No salvoes, no schoolchildren reciting poetry, no regimental bands! Isn't it marvellous, Jean-Baptiste?"

"We have travelled a long way," he said, tired, and put his head on my shoulder. "And in the end you came back to me after all."

"You have arrived, Jean-Baptiste. Yet in spite of that you are afraid of ghosts?"

He didn't answer. His head felt heavy on my shoulder.

"Fernand sleeps across your bedroom door with a pistol in his hand. What ghosts are you afraid of?"

"The ghosts of Vasa. During the Congress of Vienna the last Vasa King, the exiled one, you know, put in his claims to the throne for himself and his son."

"But that's eight years ago. The Swedes deposed him because he was crazy. Is he really crazy?"

"His policy certainly was. The allies rejected his claims, of course. They couldn't very well do anything else after the way I, during that horrible campaign——"

"Jean-Baptiste, don't let those memories torment you. The Swedes know exactly what you did for them. They know that you made their country prosperous and rich."

"Yes, yes, but the opposition——"

"Does the opposition ever mention the Vasas?"

"No, never. But let an opposition that calls itself Liberal exist, and it is only one more step to revolution!"

"Nonsense, the Swedes know what they want. You've been proclaimed and crowned King."

"And can be killed or deposed to make room for the last Vasa. He is an officer in the Austrian Army."

I decided there and then to lay that ghost. Then he would be able to sleep at all events.

"Jean-Baptiste, the Bernadotte dynasty rules in Sweden once and for all, and you are the only one who is not convinced of that."

He shrugged his shoulders.

"But unfortunately there are people who maintain that in your fear of the opposition you don't stick to the Constitution." I turned my face away. "The Swedes set great store by their freedom of the press, dearest. And every time you suppress a paper there are one or two people who might take it into their heads to compel you to abdicate."

He winced. "Is that so? There, you see that my ghosts are not imaginary ones. The Prince of Vasa——"

"Jean-Baptiste, no one ever mentions the Prince of Vasa. The only one they mention is—Oscar, the Crown Prince!"

I heard a sigh of relief. "Is that true? Look at me, is that really true?"

"No one is dissatisfied with the Bernadotte dynasty. It has come to stay. Tell Fernand to sleep from now on in his own bedroom."

When Jean-Baptiste later drew the curtains aside from the windows the park of Drottningholm lay in bright golden light.

I went up to him by the window. "As far as Oscar is concerned," he said, gently stroking my hair, "I gave him what I never had myself, a good education, education for kingship. Sometimes I feel sad that I myself shall never see him King. Come along, let's have breakfast together as we did twenty-five years ago."

In the study we stopped before Moreau's bust. "Moreau, old friend!" said Jean-Baptiste thoughtfully, and tenderly I touched his marble face. 'They don't dust very well,' I thought, 'in these royal castles.' Then we went on, clasping each other tightly.

"I am glad," said Jean-Baptiste suddenly, "that I gave in and let Oscar marry Josefina."

"If you had had your way he'd have married some King's plain daughter, and old Miss Koskull would have been his only excursion into romantic young love, you unnatural father!"

In my boudoir a great surprise awaited us. On the breakfast-table laid for two was a fine bunch of roses, red, white, yellow, and pink. A piece of paper leaned against the vase. 'Our very best wishes to Their Majesties, Marshal J.-B. Bernadotte and wife. Marie and Fernand.'

Jean-Baptiste laughed, and I cried.

STOCKHOLM CASTLE.
February 1829.

Old Princess Sofia Albertina, the last Vasa in Sweden, is dying. Since her brother's death the old Princess has been living in the so-called Crown Prince's Palace, and although Jean-Baptiste saw to it that she was regularly asked to the court table, Oscar was the only one who took any interest in her. He calls her Aunt, and says she used to give him sweets when he was a boy. Yesterday I heard him say that she was ill, and this morning one of her octogenarian ladies-in-waiting came to me with the message that it was Her Highness's last wish to speak to me— to the silk merchant's daughter, of all people!—in private.

When I came to her she was dressed in my honour in grande toilette, lying on a sofa, and she tried to get up as I entered.

"Don't trouble to get up," I said, horrified at the sight of her sallow, wrinkled skin, her hollow cheeks, and the dull stare of her eyes in their deep sockets.

Her drawing-room was full of pink roses embroidered on

purple. The poor thing had done nothing all her life but embroider roses, and always the same pattern!

She smiled at me as I sat down, and sent her ladies away.

"I am very grateful to Your Majesty for your visit," she said. "I am told that your time is very fully occupied."

"Yes," I agreed, "we are very busy." I told her about Jean-Baptiste's full days and Oscar's promotion to Admiral of the Fleet and his plans for prison reform and the book he is writing on the subject.

"A strange occupation for an Admiral," she said.

"And for a musician," I added.

She nodded, bored. Somewhere a clock was ticking.

"Your Majesty does a good deal of hospital visiting," she said unexpectedly.

"Naturally, that is one of my duties. Besides, there's lots of room for improvement." Soon that subject was exhausted in its turn, and I heard the clock ticking again.

"I am told that you speak a bit of Swedish, Madame," she said a little later.

"I'm trying to learn it, Your Highness. Jean-Baptiste has no time to learn languages, and nobody thinks any the less of him for that. But I receive all deputations in Swedish as best I can."

The Princess seemed to be asleep and she looked as white as her powdered hair. I felt very sorry for her loneliness in her last moments. Suddenly she said:

"You are a good Queen, Madame!"

"We are doing our best, Jean-Baptiste, Oscar and I."

The ghost of the malicious smile of former days flitted over her face. "You are a very intelligent woman."

I looked at her in amazement.

"Yes," she continued, "at that time when poor Hedvig Elizabeth stigmatised you as being only a silk merchant's daughter you left the room in high dudgeon, and only returned as Queen. Hedvig Elizabeth has never been forgiven for that. A court without a young Crown Princess!" She giggled gleefully. "To the end of her life Hedvig Elizabeth had the reputation of the bad mother-in-law, he he he!"

These recollections seemed to revive her. "Oscar brought the children to see me, little Charles and the new-born baby, what's his name?"

"Oscar," I said proudly.

"Charles is very like you, Madame," she said. "I should have liked children of my own, but they never found a suitable husband for me. Oscar says you would have no objection if his children married commoners. How do you imagine that would work, Madame?"

"I've never thought about that. But Princes can renounce their titles, can't they?"

"Of course they can——" She broke off and fell into another doze. Somewhere the clock was ticking. Then she spoke again.

"I wanted to talk to you about the crown, Madame."

"Which crown?" I asked, thinking that her mind must be wandering.

"The crown of the Queens of Sweden."

Her eyes were wide open, and she spoke calmly and clearly.

"You were not crowned when His Majesty was. Perhaps you do not know that we have a crown for our Queens, a very old one, not big but quite heavy. I have held it in my hand several times. You are the mother of the Bernadotte dynasty. Why won't you be crowned?"

"Because up to now nobody has thought of it," I said softly.

"But I am doing so now. I am the last Vasa alive in Sweden and I am asking the first Bernadotte to take care of the old crown."

"I don't like these ceremonies," I said.

She opened her bloodless fingers and waited for me to give her my hand in token of consent. "I have not much time left to ask."

I could not but respond to that appeal.

I remembered that at a coronation long ago I had had to carry a handkerchief on a velvet cushion, to the ringing of the bells of Notre-Dame.

Did the old Princess guess the way my thoughts had turned? "I had the memoirs of this Napoleon Bonaparte read to me." She looked at me quizzically. "How strange that the two most important men of our time should have fallen in love with you, Madame. After all, you really are no beauty!"

Then she sighed, very softly:

"A pity I was born a Vasa. I should have preferred to be a Bernadotte and marry a commoner and have some fun in life."

When I left I bowed deeply to her and kissed the old hand. The dying Princess smiled, astonished at first and then a bit malicious. For, truly, I am no beauty.

" His Royal Highness regrets that it is quite impossible for him to find a free afternoon during this week." So Oscar's lord-in-waiting reported to me.

" Tell His Royal Highness that it is a question of fulfilling a wish of his mother's." After some hesitation the gentleman disappeared.

" But, Aunt, you know that Oscar is so terribly busy," said Marceline, not quite discreetly.

Oscar's lord-in-waiting returned. " His Royal Highness regrets that it is quite impossible this week."

" Then tell His Royal Highness that I am expecting him at four o'clock this afternoon. He will accompany me on an excursion."

" Your Majesty, His Royal Highness regrets——"

" I know, my dear Count, my son regrets that he is unable to fulfil my wish. Therefore tell him that it is no longer a wish of his mother but a command from the Queen."

Promptly at four o'clock Oscar was announced, together with three gentlemen of his suite. On the sleeve of his Admiral's uniform he wore the mourning band for Princess Sofia Albertina, who had died on March 17th. I myself wore mourning.

Oscar behaved very formally, to show me how furious he was. I told him to dismiss his gentlemen, I wanted to go on this excursion without any escort. I put on my hat and we left, on foot, to Oscar's surprise and dismay.

" We are going to the Västerlånggatan," I said, and Oscar led the way. He hadn't said a word yet, he was too furious with me. But that didn't prevent him from saluting and smiling to the passers-by who recognised him and bowed on meeting him. I had pulled the mourning veil over my face and was dressed so plainly and consequently looked so uninteresting that no one thought I belonged to His Highness.

" Here is the Västerlånggatan," said Oscar at last. " May I ask Your Majesty where we are going now? "

" To a silk shop belonging to a man called Persson. I have never been yet, but it shouldn't be difficult to find."

Oscar's patience broke. " Mama, I cancelled two conferences and an audience because of your command. And where are you taking me? To a silk shop! Why don't you let the man come to you? "

" Persson isn't appointed to the court. Besides, I'd like to see his shop."

" But surely you don't need me?"

" You can help me choose the material for my coronation dress. And I want to introduce you to Monsieur Persson."

Oscar was speechless. " Introduce me to a silk merchant?"

I felt sad. Perhaps it hadn't been a good idea to to take Oscar along. I keep forgetting that my son is a Crown Prince.

" Persson was an apprentice in your grandfather Clary's shop in Marseilles. He even lived in our house," I said with emotion. " Oscar, don't you understand, there is a man in Stockholm who has known my father and my home!"

Oscar bent down to me quickly and pushed his arm through mine. Looking round, he stopped an elderly man and asked for Persson's shop. After a good deal of bowing and scraping the man managed to give Oscar the information.

It was a comparatively small shop. But I saw at once that the silks and velvets in the window were of excellent quality. Inside there were a lot of customers, prosperous middle-class women who were so busy fingering the silks they paid no attention to Oscar's uniform. Consequently we were pushed around till our turn came. Behind the counter three young men were serving, one of them with an equine face and fair hair who reminded me of the young Persson of bygone days. It was this one who asked us what we wanted.

" I should like to see your silks," I said in my broken Swedish. He didn't understand me at first, and I repeated my request in French. " I'll call my father, he speaks French very well," said the young man, and disappeared.

Looking round I noticed that we were now quite alone in front of the counter, and to my horror I saw all the other customers pressed against the wall behind me, awestruck. I heard their murmur :

" The Queen!"

They had recognised me because I had put up the veil, the better to see the silks.

At that moment a side door opened, and Persson appeared, Persson from Marseilles, our Persson. He hadn't changed much. The fair hair had turned a dull grey, the blue eyes looked no longer timid but full of quiet self-confidence, and he smiled obligingly and showed his long yellow teeth.

" Madame wishes to see some silk?" he said in French.

" Your French has gone from bad to worse, Monsieur

Persson. And to think of all the trouble I took with your pronunciation."

The long lean figure stiffened. He opened his mouth to say something, but his lower lip trembled and he couldn't speak a word.

" Have you forgotten me, Monsieur Persson?"

He shook his head, slowly, as if in a dream. I tried to help him and said cordially:

" Monsieur Persson, I should like to see your silk cloths."

He stroked his head in confusion, and said in his miserable French:

" You have really come to see me, Mademoiselle Clary!"

It was too much for Oscar: the crowded shop, the intently listening ladies, and old Persson stammering in French. " Perhaps you would be kind enough to take Her Majesty and me into your office and show us your goods there," he said.

We went through a side door into a little office full of ledgers on a high desk, and hundreds of samples lying about just as they used to do in Papa's sanctum, and I felt immediately at home. In a frame over the desk hung a yellowed pamphlet which I recognised as soon as I saw it.

" Yes, here I am, Persson," I said, and sat down on the chair by the desk. " I should like to introduce my son to you. Oscar, this is Monsieur Persson, who was your grandfather's apprentice in Marseilles."

" I am surprised," Oscar said, smiling, " that you have not been appointed Purveyor to the Court long ago."

" I have never asked for the honour," said Persson slowly. " In any case, since my return from France my reputation in certain circles has not been a good one. And that is the reason," he said, pointed to the framed broadsheet.

" What is that?" Oscar asked. Persson took it from the wall and handed it to him.

" That, Oscar, was the first publication of the Rights of Man. Papa, your grandfather, brought it home, and Monsieur Persson and I learned it by heart. When Monsieur Persson went home he asked me for the broadsheet as a souvenir."

Oscar made no answer, but went to the window, wiped the dust off the glass with the sleeve of his Admiral's uniform, and began to read.

Persson and I looked at each other. " And the Mälar is really as green as you always told me it was," I said. " I never could visualise green water. And now the green water runs under my windows!"

"How well you remember it all, Mademoi——Your Majesty!" he said hoarsely.

"Of course I remember it. That's why it has taken me such a long time to come to you. I was afraid you'd blame me for——"

"Blame you? What could I ever blame you for?"

"For being a Queen now. Because we both used to be Republicans."

Persson looked across at Oscar in alarm. But Oscar was too immersed in the Rights of Man to hear. That restored Persson's self-confidence and he whispered to me: "That was in France, Mademoiselle Clary. But here in Sweden we are both—monarchists!" Then, with another glance at Oscar, he added: "Provided that—you understand, don't you?"

I nodded. We were silent and thought of our villa and the shop in Marseilles. Then Persson broke the silence.

"The sword of the General Buonaparte hung in the hall every evening during the last weeks of my stay in your house. How I hated it!" Blood mounted to his grey cheeks as he spoke.

"Persson, you were not jealous, were you?"

He turned his eyes away. "If I had imagined at that time that a daughter of François Clary might take to life in Stockholm, I should——"

He left the sentence unfinished.

I was dumb with surprise. So he would have offered me a home and a shop here, within a stone's throw of the castle!

"I need a new dress, Persson," I said gently.

He turned his eyes back to me, and was his old self once more, grey and dignified. . . .

"What kind of dress?"

"For my coronation. You may have read that it is going to be on the 21st of August. Have you any silk suitable for a coronation robe?"

"I have, indeed. The white brocade, you remember?"

He opened the door and called his son: "François!" He explained to me that he had called his son after my father, and then told the young man to bring the white brocade from Marseilles. "You know which one I mean."

The brocade came, heavy silk with threads of real gold. I took it on my knees, and Oscar, putting down the broadsheet, came over to look at it.

"Marvellous," he said, "just the stuff you want, Mama! Is it not too heavy?"

505

" It is very heavy, Oscar. I know because I carried it to the coach for Monsieur Persson when he left."

" Your Majesty's father declared that this silk could only be used for the State robe of a Queen," added Persson.

" Why have you never offered it at court?" I wondered. " It would have pleased the late Queen immensely."

" I kept it in memory of your papa and the firm of Clary. Moreover, the brocade is not for sale."

" Not even now?" asked Oscar.

" Not even now, Your Royal Highness." Then he called for his son again: " François, pack this brocade." And then bowed to me.

" Your Majesty, may I ask your gracious permission to offer you this brocade as a present?"

I felt a lump rising in my throat, and couldn't speak.

" I shall send it to the castle at once, Your Majesty."

I looked at the space on the wall where the framed broadsheet hung, and I looked at Persson.

" If Your Majesty could wait another moment," he said. He took the frame and wrapped it in an old piece of newspaper. " Please, Your Majesty, will you accept this too? Many years ago I promised to honour it always. And I have kept my promise."

An ironic smile appeared on his face. " I have wrapped it up so that Your Majesty can safely go through the streets with it. I myself have had trouble several times in the past."

Arm-in-arm like lovers, Oscar and I made our way back to the castle. We had nearly reached it and still I hadn't managed to say what I wanted to, I searched desperately for the right words.

" Oscar, perhaps you feel we have wasted an afternoon," I began, but stopped because we had come within hearing of the sentries. " Let's go on, Oscar, I have something to say to you." And in spite of his obvious impatience I made him go as far as the Mälar bridge.

The waters roared under the bridge. ' At this time,' I thought, ' the lights of Paris begin to dance on the waters of the Seine.'

" Listen, Oscar. I have always hoped that Persson would let me have Papa's broadsheet, and that's why I asked you to come with me."

" Are you going to lecture me on the Rights of Man?"

" Yes, Oscar."

But Oscar was growing more and more irritated.

" Mama, the Rights of Man are no longer a revelation for me. Here they are familiar to every educated person."

" Then it's about time the less educated ones learned them by heart. But I want to tell you that——"

" That I am to fight for them, isn't that it?"

" Fight for them? No, defend them!"

I looked at the turbulent water under the bridge. A memory from my childhood rose in my mind: a severed head rolling into blood-bespattered sawdust.

" Oscar, much blood was shed for their sake before and after their proclamation, and Napoleon so profaned them as to quote them even in his battle orders. And many others continue to abuse and dishonour them. I want my son to stand up for them and bring up his children to do the same."

Oscar remained silent for some time. Then he took off the old newspaper in which the Rights of Man were wrapped, and let it flutter into the Mälar.

When we had reached our gate he suddenly broke into laughter. " Mama, that amorous chirping of your old adorer was magnificent. If Papa knew of that!"

On my Coronation Day.
(21st of August 1829.)

" Désirée, I implore you, don't be late for your own coronation!"

I shall never forget this sentence as long as I live, because Jean-Baptiste kept shouting it out to me without interruption as Marie, Marceline, Yvette and I kept searching feverishly through my wardrobe. In between rummaging I admired Jean-Baptiste's marvellous coronation robe, his gold chains, his strange boots with the ermine trimming.

" Désirée, are you not ready yet?"

" I can't find them, Jean-Baptiste."

" What can't you find?"

" My sins, Jean-Baptiste. I put them all down on paper, and I've mislaid the sheet."

" Good gracious, can't you remember them?"

" No, there are too many—all little ones of course. That's why I wrote them down. Yvette, have another look."

I needed my sins because I had to go to confession before the coronation ceremonies began, and Josefina was to come with me. She and I were the only Roman Catholic members of the Protestant House of Bernadotte in Lutheran Sweden. The confession was to take place in the little chapel which Oscar had installed for Josefina on the top floor of the castle, and only after the absolution would I put on my coronation robe of white and gold brocade, which Papa had once held in his hands, and drive in solemn state to the Storkyrka, the Cathedral.

Josefina came in. "Mama, it is high time." But I still couldn't find my sins. I had to call off the search for them, and we went across the drawing-room, where Oscar was waiting for me in gala uniform.

"I had no idea," said Jean-Baptiste to Oscar, "that your mama's coronation would be hailed with such enthusiasm. Look at the crowds down there."

They kept behind the curtains and peered through them.

"I am not surprised," answered Oscar. "Mama is enormously popular, you know."

"Really?" Jean-Baptiste smiled at me, and then his irritation returned and he said:

"Désirée, are you ready or not? Have you found your sins?"

No, I hadn't, and the family wasn't co-operating at all and no one wanted to lend me some of their own. But Oscar had a bright idea.

"You have been living in sin with a man for years. There is a really big sin for you to confess."

"What sin do you mean?"

"Did you marry Papa in church or in a registry office?"

"Only in a registry office."

"There you are! The Roman Catholic Church does not recognise marriages not solemnised in church. Now, hurry up."

We arrived at the chapel just in time, and returned in fearful haste and out of breath. I ran past innumerable curtseying ladies to my boudoir, where Marie, my old Marie, now bent with age, and Yvette set to work on me at once.

"Auntie, the Archbishop is waiting already outside the church," said Marceline before she let us begin.

If you study your face every day in the mirror you don't get a fright by discovering that you are old. You see it coming and get used to it. I am now forty-nine years old, and have laughed and cried so much that many little wrinkles have formed round my eyes. And there are two lines from the nose down to the corners of my mouth. They established themselves when Jean-Baptiste fought at Leipzig.

I put cream, powder and rouge on my face as *la grande* Josephine had taught me, and thought of the way the Swedes were reacting to my coronation—as if they had been waiting for just that and nothing else for years! Jean-Baptiste didn't know what to make of their enthusiasm.. Did he really think it would be enough to be married to him in order to be the Queen? Doesn't he realise that only with this coronation I have said Yes to him, finally and for ever? Jean-Baptiste, this coronation is the promise of a bride, this time given in church and at the altar, to love and obey.

Most women when they reached my age are allowed to stop being young. Their children have grown up and their husbands have reached their goal. They may be their own mistresses. Only I may not. I am only beginning. But then, it isn't my fault that I have founded a dynasty. I am the Queen now, and for once, just for to-day, I want to look like a Queen!

"How young you are, Désirée, not a single grey hair!"

Jean-Baptiste was standing behind me, kissing my hair. I laughed.

"Many grey hairs, Jean-Baptiste, but they've been dyed for the first time. Do you like it?"

There was no answer. I turned round and saw not my Jean-Baptiste but a man in a heavy ermine coat, with the circlet of the crown of the Kings of Sweden round his forehead, a great and strange King. King Charles John XIV of Sweden.

He was staring at the yellowed broadsheet on the wall. It was new to him. It is so long since he was last in my boudoir.

"What is that, my girl?" he asked.

"An old broadsheet, Jean-Baptiste. The very first publication of the Rights of Man."

He frowned.

"My father bought it many years ago when the printer's ink on it was still wet. And now this yellow bit of paper gives me strength, I wasn't born to be a Queen."

I felt tears coming, and had to powder my face over again.

"May I stay here?" Jean-Baptiste asked. He sat down by my dressing-table and pulled a sheet of paper out of his pocket while Yvette came along with the curling tongs.

"Is that your list of sins?" I asked him. "A long list?"

"No, this sheet only contains notes about the coronation ceremony. Shall I read them to you?"

I nodded, and he read the thousand and one details about heralds, pages, costumes, the order of the procession and so on. When he mentioned the deputation from Norway he said that the enthusiasm of Sweden had suggested to him the idea of a separate coronation in Norway.

" No," I said, " not, not in Norway."

" Why not?"

" Because here in Sweden I may now be Desideria, the wanted one, but not in Norway. Don't forget that you forced Norway into this union, which may last your time and Oscar's but certainly not much longer."

" The union was necessary. Do you know that you are talking high treason ten minutes before your coronation?"

" In a hundred years' time we shall both sit comfortably on a little cloud and watch the Norwegians declare their independence, and choose a Danish Prince for their King simply to annoy the Swedes, and both you and I will get a good deal of amusement out of it up there on our cloud."

Marceline and Marie rushed in now with my coronation robe. The gold threads in the white brocade had acquired a silvery sheen in the course of the years, I noticed. I put it on and looked at myself and realised that it was the most beautiful dress that I had ever seen.

Meanwhile Jean-Baptiste went on with the explanation of the coronation procession. I heard that my two Counts, Brahe and Rosen, were to bear the insignia of State, and I was glad because I had insisted that they should have this distinction, which ought to have gone to the highest-ranking ministers. Hadn't they thrown the weight of their ancient names into the scales at the time when the Swedes had had to get used to the silk merchant's daughter on their throne?

And who was going to follow the two Counts, bearing the crown on a red cushion? Miss Mariana Koskull. That, too, had been my choice. " You are not dissatisfied with my choice, are you?" I said. " It does not say anywhere that the crown must be carried by a virgin, as it does in that ancient French stipulation which Napoleon had such difficulties in fulfilling; you remember he had to find ten virgins? All that is required is a woman of the high aristocracy. That's why I suggested Mariana Koskull." I winked at Jean-Baptiste. " And for her services to the Vasa and Bernadotte dynasties!"

At that Jean-Baptiste showed sudden interest in my jewels and bent down to inspect them.

At last I was ready. Marie came to put the purple cloak round my shoulders, but Jean-Baptiste took it out of her hand and did it himself, very tenderly. Then we stood side by side in front of the big mirror.

" It is like a fairy-tale," I said softly, " once upon a time there lived a great king and a little queen. . . ."

I turned away quickly. "Jean-Baptiste, the broadsheet!"

He took the frame from the wall and handed it to me. I bent down and kissed the glass over the faded text of the Rights of Man. Jean-Baptiste's face went white with excitement.

The folding doors to the salon opened. Josefina was there with the children. The three-year-old Charles made a dash toward me and then stopped dead. "That isn't Grandmama, that is a Queen," he said and stroked the purple cloak, his face full of awe. Josefina handed me Oscar, the baby. I took him in my arms. He had beautiful blue eyes, and hardly any hair as yet. 'It's for you as well,' I thought, 'for you, the second Oscar, that I'm going to be crowned.'

The dull roar I heard coming from outside reminded me of the night when the torches lit up the Rue d'Anjou. I heard Jean-Baptiste say: "Why are the windows closed?" and "What are they shouting down there in the street?"

But I knew already, it was French. My Swedes wanted me to understand them, and they remembered what they had read about that night of the many torches. They were shouting: "*Notre-Dame de la Paix!*", "Our Lady of Peace!" I handed the baby back to Josefina quickly because I had begun to tremble uncontrollably.

The rest happened as if in a dream. I went down the marble steps, I saw Brahe and Rosen carrying the insignia, and nodded to Rosen in memory of our drive to Malmaison and of Villatte. I saw Koskull in a blue dress carrying the crown on the velvet cushion and smiling happily. I saw Oscar and Josefina enter their open carriage, and then Jean-Baptiste and I entered ours, the last of all the carriages.

"I am arriving last in church, like a bride," I said, and then the jubilant acclamations of the crowd along both sides of the streets roared into my ears.

Jean-Baptiste smiled and waved, and I wanted to smile and wave too, but I couldn't. For I heard them call for me, and for me alone. "*Länge leve Drottningen—Drottningen!*" "Long live the Queen!" I heard it and I felt that I should not be able to help crying.

In front of the Cathedral Jean-Baptiste himself arranged the folds of my purple cloak and led me to the porch. There the Archbishop and all the bishops of Sweden were waiting for me.

"Blessed be she who cometh in the name of the Lord!" the Archbishop said. The organ music rose like a great wave, and I could only think again when the Archbishop put the crown on my head. 'How heavy it is,' I thought.

It is late at night, and everybody thinks I have gone to bed to prepare myself for the festivities taking place to-morrow and the day after in my honour. But I wanted to write once more in my diary. How strange that I should have arrived at the last page to-day!

Once, many years ago, it was nothing but white empty pages and lay on my birthday table. I was fourteen years old and wanted to know what I was to write in it. Papa answered: " The story of Citizeness Bernadine Eugenie Désirée Clary."

Papa, I have written it down, all of it, and there's nothing more to be added now. The story of the citizeness has come to an end, and that of the Queen is beginning now. I shall never understand how it all came about. But I promise you, Papa, to do all I can not to bring discredit on your name, and never to forget that you were a highly respected silk merchant all your life.